THE STARS AT WAR

BAEN BOOKS by DAVID WEBER

Honor Harrington:
On Basilisk Station
The Honor of the Queen
The Short Victorious War
Field of Dishonor
Flag in Exile
Honor Among Enemies
In Enemy Hands
Echoes of Honor
Ashes of Victory
War of Honor

edited by David Weber:
More than Honor
Worlds of Honor
Changer of Worlds
The Service of the Sword

Honorverse:
Crown of Slaves
(with Eric Flint)
The Shadow of Saganami
(forthcoming)

Mutineers' Moon
The Armageddon
Inheritance
Heirs of Empire

Empire From the Ashes
(Megabook)

Path of the Fury

The Apocalypse Troll

The Excalibur Alternative

Oath of Swords
The War God's Own
Wind Rider's Oath

with Steve White:
Crusade
In Death Ground
The Stars at War *(Megabook)*
Insurrection
The Shiva Option

with John Ringo:
March Upcountry
March to the Sea
March to the Stars

with Eric Flint:
1633

BAEN BOOKS by STEVE WHITE

Demon's Gate

Forge of the Titans

Eagle Against the Stars

Prince of Sunset

The Disinherited
Legacy
Debt of Ages

THE STARS AT WAR

DAVID WEBER
&
STEVE WHITE

THE STARS AT WAR

This is a work of fiction. All the characters and events portrayed in this book are fictional, and any resemblance to real people or incidents is purely coincidental.

Crusade copyright © 1992 by David Weber & Steve White; *In Death Ground* copyright © 1997 by David Weber & Steve White

All rights reserved, including the right to reproduce this book or portions thereof in any form.

A Baen Books Original

Baen Publishing Enterprises
P.O. Box 1403
Riverdale, NY 10471
www.baen.com

ISBN: 0-7434-8841-5

Cover art by David Mattingly

First Megabook printing, August 2004

Distributed by Simon & Schuster
1230 Avenue of the Americas
New York, NY 10020

Production by Windhaven Press, Auburn, NH
Typeset by Bell Road Press, Sherwood, OR
Printed in the United States of America

10   9   8   7   6   5   4   3   2   1

CONTENTS

Crusade

CHAPTER ONE

Exiles' Return

"Is the *zeget* to your liking?"

Twenty-Sixth Least Claw of the Khan Khardanish'zarthan, Lord Talphon, combed his claws suavely through his luxuriant whiskers, and his slit-pupilled eyes glinted across the table at his liaison officer.

"Yes, thank you, Captain. And it's quite well cooked, too."

Khardanish noted Lieutenant Johansen's teeth-hidden smile with approval, for Humans often forgot that bared teeth were a challenge among his people. He knew Johansen had studied the *Zheeerlikou'valkhannaieee* carefully in preparation for this assignment, yet it was still gratifying to see such awareness of proper behavior. Not that he was quite prepared to stop teasing his guest just yet.

"I am glad," he said, "and I apologize for how long the cooks took to grasp that you would truly prefer it cooked."

"Not necessary, Captain. I console myself with the thought that a TFN chef would find it just as hard to believe *you* would truly prefer it raw."

Khardanish allowed himself the snarling purr of a chuckle. It was remarkable how well he and Johansen had learned to read one another's nuances, particularly since neither had the proper vocal apparatus to speak the other's language. Khardanish suspected he had drawn the Lorelei Patrol at least partly because he understood Terran Standard English. There was much talk of new translating software, but the current generation remained crude and imprecise . . . and used too much memory for a lowly destroyer, anyway.

The least claw had been less than enthusiastic when he heard about his new post. It was flattering for a least claw to serve, in effect, as a

3

small claw with his own squadron, but the Tenth Destroyer Squadron's four old ships hardly constituted the Navy's cutting edge, nor did the Lorelei System qualify as a critical sector. It was one of the very few systems the Khanate had succeeded in wresting from the Federation in the First Interstellar War of two Orion centuries before, but the thoroughly useless star was hopelessly indefensible (as the Terrans had proved in ISW-2), which, he suspected, was probably why the Federation had permitted his people to keep it. Lorelei had no habitable planets, and only one of its six warp points led to Orion territory; four led to Terran space, and the sixth led only to death, for no survey ship had ever returned from its far terminus. His *Znamae* and her sisters were here purely to "show the flag," as the Terrans put it.

Yet Khardanish had come to realize his duty held an importance too few of his fellows could appreciate. Most agreed that when the Federation and Khanate allied against the Rigelians in the Third Interstellar War, the Treaty of Valkha's assignment of liaison officers to all border patrols had made sense as a means of defusing potential incidents. Far fewer would admit that the contact those liaison assignments engendered remained equally desirable as a means of nurturing the still slow-growing mutual respect of the star nations' warriors.

Khardanish himself was surprised by how genuinely fond of the lieutenant he had become. He would never find Humans attractive. Their faces were flat; their ears were small, round, and set far too low; they lacked any hint of a decent pelt; and the absence of the whiskers which were an Orion's pride made it difficult to take them seriously. Even their males had only a soft, cub-like fuzz, but it was even worse in the lieutenant's case. She was a female, and the long hair which framed her face only emphasized its total, disgusting bareness. And if the Human custom of wearing body-shrouding clothing at all times was less aesthetically objectionable—at least it hid their naked skins!—it still seemed . . . odd.

But Samantha Johansen had many qualities he admired. She was observant, intelligent, and keenly sensitive to the inevitable differences between their cultures, and her military credentials were impressive. The lieutenant was only fifty-three—twenty-eight, by her people's reckoning—but she had seen the *zeget.* Her mess tunic bore the ribbon of the Federation's Military Cross, the *Valkhaanair's* equivalent, which must have been hard to come by in the fifty Terran years of peace since ISW-3. Perhaps, he speculated idly, she had been chosen for this duty by her superiors just as carefully as he was coming to believe First Fang Lokarnah had chosen him?

"Ah, Saahmaantha!" he said now. "At times, you are too much like one of my own for comfort."

"I take that as a compliment, Captain," Johansen said, chewing another slice of *zeget* appreciatively. In fact, she found it overly gamy, but it was a warrior's dish. The bear-like *zeget* was four furry meters of raw fury, the most feared predator of the original Orion homeworld, and Least Claw Khardanish had done her great honor by ordering it served.

"Do you?" Khardanish poured more wine. The Terran vintage was overly dry for his palate, but it had been Johansen's gift, and he drank it with the pleasure she deserved of him. He tilted his glass, admiring the play of light in the ruby liquid. "Then I will tell you something, Lieutenant. Do you know what we *Zheeerlikou'valkhannaieee* call our two wars with you?"

"Yes, Captain," Johansen said softly. "'The Wars of Shame.'"

"Precisely." He sipped delicately. "I find that apt even though we are now allies. We had twice the systems, ten times the population, and a navy, and you had—what? A few dozen lightly-armed survey vessels? Should not any warrior feel shame for losing to an enemy so much weaker than he?"

Johansen met his eyes calmly, and the least claw approved. Even among his own people, many would have sought to hide their discomfort with some polite nothing; this Human merely waited.

"But you were not weaker where it mattered most, Saahmaantha," he said seriously. "For your people, war was a matter for planning and discipline; for mine, it was a chance to win honor by individual bravery. Your First Fang Aandersaahn lured us into traps, ambushed us, and massed his fire to burn us down as we charged against him, and to the *Zheeerlikou'valkhannaieee* those were coward's tactics. My grandsire, the first Lord Talphon, fought in both Wars of Shame. He was an intelligent officer, one of Varnik'sheerino's protégés, but even he thought your people's way of war fit only for *chofaki*."

Johansen still said nothing, though her eyes flickered. Literally, the term meant "dirt-eaters"; figuratively, it implied beings so lost to courage and honor they could not even recognize them as concepts.

"Yet I have read his journal many times, Saahmaantha, and he learned better." Khardanish watched his guest relax. "He was not at Aklumar, but his ship was the sole survivor of the First Battle of Ophiuchi Junction, and he fought in every major engagement of the Junction Campaign. By the end, he had learned what your Federation Navy taught us so well; that the duty of a warrior must be to *win*, not to count coup. So if you are like one of us, perhaps that is in part because my people have grown more like *yours*."

"And is that a good thing, Captain?" Johansen asked.

"Yes, Saahmaantha." He refilled her empty glass and raised his own to her in the Terran manner. "We owe you much for teaching us there is no cowardice in forethought. Some might argue that point even now—they remember only the shame of defeat and prefer still to think of Humans as *chofaki*—but my grandsire died defending Tanama against the Rigelian First Fleet with a single Alliance task group, and his Terran units died with him. None fled, and the names of their commanders are inscribed among my clan's fathers and mothers in honor." He regarded Johansen levelly. "I believe he would approve of you."

"Your words do me honor, litter master," Johansen said quietly.

"True honor is in the heart which understands them, cubling," Khardanish returned the formality, then twitched his tufted ears in humor. "But listen to us! We grow too grave, Lieutenant."

"Perhaps." Samantha sipped her own wine, leaning back from the low table on the cushions which served Orions in lieu of chairs, then grinned wryly. "But if we're growing more like one another, we've paid enough along the way, sir. This very system's history is proof of that."

Khardanish nodded. A hundred and fifty Orion years before, a Terran fleet in Lorelei had cut off and trapped a third of the Khanate's battle-line. Forty years before that, an Orion flotilla had penetrated the Terran frontier undetected during ISW-1 and surprised an entire Human colony fleet here. There had been no survivors.

"Perhaps," he suggested dryly, "that is because we have *always* been alike in at least one regard, Saahmaantha." His liaison officer raised an eyebrow in the Human expression of interrogation, and he gave another chuckle. "Both of us are incredibly stubborn," he said simply.

A gentle vibration quivered through the superdreadnought *Alois Saint-Just* as Engineering ran her final drive test, and her captain watched his read-outs with profound satisfaction. There was honor in commanding even the smallest unit of Task Force One, but to command the flagship—!

He turned his eyes to the tactical display. Only *Saint-Just*'s squadron mates *Helen Borkman* and *Wu Hsin* lay close alongside, but the dots of other ships dusted the three-dimensional sphere with a thick coating of data codes, and the nav beacons marking the warp point pulsed amid the minefields and asteroid fortresses. A thrill of pride ran through him, and he forced himself to settle back, watching the chronometer tick off the last few hours.

"Captain to the bridge. Captain to the bridge."

The computer recording was both calm and unhurried; the wail of alarms was neither, and Least Claw Khardanish erupted from his quarters, still sealing his vac suit. A luckless maintenance rating bounced off a bulkhead as his captain ran right over him and bounded into the central access shaft, cursing softly but with feeling. He loved *Znamae*, old as she was, but her accommodations had been designed by eight-thumbed *zarkotga*. Destroyers had no mass to waste on intraship cars, and his quarters were the full length of the hull from her bridge. It was bad enough to take so long to reach his station, but the unseemly haste it forced upon him could not be reassuring to his crew.

He slowed abruptly as he spied the bridge hatch. By the time he reached it, he was moving with a warrior's measured, purposeful stride.

Son of the Khan Yahaarnow'ziltakan, *Znamae*'s exec, looked up with obvious relief as Khardanish dropped into his command chair and racked his helmet. He was, he noted sourly, the last to arrive. Even Johansen, whose cabin was almost as inconveniently placed as his, had beaten him this time.

"Report!" he said crisply.

"Unknown drive fields, sir." Observer First Hinarou'frikish-ahn's experience showed in her precisely enunciated report. "Bearing oh-seven-two level by oh-three-three vertical. Range approximately three-point-two light-minutes. Estimated base course two-four-nine by oh-oh-three. Data are still rough, sir, but data base does not recognize them."

"Are you certain of that bearing, Observer?" Khardanish demanded.

"Positive, sir."

The least claw darted a quick look at Yahaarnow and Lieutenant Johansen and saw his own surprise on both faces.

"Astrogation, back-plot Observation's estimated base course."

"Aye, sir. Computing now." There was a moment of silence, and when the astrogator spoke again he sounded startled. "Sir, assuming Observation's course and bearing are correct, it looks like they came from warp point six!"

Khardanish's tufted ears flicked in quick acknowledgment, but he was deeply puzzled. Point six was the warp point Lorelei's Human discoverers had named Charon's Ferry, and if no survey ship had ever gone into it and lived, how in Valkha's name could anything come *out* of it?

"Unknowns are now at two-point-nine-five light-minutes, sir. Coming up in the outer zone of your tactical display—now."

Khardanish glanced into his holo tank. Human designers preferred a more compact, flat-screen display, but Orion eyes had problems with such systems. Now he watched drifting lights blink alive, glowing the steady yellow of unidentified vessels. They blinked again, and suddenly each bore a small light code denoting its estimated tonnage.

There were twelve of them, he noted digging his extended claws into the padded armrests of his command chair. Most were no larger than his own destroyers, but the largest was a heavy cruiser.

"Come to Status One," he ordered. "Prep and download courier drones." He waited for the acknowledgments, then made himself lean back. "All right, Communications—standard Alliance challenge."

"Aye, sir."

The range was still two and a half light-minutes—thirty minutes' travel for *Znamae* under full drive—and the five-minute wait seemed eternal.

"They are responding, sir. I do not recognize—wait! Coming up from data base now." The com officer paused, then continued flatly, "Captain, they appear to be using pre-Alliance Terran communication protocols."

Khardanish looked up sharply. Pre-Alliance? That would make them at least fifty Terran years out of date!

"Com Central confirms, sir. Their protocols match those used by the Terran Federation Navy at the time of the First War of Shame."

"Lieutenant?" Khardanish looked at his liaison officer, and Johansen raised her palms in the Human gesture of helpless ignorance. Which, he thought sourly, was a great deal of help just now.

"Can you unscramble, Communications?"

"Affirmative, sir. We have no visual, but audio is coming up now."

The com link was none too clear, and there was a hiss of static under the voice, but the distorted words were recognizable.

"Unknown vessels, this is the Terran cruiser *Kepler*. Identify yourselves."

"*Khhepaahlaar?*" Khardanish's tongue twisted on the word and he frowned at Johansen. "I do not recognize the name, Lieutenant. Do you?"

"No, sir." She punched keys at her console, calling up the TFN navy list. "No ship of that name is listed in my files, either, sir."

"I see." Khardanish combed his whiskers for a moment. There might, of course, be one explanation, for one could never be certain one had located all the warp points in any system. "Closed" warp points were undetectable; they could be located only by passing through from a normal warp point at the far end. It was possible a Federation survey flotilla had done just that—that they were coming not from Charon's Ferry but from a newfound closed point on the same approximate bearing. But that would not explain unknown drive frequencies or archaic communication codes. Or why this *Kepler* was not in Johansen's data base.

He pondered a moment longer, but there was only one way to find out.

"Identify us and ask if we can render any assistance, Communications."

"Aye, sir."

"Maneuvering, slow to thirty percent." There was no point closing too rapidly. The range was less than two light-minutes now, and his old destroyers were slow; if he should have to run he wanted all the start he could get. There was another frustrating wait as the signals crossed, and then—

"You are in Terran space, *Znamae!*" the voice from the speaker snapped, and Khardanish growled under his breath. This was becoming ridiculous!

"Sir!" Observer First Hinarou's voice was sharper. "Additional drive sources detected. Two new formations. Designate them Groups Two and Three. Group Two bears one-six-four by oh-three-three, range three-point-two light-minutes; Group Three bears oh-two-eight by oh-three-two, range three-point-one light-minutes. Both are on converging interception courses!"

Khardanish's eyes slitted. That sort of spread suggested only one thing: an attack formation. The first group must have been an advanced screen, and the others had spread out behind their scouts, maneuvering beyond scanner range to position themselves to run down his squadron whatever he did.

But *why*? If they were truly Terrans, they were *allies*, and if they were *not* Terrans, how could they have known to use Terran com protocols—even ones so sadly out of date? It made no sense! Unless . . .

No one had ever come back from Charon's Ferry, but Fleet records suggested that at least some of the Terran colony fleet annihilated here had fled *down* it in a desperate bid to escape. Was it possible they had survived?

It seemed fantastic, but it might be an explanation. After all, more than ninety Terran years had passed since then. Survivors might have managed to cling to their technology. But how could colony ships survive what survey ships could not? And how could they have produced sufficient population to build this many ships? And why wait this long to return? If—

"We have tentative classifications on Group Two, sir," Hinarou said tensely. "Coming up on your display."

Khardanish looked back down and tightened internally. At least seven of those ships were capital units; three were superdreadnoughts.

"Maneuvering, come about one-eight-oh degrees. Maximum power." *Znamae* swerved in a course change so radical it could be felt even through the drive field, and Khardanish turned to Johansen. "Observations, Lieutenant?"

"Sir, they may claim to be Terran, but they don't match anything in my records. I don't know *what* they are."

"Could they be survivors of the colony fleet of 2206?"

Johansen blinked, then frowned. "I suppose it's possible, sir, but if they are, where have they been all this time?"

"I do not know, but if that *is* the case, they cannot know what has transpired since. They may even believe we are still at war."

"Sir," Observer Hinarou broke in, "we are picking up additional sensor emissions. Battle Comp estimates they are targeting systems."

"Acknowledged, Observation."

Their pursuers were far outside weapon range, but that would change. The capital ships were gaining only slowly as they cut the angle on the squadron's course, but their escorts were twenty percent faster than his ships. They would reach missile range in little over two hours, and the first group was far closer. *They* would have the range in less than eighty minutes, and it was thirty hours to the nearest warp point.

Khardanish beckoned, and Johansen crossed to his side. He leaned close to her, speaking softly.

"Either those ships truly are Terran, however and wherever they have come from, or they are not. In either case, we cannot outrun them. If they attack, we will undoubtedly be destroyed, and the consequences to the Alliance may prove disastrous."

"I understand, sir," the lieutenant said when he paused.

"But perhaps we can avoid that eventuality. So far we have used only our own com techs, and they are *Zheeerlikou'valkhannaieee*. You are Human. You must speak for us and convince them of the true state of affairs."

"I'll try, sir."

"I know you will, Saahmaantha." He waved her back to her console, then turned to his com officer. "Patch the lieutenant into your link."

"At once, sir." The communications officer touched a key, then flicked his ears to Johansen, and she drew a deep breath.

"*Kepler*," she said slowly and distinctly, "this is Lieutenant Samantha Johansen, Terran Federation Navy, aboard the Orion destroyer *Znamae*. You are *not* in Terran space. This system was ceded to the Khanate under the Treaty of Tycho. The Federation is not—I repeat, *not*—at war with the Khanate. We are allies. I say again, the Terran Federation and the Khanate of Orion are *allies*. Please acknowledge my transmission."

Lieutenant Johansen's words winged across space to the cruiser *Kepler*, and a stunned com officer relayed them to the superdreadnought *Saint-Just*.

"*What* did she say?!" The admiral commanding Task Force One stared at his flag captain in disbelief.

"That the Federation and the Orions are allies," the captain repeated shakenly.

"Holy Terra!" the admiral murmured. "It's worse than we feared possible!"

The captain nodded silently, trying to grapple with the blasphemous possibility, then shook himself.

"Shall we reply, sir?"

"Wait," his admiral commanded, rubbing his prominent nose as he thought. He was silent for several seconds, then looked back up with cold eyes. "Instruct *Kepler* to reply, Captain. Emphasize that we've been out of contact for many years. Tell this Lieutenant Johansen"—the name was an epithet in his mouth—"we must investigate her claims. Request, politely, that the Orion ships halt and permit the screen to close with them."

"Aye, sir." The captain's voice was flat with disapproval, and his admiral's eyes flickered with cold amusement.

"If the infidel agrees, we'll halt the remainder of the task force while the screen closes, and then . . ."

The long delay between Johansen's transmission and the response was agonizing, but it finally came, and all eyes on *Znamae*'s bridge turned unobtrusively to the least claw.

"Comments, Saahmaantha?" he asked quietly.

"I don't like it, Captain," she said flatly. "They don't *feel* right, but they've got the speed to catch us if we run."

"I share the lieutenant's suspicion, sir, and I must point out that if they close to such a short range, their weapons would—"

"I know, Yahaarnow," Khardanish said, "but we have small choice, and the Alliance serves both our Khan and the Federation well. If we risk our lives to preserve it, we do no more than our duty." He held the exec's eyes until his ears twitched agreement, then looked at Johansen.

"Very well, Lieutenant, inform them we will comply." He turned back to the exec. "Maintain Status One, but I want no active targeting systems."

The Orion Tenth Destroyer Squadron hung motionless, watching a handful of scanner dots close with it. The remainder of the "Terran" fleet had halted well beyond attack range, and Khardanish hoped that was a good sign, yet uneasiness simmered in his blood, and it was hard to keep his claws from twitching. The faceless com link had refused further communication until rendezvous was made, and its silence bit at his nerves.

He watched *Kepler*'s light dot. The heavy cruiser was now at eight light-seconds and closing at a leisurely two percent of light-speed with two light cruisers and three of her brood of destroyers. The other six destroyers had halted at ten light-seconds, just within standard missile range. It *looked* as if the other side was doing exactly as agreed.

"Range six light-seconds, sir," Observer Hinarou reported.

"Lieutenant, request that they come no closer until we have established visual communications."

"Aye, sir." Johansen activated her com once more. "*Kepler,* this is Lieutenant Johansen. Our commander requests that you come no closer until visual communications have b—"

"Incoming fire!" Yahaarnow snapped, and the display was suddenly alive with missile traces.

"Return fire!" Khardanish slammed his clawed fist against his armrest. "Enemy flagship is primary target!"

"Aye, sir, opening fire now!"

The Tenth Squadron belched homing missiles, but the reply was pitiful beside the holocaust racing for it, and the enemy drive fields peaked as they charged in for the kill.

"Evasive action!" Khardanish commanded, and his ships, too, leapt to full power. They swerved in frantic evasion maneuvers, and *Znamae* lurched as the first warhead burst against her shields. The energy gunners had required a moment to activate their targeting systems, but now the force beams opened up, slamming at the enemy with electromagnetic fists.

"Launch courier drones," Khardanish said softly, and his bridge crew knew their commander had already written off his entire squadron.

"There," *Kepler*'s captain said coldly. "That one's done all the talking. That's the one we want."

Courier drones spilled from the embattled destroyers, racing for the warp point beacons as nuclear flame boiled on their mother ships' shields. The squadron's overloaded point defense stations could stop only a handful of the incoming missiles, but Khardanish's own missiles were striking home, and he watched explosions crawl over the heavy cruiser's shields. The invisible blows of his force beams savaged them as well, and they were going down.

But so were his, and the light code of the destroyer *Tramad* flickered as her last shield died and the first missile impacted on her drive field.

"Target's shields are weakening," Yahaarnow reported. "One enemy destroyer streaming atmosphere. We—"

His voice broke off as a savage burst of energy swept past *Znamae*'s shields and slashed into her bows, and Khardanish's eyes went wide in shock.

"Forward armor destroyed. Life Support Three inactive. Shield Compartment Two no longer responds. Heavy casualties in Missile One."

Khardanish slewed around towards Hinarou, and the observer first's ears were flat to her skull in disbelief.

"That was an x-ray laser, Captain!"

The least claw turned back to his display, but his brain raced. That surpassed anything the Khanate or Federation could do. It took a bomb-pumped laser to produce a weapon-grade beam of x-rays at such a range, and though independently deployed bomb-pumped lasers were feasible for static defenses, they were far too cumbersome for deep-space use against targets capable of radical maneuvers at ten percent of light-speed. And how could anyone use a bomb-pumped laser *on board* a ship, anyway?! Carbon lasers were retained there because their neutrally-charged photons could pierce a ship's electro-magnetic shields, but none of them could do damage like that at *this* range!

His display wrenched his mind from its thoughts as *Tramad*'s light code suddenly vanished. Now he commanded only three destroyers— and then *Honarhae* followed *Tramad* into destruction.

"Shields down!" Yahaarnow reported as *Znamae*'s defenses crumbled under the enemy's pounding, but no fresh missiles darted in to take advantage of her nakedness. They were tearing his ships to pieces, but aside from that single laser hit, *Znamae* had taken no damage at all! Why?

"Enemy cruisers launching capital missiles!" Hinarou snapped, and Khardanish gripped his chair's armrests in fingers of steel. Capital missiles from cruisers? Ridiculous! And why wait this long and then launch extended range weapons at such close quarters?

"*Sonasha* is gone, sir," Yahaarnow said flatly. The least claw merely nodded. *Znamae* was alone, but there was no time even for grief; she would be joining her sisters soon enough.

The bridge lighting flickered as fresh energy stabbed his ship. Her shields were down, baring her to the enemy's needle beams, and the close-range precision weapons struck viciously. They ripped through her weapon bays, mangling her force beams and crippling her point defense, and the capital missiles screamed in to complete her destruction.

But they never struck. An explosion trembled through the hull, then another and another, but they were too weak for warheads. They were—

"Captain!" Yahaarnow whirled from his useless weapon console.

"Those missiles were some sort of vehicles! Their crews are blowing holes in the hull and *boarding* us!"

Khardanish stared at his exec. *Board* a starship under way? How could they even penetrate the drive field?!

"Intruders on deck eight!" a voice shouted over the intercom. "Deck seven!" "Deck five!" Pressure loss telltales burned crimson, and a sick wave of understanding swept the least claw. He had no idea how it had been done, but he knew why. They wanted his ship . . . and her data base.

More explosions bit breaches in the hull, and vac-suited boarders swarmed through them like demons, armed with automatic weapons and grenades. Destroyers carried no Marines, and *Znamae*'s pitiful stock of small arms was locked in the armory. Her officers were armed, but only with the edged steel of their *defargaie*, the honor dirks of the Khanate.

Yet *Znamae*'s crew were Orions, and they turned on their enemies with clawed fists and feet and improvised bludgeons. They were cut down by bullets, slaughtered as grenades burst in the confines of steel passages, but they did not die quite alone. A few captured enemy weapons, turning them upon their foes before they, too, went down on the blood-slick decks and the tide of combat swept over them.

A tractor beam dragged *Znamae* toward *Kepler*, and Least Claw Khardanish rose, reaching for his own *defargo* as a thunderous explosion blew the sealed bridge hatch open and hurled Yahaarnow and two of his ratings to the deck in bloody gruel. Chattering gunfire cut down still more of his bridge crew, and then the first invader leapt through the hatch.

Khardanish's eyes were slits of fury, but even through his rage he realized it had all been a lie. Whatever their attackers were, they were not Terrans! The squat-bodied invader was too stocky, his arms too long and his legs too short. The least claw's mind recorded it all as the alien's thundering autorifle swept the bridge.

Observer First Hinarou vaulted her console, *defargo* drawn, but the invader cut her down and swung his weapon towards Khardanish. The entire bridge lay between them, and even as the least claw charged, he knew he would never reach his killer.

The rifle spoke, and Khardanish went to his knees in agony, dropping his *defargo*, as slugs mangled his right shoulder and side.

The invader took fresh aim, but before he could fire, Samantha Johansen was upon him with a *zeget*'s scream, and the fallen observer's *defargo* flashed in her hand. She drove it deep, twisting her wrist savagely, and the alien went down. The lieutenant kicked the body aside, snatched up the fallen rifle, and threw herself on her belly in her enemy's blood. The weapon's function was easy enough to grasp, and she emptied its extended magazine down the passage in a single, endless burst that piled the rest of the assault team on the deck.

The silence was deafening as she stopped firing, and Khardanish heard a click of metal as she jerked a fresh magazine from the alien's body and reloaded. Blood pumped from his wounds, and he felt Death's claws grope for him, yet his mind was cold and clear as he dragged himself across the deck. Only he and Samantha remained, and more boarders would be here soon. She could never stand them off alone, and she did not know the proper codes. He must reach the engineering station before he died.

He heaved to his feet with a kitten's mewl of pain and clung drunkenly to the console. His strength was going fast, but the visual display showed what he had hoped for. *Kepler*'s tractor had drawn *Znamae* close aboard!

Fresh thunder bellowed as Samantha fired down the passage yet again. Return fire whined off the bulkheads, but she was protected by the ruins of the hatch. She could hold a moment longer.

He flipped up the plastic shield and entered the code slowly and carefully. The single red-tabbed switch was cool under his claws, and he looked at Samantha one last time. Her round-pupilled, Human eyes met his, and he saw her agreement.

"Together, clan sister!" he gasped, and pressed it home.

CHAPTER TWO

A Decision of State

The Honorable Francis Mulrooney, Terran Ambassador to the Khanate of Orion, leaned against one side of the deep window and watched the light of a sun very like Sol stream across an oddly blue lawn of "grass" whose like Terra had never imagined. The "trees" beyond the courtyard wall were feathery spires, caparisoned in the orange and yellow and fire-red blossoms of spring, and wispy creatures flapped lacy wings above them.

To Mulrooney, *Valkha'zeeranda* had always seemed a fairy wonderland. On the surface, it was hardly the proper capital world for a warrior race, yet there was a subtle undercurrent of rightness to it. He'd often wondered what "New Valkha's" first colonists had thought and felt as they left the ships which had borne them here from the world their Wars of Unification had reduced to ruin. How must they have felt to leave their breath masks and chemical detectors and radiation counters behind forever?

He stroked the deeply incised shield and crossed swords of the Khanate, graven a centimeter deep in the windowsill, then swept his gaze over the magnificent white spires and minarets of the imperial compound and knew he saw the answer. Mulrooney was one of the very few Terrans who had visited Old Valkha and seen the cyclopean fortresses which dominated pre-stellar Orion architecture like expressions of a warrior ethos in stone and mortar. New Valkha did not boast their like. As a fortress, the imperial compound equaled any planetary defense center in the Federation, yet it hid its teeth like an Orion smile. An almost tangible sense of peace hovered over its elfin beauty, perfected by the background of the Khanate's mailed fist.

And that, he told himself, was how the *Zheeerlikou'valkhannaieee*

16

saw their imperial capital. It was flowers and cold steel, the jewel in the Khan's iron crown, an eye of tranquillity in a hurricane's heart.

He sighed and turned from the window, pacing slowly back and forth. The summons had come from the *kholokhanzir*, the grand vizier, himself, and it was unusual to be kept waiting so long. Mulrooney had many contacts in the Orion bureaucracy, and he knew some major crisis had blown up with absolutely no warning. He could uncover no clue as to what it was, but the whispers of rumored disaster made an ominous counterpoint to this unprecedented delay.

The sharp rap of wood on stone interrupted his thoughts, and he turned, reminding himself just in time to avoid any quick movement which might suggest impatience. The *kholokhanzir's* personal herald met his eyes, gripping the elaborately carved haft of his gemmed pike of office. There was more than a little white in the Orion's tawny felinoid pelt, but his spine was straight and he bowed with limber dignity. Then he straightened and beckoned politely for Mulrooney to follow.

The herald led him down a sunny hall fringed by balconies with balustrades entwined in nodding tendrils of ornamental vines. It wasn't a long walk, but Mulrooney's heart was beating fast when the herald knocked at the door at its end. Two statue-still guards flanked it, armed not with ornamental, palace-duty weapons but with businesslike needle rifles and side arms. Then the herald opened the door and bowed him through.

Mulrooney entered with a crisp stride, then stopped dead. He'd expected the *kholokhanzir*, but it seemed he'd been summoned to meet another.

He recovered and moved forward once more towards the ancient Orion seated on the cushion-strewn dais in the center of the room. He was bent with age, but his silvered pelt still showed the midnight black of the noblest Orion bloodlines.

Mulrooney stopped a precise three meters from the dais and pressed his clenched right hand to his chest as he performed his most graceful bow. Then he straightened and stood silently, giving no sign of his racing thoughts, as he met the old, knowing eyes of Liharnow'hirtalkin, *Khan'a'khanaaeee* of all the Orions.

"Greetings, Ambassador," the Khan said, and Mulrooney swallowed. Orions guarded their khan's person fanatically, yet he and Liharnow were alone. It was unheard of for any person not sworn to *hirikolus* or *hirikrinzi*—much less an alien—to be allowed into the Khan's presence unguarded, and there was no protocol to guide him in modes of address, for the Khan *never* spoke directly to a foreign envoy.

"Greetings, *Hia'khan*." He hoped it was an appropriate response.

"I have asked you here to discuss a most urgent matter," Liharnow came to the point with typical Orion brevity. "It is vital that there be no misunderstanding, so I ask you to forego the courtesies of diplomacy. I shall speak my mind fully and frankly, and I wish you to do the same."

"Of course, *Hia'khan*," Mulrooney replied. He had no choice but to accept whatever ground rules the Khan chose to set.

"Thank you." Liharnow settled more comfortably into his cushions, combing his shoulder-wide whiskers, and his ears inclined forward as if to underscore his serious mood.

"Two weeks ago, the Tenth Destroyer Squadron, commanded by Lord Talphon and stationed in the Lorelei System, was treacherously attacked." Mulrooney stiffened. There could be only one Orion response to an attack they labeled "treacherous."

"The attackers apparently entered the system through its sixth warp point, the one which your astrographers call 'Chaaraahn's Ferry,' and enticed Lord Talphon into attack range with a false parley offer. The frequencies of their drive fields matched none in our Navy's data base, but they identified themselves"—the Khan's eyes locked with the ambassador's—"as Terrans."

Despite himself, Mulrooney gasped, and the Khan shifted his ears slowly, as if obscurely satisfied.

"Lord Talphon's courier drones bore our equivalent of your Code Omega. They were dispatched very early in the engagement, as it was obvious his ships could not survive. Their messages were transmitted to *Valkha'zeeranda* by the warp point relay net and reached here five days ago. During those five days, our intelligence service has analyzed Lord Talphon's report and reached certain conclusions.

"First, the attackers did employ Terran Federation Navy communication protocols, although they were of an obsolete nature. Second, the single ship name provided by the enemy was *Kepahlar*"— Liharnow did much better with the Terran name than Khardanish had managed—"and our xenologists have identified this as the name of an ancient Terran scientist. Third, all communications from the enemy were in Terran Standard English. From these findings, a board of inquiry has judged that the attackers were in fact a Terran survey force."

Mulrooney's face was white.

"There are, however, several points which puzzle me," the Khan went on levelly. "The odd drive frequencies are one such point, as also are the peculiar communications protocols employed. In addition, our intelligence arm has observed no re-deployment of additional Federation units, nor is the Lorelei System of great military value. Finally, I have reviewed Lord Talphon's last report, and I am at least partially inclined to accept his hypothesis as to his attackers' identity. I do not believe the Federation attacked the Tenth Squadron," Mulrooney's shoulders relaxed, only to tighten afresh as Liharnow finished, "but I suspect its attackers *were* Terrans."

"*Hia'khan*," the ambassador began, "I—"

"A moment, if you please," the Khan said softly, and Mulrooney closed his mouth. "Lord Talphon concluded that these unknown 'Terrans' might be descended from survivors of the Terran colonization fleet attacked in Lorelei by the Eighty-First Flotilla in 2206, who fled down 'Chaaraahn's Ferry.' If this is indeed the case, the Federation Navy and Assembly cannot, of course, have ordered the attack, yet it was still the work of Terrans.

"I make this point," Liharnow said very carefully and distinctly, "because a majority of the Strategy Board have officially advised the *Khan'a'khanaaeee* that they reject Lord Talphon's hypothesis and that, even if he were correct, that fact could not in their judgment absolve Terra of responsibility. They recommend"—he met Mulrooney's eyes once more—"that the Treaty of Valkha be immediately repudiated as the first step in a renewed war with the Federation."

"*Hia'khan*," Mulrooney chose his words as carefully as the Khan, "this is the first I have heard of any of these events. My government will be as shocked by them as your own, but I implore you to proceed with restraint. If the Khanate attacks the Federation, we will have no choice but to defend ourselves, and the consequences for both our peoples will be terrible."

"That," Liharnow said quietly, "is why I have summoned you in this irregular fashion. I have over-ruled the Strategy Board"—Mulrooney breathed in thankfully—"so far, and First Fang Lokarnah has supported my decision, but our courses of action are limited."

"First, we may accede to the demands of the Strategy Board. Second, we may punish these Terrans ourselves, as honor demands. Third, we may require the Federation to punish them. Should we accept the Strategy Board's recommendations, the result will certainly be general war. Should we punish them ourselves, we embark upon an almost equally dangerous road, for I cannot believe the Assembly would permit the Federation Navy to stand idle while we kill Terrans, regardless of their origin, for attacking the ships of a navy with whom they may believe themselves to be still at war. But, Ambassador, should we adopt the third option, the Federation may still find itself in a most unenviable position.

"You know our honor code. My warriors' blood has been shed by *shirnowmakaie*, oath-breakers who have violated their own sworn offer to parley in peace. There must be *khiinarma*, scale-balancing. I could not deny that even if I wished to, and Ambassador"—the Khan's eyes were cold—"I do not wish to. There is one and only one way in which the Federation may intercede between the *Zheeerlikou'valkhannaieee* and those who have attacked us."

"And that way is, *Hia'khan*?" It was a question, but Mulrooney's tone said he already knew the answer.

"The Federation must become *khimhok ia' Zheeerlikou'valkhannaieee*," the Khan said softly, and Mulrooney swallowed. The term had no precise Terran equivalent, but it translated roughly as "scale-bearer to the Orions." In effect, the Terran Federation must step into the Khanate's place, assuming the duty to punish those who had offended. Yet it was far more complex than that, and his brain raced as he tried to envision all the implications.

The Federation would have a free hand but no Orion assistance. From the moment Terra accepted the "scale-bearer" role, the Khanate would stand totally aloof, and the Alliance's mutual assistance clauses could not be invoked. Worse, in a way, the final resolution must be acceptable to the Khanate. The Federation might choose to be merciful or harsh, but if the Orions did not perceive the ultimate solution as one which satisfied their own honor, the *Federation* would assume the guilt which the Khan had now assigned solely to those beings who had attacked his ships, and the consequences of that did not bear thinking upon.

"*Hia'khan*," the ambassador said finally, "I will transmit your words to my government, yet I must tell you that I foresee grave difficulties. If, indeed, those who attacked you are Terrans, then the people of the Federation will find it most difficult to demand blood balance of them."

"I understand," Liharnow said gravely, "for we would find it difficult to demand *vilknarma* of *Zheeerlikou'valkhannaieee* who had been lost for two of our centuries and attacked Terran warships in ignorance of the truth. Indeed, I understand too well, and that is one reason I would prefer to place the matter in Human hands. Honor demands punishment for treachery, yet if these Terrans truly believe we are still at war, then they did well to defend their own people, however dishonorable the manner in which they did so.

"Moreover," he continued even more seriously, "I have spent my life teaching my people the Galaxy can belong neither to he who is too cowardly to fight nor to he who is too stupid to know when *not* to fight. It has not been easy, and suspicion of other races remains strong, but I do not wish to see the Treaty of Valkha torn up and lost while our peoples destroy one another. And so I make this offer not just as Liharnow but as *Khan'a'khanaaeee*.

"We have no colonies between Lorelei and our own fortifications. Should the Federation become *khimhok ia' Zheeerlikou'valkhannaieee*, the Khanate will cede the Lorelei System to the Federation and withdraw all units from its borders. We will regard the affair as an internal problem of the Federation, to be settled by the Federation, and we will renounce *vilknarma* and accept reparations and *shirnowkashaik*, acknowledgment of guilt by the offenders. My people will find this difficult to bear, for we do not equate reparations with restitution as yours do, but if I accept in their name I sacrifice only my own honor, and they will abide by my pledged oath. This I will give in the cause of peace."

Mulrooney drew a very deep breath. The Khan's offer was an enormous concession, and the ambassador allowed himself to feel cautiously hopeful for the first time since the interview had begun.

"I thank you, *Hia'khan*," he said with utmost sincerity, "and I will immediately transmit your generous offer to Old Terra."

"My heart is not generous," Liharnow said flatly. "It cries out for *vilknarma* from the *chofaki* who have done this thing. Were they not Terrans, I would crush them into dust, but I cannot heed my heart in this. It is a decision of state, and so I must decide it, so hear my oath, Ambassador. I do not hold your government responsible, and I swear upon the honor of my clan fathers and of Valkha, shield-bearer to Hiranow'khanark, that I will sheathe my claws. Whoever these *chofaki* and wherever they spring from, I declare that I will accept the Federation as *khimhok*, to act in my stead and the stead of all my people. I have spoken."

The aged Khan lowered his ears and raised one hand in dismissal, and Ambassador Francis Mulrooney turned silently to leave.

CHAPTER THREE

The Peace Fleet

Howard Anderson was in a grumpy mood as he walked through Federation Hall's huge doors onto the Chamber's marble floor. He supposed change was inevitable, but in *his* day, the Legislative Assembly had simply called its meeting place the Assembly Chamber, and the new, highfaluting, title irritated him immensely. "*Chamber of Worlds*" indeed! It was all part of the damned imperial trappings—and so was the revolting deference everyone insisted on paying *him*. He suppressed an urge to kick the lictor who escorted him almost reverently to his seat, then sat and listened to the rustling mutter as the Chamber filled.

"Hello, Howard."

Anderson looked up and smiled as a small, uniformed figure paused beside him.

"What's an honest sailor doing in this whorehouse, Chien-lu?"

"I admire the effort you put into perfecting your curmudgeonly image, Howard, but you might consider the virtue of an occasional courteous word."

"Damn it, man, I'm a hundred and fifty years old! If I can't be a cranky, difficult son-of-a-bitch, who can?"

"Given how many people feel you *are* the Federation, I might suggest a proper decorum is in order," Admiral Li Chien-lu said with gentle malice.

"Do that and I'll drop kick your scrawny Oriental ass clear to the speaker's podium!" Anderson snorted, and the admiral laughed.

"Very well, Howard. Play your silly game if it amuses you."

"Damn straight it does." Anderson thumped the chair beside him with the gnarled walking stick he affected. "Sit down, Chien-lu." His grumpy tone had become serious. "I want to talk to you." Li hesitated, and Anderson's blue eyes hardened. "*Now*, Admiral," he said softly, and Li sat with a small shrug.

"You take unfair advantage of our relationship, you know," he said mildly. "A fleet admiral is no longer an ensign on your HQ staff."

"Granted. But we've known each other longer than either of us wants to remember, and I want to know what the hell Sakanami thinks he's doing."

"Precisely what he's said." Admiral Li shrugged again. "I won't say I'd do it the same way myself, but he hasn't slipped me any secret orders, if that's what you mean."

"I wouldn't put it past Sakanami—or that vulture Waldeck—but that wasn't what I meant. I suppose I should have asked what you and the CNO think *you're* doing?"

"Howard," Admiral Li said plaintively, "why is that when *you* were President 'cheerful and willing obedience to the lawful commands of civilian superiors' was a virtue?"

"When *I* was President, you insubordinate young sprout, your civilian superiors knew what they were doing. This bunch of fuck-ups wouldn't know a sane military policy if it shot them in the ass, and you know it!"

"You know a serving officer has no right to admit that. Besides, you're far more eloquent than I. And you carry a bigger stick."

Anderson grunted and folded his hands over the head of his cane. Despite the lightness of his earlier words, he knew Li was right. Commander Anderson had won the first battle of ISW-1, and Admiral of the Fleet Anderson had ended it as chief of naval operations, a post he'd retained throughout ISW-2. In a very real sense, the Terran Federation Navy had been his personal creation, and then he'd stepped over into politics. By the time of the Third Interstellar War, he'd been serving his second term as President Anderson. Even now, when he was all but retired, he commanded a unique respect.

Unfortunately, respect and power weren't the same thing.

There'd been intrigues enough within the Fleet, but at least responsibility and the chain of command were always reasonably well defined. Politics were different. He'd never been comfortable with greasy-mouthed politicos, and he'd spent a great deal of his time in office keeping people like Sakanami Hideoshi and Pericles Waldeck *out* of office.

He sighed, feeling the full weight of his age. He supposed those two—and especially Waldeck—bothered him so because he was at least partly responsible for their existence, but they represented a new and dangerous power in the Assembly, and what Anderson didn't know about their plans worried him far more than what he did.

He'd always been unhappy over the chartered companies, yet the

Federation of a century ago could never have built the Navy *and* financed colonization without ruinous taxation. The Khanate had simply been too big to match credit-for-credit, even with humanity's greater productivity, so something had to give, and that something had been BuCol.

It had made good financial sense to license chartered companies to finance colonization as a profit-making proposition. It had freed current revenues and expanded the tax base at an incredible rate, and Anderson knew he'd been at least as strident about the need to fund the Fleet as anyone. But the companies had been too successful. The Assembly had been unable to resist turning them into money machines, offering ever greater incentives. Before the practice finally ended in 2275, some of the chartered companies had acquired virtual ownership of entire worlds.

Yet Anderson was less concerned by the planetary oligarchies the chartered companies had birthed on what were coming to be known as the "Corporate Worlds" than by the way those oligarchies were extending themselves into an interstellar political machine of immense potential power.

The chartered companies had concentrated on choice real estate in strategic star systems, which had suited the Federation's military needs by providing populations to support Fleet bases and fortifications in choke point systems. But the Corporate World oligarchs were more concerned with the economic implications of their positions. Their warp lines carried the life blood of the Federation's trade, and they used that advantage ruthlessly to exploit less fortunately placed worlds.

Anderson found their tactics reprehensible, and he was deeply concerned by the hostility they provoked among the Out Worlds, but he would be safely dead before *that* problem came home to roost. He'd done his best to sound a warning, yet no one seemed to be listening, so he'd concentrated on more immediate worries, particularly military policy.

Now that the oligarchs had it made, they were far from eager to create potential rivals, so they'd cheerfully repealed the chartered company statutes and resurrected BuCol. They'd been less interested in paying for it, however, and they'd beaten off every effort to raise taxes. Instead, their Liberal-Progressive Party had found the money by slashing military appropriations.

The Fleet was badly understrength, and the state of the Reserve was scandalous. Officially, BuShips' moth-balled Reserve should have at least seventy-five percent of Battle Fleet's active strength in each class, yet it boasted barely thirty-six percent of its authorized numerical strength . . . and less than ten percent of its authorized tonnage. And the ships it *did* have hadn't been modernized in thirty years! It was bitterly ironic, but the worlds settled under a military-economic policy of expedience were now killing the very military which had spawned them.

The LibProgs might point to the Treaty of Valkha and fifty years of peace, but Howard Anderson knew better than most that when something went wrong it usually did so with dispatch, and Battle Fleet was twenty percent understrength for its peacetime obligations. In the event of a shooting war, any substantial losses would be catastrophic.

Which, he reminded himself, straightening in his chair, was why Sakanami's current policy was the next best thing to certifiable lunacy.

"Chien-lu," he said softly, "they *can't* send that much of the Fleet into Lorelei. Not until we know exactly what we're *really* up against."

"Then you'd better convince them of it," Admiral Li sighed. "For your personal—and private—information, Admiral Brandenburg and I said the same thing. Loudly. We have, however, been overruled by the defense minister and President Sakanami. And that, as you must realize as well as I, is that."

Anderson began a hot retort, then stopped and nodded unhappily.

"You're right," he said. "I'll just have to take the bastards on again and hope. In the meantime, how's the family?"

"Well, thank you." Admiral Li's smile thanked him for the change of subject. "Hsu-ling has emigrated, you know."

"No, I didn't know, but I approve. The Heart Worlds are getting too damned bureaucratic for my taste. If I were a half-century younger, I'd go out-world myself. Where is he?"

"He and my charming daughter-in-law signed up for the Hangchow Colony, and you should see the holos they've sent back! Their planetary charter is a bit traditional for my taste, but I'm seriously considering retiring there myself."

"You do that, Chien-lu, and I'll load this ancient carcass on a ship for a visit."

"It's a deal," Admiral Li said, and grinned toothily.

" . . . and so," Defense Minister Hamid O'Rourke said, "in accordance with the President's directives, the required units have been ordered to rendezvous in the Redwing System to proceed to Lorelei in company with Special Envoy Aurelli. That concludes my brief, Madam Speaker."

"Thank you, Mister O'Rourke." Speaker of the Legislative Assembly Chantal Duval's cool, clear voice carried well. Now her image replaced O'Rourke's on the huge screen about her podium. "Is there any discussion?"

Howard Anderson pressed his call key and watched Duval's eyes drop to her panel.

"The Chair recognizes President Emeritus Howard Anderson," she said, and the mutter of side conversations ended as Anderson replaced her image on the huge screen behind her podium. Even after all these years, his ego found the attention flattering, and he propped himself a shade more aggressively on his cane as an antidote.

"Thank you, Madam Speaker. I will be brief, but I would be derelict in my duty if I did not voice my concern—my very *grave* concern—over the Administration's plans." The silence became a bit more profound, and he saw a few uneasy faces. His caustic attacks on the Sakanami-Waldeck military policies had a nasty habit of singling out delegates who'd received their kilo of flesh to support them.

"Ladies and Gentlemen, we have agreed to assume the role of *khimhok* in this confrontation between the individuals who call themselves 'Thebans' and the Khanate. As one who knows Khan Liharnow personally, I may, perhaps, have a better grasp than many of his tremendous concession in allowing us to do so, and, as President Sakanami, I see no alternative but to accept it. Yet we must be cautious. While circumstantial evidence certainly appears to confirm that the Thebans are descendants of the Lorelei Massacre's survivors, all the evidence to date is just that—circumstantial. And even if they have been correctly identified, aspects of their conduct both before and since their attack on the Tenth Destroyer Squadron cause me to have grave reservations.

"First, they have, as yet, failed to explain to my satisfaction why they refused even to consider that Lieutenant Johansen's messages outlined the true state of affairs. It is evident from the courier drones the Khanate has made available to us that they never had the least intention of making rendezvous to confirm or disprove her statements; their sole purpose was to close to decisive range and annihilate Lord Talphon's command.

"Second, they have permitted only unarmed courier vessels to enter Lorelei since our first attempts to communicate with them, and they continue to refuse all physical contact. Their visual links to our courier ships have also been most unsatisfactory, and I find these 'technical difficulties' of theirs suspiciously persistent.

"Third, they continue to refuse to explain how colony ships survived transit into the Theban System when no survey ships have done so.

"Fourth, they have *now* refused all further negotiations until we demonstrate our ability to protect them from Orion reprisals by dispatching to Lorelei sufficient forces to mount a creditable defense of the system. Coming after their steadfast refusal to permit even a single destroyer into the system, this seems a trifle peculiar, to say the very least."

He paused to gauge the effect of his remarks. One or two faces looked thoughtful, but most were bored. None of what he'd said, after all, was new.

"I can readily understand that a colony which has been isolated for almost a century would be cautious. I can even understand a certain degree of paranoid intransigence, given the traumatic circumstances which carried their ancestors to Thebes in the first place. What I do *not* understand is why that cautious culture should now obligingly invite us to send no less than thirty percent of Battle Fleet to their very doorstep. It is all very well to call it a major step forward, but it is a step which appears to make very little sense. If they are truly beginning to feel more confident, why do they not invite one of our harmless, unarmed courier craft to make the first contact? Surely that would be the rational approach. *This* sounds entirely too much like their offer to Lord Talphon."

This time, he saw some concern in his audience when he paused.

"Certainly it would be insane of any single planet to challenge both the Orions and us, but we may err seriously if we assume they are rational by normal standards. Were the Fleet up to strength, I might feel less concern, but the Fleet is *not* up to strength, and we can neither be certain what a potentially irrational culture may do nor risk substantial Fleet losses."

He paused once more, wondering if he should state his case even more strongly, then decided against it. The LibProgs already called him a senile crackpot in private.

"Madam Speaker, while military and diplomatic policy fall within the purview of the Executive, the Constitution grants the Assembly an oversight role, specifically confirmed by the Executive Powers Act of 2283. I therefore move that this Assembly instruct the Administration to hold its 'Peace Fleet' at readiness in Redwing pending a fresh approach to the Thebans, and that the Thebans be informed that the Federation requires direct, face-to-face contact before any Federation warship enters the Lorelei System. If these people are sincerely eager to rejoin the rest of humanity, they will accept. If they are not sincere, it would be the height of foolhardiness for us to expose so substantial a portion of our Navy to risk without overwhelming support.

"Thank you."

He sat in silence, and Speaker Duval's image reappeared.

"It has been moved that the Administration be instructed to hold the 'Peace Fleet' in Redwing until such time as the Thebans agree to direct contact with Federation negotiators," she said clearly. "Is there a second?"

"Madam Speaker, I second the motion." It was Andrew Spruance of Nova Terra, one of Anderson's Conservative Party allies.

"Ladies and Gentlemen of the Assembly, the motion has been seconded. Is there any debate?" An attention chime sounded almost instantly, and Duval looked up. "The Chair recognizes the Honorable Assemblyman for Christophon."

"Thank you, Madam Speaker." Pericles Waldeck, the LibProg Assembly leader and Anderson's personal *bête-noire*, smiled from the screen. "As the distinguished President Emeritus, I will be brief.

"No one in this Chamber can match President Anderson's lifetime of experience. As both war hero and statesman, he deserves our most serious attention. In this instance, however, I am unable to agree with him. Prudence, certainly, is much to be admired, but President Sakanami has been prudent. Three months have passed since the regrettable attack on the Orion squadron—three months in which no Theban vessel has attempted to depart the Lorelei System or fired upon any of our courier craft within it. They have been cautious, true, and perhaps less than courteous and forthcoming by our standards, but let us remember their history. Is it reasonable to expect any culture which began in massacre and desperate flight from the Orions, which must have spent virtually an entire century in preparation to return and, if necessary, confront those same Orions, to react in any other way?

"I am not well versed in technical matters, but many experts have agreed that the communications problems cited by the Thebans are, indeed, possible, particularly when technologies attempt to interface once more after a ninety-one-year separation. And their sudden about-face in requesting a powerful Fleet presence does not strike me as inconsistent. After all their people have endured, an element of 'show me' must be inevitable where their very survival is concerned.

"Finally, let us consider the strength President Sakanami proposes to commit to his Peace Fleet. We will be dispatching twenty-one capital ships, fifteen fleet and light carriers, and a strong escort of lighter units. The Thebans have shown no reluctance to allow our couriers to approach Charon's Ferry, and their fleet strength in Lorelei has never exceeded seventy vessels, only twelve of them capital ships. While this is an impressive strength for any isolated system—indeed, a strength which, following the Thebans' reunification with the rest of humanity, will do much to repair the weakness which President Anderson has often decried in our own Navy—it cannot be considered a serious threat to the Peace Fleet.

"With all of this in mind, and conceding every argument which urges caution, I cannot support President Anderson's contention that still more caution is required. Let us not jeopardize the chance to achieve a quick and peaceful resolution by an appearance of irresolution. Ladies and Gentlemen of the Assembly, I ask that President Emeritus Anderson's motion be denied.

"Thank you."

He sat, and Anderson leaned back, his own face expressionless, as the LibProg steamroller went smoothly to work. A dozen delegates rose to endorse Waldeck's words. They couldn't have been more respectful and deferential towards the Federation's "Grand Old Man," yet their very deference emphasized that he was an *old* man—one, perhaps, whom age had rendered alarmist.

And, he was forced to admit, many of their arguments made sense. A dangerously complacent sense, perhaps, but one against which he could offer little more than instinct. It might be an instinct honed by over a century of military and political service, but it couldn't be quantified as ship strengths could, and it wasn't enough to convince the Liberal Democrats or the handful of Independents to join his Conservatives in bucking a powerful president and his party under the terms of an act whose constitutionality had always been suspect. . . .

The final vote rejected his motion by more than three to one.

CHAPTER FOUR

A Slaughter of Innocents

Fleet Admiral Li Chien-lu frowned as Special Envoy Victor Aurelli entered his private briefing room and sat. Aurelli's patrician face wore a faintly supercilious smile, and Li was hard pressed to keep his frown from becoming a glare as he placed a memo chip on the conference table.

"Thank you for coming so promptly, Mister Aurelli," he said.

"You sounded rather emphatic," Aurelli replied with a slight shrug.

"I suppose I did. And if I did, Mister Aurelli, *this*"—Li tapped the chip sharply, eyes suddenly dagger-sharp—"is to blame."

"I take it those are my modest amendments to your . . . battle plans?"

"No, Mister Aurelli, they're your unwarranted intrusion into my standard operational directives."

Two pairs of eyes locked across the conference table, and there was no affability in either.

"Admiral," the envoy finally broke the silence, "this is a diplomatic mission, not an assault on a Rigelian PDC, and I do not propose to permit you or anyone else to jeopardize its success. This crisis is too grave to justify offering gratuitous insult to Theban sensibilities."

"Considering those same Thebans' record to date," Li returned coldly, "I fail to see how any prudent deployment of my forces could be deemed a 'gratuitous insult' to their gentler natures. And, sir, while you may command the mission, *I* command this task force."

"Which is a subordinate component of the over-all mission, Admiral. I direct your attention to paragraph three of your orders."

Aurelli's gentle smile made Li wish briefly that they were on one of the Out Worlds which had resurrected the code duello.

"I am aware of my instructions to cooperate with you, sir, but Fleet orders are for a flag officer's guidance. If in his judgment the situation on the spot requires prudent and timely precautions not visualized when those orders were written, he is expected to take them. And, Mister Aurelli, this latest Theban 'request' requires the precautions laid down in my ops order."

Aurelli sighed. The admiral was a typical Academy product: dedicated, professional, and utterly unable to see any further than his gunnery console. Of course the Thebans were acting irrationally! What else could anyone expect from a colony with their history? How would Admiral Li have felt if a "negotiator" allied with the Rigelians had told *him* the Third Interstellar War was all a misunderstanding?

That was why this was too important to botch by letting the military fumble around in charge of it.

"Admiral Li," he said, "you may not believe this, but I sympathize with your concerns. As a military commander, it's your duty to project possible threats and counter them. I accept that. But in this instance, I must insist that you follow the instructions I've given you."

"No." Aurelli's eyebrows rose at Li's flat refusal. "The Thebans have 'requested' that we rendezvous with them on their warp point with our entire strength. That will place my carriers and battle-cruisers twenty hours from the nearest friendly warp point. My battle-line units will be over a full day from it. I will not place my ships and my people in a position from which they cannot withdraw in the event of hostile action."

It was Li's turn to lean back and glare. Victor Aurelli was an ass. The sort of idiot who chopped away at every military budget on the theory that if the Fleet could do its job—somehow—last year, it could do it with a bit less this year. And now he wanted a third of Battle Fleet to advance beyond withdrawal range into a star system occupied by a fleet which had already demonstrated that it would shoot a man out from under a flag of truce?

"Admiral, have you detected any additional Theban units?"

"No, but a star system is a very large haystack. Against a ship with powered-down systems, our scanners have a maximum detection range of under five light-minutes under ideal conditions. The entire Orion Navy could be out there, and without a proper network of scan sats we'd never know it."

"But you have *not* detected any additional units?" Aurelli pressed, and Li shook his head curtly. "And if there were any such units, could they enter attack range without being detected?"

"Not without better cloaking technology than we know of," Li admitted.

"Excellent. Then whether there are additional Theban warships or not, we need concern ourselves immediately only with those we can detect. Given that, would you say you were confident of your ability to engage and defeat, if necessary, the forces you've so far identified?"

"Given that they have no radical technical or tactical surprises for me, and that there are no additional hostile forces hidden away, yes."

Aurelli hid a sigh. Why did the military always insist on qualifiers? They used the same worn-out tactic every time they demanded a bigger budget. If the Orions do this, if a new Rigelian Protectorate turns up, if the Ophiuchi do that, if, if, if, *if!*

"Admiral, if you were defending the Centauris System and the sole warp point to Sol, would *you* allow a hostile force into Centauris instead of trying to stop it at the warp points?"

"Under some circumstances, yes," Li said surprisingly. "If my forces were strong enough to defeat the enemy in a head-on engagement but too weak to block all potential entry warp points, I would concede the warp points rather than risk being defeated in detail. And"— his dark eyes stabbed the envoy like a force beam—"if I could, I'd suck the hostiles too deep in-system to run before I let them know I had the strength to smash them."

"I'm not going to argue anymore, Admiral." Aurelli's voice was cold. "You will muster the entire task force—not just a screen of cruisers and battle-cruisers—and advance to Charon's Ferry. You will rendezvous with the Thebans, and you will refrain from potentially provocative actions."

"Sir, I must respectfully refuse to do so," Li said equally coldly.

"You have no choice." Aurelli's thin smile was dangerous as he reached inside his jacket. "President Sakanami anticipated that there might be . . . differences of opinion between the military and civilian components of this mission, Admiral Li, and he took steps to resolve them."

Li unfolded the single sheet of paper, and his face tightened. The orders were crisp, cold, and to the point, and he refolded them very carefully before he returned them to the envelope.

"Do you really think they'll do it?"

First Admiral Lantu glanced at Fleet Chaplain Manak as he spoke, and the churchman shrugged. His yellow eyes were thoughtful as he stroked his cranial carapace, and his ring of office glinted on his three-fingered hand.

"Yes," he said finally. "I had my doubts when the Prophet decreed it, but Holy Terra works in mysterious ways. It would seem the infidels have been blinded by our words."

"I hope you're right," Lantu grunted, turning back to his large-scale nav display. The light dots of the infidel task force moved steadily towards him, led by the single destroyer squadron he'd sent out as guides and spies. It was hard for Lantu to believe anyone could be this stupid.

"I believe I am," Manak replied with the serenity of his faith. "The cursed Orions fell into your snare, my son. If the Satan-Khan's own children can be taken so easily, should not the apostate fall still more easily?"

Lantu didn't reply. Satan's children or no, those Orions had shown courage. It had been obvious from the initial reports that the boarding attack had been a total surprise. There'd been no hope of organized resistance, yet somehow *Znamae*'s bridge officers had held long enough to blow their fusion plants . . . and take *Kepler* with them.

He glanced at the huge portrait of the Angel Saint-Just on the flag bridge bulkhead and closed his inner eyelids in sympathy. How must the Holy Messenger feel to see his own people brought so low?

Admiral Li sat on the superdreadnought *Everest*'s flag bridge and ignored Victor Aurelli. Neither training nor personality would let him show his contempt before his officers, but he was damned if he'd pretend he liked the man.

"Coming into scan range of the Ferry now, sir," his chief of staff reported. "The drive source count looks consistent."

"Thank you, Christine. Any new messages from the Thebans?"

"None, sir."

Li nodded and watched his display. The "Peace Fleet" continued its stately advance at four percent of light-speed, and he tried not to think of how far from home they were.

"Hmmmm . . ." Admiral Lantu studied the images relayed from his flanking destroyers, then gestured to his flag captain. "Look there. See how carefully they're protecting those units?"

"Yes, sir." Captain Kurnash rubbed the ridge of his snout, staring at the ships at the center of the infidel formation. "Those are the ones that carry the small attack craft, sir."

"I know." Lantu drummed on the arm of his command chair and thought. Their contact vessels had watched the infidels closely since they'd entered Lorelei, and he'd viewed the reports on those small craft with interest. Their routine operations had shown they were fast and highly maneuverable, though he had no idea what their maximum operating range might be or what weapons they carried. Missiles, most probably, but what sort of missiles? The People had nothing like them, and the lack of any sort of comparative meter-stick bothered him.

"I think we'd better deal with them first, Kurnash," he said at last. "Can we get salvos in there?"

"Certainly, sir. We won't be able to get to beam range immediately, but if they really wanted to protect them, they should have left them out of missile range."

"Thank Terra for Her favors, Captain, and get your revised fire plan set up. Oh, and send a drone to the reserve with the same instructions."

"Approaching rendezvous," Commander Christine Gianelli reported. "Range to Theban flagship fifteen light-seconds. ETA to contact six minutes."

"And the Thebans' status?" Li asked sharply.

"Shields down, as our own. We're picking up a lot of primary and secondary sensor emissions—mostly point defense tracking stations, though CIC thinks some may be targeting systems—but no Erlicher emissions, so at least they aren't warming up any force beams or primaries."

"Thank you." Li turned his chair to face Aurelli at last. "Mister Envoy, we are coming onto station," he said with cold formality. "I suggest you hail the Theban representatives."

"Thank you, Admiral, I think that would be an excellent idea," Aurelli said smugly, and Li nodded curtly to his com officer.

"The infidels are hailing us, Holiness."

Fleet Chaplain Manak glanced at his assistant and nodded.

"Are the computers ready?"

"They are, Holiness."

"Then we shall respond." Manak glanced at Admiral Lantu. "Are you ready, my son?"

"We are, Holiness." Manak noted the tension in Lantu's eyes and smiled. He'd watched the admiral grow to adulthood and knew how strong he was, but even the strongest could be excused a bit of strain at such a moment.

"Be at ease, my son," he said gently, "and prepare your courier drone. We shall give the infidels one last chance to prove they remain worthy of Holy Terra. If they are not, She will deliver them into your hand. Stand by."

"Standing by, Holiness."

"Greetings, Mister Aurelli. My name is Mannock."

The voice was clear, despite the poor visual image, and Victor Aurelli wondered what mix of colonist dialects had survived to produce its accent. The Standard English was crisp, but there was a hard edge to the vowels and a peculiar lisp to the sibilants. Not an unpleasant sound, but definitely a bit odd. And this Mannock was a handsome enough fellow—or might have been, if not for the flickering fuzz of those persistent technical problems.

"I'm pleased to meet you, sir," he replied, "and I look forward to meeting you in person."

"As I look forward to meeting you." The poor signal quality prevented Aurelli from noticing that the computer-generated image's lips weren't quite perfectly synchronized with the words.

"Then let us begin, Mister Mannock."

"Of course. We are already preparing to initiate docking with your flagship. In the meantime, however, I have a question I would like to ask."

Of course, Mister Mannock. Ask away."

"Do you"—the voice was suddenly more intent—"accept the truth of the Prophet's teaching, Mister Aurelli?"

Aurelli blinked, then frowned at the com screen.

"The teaching of *which* prophet, Mister Mannock?" he asked . . . and the universe exploded in his face.

"Incoming fire!" someone screamed, and Captain Nadine Wu, CO of TFNS *Deerhound*, stared at her display. Missiles were coming at her carrier—not one, or two, or a dozen, but scores of them!

"Impact in eighteen seconds—mark!" her gunnery officer snapped. "Weapons free. Stand by point defense."

"Launch the ready fighters!" Captain Wu ordered, never looking away from her plot. The stand-by squadron might get off before those missiles struck. No one else would.

"Oh, dear God!"

The anguished whisper came from Victor Aurelli, but Admiral Li had no time to spare the envoy.

"Execute Plan Charley!" he barked, and his answering missiles whipped away. But he needed time to power up the shields and energy weapons Aurelli had forbidden him to activate on the way in, and *Everest* trembled in agony as the first warheads erupted against her naked drive field.

"Captain Bowman reports we're streaming air, sir," Gianelli reported. "Datalink gone—we're out of the net."

"Acknowledged. Get those beams up, Christine! We need them badly—"

"Energy fire on *Cottonmouth*!" Li turned to his ops officer in surprise. Energy fire? How? They hadn't picked up any Erlicher emissions, so it couldn't be force beams, and the battleship was too far out for effective laser fire.

"Specify!"

"Unknown, sir. It appears to be some sort of x-ray laser."

"*X-ray laser?*" Li stole a second to glance at his own read-outs and winced as the impossible throughput readings registered.

"*Cottonmouth* is Code Omega, sir," Gianelli reported flatly. "And the carrier group's taking a pounding. *Deerhound* and *Corgy* are gone. So is *Bogue*, but she got about half her group off before they nailed her."

"Many hits on enemy flagship," Gunnery announced, and Li watched *Saint-Just*'s dot flash and blink. His missiles were getting through despite her readied point defense, but her armor must be incredible. Her shields were still down and fireballs spalled her drive field like hellish strobes, but she wasn't even streaming atmosphere yet!

"Admiral Li!" He looked up at his Plotting officer's summons. "We're picking up additional drive fields, sir—they're coming out of the Ferry!"

Dispassionate computers updated the display silently, and Li looked at the destruction of his task force. They must have had a courier drone on the trips, ready to go the instant Aurelli fumbled their question. Now the rest of their fleet—the fleet no Terran had ever seen—was coming through, and six more superdreadnoughts headed the parade.

He swore silently and ran his eyes back over his own battered force. The carriers had taken the worst pounding. Half were gone and most of the rest were cruelly mauled—the bastards must have gunned for them on purpose. His surviving units were getting their shields up at last, but most of the capital ships were already streaming air. At least half of them must have lost their datalink, which meant they'd be forced to fight as individuals against trios of enemy ships whose fire would be synchronized to the second. Worse, it was already obvious the "Peace Fleet's" supposed numerical advantage was, in fact, a disadvantage.

They'd timed it well. If he'd been only a little closer to the Ferry, he might have been able to bull through and sit on it, smashing their reserves as they made transit. As it was, he couldn't quite get there in time, and trying to would only put him closer to those damned lasers. They were almost as long-ranged as his force beams and, unlike force beams, they could stab straight through his shields. If he got even closer to them—

"Pull us back, Christine." He was amazed he sounded so calm.

"Aye, aye, sir," his chief of staff said levelly, though she knew as well as he that backing off the warp point was tantamount to admitting defeat.

If only more of his fighters had gotten into space! The ones which had launched were doing their best, but once their missiles were expended they would have only their single onboard laser mounts, because there would no longer be any hangar decks to rearm them. Only *Elkhound* and *Constellation* had gotten their full groups off, and even now heavy missile salvos were bearing down on both frantically evading carriers.

"*Sir!*" The utter disbelief in Gianelli's voice wrenched his head around. She sat bolt-upright at her console, her face white. "*Greyhound* reports she's being *boarded*, sir!"

"Ramming Fleet in position, Admiral. First *samurai* salvos away.

"Thank you, Plot. Captain Kurnash, where are my shields? I—Ahhhh!"

Saint-Just's shields snapped up, and Admiral Lantu grinned fiercely. These infidels clearly had no lasers to match his own. He didn't know what those long-ranged energy weapons of theirs were, but they couldn't reach through a shield as his could, and the massive armor his ships mounted as an anti-laser defense had served them well. The damage in the first exchange had gone in the People's favor by a wider margin than he had dared hope.

"They're pulling back, sir."

"I see it, Plot. Maneuvering, the fleet will advance."

"Aye, aye, sir."

Li Chien-lu shut it all out for a moment, forcing himself to think.

That first deadly salvo had gutted his carriers and blown too many of his capital ships out of their datanets, and the enemy's ability to board ships under way made an already desperate situation hopeless. Captain Bowman had *Everest*'s Marines racing for the armories, but they would be pathetically out-numbered when those "capital missile" vehicles got around to her. In a stand-up fight with the strength bearing down on them, his task force would be annihilated in thirty minutes of close action.

"Commander Gianelli."

"Yes, sir?"

"Order all escorts, battle-cruisers, and carriers to withdraw. The battle-line will advance and attack the enemy."

"Aye, aye, sir."

Admiral Li turned back to his plot as his battered formation unraveled. One or two battle-cruisers ignored the order, their drives already too damaged to run, and he doubted very many of those fleeing units would escape, but—

"What are you *doing*?!" A hand pounded his shoulder, and he turned almost calmly to meet Victor Aurelli's stunned eyes.

"I'm ordering my lighter units to run for it, Mister Aurelli."

"But . . . but . . ."

"They may have the speed for it," Li explained as if to a child. "We don't. But if we can make these bastards concentrate on us while the others run, we can at least give them a chance."

"But we'll all be *killed*!"

"Yes, Mister Aurelli, we will." Li watched his words hit the envoy like fists. It was very quiet on the bridge, despite the battle thundering about *Everest*'s hull, and the admiral's entire staff heard him as he continued coldly, "That's why I'm so glad you're aboard this ship."

He turned away from the terrified civilian to Commander Gianelli.

"Let's go get them, Christine."

CHAPTER FIVE

"A *khimhok* stands alone, Mister President"

Howard Anderson switched off his terminal and rose, rubbing his eyes, then folded his hands behind him and paced slowly about his small study.

During his own naval career, courier drones had been the only way to send messages between the stars, but the slow extension of the interstellar communications relays was changing that. No com signal could punch through a warp point, but drones could, and deep-space relays could beam their contents across the normal space between warp points at light-speed. Their cost tended to restrict them to wealthier, populous systems, but the Federation had taken pains to complete links all along its frontier with the Khanate.

Which meant Old Terra had learned of the disaster in Lorelei ten times as quickly as it might once have . . . for what it was worth.

He looked around his study unseeingly. Eighty percent of the "Peace Fleet" had died, but *Everest*'s Omega Drones had gotten off just before she blew her fusion plants. The data base download had included Chien-lu's log, and Anderson's fury had burned cold as he read the thoroughly illegal bootleg copy an old friend had passed him.

He picked up the message chip in age-gnarled fingers and wondered what the summons meant. Perhaps Sakanami had discovered he knew and meant to shut him up? If so, he was about to discover the limits of the presidency's power.

The aide rapped on the ornate doors, then opened them and stood aside, and Anderson stepped wordlessly into a magnificent office.

39

Its splendor was an expression of the power of the man in the president's chair, but he was unimpressed. He'd sat in that chair himself.

He stumped across the sea of crimson carpet, leaning on his cane. It was less of an affectation than it once had been. He'd been in his fifties before the antigerone treatments became available, and his body was finally beginning to fail. But his eyes remained as sharp as his brain, and they flitted busily about as he advanced upon his waiting hosts.

Sakanami Hideoshi sat behind the big desk, expressionless as a *kabuki* mask. Vice President Ramon Montoya and Hamid O'Rourke sat in armchairs by the coffee table, Pericles Waldeck stood gazing out the windows with ostentatious unconcern, and Erika Van Smitt, leader of the Liberal Democrats, sat across the coffee table from Montoya.

Quite a gathering, Anderson mused, choosing a chair beside Van Smitt. Add himself, and the people in this room represented the Administration and over ninety percent of the Assembly.

"Thank you for coming, Howard," Sakanami said, and Waldeck turned from the window with a smile. Anderson met it stonily, and it faded. The silence stretched out endlessly until Sakanami finally cleared his throat.

"I've asked you here because I need your advice, Howard."

"That's a novel admission," Anderson said, and the president winced.

"Please, Howard. I realize how you must feel, but—"

"I doubt very much," Anderson's voice was cold and precise, "that you have the least idea how I feel, Mister President." *If you did, you'd've had me searched for weapons, you son-of-a-bitch.*

"I—" Sakanami paused. "I suppose I deserved that, but I truly do need your help."

"In what way?"

"I need your experience. You've led the Federation through three wars, both as an admiral and as president. You understand what the Fleet needs to fight with and what it takes to produce it. I'd like to create a special cabinet post—Minister for War Production—and ask you to assume it."

"And what would the duties of this post be?"

"You'd be my direct representative, charged with rationalizing demand and output. If you took the post, I'd ask you to go out to Galloway's World. Admiral Antonov will be taking command in the Lorelei Sector, and I want you to help him coordinate the operations of the Fleet yard with its civilian counterparts before he ships out. Are you interested?"

"Would I retain the right to speak my mind, publicly as well as privately?" Anderson was surprised and—he admitted it—excited by the offer.

Sakanami glanced at Waldeck, then nodded firmly. "I couldn't expect the full benefit of your experience if you didn't."

"Then I accept, Mister President," Anderson said. His voice was still cold, but he was beginning to wonder if he'd misjudged Sakanami.

"Good. Good! And there's another thing I need from you, Howard. You're the only man on Old Terra who's ever personally met Khan Liharnow, and a message from you will carry more weight than one from me."

"A message to Liharnow?" Anderson's eyes narrowed once more. They'd shown him the carrot, now they were about to tell him how high he had to jump to get it. "What message?"

"We haven't released the report, but ONI has finished its analysis of Admiral Li's drones," O'Rourke answered for Sakanami. The defense minister faltered as Anderson turned his basilisk gaze on him, then continued.

"You must have heard rumors the Thebans aren't human after all. Well, we have positive confirmation they aren't. The battle-cruiser *Scimitar* got away, but not before she was boarded. The Thebans have some sort of personnel capsule—something like a short-ranged capital missile—that lets them literally shoot small boarding parties at a ship. They have to knock the shields down first, but they carry drive field penetrators like fighters and small craft. ONI puts their maximum range at about eight light-seconds.

"Anyway, *Scimitar*'s Marines took out her boarders, and the bodies are definitely non-human." He paused, as if that explained everything, and Anderson frowned. Obviously they didn't realize he'd already seen the original reports, but what were they driving at?

"I fail to see," he said into the expectant silence, "what that has to do with my acquaintance with Liharnow."

"Surely it's obvious that this changes everything, Howard." Pericles Waldeck's patronizing manner was one of several reasons Anderson detested him.

"How?" he asked coldly.

"Mister Anderson"—O'Rourke seemed stunned by his obtuseness—"we lost eighty percent of Admiral Li's force—over ninety percent of its tonnage, since none of the battle-line got away. That's more than a quarter of Battle Fleet!"

"I'm familiar with the figures, Mister O'Rourke."

"Well, don't you see, we agreed to intervene and handle the situation alone because we thought we were dealing with *humans*! We're not—and we don't have the least idea how powerful these Thebans really are. They *said* they had only one system, but they could have dozens. We need to invoke the Alliance and get the Orions in here to help!"

Anderson stared at him.

"We can't," he said sharply. "It's absolutely out of the question."

"Howard," Sakanami stepped into the breach, "I don't think we have any choice. It'll take us months to redeploy the Fleet, and if we do it'll leave the frontiers almost naked. We need the Orions."

"Don't you understand the Orion honor code?" Anderson demanded. "A *khimhok* stands alone, Mister President. If you ask Liharnow for help now, you're rejecting the role you *asked* him to let you assume! The best we can hope for is that he won't hold us responsible if the Thebans hit him again."

"But we accepted the role because we thought the Thebans were humans, and they aren't," Waldeck explained with elaborate patience.

"Which doesn't matter a good goddamn!" Anderson shot back. "Jesus, haven't you even *talked* to your xenologists?! To an Orion, an obligation is an obligation. If he makes a mistake, takes on a responsibility because of a misunderstanding, that's his problem; he'll handle it anyway or die trying."

"I think you're overreacting," Sakanami said.

"Like hell I am! Damn it, Liharnow put his own honor on the line to let you handle the Thebans! You go to him with an idea like this, and you'll have the fucking Orion Navy on your back, too."

"I find your language offensive, Howard," Waldeck said coldly.

"Well, fuck you and the horse you rode in on!" Anderson retorted. "I'll help clean up your goddamn mess, Wonder Boy, but I'll be damned if I help you make it any worse!"

"Howard—" Erika Van Smitt started pacifically.

"You stay out of this, Erika! All you did was support the Administration—don't screw up now and get roped into *this* insanity!"

"I've had just about enough of you, Anderson," Waldeck grated. "You *and* your holier than thou criticism! It's always the civilians, right? Always *our* fault! Well, Mister Anderson, this time your precious Fleet's in it up to its gold-braided ass!"

Anderson met the younger man's eyes contemptuously. Their enmity cut far deeper than mere politics—it was personal and implacably bitter. Waldeck would never forget that CNO Anderson had personally seen to it that Admiral Solon Waldeck was court-martialed and shot after ISW-1 for allowing the Orions to capture a copy of the Federation's entire astrogation data base . . . and attempting to conceal the fact. Other branches of the Waldeck clan had provided many a flag officer as distinguished as any family could wish, but Solon had been Pericles Waldeck's grandfather.

Now Waldeck's florid face darkened as the famous Waldeck temper roused. Sakanami looked alarmed and reached out a hand, but Waldeck ignored it.

"You're riding pretty high right now, aren't you, Mister Minister for War Production? All fired up to 'help' us after you warned us and we went right ahead and put our foot in it, right?"

"Something like that," Anderson said coldly.

"Well, just remember this—it was your precious Navy admiral who decided to take his task force right onto Charon's Ferry and got his command shot to hell! You remember *that* when you tell us what we can and can't do to get out of the mess *he* made!"

Anderson's lined face went white, and Waldeck's eyes glowed. But he'd misread the old man.

"You goddamned lying son-of-a-bitch!" The ex-president was on his feet, age forgotten in his rage, and the taller, younger man retreated a half-step in shock.

"*Howard!*" Sakanami's face was distressed as he stood behind his desk.

"You get this shit-faced fucker out of my face or I'll ram this cane up his goddamned ass!" Anderson roared, and started for Waldeck.

"Mister Anderson!" O'Rourke had more guts than Anderson had guessed, for it was he who seized his arm to hold him back. "*Please*, Mister Anderson!"

Anderson stopped, quivering in every muscle, shocked by his own loss of control. He dragged in deep, shuddering breaths, and Waldeck recovered some of his lost composure.

"I'll overlook your outburst," he said coldly, "because I know you and Admiral Li were close. But he was in command, and he took his entire force into a position it couldn't possibly escape from. If he hadn't, we wouldn't *need* the Orions. So whether you approve or not, we're going to ask for them."

"I see." Anderson's voice was ice, and President Sakanami shifted uneasily as he turned his cold blue eyes upon him. "I'd wondered who really pulled the strings in this administration. But this time he's wrong."

"I—" Sakanami began, but a savage wave cut him short.

"Understand me. You will *not* ask the Orions for help. If you try it, I'll move for your impeachment."

A moment of shocked silence hovered in the office, then Waldeck spoke.

"On what possible grounds?" he asked tightly.

"The truth, Piss Ant," Anderson said contemptuously. "And I'll *enjoy* nailing you to the cross where you goddamned well belong."

"How?" Waldeck sneered.

"By producing the secret orders this administration handed Victor Aurelli after assuring the Assembly there *were* no such orders," Anderson said very softly.

He saw the shot go home, but Waldeck recovered quickly and managed a bark of laughter.

"Preposterous!"

"Mister President," Anderson turned to Sakanami, "I apologize for my intemperate language, but not for the anger which spawned it. I am in possession of a copy of Admiral Li's log. In it, he recorded the orders he received over your signature, placing Aurelli in command of the military as well as the diplomatic aspects of his mission, and also the orders he was given *by* Aurelli . . . and obeyed under protest. I leave it to you to estimate the effect of that log entry in the Assembly and press."

"You wouldn't dare!" Waldeck spluttered. "We'd—"

"Pericles, shut up." Sakanami's voice was cold, and Waldeck's mouth snapped shut in astonishment. Anderson was almost equally astonished as the president sat back down and turned his chair to face all of them.

"He's right," Sakanami continued in the same hard voice. "I should never have issued those orders to Li, whatever you and Aurelli thought."

"But, Hideo—"

"Be quiet," Sakanami said icily. "You may be the majority leader in the Assembly, but I'm not letting you cut this administration's throat by pushing Howard into making good on his threat."

"But we *need* the Orions!" Waldeck said desperately.

"Perhaps. But what if Howard's right about the Khan's reaction? The last thing we need is to bring the Orions in on the wrong side of a three-cornered war!"

"But, Mister President—" O'Rourke began.

"Please, Hamid." Sakanami raised a hand. There was no affection in the gaze he turned on Anderson, but there was a cold respect. "I'll make you an offer, Howard. I will consult ONI's xenologists before I proceed with any message to the Khan. If they concur with you, no such message will be sent, nor will I assign public blame for what happened at Lorelei to Admiral Li. In return, *you* will promise not to publish his log entries until after we're out of this mess. Is that acceptable?"

"Yes," Anderson said shortly. He felt like a traitor, but he knew the people at ONI. They would never support the idea of calling in the Orions, and that had to be headed off at any cost. Even Chien-lu's name.

"Then I think that concludes our business. Thank you."

Anderson nodded curtly and turned for the door, but Sakanami's voice stopped him.

"By the way, Howard, how soon can you ship out for Galloway's World?"

He turned back quickly, his face showing his surprise, and the president laughed sharply—a laugh that took on an edge of true humor at the matching surprise on Waldeck's face.

"You've always taken your politics too personally, Howard. I don't like you, and you don't like me, but I really do need your experience."

"I don't—" Anderson began, but Sakanami stopped him.

"Don't say it. Instead, reflect on your little victory here. You may not win the next round, but you called the tune today. Maybe you were even right. But whether you were or not, and whether or not I give in next time, I need you. So take the goddamned job. Please?"

Anderson stood irresolute for one more moment, watching the hatred on Pericles Waldeck's face and visualizing the inevitable battles if he took the post. But Sakanami was right—damn him. The situation was too grave to withhold any service he could give, and he nodded slowly.

CHAPTER SIX

The Path of the Storm

First Admiral Lantu stood on the bridge of the superdreadnought *Hildebrandt Jackson*, double-jointed arms crossed behind him, and contemplated his visual display. The Alfred System was a distant G0/ K2 binary, and each component had a habitable planet, yet only one was inhabited. Alfred-A IV, known to its inhabitants as New Boston, was on the dry side, but it lay within forty hours of a warp point. Alfred-B I, though suitably damp, was over a hundred hours from the nearest warp point—almost two hundred from the next closest. Lantu tended to agree with the infidels; there was little point wasting time going to Hel when Boston was so much closer to hand.

He rocked on his wide feet, watching another wave of shuttles slice into the planetary atmosphere. The space about New Boston was crowded with the ships of First Fleet of the Sword of Holy Terra, but he was beginning to think his concentration of firepower might be a bit excessive. Most of the survivors of the infidels' massacred fleet had escaped through the closest warp point, to the starless nexus JF-12 and the Blackfoot System. First Fleet's battle-line, headed by six superdreadnoughts and nine battleships, had encountered exactly five small frigates in Alfred, and those had fled at high speed. Lantu didn't blame them; there'd been no point in those ships sacrificing themselves to defend an unfortified world.

He shook his head at the blue and green planetary jewel on his display. There were over a million infidels on that gem, and not even a single missile platform to protect them. Incredible.

He settled into his command chair. Most of the infidels had blown their fusion plants when his *samurai* infantry sleds swamped them with boarders, but they'd fought well first. Captain Kurnash's beloved

Saint-Just would be in yard hands for months, and her sister *Helen Borkman* would never fight again. The ferocity with which the infidel battle-line had turned on him, forcing him to let many of their light ships escape despite his initial success, had dismayed him. The Synod was pleased, but it saw only the destruction *he'd* wreaked without grasping what it had taken for the infidels to strike back so fiercely after their surprise, and the Church's obvious contempt for its enemies worried him.

Yet even he found the total lack of defenses in Alfred . . . odd. Most of their Lorelei prizes had managed to dump their data bases before they were taken, but Thebes had learned much. Among other things, they'd learned of the "Treaty of Tycho," and Lantu was inclined to concede that only demonic influence could account for its irrationality. The original assumption that the accursed Khanate had conquered humanity might have been an error, but the infidels had certainly been seduced into apostasy somehow. How else could a victorious Federation not only have concluded peace with the Satan-Khan but *suggested* a prohibition against fortifying "transit" systems along their mutual frontier? It was insane enough not to destroy their enemies when they lay prostrate, but this—!

Lantu shook his head again, baffled. Of course, there were those none-too-clear references to "The Line." The Redwing System, five transits beyond Alfred, was its closest outpost, and he gathered from the scanty data that the infidels regarded it as a formidable obstacle, even though its fortifications were eighty and ninety Terran years old. But he and First Fleet would cross that bridge when they came to it. In the meantime, the shipyards could take the prizes apart and analyze away to their heart's content while Lantu tidied up by occupying all the systems the infidels had so obligingly left totally undefended.

Sergeant Angus MacRory of the New New Hebrides Peaceforce ran a hand through his wet, dark hair. His brown uniform was streaked with sweat, and his calloused palms stung. His world was digging in, but they were almost as sadly deficient in construction equipment as they were in weapons.

He laid aside his pick and climbed out of the weapon pit to survey his handiwork while tools clinked all about him. New Hebrides' (natives routinely dropped the official first "New" of their planet's official name) pseudo-coral islands made digging hard, but his painfully hacked-out hole was well placed to cover New Lerwick's single airfield—for all the good it might do. Angus had been a Terran Marine Raider for seven years before the home-hunger drew him back, and though he didn't intend to admit it to his fellows, he knew their efforts were an exercise in organized futility. Not that they needed telling. Peaceforcers were policemen, ill-equipped for serious warfare.

Corporal Caitrin MacDougall leaned on her shovel beside him. She was tall—rivaling his own hundred and ninety centimeters—and broad-shouldered for a woman. Short, red-gold hair dripped sweat under her uniform tam-o-shanter, her snub nose was smeared with dirt, and she was as weary as Angus, but she grinned tiredly as their eyes met.

"Deep enough?" she asked.

"Aye," Angus replied. "Or if no, it's no gang deeper."

"You've got that right." Caitrin held a doctorate in marine biology, and six years of study on New Athens had muted her New Hebridan burr.

"Weel, let's be gettin' the sandbags filled." Angus sighed, reaching for his own shovel. "And if we're dead lucky, Defense Command may even find us a wee little gun tae put in it when we've done."

Captain Hannah Avram, TFN, stepped into the destroyer *Jaguar*'s briefing room. Commodore Grissom was bent over the holo tank, watching its tiny dots run through yet another battle problem, and she had to clear her throat loudly before he noticed her.

"Oh, hi, Hannah." He waved at a chair and put the tank on hold as he swung his own chair to face her.

"You sent for me, sir?"

"Yep. What's the status of your repairs?"

"We've got all launchers back on line, and one force beam. Shields are at eighty-six percent. Her armor's a sieve, but the drive's in good shape and datalink's back in . . . sort of."

"'Bout what I expected," Grissom murmured, tugging at his square chin.

How the heavy-set commodore managed to sound so calm baffled Avram. His pathetic "New New Hebrides Defense Fleet" was a joke. Her own *Dunkerque* and her sister *Kirov*, all that remained of the Ninth Battle-Cruiser Squadron, were his heaviest ships. Admiral Branco, the Ninth's CO, hadn't made it out of Lorelei, and *Dunkerque* and *Kirov* were here only because they'd been cut off from the JF-12 warp point. Grissom had three cruisers—a heavy and two lights—and two destroyers to support them. That and a hodgepodge of twelve Customs Patrol frigates and corvettes.

"As I see it, I don't have a hope in hell of holding this system, Hannah," Grissom said, finally admitting what she'd known all along, "but we have to make the gesture."

He leaned well back, folding his hands on his ample belly and frowning up at the deckhead.

"There are six and a half million people on New New Hebrides, and we can't just abandon them. On the other hand, the Thebans have a lot of warp points to choose from in Lorelei, and I figure it's unlikely they'll just race off in all directions when they can't be certain how quickly we can regroup.

"If they were coming straight through, they'd already be here. They aren't, which may mean they're being cautious and methodical, and *that* means they may probe with light forces before they come whooping through the Alfred warp point. If they do, we might just manage to smack 'em back through it and convince them to go pick on someone else until Fleet can get its act back together and rescue us. That's a best chance scenario, but it looks to me like we've got to play for it and hope, right?"

He straightened quickly, eyeing her intently, and Avram nodded.

"Right," he grunted, and flopped back. "Okay, I'm giving you a brevet promotion to commodore and putting *Kirov, Bouvet, Achilles*, and *Atago* under your command." Avram sat a bit straighter. That was his entire battle-cruiser and cruiser strength. "I'll hold the tin cans and small fry right on the warp point to pound 'em as they make transit, and I want the cruisers close enough to use their force beams, but keep *Dunkerque* and *Kirov* back."

He paused, and Avram nodded again. Her battle-cruisers were *Kongo*-class ships with heavy capital missile batteries and weak energy armaments. They were snipers, not sluggers, and keeping them well back would also keep her wounded armor away from those godawful lasers.

"It's my duty to defend this system, Captain," Grissom said more somberly, his black face serious, "but I can't justify throwing away battle-cruisers when I figure they're worth more than superdreadnoughts were a month ago. So if I tell you to, your entire force will shag ass out of here."

"Yes, sir," Avram said quietly.

"In that case, you'll be on your own, but I recommend you make for Danzig." Avram nodded yet again. Danzig was in a cul-de-sac, a single-warp point system not covered by the Treaty of Tycho's prohibition against fortifying "transit" systems. It was fairly heavily industrialized, too, and Fortress Command had erected respectable warp point defenses.

"If you can help the locals hold, you'll suck off enemy forces to seal your warp point. More important, there are fifteen million people on Danzig. It'll be your job to protect them, Captain."

"Understood, sir. If it happens, I'll do my best."

"Never doubted it, Hannah. And now"—Grissom propelled himself explosively from his chair—"let's go find a tall, cold drink, shall we?"

✧   ✧   ✧

Admiral Lantu rechecked his formation as Chaplain Manak's sonorous blessing ended. The tricky thing about warp point assaults was sequencing your transits so no two units emerged too close together and overlapped in normal space. That resulted in large explosions and gave the enemy free kills, which meant an alert defender always had an important edge. You had to come through carefully, and if he had the firepower he could annihilate each assault wave as it made transit.

Lantu doubted there was that much firepower on the other side of this warp point, but there could be enough to make things painful.

"All right, Captain Yurah," he told *Jackson*'s captain. "Execute."

"They're coming through, Skipper."

Acting-Commodore Avram acknowledged her exec's report as her tactical display lit with the first red dots. Grissom's light craft were a loose necklace around the warp point cursor, already launching while she waited impatiently for her own scanners to sort out the targets.

Aha! The symbols changed, shifting to the red-ringed white dots of hostile destroyers, and Grissom's ships were concentrating on the leaders.

"Gunnery, take the trailers!" she snapped, and *Dunkerque* bucked as the first salvo of capital missiles spat from her launchers and external ordnance racks.

Angus MacRory looked up from his hole. Night hung heavy over New Lerwick, lit only by the wan glow of Brigit, the smallest of New Hebrides' three moons, and the sudden glare tore at the eye. Searing pinpricks flashed and died against the cold, distant stars, and his lips tightened. Caitrin slid into the hole beside him, one hand gripping his shoulder bruisingly, as they watched their threadbare defenders meet the foe.

"Execute Plan Beta," Lantu said quietly to Captain Yurah. The first destroyer should already have returned if there was no resistance.

"Aye, sir," Yurah replied, and the battleship *Mohammed* moved forward.

"*That's* no destroyer, Skipper!" Commander Dan Maguire said, and Hannah Avram's heart sank as the crimson-on-crimson of a hostile capital ship burned in her plot. Another appeared behind it, and another.

The commodore's scratch team had done well against the first wave.

Six destroyers had been blasted apart in return for a frigate and heavy damage to a corvette and one precious Terran destroyer, but this was no probe.

Her display flickered and danced with the violence of warheads, force beams, and the deadly Theban lasers, and Terran units vanished with dreadful, methodical precision. Capital missiles from her battle-cruisers blanketed the lead battleship, pounding down her shields and savaging her armor, but it wasn't going to be enough. "Personal signal from Flag, sir."

Avram punched a stud, and Grissom's broad, dark face appeared on her com screen.

"All right, Hannah," he said. "Shag on out of h—"

His signal chopped off, and Hannah Avram's contralto was harsh.

"Execute Dunkirk, Maneuvering." Her lips thinned. "Gunnery, maintain fire on Target One until we lose the range."

"Jaysus!" someone murmured beside Angus's hole. The explosions had died away briefly, only to erupt with fresh violence minutes later. Waves of nuclear flame billowed, far hotter than before, and the Navy couldn't possibly throw that many missiles with what Angus knew they had out there.

The silent, white-hot flashes continued for perhaps two minutes, then began to scatter and die. A cluster of them sped off across the system as some of the defenders retreated under fire in a desperate effort to reach the Sandhurst warp point. Smaller clusters flashed and faded, and he clenched his fists. The enemy was picking off the cripples, but one glaring spark was bigger and brighter than any of the others. Someone was kicking hell out of something big up there, he thought fiercely, pounding it again and again and—

The spark suddenly flared still bigger, expanding in an eye-aching boil of light.

"They got one o' the bastards," he said softly.

Admiral Lantu read the message flimsy, then looked up at Yurah. "Break off the pursuit, Captain."

"But, sir, we've got eight cruisers and six battle-cruisers after them. They can't—"

"You may overhaul the cruisers, Yurah, but not the battle-cruisers, and you'll lose more than you'll gain in the chase. Break off."

"Aye, sir." Yurah sounded a bit rebellious, but Lantu let it pass, unable to blame him for wanting the kills. He'd gotten one of the lights, but infidel cruisers mounted more launchers; they were giving almost as good as they got. Lantu could still have them in the end—his ships had to score a crippling drive hit eventually—but meanwhile the infidel battle-cruisers were pounding their pursuers with those damnable long-ranged missiles.

The yards back home were putting matching weapons into production, helped by the fact that they, too, used standard Terran units of measure and tech notations, but he didn't have any yet. And, as he'd told Yurah, he'd lose more than he gained without them. Just as he'd already lost *Mohammed*.

He folded his arms behind him once more, rubbing his thumbs against his shoulder carapace. A single battleship, one heavy cruiser, and six destroyers wasn't an exorbitant price for an entire star system, but he was bothered by how well the infidels had done. Most of their minuscule ships hadn't even had datalink, yet he'd lost eight ships, and the damage reports from *Karl Marx* and *Savanarola* sounded bad. If the infidels ever managed to assemble a real task force, things might get nasty.

He shook himself out of his gloomy thoughts and glanced at Yurah. "Shape your course for New New Hebrides, Captain."

Dawn bled crimson over New Lerwick Island, and Sergeant MacRory sat in his hole with his com link. There was no sign of the invaders here—which was just as well, since Major Carmichael had never gotten his promised heavy weapons—but there was heavy fighting elsewhere. New Hebrides was a world of archipelagoes and small continents, and her people were scattered too thinly to prevent the enemy from landing unopposed in far too many places. But the enemy wasn't interested in unopposed landings; he was dropping his troops right on top of the population centers.

The civilian com channels were a madhouse of civil defense signals, frantic, confused queries, and Theban broadcasts in perfect Standard English. Angus couldn't make much sense of the latter; they seemed to consist mainly of weird commands for all "infidels" to lay down their weapons in the name of "Holy Terra," and wasn't that a fine thing for aliens to be telling humans?

But the Peaceforce channels were clear . . . and filled with horror. The main landing had apparently been over the capital of New Selkirk on the continent of Aberdeen. The first few shuttles had fared poorly against the capital's hastily cobbled-up defenses, but the Thebans had put a stop to that. Two-thirds of New Selkirk had been obliterated by a kilotonne-range nuke, and there were reports of other nuclear attacks, apparently called in from orbit anywhere the defenders denied the Thebans a foothold.

MacRory leaned back in his hole, tam-o-shanter covering his eyes, and hatred and helplessness coursed through him. How the hell were they supposed to fight that sort of firepower in the hands of someone ruthless enough to use it so casually? He was thankful they hadn't come to New Lerwick yet, for he had no more desire to die than the next man, but he knew. The planetary president had died in New Selkirk, but as soon as the surviving government could reach a com, they would have no choice but to order a surrender.

He ground his teeth and tried not to weep.

CHAPTER SEVEN

The Faith of Holy Mother Terra

Archbishop Tanuk smothered his impatience as his shuttle entered the atmosphere of his new archbishopric, but try as he might, he could not suppress his pride.

A century before, the Angel Saint-Just had set forth to claim this very world for Holy Terra. Now the Holy Messenger's true People would complete his mission, even if they must wrest it from his own apostate race, and the Synod had elevated the son of a lowly mining engineer to the primacy of New New Hebrides to oversee that completion.

He folded his hands, watching his amethyst ring catch the cabin lights, and the incised sigil of Holy Terra glittered like a portent.

Angus MacRory tried to hold his head erect as he marched with the survivors of the New Lerwick detachment, coughing on the dust of their passage. The day was hot for Aberdeen—almost twenty degrees Celsius—and they were far from the first to make this march. Thousands of feet had churned the surface to ankle-deep powder, and their guards' odd, three-wheeled motorcycles trailed thick plumes as they rode up and down the column. Those bikes might look silly, but they made sense; the Thebans' short, stumpy legs would be hard-pressed to match even their prisoners weary shuffle.

One of them puttered closer. He—at least Angus assumed it was a male—was dark skinned, his face covered with a fine, almost decorative spray of scales. His dark green uniform and body armor couldn't hide the strange angularity of the bony carapace covering his shoulders, and the smaller carapace over the top and back of his head gleamed under the sun. His amber eyes reminded Angus of a German

Shepherd, but his blunt, vaguely wolf-like muzzle ended in flared, primate-like nostrils, and his large, powerful teeth were an omnivore's, not a carnivore's.

Angus had examined his captors carefully, and the first thing he'd thought of was an Old Terran baboon. The aliens' torsos were human-size but looked grotesque and ungainly perched on legs half as long as they should have been—an impression sharpened by their over-long arms. Yet they weren't baboons or anything else Old Terra had ever seen. Their limbs appeared to be double-jointed; their ankles sprang from the centers of broad, platform-like feet; they had three fingers, not four; and their thumbs were on the outsides of their hands, not the insides.

They were ugly little boggits. But though they might look like clumsy, waddling clowns and their planetary combat gear might be obsolescent by the Corps' standards—indeed, from what he'd seen, he suspected it wasn't quite as good as that issued to the paramilitary Peaceforcers—they were backed by starships and nukes. That was all the edge they'd needed to smash New Hebrides' pathetic defenses in less than eighteen hours, and their quick, ruthless organization of their prisoners soon finished off his amusement.

The officers and both chaplains had been singled out and marched away even before they'd been shipped over to the mainland, and Sergeant-Major Macintosh had been shot two days ago for jumping a guard. They'd passed a line of civilian prisoners separated into three groups—men in one, women in another, children in a third—and the weeping bairns had pushed the big sergeant-major over the edge. Macintosh's death had also made Angus the senior surviving noncom, and he tried to keep himself alive by reminding himself others depended upon him.

Unlike the civilians, the military POWs hadn't been segregated by sex. He didn't know if that was a good sign or a bad, but as he'd told the others, if they'd meant to shoot them all, they could've done it on New Lerwick instead of shipping them clear across the Sea of Forth.

He lowered his eyes to Caitrin MacDougall's shoulders as she trudged along in front of him and tried to believe it himself.

"Welcome, Your Grace." Father Waman bent to kiss Tanuk's ring.

"Thank you, Father, but let us waste no time on ceremony. We have much to do in Holy Terra's service."

"I've made a start, Your Grace, if you'd care to read my report . . . ?"

"A brief verbal summary will do for now." Tanuk waved the priest to a chair and settled back behind his own desk.

"Certainly, Your Grace. The leaders of the heresy have already been executed." Waman gestured distastefully. He'd been astounded by how stunned the infidel priests and government leaders had looked as they were lined up to be shot. The military officers had seemed less surprised.

"Of course," Tanuk said a bit impatiently. "And the others?"

"That will take time, Your Grace. The infidels aren't gathered in large cities but spread out in towns and villages. Almost half live on one and two-family farms and aquaculture homesteads, but we've made a start, and the children are being segregated as you instructed."

"Excellent. If we can reach them young enough, perhaps we can wean them from their parents' apostasy."

"As you say, Your Grace. The ministers of Inquisition have completed their first re-education camps. With your permission, I've instructed Father Shamar to begin with the captured military personnel."

"Indeed?" Tanuk rubbed his muzzle. "Why?"

"I believe they will be the ones most steeped in fallacy, Your Grace. I fear few will recant, but we may learn much from them to guide us when we turn to the civilians. And if some sheep must be lost, best it should be such as they."

"I see." Tanuk frowned, then nodded. "So be it. You've done well, Father, and I shall report it to the Synod with approval. Continue as planned and inform Father Shamar I look forward to his first reports."

At least there were beds. For the first time in over a week, Angus wasn't sleeping on the ground, and he was clean, for the POWs had been herded into communal showers on arrival at the camp. Their captors still made no distinction between male and female, and he'd been forced to deploy his small washcloth with care as he and Caitrin bumped under the spray. He was eight years older than she, and he'd known her all her life, but he'd been away for four years before she left for New Athens, and she'd only returned last spring. The beanpole adolescent he remembered had vanished, and his body had been intent upon betraying his awareness of the change.

Yet it was hard to remember that pleasant tide of embarrassment as he lay on his hard, narrow cot. All the surviving noncoms shared one hut, and Caitrin lay two cots down, but his mind was full of what he'd seen of the camp.

It was near ruined New Selkirk, at the foot of the New Grampians, the rugged mountain spine of Aberdeen. New Hebrides' islands had been formed by eons of pseudo-coral deposits, but the continents were granite. The mountains had been air-mapped yet remained mostly unexplored, for the New Hebridans were a coastal folk. If he could slip his people away into the Grampians . . .

He snorted bitterly in the dark. Certainly. Just slip away—past three electrified fences and guards with automatic weapons. True, they seemed a bit casual, without a single proper weapon emplacement in the place, yet that gave him no hope. There were some good lads and lasses caged up with him—not Marines, but good people—and if he could have gotten his hands on a weapon it might have been different, but that was wishing for the moon.

No, he could only wait. Wait and hope . . . and maybe pray a bit.

"I am Yashuk," the alien announced, "and I am your teacher."

Angus and Caitrin exchanged speaking glances. Yashuk stood on a dais that brought his head to human height, and the two manacled humans sat in low chairs. Angus found the effort to place them at a disadvantage fairly crude, yet there'd been something peculiarly demeaning in submitting to the armed guards who'd split the non-coms into handcuffed pairs and marched Caitrin and him away to this small room.

He looked back at Yashuk. The alien wore a violet-colored, hooded robe, like a monk's, but there was nothing monkish about the businesslike machine-pistol at his side. A purple-stoned ring flashed on his narrow hand as he gestured with a thick metal rod, and the rheostats on that rod's grip made Angus uneasy.

He realized Yashuk had fallen silent, his head cocked, and wondered if he was showing impatience.

"To teach us what?" Caitrin asked. It seemed to be the right question, for Yashuk nodded almost approvingly.

"It is well you ask." Angus hid a grin. Yashuk's Standard English was better than his own, despite his elongated palate, and his pomposity came through perfectly.

"You have been seduced into apostasy," the Theban continued. "Your race has fallen into sin, abandoning the way of Holy Terra to commune with the Satan-Khan. As the Angel Saint-Just brought enlightenment to my world, so now I return the Holy Messenger's gift to his own race."

Angus blinked. Yashuk seemed to feel his gibberish meant something, but what was an "Angel Saint-Just"?

"Excuse me, Yashuk"—it was Caitrin again, and Angus was content to let her speak; he'd never been very verbal even with other humans, and she was the one with the fancy education—"but we don't understand you."

"I know this," Yashuk said smugly. "The Truth has been concealed from you, but I shall open your eyes. Listen, and heed the word of Holy Terra."

He drew a small book from his robe and cleared his throat with a very human sound, then began to read.

"For ages, the People dwelt in darkness, worshiping false gods, and nations warred each upon the other for empire and the wealth of their world.

"Yet they were not suffered to remain in darkness, for in the Year of Annunciation, the Holy Messenger came upon them. Saint-Just was his name, and he was sent by Holy Terra as Her Angel to lead the People into light.

"But the Satan-Khan, who hates Holy Terra and all Her children, harried the Angel's fleet, destroying its ships, so that only three of the Messenger's vessels ever touched the soil of the world the Holy One named Thebes. On the Island Arawk they landed, and they were *Starwalker*, *Speedwell*, and *John Ericsson*. Scarcely ten score Messengers survived the Satan-Khan's attack, and they were sorely wearied and afraid when they came to the People.

"Yet great was their mission, and the Angel Saint-Just went forth among the People, sharing with them the science of Holy Terra. As children they were before Her knowledge, but freely he gave of it to them.

"Now other nations were afraid and sought to smite down the Messenger and the People of Arawk, but the Messenger and his Companions aided those who had received them. The guns and tanks of Arawk's enemies withered before the weapons Holy Terra placed in the hands of those who had succored Her Messengers, and their foes were brought low.

"But even in that moment of triumph, the Satan-Khan struck, sending a terrible pestilence upon the Holy Ones. Not one of all the People died, but only the Holy Ones, and the pestilence slew and slew until only the Angel Saint-Just and less than a score of his fellows lived, and they sorrowed for all the Satan-Khan's despite had slain.

"Yet they lived, and they gathered to them disciples, among them Sumash, Prince of Arawk, and taught them the Faith of Holy Terra. And the Angel Saint-Just said unto Sumash, 'Learn of Holy Terra's arts and gather your people, that they may gird themselves, for the day shall come when they will be called by Holy Terra to return the gifts She has given. The Satan-Khan presses Her sore, and it may be She shall fall even into his hand, but your people shall become the People of Holy Terra even as my own. They will go to Her as sons, mighty in Her Faith, and smite the Satan-Khan. They will raise Her up once more, and woe be unto the unbelievers in that day, for they shall be gathered up and cast into the Fire forever.'

"Thus the Holy Messenger taught Sumash, and he learned all the Angel Saint-Just set before him. He mastered *Starwalker*'s Holy Records and grew mighty in the knowledge of Holy Terra, yet always he remembered he was but Her humble servant, and greatly did he please the Messenger.

"Yet in the Eighth Year of the Holy One, the Satan-Khan's pestilence returned, more terrible than before, and slew even the Angel Saint-Just and all his Companions.

"Great was the despair of the People when the Messengers were taken from them, and some among the disciples proved false and turned from the Holy One's teaching of jihad, but a vision came upon Sumash. Holy Terra Herself appeared unto him, anointing him as Her Prophet and the Messenger's Sword, and he cast down the faint of heart and drove them from *Starwalker*. And when they went among the People, preaching sedition against him, the Prophet came upon them in terrible wrath, and he slew them for their apostasy."

Yashuk drew a deep breath, almost a sigh, and closed his book.

"Thus did the Angel Saint-Just come to Thebes and charge the People with their holy task," he said reverently, and Angus gaped at him.

"But, Yashuk," Caitrin said softly and carefully, "we've never heard of the Angel Saint-Just, nor of the Faith of Holy Terra."

"We know this," Yashuk said sorrowfully. "We have scanned your records, and the Faith has been extirpated root and branch. Even as the Holy One foretold, the Satan-Khan has brought Holy Terra to the dust and seduced Her own children into sin."

"Like hell," Angus grunted. "We kicked the Tabbies' arse!"

"You will not use such language to me," Yashuk said sternly.

"Get knotted!" Angus snarled. "An' as fer that load o' crap yer peddlin', I—"

Yashuk's yellow eyes flamed. His rod hummed, and Angus screamed and arched up out of his chair. Molten lead ran down his nerves, and torment hurled him to the floor, twisting and jerking, teeth locked against another scream.

Agony tore at him forever before it ended with the quiet snap of a released switch. He grunted in anguished relief, consciousness wavering, and Yashuk's voice was colder than the gulfs between the stars.

"Be warned, infidel. For the Messenger's love, we will teach you Truth once more, but if you cling to apostasy, then even as he foretold, you will be cast into the Fire, and all other unbelievers with you. Return to your Faith and embrace Holy Terra, or you will surely die."

Angus wasn't particularly religious, and he knew it was stupid to defy Yashuk, but there was too much Highlander in his heritage. The agony of the rod's direct neural stimulation punished every defiant word, and his brawny body grew gaunt, yet the grim denial in his hollow, hating eyes never wavered.

It seemed Yashuk's stubbornness matched his own. Half the non-coms vanished within a week, "cast into the Fire" by less patient "teachers," but he refused to admit Angus might defeat him, though Angus had no doubt the alien would already have sent him after the others if not for Caitrin.

She sought desperately to divert Yashuk, tying him up in conversation, seeking "enlightenment," and her keenly probing questions seemed to delight the alien. On a good day she could divert him into an hours-long explanation of some abstruse theological distinction while Angus sat quietly, gathering his strength as she watched him from the corner of one anxious eye. He knew she regarded Yashuk's drivel exactly as he did, despite her exasperation with his own stubborn, open rejection, but they were different people. She had the gift of words, the ability to dance and spar. Angus didn't, and even though enough defiance must exhaust even Yashuk's patience, he couldn't pretend.

It was the way he was.

"I weary of you, infidel," Yashuk said coldly, tapping his rod as he glared at Angus. "Caitrin seeks knowledge, yet you hold her back. You cling to your darkness like the Satan-Khan's own get! Will you die for it? Will you see your soul cast into everlasting damnation before you return to your Holy Mother?"

"Aye? Weel, I've had aboot enow o' *yer* drivel, tae," Angus said wearily, matching glare for glare. He was weary unto death, and a darkness had begun to grow in his brain. Not the darkness Yashuk yammered about, but despair. He knew Caitrin had not yet professed her "conversion" only because she was protecting him. But she'd felt the rod twice in the last two days for defending him too openly, and enough of that would get *her* killed.

"I've had you *and* yer maunderin'," he said now, coldly. " 'Holy Terra' my left nut!"

"*Blasphemy!*" Yashuk screamed, and the dreadful rod whined.

Angus shrieked. He couldn't help it, couldn't stop the screams, yet within his agony was a core of gratitude. This was the end. This would kill him and set Caitrin free to—

His torment died in a high-pitched squeal; not his, but another's. Reaction's heavy hand crushed him to the floor, but he rolled his head and opened his eyes, then gaped in horror.

Somehow Caitrin had reached Yashuk while the alien concentrated on him. Now her wrists were crossed behind his neck, and the chain between them vanished into his throat.

Yashuk writhed, one hand raking bleeding furrows in his throat as it scrabbled at the chain. The other reached back, and his incredibly long arm clubbed her with his rod. Angus heard her grunt in anguish as the blows crunching into her ribs lifted her from the floor, but she held on grimly, and her forearms tightened mercilessly.

Angus groaned and dragged his hands under him, but he had no strength. He could only watch their lethal struggle while the alien's face darkened and his squeal became a strange hoarse whine. He smashed his cranial carapace into Caitrin's face again and again. Blood ran from her mouth and nose, and her knees buckled, but Yashuk was weakening. He stumbled to his knees and dropped the rod to paw at the chain two-handed in a weak, pathetic gesture. His limp hands flopped to the floor, and she braced a knee in his spine, her face a mask of blood and hate, and wrenched the chain still tighter.

She held it until the last light faded from the bulging yellow eyes, and then she collapsed over the body of her foe.

Caitrin MacDougall opened swollen eyes, blinking as Angus's face swam above her, and stifled a whimper as simply breathing grated broken ribs.

"Bloody fool," Angus said softly. His brogue was more pronounced than ever as he dabbed at her face with a damp cloth from somewhere.

"Me?" she whispered through split, puffy lips. "He'd have killed you this time, Angus."

" 'Twas what I wanted, ye great twit. Ye took tae many chances fer me, lassie."

"Well, we've both blown it now," she sighed. She tried to sit up and collapsed with a moan. "What're you still doing here?"

"I cannae leave ye," he said reasonably.

"You're going to have to. If you move fast, you might even make it as far as the wire, but with me to slow you down—"

"Hisht, now! Ye'll no have tae run. We'll see tae that."

"We?" She rolled her head and gaped at the crowd of brown-uniformed men and women. Each of them seemed to be holding a Theban machine pistol or assault rifle. "What—?"

"Yon Yashuk had our handcuff keys and a knife, Katie," Angus said with an ugly smile, "and no a one of 'em expectin' an 'infidel' tae be runnin' aboot loose. I slipped around ahind the spalpeens and picked off a dozen o' our wee 'teachers.' They've had nowt tae worry at fer tae lang, and when I threw a dozen pistols in the hut door, weel. . . ."

He shrugged as if that explained everything, and Caitrin gawked at him.

"Do you mean you lunatics—?"

"Aye, lassie, we've taken the whole damned camp, and we started wi' the com shack. Sae just lie easy, Katie girl. We've a stretcher here, and ye're comin' wi' us!"

CHAPTER EIGHT

A Question of Authority

Senior Chief Petty Officer Hussein watched Captain—no, he reminded himself, *Commodore*—Avram stalk into *Dunkerque*'s boat bay and felt sorry for whoever the Old Lady was going to meet.

He sprang to attention with alacrity. The sideboys did the same, but Commodore Avram hardly seemed to notice. She saluted the Federation banner on the forward bulkhead with meticulous precision as the bosun's pipe shrilled, then stepped silently into her cutter, and the atmospheric pressure in the boat bay dropped by at least a kilo to the square centimeter as its hatch closed. It departed, sliding through the mono-permeable force field at the end of the bay, and Chief Hussein shook his head sadly.

Some poor bastard dirtside was about to grow a new asshole.

Hannah Avram sat on her fury and made herself lean back as the cutter headed for Gdansk, the capital city of New Danzig. Despite her preparations, her position was unbelievably fragile, and venting her volcanic anger would do more harm than good, but still—!

She smoothed the cap in her lap and smiled unwillingly as she stroked the braid on its visor. That was the single card she had to play, and she'd built her entire strategy on it. And it helped enormously that Commodore Hazelwood was such a gutless wonder.

She shook her head, still unable to believe either the situation or how much she'd already gotten away with. Richard Hazelwood came from a distinguished Navy family, but now that she'd met him she understood how he'd gotten shunted off to Fortress Command in a system no one had ever dreamed might actually be attacked. She doubted Hazelwood would blow his own nose without authorization—in triplicate!—from higher authority.

Her arrival in Danzig with what was left of the New New Hebrides defenders—her own ship, *Kirov*, the heavy cruiser *Bouvet*, and the light cruiser *Atago*—had been bad enough. They hadn't even been challenged until they'd been in-system over two minutes! God only knew what *Thebans* might have done with that much time, and Hannah Avram had no intention of finding out. That was one reason *Kirov*, *Bouvet*, and *Atago*, along with the six destroyers which constituted Danzig's entire mobile local defense force, were sitting on the warp point under Captain Yan, *Kirov*'s skipper.

The only good thing about the entire bitched-up situation was that Hazelwood was such a wimp he hadn't even questioned her brazen usurpation of his authority. He'd been overjoyed to let her shoulder the responsibility by exercising a Battle Fleet commodore's traditional right to supersede a Fortress Command officer of the same rank. Of course, that assumed the Battle Fleet commodore in question was a *real* commodore and not simply a captain who'd been "frocked" by a desperate superior. Hannah had a legal right to the insignia she now wore, but her rank certainly hadn't been confirmed by Fleet HQ. It hadn't occurred to Hazelwood to ask about that, even though his personnel files had to list her as a captain, and she wasn't about to mention it to him.

Only her staff knew her promotion had been signed by Commodore Grissom rather than some higher authority, and she'd used the week since her arrival well, getting personally acquainted with all of Danzig's senior officers. For the most part, they were a far cry from their erstwhile CO, and they were delighted by her assumption of command.

But now that Hazelwood had gotten over his immediate panic he was proving a real pain in the ass. The man commanded a dozen Type Three OWPs, for God's sake! Admittedly, his forts were a lot smaller than The Line's, but they were still more powerful than most battleships and covered by a minefield whose strength had surprised even Hannah. He was also responsible—or had been, until she took the burden off his shoulders—for the protection of fifteen million Federation citizens. Yet he wanted to send out a courier ship to discuss "terms" with the Thebans!

She gritted her teeth against a fresh flare of anger. Bad enough to have an idiot as her second in command, but Hazelwood also had close ties to the local government. Well, that was to be expected after he'd spent six years commanding their defenses, but it also meant they were prepared to back him. Indeed, she suspected President Wyszynski had actually put Hazelwood up to it. Or it might have been Victor Tokarov. In fact, it sounded more like Tokarov than Wyszynski.

The president might, on a good day, have the independence to decide what color to paint his office without running it by the manager of the Cracow Mining Company. Danzig had been settled by Polish neo-ethnicists fifty years ago, but the planet's incredible mineral wealth had brought New Detroit's Tokarov Mining Consortium in almost from the beginning, which had contributed immensely to the speed of Danzig's industrialization. It had also moved the planet firmly into the Corporate World camp.

Backed by Tokarov money, Wyszynski could be re-elected planetary president three months after he died. Conversely, of course, if he irritated the Tokarov interests, he couldn't be elected dog-catcher. Assuming, that was, that there were enough dogs on Danzig to *need* a dog-catcher.

The more she thought about it, the more convinced she'd become that Tokarov had originated the suggestion. It was just the sort of brilliant idea to appeal to a business-as-usual financier. But neither Tokarov, Wyszynski, nor Hazelwood—damn him!—had been at Lorelei or New New Hebrides. They'd make out better negotiating with a saber-toothed tiger . . . or a *zeget*.

The cutter's drive changed note as it settled towards the pad, and she looked out the armorplast view port at the spaceport's orderly bustle. A dozen local shuttles full of additional mines were about ready to lift off, and there were another dozen Fleet personnel shuttles spotted around the pads. Most had their ramps down, and she could just see a platoon of Marines marching briskly off towards their waiting ground transport.

Her lips quirked wryly as she turned away from the view port. Her newest idea had horrified most of her fledgling staff, but they'd come through like champs. Danny had worked like a Trojan with Commander Bandaranaike, her legal officer, as well as finding time to handle the logistical side. And, she supposed, she might as well be hanged for a sheep. Besides—her smile vanished—Commodore Grissom had charged her with the defense of Danzig. If he could go down fighting knowing it was futile in defense of less than half as many people, then she could damned well do the same for Danzig's.

Even if she had to do it in spite of their government.

Victor Tokarov watched Commodore Avram walk in. She laid her briefcase neatly on the conference table, then sat and set her cap equally neatly beside it. She was smiling, but Tokarov had attended too many outwardly affable business meetings, and the good commodore's over-controlled body language spoke volumes. He could teach her a thing or two about stage-managing meetings. Not that he had any intention of doing so. Or perhaps, in a way, he did, he thought with a hidden smile.

President Josef Wyszynski nodded pleasantly to her. Commodore Hazelwood did not, but he'd made it clear he intended to distance himself from the entire discussion. It was a pity, Tokarov thought, that it was Avram who was the newcomer. She had so much more to recommend her as an ally, aside from her foolish insistence on "defending" Danzig. No single system could stand off the juggernaut which had smashed Battle Fleet at Lorelei and driven this deep into the Federation so quickly. Far wiser to make bearable terms locally, preserving Danzig's industrial infrastructure—and people, of course—from pointless destruction. The Navy would get around to rescuing them sooner or later, after all.

"Thank you for coming, Commodore," Wyszynski said. "I appreciate your taking the time from your busy schedule."

"Not at all," Hannah said with a tight smile. "I'd planned on paying a call as soon as convenient. I do rather regret pulling *Dunkerque* off the warp point at this particular moment, but I'd have had to turn her over to the local yard for permanent repairs sometime soon, anyway."

"Uh, yes, I see." Wyszynski cleared his throat. "Turning to the point which, I believe, Commodore Hazelwood has raised with you, it seemed a good idea for the planetary government's viewpoint to be—"

"Excuse me, Mister President," Hannah said calmly. "I presume you're referring to Commodore Hazelwood's suggestion that we seek a negotiated local *modus vivendi* with the Thebans?"

Wyszynski seemed a bit taken aback by her interruption, but he nodded. "Well, I'd hardly put it in quite those words, but, yes. I understand you oppose the idea, and of course, as the senior officer in Danzig you have every right to make your own tactical dispositions, but we feel—"

"Excuse me again, sir," Hannah interrupted, and Tokarov gave her high marks for tactics as she crowded the president, throwing him off stride and asserting her own authority. "Such negotiations—which, I feel I must point out, have *not* been authorized by President Sakanami or the Legislative Assembly—represent rather more than a simple tactical decision."

"Well, we know *that*," Wyszynski replied a bit tartly. "But President Sakanami is on Old Terra, not here."

"True. On the other hand, sir, any negotiations with a hostile power lie strictly within the purview of the Federal government, not of member planets. I direct your attention to Article Seven of the Constitution."

Wyszynski's mouth opened, and his eyes darted to Tokarov. The mining director swallowed a frown, but it was clear more direct action was in order.

"You're quite correct, Commodore. But while I realize I'm present solely as an economic and industrial advisor, I think President Wyszynski's point is that the Constitution makes no provision for a planet which finds itself cut off from the rest of the Federation *by* a hostile power. And Danzig, as a Federated World, has no Federal governor and hence no official representative of the Federal executive."

"I see." Hannah cocked her head thoughtfully. "Your point is that with no such official the planetary government must—strictly as an emergency measure—create its own foreign policy until contact with Old Terra is regained?"

"Exactly," Wyszynski said quickly.

"I see," Hannah repeated. She shrugged slightly and opened her briefcase. "Actually, gentlemen, I didn't come specifically to discuss this point. I'd intended to give you this"—she handed over a document chip folio—"which details my planned repair and construction policy. Given Danzig's industrial capacity, I believe we can easily triple the density of the present warp point minefields within two months. After that, I'd like to get started on the construction of destroyers and light carriers. I doubt we'll have time for anything much heavier, and the local population would be strapped to provide crews if we did. In respect to that point, it occurs to me that we may have to introduce conscription—on a hostilities-only basis, of course—and I'd intended to discuss that with you, as well."

Her listeners stared at her in shock. Even Tokarov's jaw had dropped just a bit, and she smiled at them.

"Still, if you feel we must resolve this negotiations question first, I am, of course, at your service."

Wyszynski blinked. Avram's fast, unpredictable footwork was hardly what one expected from a bluff, apolitical TFN officer. For his part, Tokarov eyed the commodore with new respect. She might not be very good at hiding emotions, but he made a mental note against equating that with lack of guile. Poor Josef was obviously uncertain how to proceed, so it looked as if it was going to be up to him.

"Speaking for Danzig's industrial interests, we'll certainly be glad to take the fabrication side of your requests under advisement. But I really think we have to determine whether or not such a program would accord with the government's intention to seek a cease-fire with the Thebans."

"Not really, Mister Tokarov. You see, there will *be* no negotiations."

"I beg your pardon?" Wyszynski demanded, swelling with outrage.

"With all due respect, Commodore, this is a political question—and a legal one, of course—but certainly not a military one."

"On the contrary, sir." The steel glinting in Hannah's brown eyes gave Tokarov a sudden feeling of dread. "It most certainly is a military question. On the other hand, I wasn't speaking to its purely military aspects. I was, in fact, addressing those same legal and political points you just referred to."

"In what way, Commodore?" Tokarov asked.

"In this way, Mister Tokarov." She extracted another document from her briefcase, this time a printed hard copy, and handed it across the table to him. He looked down at it in some surprise.

"This seems to be a copy of the Articles of War," he said, playing for time and trying to deduce her intent.

"It is. If you'd take a look at Article Fifty-Three, please?" He thumbed pages, and those steely brown eyes shifted to Wyszynski like *Dunkerque*'s main battery. "Since we have only one copy, I'll save a bit of time by citing the relevant passage for you, Mister President. Article Fifty-Three says, and I quote, 'The senior Naval officer present shall, in the absence of guidance from the relevant civil authorities, exercise his discretion in the formulation of local military and supporting policies, acting within the understood intent of previously received instructions.'"

Tokarov stopped turning pages. He didn't doubt she'd cited correctly, but he still didn't see where she was headed. Which didn't prevent a sudden sinking sensation. Commodore Avram looked entirely too sure of herself. She had something nasty up that silver-braided sleeve of hers.

"I fail to see," President Wyszynski said, "the relevance of that article, Commodore. We're not discussing military policy, except, perhaps, in the most indirect fashion. We're talking about a political decision made by the duly constituted local authorities. In fact, I believe we *are* the 'relevant civil authorities' in this case!"

"With all due respect, Mister President, I must disagree," Hannah said coolly, and Wyszynski gaped at her. "The document I've just cited from is the legal basis of the Federation Navy. It is not merely a military document; it is also a *legal* document, drafted by the Admiralty but approved and enacted by the Legislative Assembly and, as such, constitutes a portion of the legal *corpus* of the Federation, not of any single member planet. Under Article Two of the Constitution, Federal law, where existent, supersedes locally enacted law. As such, I am not bound by your wishes, or those of Mister Tokarov, in the formulation of my own 'military and supporting' policy. In fact, I am a direct representative of the Federal government. Wouldn't you agree?"

"Well, I . . . I suppose that *sounds* like it makes sense, in a way. Not," Wyszynski added hastily, "that I've ever seen any documentation on the point. And constitutional law is hardly my strong suit. I'd hesitate to make any rash pronouncements or commitments."

"I realize that, sir, and I am, of course, equally desirous of maintaining a scrupulous adherence to the law of the Federation. Accordingly, I discussed this very point at some length with my legal officer before I left to attend this meeting. At her suggestion, I refer you to *Hargood-vs.-Federation* and *Lutwell's World-vs.-Federation*. In both cases, the Supreme Court determined that the senior Navy officer present was, in fact, directly representative of the Federal government. I'm certain your own Attorney General could provide you with copies of those decisions."

"All right, then," Wyszynski said. "But I still fail to see how your authority to determine military policy applies to a purely political question like negotiations with the Thebans!"

"I invite your attention once more to the relevant portion of Article Fifty-Three, sir." Hannah smiled. Why, she was actually beginning to enjoy herself! Odd. She'd never *thought* she had a sadistic streak.

"*What* 'relevant portion'?" Wyszynski snapped.

"I refer," she said softly, "to the specific phrase 'military and *supporting* policies.' I submit to you, sir, that my intention to defend Danzig and prevent any Theban incursion therein, which is clearly a military policy and hence within *my* jurisdiction, precludes any negotiation with the enemy. And, as the proper authority to determine policies in support of my military intentions, I must ask you to abandon any idea of those negotiations and, instead, turn your attention to my industrial requirements."

"Now just a moment, Commodore!" Tokarov said sharply. "You can't seriously suggest that we allow a military officer to dictate to a duly elected planetary government!"

"That, I'm afraid, is precisely what I'm suggesting, Mister Tokarov," Hannah said flatly, "though 'suggest' is, perhaps, not the proper word. I am *informing* you of my decision."

"This—this is preposterous!" Wyszynski blurted. "Why, you haven't got any more legal right to issue . . . issue *diktats* to civilian authorities than . . . than . . ." He slid to a halt, and Tokarov looked at Hannah with narrow eyes, all humor vanished.

"I believe President Wyszynski means to point out that while you may represent the Federal military, you have no *civilian* authority, Commodore," he said coldly.

"On the contrary." Hannah pulled out another thick book. It thudded onto the table, and Tokarov's eyes dropped to the cover. *Admiralty Case Law of the Terran Federation, Vol. XLVIII*, it said.

"And what, if I may ask, does *this* have to say to the matter?"

"Under Admiralty law, Mister Tokarov, the senior Federation Navy officer present becomes the Federation's senior *civil* officer in the absence of proper civilian authority. I refer you to *Anderson-vs.-Medlock, Travis, Suchien, Chernov, et. al,* otherwise known as 'The *Starquest* Case.' Since we have all just agreed there is no local Federal authority in Danzig, I have no option but to consider myself acting in that capacity. This"—she extracted yet another document from the deadly magazine of her briefcase—"is a proclamation drawn up by my legal officer and myself. It announces my assumption of civil authority as Governor of the Danzig System in the name of the Federal government."

"You're insane!" Hazelwood blurted, speaking for the first time. "That's patently illegal! I refuse to listen to this driv—"

"Commodore Hazelwood," Hannah said very, very softly, "you are in violation of Articles Seven, Eight, and Fourteen of the Articles of War. I am your superior officer, and you will bear that in mind and address me as such or I'll have your commission. Do you read me, Commodore Hazelwood?"

Hazelwood wilted into a confused welter of dying half-sentences, and Hannah turned back to Tokarov, dropping all pretense that anyone else in this room mattered.

"Commodore Hazelwood has just been relieved—on my authority—of his duties as Sky Watch commander." She glanced at her watch. "One hour ago, Captain Isaac Tinker turned command of *Bouvet* over to his exec and assumed Commodore Hazelwood's duties to free the commodore to act as my personal liaison with Danzig's industrial complex. I'm certain he'll carry out his new duties in the exemplary manner in which he carried out his previous responsibility for Fortress Command."

"You won't get away with this, Commodore," Tokarov said quietly.

"Governor, please," Hannah replied calmly. "I am, after all, speaking in my civilian persona. And I've already 'gotten away' with it, sir. With the exception of one or two defeatists, the officers and enlisted men and women of the Navy have no interest in negotiating with the Thebans. Nor, I might add, do the officers and enlisted people of the Marine detachments."

Tokarov swallowed, eyes suddenly very wide, as she reached into that deadly briefcase yet again. She extracted a small handcom and activated it.

"You may come in now, Major," she said into it, and the conference room doors opened. Ten Marines in unpowered body armor stepped through them, bayoneted assault rifles ostentatiously unthreatening in their hands. They took up properly deferential positions against the wall, paying absolutely no attention to the people sitting around the table.

"Now, gentlemen," Hannah's voice drew their pop-eyed stares from the silent Marines as she closed her briefcase with a snap, "I believe that completes our business."

"This—this is mutiny! *Treason!*" Wyszynski blurted.

"On the contrary, Mister President. This is a constitutional transfer of authority, in exact accordance with the legal precedents and documents to which I have drawn your attention."

"That's nonsense!" Tokarov's voice was more controlled, but his eyes were just as hot. "This is a brazen use of force to circumvent the legitimate local authorities!"

"That, Mister Tokarov, is a matter of opinion, and I suggest you consult legal counsel. If I've acted beyond the scope of my authority, I feel certain the Admiralty and Assembly will censure me once contact with those bodies is regained. In the meantime, we have a war to fight, and the organs of the Federal authority in this system— the Fleet and Marine units stationed herein—are prepared to do their duty, under my orders, as per their oaths to protect and defend the Constitution of the Terran Federation. Which, I'm very much afraid, makes your objections irrelevant."

"You'll never get away with this. My people won't stand for it, and without us, there's no industrial base to support your insane policy!"

"On the contrary, sir. Your managerial personnel may, indeed, refuse to obey me. Your labor force, however, *won't* refuse, and you know it. In the meantime, Marine units are on their way to your offices and major industrial sites even as we speak, and any act of sabotage or active resistance will be severely dealt with. You may, of course, at your discretion, elect to employ passive resistance and noncooperation. I should point out, however, that such a decision on your part will have the most serious postwar repercussions if, as I confidently expect, my actions are retroactively approved by the Assembly."

She held his eyes unblinkingly, and something inside him shied away from her slight, armor-plated smile. She waited a moment, inviting him to continue, and his gaze dropped.

"I believe that's everything then, gentlemen," she said calmly, standing and tucking her cap under her arm. "Good day."

She walked out amid a dead, stunned silence.

CHAPTER NINE

Ivan the Terrible

The VIP shuttle completed its approach run and settled on the landing platform with a sort of abrupt grace that would have looked inexplicably *wrong* to anyone who'd lived before the advent of reactionless, inertia-canceling drives. Its hatch slid open and a solitary passenger emerged into the light of Galloway's Sun.

Fleet Admiral Ivan Nikolayevich Antonov was of slightly more than average height but seemed shorter because of his breadth, thickness, and—the impression was unavoidable—density. His size, and the way he moved, suggested an unstoppable force of nature, which was precisely what his reputation said he was. But he stopped at the foot of the landing ramp and saluted, with great formality, the frail-looking old man in civilian clothes who headed the welcoming committee. One didn't ordinarily do that for a cabinet minister . . . but Howard Anderson was no ordinary cabinet minister.

"Well," Anderson growled, "you took your sweet time getting here, EYE-van."

"My orders specified 'Extreme Urgency,' sir," the burly admiral replied in a rumbling, faintly accented basso. "I had certain administrative duties to attend to before departure . . . but Captain Quirino is speculating about a new record for our route."

"So what are you doing standing around here now with your thumb up your ass?" was the peevish reply. The other dignitaries stiffened, and the painfully young ensign beside Anderson blanched. "Let's go below and make all the introductions at once. You already know Port Admiral Stevenson . . . he'll want to welcome you to The Yard." Ever since the First Interstellar War, the sprawling complex

71

of Fleet shipyards and installations in the Jamieson Archipelago of Galloway's World had been called simply that.

"Certainly, sir," Antonov replied stonily.

Anderson led Antonov in mutual silence towards the luxuriously appointed office that had been set aside for his private use. The ensign who'd hovered at the old man's shoulder throughout the formalities scurried ahead to the door, but Anderson reached out with his cane and poked him—far more gently than it looked—in the back.

"I'm not yet so goddamned feeble I can't open a door, Ensign Mallory!" His aide stopped dead, face flustered, and Anderson shook his head in exasperation. "All right, all right! I know you meant well, Andy."

"Yes, sir. I—"

"Admiral Antonov and I can settle our differences without a referee," Anderson said less brusquely. "Go annoy Yeoman Gonzales or something."

"Yes, sir." Mallory's confusion altered into a broad smile, and he hurried away . . . after punching the door button. Anderson growled something under his breath as the panel hissed open, waved Antonov through, and used his cane to lower himself into a deeply-padded chair.

"*Puppy!*" he snorted, then glanced at Antonov as he settled back. "Well, so much for your introductions—and thank *God* they're over!"

"Yes," Antonov agreed as he loosened his collar and shaped a course for the wet bar. "Upholding your image as an obnoxious old bastard must be almost as great a strain as serving as the public object of your disagreeableness. Don't they keep any vodka here? Ah!" He held up a bottle. "Stolychnaya, this far from Russia!" He looked around. "No pepper, though."

Anderson shuddered. "Make mine bourbon," he called from the depths of his chair, "if there is any. Do you know," he went on, "what the problem's been with the TFN from its very inception?"

"No, but I have a feeling you're going to tell me."

"Too many goddamned Russkies in the command structure!" Anderson thumped the floor with his cane for emphasis. "I say you people are still Commies at heart!"

Anderson was one of the few people left alive who would even have understood the reference. But Antonov knew his history. His eyes, seemingly squeezed upward into slits by his high cheekbones in the characteristic Russian manner, narrowed still further as he performed a feat most of his colleagues would have flatly declared impossible: he grinned.

"Also too many capitalistic, warmongering Yankee imperialists," he intoned as he brought the drinks (and the vodka bottle). "Of which you are a walking—or, at least, tottering—museum exhibit! These last few years, you've actually begun to *look* a bit like . . . oh, what was the name of that mythological figure? Grandfather Sam?"

"Close enough," Anderson allowed with a grin of his own.

It was an old joke, and one with a grain of truth. The Federated Government of Earth, the Terran Federation's immediate ancestor, had created its own military organization after displacing the old United Nations at the end of the Great Eastern War. Twenty years later, China accelerated the process with her abortive effort to break free of the FGE. Not only did the China War have the distinction of being the last organized bloodletting on Old Terra, but it had encouraged the FGE to scale the old national armed forces back to merely symbolic formations . . . quickly.

Since the Chinese military had no longer existed, the Russian Federation and the United States had possessed the largest military establishments, and hence the largest number of abruptly unemployed professional officers. Inevitably, the paramilitary services that were later to become the TFN had come to include disproportionate numbers of Russians and the "American" ethnic melange in their upper echelons. Even now, after two and a half centuries of cultural blending had reduced the old national identities largely to a subject for affectation (on the Inner Worlds, at least), the descendants of the two groups were over-represented among the families in which Federation service was a tradition.

"I'm starting to feel about as old as a mythological figure," Anderson went on. "You're looking well, though."

It was true. Like other naval personnel who had declared their intention of emigrating to the Out Worlds later, Antonov had had access to the full course of antigerone treatments from an early age. At seventy-two standard years, he was physiologically a man in his early forties. He shrugged expressively and settled into the chair opposite Anderson's.

"I keep in condition. Or try to. For an admiral, it's about as hard as for this damned peacetime Fleet." He scowled momentarily, then gave Anderson a reproachful look. "But we're wasting perfectly good drinking time! Come on, Howard! *Ty chto mumu yebyosh?*" He raised his glass. "*Za vashe zdorovye!*"

They drank, Antonov tossing back his vodka and Anderson sipping his bourbon more cautiously, muttering something inaudible about doctors.

"That's another thing about you Russians . . . if you want to tell a man to drink up, why not just say so? 'Why are you fucking a cow?' indeed! Well, I'll say this much for you: your language is rich in truly colorful idioms!"

"Rich in every way!" Antonov enthused, refilling his glass. "Ah, Howard, if only you knew the glories of our great, our incomparable literature—"

"I read a Russian novel once," Anderson cut in bleakly. "People with unpronounceable names did nothing for seven hundred and eighty-three pages, after which somebody's aunt died."

Antonov shook his head sorrowfully. "You are hopelessly *nekulturny*, Howard!"

"I'll *kulturny* you, you young upstart!" Anderson shot back with a twinkle. For an instant, the decades rolled away and it was the time of the Second Interstellar War, when Commander Nikolai Borisovich Antonov, his Operations officer, had learned of the birth of a son on the eve of the Second Battle of Ophiuchi Junction. They'd all had a little more to drink that night than they should have, but Nikolai had survived both the vodka and the battle. And toward the end of the Third Interstellar War, President Anderson had met Vice Admiral Antonov's newly commissioned son . . . who now sat across from Minister of War Production Anderson, tossing back his vodka so much like Nikolasha that for an instant it seemed . . .

Too many memories. We are not meant to live so long. Anderson shook himself. *That's enough, you old fart! Next you'll be getting religious!*

Antonov, watching more closely than he showed, sensed his change of mood, if not its cause. "How bad is it, really, Howard?" he asked quietly. "Even these days, the news is always out of date. I don't know much beyond what happened to Admiral Li."

"Then you know we've lost a third of the Fleet," Anderson responded grimly. "What you may *not* know yet, is that ONI's latest estimate, based on scanner reports from the Lorelei survivors, is that the Thebans actually deployed a fleet stronger than Chien-lu's was."

Antonov's eyes became very still, and Anderson nodded.

"Right. So far, we've actually observed twelve super-dreadnoughts, eighteen battleships, and twenty-odd battle-cruisers, and I'm willing to bet there's more we *haven't* seen. They seem a bit weak in escort types, but that still gives them effective parity with our entire surviving battle-line, though we haven't seen any sign of carriers yet. On the other hand, we lost an even larger proportion of our carriers than we did of our battle-line, and, of course, they're concentrated with the interior position and the initiative. You can infer the strategic situation *that* leaves us with."

He pushed himself erect with his cane, reaching across the desk for a remote-control unit, and touched a button. A wall vanished, giving way to a holographic display of warp lines.

"It's at least as bad as you think, Ivan." (Preoccupied, he forgot to mispronounce the name.) "At the rate the Thebans—whoever or whatever they are—have pushed on from Lorelei; they're two or three transits out in all directions by now. All *our* directions, that is; they've stopped well short of the Orion border fortifications for the moment...another mystery, but one complication we don't have to worry about. Yet." He fiddled with the control, producing a pair of cursors which indicated two systems: Griffin and Redwing. "Some of Chien-lu's survivors are still picketing the approaches, and the way they're spreading out is attenuating some of their numerical advantage, but we don't have anything with a prayer of stopping them short of The Line.

"Now for the good news, such as it is. Our Ophiuchi allies have agreed to help. They're not going to commit forces to actual combat against the Thebans—they're a *long* way off, and the proper role of a *khimhok's* allies is a pretty fuzzy area—but they're arranging to take over some of our border obligations. That'll let us shift a lot of what's left of the Fleet to this sector, but it'll take time to concentrate our forces, and new construction is going to take even longer. For now, your 'Second Fleet' will have to depend largely on the mothballed units here at Galloway's World...such as they are. The big question concerns priorities in reactivating them." He raised an eyebrow, inviting comment.

"The *Pegasus*-class light carriers first," Antonov responded without hesitation. "And, of course, the reserve fighter squadrons."

"That decision didn't take long," Anderson remarked with a smile. "Are you certain? Those ships are as obsolete as dodoes, and they weren't anything much even in their day. Just very basic fighter platforms built early in ISW-3 . . .

" . . . for an emergency not unlike this one," Antonov finished for him. "As you've so rightly—and publicly—pointed out, my trip here took a while, so I've had time to think. Two points: first, we have more *Pegasus* class than anything else in the Reserve and they're relatively small. Coupled with their austerity, that means they can be reactivated more quickly than fleet carriers or battle-line units...and time is of the essence. We have to use what we have and what can be made ready in the next few weeks.

"The second point," he continued with a frown, "is a little more speculative. But from the courier drones Khardanish and Admiral Li were able to send off, it seems clear the Thebans don't have strikefighters and that Admiral Li, due to the circumstances in which he found himself, was unable to employ his fighters effectively. Taken together, these two facts suggest to me that the Thebans may not take fighters seriously. This attitude—while it lasts—could give us an advantage. But if we're to seize it, we have to deploy all the fighter assets we can in as short a time as possible."

"Very cogently put," Anderson approved. "As a matter of fact, I just wanted to hear your reasoning . . . which, it turns out, parallels mine. You must have noticed all the work going on in the orbital yards. The first three *Pegasuses* will recommission in a few days, with more on the way."

Antonov looked like a man who'd had one of several heavy weights lifted from his shoulders. "Actually, you forgot a couple of lines of good news." He smiled at Anderson's quizzical look. "Not even Russians are *always* gloomy, Howard. I'm referring to a few new developments which fortunately were already in the R&D pipeline. Captain Tsuchevsky's last post before joining my staff was assistant project officer on the strategic bombardment program to increase capital missile range, and he's given me a glowing report on the possibilities. Add that to this new missile with warp transit capability—whatever they've decided to call it—and the new warheads . . ."

"Right, right," Anderson interrupted, "but you're going to have to fight your first battle without any of the new hardware."

"Understood. But you know the old saying about light at the end of the tunnel." He paused. "There's something else that could mean even more to us . . . *if* it exists. In which case it's still classified 'Rumor' even for a fleet admiral. But one does hear things about a new breakthrough in ECM." He left the statement hanging.

"So one does. I'll look into it and see if there's anything to the rumor." Anderson was all blandness, and Antonov merely nodded. They understood each other.

"And now," Anderson said briskly, "there's someone I want you to meet." He touched another button. "Ask Lord Talphon to come in," he said.

Antonov's mouth didn't quite fall open, but his expression constituted the equivalent. Before he could formulate a question, a side door slid open to admit a tall Orion whose fur was the jet-black of the oldest noble bloodlines rather than the more usual tawny or russet shades. Antonov recognized his jeweled harness as being of the most expensive quality and noted the empty spots from which insignia of military rank had been removed.

"Admiral Antonov," Anderson said formally, "permit me to introduce Twenty-Third Small Claw of the Khan Kthaara'zarthan, Lord Talphon."

The massive admiral rose and performed the small bow one gave an Orion in lieu of a handshake.

"I am honored to greet you, Admiral Antaanaaav," Kthaara said, returning his bow just as gravely.

His voice was deep for an Orion, giving an unusual, almost velvety rumble to the gutturals of his language. Antonov was widely recognized as one of the TFN's "Tabby experts"—which, he knew, was one reason he'd been tapped to command Second Fleet—and now he savored Kthaara's patrician enunciation. Others might refer to the Orion language as "cat fights set to bagpipes" and bemoan the facts of evolution which made it impossible for the two species to reproduce the sounds of one another's languages, but not Antonov. He would have preferred to be able to speak Orion himself, but he differed from most of his fellows in the fact that he actually liked the sound of Orion voices. Which, Anderson had always maintained, was a perversion only to be expected from anyone who thought *Russian* was Old Terra's greatest language.

"Mister Aandersaahn is not altogether accurate concerning my status, however," Kthaara continued, "for I have resigned my commission, though it is true that I have been Lord Talphon and *Khanhaku'a'zarthan* since my cousin Khardanish died without issue."

Understanding dawned. "Please accept my condolences on the death of your cousin. He was a victim of treachery"—Antonov knew what that meant to an Orion—"but he died well."

"Thank you, Admiral," Kthaara reciprocated. "The circumstances of his death are the reason for my presence here. The *Khan'a'khanaaeee's* agreement to accept the Federation as *khimhok* satisfies the honor of our *race*, but I, as an individual and as Lord Talphon and—especially—as *khanhaku* of my clan, carry a special burden. Thus the *Khan'a'khanaaeee* has allowed me to set aside my military duties until this burden is lifted. I come to you as a private individual, to volunteer my services in the war against my cousin's killers!"

"Before you say anything, Ivan," Anderson put in, "Lord Talphon brings with him a certification from the Khan himself that he can act as an individual without compromising the Khanate's *khimhok* neutrality. And, I might also point out, he's regarded in the KON as one of their leading experts on strikefighter tactics."

Antonov scowled. The flower of the Federation's fighter jocks had perished with the "Peace Fleet," and now he was being offered the services of one of the top . . . he might as well say "people" . . . of a navy that specialized in fighters with a fervor that wasn't entirely based on cost/benefit rationality as humans understood it. For all of Orion history, their honor code had regarded personal combat as its only truly honorable expression. The Tabbies hadn't really been happy since the First Interstellar War, when small spacecraft had ceased to be effective combat units—a warrior with 150,000 tonnes of superdreadnought wrapped around him was hardly a warrior at all. The invention of the deep-space fighter had allowed them to be themselves again, and even the most prejudiced TFN officers admired their mastery of fighter tactics.

Yes, Antonov thought, *I can use him.* And, of course, to refuse his offer could hardly help Federation-Khanate relations, which needed all the help they could get, at the moment. But . . .

"Lord Kthaara," he began awkwardly, "I fully appreciate the significance of your offer, and I am grateful for it. But there are difficulties. As I don't need to tell you, any military organization has its professional jealousies . . . which can only be inflamed by bringing in an outsider to fill a billet as high as your rank and experience warrant. . . ."

"Rest assured, Admiral," Kthaara interrupted, "I will serve in any capacity you can find for me. If you want me to pilot a fighter, or operate a weapons console, I will do it."

And that, Antonov reflected, said a great deal about how serious Kthaara was. His clan had a high reputation, even among Orions, for the warriors it produced. Most Orion clan names and titles of nobility were identical, commemorating the heroism in battle which had earned their first Clan Father his lordship; the *khanhaku* of Clan Zarthan bore a secondary title, which was a proud honor indeed. For Kthaara to accept such a subordinate position was an almost unheard of concession, but even so . . .

"Unfortunately, that isn't the only problem." Antonov took a deep breath. "Our races have been allies for fifty Terran years, but it is an alliance that many in the Navy are still uncomfortable with. You see, fighting you was the TFN's reason for coming into existence in the first place. Before we met you, our Federation had no real military forces at all. The humans of that era believed that war was something that would never happen again . . . that any advanced civilization, anywhere, *must* be nonviolent."

"Why did they think that?" Kthaara asked, genuinely curious.

"Er . . . never mind. The point is, and I must be blunt, that dislike of your race is something of a tradition in the TFN. I regret that this is the case; but it is my duty to consider the effect the prejudices of others may have on the morale and effectiveness of my forces."

"Admiral, I fully understand. There are those among my race who still think of Humans as *chofaki*, in spite of the history of the Third Interstellar War . . . and in spite of Humans like my cousin's liaison officer, whom I believe you knew."

"Lieutenant Johansen?" Antonov was surprised anew. "Yes, I knew her; she served with my staff before her posting to Lord Khardanish's squadron. She was a fine officer. But—"

"A fine officer whom you encouraged to perfect her understanding of the Tongue of Tongues," Kthaara agreed with the Orion ear flick of acknowledgment. "Which is why I think you will be interested to know that her name has been entered among the Mothers in Honor of Clan Zarthan. My cousin, in his last courier drone, requested this . . . and made clear that she was fully deserving of it, that none of the *Zheeerlikou'valkhannaieee* could have better satisfied the demands of honor than she." He drew himself up. "I myself may do no less!"

For a moment, two pairs of eyes produced by two altogether separate evolutions met. Then Antonov spoke gruffly.

"Commissioning a foreign citizen is a little irregular, but with the good offices of such a dignitary as the Minister of War Production . . ."

Anderson smiled beatifically.

Admiral Antonov's staff contained an unusually high proportion of "Tabby experts." Despite that, and even though they'd known about it in advance, they couldn't quite hide their reaction when he entered the briefing room with a Whisker-Twister wearing a harness of TFN black-and-silver with the insignia of a commander in tow.

"As you were," Antonov rumbled, then continued matter-of-factly. "I would like to introduce Commander Kthaara'zarthan, who will be serving as Special Deputy Operations Officer of Strikefighter Operations." The title had been hammered out hours before, and the rank was a diplomatic courtesy. (The legal officer had been brought to the edge of a nervous breakdown by Kthaara's polite but relentless insistence that he was in no sense a diplomatic representative.) But none of that mattered. If Ivan the Terrible said the Tabby was a commander, then the Tabby was a commander. Very simple.

"Now," Antonov continued, with the air of a man who has made the most routine of announcements, "Lieutenant Commander Trevayne has prepared an intelligence update." He gestured to the intelligence officer, who activated a warp line display.

Winnifred Trevayne's face was dark, but her features were sharply chiseled and her speech held not a trace of the lilt an ancestor had brought from Jamaica in the late twentieth century; it was all clipped, upper-middle-class British.

"Thank you, Admiral. The Thebans have, at last report, secured the Laramie System." There was no reaction from the others; the news wasn't unexpected, and they were inured to shock by now. Trevayne summarized the fragmentary reports of fleeing survivors, adding: "This, combined with their known presence at QR-107, puts them in a position to attack Redwing along either—or both—of two axes. We do not know if they are in the same position vis-a-vis Griffin; the Manticore System has fallen, but at last report the Basil System had not."

"Thank you, Commander," Antonov said impassively. Then he addressed the room at large. "We now face the decision we knew must come. The Thebans have reached The Line at two points. They must know from captured data that they are finally about to run into something hard. Since there has been nothing stupid about their conduct of the war so far, we must assume they will concentrate their forces accordingly. The question is: will they attack Griffin or Redwing?" His voice seemed to drop an octave. "We must assume that their captured navigational data is complete. If so, they know Redwing is on the direct line to Sol. On this basis, I believe that Redwing is where they will attack. But, since we cannot be certain, I have no option but to divide our forces."

No one spoke. Antonov had invited neither comment nor advice. He'd taken the entire terrifying responsibility on his own massive shoulders.

"I will," he resumed, "take personal command of the Redwing task force. Captain Tsuchevsky," he said, turning to his chief of staff, "signal Vice Admiral Chebab. He will be taking the other task force to Griffin." Everyone present knew that dividing Antonov's new "Second Fleet" would result in two contingents whose size could scarcely justify the term "task force."

"And now, ladies and gentlemen," Antonov continued, "I believe we have a long night ahead of us."

CHAPTER TEN

"To Smite the Infidel..."

First Admiral Lantu watched the display as the destroyer slipped into orbit about Thebes, and frowned. He was too dutiful a son of the Church to begrudge the Synod's orders to return and confer, yet he found himself resenting the priceless time it took.

So far, the infidels had failed to mass a proper force against either First or Second Fleet, but he'd spent too many hours poring over captured data to expect that to continue. He'd smashed far more of their fleet in Lorelei than he'd dared hope, but they had reserves. And the Federation had grown far vaster than the Synod had believed possible. The infidels had found some way to make colonies spring up like weeds since the Year of the Annunciation, and Holy Terra's Sword must strike deep, and soon, or be overwhelmed.

He sighed heavily, and Fleet Chaplain Manak chuckled beside him. "Patience, my son," he murmured.

"Is it so obvious?" Lantu asked with a grin.

"To one who has watched you grow from childhood? Yes. To the Synod? Perhaps not, if you keep your wits about you."

"I'll bear it in mind," Lantu said softly.

The chairs in TFS *Starwalker*'s briefing auditorium were uncomfortable for Theban legs, but no one had ever even considered replacing them. The Synod of Holy Terra sat in state in its hallowed meeting place, eyes bright as Lantu entered with a measured tread and genuflected to the Prophet. He basked in their approval, yet he felt tension hovering like smoke.

"The blessing of Holy Terra upon you, my son," the Prophet said sonorously. "You return on the wings of victory, and we are well pleased."

"I thank you, Your Holiness," Lantu murmured, and the Prophet smiled.

"No doubt you begrudge time away from your fleet, First Admiral." Lantu glanced up in surprise, and the Prophet's smile grew. "That is only to be expected of a warrior, my son. We are not all"—the Prophet's glance rose to brush the grizzled bishops and archbishops— "too old and weary to understand that." There was a mutter of laughter, for the Prophet was even younger than Lantu.

"Yet it was necessary to recall you briefly. You are our warlord, the anointed champion of Holy Terra, and we require your advice."

"I am at your disposal, Your Holiness."

"Thank you." The Prophet gestured at a chair beside him. "Please, be seated, and I will explain our quandary."

Lantu obeyed, though he would have preferred to remain standing. It seemed impious to sit in the Prophet's presence.

"Now," the Prophet said briskly, "there has been some lively debate in this chamber, First Admiral. Your victories in Lorelei began our jihad with great success, yet success sometimes breeds dissension."

Lantu swallowed unobtrusively and looked out from the stage to find Manak. As First Fleet Chaplain, the old man was second only to the Prophet in rank, and his smile was comforting.

"The Messenger himself warned that Holy Terra might fall into the Satan-Khan's power, yet none of us ever truly anticipated the horror you discovered, my son," the Prophet continued, "and the truth has thrown us into turmoil. Our goal was to launch our jihad against the Satan-Khan, but the discovery of the Federation's apostasy divides us over how best to proceed. One portion of the Synod believes we should return to our original plan; another believes we must first crush the apostate. Both are infidel, so there is merit on both sides, and since we have not reached consensus, we ask you to speak your mind. Tell us how *you* think best to smite the infidel."

Lantu had suspected what they would ask, but the Prophet gave no sign of his own opinion, and the admiral gathered his thoughts with care.

"Your question is difficult, Your Holiness, and Holy Terra did not call me to the priesthood, so I can speak only to its military aspects. Is that satisfactory?"

"It is."

"Thank you, Your Holiness. In that case, I would begin by setting forth the military position as I now understand it.

"So far, we have occupied ten of the apostates' star systems and four of their starless warp junctions. We've also taken three unpopulated star systems from the Satan-Khan, which brings us almost into contact with the permanent fortifications of both of our enemies. Only one apostate system—Danzig—has withstood us. We could take Danzig, but the system's warp point is heavily fortified; our initial probe was thrown back with heavy losses, and I have decided against further attacks until we can deal decisively with the infidels' remaining fleet strength. The cost of Danzig's final conquest, though not unbearable for the capture of an entire star system, will be high. Indeed, no matter which direction we next strike, we will confront permanent defenses and, I fear, pay a high price to break through them. It is for that reason that I wish to defer attacks against nonessential objectives in the immediate future.

"Our losses to date are not severe in light of our achievements: a superdreadnought, four battleships, seven battle-cruisers, five heavy and light cruisers, and a dozen or so destroyers. Several more ships are under repair, but most of our losses will be made good by the repair of our prizes."

He paused and folded his hands before him.

"Before I continue, Your Holiness, may I ask Archbishop Ganhad to explore the question of weapons production for us?"

"Of course." The Prophet gestured for the stumpy old archbishop, the Synod's Minister of Production, to rise.

"Thank you, Your Holiness." Lantu turned to Ganhad. "Your Grace is more knowledgeable than I. Could you explain briefly to the Synod how what we've learned of the infidels' weapons affects our own production plans?"

"I can." Ganhad turned to face his fellows. "The infidels have attained a generally higher level of technology than the People," he said bluntly. "The gap is not tremendous, and some of our weapons surpass theirs, yet it exists.

"They have no equivalent of our *samurai* sleds, nor have we seen any equivalent of our Ramming Fleet, and their lasers, while somewhat more sophisticated in manufacture, are much less powerful and shorter ranged than our own.

"It would appear that they possess only four major weapon systems which we do not, and one is merely a highly refined development of another.

"First of these is the so-called 'capital missile,' which marries a long-ranged drive and powerful seeking systems with a heavy warhead. Such weapons can engage us from beyond our own range, and they carry ECM systems which make them difficult for point defense to stop. Accordingly, we've made their development our first priority, and our own capital missiles will begin reaching the fleet shortly.

"Second are the attack craft they call 'fighters.' These are one- and two-man craft, armed with short-ranged missiles and light lasers, capable of operating up to several light-minutes from their carriers. Their data base and tactical manuals indicate that they think highly of this weapon, but it has not proven effective in any of our engagements. Further, the infidels have developed the 'AFHAWK'—a small, high-speed missile with a light warhead but very sensitive homing systems—for anti-fighter defense. This weapon is ingenious but straightforward and is already in production. In light of the inefficacy of their fighters to date and our possession of the AFHAWK, we've given development of our own fighters a low priority.

"Third is the device they call a 'force beam.' While somewhat longer-ranged than our lasers, with a better power-to-mass ratio, it is simply a powerful Erlicher generator—or tractor beam—of alternating polarity. In essence, it wrenches its target apart by switching from tractor to presser mode in microsecond bursts. Although it cannot penetrate intact shields as lasers can, it remains a most formidable weapon. Since, however, it is no more than an application of technology we already possess, we can put it into production rapidly if we so desire.

"Fourth, but perhaps most important, is their 'primary' beam. In simplest terms, this is merely a vastly refined force beam so powerful and focused as to overload and penetrate shields locally. In addition, its power is sufficient to punch through the thickest armor or, indeed, anything in its path. It is slow-firing and its focus is extremely narrow— no more than four or five centimeters—but that is quite sufficient to disable any system. Since, however, it is basically only a powerful force beam, development of the one should lead naturally to development of the other, and we expect to have both in production shortly, although we will assign a higher manufacturing priority to the primary in light of our laser weapons' superiority."

He turned to Lantu with a courteous bob of his head.

"I trust that covers your question, First Admiral?"

"It does, indeed, Your Grace." Lantu chose not to mention that his own reports had suggested giving rather more priority to the fighter. The infidels hadn't yet had a chance to employ them as their tactical doctrine decreed, and the prospect of facing swarms of small, fast attackers operating from ships he couldn't reach was an unpleasant one. But development and production facilities had to be prioritized somehow, and a warrior—as he'd been rather pointedly told—fought with the weapons he had, not the ones he wished for.

He turned back to the task at hand.

"As I see it, Your Holiness, we have two strategic options and, within them, two operational problems.

"First, we may attack the Satan-Khan. This must, of course, be our ultimate goal. Until he's defeated, Holy Terra can never be safe, yet he has so far been content to let us smite the apostate unhindered. No doubt he finds this entertaining, but it may well prove his downfall.

"Second, we may continue to attack the apostate, and this, I think, is the wiser choice. We've occupied three of their inhabited worlds, and all we've seen suggests that it shouldn't be difficult to convert their industrial plants to our own use. If, in addition to this, the Holy Inquisition can bring substantial numbers of infidels to recant and embrace the True Faith, we will acquire large additions to our labor force. Finally—forgive me, I realize this is a spiritual consideration, yet it must be mentioned—we may liberate Holy Terra Herself much more rapidly if we continue to advance towards Her.

"If the Satan-Khan is prepared to allow us to defeat the Federation and add its industry to our own, then his own conceit will be his undoing."

He paused and saw Manak's approving nod. More importantly, he saw several other prelates nodding slowly.

"That is well-argued, my son," the Prophet said softly. "But what of these operational problems you mentioned?"

"Your Holiness, we've driven as far into infidel space as we can without confronting their fortifications. I lack sufficient data on what they call 'The Line' to evaluate its strength, but while the forts are quite old, the infidels seem to consider them powerful, which suggests they've been refitted and updated heavily. Certainly the only fortifications we've actually encountered—those of the Danzig System—are, indeed, formidable.

"Further, we know their reserves have not yet been committed. I would feel happier if they had been, preferably in bits and pieces we might defeat in detail. Instead, the infidels seem intent on gathering strength for a heavy blow.

"Our problems thus are, first, whether or not to continue to advance and, related but separate, *how* we shall advance.

"At the moment, we have near parity with the infidels, and no other sectors to guard. We are concentrated, if you will, to an extent they cannot match. But if we suffer heavy losses, we may forfeit that advantage.

"On the other hand, we occupy systems they must eventually seek to regain. I suggest, therefore, that we stand temporarily on the defense and let them come to us in order to eliminate as much as possible of their reserves before we assay 'The Line.' "

"Stand on the defense?!" An elderly bishop jerked upright in shock. "When you've defeated them so easily at every attempt?"

Lantu glanced at the Prophet, who nodded for him to reply.

"Forgive me, Your Grace, but to date we've had the advantage of surprise and overwhelming numbers against naked warp points. Contested warp point assaults will be costly, particularly if we attack fleet units supported by fixed defenses. If, on the other hand, we revert to a defensive stance, we invite their attack and *we* hold the defender's advantage."

"So your defensive stance is actually an offensive one?" Manak asked.

"Exactly, Holiness," Lantu said gratefully.

"Yet you yourself point to their greater resources!" the bishop protested. "If we yield the initiative, may they not assemble such force as to overwhelm us, defensive advantage or no?"

"That is, of course, possible, but the infidels are not wizards. It takes time to build ships, and if much time passes without an attack, we may rethink our own deployments. But it seems wiser to me to tempt them into a mistake than to make one ourselves."

"Hmph!" the bishop snorted. "These are not the words I expected of a warrior! You say our losses are scarcely a score of ships, while they have lost many times that many—is this not a sign their apostasy has sapped their ability to fight? With Holy Terra at your side, do you fear to confront so contemptible a foe?"

Lantu bit off a hot retort as he recalled the stubborn, hopeless fight of the infidel battle-line at Lorelei. Whatever else it was, the Federation was *not* a "contemptible foe," but he must be wary of charges of cowardice.

"Your Grace," he said carefully, "with Holy Terra at my side, I fear neither to confront any foe nor to die. I only advocate caution. We have won great victories against a powerful enemy; I would not see them thrown away through overconfidence."

He dared say nothing stronger, but he saw disagreement on the bishop's face—and others—and his heart sank. The Synod hadn't personally faced the infidels. They had only his reports, and the bishop hadn't seen—or had ignored—the warnings he'd tried to give.

"Thank you, my son," the Prophet said expressionlessly. "You have spoken well. Now we ask you to retire while the Synod debates."

"Of course, Your Holiness." Lantu effaced himself and left, trying not to let his apprehension show.

More than an hour passed before Manak rejoined Lantu in the small antechamber. The old churchman's expression was heavy as he beckoned to Lantu, and the admiral fell in beside him as he headed for *Starwalker*'s ramp. The chaplain rested one hand on his shoulder and shook his head.

"They've heeded you, in part. We will let the Satan-Khan wait. It makes good sense to gain the Federation's resources, and it is our duty to reclaim the apostate for the Faith, so you left little to argue on that point. But they reject your proposal to stand on the defensive."

"But, Holiness—"

"Hush, my son." Manak looked about quickly, then spoke in a softer voice. "I expected that to come from old Bishop Wayum, but the Prophet himself agreed. The matter is closed. We will continue the attack."

"As the Synod decrees," Lantu murmured, but he closed his inner eyelids in disquiet as he descended *Starwalker*'s sacred ramp.

CHAPTER ELEVEN

"The Line will hold!"

"Attention on deck."

The assembled officers rose silently as Admiral Antonov entered the briefing room, accompanied by Kthaara and Captain Tsuchevsky.

"As you were." The admiral's bass voice was quiet—ominously so, Tsuchevsky thought. He'd known Antonov for years, and he knew the signs. In particular, he noted that the boss's faint accent was just a trifle less faint than usual.

"Commodore Chandra," Antonov addressed the CO of Redwing Fortress Command, "I have reviewed your proposals for defensive dispositions. I believe the essence of these is that all orbital fortresses be tractored to within tactical range of the Laramie and QR-107 warp points, there to fight a delaying action while Second Fleet covers the evacuation of essential personnel to Cimmaron."

"Correct, sir," Chandra acknowledged. He and the others were actually showing relief at Antonov's calm and measured tone, Tsuchevsky noted with a kind of horrified fascination. "Of course," Chandra babbled on, "I've given a high priority to detaching part of Second Fleet's assets to cover the Novaya Rodina warp point during the withdrawal. I was certain this would be a matter of special concern to you and—" an unctuous nod "—Captain Tsuchevsky."

"I took note of this, Commodore. I also took note," Antonov continued just as emotionlessly, "that the 'essential personnel' to be evacuated included the upper management levels of the Galloway's World industrial interests with branches here . . . as well as everyone in this room." The increase in volume was so gradual only the most sensitive souls perceived it. Chandra was not among them.

"Er, well, Admiral, there are, after all, a hundred and fifty million people on Redwing. Since we can't possibly evacuate all of them, we have to consider who among those we *can* evacuate will be most useful to the war effort, so certain hard choices . . . yes, Hard Choices . . . must be made. And, obviously, special consideration must be given to—"

"You are relieved, Commodore." Antonov's voice cut Chandra's off as if the latter hadn't existed. "There is a courier ship leaving for Terra at 22:00; you will be on it . . . along with my report to Admiral Brandenburg."

Chandra blinked stupidly. "But, but, Admiral sir, I only . . ."

"Do you wish to add insubordination to charges of incompetence and cowardice, Commodore Chandra?" Antonov wasn't—exactly—shouting, but his voice had become a sustained roar from which everyone physically flinched, "*Yob' tvoyu mat'!*" Realizing he'd lapsed into Russian, he obligingly provided a translation. "Fuck your mother! Get out of here and confine yourself to quarters until departure, you worthless *chernozhopi!*"

Chandra's staff sat paralyzed as he stood clumsily, face pale, and then stumbled from the room. Tsuchevsky sighed softly in relief that Antonov hadn't continued his translation—the fine old Russian term of disapprobation "black ass" might have been even more offensive than the admiral intended. Every other face was blank . . . except Kthaara'zarthan's. The Orion watched Chandra with a grin that bared his ivory fangs.

"Now," Antonov continued, not quite as loudly (one could merely feel the vibrations through the soles of one's feet), "the rest of you will continue in your present duties . . . on a probationary basis, contingent upon acceptable performance of those duties. And I trust I have made clear my feelings on the subject of defeatism." His voice lost a little volume but became, if possible, even deeper. "There will be no more talk of retreats or evacuations! The Line will hold! As of now all leaves are canceled. Captain Lopez!" That worthy jumped in his chair. "You are now a commodore. You should regard this not as a promotion but as an administrative necessity for you to assume Commodore Chandra's duties. You will coordinate with Captain Tsuchevsky to schedule operational readiness exercises around the redeployment of this system's defenses." He activated the room's holographic unit and indicated the orbital works surrounding the Laramie and QR-107 warp points. "All of these fortresses are to be tractored —*here.*" The cursor flashed across the planetary system to the Cimmaron warp point.

The Fortress Command staff's shock was now complete. Lopez found his tongue. "But, sir, what will we use to defend the Thebans' entry warp points? And what about the Novaya Rodina warp point?"

"Nothing is to defend the ingress warp points, Commodore,"

Antonov rumbled. "If we try to defend them, not knowing which the Thebans will choose, we must divide our forces. And even if we stop them, they will simply bring in reinforcements and try again. And *they* have reserves available now." He glared around the table. "I will attempt—*one more time*—to make myself clear: this is not a delaying action. Our objective is to *smash* the Thebans! If any one of you fails to understand this, or to carry out my orders, I'll break him."

"As for the Novaya Rodina warp point," Antonov continued after a pause of a few heartbeats, "its defenses are not to be reinforced. Novaya Rodina is a major warp nexus—but mostly of warp lines leading to uninhabited systems. The Thebans must know this. And, so far, they've consistently advanced toward the Inner Worlds. I believe they will continue to do so."

The briefing room was silent again, but this time not entirely from fear. Everyone present knew Antonov had relatives on Novaya Rodina . . . and that Pavel Sergeyevich Tsuchevsky was one of the first native-born citizens of that fledgling colony.

"And now," Antonov resumed, "we have much planning to do. In particular, it is necessary that Fortress Command and Second Fleet coordinate fighter operations. Commander Kthaara'zarthan will be in charge of this project." He paused, then continued in the calm, low voice no one in the room was ever likely to misinterpret again. "Is this a problem for anyone?"

The disorientation of warp transit faded as *Hildebrandt Jackson* followed her escorts into Redwing, and First Admiral Lantu watched the superdreadnought's displays confirm his advance elements' incredible report. The warp point was undefended.

It was anticlimactic . . . and disquieting. Holy Terra's warriors had prepared themselves for Her sternest test yet: an assault on a warp point of the infidels' long-established, much-vaunted "Line." But already his scouts were proceeding unmolested across the system as his capital ships emerged into an eerie calm which shouldn't exist.

"I don't like this, Holiness," he said, but quietly. His subordinates must not see his uncertainty. "All our data speaks of massive fortifications at *all* of Redwing's warp points, and simple sanity says the infidels *must* commit their available mobile forces to its defense. So where are they?"

"Ah, my son, who can fathom the minds of the apostate?" Manak said too calmly. *He* knew better than to fall into the Synod's complacency, and Lantu started to say so, then paused before the unspoken worry in the prelate's eyes. The Fleet Chaplain wasn't getting any younger, he thought with a sudden pang.

"Holiness. First Admiral." Lantu looked up at Captain Yurah's voice.

"The scouts have reached sensor range of the other warp points. They're downloading their findings now, and—"

The flag captain paused as fresh lights awoke in the master plot's three-dimensional sphere. Most of them were concentrated at one point.

"So," Lantu murmured. "*That's* where they went, Holiness! The infidels have tractored everything but the planetary defenses to our projected *exit* warp point. It would seem they've anticipated our objectives . . . but why not contest our entry transit?" The first admiral rubbed the bridge of his muzzle unhappily. "Even their energy weapons could have hurt us badly at a range that low. It makes no sense. No *military* sense," he added. "Surely even heretics . . ."

"Remember, my son, that these fortifications are old. Indeed, they date almost from the days of the Messenger! Perhaps they're feebler than we thought." Lantu carefully took no note of Manak's self-convincing tone, but the fleet chaplain frowned. "Still, perhaps it would be wise to wait until after they've been reduced before detaching units against the planet."

"I agree, Holiness. Captain Yurah, inform Commodore Gahad that the Fleet will execute deployment Plan Gamma. He is not to detach his task group without my specific instructions."

"Aye, sir," Yurah confirmed, and Lantu watched his display as First Fleet of the Sword of Holy Terra advanced steadily towards the clustered fortresses. He didn't like it, but the Synod's instructions left him no choice.

"Enemy fleet is proceeding towards the Cimmaron warp point, Admiral."

Antonov grunted. They'd had some bad moments as the Theban scouts approached within scanner range of this stretch of the asteroid belt between the system's gas-giant fourth and fifth planets. But the scouts had been mesmerized by the mammoth orbital forts. They hadn't been looking for ships with their power plants stepped down to minimal levels, lurking amid the rubble of an unborn planet.

He looked around the improvised flag bridge of TFNS *Indomitable*. A *Kongo*-class battle-cruiser wasn't intended to serve as a fleet flagship, and accommodations for his staff were cramped. But there'd been no question of flying his lights on one of the capital ships holding station in the Cimmaron System, thirty-two light-years distant in Einsteinian space but an effectively-instantaneous warp transit away, awaiting the courier drone that would summon them when the moment was right. No, he would live or die with the ships that would be trapped in Redwing if his plan failed and the Thebans secured its warp points.

Kthaara approached. "Admiral, they are nearing Point Staahlingraad." He gestured at the scarlet point in the navigational display.

Antonov nodded, watching from the corner of one eye as Kthaara's ears flattened and his claws slid from their sheaths. Labels like "Felinoid" were usually misleading, he thought; an Orion, product of an entirely separate evolution, was less closely related to a Terran cat than was a Terran lizard, or fish, or tree. The resemblance was mere coincidence, bound to happen occasionally in a galaxy of four hundred billion suns. But Kthaara was nonetheless descended from millions of years of predators . . . and Antonov was just as glad humans weren't this day's prey.

"Commodore Tsuchevsky," he said unnecessarily, "when Thebans reach Point Stalingrad, you will bring fleet to full readiness and await my word."

"Understood, Admiral." Tsuchevsky knew how much strain the boss was under when he started voicing redundant orders . . . and when his Standard English started losing its definite articles.

"Commander Kthaara," Antonov continued, "you will order our fighter launch at your discretion, within parameters of operations plan." Once that would have been unthinkable, but not after the past few weeks' exercises. There might still be officers who didn't accept the Whisker-Twister; none of the fighter jocks were among them.

He settled back in his command chair and waited.

Aboard the command fortress, other eyes watched the Thebans approach Point Stalingrad. They reached it.

"Launch all fighters!"

Commodore Lopez committed Fortress Command's full fighter strength, and, for the first time, the TFN's fighters hurled themselves at the Thebans in a well-organized, well-rehearsed strike from secure bases.

Lantu hunkered deeper into his command chair as his tactical sphere blossomed with new threat sources. He'd been afraid of this. Those well-ordered formations were a far cry from the scrambling confusion he'd faced at Lorelei, and they might explain why the infidels had conceded the entry warp points. It was clear their fighters had even more operational range than he'd feared—enough, perhaps, to fall back and rearm to launch a second or even a third strike before First Fleet could range on their launch bays.

But First Fleet wasn't entirely helpless, he reminded himself grimly.

Lieutenant Allison DuPre of Strikefighter Squadron 117 led Fortress Command's fighters towards the enemy, hoping Admiral Antonov and the Tabby were right about Theban underestimation of their capabilities. They'd better be. She was one of the very few veteran pilots Fortress Command had, and they'd need every break—

Her wingman exploded in a glare of fire.

"AFHAWKs!" she snapped over the command net. "Evasive action—now!"

Only then did she permit herself to curse.

Lantu watched the first infidel fighters die and thanked Holy Terra Archbishop Ganhad had agreed to make AFHAWK production a priority, but he didn't share his staff's satisfaction. The kill ratio was far lower than predicted; clearly the infidels had devised not only an offensive doctrine to *employ* the weapon but defensive tactics to *evade* it, as well. No wonder their tactical manuals stressed that the best anti-fighter weapon was another fighter!

The survivors streamed forward past the wreckage of their fellows. They would be into their own range all too soon.

Lieutenant DuPre's surviving squadron spread out behind her, settling into attack formation, and she felt a glow of pride. They might be newbies, but they'd learned their stuff. And the Tabby had known a few wrinkles even DuPre had never heard of. She watched her display as the cursor marking their initial point flared. Any moment now—

There!

"Follow me in!" she snapped, and massed squadrons of fleet little vessels screamed through a turn possible only to inertia-canceling drives. They howled in, streaking in through the last-ditch fire of lasers and point defense missiles, breaking into the sternward "blind spots" of ionization and distorted space created by the Theban capital ships' drives.

One-Seventeen lost two more fighters on the way in . . . including Lieutenant DuPre's. But the three survivors broke through into the blind spots where no weapons could be brought to bear. And then, at what passed for point-blank range in space combat, their weapons spoke, coordinated by their dead skipper's training and energized by vengeance.

Lantu kept his face impassive, but he heard the fleet chaplain's soft groan as the infidels broke through everything First Fleet could throw. Their weapons were short-ranged and individually weak, but they struck with dreadful, beautiful precision. Entire squadrons fired as one, wracking his ships' shields with nuclear fire, then closing to rake their flanks with lasers as they streaked forward past the slow, lumbering vessels. None of them had targeted *Jackson*, but the superdreadnought *Allen Takagi* was less fortunate. Her shields went down, and even her massive armor yielded to the insistent pounding of her attackers. She faltered as a drive pod exploded, but she lumbered on, bleeding atmosphere like blood.

"They're breaking off, sir," Yurah reported, but the admiral shook his head. They weren't "breaking off." They'd executed their attack; now they were withdrawing to rearm for another.

"Sir, *John Calvin* and *Takagi* can no longer maintain flank speed. Shall I reduce Fleet speed to match?"

"Negative. Detail extra escorts to cover them and continue the advance at flank. We've got to hit those forts as soon as possible."

"Aye, sir."

"Admiral," Tsuchevsky reported, "the Fortress Command fighters are fully engaged. The enemy has sustained heavy damage and seems to be detaching some destroyer formations for fighter suppression— a task for which"—he added with satisfaction—"they clearly lack the proper doctrine and armament. But their heavy units are proceeding on course for the warp point. They'll be within capital missile range of the fortresses shortly."

Antonov nodded as he stared fixedly at the system-wide holo display. To communicate with the fortresses would be to risk revealing himself. He could only trust that Lopez would play his part.

"Commodore Tsuchevsky," he spoke distinctly and formally, "Second Fleet will advance."

The deck vibrated as *Indomitable*'s drive awoke. On the view screens, the drifting mountain that had concealed her slid to one side, revealing the starry firmament, and reflected starlight gleamed dimly as other ships formed up on the battle-cruiser while the last fighter warheads flashed like new, brief stars amid the Theban fleet.

Antonov sat back and heaved a sigh. Then he leaned over and spoke in Tsuchevsky's ear. "Well, Pasha, we're committed. Let's hope Lopez doesn't have his head too far up his ass."

"Da, Nikolayevich," Tsuchevsky replied just as quietly.

Fortress Command's fighters fled back to their bases to rearm, pursued by a badly shaken Theban fleet. Few ships had been destroyed— the orbital forts had too few fighters for a decisive strike, as Kthaara had observed with exasperation—but many were damaged. Some were injured even more seriously than *Calvin* and *Takagi*, and keeping formation was becoming a problem, but Lantu pressed on at his best speed. He wanted very badly to get within missile range and smash those looming fortresses before they relaunched their infernal little craft for a second strike . . . if he could.

His fleet entered capital missile range, and he braced himself again as the big missiles began to speed toward First Fleet.

The Thebans had encountered those missiles before; what they hadn't encountered were the warheads Howard Anderson had somehow managed to get to Redwing ahead of all realistic schedules. Not many of them, but a few. And as one of them came within a certain distance of its target, a non-material containment field collapsed, matter met antimatter, and the target ship experienced something new in the history of destruction. The field-generator was so massive that little antimatter could be contained—but even a little produced a blast three times as devastating as a warhead of comparable mass that relied on the energies of fusing deuterium atoms.

Some Thebans panicked as the hell-weapons crushed shields with horrible ease and mere metal vaporized . . . but not on Lantu's flag bridge. Face set, the first admiral ordered still more speed, even at the expense of what remained of his formation. There was no doubt now. He *had* to close the range and stop the terrible fighters and missiles at their source. And the new technology *must* be captured and turned to the use of Holy Terra. But even as he passed the word for the boarding parties to prepare themselves, infidel superdreadnoughts began to emerge ponderously from the Cimmaron warp point and the first rearmed fighters spat from the fortresses.

All of which meant that neither organic nor cybernetic attention was directed sternward in the direction of the barren asteroid belt they'd passed earlier. So the small fleet of carriers and their escorts that proceeded in First Fleet's wake went unnoticed.

Indomitable's flag bridge was silent. Antonov intended to take full advantage of Kthaara's instinct for fighter operations, so the Orion must be given the free hand he'd been promised. As was so often the case, once battle was joined the commanding officer's role was largely reduced to projecting an air of confidence.

Suddenly, Kthaara spoke a string of snarling, hissing noises to his assigned Orion-cognizant talker. The talker passed the orders on in the name of Fleet Command, and two fleet carriers and nine *Pegasus*-class light carriers launched their broods as one.

The thermonuclear detonations surrounding the battling Theban ships and Terran fortresses were dwarfed less and less often by the greater fires of negative matter, Lantu noted as he ordered the *samurai* sleds launched. Holy Terra was merciful; the infidels' supply of their new weapon was clearly limited. But his relief was short-lived.

"First Admiral! Formations of attack craft are approaching from astern!" Fresh lights blinked in the display sphere to confirm the incredible report, and Lantu blanched. The fortresses' fighters looming second strike would, at these ranges, arrive and be completed just before these mysterious newcomers struck, and understanding filled him. There *were* mobile infidel units; somewhere behind him was a fleet of unknown strength, in position to pin him against The Line like an insect pressed against glass.

He did what he could, cursing himself fervently for not having paid still more attention to the infidels' tactical manuals. A few minutes' desperate improvisation with his maneuvering officer rearranged his ships—some of them, at least—to cover one another's blind zones, producing a ragged approximation of the classic echelon type of anti-fighter formation. There were too many uncovered units, too many weak spots, but at least his ships could offer each other *some* mutual support. And, he reminded himself, his boarding parties should reach their objectives any time now. . . .

Gunnery Sergeant Jason Mendenhall, Terran Federation Marine Raiders, led his squad through the outermost spaces of the command fortress. Though normally the realm of service 'bots, these passages were designed for human accessibility if the need arose, so the Marines moved under artificial gravity through passageways that were large enough to accommodate them . . . barely.

There was no way they could have made it through inboard spaces in the old powered armor, the sergeant reflected. It had served well enough in the Third Interstellar War, but it could never squeeze into these close quarters. Which, after all, was exactly why this handier new version had been designed—and thank God for it! The designers had never expected to repel boarders in deep space *(Eat your hearts out, pirates of the Spanish Main!)*, but now that they knew. . . .

Some R&D smartass with an historical bent had resurrected the name "zoot suit" early in the development program, and the official term "Combat Suits, Mark V" had somehow been altered to "combat zoots." Mendenhall didn't care what anyone called them. He didn't even care how badly he stank inside one. He'd seen the demonstration of assault rifle bullets bouncing off a zoot . . . and he knew the capabilities of the weapon he carried.

The dull *whump! of* an explosion came around a corner, and air screamed down the passageway, confirming Tactical's projection of where the Thebans would breach the hull. Sergeant Mendenhall waved his troopers flat against the bulkhead. They didn't have long to wait before their helmet sensors picked up the sounds of the advancing boarders through the rapidly thinning air. Mendenhall grunted in satisfaction and motioned the squad forward, then swung his combat-suited body around the corner with his weapon leveled.

He was prepared for the appearance of the Theban he confronted, but the Theban was not prepared for a two-and-a-half-meter-tall armored titan out of myth. He was even less prepared for the looming troll's weapon. The center of its single-shot chamber contained a hydrogen pellet suspended in a super-conducting grid, and now converging micro-lasers heated the pellet to near-fusion temperatures. The resulting bolt of plasma was electromagnetically ejected down a laser guide beam, leaving a wash of superheated air that would have fried a man protected by anything less than a combat zoot. Mendenhall wore such a zoot; the Thebans did not.

The gout of plasma engulfed the lead boarder, and his brief, terrible scream ended in a roar of secondary explosions as the heat ignited the ammunition he was carrying.

Most of his fellows died almost as quickly as he, their vac suits' refrigeration systems overwhelmed by a thermal pulse that seared the bulkheads down to bare alloy, and the survivors were stunned, frozen for just an instant as the rest of Mendenhall's squad deployed and opened fire. Not with plasma guns but with cut-down heavy anti-personnel launchers that fired a rapid stream of hyper-velocity rockets—powered flechettes, really. Theban vac-suits had some protective armor, but against the weapons the Marines' exoskeletal "muscles" let them carry, they might as well have been in their skivvies.

It was a massacre, but the Thebans didn't quite go alone. One of them carried a shoulder-fired rocket launcher to deal with blast doors and internal bulkheads, and Gunny Mendenhall's combat zoot received, at point-blank range, a shaped-charge warhead designed to take out a heavy tank.

First Admiral Lantu fixed bitter eyes on the tactical display as he listened to Captain Yurah. Not a single boarding party had reported success, and the brief snatches of their frantic battle chatter were the last datum he needed. Another ambush, he thought coldly. First Fleet had stumbled into ambush after ambush, and the fact that he'd warned against the attack only made his bitterness complete.

The Line's fighters had struck hard . . . and the mystery fighters had struck harder. *Takagi* was gone. *Calvin* was practically immobile. Other ships were almost as badly damaged, and the fighters which had wreaked such havoc were already returning to the shadowy carriers hanging at the very edge of detectability. They'd suffered less losses than those from the fortresses, too, for they'd *started* in First Fleet's blind spot. Nor did he dare turn to deprive them of their tactical advantage while he engaged The Line; allowing those demonic fortresses to fire their far more powerful missiles into that same blind spot would be suicidal. Worse, the capital ships from Cimmaron, though few in number, were starting to make a difference in the energy-weapon slugging match which now raged with the fortresses.

And the supply of AFHAWKs wouldn't last forever.

"Holiness, we must disengage," he said quietly, and Manak stared at him with shocked eyes. "The infidels have trapped us between the fortresses and their carriers; if we don't break off, our entire fleet may be destroyed."

"We can't, my son! Our losses are heavy, but if we reduce the fortresses—secure the warp point—the *apostate* will be trapped, not us!"

"I wish it might be so, Holiness," Lantu said heavily, "but Cimmaron is also fortified. Even if we crush The Line, its forts will be waiting when we make transit. And if we *don't* make transit, the infidel carriers will pick our bones while we squat amid the wreckage. But even if we held the warp point, we could never trap their ships, Holiness; their carriers are as fast as our fastest units, their fighters out-range our best weapons, and they can always withdraw on Novaya Rodina."

"But the Synod, Lantu! The Prophet himself decreed this attack—how will we explain to the *Synod*?"

Lantu's head lifted. "*I* will explain to the Synod, Holiness. This fleet is my command; Holy Terra has trusted me not to waste Her People's lives, and persisting blindly will do just that. The decision is mine alone; if it is faulty, the fault will be my own, as well." Yet even as he said it, Lantu knew, guiltily, that he didn't believe it. The fault lay with those who had ignored his counsel and commanded him to execute a plan in which he did not believe. With those who'd fatuously assumed generations-old orbital forts hadn't been upgraded and modernized. Those for whom his fleet had sacrificed so much . . . and would now be required to make still one more sacrifice—

"No." Manak touched his arm. "You are our First Admiral, but I am Fleet Chaplain. The decision is mine, as well, and—" he met Lantu's eyes levelly "—it is the right one. *We* will explain to the Synod, my son. Do what you must."

"Thank you, Holiness," Lantu said softly, then drew a deep breath and turned to his communications officer. "Connect me with Admiral Trona," he said in a voice of cold iron. "It will be necessary for the Ramming Fleet to cover our withdrawal."

Commodore Lopez looked about the command center, watching people as weary as he try to coordinate damage control in the blood-red glow of the emergency lights. Surely, he thought, this battle could not go on.

It couldn't. A tired cheer went up as the Theban fleet began to swing away. Lopez started to join it, but an anomaly on the battle plot caught his eye. Why were those battle-cruisers and heavy cruisers detaching from the withdrawing enemy and moving toward his forts at flank speed?

It is practically impossible for one starship to physically ram another, given the maneuverability conferred by reactionless drives. Even if one captain is suicidal enough to attempt it, the other can usually avoid it with ease. And, in the rare instances in which it can be contrived, the damage to both ships is almost invariably total, unless one vessel's drive field is extraordinarily more massive than the other's. It is not a cost-effective tactic, for a warship heavy enough to endure a defender's fire while closing *and* to smash a capital ship is too valuable a combat unit to expend on a single attack, however deadly.

But the Thebans had found a way. It cost them something in speed and power efficiency, but in return they could manipulate the drive field itself, producing a "bow wave" or spur which was, in effect, an electromagnetic ram. The TFN had never imagined such a thing, for even with the ram, damage aboard the attacking vessel was dreadful as abused engine rooms consumed themselves, and the attack was still fairly easy for a mobile unit to avoid.

But The Line's fortresses weren't mobile.

The cruisers of the Theban Ramming Fleet were crewed by the most fanatical members of the Church of Holy Terra. They carried little except the mammoth machinery required to deform a drive field . . . and assault sleds set for automatic launch after ramming.

"Admiral," Tsuchevsky spoke urgently, "the fortresses have taken heavy damage from this new attack system and their Marine detachments are again engaged with boarders. Our second strike is just entering attack range . . . they could be diverted against the ramming ships that haven't reached their targets. . . ."

Antonov cut him off with a chop of his hand. "No," he said, loudly enough to be heard by his entire staff. "That's what the Thebans want. The fortresses will have to defend themselves as best they can. Our first priority must be their capital ships. Every one of those that escapes, we'll have to fight again one day." He'd been as shaken as anyone else by the Thebans' latest manifestation of racial insanity, but he couldn't show it. "The fighters will proceed with their mission."

Kthaara looked at him oddly, clearly thinking the admiral would have made a good Orion. Antonov knew his human officers were thinking precisely the same thing.

It was over. The Theban survivors had completed their skillfully directed withdrawal from the system, and Second Fleet had rendezvoused with the fortresses to lend whatever aid it could. Antonov looked expressionlessly at the scrolling lists of confirmed dead . . . the many dead. Including Commodore Antonio Lopez y Sandoval, killed at his station when a Theban battle-cruiser disemboweled his command fortress with a spear of pure force.

He heard a voice from the group of staffers behind him and turned around. "What is it, Commander Trevayne?"

"I was just thinking, sir," the intelligence officer replied softly, "of something a countryman of mine said centuries ago. 'Except for a battle lost, there is nothing so terrible as a battle won.'"

Antonov grunted and turned back to the names on the phosphor screen.

CHAPTER TWELVE

Like the Good Old Days

The ground car settled as pressure bled from the plenum chamber, and the passenger hatch unsealed itself. Howard Anderson climbed out unaided and stumped past Ensign Mallory on his cane, glad the earnest young man had finally learned not to offer assistance. Even an aide with a bad case of hero worship could learn not to coddle his boss if he was chewed out enough, and all ensigns should be pruned back occasionally. It served them in good stead later.

Mallory scurried ahead to punch the elevator button, and this time Anderson gave him a brief nod of thanks as he stepped into it. He regretted it almost instantly when the ensign beamed as if, Anderson thought sourly, he were wagging the tail he didn't have. Then his thoughts flicked away from Mallory and he stood silently, drumming gently on the head of his cane as floor lights winked. If ONI had found what he expected, he was going to tear someone a new asshole . . . and enjoy it.

The elevator stopped, and the old man and the young stepped out. An unbiased witness might have reflected on how much the ensign looked like a vastly younger version of his boss, but if that had been suggested to Anderson he would have felt a bit bilious. He liked young Mallory, but it would have wounded his *amour-propre* to remember ever having been *that* green.

"Those reports ready, Andy?" he asked as they neared his office.

"Yes, sir."

"Good."

His office door opened, and he waved Yeoman Gonzales back down as she started to shoot upright. She settled back with rather more

101

aplomb than Mallory would have shown, and he spared her a smile as he passed on his way to the inner office.

He shooed Mallory out of the room as he switched on his terminal. His gnarled fingers tapped at the keyboard with surprising agility, and his blue eyes hardened as a file header appeared.

"Why, hello, Mister Anderson. This is a pleasant surprise."

Lawrence Taliaferro stood as the Minister for War Production entered his sumptuous office. He was a chunky man, going rapidly to fat, with a broad face. At the moment his gray eyes were wary, and Anderson wondered idly how many different reasons Taliaferro had to worry. Probably quite a few, but the one which brought him here would do for starters.

"Thank you," he said graciously, sitting as Taliaferro personally drew a comfortable chair closer to his desk.

"Not at all. Not at all. May I offer refreshment?" Taliaferro's finger hovered over his call button, but Anderson shook his head. He found the Corporate World nobility's ostentatious employment of personal servants distasteful. Besides, he approved of the Orion habit of never accepting food or drink from *chofaki*.

"Well, then!" Taliaferro said brightly. "What brings you here, Mister Anderson? Anything we can do for you would be an honor."

"Why, thank you again," Anderson said genially. This was the first time he'd actually met Lawrence Taliaferro. The Taliaferro Yard had done a good job reactivating Antonov's ships, but so they damned well should have. They owned half the Jamieson Archipelago in fee simple after forty years of gobbling up chunks of their competitors. Even for a world whose constitution enshrined monolithic capitalism, the Taliaferros were over-achievers.

He eyed his host thoughtfully. Lawrence was the grandson of Winston Taliaferro, founder of the family empire. Anderson remembered Winston well from ISW-1, and he considered it a great pity the old man had died before antigerone therapy became available. He'd been a hard, merciless old pirate, but he'd been a *man*. And for all his ambition, he'd never, to Anderson's knowledge, played fast and loose with the safety of the Terran Federation. Fortunately, the population of Galloway's World had grown enough that Lawrence would have to agree to emigrate if *he* wanted the antigerone treatments.

Taliaferro fidgeted under those thoughtful, silent old eyes, feeling betrayed after all the credits he'd contributed to Sakanami Hideoshi's campaign chest. He knew they were at war, but had it really been necessary to send this horrible old dinosaur to *his* world? And what brought the old bastard here now? Those bright blue eyes were like leveled missiles, summoning up a long mental list of the Taliaferro Yard's hidden infractions.

"Mister Taliaferro," Anderson said finally, "I've been reading some interesting technical reports in the past few days. Some very exciting ones."

"Oh?" Taliaferro relaxed just a bit.

"Yes, indeed. There've been a lot of changes since my day. If I'd had some of the new hardware at Aklumar or Ophiuchi Junction, well . . ." He shrugged, and Taliaferro beamed.

"Yes, we're rather proud of our achievements. Our men and women in uniform deserve the very best, and—"

"I quite agree," Anderson interrupted smoothly, "and now that we've got the Reserve reactivated and cleared the decks, as it were, I've been considering the prioritization of new construction. It looks like a lot of credits will be flowing through The Yard and Galloway's World generally. A lot of credits."

"Oh?" Taliaferro repeated, sitting straighter, and avarice gleamed in his eyes. Anderson observed it with pleasure.

"Indeed. And I want to personally inform you of the disbursement plan which will cover the Taliaferro Yard's share of the preliminary work."

"Why, that's very kind, sir. I'm sure—"

"In particular," Anderson said affably, "of why the Taliaferro Yard will be performing the first one-point-five billion credits of work gratis."

"*What?!*" Taliaferro jerked up out of his chair, eyes bulging, and the old man smiled coldly. "You can't—I mean, we . . . *Preposterous!*"

"On the contrary, Mister Taliaferro," Anderson's suddenly icy tone cut like a flaying knife, "I'm being quite lenient."

"But . . . but . . ."

"Sit down, Mister Taliaferro." The industrialist collapsed back into his chair, and Anderson leaned forward on his cane. "I've been most impressed by your R&D on new ECM systems. Your people are to be commended. If I'm to believe the evaluation of BuShip's technical personnel, they've achieved a breakthrough into a whole new generation of electronic counter measures. A single installation which can not only provide both fire confusion and deception ECM but also substantially negate hostile fire confusion *and*, if the test results are to be believed, actually cloak a ship. Invisibility at ranges as low as eleven light-seconds, Mister Taliaferro. A priceless tactical advantage."

"Well, of course," Taliaferro said, "but there have been—"

"I'm aware of the 'difficulties' you've encountered," Anderson said softly. "What *you* may not be aware of is that under its war powers, the Office of Naval Intelligence plays a much broader oversight role and examines all sorts of things it's legally barred from exploring in peacetime. Including the records of military suppliers."

Taliaferro paled, and Anderson smiled thinly.

"Since November 2294," he continued precisely, "the TFN has disbursed to the Taliaferro Yard over a billion credits for R&D on next-generation ECM. I find that very interesting, since ONI has obtained in-house reports from your own technical staff indicating that on November 18, 2294, their equipment surpassed Fleet specs under field conditions."

"But we needed more tests, and—" Taliaferro said in a sick voice.

"You always do," Anderson said coldly. "In some ways, I suppose, it's just as well. The new systems would've done Admiral Li little good in the . . . tactical position he faced in Lorelei, and no doubt the enemy would have obtained specimens. Since then, however, your actions have undoubtedly cost hundreds if not thousands of lives by depriving the Fleet of a system it needs desperately. Moreover, according to your last funding request to BuShips, you require another thousand megacredits for 'crash development' to get the system operational. Rather greedy of you, Mister Taliaferro. First you steal a billion credits by suppressing test results, and then you propose to extort *another* billion as your kilo of flesh for turning an already operational system over to the Fleet after another six months of 'development.'"

"You can't prove that!"

"Oh, but I can. And if I have to, I will. Complete documentation is already in my files and those of ONI on Old Terra."

"But what you're saying—! It would ruin us!"

"No, it won't. You'll miss quite a few dividends, but if we turn it over to the Procurator's Office, the fines will be at least twice as high. And, of course, you'll spend the next few decades in prison."

"But BuShips authorized every step of the program!"

"I know. Did I mention that Vice Admiral Wilson is en route to Old Terra to face a general court martial?" Taliaferro's pudgy body wilted. "I'm still awaiting the final ONI report on exactly how BuShips came to award you this development contract in the first place. I'm fairly certain we'll find Admiral Wilson at the bottom of that, too, and I have no more doubt of his trial's verdict than you do. But we don't have time to waste, and I imagine that if you comply with my modest arrangements now, the post-war government won't do much more than slap your wrist with a few megacredits of fines."

"I can't—" Taliaferro began, then stopped and slumped as arctic blue eyes bored into him. "All right," he said dully. "You win."

"Thank you, Mister Taliaferro. The first work orders will be in your hands by this afternoon."

Anderson stood, leaning on his cane, and Taliaferro made no effort to rise. He only stared at the old man with mesmerized eyes, and Anderson paused.

"Before I go, let me just add that I knew your grandfather and your father. They were both experts at squeezing the last centicredit out of a contract, and we had our run-ins in the good old days, but neither of them would have been stupid enough to try this. Perhaps you might consider that if neither of *them* ever won a round with me, it'll be a cold day in Hell before a miserable little piss ant like you does. Good day, Mister Taliaferro."

He felt more spry than he'd felt in decades as he left the office and headed for the next unfortunate industrial magnate on his list.

Commodore Angelique Timoshenko, acting head of the TFN's Bureau of Ships, pressed a button on the work table. A schematic glowed to life on its surface, and her slender finger tapped a blinking line.

"There it is, sir," she said crisply, and Howard Anderson nodded. She was, he reflected, a far cry from her late, unlamented boss. Though young for her rank, and even more so for her new position, she was as brilliant as she was attractive. And no shrinking violet, either. Antonov had addressed her as "Commodore Timoshenkova" when they met, and she hadn't turned a hair as she politely—but firmly—corrected him. Her family had left Russia and its naming conventions behind in the second decade of the twentieth century, but it still took nerve for a junior to correct Ivan the Terrible.

"So that's how they do it," he murmured.

"Yes, sir. Ingenious, isn't it?"

"And goddamned dangerous," he growled.

"No question about that," Timoshenko agreed.

Anderson straightened thoughtfully. He was no longer as up to date technically as he would have liked, but sixty years in naval command gave a man a fair grasp of basic principles. If he couldn't be on a flag bridge, watching BuShips tear into the first specimens of captured Theban equipment was the next best thing, and this showed an audacious—if risky—ingenuity that appealed to him, even if an enemy had thought of it first.

He pursed his lips, remembering his own reaction to the force beam. That had been an Orion development during ISW-1, but, fortunately, they'd committed it in driblets. By the time they'd had it ready for mass production and called in their feet for refit, the TFN had known about it and been producing its own version—and had carried through and produced the primary *before* the Orions.

"They must have the occasional accident," he observed now.

"Yes, sir. This gives them a hellacious throughput, but their mag bottle technology's cruder than ours, and it takes an *extremely* dense field. If it hiccups—blooie!"

"Agreed." The commodore was probably understating, but it certainly explained how the Thebans could produce a bomb-pumped laser without a bomb. They didn't; they simply detonated the bomb *inside* their ship.

He frowned at the schematic, tracing the lines of light with a finger. Each laser-armed Theban ship contained at least one installation walled with truly awesome shielding, all wrapped around a mag bottle many times as dense as that of a standard fusion plant containment field. When they fired those godawful lasers, they detonated a nuclear warhead inside the mag bottle, which trapped its explosive power but not its radiation. Heavily armored and shielded conduits focused and channeled that dreadful radiation, delivering it to up to four laser projectors. But it all depended on the containment field, for, as Timoshenko said, if that field faltered, the firing ship would die far more spectacularly than its intended victim. And even with it, the detonation chamber—and everything within meters of it—must quickly become so contaminated that total replacement would be required on a fairly frequent basis.

"Do you have any projections on their failure rate?"

"They're rough, but it may be as high as three percent. The system's supposed to shut down when the fail-safes report field instability, but it may fail catastrophically in about ten percent of those cases. Call it point-three percent, maybe a little less, for a serious event."

"Um. I don't know if I want to incorporate anything that . . . fractious into our own ships, Commodore."

"I don't think we have to." Timoshenko touched a button on the work table and the schematic changed to a modified TFN blueprint.

"I'd say they've adopted this expedient because lasers were the best energy weapon available as of the Lorelei Massacre. It looks to me like they simply never considered the potential of the force beam, so they concentrated all their efforts on improved lasers, whereas we were diverted from the whole laser field, in a way, by other developments. In a sense, we've neglected their chosen field just as they've ignored ours."

"Which means?"

"Which means, sir, much as I hate to admit it, that we've overlooked quite a few potentials of our own systems. Our technology's better, and I think we can substantially improve on their current approach, but we're going to need at least several years of R&D before I'd be prepared to recommend it. In the meantime, however, we can improve the performance of our standard shipboard lasers dramatically.

We won't be able to match their maximum effective range, but I think we can actually improve on their effective throughput figures, at least on a power-to-mass ratio."

"And how will we do that?" Anderson's eyes glinted at Timoshenko's enthusiasm; he'd always enjoyed watching bright people solving difficult problems.

"Like this," Timoshenko said, tapping the schematic, "by using a pair of heterodyning lasers in exact wavelength de-synchronization. Originally, we thought we'd need two separate projectors, but now that we've looked into it a bit, we think we can mount a pair of emitters in a single projector about fifty percent larger than a standard laser mount—the same size as a capital force beam, in other words. At shorter ranges, we should get very nearly the same destructive effect they do, without the potential for disaster built into their system. And without the need for all their shielding or to replace expendable lasing cavities between shots, the mass required for each projector will be less than fifty percent of theirs. We won't have as much range, but effectively, we can squeeze twice as many weapons into the same hull."

"That many?" Anderson was impressed, but he'd been a field commander waiting on the backroom types in his time. "How long?"

"The big problem's going to be maintaining optimum frequency control as the lasers heat up under repeated firings, but Commander Hsin is working on it. I've studied his reports, and it looks like we can handle most of it with modified Tamaguchi governors. Most of the changes will be to software, not hardware, if he's on the right track, and I think he is. So, assuming he can get the modified governors up and running as estimated, and given that most of what we're talking about is simply a new application of existing technology, I think we could have the first unit ready for testing in about five months. From successful test date to production would take another three to four. Call it eight months—ten at the outside."

"And to put this bomb-pumped system into production unchanged?"

"We might save three months. I don't think we could cut much more than that off it."

"All right." Anderson took his cane from the work table and headed for the door, gesturing for her to accompany him. "I'm inclined to think you're onto something, Commodore, but money's no problem, and neither is manufacturing priority. Push both systems full bore."

"Yes, sir. And this 'ram' generator of theirs?"

"Let it lie for now. It won't help forts, and Admiral Antonov seems to feel his mobile units can handle it with evasive maneuvering and anti-drive missiles now that he knows about it."

"Yes, sir."

"I'm impressed, Commodore," he said, pausing at the door and offering his hand. "I wish I'd had you around ninety years ago."

"Thank you, sir. I take that as a compliment."

"You should," he snorted cheerfully.

CHAPTER THIRTEEN

The Blood of Patriots

This time Lantu had company as he awaited the Synod's pleasure. Fleet Chaplain Manak sat beside him . . . and two cold-eyed, armed Church Wardens flanked them both.

Lantu sat very erect, pressing his cranial carapace against the bulkhead behind him, and tried to ignore the Synod's policemen. He'd always found Wardens vaguely distasteful—had some intuition warned him he might someday find himself under their inspection?

His eyes tried to stray to Manak again. The fleet chaplain worried him, for Manak was old, and he was taking this waiting, grinding tension poorly. He sat bent-headed, inner lids closed and arms crossed before him. They'd been separated for days, yet his old friend had said not a single word in the dragging hours since the Wardens had "escorted" them here.

He sighed internally, maintaining his external impassivity. They'd known their retreat might rouse the Church's ire, but he hadn't counted on the heat of the Synod's reaction. It wasn't as if his fleet had been destroyed, after all. True, a disturbing percentage of the battle-line was in yard hands, but his withdrawal had prevented far worse, and he'd managed it in the face of massed fighter attacks launched from ships so distant his own vessels could hardly even *see* them!

Yet the Quaestors' harsh questions had ignored his achievement in preserving Terra's Sword, and he knew their attitude reflected the Synod's. The churchmen saw only that he'd failed to drive the Sword home in The Line's vitals, and it seemed the fact that he'd warned them of the danger ahead of time only made them angrier. Certainly the Quaestors had harped on that point, asking again and again if he had not gone into battle *expecting* defeat and so fled prematurely.

109

Lantu had answered calmly, yet he labored under a keen sense of injustice. He'd been overruled and ordered to attack by the Synod and the Prophet himself, so why must he and Manak bear the stigma of failure?

Because, a small, still voice whispered, you're a single admiral and Manak a single prelate. You're expendable; the Synod isn't.

The hatch opened, and the soft, sudden sound startled even Manak into looking up. A Warden major stood in the opening.

"First Admiral. Fleet Chaplain. The Synod requires your presence."

The approval of Lantu's last appearance before the Synod was notably absent, and cold eyes burned his back as he followed Manak down the central aisle. The Prophet's white robes were a flame, but the violet stole of the Holy Inquisition was a dark, dangerous slash of color across them.

Lantu raised his head proudly but not arrogantly. The Prophet's regalia indicated his readiness to pronounce judgment *ex cathedra*, with the infallibility of Holy Terra Herself, and the admiral was prepared to submit to Her will. Yet he'd done his best. Any error resulted from his effort to serve Her to the very best of his merely mortal ability.

"First Admiral Lantu," the Prophet said sternly. "Fleet Chaplain Manak. You have been summoned to hear the judgment of Holy Terra on your actions at the Battle of Redwing. Are you prepared?"

"I am, Your Holiness." Lantu was pleased by how firmly his reply came, and shocked by the slight quaver in Manak's echoing response.

"It is the judgment of Holy Terra that you have failed Her holy cause. It is Her judgment that if you had pressed your attack, trusting—as you ought—in Her guidance and support, Her Sword would have smitten the infidels' defenses into dust and that, once those defenses were breached, you would have trapped the infidels' ships behind your own, to be crushed by Second Fleet. By your weakness and lack of faith, you have failed Her most holy Self, and imperiled Her jihad."

Lantu swallowed, but his eyes refused to waver. Beside him, Manak's shoulders hunched in misery.

"Your lives are forfeit," the Prophet continued inexorably, "yet your past actions stand to your credit, and Holy Terra is merciful. Thus you will be given an opportunity to atone in Her eyes.

"Our Holy Inquisition has not prospered on New New Hebrides. As this world was the original goal of the Messenger, we must strive mightily to return its apostate people to the Faith, yet they have not only rejected Holy Terra's message but raised armed, unholy resistance against Her. You, First Admiral, are a military man. You, Fleet Chaplain, are a shepherd of the Faith. It shall be your task to aid Archbishop

Tanuk in bringing these infidels once more into Holy Terra's arms. Success will atone for your recent actions; failure will not be tolerated by Holy Terra.

"Holy Terra has spoken." The Prophet brought his crosier's heel sharply down upon the stage, then moved his eyes to the Warden major. "Escort the admiral and chaplain to their shuttle, Major," he said softly.

Angus MacRory finished field-stripping the Shellhead grenade launcher and reached for his cleaning kit. It was cool under the long, streamer-like leaves of the massive banner oaks, and he was grateful for his warm civilian jacket. It was hardly proper Peaceforce uniform, but it was immaculately clean, and the sergeant's chevrons pinned to its collar were polished.

Caitrin dropped down across the blanket from him and picked up the old toothbrush, working on the action as he swabbed the launcher's bore. Her long fingers had become as rough as his own, and her hands were equally deft.

He watched her, not exactly covertly but unobtrusively. Her red-gold hair was longer now, gleaming in a short, thick braid from under her sadly tattered tam-o-shanter. Its decorative pom-pom had been snatched away by a bullet, but, unlike Angus, she'd found an almost complete uniform when they raided the New Glasgow Peaceforce supply dump. They'd lost six men and two women on that one, but the guns they'd recaptured had been worth it.

"The com shack's picked up something," she said after a moment.

"Aye?" Angus raised the launcher's barrel and squinted down its gleaming bore. The guerrillas never used coms, and the Shellheads seemed not to have considered that they might have any. They certainly didn't have any decent sense of communications security, anyway.

"There's a security alert in the New Greenock sector. Someone important's making an inspection of the camps Monday."

"Are they, now?" Angus murmured. He laid the launcher barrel across his thighs, and she smiled as he met her eyes thoughtfully.

The guerrillas had done far better than he'd dared hope. A dozen bands now operated from the mountainous continental interiors. They couldn't reach the islands—they were too far away and too small to dodge patrols—but fishing boats still operated under the Shellheads' supervision, for people had to be fed, and they managed an occasional crossing between continents.

Angus had never expected to find himself the senior commander of his home world's defenders. It had just . . . happened. Was it his Marine training coming to the fore? More likely it was simply the fact that none of the Peaceforce's officers survived and that he'd managed to last this long. He'd never been to OCS, but his own tactical ability had surprised him, though he relied heavily on Caitrin as his exec.

His unalterable rule that no recruit with relatives in the Occupied Zones would be accepted for operations had served them well in decreased vulnerability to reprisals, yet it held their numbers down. His own band, built around the re-education camp escapees and civilians picked up since, numbered scarcely six hundred, with barely another thirty-five hundred spread among the other bands, and to pit four thousand people against an occupation force backed by orbiting warships was lunacy. He knew that, but just as he'd been unable to pretend with Yashuk, he was unable to consider not fighting back. The Shellheads couldn't do anything much worse than they already had, and he was damned if they were going to have it all their own way.

Caitrin understood that. In fact, she understood *him* better than anyone else ever had, and she had an uncanny ability to extract the kernel of his plans from his sparse descriptions and make others understand them, as well. Surprisingly, perhaps, he understood *her* just as well. Despite very different personalities and educations, they'd fused in some mysterious way into a whole greater than its parts, and the strength of her amazed him. It was she who had first confronted their feelings for one another—something he would never have dared to do—which explained how they'd become lovers.

"Ammo?" he asked now.

"We've got four units of fire for our own small arms," she replied without consulting her notebook. "About three-and-a-half for the captured Shellhead weapons. The mortar section lost a tube at Hynchcliffe's farm, but they've got two units of fire with them and about five times that back at Base One. The Scorpion teams are down to about a dozen rounds, but we could hit that dump at Maidstone for as many Shellhead SAMs as we can carry."

"Um." He wished he had more mortar ammo, but fetching it from Base One would take too long. The mountains slowed even the colonists' Old Terran mules to a crawl, but they were the guerrilla's friends, too rugged and heavily forested for Shellhead GEVs and infantry bikes, and Shellheads on foot could never keep up with the longer-legged humans. Their choppers were another matter, but the Scorpion teams had taught them circumspection. Unfortunately, they were running out of Scorpions.

In fact, they were running out of *all* military ammunition. They'd hit all the Peaceforce armories they could, but the Shellheads had caught on to that one fairly quickly and simply destroyed their stockpiles of captured weapons. By now, half the guerrillas' human-made small arms were civilian needle rifles, ill-suited to military targets. Their tiny projectiles relied on incredible velocities for effect, and while a single hit could reduce a limb to jelly, they lacked the mass to punch through body armor.

Fortunately, captured Shellhead weapons were taking up the slack. The troop reminders stamped on them—in English—helped, but they weren't really necessary, since the weapons themselves were based on original (if venerable) Terran designs. Awkward dimensions posed a much greater problem, for the Shellheads' over-long arms put triggers and butt plates in odd places. A determined man with a hacksaw could do a lot about that, but safeties placed for thumbs on the wrong side of the hand were another matter.

"Aye," he said finally. " 'Tis a gae lang way, but we can do it. Send runners tae Bulloch and Ingram—there's nae time fer the others. Sean can hit Maidstone; after that, 'twill be a repeat o' the Seabridge raid."

"I'll get right on it." Caitrin rose and walked away, and Angus watched her with a smile, confident she understood exactly what he intended. She was a bonny lass, his Katie.

Archbishop Tanuk's tilt-engine vertol sliced cleanly through the air, five minutes from the Inquisition's New Greenock camps, as the prelate ignored Father Waman and his staff and peered moodily out a window.

These infidels were incredibly stubborn. Even the handful who'd professed the Faith were riddled by secret heretics, and the terrorist renegades in the mountains were true devils. Their raids had grown increasingly audacious—they were even infiltrating and attacking the People's housing areas! He'd come to them in love, prepared to be stern to restore their souls to Holy Terra, but they clung to their blindness. The infidels outside the Occupied Zones still hid their heretical priests, and it was almost as bad *inside* the OZ. Just last week he'd learned three "converts" who'd been allowed to help manage the New Selkirk camps were in contact with the terrorists. Unfortunately, they'd helped almost four hundred infidels escape before they were executed.

The most stringent counter-measures seemed useless. Colonel Fraymak's garrison was doing its best, but these mountains were impossible, and his helicopter and vertol strength had taken dreadful losses. The archbishop had hardened his heart and authorized Warden Colonel Huark to shoot hostages and even entire villages as reprisals, but it only seemed to make these infernal heretics more determined to cut his soldiers' throats in the dark!

He rubbed his ring of office and sighed. He was Holy Terra's servant, and somehow She would help him bring his charges back to Her, but it was hard. He feared even sterner measures would be required, and made a mental note to remind Father Shamar to provide his Inquisitors with infidel lie detectors. Perhaps they could at least sort out the honest converts that way. And if they could do that, then—

His aircraft lurched suddenly, and he looked up questioningly as his military aide hurried back from the cockpit.

"Your Grace, New Greenock is under attack! The terrorists have cut their way through the perimeter and taken out the main barracks with mortars. Now they're—"

The aide broke off, gaping out the window, and Tanuk turned quickly. The last thing he ever saw was a Scorpion missile streaking towards him.

CHAPTER FOURTEEN

Options of War

The wide armorplast view port was partly blocked by Ivan Antonov's bulk as he stared at the panorama before him. Redwing's orbital yards seethed with activity such as they had not known since their original erection for the sole purpose of building The Line as men and machines swarmed over the torn and blistered skins of wounded orbital fortresses, and the light of laser welders flickered as the work of repair went on in shifts around the clock.

In some cases, those repairs looked all too much like rebuilding . . . but in the Federation's present pass, none of them could be written off. And the fortresses that had gotten off lightly enough to be considered operational by the elastic definitions that obtained these days had already been tractored to the QR-107 warp point, for the trap he'd sprung on the Thebans could be sprung only once.

At least the more-or-less operational fortresses were being reinforced by more and more mobile units as the Federation's unimaginable industrial potential was gradually mobilized. Antonov watched a newly-arrived *Thunderer*-class battleship slide into orbit, fresh from moth-balls and bristling with old-fashioned but still lethal energy weaponry. He was glad to see her; there had been few ships of her weight in the Reserve, and she was one of the few heavy units that had yet reached Redwing. Most of his gradually increasing trickle of reinforcements were still of the lighter classes.

Even more welcome were the lowly freighters carrying more anti-matter warheads . . . and also something new. The great problem of space warfare since the chance discovery of warp points—those ill-understood anomalies in space/time that allowed instantaneous transit

at an insignificant energy cost—had been an assault against an alerted
defense. Even when a fleeting edge of surprise could be seized, attacking
ships emerging one by one from a warp point into concentrated
defensive firepower were at such a disadvantage that military historians could only compare them to infantrymen advancing across an
open field of Flemish mud against machine-gun emplacements. Indeed,
they were in even worse case, for these defenders could not be "prepared" by bombardment; nothing as small as a missile could carry the
necessary instrumentation for a warp transit *and* a controlled attack.

But now a way around the conundrum had been found, thanks to
new developments in artificial intelligence. (Could the "sentient computers" of the early—and vastly over-enthusiastic—computer pioneers
be far away? Antonov rather hoped they were.) An unmanned carrier
pack, smaller than any starship but far larger than a missile, could make
a one-time warp transit and release its trio of "SBMHAWK" missiles
against preprogrammed classes of targets. The missiles' "homing all the
way killer" guidance circuits did the rest. Commodore Timoshenko
promised eventual production of reusable packs with better on-board
systems and larger missile loads, but even this early version would be
an immeasurable advantage, and they'd begun arriving at Redwing at
last . . . a few of them. Always too few.

Pavel Tsuchevsky approached from his right. "That fort there was
one of the hardest hit to survive at all," he said grimly, pointing to
a hulk whose original shape was barely discernible. "A second rammer
got through after the impact of the first overloaded its shields and
station-keeping drive. Most of its crew were killed by the concussion—
we've never thought it was worthwhile to install first-line inertial
compensators on forts. They're not exactly intended for high-gee
maneuvering."

"But they held," Antonov growled.

Winnifred Trevayne stepped up to the left. "By the time the last
waves of boarders arrived, many of the Marines had exhausted their
zoot power cells," she said sadly. "They had to switch to ordinary battle
dress. From what I've heard in the debriefings, the fighting was
indescribable . . . toward the end, it was actually hand-to-hand."

"But they held," Antonov rumbled from deep in his cask of a chest.

Kthaara'zarthan spoke from directly behind him. "Most of the
Fortress Command fighters managed to launch before the rams hit.
They did what they could to blunt the attack, but many had to launch
before they had rearmed. At least one managed to physically ram a
Theban ship; he could not destroy it outright, but he left it unable
to complete its attack run. Our report recommends the pilot for the
Golden Lion of Terra." The last four words were barely understand-
able, but the tale flowed out naturally in the Tongue of Tongues, which

throughout history had been a medium for such tellings. "We believe at least two other pilots did the same, but their mother fortresses were destroyed. Without the fortress records, we cannot identify them to record their names in honor as they deserve."

A raised hand showed its claws and clenched, sinking those claws into its fisted palm. Bright drops of blood welled as it opened in ritual salute.

"They fought as *farshatok*," he said softly. "When it was over, there were fewer usable recovery bays than there were fighters. By the time our carriers returned, many had exhausted their life support."

"But they held!" Antonov's voice was a deep, subterranean sound, welling up like magma from beneath the crust of one of humankind's planets. He turned heavily to face the half-circle of his subordinates.

"We've given the Thebans their first check, and they seem to have reverted to a holding operation in QR-107. Now, we don't know anything about their philosophy, or whatever is driving them, but their behavior so far suggests fanaticism of some stripe or other." He glanced at Winnifred Trevayne, who nodded. "If they're like human fanatics, they deal well with success, but poorly with defeat. After all, they *expect* success; their ideology tells them they alone understand the will of God, or"—a wry expression, almost a wince—"the dynamics of history, and that this enables them to ride the wave of the future. Failure is inexplicable, and shakes their faith."

He drew himself up against the backdrop of the stars, the mammoth orbital constructs, and the lovely blue-white curve of Redwing II.

"It is therefore essential we maintain pressure on them, remind them that they have lost the initiative. We remain too weak in heavy units to risk a decisive fleet action; but we can, and will, conduct a series of nuisance raids into QR-107, using our light carriers. I imagine," he added with a wintry, closed-lipped smile for Kthaara, "their earlier contempt for fighters has now turned into a very healthy fear, and that they're still feeling their way toward effective anti-fighter tactics."

Tsuchevsky cleared his throat. "Also, Admiral, the new SBMHAWKs give us a unique opportunity to clear the warp point for the raiders. The carriers and their escorts can be loose in QR-107 space before the Thebans understand what's happened!"

Antonov shook his head. "No, Pavel Sergeyevich. I know, it's tempting to give the SBMHAWKs an operational test . . . and, of course, reduce our casualties. But then the Thebans would know about the weapon. The shock value would be gone, and they could start to develop counter-measures. No, the system cannot be used at all until circumstances are such that it can be used to decisive effect."

Tsuchevsky looked almost mutinous. "But, Admiral . . . we used the antimatter warheads as soon as we had them. . . ."

"With great respect, Captain Tssssuchevssky," Kthaara cut in, "the circumstances are different. Our ability to hold this system was very much in doubt. We had to take every possible advantage, and the new warheads may have made the difference. Now, we have won the luxury of . . . I believe the Human expression is 'Playing our cards close to our chest.' And the need to make decisive use of a new weapon is a lesson the *Zheeerlikou'valkhannaieee* learned well from the Federation in the Wars of Shame. Yes," he raised a blood-dotted, unhuman hand, forestalling Tsuchevsky's protest, "we will lose more people this way. But . . . they are Warriors."

There was silence. There were no anti-Orion bigots in this group, but the fact remained that Kthaara was dispassionately discussing *human* deaths. And yet . . . everyone knew the bond that had formed between the big Tabby and Second Fleet's fighter pilots, many of whom would die if the SBMHAWKs weren't used. And everyone knew better than to think for a moment that he would ever play "yes-man" for the Admiral.

There was no further protest.

Second Admiral Jahanak entered *Hildebrandt Jackson*'s briefing room with Fleet Chaplain Hinam. His new staff, headed by Flag Captain Yurah, rose expressionlessly, but Jahanak felt their resentment.

He understood, and he knew how much worse it would have been had the Synod followed its first inclination to strip Lantu of his rank and name Jahanak First Admiral in his stead. His own jihad had been respectable, but scarcely as brilliant as Lantu's, and these officers had shared the first admiral's heady triumphs. And his defeat . . . if defeat it was.

Jahanak had his own thoughts on that, but no intention of voicing them. Unjust as Lantu's disgrace might be, there was no point refusing to profit over a matter of principle which could help neither of them in the end.

He took his place at the head of the table, Hinam at his right hand, and looked down its length at Captain Yurah. The flag captain looked back with just a trace of . . . defiance? No, not quite that, but something akin.

"Gentlemen," Jahanak's voice was brisk but precise, "we shall shortly be reinforced by a third of Second Fleet. Our own damaged units will be reassigned to Second Fleet as they're repaired, but until then Second Fleet will, of course, be understrength. First Fleet, on the other hand, will be restored to full strength, and large additional stores of AFHAWKs are being forwarded to us. So reinforced, my orders—*our* orders—are to resume the offensive and secure the Redwing System as soon as practicable."

He carefully did not note the flinch which ran around the assembled staff officers, but there was frank dismay on several faces. He felt Fleet Chaplain Hinam bristle and unobtrusively touched the churchman's arm under the table. Unlike the Synod, Jahanak didn't believe Lantu's staff had been "infected" by his "defeatism." He knew too many of these officers, just as he did Lantu; if they were dismayed—even frightened—they had their reasons.

He laid his hands on the table and studied them, weighing the staff's reaction against his own evaluations. And, he admitted, against its bearing on his own position.

"I've read your reports . . . and First Admiral Lantu's," he said finally, and Captain Yurah seemed to relax slightly as he spoke Lantu's name with no trace of condemnation. Lantu always had inspired intense personal loyalty, Jahanak reflected without bitterness. His own strengths lay in more calculated maneuvers. "I ask you now if you would change—or expand upon—anything you said in them. Captain Yurah?"

"I would expand only one point, Second Admiral," the flag captain said flatly, "and that is to emphasize even more strongly the danger represented by the infidels' fighters. Our tonnage advantage over their mobile units was on the order of five-to-one, but even with due allowance for the destruction inflicted upon their fortresses, our damage was at least three times theirs. Had the first admiral not withdrawn"—he met his new commander's eyes levelly—"the Sword would *have* no First Fleet."

"I see." Jahanak glanced around the other faces. "Would anyone disagree with the flag captain?" No one spoke, and he gave a wintry smile. "I assure you, gentlemen—neither Fleet Chaplain Hinam nor I will hold honesty against you. No one has more respect for the Synod than I, but *you* are the officers who confronted these fighters. If you agree with Captain Yurah, say so."

The silence lingered a moment longer, then died in a soft rumble of agreement, and Jahanak sat quietly, listening as much to how his officers spoke as to what they said. His face showed nothing, but his hands folded together on the table as he absorbed the staff's intensity.

"Very well." He brought their comments to a close at last and glanced at Fleet Chaplain Hinam from the corner of one eye, but Hinam was carefully expressionless, refusing to challenge him. Jahanak hid his wry amusement. There were advantages in claiming the First Prophet as an ancestor.

"In all honesty, gentlemen, what you say only confirms my own initial impression. Before accepting this command, I strongly endorsed First Admiral Lantu's request that development of our own fighters be given absolute priority." Captain Yurah's eyes lit, and Jahanak nodded slightly. "That request has been granted. Archbishop Ganhad informs me it will take time—I understand the major difficulty lies in duplicating the infidels' small fusion plants—but the process is under way.

"With that in mind," he said more briskly, "it is certainly our duty to advise the Synod of prudent strategic decisions enforced by our existing weapons mix. As it stands, the infidels are able to strike from ranges far beyond our own. If they possess sufficient fighters—and we must assume from Redwing that they do—they can afford to exchange them for capital ships in quite large numbers. Until our own fighters can interdict them short of the battle-line, we must assume the infidels will welcome battle in deep space, where they can make full use of their range and speed advantage over our stronger battle-line. Does this accurately reflect your joint view of the situation?"

There were relieved nods, and Jahanak smiled faintly.

"In that case, I shall recommend to the Synod that we assume a defensive stance until such time as our own fighters become available. QR-107 is a starless nexus—useless to us but an ideal battle-ground for the infidels—and, of course, we have no fortifications to support our mobile units in defending the QR-107-Redwing warp point. To hold against a determined attack would require the forward deployment of our battle-line, but this would place our slowest, most powerful, least expendable vessels far from retreat should the infidels muster sufficient firepower to break through in strength.

"In view of these facts, I intend to withdraw our battleships and superdreadnoughts to Parsifal and cover the warp point with lighter units—specifically with *Nile*-class light cruisers and *Ronin*-class battle-cruisers. With their heavy missile armaments, they can deliver massive AFHAWK fire should the enemy enter QR-107."

He paused, feeling Hinam's unspoken opposition. His major concern was easing the hostility of his staff, but even so . . .

"Understand me, gentlemen," he said crisply. "We are *not* surrendering this nexus without a fight. I intend to bleed each infidel sortie from Redwing and, at the same time, gain experience against the fighter threat. We must evolve proper anti-fighter tactics before we once again expose capital ships to their attack, and this nexus will provide both our laboratory and a forward picket for our battle-line in Parsifal. I would prefer to implement the Synod's wishes and launch a new and immediate attack on Redwing. Given the situation, I do not believe this to be possible. We shall therefore convert our disadvantages into advantages while building the weapons we need for the new attack we most assuredly *will* launch against The Line."

The eyes which met his now were almost enthusiastic, and he smiled.

"Thank you, gentlemen. Please return to your duties. I want

complete status reports on your departments in two hours. Dismissed."

He watched the hatch close behind the last of his staff before he turned to Hinam with a wry expression.

"I gather my battle plan fills you with less than total enthusiasm, Holiness?"

"It does not fulfill the Synod's bidding, Second Admiral," Hinam said frostily. "The Prophet will not be pleased."

"And do you think *I* am pleased?" Jahanak asked more acidly. "Holiness, I am but mortal, as is my staff. Indeed, even the Synod and the Prophet are mortal . . . and fallible." Hinam swelled with indignation, and Jahanak smiled thinly. "Recall, Holiness," he said softly, "that even my holy grandsire met occasional failure in Holy Terra's service."

Hinam's mouth closed with a snap, and Jahanak hid a grin. His kinship to the First Prophet wasn't a card he dared play often, but when he did, it was with effect.

"As mere mortals, Holiness Hinam," he went on calmly, "we can but offer Holy Terra our best. You saw my staff's initial reactions. They served First Admiral Lantu—as I, myself, have—and they've learned to expect victory in Holy Terra's cause. They don't understand what happened, but they can't believe—or won't, perhaps—that it was Lantu's fault, nor do I know that I blame them. *I* wouldn't have believed he would retreat from the Satan-Khan himself, yet he withdrew. And, Holiness, anything we may do for the jihad begins from that point . . . and depends upon those officers. I *must* enjoy their support, and I won't win it by casting aspersions upon the officer they believe saved their Fleet for Holy Terra's further service."

"I . . . can see that," Hinam said unwillingly. "Yet to take it upon yourself to alter the Synod's strategy is—"

"Is one of the functions of a flag officer, Holiness," Jahanak interrupted as he sensed victory. "I don't challenge the Synod's essential strategy, but they cannot be as well aware of the severity of the situation as we who directly confront it. Had Lantu done his duty and secured Redwing, thus breaking The Line decisively," Jahanak felt a brief twinge at his own words but continued smoothly, "then I could do *mine* by continuing the advance. As it is, I dare not expose our battle-line to the infidels' fighters. Too many of our ships are out of action to confront fighters *and* fortresses until we have carriers of our own. I'm sorry, Holiness, but my sorrow can't change facts. I must gain my officers' trust; renew their courage and faith in Holy Terra, and build my own strength before I once more challenge The Line. The Synod," he finished gently, "will thank neither of us if we compound Lantu's failure by a more serious one of our own."

The fleet chaplain sat silent, staring down as he turned his ring of office on his finger. Jahanak leaned back, waiting patiently. Given his birth, he'd seen more of senior churchmen than most officers, and he felt confident of Hinam's final reaction.

"Very well," the chaplain sighed at last. "I don't like it, and the Synod will be displeased, but perhaps you're right. I will support you in this, Second Admiral." He raised his head and tried to put a glint of steel into his gaze. "For now."

"Thank you, Fleet Chaplain," Jahanak said gratefully . . . and carefully kept the laughing triumph from his own yellow eyes.

Ivan Antonov tried again.

"You see," he began as he poured another round for himself and Kthaara, "your race's unity came after a series of wars that almost destroyed it. Whole nations and cultures vanished, and those that were left were smashed down to bedrock. So when one group finally established control over what was left of your home planet, it was able to remake the entire race in its image. Culturally, the slate had been wiped clean." He paused, saw that Kthaara understood the expression, then resumed.

"So all Orions today share a common language and culture. We got off lightly by comparison. Our Great Eastern War was destructive enough, but not on the scale of your Unification Wars—there was no wholesale use of strategic nuclear weapons, and we avoided biological warfare entirely. So our cultural diversity survived our political unification, and today we still cling to what's left of it. Some of us," he added, raising his glass, "more than others. *Za vashe zdorovye!*"

"*T'chaaigarna,*" Kthaara responded, and tossed off his vodka. Alcohol affected the two species in the same way, and both had surrounded its use with traditions, including the according of special prestige to imports. Since the Alliance, the Orion upper classes had acquired a fondness for bourbon. At least, Antonov thought, he'd managed to cure Kthaara of *that.*

"*I* think, perhaps, you overstate the consequences of the Unification Wars somewhat," the Orion said, claws combing his whiskers thoughtfully. "Unlike Old Terra, we had enjoyed a single world-state within our own recorded history, long before we ever discovered the scientific method. Yet it is true our cultures were far more diverse before their differences were overwhelmed by the survival imperatives which followed the Wars."

"Precisely," Antonov replied, leaning over the table. "But that *didn't* happen to humans."

"Yes," Kthaara said slowly, "and it explains much we find

incomprehensible about you—and not just the idea that an advanced, united race can have so many different kinds of personal names! My people have always looked at your pluralism and seen chaos, but now much becomes understandable—including your notorious inventiveness." His tooth-hidden smile reminded Antonov anew that the Orion face (like humanity's, and unlike Terran cats') had evolved as a tool of self-expression.

"That has always been hard for us to understand. Naturally, we could never accept the idea that you were simply more intelligent, nor was there any scientific evidence for such a notion. My sire, Kornazh'zarthan, had a theory, which I see now was correct—though he used to get into terrible arguments with my grandsire, the first Lord Talphon! He believed your secret was your unimaginable diversity. What a constant creative tension it must generate! And what an incredible range of options it must open to each individual: a banquet of novel perspectives and modes of thought!" He sighed, an almost startlingly human-like sound. "Thus it must have been on Old Valkha once, before the Unification Wars. We have lost much."

They were both silent for a space, gazing out the transparent view port in Antonov's quarters, one of the privileges of rank the admiral most treasured. Kthaara had become a frequent visitor here during his and the admiral's off-duty hours. Socially, his position was ambiguous: still officially a mere commander in an ill-defined staff position, but with the "permanent rank" of small claw of the khan (approximately a commodore) and more and more Antonov's *de facto* fighter commander. Anyway, Antonov liked him.

The communicator chimed, and Captain Tsuchevsky's face appeared in the screen as Antonov keyed acceptance.

"Admiral, the debriefs from our latest QR-107 raid are complete. They seem to confirm what we've seen the last few weeks. The Thebans aren't seriously opposing entry by small groups of raiders, now that we've demonstrated we have enough battleships to clear the warp point of any defense they seem inclined to mount just now. At the same time, we've encountered enough opposition deeper in to make it appear the enemy could fight a major fleet action if we force one by entering the system in strength. I'll download the full report later."

Kthaara leaned forward into a near-crouch, mobile ears twitching in a way Antonov had come to recognize. "So, Admiral, they are willing to continue this war of raids and counter-raids, gaining experience in anti-fighter operations and thinking we lack the strength to seek a full-scale fleet engagement." The ears flattened. "So perhaps now is the time to force such an engagement! We could brush aside the light forces on their side of the warp point and transit our new fleet carriers before they realized what was happening!" Beneath all of Kthaara's sophistication lay an elemental Orion, Antonov reflected. When a large-scale decisive battle beckoned, the philosophical detachment which had recognized the need to defer use of the SBMHAWKs went by the boards, a feeble thing to set against the instincts of all Orion history and prehistory.

"No," the admiral said slowly. "The new Theban commander—and I'm convinced they have a new one—is trying to gauge our strength. We'll let him think we don't have enough of the big carriers to risk a pitched battle yet. For now, we'll continue our probes and raids as planned." He smiled at the disappointment which confronted him. "Remember what you've told me of the lessons of the Wars of Shame, Kthaara'zarthan!"

Kthaara relaxed, seeming to deflate a bit.

"You are correct, of course, Ivaaan'aantaahnaav," he said with the same surprisingly expressive smile as before, and reached for his vodka glass once more.

CHAPTER FIFTEEN

The Stewards of Holy Terra

"Your presence honors us, First Admiral."

Colonel Fraymak's respect actually seemed genuine, Lantu thought. Perhaps it was. Despite his disgrace, the Ministry of Truth had labeled his last campaign a resounding triumph, though it hadn't occurred to him the Church might lie to its own warriors. He toyed with the notion of telling Fraymak the truth, then pushed the thought aside. It would only undercut his own authority, and he disliked his own strange, base temptation to shake the colonel's faith.

"Thank you, Colonel," he said, "but our work is cut out for us. Have you caught up with the terrorists who killed Archbishop Tanuk?"

"Ah, no, First Admiral." Fraymak looked out the window of Lantu's new and luxurious—*very* luxurious—office, and frowned. "In fact," he continued unhappily, "I don't expect to, sir."

"No?" Lantu rocked back in his chair and stroked his cranial carapace. It took a certain courage to make that sort of admission to a superior who'd been on-planet barely three hours. "Why not, Colonel?"

"Sir," the colonel focused his eyes above Lantu's head like a first-year cadet, "I have one reinforced infantry brigade, supported by one light armored regiment and two vertol battalions. That's not enough to garrison the re-education camps *and* organize reaction teams on a planetary scale."

"Why should you have to garrison the camps?" Lantu asked in some surprise. "They're the responsibility of the Inquisition and Wardens."

"The archbishop . . . requested"—Lantu noted Fraymak's careful phrasing—"that I assist the Wardens, sir." His suddenly lowered eyes met Lantu's. "That was right after the New Selkirk inmates massacred the Warden guard force and escaped *en masse*."

"I see." Lantu stroked his carapace even more thoughtfully. No one had reported *that* little fiasco to Thebes. "So basically we're just chasing around behind the infidels after they hit us?"

"Unfortunately, that's a fair way to put it, sir."

"How many terrorist groups are we talking about, Colonel?"

"We're not certain. None of the New Hebridans still awaiting re-education ever see anything, of course, but our best estimate is between seven and fifteen major groups. There are at least three here on Aberdeen, two on Scotia, and one each on Hibernia and New Gael. So far, there are none on the islands, but even with confiscated transport, I can't move troops around quickly enough to cover all four continents."

Lantu ran the tip of a letter-opener over the map on his desk, hiding a wince at the contour lines of the continental interiors. No wonder the colonel had problems. "And they hit targets near the mountains, then pop back into them and laugh at you, right?"

"Yes, sir." Fraymak made no effort to hide his relief at Lantu's understanding tone, but he shifted uncomfortably for a moment before he continued. "And, sir, with all due respect to the archbishop and Father Shamar, I don't really believe we should consider them 'terrorists.'"

"No?"

"No, sir. They hit mainly military targets, sir, and they've got excellent tactics. They're short on heavy weapons, but that actually lets them move faster and through rougher terrain. By now, about half their weapons are captured equipment. Every time I stick a squad or a platoon out on its own to cover the Wardens, I might as well be handing that many weapons over to them," he ended bitterly.

"I understand, Colonel, but we're here to support the Church, not vice-versa." The colonel nodded, and Lantu dropped his letter-opener. "Have we considered moving our installations out of reach from the mountains?"

"We can't, sir. The continental coastal strips are barely two hundred kilometers wide and heavily forested, and these trees are incredible; a mature 'banner oak' stands over ninety meters, with foliage too dense for thermal scan penetration. The guerrillas don't *have* any heavy equipment, so there aren't any electronic emissions and magnetic detectors are virtually useless. Small parties just filter through the trees, link-up, hit their targets, then disappear again. It's like trying to spot fish in muddy water, sir."

Lantu understood the colonel's frustrated professionalism perfectly. The late archbishop had scattered his troopers in penny-packets, and the terrorists—guerrillas, he corrected himself, mindful of the colonel's point—held the initiative. All Fraymak could do was react *after* he was hit.

"I assume they have bases. Can't we even locate them?"

"Warden Colonel Huark raised that same point, sir," Fraymak said tonelessly. "The answer is no. These mountains are riddled with caves and deep valleys. Without more scan sats, I can't even cover the valleys adequately, much less spot them through thirty or forty meters of rock."

"Colonel Huark raised the point?" Lantu was surprised. The Warden colonel hadn't impressed him when he greeted his shuttle.

"Yes, sir," Fraymak said even more tonelessly. "I believe he intended to call in nuclear strikes on them."

Now that I can believe. It's just the sort of idiocy a Warden would come up with. I'm surprised he hasn't suggested a saturation bombardment of the entire continental interior! Lantu started to say as much, then stopped. It would only be another attempt to shake Fraymak's faith. Besides, the colonel's expression made him half-afraid Huark had suggested just that.

"I think," he said instead, "that we have the resources—properly used—to kill this fly with a slightly smaller sledgehammer, Colonel."

"Yes, sir!" The colonel's profound relief made Lantu smile.

"All right. I think we'll begin by informing Colonel Huark that camp security is *his* responsibility. Pull in your men and organize battalion-sized reaction forces, then work out a deployment grid that gives us optimum response time to all our own installations."

"Yes, sir." The colonel paused, manifestly struggling with himself, then took the plunge. "Uh, sir, while I agree whole-heartedly with your orders, I think I should point out that we're going to get hit hard, at least initially."

"Why?"

"The Wardens aren't—well, they aren't very good at security, sir, and the guerrillas *really* hate them. Especially the extermination squads."

"The what squads?" Lantu asked very quietly, and Fraymak swallowed.

"The extermination squads, sir. They're special units."

"So I gather. But what, exactly, do they do, Colonel?"

"They're in charge of reprisals, sir," Fraymak said uncomfortably.

"Reprisals." The single word came out with glacial coldness.

"Yes, sir. Counter-reprisals, really." Lantu crooked his fingers, inviting the colonel to continue. "The guerrillas make a point of hitting installations near the camps with the highest execution totals. They . . . don't leave much behind when they do. So Warden Colonel Huark and Father Shamar organized the extermination squads. Whenever we get hit, they pick out hostages or a village that hasn't been brought in for re-education yet and they, well, they *exterminate* them, sir."

Lantu closed his eyes, and his own words about supporting the

Church were bitter on his tongue. How could something like *that* serve
Holy Terra? He sat very still for a moment before he opened his eyes.
"Well, Colonel Fraymak, you're under my orders, not Colonel Huark's,
and we'll do this my way. Adjust your deployment to cover dependent and civilian housing, but the *extermination* squads are just going
to have to look after themselves."

"Yes, sir." The colonel's gaze met his with grim satisfaction before
he executed a snappy salute and withdrew.

Lantu watched the door close and shook his head. Extermination
squads. Sweet Terra, no wonder this planet was a shambles!

Not until much later did he realize Fraymak hadn't used the word
"infidel" once.

"First Admiral?"

Lantu looked up at his secretary's soft, sweet voice and smiled.
Hanat was tall for a Theban woman, her head reaching almost chest-
high on him, and he'd instantly recognized who really kept things
moving around here. She was a curious blend of the efficient and the
traditional, managing somehow to handle everything that crossed her
desk without ever overstepping the bounds which would set an old-
fashioned male's teeth on edge.

"Yes, Hanat?"

"You were due in the fleet chaplain's office ten minutes ago."

"What?" Lantu looked at his chronometer and grimaced. "Damn.
Excuse me," he apologized automatically, and she laughed softly. "Fortunately, I've known him a long time—I doubt he'll have me shot just
yet." He stood and took down his pistol belt, buckling it distastefully.
He shouldn't have to walk around armed inside the HQ compound.

"Don't forget your meeting with Colonel Huark at fourteen-thirty,
either," Hanat admonished.

"As if I could." Lantu didn't bother to conceal his opinion of the
Warden. "Did you get those figures to the fleet chaplain?"

"Yes, sir," she said with revulsion. That was why he didn't hide his
contempt for Huark from her. "You were right. They're twelve percent over Archbishop Tanuk's execution ceiling."

"Terra!" Lantu muttered. "Well, I'll read them when I get back. Copy
the data to my computer while I'm out."

"Of course." She reached out to adjust his pistol belt's buckle.
"There. Can't have my boss looking sloppy."

Lantu grinned at her and walked out of the office, humming.

"Sit down," Manak invited, and the admiral dropped into a chair.
His pistol caught on its arm, and he muttered a curse as he wrestled
with it.

"Language, my son. Language!" Manak's gentle mockery made Lantu feel better. The old chaplain had been monosyllabic and despondent for days after their conviction by the Synod. Even now there was little of the old sparkle in his eyes, and Lantu sometimes thought he sensed a disquieting brittleness about his inner strength. Lantu had been a baby when his parents died, and the fleet chaplain had raised him as his own son. Seeing him so cavalierly reduced was one more coal in the admiral's smoldering resentment.

"Sorry," he said, then sighed in relief as the pistol came unsnagged. "Holy Terra, I *hate* having to wear this thing."

"As do I." Manak frowned and looked around what had been Archbishop Tanuk's office. Its splendid luxury had yielded to the fleet chaplain's spartan hand, and Lantu found its present austerity far more comfortable.

"I've received word from the Synod," Manak continued. "They've decided—for the present, at least—to confirm me as acting archbishop." He snorted. "I imagine none of the regular bishops wanted the job."

"Wise of them." Lantu was careful to limit the bite in his tone.

"Unhappily true. But that means *I* set policy now, and that's what I wanted to see you about. Colonel Huark and Father Shamar have both protested your new deployment orders."

"I'm not surprised, Holiness, but if they want to stop these attacks instead of just responding to them, then—"

"Peace, my son. I know you too well to question your judgment . . . unlike some others." The fleet chaplain's face was momentarily bitter, but he shook the expression aside. "I've told them you have my full support. In return, I'm going to need yours, I think."

"Oh? In what way, Holiness?"

"I've read the report your charming secretary put together." Manak smiled slyly, and Lantu grinned—Manak had badgered him for years about his duty to take a wife as Holy Terra expected—but the churchman sobered quickly.

"You're right. The execution totals are far too high, even excluding reprisals. If your figures are as accurate as I expect, we've killed almost thirteen percent of the population. That is *not* the way to win converts."

Lantu nodded feelingly.

"What you may not realize," Manak went on, "is that our conversion rate—our *claimed* conversion rate, I should say—is under five percent. I find that truly appalling. Surely infidels should be willing to at least *pretend* conversion to escape death."

"They're stubborn people, Holiness," Lantu said mildly.

"Indeed they are, but this is still highly disturbing."

"I suspect, Holiness," Lantu said cautiously, "that the Inquisition has been . . . over zealous, let us say, in its use of punishment."

"Torture, you mean," Manak corrected bitterly, and Lantu relaxed. That sounded like the Manak he knew and respected. "One shouldn't speak ill of the dead, perhaps, especially not of martyrs in the cause of Holy Terra, but Tanuk never could tell right from left without an instruction book."

"I never knew the archbishop—"

"You missed very little, my son. His faith was strong, but he was ever intolerant. It's one thing to carry the jihad home against the infidels; it's quite another to slaughter them out of frustration, and that's precisely what the Inquisition is doing. If they prove impossible to reclaim, then we may have no option, but the Inquisition will win more converts with love than with hate. And whatever they may have become, they are still of the race of the Messenger. If only for the love we bear him, we must make a true effort to restore them to their Faith."

"I agree, Holiness. But I think our problem may be more difficult than simply *restoring* their Faith."

"Oh?"

"Holiness," Lantu considered his next words carefully, "I've been studying the planetary data base ever since we got here. There are many references to Holy Terra, but only as another world—the mother world, to be sure, but with no awareness of Her divinity. Could the infidels be telling the truth when they say they never heard of the Faith, much less rejected it?"

"Of course they are." Manak sounded a bit surprised. "I thought you understood that, my son. The Satan-Khan's influence is pervasive. All references to the Faith have been suppressed."

"But, Holiness," Lantu said cautiously, "I see no gaps, no evasions. Could something so profound be suppressed so tracelessly?"

"Lantu, this planet was settled nine years *after* their apostate Treaty of Tycho. Believe me, it wouldn't be difficult to delete all reference to the Faith from a colonial data base and keep it deleted. When we liberate Holy Terra, we'll find the evidence."

He sounded so positive Lantu merely nodded, but the admiral found his very assurance disturbing. The Church had always been zealous to protect its children from spiritual contamination, which was why access to the original Holy Writ in *Starwalker's* computers was so restricted. But Manak's confidence suggested something else. Was it possible he knew how simple it would be to suppress data because it had already—?

He chopped off that dangerous thought in a hurry.

"Getting back to my original point, though," Manak continued, "I'm going to disband the extermination squads—which Huark will hate— and I'm going to cut Archbishop Tanuk's camp execution levels in half. Shamar will hate that, and he'll hate it even more when I send in chaplain inspectors to limit his use of torture and make sure he abides by *my* quotas. They've both got powerful sponsors in the Synod, too; that's why I need your support."

"You have it, of course. What do you need me to do?"

"Just stand around and look efficient," Manak said dryly. "I'm basing my case on military expediency by arguing that a reduction in 'punishment' and the death totals will undermine popular pressure to support the terrorists."

"I see." Lantu fingered his muzzle. "It should have that effect, to some extent, at least. But it won't end it, Holiness."

"I know, but if I can justify it militarily long enough to raise the conversion rate, I won't need to justify it on any other grounds."

"I see," Lantu repeated, nodding with renewed respect. "And if I should just happen to score a few successes in the field—?"

"Exactly, my son," Manak said, and smiled.

"Jaysus!" Angus MacRory threw himself flat as yet another vertol swept overhead. A cluster of armored GEVs snorted through the underbrush like a herd of near-hippos barely a klick down-slope, and he heard the putter of infantry bikes following the paths the GEVs had flattened.

"My sentiments exactly," Caitrin muttered, and raised herself cautiously, peering uphill. "I think the rally point's still clear."

"Aye, and let's hope it *stays* clear." Angus drew the AP clip from his grenade launcher and replaced it with one of shaped-charge HEAT grenades. They had enough punch to deal with a lightly-armored GEV . . . assuming they got past the reactive armor's explosive strips first.

The thick smoke billowing through the canopy of distant treetops on the lower slopes had been a Shellhead extermination center, and Angus hoped the hostages they'd released had made a clean getaway. The guerrillas' civilian supporters were waiting to spirit them out to isolated farmsteads beyond the OZ, and they should be safe there. If they ever *got* there.

The speed of the Shellhead reaction had been almost as astounding as its strength. There must be at least two companies out there, and they'd dropped out of the sky before he and his people had gotten more than fifteen kilometers from the site of the raid. Fortunately, the Grampians thrust a stony tentacle close to the coast here, but—

He looked up as a rocket motor snarled and a captured Shellhead

SAM raced for a lumbering personnel vertol. Its proximity fuse exploded close to the port engine, and the aircraft lurched away, trailing smoke. Angus smiled grimly. They weren't going to find any handy clearings to set that beastie down in.

His smile vanished as a heavily-armored attack helicopter darted at the SAM team's position. A ripple salvo leapt from its rocket pods, followed by a hurricane of tracers. Then the chopper flashed over the spot, and the orange glare of napalm belched through the shattered trees.

Unless that team had been very, very lucky, it was dead. These new, powerful response teams were going to make things ugly.

"Weel, let's gae," he sighed, waving for Caitrin to proceed him while he lay still to cover her. She darted to their next chosen bit of cover, and he rose, jogging quietly past her.

It had to be the new Shellhead military type. The one called Lantu. The Shellhead com techs had finally begun to develop an awareness of basic security—probably another gift from this Lantu—but the resistance was still picking up enough to identify its new foe.

It might, Angus mused as he flopped down behind a fallen tree and waited for Caitrin to lope past him, be worthwhile to see if they couldn't find a way to send him to join Archbishop Tanuk.

CHAPTER SIXTEEN

The Blood of Warriors

The surge of the electromagnetic catapult, the queasiness of departure from the ship's artificial gravity, the indescribable *twisting* sensation of passage through the drive field, the instant of disorientation as "up" and "down" lost all meaning in the illimitable void of space (lacking even the reassuring reference point of a sun in this segment of nothingness men had labeled "QR-107"), the familiar grip of the fighter's drive as it assumed control of acceleration and inertia—all were behind him now. Kthaara'zarthan stretched out as far as the confines of the Human-designed fighter's cockpit allowed, then relaxed, muscle by muscle, and heaved a long sigh of contentment.

The Humans had modified the cockpit of this fighter to accommodate him and link with his Orion-designed life support suit months before. He had taken her on practice runs in Redwing until she responded like an extension of his own body, with a smoothness of control that could hardly have been bettered by that "direct neural interfacing" of which the Khan's researchers (and, he had been amused to discover, the Humans', as well) had blathered for centuries without ever quite overcoming those irritating little drawbacks which would kill a pilot outside the safe confines of a laboratory. Especially in the stress of battle.

He snorted into his helmet—a very Human sound of amused disgust that ended in a high-pitched sound no Human could have manufactured. He would believe in neural interfacing when one of those *droshokol mizoa-haarlesh* who preached its virtues were willing to risk their own pelts flying it in combat. Which, he reflected, nudging his controls with sensual pleasure, was not to say he would welcome

133

it, for it was difficult to believe anything could equal the sheer delight of holding his fleet little vessel's very soul between his claws. Yet not even this pleasure could substitute for personal combat against his cousin's killers. Even the Humans—some of them, at least—could understand that.

Humans. Kthaara gave the clicking sound equivalent of a man's rueful headshake. Who could understand them? He had seen them in battle, and he would have words for the next cub of his clan who called them *chofaki*. Yes, and more than words, if more was required. But the fact remained that there was no understanding them, with their wildly inconsistent ethics and their seemingly limitless capacity for self-deception. Howard Anderson had once quoted to him from a Human philosopher: "We have met the enemy, and he is us." A great philosopher indeed, Kthaara had acknowledged. Truly, Humans were a race forever at war with themselves—at once the source of their unique vitality and the price they paid for it. The *Zheeerlikou'valkhannaieee*, knowing precisely who and what they were, could see the universe precisely as it was; their follies resulted from inability to subordinate their innermost nature to some bloodless balancing of advantage and disadvantage, and not from the strange tendency of most Humans to painstakingly construct an unreal universe and base their actions thereon. Not all Humans— certainly not Ivan Antonov.

There was, of course, another barrier to empathy with Humans which no well-bred Orion would ever dream of revealing to them. Besides, Kthaara was a cosmopolite; he had long since learned to overcome the physical revulsion any normal mind must feel in the presence of such a species. But it was hard. It would have been better if they were completely hairless; their spotty, patchy growth made them look diseased. It was fortunate they had the decency to keep their bodies covered with fabric . . . most of the time.

He had learned that since their industrial revolution they had abandoned their nudity taboos. Well, most of them had, at any rate, he amended, marveling anew at the multiplicity of utterly incompatible value systems Humanity embraced. It was maddening. Each time he thought he had brought a definitive idea of what Humans believed within claws' reach, he discovered yet *another* level of disagreement within their complex melange of cultures. He still couldn't imagine how *they* kept track of it, much less how any rational species could be expected to do so. And those who had discarded the traditional religious view of the naked human body as an obscene sight were actually proud of themselves. Kthaara couldn't imagine why.

Yet the faces were the worst, flat, without the slightest trace of a muzzle, with eyes and mouth surrounded by bare and unmistakably wet-looking skin. The males, in obedience to the dictates of current fashion, made it even worse by shaving what facial hair they did possess in an odd and perverse throwback to primitive self-mutilation.

But give them their due: though they might not be aware of their own ugliness, they at least recognized the handsomeness of the Orions—which must, he reflected, be intrinsically obvious to any truly sensitive mind! He had, however, been taken aback to learn that the Human reaction to his own species was due in part to a pleasing and comforting resemblance to a Terran domestic animal!

He shook loose from the thoughts as he maneuvered his fighter into place in the strike formation. Excessive concern with appearances was an adolescent characteristic few Orions completely outgrew until old age. But it, too, could be overcome. He reflected on the insignificance of the physical body that housed an Ivan Antonov, and thought back to the staff conference that had led to his presence here. . . .

"No, Admiral Berenson," Antonov had said implacably. "This has been discussed before. Our probes have established that the ingress warp point is covered by light craft, supported by nothing heavier than battle-cruisers. The SBMHAWKs must not be used until we reach a warp point defended by heavy units."

"With great respect, Admiral," the commander of Second Fleet's light carriers replied, not sounding particularly respectful, "we have to fight our way through QR-107 before we can even reach such a warp point! And I cannot answer for the ability of my units to contribute much to that end after the losses they're bound to take in forcing the warp point under the present plan." He drew a deep breath. "Sir, I believe an unused weapon is a useless weapon. As you've so rightly pointed out, we know exactly what ship classes are waiting on the other side of the warp point. This makes the situation ideal for SBMHAWK deployment; they can be programmed with precision."

Antonov scowled. He could count on solid support from his own staff on this—Tsuchevsky had come around to Kthaara's way of thinking. But Berenson, a relatively recent arrival who possessed a solid reputation as a fighter pilot and commander of fighter pilots, remained unconvinced.

"Our battle plan has been formulated with an eye to minimizing losses to your light carriers, Admiral," Antonov replied in his very best effort at a conciliatory tone of voice. "Of course, the fighters can expect a certain percentage of casualties, but our assessment is that these should be within acceptable levels—"

"'Acceptable levels,' Admiral?" Berenson cut in, shocking even his own supporters in the room. (*Nobody* interrupted Ivan the Terrible.)

He glanced at Kthaara, who was known to have been one of the plan's principal authors, then back to Antonov. "Perhaps, sir, what we need here is a *human* definition of 'acceptability'!"

"*Yob' tvoyu mat'!*" Antonov exploded, with a volume that seemed to cause the entire orbital fortress to vibrate. Even Berenson flinched visibly. "Who the fuck ever told you this was safe occupation? It is objective that matters. We—all of us—are expendable. Your pilots understand that even if you don't, you motherless turd!" He paused, then continued in a mere roar. "I have broken bigger men for less cowardice than yours, Admiral! For cowardice in face of enemy, I swear I will have anyone—whatever his rank—shot! If you feel you cannot carry out plan as it stands, it is your duty to so inform me, so I can replace you with someone who can. Do I make myself clear?"

"Perfectly clear, Admiral." Berenson's face was paler by a couple of shades, but he hadn't gone into a state of shock like almost everyone else in the room. "Your orders will, of course, be carried out to the letter."

"Good." Antonov rose. "This meeting is adjourned. Captain Tsuchevsky and Commander Kthaara, please accompany me to my quarters."

Once the three of them were in the elevator, Antonov sighed deeply, knowing what was coming next.

"You're going to have a stroke one of these days, Ivan Nikolayevich," Tsuchevsky scolded sternly, and Antonov held up his hand wearily.

"I know, I know, Pasha. I promise I'll stop losing my temper." He glanced at Kthaara, who was looking ill at ease, and smiled faintly. "What, nothing about your request?!"

The Orion relaxed slightly. "This is hardly the time, Admiral. I find I owe you an apology." Antonov raised an inquisitive eyebrow, and Kthaara explained bleakly. "I now understand what you meant at our first meeting when you spoke of the problems I would cause you."

"Oh, that!" Antonov gave a sound halfway between a laugh and a snort. "Don't give it another thought. You see, Berenson was talking about me as much as he was about you."

"I know there are those among your officers who feel you understand my race all too well—better than a Human has any right to," the Orion replied slowly. "They may have a point." A sudden carnivore's grin signaled the mercurial mood-shift the two humans had come to know so well. "So perhaps it is time to renew my request!"

A low moan escaped Antonov.

"Kthaara, you can't really be serious," Tsuchevsky put in. "You know better than most what a problem command-and-control poses in strikefighter operations, even under the best circumstances! And you know you can't take your talker along in a single-seat vehicle!"

"Command-and-control is not a factor, Paaavaaaal Saaairgaaiaavychhh," replied Kthaara (who'd been around these two long enough to grasp the nuances of modes of address), "for I seek to command no one. It will be enough if I am assigned to a squadron whose commander understands the Tongue of Tongues, so that I will be able to report to him."

Antonov gazed narrowly at the being who stood before him like Nemesis, overhead lights gleaming on midnight fur. "Do I understand, then, that you're requesting to take part in the coming battle as a common fighter pilot? And do *you* understand how much more good you could do—how much more damage you could do the Thebans—on the flag bridge?" He drew a deep breath. "Kthaara, as much as I'd hate to see you do it, I must tell you you could go home to Valkha right now and know you'd avenged your cousin many times over by what you've already contributed. You don't need to do this!"

"Yes, I do, Admiral." Kthaara's reply was quiet, but the elemental predator looked out of his slit-pupilled eyes. "You know I do. I have only planned and organized the killing of Thebans by others. No amount of this can meet the demands of honor. Ever. This may be unreasonable . . . but honor itself is unreasonable."

A couple of heartbeats of brooding silence passed before Antonov spoke, with the kind of gruffness that told Kthaara he'd won. "Well, if you must play the fool, I believe Commander Takashima understands Orion well enough. . . ."

The emergence of the first wave of *Pegasus*-class light carriers from warp told the Theban defenders of QR-107 another raid was underway. The second group, and the third, made them wonder. They'd expected any major infidel incursion to be led by battleships. But Ivan Antonov was still hoarding his battleships.

At any rate, Admiral Tharana, CO of the light covering forces and fifteen *Ronin*-class battle-cruisers that supported them, knew his duty. He reported the attack to fleet command, five-and-a-quarter light-hours away near QR-107's other warp point. Then, while his messages winged across the endless light-minutes, his units converged on the invading carriers, which were their primary targets. Their new anti-fighter training told them fighters with their bases destroyed were only temporary threats, but Antonov also knew that. On his orders, the light carriers now performed an old trick—one that was an Orion favorite and, in particular, of Kthaara'zarthan.

The reactionless drive didn't really cancel inertia, and Berenson's carriers couldn't instantaneously reverse direction without loss of velocity like those "flying saucers" Terrans had been wont to observe during the decades of endemic mass hysteria preceding the Second

Millennium. But they could (and did, immediately after launching their fighters) make a far tighter 180-degree turn than would have been imaginable in the days of reaction drives, and vanished back into the warp point, leaving the fighters to slash into badly bewildered Theban formations. Back in Redwing space, they swung about again, paired off with *Scimitar*-class battle-cruisers, and returned to the carnage of QR-107 in time to retrieve and rearm their fighters.

It was the kind of complex tactical plan which ordinarily invites disaster by requiring a degree of precision which cannot be counted upon in the field. It worked because it was conceived in the cross-fertilization of two winning—but very different—traditions, practiced to exhaustion under the lash of Ivan Antonov's will, and executed by David Berenson, whose abilities were such that Antonov had to tolerate him. The Thebans were thrown onto the defensive against an enemy whose strength grew steadily as more and more ships emerged. By the time Admiral Tharana finally exercised the discretion the communications lag had forced Second Admiral Jahanak to grant him, it was almost too late.

The battered Theban survivors withdrew from the vicinity of the warp point, and as they did, it became harder and harder to render accurate reports of the number and tonnages of the arriving infidel ships. But it wasn't until his rampaging fighter squadrons had driven them out of scanner range altogether that Antonov allowed certain ships to disappear.

Electronic countermeasures had always been a crucial element of space combat, in which the unaided human eye was largely useless. Early-generation ECM suites had operated purely in fire-confusion mode; their only function was to make the ships that carried them more difficult targets, for the massive energy signature of an active drive field was simply impossible to hide. Later systems could play more sophisticated games with enemy sensors and make a ship seem, within limits, to be significantly more or less massive, but no one had ever been able to devise a way of concealing from today's broad-spectrum active and passive sensor arrays the fact that *something* was out there. Until now.

The new system was hideously expensive, and too massive for small ships, but its capabilities were on a par with its cost and tonnage penalty. It could perform all the functions of the earlier-generation systems and more for any ship which mounted it. Sophisticated computers wrapped a force field bubble about the betraying energy signature of its drive field—a very unusual bubble which trapped the energy that turned a starship into a brilliant beacon and radiated it directly astern, away from hostile scanners. Other, equally sophisticated computers monitored the strengths and frequencies of active enemy sensors, playing a fantastically complex matching game with their frequency shifts and sending back cunningly augmented impulses to blind their probing eyes. For the first time since humanity had abandoned primitive radar, true "stealth" technology had become feasible once more.

It wasn't infallible, of course. Though passive sensors were useless against it, active sensors had been found to be able to penetrate the ruse between fifteen and twenty percent of the time. But active scanners were far, far shorter-ranged, and that success rate had been achieved in tests whose participants had known exactly what they were looking for. Against an enemy who didn't even suspect the device's existence . . .

Thus it was that Antonov's eight *Wolfhound*-class fleet carriers ceased masquerading as light cruisers. They vanished from the ken of detection instruments and split off from the emerging Terran formation, advancing deep into the void of QR-107 on a wide dog-leg, unaccompanied by their usual escorts and protected only by the invisibility conferred by a new and untried system.

Second Admiral Jahanak's thumb caressed the switch on his light pencil in an unconscious nervous gesture as he waited. Tharana had waited overlong to break off, he thought sourly. But sufficient light units remained to maintain a scanner watch over the advancing infidel fleet while Tharana's surviving battle-cruisers fell back on the main body at maximum. Now Jahanak watched Captain Yurah listening intently to the voices in his earphone and possessed his soul as patiently as he could.

"Second Admiral. Holiness." The flag captain paused to nod politely to both of his superiors and Jahanak managed not to snap at him. "Admiral Tharana's reports indicate this is a major attack. His units have been pushed back to extreme scanner range, but he estimates the enemy's strength at approximately six superdreadnoughts, twelve battleships, nine battle-cruisers, and twelve to fourteen light and heavy cruisers. They appear to be accompanied by eighteen to twenty destroyers and eight to ten of their cruiser-size carriers. They are advancing directly towards us at five percent of light-speed. ETA is approximately ninety-three hours from now."

"Thank you, Captain." The switch on Jahanak's light pencil clicked under his stroking thumb, and he switched it quickly off again, then slipped it into his pocket. It would never do, he thought sardonically, to admit he, too, could feel anxiety.

"Well, Holiness," he turned his command chair to face Hinam, "it seems the infidels are finally seeking a decisive battle. The question is whether or not we grant it to them."

Hinam leaned forward, looking alarmed. "Surely, Second Admiral, there can be no question! The infidels are so inferior in both numbers and tonnage that not even the diabolical weapons their satanically-inspired cunning has allowed them to develop can . . ."

Jahanak tuned it out, maintaining a careful pose of grave attention, and thought hard. Yes, they were obviously counting on their fighters and those incredible new warheads to make up the force differential. But how many fighters could they have? The reports from the fighter-development project back on Thebes gave him a fair idea how much carrier tonnage it required to service and launch each fighter. The approaching fleet included only cruiser-size "light carriers" such as had been encountered at Redwing, and not many more of them than had been engaged there. Was the enemy's supply of fighters—or pilots—subject to some unsuspected limiting factor?

It seemed unlikely from captured infidel data, but there clearly couldn't be enough fighters aboard that handful of carriers to even the odds between the two fleets. Especially not here, where there could be no ambush and the infidel fighters would have to approach from ahead, through the entire range of his AFHAWKs. Of course, the enemy's antimatter warheads would be a problem, but the infidels couldn't know his *Prophet*-class battleships and the refitted *Ronin*-class battle-cruisers he'd held back from the warp point now carried copies of their own long-range missiles—as did the external racks of all his other capital ships, as well. If their previous tactics held good, they would close to just beyond standard missile range in order to maximize accuracy, allowing him to get in the first heavy blows, and once they closed to laser range—

Yet the infidel who'd commanded at Redwing was manifestly no fool. Still, one didn't have to be a fool to fall victim to overconfidence. . . .

He realized Hinam had stopped for breath, allowing Yurah to resume. "Only one thing bothers me," the flag captain frowned. "There seems to be a discrepancy between the ship counts reported during the earlier stages of the battle and the ones we're getting now. A few light cruisers seem to be missing from that formation."

"The earlier reports were confused and contradictory," Hinam declared dismissively. Which, Jahanak knew, was true. "And the infidels could now be using ECM in deception mode to confuse us." He turned to Jahanak, eyes bright. "This is your hour, Admiral! Don't spurn the chance Holy Terra has offered—seize it!" His gleaming eyes narrowed shrewdly. "The Synod will hardly complain about minor past deviations from policy on the part of the hero who smashes the main infidel fleet!"

Jahanak hid an incipient frown. Little as he liked Hinam, the fleet

chaplain's last point had struck home. A decisive victory would vin-
dicate his strategy, demonstrating that he'd been right and the Synod
wrong. (Oh, of course he wouldn't put it that way. But everyone would
know.) He lifted his head and spoke urbanely.

"As always, Holiness, I am guided by your wisdom in all things.
Captain Yurah, the battle-line and all supporting elements will engage
the enemy as per Operational Plan Delta-Two."

"At once, Second Admiral!" Yurah's eyes blazed, and Jahanak smiled,
remembering the hostility of their first meeting. The flag captain's
eagerness augured well.

The second admiral leaned back, watching his display as the fleet
moved forward. Forward, but not too far forward. They'd had time
to consider, to plan for all contingencies that might arise in QR-107,
and now the Sword of Holy Terra unsheathed itself with practiced
smoothness.

Eleven superdreadnoughts, fourteen battleships, and thirty battle-
cruisers took up their positions, screened ahead and on the flanks by
massed cruiser flotillas and destroyer squadrons. Even if those carriers had lost no fighters at all in breaking into QR-107 (and they
had lost, Jahanak thought coldly), they wouldn't be enough to even
those odds. Not against ships who knew, now, what fighters could
do . . . and what to do about them, in turn.

Yet it wouldn't do to become overly confident himself. That was
why he'd selected Delta-Two, which wouldn't take his battle-line overly
far from the Parsifal warp point. If the infidels were foolish enough
to come to him, he would oblige them by crushing them, but his fleet
represented too much of Terra's Sword to risk lightly.

The two fleets swept closer and closer, and the phantom carriers
swung wide around the ponderous Theban formation, circling until
they entered its wake, cutting between it and the Parsifal warp point.
They had plenty of time to position themselves before the two battle-
lines drew into capital missile range. And just as the opening salvos
were being exchanged, two hundred and forty fighters, piloted by two
hundred and thirty-nine humans and Kthaara'zarthan, entered the
Theban battle-line's blind zone from nowhere.

Kthaara felt an almost dreamy sense of fulfillment as his squadron charged up the stern of the Theban super-dreadnought. The
massive vessel, warned by frantic reports from its screening units, began
an emergency turn—slow and incredibly clumsy compared to a
fighter . . . and too late. Far too late. His fighter shuddered, slicing
through the curdled space of the huge ship's wake, closing to a shorter
range than he'd ever thought possible. His entire being, focused on

his targeting scope, willed his heavy, short-ranged close-attack missiles through the wavering distortion of this unreal-seeming space as
the 509th Fighter Squadron fired.

Neither he nor his Human *farshatok* could miss at this range—
electromagnetic shielding and drive field alike died in a searing cluster
of nuclear flares, and the stern of the mammoth ship seemed to bulge
outward, splitting open in fissures of hellfire, as a warhead Kthaara
was certain was one of his made the direct physical hit no mobile
structure could withstand. No human who heard it would ever forget his banshee howl of vengeance.

"Let's keep the noise down," Commander Takashima called as they
pulled up with a maneuverability possible only to craft such as theirs.
There was no reproach in his voice—his understanding of the Tongue
of Tongues, and those who spoke it, had turned out to be far less
superficial than Antonov had implied. "Good job, everyone. Let's get
back to the barn and—"

Takashima's voice died in a burst of static as the glare of his exploding
fighter almost overloaded their view ports' automatic polarization. It
faded, revealing the Theban light cruiser that had, by who knew what
fanatical efforts, managed to swing about and come within AFHAWK
range on a converging course that would soon bring it close enough
to use its point defense lasers, as well.

"Evasive action!" The voice in Kthaara's helmet phones was that
of the squadron ops officer, a painfully young lieutenant. (But he also
understood the Tongue of Tongues, Kthaara had a split second to
reflect; yes, perhaps Antonov's choice of a squadron to attach him
to hadn't been so casual after all.) "Back to the ship—fast!"

"A course for the ship will carry us directly through the Theban's
optimum AFHAWK envelope, Lieutenant Paapaas," Kthaara said without
having time to reflect. "We can turn about and outrun him, but such
a course will take us further from the carrier than we can afford to get."
Let's see . . . how to put this? "May I suggest that the squadron reform
on me, as I seem to be in the best position to . . ."

"Certainly, Commander!" Pappas couldn't quite keep the gratitude
out of his voice. Kthaara waited for him to give the other pilots the
order, then wrenched his fighter around and accelerated directly towards
the Theban, corkscrewing madly. He had time to see that Pappas and
the others were glued to him, and to feel a kind of pride in them that
couldn't be put precisely into any Human language.

The Theban crew were new arrivals; they'd trained intensely and
listened to the stories of the veterans of Redwing. But they'd never
actually faced fighters. And they were shaken to the core by what Holy
Terra was allowing to happen to their fleet. Their point defense should
have taken toll of these fighters that so unexpectedly swept past them

at an unthinkable relative velocity, clawing their ship's flanks with lasers. But in less than an eye-blink the little crafts were in their blind zone, receding rapidly . . . and Kthaara saw that all four of his companions were still with him.

He was, he decided, really getting too old for this.

"But where *are* they?" Hinam's voice wavered on the edge of hysteria as he stared over the scanner crews' shoulders, searching as they for the carriers to which the mysterious fighters had returned. "Where—"

"Be silent," Jahanak said curtly. Shock had the desired effect—fleet chaplains simply weren't spoken to that way. But on this flag bridge at this time, no one noticed. Hinam subsided, and Jahanak continued to absorb reports that told of the light carriers' massed fighter launch—a launch whose delay was no longer quite so inexplicable. Those fighters would hit his badly shaken fleet while the first attackers were rearming aboard their phantom carriers, and dealing with this fresh strike would require a compact formation which couldn't spread out to search for the invisible ships which had launched the first one. Meanwhile, the infidel battle-line was keeping scrupulously out of laser range and continuing the long-range capital missile duel in which their antimatter warheads nearly canceled out his own more numerous launchers.

"Signal to all units, Captain Yurah. Withdraw immediately and transit to Parsifal." This contingency had also been planned for. Turning to meet Hinam's stricken gaze, he continued smoothly. "It would seem, Holiness, that we've achieved our minimal objective of learning more about the infidels' capabilities and lulling them into overconfidence before unleashing our own fighters upon them. We can thus withdraw to Parsifal . . . as we intended to do all along."

Hinam stared at him, then shifted his gaze to a repeater screen showing the fleet's damage reports, then stared back at Jahanak again, as at a lunatic. He tried to speak but failed, and Jahanak went on remorselessly.

"You will, of course, be able to help explain our true intention in seeking this battle—as you urged my staff and myself to do—to the Synod." His eyes held the fleet chaplain's for a cold, measured heartbeat before he continued thoughtfully. "It is, after all, essential that we present a consistent report to avoid any possible misunderstanding on the Synod's part. Wouldn't you agree, Holiness?"

He turned away from the now speechless fleet chaplain and gave his attention to the battle. Yes, Hinam would go along, if only out of self-preservation. That, and the occasional, judicious mention of his own lineage, should get them past this debacle, in spite of the hideous losses his fleet still must take. Thank Holy Terra they hadn't ventured too far from the Parsifal warp point. The fighters from the cloaked carriers would only have the opportunity for one more strike before his survivors were through the warp point to the safety of Parsifal.

The lighter, faster Terran units, including Berenson's command, were already closing in on the Parsifal warp point, surging ahead of the lumbering battle-line when the battle had turned into a pursuit, and the cloaked fleet carriers, having dodged the retreating Thebans with almost ludicrous ease, moved to join them. The only living Thebans in QR-107 were the scattered light units that hadn't made it through the warp point with the main body, and which were now being hunted down.

Kthaara—just arrived by cutter aboard Antonov's new flagship—entered TFNS *Gosainthan*'s flag bridge to see Rear Admiral Berenson's face, contorted with suppressed fury, filling the main com screen.

"Your orders have been carried out, Admiral," Berenson was saying through tightly compressed lips. "Three *Shark*-class destroyers have been detached, and have now transited the warp point. No courier drones have been received, as yet. Wait." He turned aside, listened to someone off-screen, and spoke briefly. Then he turned back, and the fury in his face had congealed into hate. "Correction, Admiral. A courier drone—*one*—has returned from Parsifal. I have ordered its data downloaded to the flagship." Even as he spoke, the information appeared on a screen. "You will note," Berenson went on in a tightly controlled voice, "that it concludes with a Code Omega signal for all three ships."

Antonov, face expressionless, studied the data. "Yes," he finally acknowledged in a quiet voice. "I also note that they were able to record for the drone their sensor read-outs on the Theban defenses." Kthaara saw it, too; the shocking total of orbital fortresses in whose teeth the three destroyers had emerged into Einsteinian space. Antonov continued just as quietly. "You said it yourself, Admiral Berenson, at the last staff conference: to employ the SBMHAWKs with maximum effectiveness, we need to know exactly what is waiting at the other end of the warp line. We now have that information. And, as *I* said on the same occasion, it is the objective that matters." As the message crossed the few light-seconds that still separated them, he cut the connection. Then he turned to face Kthaara.

"You look like shit," was his greeting. For once, the Orion hadn't taken time to groom himself.

"So do you." Nothing ever really wore Antonov down; he was like planetary bedrock. But he was showing a certain undeniable haggardness.

"I heard what you did out there." Was it possible the Human smiled, a trifle?

"I saw what you just did here." Kthaara spoke seriously, but he, too, showed the beginning of his own race's smile. "You are more like my people than even Baaaraaansaahn thinks. And that is why . . ." He seemed to reach a decision. "You know of the oath of *vilkshatha*, do you not?"

Antonov blinked at the seeming irrelevancy. "Of course. It's the 'blood binding' that makes two Orion comrades-in-arms members of each other's family."

"Correct: two *farshatok* of the *Zheeerlikou'valkhannaieee*. To my knowledge, the ceremony has never involved a member of any other race. But as Humans say, there is a first time for everything . . . Ivaaan'zarthan!"

For a couple of heartbeats, Antonov was as motionless as he was silent. Then he threw back his head and bellowed with gargantuan laughter.

"Well," he managed when he had caught his breath, "I hope you know what you're doing . . . Kthaara Kornazhovich!"

CHAPTER SEVENTEEN

"I need those ships!"

The Marine honor guard clicked to attention in the echoing spaces of the superdreadnought *Gosainthan*'s boat bay, and Antonov stepped forward to the VIP shuttle's ramp. "Welcome to Redwing, Minister."

Howard Anderson didn't acknowledge the greeting. He merely stared, then pointed with his cane. "And just what the hell is *that*?"

"I believe it's my face." Antonov was all imperturbability. Anderson was not amused.

"You *know* what I mean!"

"Oh, *that*." Antonov rubbed his jaw. At least the stubble phase was past. It was getting almost fluffy. "Well, I've always wondered what I'd look like with a beard. Somehow, it just came up in conversation with Commander Kthaara'zarthan." He gestured in the direction of the big Orion, who was looking insufferably complacent. "He urged me to try it, just to see how it would turn out. I think it's coming along rather well, don't you?"

"You look," Anderson replied, eyeing the burgeoning facial hair with scant favor, "like something out of an early twentieth-century political cartoon about Bolsheviks!" Then he glanced at Kthaara again. There was, he decided, no other way to describe it: the Orion looked like he'd swallowed a canary built to scale.

"Well," Anderson sighed, setting down his empty glass with a click. "Congratulations, Ivan. I don't need to tell you what you've accomplished here." Antonov, silhouetted against his stateroom's view port, gave an expressive Slavic shrug.

"We've been lucky. And part of our luck has been the new hardware you've sent us—especially the new ECM. Trying to guess what

Father Christmas will pull out of his bag next has become the Fleet's favorite pastime."

"Ho, ho, ho! Well, as it happens, I *do* have a little something to satisfy your curiosity. I'm sure you've read the preliminary reports on how the Thebans manage to produce those lasers of theirs?" Antonov nodded. "And may I assume you're not particularly wild about the thought of exploding nukes rolling around the insides of your own ships?"

"You may, indeed." There was very little levity in Antonov's rumbling voice. "But if there's no other way to match their beams—" He broke off with another expressive shrug.

"Ah, but there is another way!" Anderson looked briefly very like Kthaara'zarthan as he smiled. "What would you say to a laser with about seventy-five percent of the Thebans' range, no bombs, and damned near two-thirds again as many projectors per tonne?"

"*Bozhemoi!*" Antonov said very softly and sincerely. "There truly is such a weapon?" Anderson nodded smugly, and the admiral grinned. "Then Father Christmas has outdone himself, Howard!"

"No, this time it's *Mother* Christmas," Anderson corrected. "In the form of Rear Admiral Timoshenko. She calls them 'hetlasers,' and I saw a full-scale field test just before I personally rammed her promotion through the board. You should have heard old Gomulka howling about promoting her out of the zone!" His eyes gleamed with fond remembrance.

"They don't pack quite as much punch per projector, but the numbers more than make up for it across their range, and I've had BuShips modify the plans for the new superdreadnoughts and battleships. I'm afraid it'll put our building schedules back a couple of months, but I was pretty sure you'd think it was time well spent."

"Indeed," Antonov nodded. "The only real tactical advantage the Thebans have left is in energy-range combat. With that gone, and with an initial SBMHAWK bombardment, there's no way they'll be able to keep us out of Parsifal. And we haven't used the extended range capability of the standard SBMs yet, either; as far as they know, their missiles' range will match ours, now that they've developed capital missiles of their own."

He paused and frowned slightly. "But, Howard, under the schedule you've just outlined, we'll have enough SBMHAWKs long before we have enough new capital ships. And the longer we wait, the more time they'll have to strengthen their defenses. Why not refit my existing heavy ships with hetlasers now?"

"That's been thought of, of course. But withdrawing your battlewagons to Galloway's World for refitting—even in shifts—will mean going on the defensive for now in QR-107."

Antonov looked at him sharply. "Why, of course, Howard—by definition. The whole purpose is to enable us to break into Parsifal without crippling losses, so naturally we won't be attacking until the work is completed. Besides, we've already taken up a mobile defensive posture that doesn't involve capital ships. Rear Admiral Berenson is in command there now, with the cloaked *Wolfhounds* as well as his own light carriers, disposed to sting the Thebans to death if they try to counterattack from Parsifal. Surely," he went on, looking unwontedly concerned, "you understand—"

"Of course *I* understand, Ivan. Whatever you think, I'm not senile yet. I only mentioned the point because of political factors."

"*Political* factors?" Antonov started to take on a dangerous look. "What political factors? We're talking about a military decision!"

Humanity had left instantaneous communications (and the tendency to micro-manage military operations to death) on Old Terra, and the Federation had always granted its admirals broad authority to run wars on the Frontier. If it hadn't, it would long ago have been replaced, as a simple matter of natural selection, by a polity that did.

"Remember, Ivan," Anderson said, "this isn't a normal situation. Having gotten us into this mess in the first place, the politicos are still shitting their pants. Once we unmistakably gain the military upper hand, I expect them to turn vindictive; at present, they're merely scared, and they won't respond well to any suggestion of 'irresolution' on the military's part! Trust me—I'm talking from seventy years of political experience."

"Experience I don't envy you in the slightest!" Antonov snapped. He visibly controlled himself. "Look, Howard, surely even politicians can understand an elementary matter of military necessity like this—at least after you explain it to them. Can't they?"

Anderson laughed shortly. "Not these fuck-ups. And don't count on my explanations doing much good—at least as far as Waldeck goes. You know he hates me about as much as I do him."

"*Sookin sin!* Son-of-a-bitch! So the military objective—and the lives of my people—are secondary to enabling gasbags like Sakanami and slime molds like Waldeck to evade the consequences of their own stupidity?"

Anderson gave a theatrical wince. "I *do* wish you wouldn't say things like that, Ivan! Where's your respect for properly constituted civilian authority?"

Antonov exploded into a spate of Russian, and the little Anderson understood made him just as glad he didn't understand the rest. Finally, the massive admiral calmed down sufficiently to communicate in Standard English.

"Why am I even surprised? Mass democracy! Ha! The divine right of political careerists!" He glowered at Anderson. "Does such a regime even deserve to survive?"

"Hey," Anderson said, alarmed. "Don't go Russian-nihilistic on me, Ivan! Not now!"

Antonov let out a long breath. "Oh, don't worry, Howard. I'll follow orders. But," he continued grimly, "in order to do so, I need those ships. You'll just have to explain the facts of life to Sakanami and Waldeck and even that cunt Wycliffe." (This time Anderson's wince was sincere.) "If my battle-line has to go into Parsifal without hetlasers, or if I have to wait for the new construction, the losses will make them *really* shit in their pants." He leaned forward, and his voice dropped even deeper than was its wont. "I need those ships!"

"Well," Anderson said mildly after a heartbeat or two, "we'll just have to see what we can do about getting them for you, won't we?"

The cloud-banded blue dot swelled on TFNS *Warrior*'s visual display, and the light cruiser's captain turned to the old man at the assistant gunnery officer's station.

"You know, Admiral, it's eight years since I last saw Old Terra. She sure is pretty, isn't she?"

"Indeed she is, Captain. And thank you for letting me watch. It's been a lot more than eight years since *I* last saw her from a command deck."

"In that case, Admiral, would you care to take the con?"

Commander Helen Takaharu smiled, and Howard Anderson grinned back like a schoolboy. Then his grin faded.

"No, Captain. Thanks for the offer, but I'm afraid it's been too long. Besides, I'm not really an admiral anymore."

"You'll always be an admiral, sir," Takaharu said softly, "and I'd be honored if you accepted."

Color tinged Anderson's cheeks, but for once he felt no ire. There was no sycophancy in Takaharu's voice. He hesitated.

"Please, sir, I know I speak for *Warrior*'s entire crew."

"Well, in that case, Captain Takaharu," he said gruffly, "the honor will be mine." He stood, and Takaharu rose from her command chair.

"I relieve you, sir," he said.

"I stand relieved," she replied crisply. He settled into her chair, and she moved to stand at his shoulder, her face creased in a huge smile.

"Maneuvering, stand by for orbital insertion."

"Standing by, aye, Admiral," the helmsman replied, and Howard Anderson stroked the command chair's armrests almost reverently.

"Out of the question," Irena Wycliffe said sharply. "Totally out of the question! I'm astonished Admiral Antonov could suggest such a thing."

Anderson leaned back and looked around the conference room. Hamid O'Rourke looked unhappy and avoided his eyes, and several other ministers fidgeted uncomfortably.

"Ms. Wycliffe," he said at last, "I fail to understand exactly which aspect of the Ministry of Public Welfare qualifies you to hold such a pronounced opinion?"

Wycliffe flushed and glanced angrily at the president. In point of fact, she wasn't expressing *her* opinion. She was one of Pericles Waldeck's closest supporters, his eyes and ears—and mouth—in the Sakanami Cabinet.

"I may not have your own long—and long *ago*—military experience, Mister Anderson," she shot back, "but I'm quite conversant with the course of *this* war! Admiral Antonov held Redwing by the skin of his teeth, and now, when he's finally pushed the Thebans back at last, he wants to *weaken* his forces? Even I know the thing for the Thebans to do is counterattack as quickly as possible!"

"Ladies and gentlemen, please!" Sakanami intervened mildly. "This is not a question to settle on the basis of personalities." He glanced at both disputants. "I trust I make myself clear?"

Anderson snorted in amusement and nodded. Wycliffe distributed her glare almost impartially between him and the president.

"Now, then," Sakanami continued. "Admiral Antonov is entitled to make his own tactical dispositions. No one disputes that. But I do feel we have a right to question the wisdom of such a fundamental strategic redistribution. Admiral Brandenburg?"

The chief of naval operations was a spare, white-haired man. Seventy years younger than Anderson, he actually looked older as he sat quietly erect in his space-black and silver uniform. Five years as CNO had taught him the tricks of the political jungle, but he'd commanded a task force himself in ISW-3, and he frowned thoughtfully.

"As a rule, Mister President, the commander on the spot usually has a clearer appreciation than GHQ, and Antonov's record to date certainly seems to suggest he knows what he's doing. I suppose there is a possibility of a counterattack, but as I understand it he's not talking about pulling the battle-line back *en masse*, is he, Howard?"

"No. He wanted to, but I convinced him it'd cause undue concern"—Anderson grinned wryly—"back home. Besides, Fritz, we're heavily committed to the new construction programs. We can only free up the space to handle about a third of his battle-line at a time without disrupting things, so we're talking about a temporary reduction, not a total rollback."

"Indeed?" Wycliffe put in. "But it's actually a *two-thirds* reduction, isn't it?"

"It is," Anderson agreed with unruffled calm. "One-third of his units

will be put into yard hands immediately; the next third will start back
to Galloway's World when they're finished. They'll pass one another
en route, but for some weeks Second Fleet's battle-line will, indeed,
be at one-third strength."

"Still," Brandenburg mused, "we're talking about a fleet defending
a starless nexus, with no need to mount a warp-point defense."

"Which doesn't mean those ships won't be needed!" Wycliffe turned
to Sakanami. "Mister President, such a policy would cause great disquiet in the Assembly. Important people will ask questions."

"Let them," Anderson said coldly.

"Oh, that's a wonderful idea! Wars, Mister Anderson, are not fought
only on the front lines—and military people aren't the only ones with
a stake in their outcome!"

"No, just the ones who do the dying," Anderson said even more
coldly, and Wycliffe jerked back as if he'd slapped her. He pressed his
advantage.

"Look, Fritz has already pointed out we've got plenty of depth and
no population to defend. Any counterattack will be met with a mobile
defense, not a point-blank battle on top of a warp point! Admiral
Antonov is confident his fighters can stop any Theban attack cold,
and I concur. Fritz?"

"On the basis of the reports I've seen," Brandenburg said mildly,
"I'd certainly have to agree. In a mobile defense, the sluggers would
only slow him down, anyway. He'd need carriers and fighters to pound
them as they try to close, and carriers need escorts who can keep up
with them."

"I see." Sakanami rubbed the conference table gently, then raised
his fingers, as if inspecting them for dust. "Hamid?"

"I"—O'Rourke shot Wycliffe an unhappy glance—"have to agree
with Admiral Brandenburg. If we're going to stand on the defensive
in QR-107, the battle-line would definitely play a secondary role."

"But that raises another point." Anderson shook his head. Whatever else she was, Irena Wycliffe wasn't a quitter. "Should we even be
talking about standing on the defensive? Why isn't Second Fleet
pushing forward into Parsifal right now?"

"Because," Brandenburg's voice was unwontedly caustic, "a lot of
people would die, Ms. Wycliffe. In a warp point assault, the enemy
is right on top of you as you make transit. They'd be at their most
effective range and working right through our shields from the outset; without matching weapons, *we'd* have to pound their shields flat
before we could even get at them." He snorted. "That's why Antonov's
insisting on this refit! Or would you prefer for him to wade right in
and lose more ships and people than he has to?"

"Fritz is right, Mister President," Anderson said. "We could probably take Parsifal now, but the battle-line would take murderous punishment. They still will, even with the new lasers, but at least they'll be in position to reply effectively. You may face some political questions now, but what are your options? Push ahead too soon and get our people killed? Or wait till we have enough *new* ships for the attack—possibly as much as a year from now? At the moment the Thebans don't have any fighters, but give them that much time and they will. In which case"—he looked steadily at Wycliffe—"our losses will be even higher."

"I have to agree with Mister Anderson and Admiral Brandenburg." O'Rourke took the plunge at last.

"Why?" Wycliffe's cold tone warned of more than military consequences for Hamid O'Rourke if he crossed Pericles Waldeck.

"Because they're right," O'Rourke said sharply. "And if there are questions in the Assembly, I'll say so there. It's important to launch heavy, properly prepared attacks, and this is the quickest way to accomplish that. Mister President," he turned to Sakanami, "Admiral Antonov is right."

"Very well," the president said calmly. "If that's the opinion of the Chief of Naval Operations, the Minister for War Production, and the Defense Minister, the question is closed. Now, the next item on the agenda is—"

Anderson sat back. It had been easier than he'd expected after all. He'd known Brandenburg would support him, but he hadn't expected O'Rourke to overcome his fear of Waldeck's revenge. It seemed he owed the man an apology, and he made a mental note to deliver it in person.

CHAPTER EIGHTEEN

No Sae Bad . . . Fer a Shellhead

The vertol's cockpit was less impressive than a flag bridge, and he might become dead very quickly if he stumbled over a guerrilla SAM team, but it was worth it to get away from HQ. Or, Admiral Lantu amended wryly as the craft turned for another sweep, it had been *so* far. He knew it worried Fraymak, but he refused to be a mere paper-pusher. Besides, flying an occasional mission gave him at least the illusion of commanding his own fate.

Unlike many Fleet officers, Lantu was an experienced vertol pilot, and he habitually took the copilot's station. Now he leaned to the side, pressing his cranial carapace against the bulged canopy to peer back along the fuselage. A pair of auto-cannon thrust from the troop doors, and there were rocket pods under the wings, but the vertol's sensor array was their real weapon. It probed the dense forest below with thermal, electronic, and magnetic detectors, its laser designators ready to paint targets for their escorting attack aircraft, not that Lantu expected to find any. The guerrillas knew what they were doing, and it was the Satan-Khan's own task to get any reading through these damnable trees, especially once they split back up into small groups. But at least his sensors *forced* them to break up and stay broken up . . . he hoped.

It was a frustrating problem. How did he know if he was winning? Body counts were one way, but the guerrillas seemed to have an inexhaustible supply of recruits, thanks to Colonel Huark and the late archbishop. The lower incidence of attacks might have been a good sign, if their larger assault parties weren't gaining in firepower what they lost in frequency and proving a nastier handful for any reaction teams that managed to catch them.

Lantu sighed. The jihad's initial force structure had badly underestimated the need for ground troops, and replacing the Fleet's climbing losses took precedence over increases in planetary forces. And it seemed New Hebrides, for all its spiritual importance, had been demoted in priority as the general situation worsened. Replacements slightly outpaced losses—Fraymak's command was essentially an understrength division now—but there were never enough troops, for the colonel's comments about fish in muddy water had been accurate in more than one sense.

Pattern analysis convinced Lantu the guerrillas' active cadres were small, and prisoner interrogations seemed to confirm that, but without more troops, he couldn't expand the occupation zones, and beyond the OZs they simply vanished into the sparse general population. Even within them, they were hard to spot, and Fraymak couldn't put checkpoints *everywhere*. Nor, despite Huark's suggestions, could he provide sufficient guards to confine all the locals in holding camps. Moreover, he had to feed these people—and his own—somehow, and the agricultural and aquacultural infrastructure was too spread out for centralized labor forces.

He knew he was hurting them, but how *much?* Certainly not enough to stop them; the destruction of the New Perth Warden post which had sparked this search and destroy mission proved that. But at least there'd been only two more raids on civilian housing, and that was sufficient improvement for Manak to continue his more lenient re-education policies.

Lantu sat back, eyes skimming the treetops, and chuckled mirthlessly. Here he was, hunting guerrillas in the hope of killing a few of them in order to justify *not* killing their fellows in the Inquisition's camps! Holy Terra—if, as he was coming to doubt, there *was* a Holy Terra—must have a warped sense of humor.

Angus MacRory sweated under the thermal canopy and held his field glasses on the vertol. The old-fashioned glasses had none of the electronic scan features which might have been detected, and he hoped none of his SAM teams got itchy fingers and gave *their* position away. Five or six men and women might not be an unreasonable trade for an aircraft loaded with sensors and heavy weapons . . . if you had the people to trade.

He lowered his glasses and gnawed his bushy mustache. These new Shellhead operational patterns were enough to worry a man. He'd lost fifty-one people in the past two months—not many for a Marine division, but an agonizing total for his light irregulars. He had another twenty seriously hurt and twice that many walking wounded, but at least Doctor MacBride's deep-cave hospital camp was virtually impossible to spot.

His teams were still exfiltrating, but by now most of them could have given lessons to Marine Raiders. Unless the Shellheads got dead lucky, they wouldn't spot any of them, so he judged the raid had been a success. Yet he knew he'd picked New Perth because it could be hit, not for its importance. Clearly Admiral Lantu had other priorities than protecting Wardens too clumsy to protect themselves, which—despite the satisfaction of killing those particular vermin—was worrisome. It was only a matter of time before Lantu began using Wardens for bait . . . if he hadn't already. This particular response team had arrived suspiciously quickly even for him.

Angus tipped his bonnet to his opponent. Before he'd turned up, the momentum had been with the Resistance, and though Angus had never expected to *win* the damned war, he'd thought he might keep the bloody Shellheads on the defensive until the Fleet returned. Now he was being forced to plan operations so carefully the bastards were free to do just about as they liked within the Zones, and that wouldn't do at all, at all.

He could replace personnel losses, but newbies required training and he was short on arms. Those the New Perth Wardens no longer required would help, yet he needed to hit a real arms dump, and Lantu was being difficult. Still, the Shellies had just rebuilt their Maidstone base, and the New Rye ran right down to it. If he could divert the Knightsbridge response force . . .

He frowned. Yes, it might be done. It wouldn't be as effective as, say, picking off Admiral Lantu, but it would help.

Lantu walked wearily into his office and hung up his body armor, smiling tiredly in answer to Hanat's greeting.

"Any luck?" she asked.

"There are times," Lantu said feelingly, "when I'm inclined to accept Father Shamar's theories of demonic intervention."

"No luck, then," she observed as she poured him a cup of hot *chadan*. He took it gratefully, pressing a chaste kiss to her cranial carapace, and slumped behind his desk.

"No, no luck. Whoever's running them knows what he's doing."

"Among these people"—like Fraymak, Hanat never said "infidel" anymore; then again, neither did Lantu—"it might just be a *she*."

"So it might. Jealous?"

"Maybe," she said, then laughed at his expression. "I'm not about to ask for a rifle, First Admiral. Their women have the size for it and ours don't. It's just that there are things I *could* do as well as a man."

"Yes," Lantu considered the heretical thought, "yes, I suppose so. But—"

"But Holy Terra expects Her daughters to produce children—preferably sons—for Her jihad," Hanat said in a dry, biting tone.

"Hanat," Lantu said very seriously, "you can say such things to me, here, because I have my office swept by my own people every day. Don't ever say them where Colonel Huark might hear of it."

"I won't." She bent over his desk and sorted data chips. "Here are those reports you asked for, First Admiral. And don't forget your meeting with the Fleet Chaplain at fifteen hundred."

He nodded, and she headed for the door, but his voice stopped her.

"There *are* things you could do as well as any man in the service, Hanat. Would you really like to do them?"

"Yes," she said, without turning. "Yes, I wish I could." She opened the door and left, and Lantu watched it close behind her.

"Do you know," he said softly, "I wish you could, too."

" . . . so your people will hit the MacInnis Bay fuel depot." Caitrin MacDougall tapped the plastic laminate of a New Hebrides Fisheries map with a bayonet and met Tulloch MacAndrew's frowning eyes. "Mortar the dump and rocket the guard shacks, but the main thing is to raise enough hell to draw the Knightsbridge battalion after you. When you do, bury the tubes, hide your equipment, and move deeper into the Zone, not out. With luck, they'll sweep towards the Grampians looking for you. Got it?"

"Aye, but that's no tae sae I like it. If we're tae draw the buggers oot, let's hit 'em here." Tulloch tapped a spot on the map even further from Maidstone, but Angus shook his head.

"Nay, Tulloch. If yon Shellies are willin' tae break up their 'extermination squads,' I'm willin' tae stop hittin' their housing."

"Then ye're a fool." Tulloch was as blunt as Angus himself. "Aye, I ken they've stopped 'reprisals,' but it's done nowt tae stop the killin' in the camps."

"It may not have stopped it, but the execution levels have dropped by almost seventy percent."

"Ant' grateful I am, Katie," Tulloch agreed, "but sae lang as they gae on killin' us, I'm game t'gae on killin' *them.*"

"I hear ye, Tulloch," Angus said quietly. "And sae we will, but not today. I've a thought aboot that, but I need time tae work it oot."

His eyes held Tulloch's until MacAndrew nodded slowly.

Lieutenant Darhan cringed in his hole as the infidel mortars ripped off another four-shot clip. Ninety-millimeter rounds walked across the vehicle pool with metronome precision and a distinctive, easily recognized "Crack!" They were hitting him with weapons shipped here from Thebes, and doing it as well as he could have done himself.

The infidels must have scouted the base carefully—they'd probably watched it going up, for Terra's sake!—and the first rockets had taken out both com huts and the alternate satellite link aboard the command GEV. Captain Kyhar had gone up with his vehicle—dropping command on him—and Darhan didn't know if he'd gotten off a message before he died. But he did know none of his short-range tactical coms could if Kyhar hadn't.

His perimeter was already too big for his two platoons, and rockets and mortars had chewed up his own heavy weapons with malignant precision. One machine-gun had gotten two infidel sapper teams that rushed the wire too soon, but its crew had died in a hurricane of fire when they did.

A crackling hiss lifted his head out of the hole with a curse as rockets smoked over the perimeter, towing assault charges. The flexible cables unfolded their wing-like charges over the wire, then detonated. The glare of HE not only blew the wire but cleared the mines in the gaps, and the mortars shifted back, dropping visual and thermal smoke to hide the holes.

"They're coming through the wire in Alpha Sector!" Darhan barked into his hand com. "Reserve to Alpha Two *now!*"

His small reserve force scuttled through the carnage on short, strong legs, and he pounded the dirt as he urged them to greater speed. If the infidels broke through, they could swamp him by sheer weight of numbers, and—

The smoke screen lifted, and Darhan gaped at the breached wire. There wasn't an infidel in sight! But why—?

A fresh roar of assault charges shook the base, and he whirled in horror as Sergeant Targan came up on the com.

"Gamma Sector! Wire breached in Gam—"

Darhan was already running, screaming for the reserve to follow him, when the sergeant's voice cut off with sickening suddenness. He stumbled over mangled dead and wounded, eyes slitted against the smoke as dirt and flame erupted all over Gamma Sector, and a tall, long-legged shape loomed before him. His machine-pistol chattered viciously and the shape went down, but there was another behind it, and something smashed into Darhan's body armor with terrific force. The blow slammed him onto his back, stunned and breathless, and an infidel loomed out of the smoke. She was short for a human, black hair streaming in a wild mane, and the bayonet on her Theban rifle pricked the base of his throat.

"Be *still*, ye miserable boggit!" she snarled, and he went limp, not knowing which hurt worse—the terrible ache in his bruised body or failure.

✧　　✧　　✧

Colonel Fraymak tugged on his muzzle in puzzlement. MacInnis Bay was further from the mountains than the guerrillas normally struck, and the attack pattern was . . . odd. Their short, vicious bombardment had scored heavily, killing or wounding a third of the guards and torching thousands of liters of fuel, but why hadn't they exploited that success? Had something gone wrong from their side and forced them to break off? But MacInnis Bay was in one of the rare timbered-off areas; his scouts should have found some sign of the raiders before they all got back under cover of the forests, for Terra's sake.

"Still nothing?"

"No, sir." Major Wantak shook his head. "I've sent in additional units from New Bern. This far into the Zone, we ought to be able to spot *something* before they get away."

Fraymak paused, arrested by how Wantak's comment echoed his own thoughts. Something about what his exec had said . . .

"Satan-Khan!" he hissed. Wantak recoiled from the venomous curse, and Fraymak shook himself. "It's a diversion! They *wanted* to draw our reaction!"

"But—" Wantak broke off, cranial carapace gleaming under the CP lights as he cocked his head. "It makes sense, sir, but what are they diverting us *from*? We haven't had any reports of other attacks."

"No." Fraymak was bent over the map table, scrolling quickly through the projected map sheets until he had the Knightsbridge sector. "But whatever they're after, they drew Lieutenant Colonel Shemak's force first." He slapped the table, yellow eyes narrow in thought. There were over a dozen likely targets in the sector, from reeducation camps to the Maidstone depot.

"Get on the satellite net. I want a status report from every unit in the Knightsbridge sector right now!"

Lieutenant Darhan squatted in the dust on short, folded legs with the survivors of his command. Most of the infidels had already vanished into the heavily-timbered slot of the Rye River valley, leading sturdy Terran mules and New Hebridan staghorns laden with ammunition, small arms, and rocket and grenade launchers. He'd seen Theban camouflage sheets draped over the weapon loads, and he wished to Holy Terra the quartermaster had never shipped them in. Designed to foil the thermal and magnetic detectors the infidels didn't have, they worked quite well against those the People *did* have.

The last raiders ringed his survivors, and he wondered why they hadn't already been shot. As far as he knew, the infidels never left anyone alive. Of course, they usually hit Wardens, not regulars, but even so. . . .

A pair of infidels waded through the debris towards him. The man was big, brawny, and dark, and Darhan had seen enough infidels by now to know he was older than the almost equally tall woman beside him. The lieutenant noted the polished chevrons on the man's collar as they drew nearer.

"Ye're the senior officer?" the man demanded, and Darhan nodded. "Good. We're gang now, but I've summat fer ye tae gi' Admiral Lantu."

Darhan blinked both sets of eyelids. Did that mean they *didn't* mean to kill him?

"Here." Darhan took the envelope numbly, and the man touched his tattered bonnet in a jauntily-sketched infidel-style salute. The lieutenant responded automatically, and the man grinned, then waved his Theban grenade launcher at his followers, who faded into the trees behind him.

Lieutenant Colonel Shemak's battalion came screaming in from the south forty-five minutes later.

"It might have been worse," Manak sighed. "At least they didn't massacre their prisoners."

"True, Holiness." Lantu once more debated telling his old mentor about the message the guerrillas had left with Lieutenant Darhan. Once he would already have done so, but Manak grew more brittle with every day, as if his natural aversion to following in Tanuk's footsteps was at war with an increasing desperation. His fulminating diatribes against Admiral Jahanak, for example, were most unlike him. He seemed to be retreating into a spiritual bunker and venting his fury and despair on purely military matters to avoid any hint of doctrinal weakness.

"Perhaps they truly are learning from our own restraint," the fleet chaplain mused.

"Perhaps," Lantu agreed. He folded his arms behind him and wrinkled his lips in thought. "Holiness, I would like to propose something which, I fear, Father Shamar and Colonel Huark will hate."

"I wouldn't worry about that," Manak said with a ghost of his old humor. "They're already about as upset as they can get."

"In that case, Holiness, I'd like to put at least a temporary halt to any further executions for heresy."

"What?" Manak looked up quickly, his voice sharp. "My son, we can take no chances with the Faith!"

"I'm not proposing that we should, Holiness," Lantu said carefully. We have a double problem here. Certainly we must win the infidels"—the word tasted strange these days—"for the Faith, but to do so, we must hold the planet without killing them all. The degree to which we've already relaxed the Inquisition's severity seems to have brought an easing in the ferocity of the guerrillas' tactics, as witnessed by the lower incidence of attacks on civilian housing and the fact that Lieutenant Darhan and his troops weren't shot. I believe the Fleet's manpower requirements will grow even greater in the immediate future, so substantial reinforcements here seem unlikely. If only as a temporary expedient to reduce the burden on our own troops, a ruling—even a conditional one—that infidels will be executed only for specific violations of regulations might be most beneficial."

"Um." Lantu felt a chill as Manak looked down at his hands. Just months ago, the old churchman would not only have recognized his true goal but helped achieve it. Now the thought of tying the camp firing squads' hands actually upset him, but he nodded slowly at last.

"Very well, my son, I will inform Father Shamar that—purely as a matter of military expedience—infidels are to be executed only for active infractions. But—" he looked up sharply "—*I* will decide what constitutes an infraction, and if the *terrorists*"—the gentle stress was unmistakable—"begin attacking non-military targets once more, I will rescind my decision."

"I think that's wise, Holiness."

"That is because you have a good heart, my son," Manak said softly. "Do not permit its very goodness to seduce you from your duty."

A sharper, colder chill ran down Lantu's spine, but he bent his head in mute acquiescence and left silently.

Hanat was waiting anxiously in his office. Unlike anyone else at HQ, she'd read the guerrillas' message. Now she watched him silently, her delicate golden eyes wide.

"He's agreed to suspend executions for simple apostasy," Lantu said quietly, but she didn't relax. Instead she seemed to tighten even further.

"Are you sure this is wise, Lantu?" She seemed unaware she'd used his name with no title for the first time, and he curled one long arm about her in a little hug.

"No," he said as lightly as he could. "I'm only sure I have to do it. And at least we know who their leader is now."

Hanat nodded unhappily, and he hugged her again, more briskly, before he sat and reached for pen and paper. This was one message he dared not trust to any electronic system.

"Weel, now," Angus murmured, as he refolded the letter Tulloch MacAndrew had delivered to him. His burly, beetle-browed subordinate still seemed amazed to be alive, much less back among his fellows. It was pure bad luck he'd been scooped up by the Shellhead checkpoint, but Angus recognized the additional, unspoken message of his release as Lantu's courier.

"He's agreed?" Caitrin asked.

"Aye. That's tae sae he's convinced his ain boss tae stop the killin's fer aught but actual resistance sae lang as we keep our word tae engage only military targets. And—" Angus chuckled suddenly "—he'd nowt tae sae at all at all aboot the Wardens we might chance upon."

His gathered officers laughed. The sound was not pleasant.

"D'ye think he means it?" Sean Bulloch asked skeptically.

"Aye, I do," Angus said. "He's a braw fighter, this Lantu, but he seems a trusty wee boggit. He's no sae bad at all . . . fer a Shellhead."

CHAPTER NINETEEN

"We must all do our duty, Admiral Berenson."

"Before we begin," Ivan Antonov rumbled, eyes sweeping his assembled officers, "Commander Trevayne has prepared an intelligence update based on new findings. Commander."

"Thank you, Admiral." The newly promoted intelligence officer rose. In an era when defects of eyesight had not been biochemically corrected, Winnifred Trevayne would surely have had a pair of spectacles perched on the end of her nose, the better to peer over them at her class. "As you all know, the Thebans have always followed a policy of destroying their ships to avoid capture. On the few occasions when they've been prevented from doing this, they have nonetheless suicided as individuals after activating an automatic total erasure of their data bases. So we've been able to ascertain their physiology but little else, other than their seemingly inexplicable use of Standard English and of ship names from human history and languages.

"Now, however, we've finally had a spot of luck. One of the Theban destroyer squadrons trapped in QR-107 managed to avoid interception far longer than any of the others, largely by hiding where we never expected to find them: on the deep-space side of the Redwing warp point. They might be hiding still, if their commander hadn't elected to launch a virtual suicide attack on the fleet train and run straight into the convoy escorts. Most of them were destroyed, but one of them took a very lucky—from our viewpoint—hit which set up a freak series of breakdowns in its electronics, involuntarily shutting down its fusion plant and also crippling the crew's ability to lobotomize the computer. With no power, they couldn't evade, and our

162

Marines got aboard." She turned to Antonov. "Incidentally, Admiral, our report specifically commends Captain M'boto, the Marine officer who led the boarding party. He not only secured their fusion plants before they could restore power but also dispatched a hand-picked force directly into their computer section, which prevented them from physically destroying their data. There were, as usual, no prisoners—but we're now in possession of priceless information. Far from complete information, of course ... but I'm now in a position to tell you what this war is all about."

A low hubbub arose, stilled as much by everyone's eagerness to hear more as by Antonov's glare. They all knew about the captured Theban destroyer, but Trevayne had been playing its significance very close to her chest. This was due partly to a natural reticence that her profession had only reinforced, and partly to sheer inability to credit her own findings and conclusions. Only Antonov had heard what she was about to reveal.

She began—irrelevantly, it seemed—with a story most had heard many times: the colony fleet, bound for New New Hebrides in the darkest days of the First Interstellar War, all but wiped out in the Lorelei system, whose survivors had fled down Charon's Ferry from whence no ship had returned before or since. But the tale took a new twist as Trevayne neared its end.

"Now we know why the early survey ships hadn't returned," she stated flatly. With unconscious drama, she activated a holo display and gave them all their first glimpse of the Thebes System. "As you will note, the Theban end is a closed warp point inside an asteroid belt." She held up a hand to still her audience's incredulous sound. "Yes, I know it's a freakish situation—possibly unique. But, as you can see, that system is bloody *full* of asteroids, as is often the case with binaries; the secondary sun's gravitation prevents planetary coalescence throughout a far wider region than does a mere gas giant. At any rate, the point is that those colony ships—big brutes equipped with military-grade shields because of the war—survived the meteor impacts which pulverized small survey ships with prewar meteor shielding."

Most of the officers sat speechless, dealing as best they could with a surfeit of new facts. Berenson was the first to make, and accept, the logical conclusion.

"So, Commander," he grated, leaning forward as if to come physically to grips with the unknown. "You're telling us those colonists—or, rather, their descendants—are behind this war? That this is why the Thebans speak Standard English? I suppose it would account for the ship names from human history ... but what about the ships with human names no one can identify?"

"As a matter of fact, Admiral, it was those names that put me onto the scent—those and repeated references to an 'Angel Saint-Just' in the Theban religious material of which the data base is full. I was afraid I was going to have to send back to Old Terra, but fortunately the archives at Redwing contain exhaustive personnel records of the old colonization expeditions in this region. A computer search of that fleet's complement turned up all those ship names—and one Alois Saint-Just."

Her eyes took on a faraway look. "Finding specific information on Saint-Just himself wasn't as hard as it might have been, as he seems to have made an impression on everyone who met him. A xenologist by profession, he was also a student of history, with a particular interest in ancient Egypt; hence the name 'Thebes.' He had many other interests as well." Her voice grew somber. "A brilliant man—and a very troubled one. He was obsessed with a foreboding that Terra was going to lose the war—a not unreasonable supposition at that time." She shot an apologetic glance at Kthaara, who sat listening impassively. "After he disappears from sight, we're thrown back on inference from the Theban religious references. But there are so *many* references we can form a pretty clear picture of what happened.

"The survivors, led by Saint-Just, found a Theban society on the threshold of the Second Industrial Revolution, but whose *ancien regime* was still in political control, and which had retained an unhealthy predilection for religious mania. They landed on a largish island-nation, to which—in direct contravention of the Non-Intercourse Edict of 2097—they gave modern technology so that it could forcibly unify the planet into a world-state, a potential ally for the Federation against the Khanate.

"The plan worked—up to a point. Then most of the humans died of what must have been a Terran microorganism that mutated in the new environment. Saint-Just and a few others lived, but they were so few they became more and more dependent on high-ranking Thebans, especially a noble named Sumash. He seems to have been of an unusually mystic bent even for a Theban, and he must have regarded himself as Saint-Just's chief disciple. I like to hope Saint-Just himself hadn't come to think in these terms, but we'll never know . . . for shortly, the same bug returned, in an even more virulent form, and killed all the remaining humans, leaving Sumash to his own devices.

"The colony ships' data bases must have held lots of Terran religious history. Using this for raw material, Sumash proceeded to manufacture a theology in which Saint-Just and the other humans had been messengers sent by God to bring the fruits of technology to Thebes, and the Orions who'd killed so many of these benefactors"—(another embarrassed glance at Kthaara)—"became the minions of the devil, led by the 'Satan-Khan.' Saint-Just had explained that the Orions were in control of Lorelei, at the other end of the warp line, so Sumash—the 'First Prophet,' as he's now remembered—proscribed all outside contact until Thebes was capable of mounting a full-scale jihad—"

"—which has now commenced," Berenson finished for her grimly. "But, Commander, if we humans are some kind of angels according to this crazy ersatz religion, why have the Thebans attacked *us?*"

"As often happens, Admiral, this religion took unintended turns after its founder's death. In particular, there was a shift of emphasis from *humans* to *Terra* as the fountainhead of enlightenment. It must have been a shock for them, finally emerging into Lorelei, to hear a *human* voice challenging them from an Orion warship. Clearly, the Angel Saint-Just's worst fears had been confirmed: his own race had been conquered or seduced by the Satan-Khan, leaving the Thebans standing alone as the true children of Holy Mother Terra."

This time it was Tsuchevsky who grasped it first. "Good God, Winnie! Are you telling us the Thebans' goal is to . . . to *liberate* Terra— from the *human race?*"

Trevayne nodded slowly. "I'm afraid that's exactly what I'm telling you—as insane as it may sound."

"But it's absurd!" Berenson's outburst shattered the stunned silence. "They must have learned by now, in the human systems they've occupied, that we *won* the First Interstellar War, and that we've never heard of any religion of 'Holy Mother Terra'!"

"I'm afraid, Admiral, that you underestimate the True Believer mentality's capacity for convoluted rationalization. The facts you've cited merely 'prove' the Satan-Khan and his human quislings have succeeded in reducing humanity to a state of hopeless apostasy by falsifying history and expunging all memory of the true faith!"

Antonov's basso sounded even deeper than usual in the flabbergasted stillness that followed. "Thank you, Commander . . . and congratulations on a brilliant piece of intelligence analysis." Everyone knew Antonov wasn't given to—nor, it was widely believed, capable of— fulsome praise. "However, the data on the Lorelei defenses are of more immediate military interest."

"Of course, Admiral." Trevayne manipulated controls and the holo projection changed to display Lorelei's five uninteresting planets, its six considerably more interesting warp points . . . and what appeared to be a rash of red dots infesting the regions of the four warp points connecting with Federation space.

"You realize, of course," Trevayne began earnestly, indicating the read-out of the warp point defenses, "that these data are somewhat out of date and therefore almost certainly on the conservative side, as the Thebans have had time to . . ." Her voice trailed off as she saw the needlessness of what she was saying. They were impressed quite enough by the raw data.

"This changes things," Antonov stated quietly. "The defenses of Lorelei are at least twice as powerful as we'd believed possible. But that was before we realized how heavily industrialized Thebes is, or what kind of fanaticism is driving them. And Lorelei is, after all, their final line of defense outside their home system. To break these defenses, we must hold one surprise in reserve." He gazed directly at Berenson. "I have therefore decided that we will forgo use of the SBMHAWKs at Parsifal and rely on our hetlaser-armed capital ships, as soon as sufficient of them become available, to break into that system."

The room was deathly silent. Antonov had invited neither discussion nor questions. But Berenson rose slowly to his feet. For several heartbeats, he and Antonov stared unblinkingly at each other. When he spoke, it was in an anticlimactically quiet tone—almost a *pleasant* tone, compared to the explosion they'd all anticipated.

"A point of information, Admiral. Are we to understand that the entire rationale for sending the crews of three destroyers on a suicide run into Parsifal has now become . . . inoperative? That those crews died for absolutely nothing?"

"Hardly, Admiral Berenson." Antonov's voice was equally quiet and controlled. This clash of wills had reached a level at which mere noise was superfluous. "Intelligence information has uses other than programming SBMHAWK carrier packs. Tactically, that information will be priceless to us when we attack. Those crews did their duty . . . as we must all do our duty, Admiral Berenson."

"Of course, Admiral. Our duty. I will assuredly do my duty. I will also send a personal message to Admiral Brandenburg stating for the record my feelings concerning your conduct of this campaign. That, too, is part of my duty, as I conceive it."

Again, the entire room braced for Apocalypse. Again, they were both disappointed and relieved. Antonov only looked somberly at Berenson for a long moment, then let his face relax into what looked very much like an expression of grudging respect. "You must do as you feel you must, Admiral Berenson," he said slowly. "As I must."

One month later, Antonov stood on *Gosainthan*'s flag bridge, gazing at a view screen that showed wreckage drifting among the unfamiliar constellations of Parsifal.

That wreckage was unusual. Space battles seldom left visible evidence, so vast were the volumes in which they were fought. But the floating, tumbling aftermath of what had just occurred about the QR-107-Parsifal warp point was so thick it hadn't yet had time to dissipate even in these trackless outer reaches of the system.

The Thebans had been positioned to face the kind of attack they'd experienced at QR-107, with laser-armed fortresses close to the warp point and mobile forces further away, at maximum effective AFHAWK range. The former were to smash the infidel carriers as they emerged, the latter to pick off their fighters as they launched. Instead, the assault had been led by refitted *Thunderer-* and *Cobra*-class battleships, supported by equally refitted *McKinley*-class superdreadnoughts, and two fleets, equipped with the most destructive laser armaments in the history of Galactic warfare, had fought it out at close energy-weapon range. It had been submachine-guns at ten paces: an orgy of mutual destruction in which defense had been largely irrelevant. The missile-armed Theban ships and fortresses had done what they could, pouring fire into the already superheated furnace of battle, and the losses among the first Federation waves had been appalling. But as Antonov had continued to unflinchingly commit wave after wave, the superior numbers of the Federation's hetlasers had begun to tell. Only when the defense was clearly broken had the carriers begun to make transit. Faced with a combination of fighters and the rearmed capital ships, Jahanak had elected to cut his losses, withdrawing his mobile forces to the Lorelei warp point and leaving the surviving fortresses to cover his disengagement.

Now Berenson's carriers and their cruiser/destroyer screen were harrying the retreating Thebans across the Parsifal system as Antonov listened with half an ear to the reports of the reduction of the last of the fortresses.

"Preliminary reports indicate we may have secured some current data, Admiral," Winnifred Trevayne was saying. "This will enable us to update our estimates of Lorelei's defenses."

"Yes." Antonov spoke absently. He continued for a moment to gaze at the drifting wreckage. Then, abruptly, he swung around and activated a holo representation of Lorelei and motioned for Tsuchevsky and Kthaara to join them.

"Look here: the fortresses are heavily concentrated at the warp point connecting with this system, and I doubt if that's changed since these data were current. And that's bound to be where most of their mobile forces will concentrate after they're through running. After all"—he changed the display to a warp line schematic—"that's our most direct line of advance on Thebes itself. So they expect us to advance directly from here to Lorelei.

"But," he continued, maneuvering a floating cursor, "there is an alternate route to Lorelei: through this system's third warp point to

Sandhurst, then to New New Hebrides—stupid name!—then to Alfred, and finally to Lorelei, through"—he reactivated the display of Lorelei—"*this* warp point, which is naturally the least heavily defended."

Kthaara looked skeptical. "But, Admiral, the delay . . ." he began. The direct approach was programmed into his genes.

"But," Tsuchevsky cut in, "think of the advantages. There are colonies in Alfred and New New Hebrides, and also in Danzig, whose only warp access is through Sandhurst. We'll be able to liberate those populations all the sooner."

"Eh?" Antonov looked up absently. "Oh, of course, Pasha. To be sure. But," he continued, his voice gaining in enthusiasm, "the point is that we'll force the Thebans to shift their defenses in Lorelei to meet a new threat, spreading their forces thinner. Remember, they won't be able to weaken the defenses of the Parsifal warp point too much; for all they'll know, the whole operation is a feint."

And so it was decided. Leaving a sufficient force in Parsifal to keep the Thebans guessing, the main strength of Second Fleet would advance through the Sandhurst warp point as soon as battle damage could be repaired and munitions replaced.

The human warships departed, moving onward to prepare for the next assault. In their wakes, the wreckage continued to drift, eventually dispersing by random motion into the infinite gulf between the stars, leaving nothing to show the battle had ever taken place.

CHAPTER TWENTY

Complications

The warp point at the Sandhurst end of the Parsifal-Sandhurst warp line lay nearly six light-hours from Sandhurst's orange-yellow G8 primary, which barely showed as a first-magnitude star at such a distance. It seemed even further to Ivan Antonov.

He'd been impatient enough after the numerous delays in repairing the ships damaged in the brutal Parsifal slugfest. Now, with the weak orbital fortresses that had guarded the warp point reduced to cosmic detritus and his fleet proceeding on a hyperbolic course toward the New New Hebrides warp point on the far side of the local sun, the less than 0.06 c his battle-line must maintain seemed excruciatingly slow.

Berenson was luckier, he brooded. The rear admiral led the faster screening force well in advance of the main body: battle-cruisers and heavy cruisers, sweeping ahead of the light carriers and their escorts. Fortunately, Sandhurst's third planet—a gas giant nearly massive enough to be a self-luminous "brown dwarf"—wasn't presently in such an orbital position as to complicate astrogational problems. And the asteroid belt it had created wasn't quite on the fleet's course and presented no hazards.

He tried to shake loose from his mood. *Stop being such an old woman, Ivan Nikolayevich!* There was no sign of mobile forces in the system; they must still be sitting in Lorelei, awaiting a direct attack from Parsifal. They'd shit in their pants—or whatever Thebans did—when the pickets at the Sandhurst-New New Hebrides warp point fled to Lorelei with the news. The absence of any opposition beyond the few fortresses was a clear indication he'd taken them completely by surprise, and if any mobile units were foolish enough to advance from Lorelei in the face of his fighters, his wide-ranging scout ships—already crossing the far edge of the asteroid belt ahead of Berenson's screen—would detect them and give him plenty of time to bring his fleet to general quarters.

Still, as he watched the lights on his display representing Berenson's ships approach the inner fringes of the asteroid belt in the scouts' wakes, he couldn't rid himself of a nagging worry—a feeling there was something he should have remembered.

Then it came to him.

Second Admiral Jahanak also watched a display, this one a holo sphere aboard the battle-cruiser *Arbela*, but his showed more than Antonov's. It showed the Theban ships concealed in this cluster of asteroids, not far from the New New Hebrides warp point.

He forced himself to relax. Things had been . . . difficult since his retreat from Parsifal. The Synod, merely restive before, was now in an ugly mood. His explanations that he'd never really wanted to fight so far forward were beginning to wear as thin with the panicky prelates as his references to his grandsire.

The situation had its compensations, though. He'd been able to argue that the forces sitting in the Manticore System watching the smaller infidel fleet in Griffin were more needed to defend Lorelei, so at least there were some reinforcements. Those, and the few captured infidel carriers which were even now being converted to bear Holy Terra's first operational fighter squadrons, let him feel secure at last about holding Lorelei and gave him enough freedom to search for an action to satisfy the Synod's constant, hectoring demands that he Do Something. But what?

The infidels' unexpected failure to stick their heads into the trap of Lorelei's fortresses and fleet units from Parsifal had suggested one possibility. Could it be they meant to take the Sandhurst-New New Hebrides-Alfred route instead? The notion contradicted their own tactical manuals' insistence on following the shortest possible route wherever possible, but whoever was commanding the infidel forces seemed not to have read those manuals, judging from his earlier tactics.

And if they *were* taking the longer route, it would be as well to at least try to reduce their carrier strength along the way. If they weren't, a strong force at Sandhurst would be well-placed to slice in behind any force that might depart Parsifal for Lorelei.

Thus it was Jahanak had led his battle-cruisers and an escorting force of lighter units to Sandhurst, where he'd discovered this asteroid cluster. (Contrary to the mental picture many have, asteroids are sparse in asteroid belts. Yes, there are millions of them, but only where they cluster do conditions even approach those depicted in popular entertainment.) Fleet Chaplain Hinam had been upset by his decision not to support the warp point fortifications, but the cluster had been decisive. It was big enough to conceal his entire force in a volume of space small enough for light-speed command and control to be practical, and close enough to the New New Hebrides warp point for him to strike and run. Besides, sacrificing the fortresses might even convince the infidel commander that his strategy of misdirection had worked.

Now, looking into *Arbela*'s holo sphere, he knew Holy Terra was with him. The infidel carriers that were his target had crossed the system to him, escorted by nothing heavier than destroyers, and were proceeding well behind the screen of cruisers. And the main infidel strength lumbered along too far in the rear to affect the outcome of the kind of battle he meant to fight.

"Second Admiral," Captain Yurah, who'd assumed command of *Arbela* (Jahanak had enough problems without having to break in a new flag captain) indicated the holo sphere, where the enemy cruisers were already receding from the asteroids, "the infidel carriers are nearing the closest approach to which their course will bring them."

Jahanak nodded. He wanted those carriers very badly. Of course, he had no way of knowing which of them carried the new cloaking device as they swept along at normal readiness. But if he could close with them before they could engage it, surely his sensor crews, working at short range and knowing the locations and vectors of what they were looking for, could penetrate it. The Satan-Khan-spawned thing wasn't magic, whatever they were saying on the lower decks!

He glanced sideways at Hinam as his thoughts reminded him of his fleet's morale problems. The fleet chaplain sat slumped in the listless posture which had become habitual for him since the battle of QR-107. He hadn't been giving much trouble lately—even his protests against leaving the fortresses unsupported had been halfhearted and *pro forma*—but he hadn't been much help, either. And the enlisted spacers had never needed spiritual reinforcement as much as they did now. Well, perhaps Hinam could be roused from his torpor.

"Holiness," he said briskly, "we'll be attacking momentarily. Do you wish to speak to the crews?" He glanced at Yurah to confirm that the fleet's com net was clear of any vital tactical data. The whisker lasers were virtually undetectable but could bottleneck communications badly. The flag captain checked his status board and nodded, and Jahanak indicated the fleet chaplain's communications console. Terra! Who would have believed he would ever have *wanted* Hinam to open his mouth?

The fleet chaplain stirred sluggishly, a faded memory of the old fire flickering in his eyes. He leaned forward, pressing the com button and hunching over the pickup, and spoke in the low, rasping voice which had replaced his one-time certitude.

"Warriors of Holy Terra," he began, "the infidels have been delivered into your hand at last. Their victories from Redwing to Parsifal and the Satan-Khan's unclean influence may fill them with false confidence, but they are empty as the wind before those filled by the Faith."

He paused as if for breath, and his eyes burned brighter. His voice was stronger, more resonant, when he resumed.

"Warriors of Holy Terra, we know—even as the ancient *samurai* who served Mother Terra in the days of the Angel Saint-Just—that death is lighter than a feather but duty to Her is as a mountain. Brace yourselves to bear that weight, knowing that She will give you of Her own holy strength in Her service! Even now Her foes approach the Furnace She has prepared for them, and you have been honored by Her trust, for it is to you She turns to thrust them into the purifying Fire! Gird your loins, Warriors of Holy Terra! Set your hands upon the hilt of Holy Terra's Sword, for the time is come to drive it home at last! The Jihad calls us! Advance, knowing that victory awaits!"

Hinam thundered his final words into the pickup with all the old fire, all the old faith, and his eyes blazed like yellow beacons as he released the button and leaned back in his chair.

"Thank you, Holiness," Jahanak murmured. "Your words have been an inspiration to us all." *At least I* hope *they'll do some good.* He frowned at the sphere as the infidel carriers reached the predetermined closest point on their course past *Arbela* and her consorts.

"Captain Yurah," he said more crisply, "begin the attack."

The order was passed, and he sat back with a sigh. Yes, it would be good to repay the infidels in their own coin, springing the same sort of trap they'd sprung on Lantu at . . .

. . . Redwing! It was like an explosion in Antonov's brain.

"Captain Chen!" he shouted at his flag captain. "Sound general quarters! And have communications raise Admiral Berenson. Tell him—"

It was too late. Even as he spoke, input was automatically downloaded to the silicon-based idiot savant that controlled his display, and the red lights of hostiles sprang into life, sweeping out of the asteroid belt and into energy-weapons range of the light carriers seventy-five light-seconds in the wake of Berenson's cruiser screen.

Berenson had already seen it—his scanners suffered from little time lag here as the Thebans erupted into his carriers at what passed for knife-range in space combat. Furiously, he ordered his command to general quarters and began to bring his ships about. But even with reactionless drives, a complete course reversal took time. Too much time, and he watched, nauseated, while the Thebans savaged the virtually unarmed carriers that frantically tried to launch as many of their fighters as possible.

"Admiral," Tsuchevsky's voice was harsh, "the Thebans seem to have their entire battle-cruiser strength here, with escorts. They're still concentrating on what's left of our light carriers, but they've managed to slip between them and the cruisers. They're forcing the carriers away from the screen. Admiral Berenson is cutting the angle and closing, but he still hasn't been able to bring his battle-cruisers into capital missile range. The fleet carriers have gone into cloaking mode, and are advancing at maximum speed, as per your orders."

Antonov nodded absently. Thank God he'd kept the big carriers with the battle-line! It occurred to him that the Thebans had never seen his fleet carriers; they probably thought the ships with the mysterious cloaking ability were among the light carriers in the van, which would help account for their single-minded pursuit of those vessels. And they'd cleverly positioned themselves close enough to the New New Hebrides warp point to get away before his battle-line— slower than their slowest ship—could close to effective missile range. Or what they *thought* was effective missile range. . . .

"Order the fleet carriers to come as close as they can to the egress warp point. They can get fairly close to the battle—the Thebans won't be scanning open space for them. They're to launch all fighters as soon as the Thebans start to break off the engagement. And no, Kthaara, there's no time to get you aboard one of them!" He smiled grimly. "Our options appear to have narrowed. We can no longer concern ourselves with concealing the full capabilities of the SBMs. Signal Admiral Berenson that he is authorized to use them at their maximum range."

The order went out, and at effectively the same instant as Berenson's acknowledgment was received, the scanners showed the strategic bombardment missiles speeding from his battle-cruisers toward targets at their full range of twenty light-seconds.

Jahanak cursed as his ships began to report hits by missiles launched by the infidel battle-cruisers from beyond capital missile range. There weren't enough of them, and the range was too extreme, for them to do catastrophic physical damage. Their damage to his calculations was something else again. If mere battle-cruisers had this new weapon (*another* new weapon!) he had to assume the oncoming battle-line also had it, and in far greater numbers. And that meant his estimate of how soon that battle-line would become a factor had suddenly become *very* suspect.

Even more unsettling was the failure of any of the light carriers to fade out of his sensors' ken. Five of them had already been destroyed; surely the survivors would go into cloak when the alternative was destruction—*if they could.* Clearly, the ones with the cloaking capability were elsewhere. But where?

"Captain Yurah, the fleet will disengage and retire to New New Hebrides!"

The few fighters the light carriers had managed to launch had already shot their bolt; they wouldn't be able to mount an effective pursuit. And passing the infidel battle-cruisers at energy-weapons range held no terror. There was no indication from the intelligence analyses of the Battle of Parsifal that anything lighter than a battleship had been fitted with the new heterodyne-effect lasers, and if the infidel screen cared to exchange energy fire with his beam-heavy *Manzikert*-class battle-cruisers, it would be their last mistake. It was more than slightly infuriating to have sprung his trap so successfully and still fail to destroy the carriers he'd sought, but his ships *had* shattered the infidels' light carriers. Even as he watched his display, another carrier's light dot vanished, and most of those which survived would require lengthy repairs. Even if total success had eluded him, he'd still struck a weighty blow.

But then he glanced at Hinam. The fleet chaplain had sunk into his earlier lassitude, and suddenly, unbidden, there came to Jahanak the shades of a kindly cleric who'd taught him the grand old tales in his childhood, and another who'd been there when the first child of his young adulthood died in infancy. He reached out and laid a four-fingered hand on the fleet chaplain's arm.

"We haven't been defeated, Holiness," he said with unwonted gentleness. "We've inflicted crippling casualties on the infidel light carriers in return for trifling losses. Now we must retire, as we'd planned to do." And why, he wondered, should a simple statement of truth not *sound* like the truth? Were words tainted by use as rationalization, even as a whore was forever tainted despite a subsequent lifetime of virtue? Of course, came the unwanted thought, that analogy suggested it was people, not words, that became tainted, but . . .

The question became academic for Jahanak when hundreds of infidel fighters swept out of nowhere and streaked through space toward the blind zones of his retreating starships.

By the time Antonov's battle-line came within energy range, there was little for it to do besides help recover fighters whose light-carrier bases no longer existed. Of the eleven carriers Berenson had once commanded, only four remained, and all but one of the survivors were badly mauled. Nor, despite the SBM and its cloaked fleet carriers, had Second Fleet repaid the Thebans with proportionate damage. For the first time since Redwing, the enemy had scored a clear and punishing success, and it hurt all the more after the Federation's string of victories.

True, the fleet carriers' fighter squadrons had exacted a terrible revenge, but they'd had to break through the escorts before they could even reach the battle-cruisers, and there hadn't been time to rearm after their first strike and make it decisive. Berenson's screen had also wrought havoc, but his lack of hetlasers had forced him to remain at missile range. Again, his blows, though vicious, hadn't been decisive. The enemy heavy cruisers and escorts had paid dearly, but most of the battle-cruisers had escaped, though many trailed atmosphere as they vanished into the warp point, leaving a victorious but shaken Federation fleet in undisputed possession.

Kthaara, watching discreetly on *Gosainthan*'s flag bridge as Antonov and Berenson carried on a conversation that could now be conducted without annoying time lags, reflected anew on the impossibility of really grasping subtleties of expression in a race so very alien. It was as if *both* admirals were savoring the unaccustomed sensation of feeling crestfallen. Antonov, in particular, was as close to seeming awkward as the Orion had ever seen him.

"Well, Admiral Berenson," the bear-like Fleet Admiral rumbled, "it would appear this route to Lorelei involves . . . unanticipated complications." He looked like he'd bitten into a bad pickle. "It would also seem that we are not quite so free to decide when and where to commit new weapon systems as we—as *I*—may have supposed."

"So it would seem, sir." For just an instant, Berenson's face unmistakably wore the expression Kthaara had learned to recognize as meaning "I told you so!" But only for an instant. "I suspect we may all have been guilty of cockiness—of underestimating the Thebans."

"Yes." Antonov nodded grimly. "But *never* again! To begin, we mustn't assume there are no surprises waiting in Danzig. We don't know what the Thebans may have left behind there, so we can't leave it in our rear, uninvestigated. I'd hoped to seal it off and let its occupying force wither on the vine, but much as I'd like to push on immediately to New New Hebrides before the Theban survivors can reorganize themselves there, we will first proceed to the Danzig warp point and send a scouting force through. After taking *all* precautions against a counterattack!"

"Agreed, sir," Berenson said. "Shall I detail the scouts?"

"If you would," Antonov replied. "I'll be attaching the fleet carriers to support you. The battle-line will leave a covering force for the

New New Hebrides warp point and follow your screen." He smiled grimly. "If anything comes out of that warp point, Admiral, it won't be going back into it again."

"Absolutely, sir," Berenson said. And, for the first time in Kthaara's memory, the two admirals smiled at one another.

CHAPTER TWENTY-ONE

Without Authorization

Hannah Avram sat on her flag bridge, scanning the latest shipyard report, and marveled yet again at the change the past dreadful months had wrought in Richard Hazelwood. The uncharitable might argue, she supposed, that his complete loss of support from the planetary government had left him no choice but to join her own team, but Hannah thought differently. He'd been sullen and uncooperative for a month or so after what President Wyszynski persisted in referring to as her *coup d'etat*, but he'd seemed to come alive after Danzig's defenders smashed the first Theban probe of the system without losing a single ship.

They'd done almost as well against the second, but they'd paid to stop the third. She glanced around her bridge with a familiar stab of anguish. She'd made too many mistakes the third time, starting with her hesitation in opening fire. The assault had been led by *Kongo*-class battle-cruisers, undoubtedly (in retrospect) captured at Lorelei, and the sudden appearance of Terran ships had confused her just too long. They'd gotten off their initial salvos while she was still convincing herself they weren't a relief force.

Worse, she should have realized the Thebans would develop their own capital missiles. She hadn't, and the heavy external ordnance salvos of those leading ships had blown her beloved *Dunkerque* apart. *Kirov* had survived, though badly damaged, and *Dunkerque*'s casualties had been mercifully light—over two-thirds of her crew had survived—but her ship's destruction had been agony . . . and it had been Dick Hazelwood, of all people, who'd helped her put it into its proper perspective.

She still remembered Maguire's astonished expression when

Hazelwood chewed her out—respectfully, but without a ghost of his old wimpiness. She'd been hagridden with guilt for having hesitated, and for having decided against building additional capital missile-armed units as a first priority. That decision had left *Dunkerque* and *Kirov* to fight alone against the Thebans' initial long-ranged salvos as their battle-cruisers squatted atop the warp point, and her confident assumption of a monopoly on capital missile technology meant she'd loaded her own XO racks solely with offensive weapons.

She hadn't included any EDMs in her external loads, and that had sealed *Dunkerque*'s fate. The enhanced drive missiles created extensions of a starship's drive field, interposing those false drive fields to fool incoming missiles' proximity fuses into premature detonation . . . and there hadn't been any. She'd skimped on them, "knowing" her battle-cruisers were beyond reach of any Theban weapon and desperate to throw the heaviest initial salvos she could. And so her ships had been shattered before their shorter-ranged consorts could close to effective range and the forts could come fully on-line, and her own survival had seemed an utterly inadequate compensation.

But Hazelwood had seen more clearly than she. He'd accepted that she'd made mistakes, but it had also been he who pointed out that her insistence on reinforcing the minefields had been decisive. Danzig's minelayers had more than quadrupled the original density of the fields, and though no one could emplace mines directly atop an open warp point, where they would be sucked in and destroyed by the point's gravity stresses, their strength had prevented the Thebans from advancing in-system. Penned up on top of the warp point, they'd been unable to employ effective evasive maneuvering, and their concentration on her battle-cruisers had given the forts time to bring their own weapons—and defenses—to full readiness. The result had been the destruction of eight Theban battle-cruisers, four heavy cruisers, and six light cruisers in return for *Dunkerque*, *Atago*, three destroyers, and heavy damage to *Kirov* and two of the forts. And that, as Commodore Richard Hazelwood had finished acidly, was a victory by anyone's standards!

He'd been right, of course, and Hannah was grateful for his support. Just as she was grateful for the way he'd torn into his duties as her construction manager. He should, she thought, have been assigned to BuShips instead of Fortress Command from the beginning, for he certainly seemed to have found his niche, and he'd taken a far from hidden satisfaction in cracking the whip over Victor Tokarov and friends. His personal familiarity with the Danzig System's economic and industrial sectors told him where all the bodies were buried, and he'd exhumed the ones most useful to her with positive glee. Indeed, to her considerable surprise, she and Dick Hazelwood had become friends—a possibility she would flatly have denied when she first met him.

She turned her attention back to her screen, finishing his latest report. Her new flagship, the battle-cruiser *Haruna*, and her sisters *Hiei*, *Repulse*, and *Alaska*, were the largest units the Danzig yards had yet produced. When her fourth sister, *Von der Tann*, was commissioned next month, they and *Kirov* would give her a solid core of capital missile ships. She wished they had some true battle-line units with proper energy armaments—each Theban attack had been more powerful than the last, and she was acutely nervous over what they might come up with next—but there were limits to her resources. Committing so much of her limited yard space to the battle-cruisers was risky enough, and about as far as she could go.

At least she'd managed to build an impressive number of lighter units to support them. It could hardly be called a balanced fleet, but there was only one possible warp point to defend, and her "light forces" packed a hell of a defensive wallop. There were over thirty destroyers, uncompromisingly armed for close combat, with far lighter shields and far heavier armor than BuShips would have tolerated before meeting Theban lasers. And backing them were the real reason she'd come to think Hazelwood had missed his calling in Fortress Command: fourteen *Sand Fly*-class carriers built to his personal specifications.

They weren't the fleet or even light carriers of Battle Fleet, but tiny things, no larger than destroyers and thus suitable for rapid production. Their strikegroups were smaller than an *Essex*-class light carrier, but they were as big as the old *Pegasus* class, and they'd had time—thank God!—to bring their training up to standard. With the handful of local defense fighter pilots as a nucleus, they'd expanded their fighter strength at breakneck speed, and Danny Maguire had found a way to maximize their available flight decks by borrowing from the Rigelian Protectorate's ISW-3 tactics. Hannah had over three hundred fighters based on Danzig, the orbital forts, and a clutch of scarcely mobile barges. If battle was joined, she'd use the old Rigelian shuttle technique, staging them through her small carriers to strike the enemy. It was going to require some fancy coordination, but the exercises had been encouraging.

She sighed, closed the report file, and leaned back in her chair, running her fingers through her hair. With Dick to run the yards, Captain Tinker to run Sky Watch, and Bill Yan to deputize as her fleet commander, she'd been able to turn to the political side of her "Governor" role. She'd been lucky there, too. Commander Richenda Bandaranaike had proved a stellar legal gymnast, as devious as she was brilliant, and half of Hannah's civilian duties consisted of little more than confirming her recommendations. It had been a chastening experience for Wyszynski and Tokarov to confront Richenda's implacable ability to do whatever the governor wanted and then find some perfectly plausible legal justification for it.

The hardest part, as she'd feared from the beginning, was manpower. Danzig's population wasn't all that big, and manning and supporting her steadily growing naval force had strained it badly, but she'd been pleasantly surprised by the locals' response. Tokarov money or no, the old, defeatist planetary government was going to find the next election a painful experience, she thought gleefully. Wyszynski continued to cooperate as grudgingly as possible, beginning every discussion with a protest of her "patently illegal usurpation" of authority, but Danzig's citizens clearly disagreed. She hadn't even had to resort to conscription; volunteers had come forward in numbers too great for her limited training facilities to handle.

She stretched and checked the chronometer, then grinned tiredly and punched for another cup of coffee. It was late, and however capable her support team, there were never enough hours for everything. Assuming full responsibility for the political and military governance of an entire star system was even more wearing than she'd anticipated. Sometimes she almost hoped the Admiralty and Assembly *would* disapprove her actions. Once they cashiered her, she might actually get to sleep for six hours in a row!

Her steward appeared with the coffee as she turned to the next endless report, and she sipped gratefully. God, she was tired. And—

She jerked upright, cursing as coffee sloshed over her tunic. The shrill, teeth-grating atonality of the alarm blasted through her, and she shoved her reader display viciously aside, jerking her chair around to face Battle Plot.

The light codes of her own units flickered and changed as they rushed to general quarters with gratifying speed, but her attention was on the dots emerging from the Sandhurst warp point. Just as the last Theban attack had included those damned *Kongos*, the six lead ships of this attack were obviously more prizes. CIC identified them as *Shark*-class destroyers, and Hannah's lips twisted in a snarl. *Not this time, you bastards!*

"Dan! Switch the mines to manual override!" If the Thebans had managed to put their prizes' IFF gear back into commission, the mines wouldn't attack without specific commands to do so.

"Aye aye, sir. Switching now."

"If they stay out of the mines, we'll take them with missiles. No point losing fighters or taking damage by closing into their shipboard range."

"Understood, sir." Maguire studied his own console for a moment. "We've got a good set-up, sir."

"Then open fire," Hannah said softly.

❖   ❖   ❖

Captain Georgette Meuller, CO of Destroyer Squadron Nineteen, stared at her display in disbelief. Like every other member of DesRon 19, she'd entered the Danzig warp point expecting to die. Oh, there was always a chance of catching the defenders so totally off guard they could run before they were engaged . . . but not much of one. And unless they did, there was no way any of them were getting back to Sandhurst alive. Yet she'd understood why they had to go. But this—!

There were dozens of ships out there . . . and they were all Terran! Even the forts were still intact! It was impossible. Danzig had been cut off for twenty-five standard months, and there'd only been a half-dozen tin-cans to support the forts before the war. Where in God's name had they all *come* from?

"Sir!" Her senior scan rating's voice snatched her from her thoughts. "Those battle-cruisers have locked on their targeting systems!"

Georgette swung towards her com section.

"Raise their CO for me—quickly! Send in clear!" Her communications officer didn't bother to reply—she was already stabbing keys as the scan rating paled. "They're *launching*!"

"First salvo away," Commander Maguire reported tensely. "Impact in twenty-five seconds."

Hannah grunted, watching her display narrowly. *You bastards are dead. You should've known better than to send tin-cans through without support. Were you that sure you could sucker me again?*

"Sir!" It was her communications officer. "I'm receiving an emergency hail!"

Hannah nodded. The Thebans had already demonstrated their ability to masquerade as humans over the com, and if they could confuse the defenders, even if only long enough to complete their scans and send back courier drones with exact data on the defenses, the advantage for their follow-on echelons would be incalculable.

"What sort of hail?" she asked almost incuriously.

"They say they're Terrans, sir. It's from a Captain Meuller."

"What?!" Hannah leapt from her command chair and vaulted Maguire's console like a champion low-hurdler. She landed beside the com officer, grabbing his small screen and wrenching it around to stare at the face of her best friend from the Academy.

Georgette Meuller watched the missiles tearing down on her command. There wasn't time. Not to convince whoever had fired them they were friendly units. She and her people were going to die after all.

"Stand by point defense!" she said harshly, knowing it was futile. Laser clusters trained onto the hurricane of destruction streaking towards her, and she bit her lip. A handful of capital missiles vanished in the fireball intercepts of defensive missiles, but not enough to make any difference at all, and she tightened internally as the lasers began to fire.

And then, with the lead missile less than ninety kilometers from impact, the visual displays polarized in a tremendous glare of eye-tearing light as more than eighty capital missiles self-destructed as one.

Haruna's cutter completed its docking maneuvers, the hatch slid open, and a tall, slender woman in the uniform of a commodore stepped through it. The bosun's pipe shrilled and the sideboys snapped to attention as Hannah Avram saluted the flag on the boat bay bulkhead, then turned to salute the stocky captain who awaited her. She'd never met Pavel Tsuchevsky, but they'd spoken over the com when he received her formal reports for his admiral. Now, as their hands fell from their salutes, her sinking sensation returned. The fact that Admiral Antonov hadn't come to greet her, coupled with his silence since receiving those same reports, was ominous.

"Commodore Avram." Tsuchevsky's voice was carefully neutral. "Admiral Antonov would appreciate your joining him in his staff briefing room. If you'll accompany me, please?"

Hannah nodded and fell in beside him, schooling her features into calmness and biting off her burning desire to ask questions. The answers would come soon enough—possibly *too* soon—but she was damned if she'd let anyone guess how anxious she was.

The intraship car deposited them outside the briefing room, and Tsuchevsky stood courteously aside to let her enter first. At least they were going to let her go on pretending to be a commodore until the axe fell. She'd never met Admiral Antonov, either, but from his reputation he was probably looking forward to chopping her off at the ankles in person.

Ivan Antonov looked up, face hard, as she stopped before the conference table, cap under her arm.

"Commodore Avram, reporting as ordered, sir," she said crisply, and he nodded. For the first time in two years, she was acutely aware of the insignia she wore as the admiral studied her coldly. He sat at the table, square-shouldered and unyielding, flanked by a dark-faced female commander and—Hannah just barely avoided a double-take—an Orion?

She wrenched her attention back from the Tabby and stood tautly at attention, wondering what Antonov had made of her reports. The complete lack of explanations which had accompanied his orders to rendezvous with *Gosainthan* in Sandhurst suggested one very unpleasant possibility. He was known for his own willingness to break the rules, but also for his ruthlessness, and as she faced him in silence she knew exactly why people called him "Ivan the Terrible."

"'Commodore,'" his voice was a frigid, subterranean rumble, "do you realize how close you came to killing twelve hundred Fleet personnel?"

"Yes, sir." She locked her eyes on the bulkhead above his head.

"It might be wise," he continued coldly, "to double-check your target identification in future."

"Yes, sir," she said again when he paused. What else could she say? It was grossly unfair—especially after the Thebans had mousetrapped her once before in just that way—but perhaps it was understandable. And she still felt nauseated at how close she'd come to killing Georgette's entire squadron.

"I suppose, however," Antonov went on stonily, "that we might overlook that in this instance. I, after all, had not considered the possibility that there might not be Thebans on *your* side of the warp point, either. Had I done so, I might have sent through courier drones instead of destroyers, and this entire unfortunate affair might never have risen."

"Yes, sir," she said again.

"So," he said, "let us turn our attention instead to your other actions. It was, I trust you will admit, somewhat irregular of you to supplant another Fleet officer senior to you? But, then, you never bothered to inform him he *was* senior, did you?" Hannah said nothing, and the flint-faced admiral smiled thinly. "Then there were your fascinating, one might almost say precedent-shattering, interpretations of constitutional law. Your legal officer must be most ingenious."

"Sir, I take full responsibility. Commander Bandaranaike acted solely within the limits of my direct orders."

"I see. And is the same true of the Fleet and Marine personnel who assisted you in forcibly supplanting the planetary government? A planetary government, I might add, which has already requested your immediate court martial for mutiny, treason, insubordination, misappropriation of private property, and everything else short of littering?"

"Yes, sir," Hannah said yet again. "My personnel acted in accordance with my orders, sir, believing I had the authority to give those orders."

"Do you seriously expect me to believe, 'Commodore,' that none of your officers, none of your personnel, ever even suspected you were acting in clear excess of your legitimate authority? That *no one* under your command knew Commodore Hazelwood, in fact, outranked you?"

"Sir, they knew only that—" Hannah broke off and bit her lip, then spoke very, very carefully. "Admiral Antonov, at no time did I inform any of my personnel of the actual circumstances under which I was breveted to commodore. Under the circumstances, none of my officers had any reason to question my authority to act as I acted. I cannot speak to their inner thoughts, sir; I can only say they acted at all times in accordance with regulations and proper military discipline given the situation as it was known to them. And, sir, whatever your own or the Admiralty's final judgment as to my own behavior, I believe any fair evaluation of my subordinates' actions must find them to have been beyond reproach."

"I appreciate your attempt to protect them, 'Commodore,'" Antonov said coldly, "but it is inconceivable to me that not even the members of your staff were aware of the true facts and that you were, in fact, acting entirely on your own initiative without authorization from any higher authority." Hannah stiffened in dismay, and her eyes dropped to his bearded face once more. Dropped and widened as that stony visage creased in a wide, gleaming smile that squeezed his eyes almost into invisibility.

"Which means, *Rear Admiral* Avram," he rumbled, "that they are to be commended for recognizing the voice of sanity when they heard it. Well done, Admiral. Very well done, indeed!"

And his huge, hairy paw enveloped her slim hand in a bone-crushing grip of congratulation.

CHAPTER TWENTY-TWO

Knight Takes Queen

Angus MacRory's stomach rumbled resentfully as he waded through the cold mist, cursing softly and monotonously. The fog offered concealment from Shellhead recon systems, but its dripping moisture made the mud-slick trail doubly treacherous, and his next meal was ten hours overdue.

Caitrin skidded ahead of him, and he bit his lip anxiously as she caught herself and slogged wearily on. That was another worry, and he scrubbed sweat and mist irritably from his face.

New Hebrides had slipped into winter, and the Fleet had not returned. Prisoner interrogations said the Shellhead navy was in a bad way, but unless the Federation got back to New Hebrides soon, there would be no Resistance to greet it.

Angus cursed again, telling himself that was his empty belly talking. Yet he knew better. Admiral Lantu was finally winning, and the weather was helping him do it.

New Hebrides' F7 sun was hot but almost eighteen light-minutes away, which gave the planet a year half again as long as Old Terra's neighbor Mars and cool average temperatures. Its slight axial tilt and vast oceans moderated its seasons considerably, but winter was a time of fogs and rainy gales. There was little snow or ice, yet the humid cold could be numbing, both physically and mentally. Worse, the titanic banner oaks were deciduous. Their foliage had all but vanished, and that, coupled with the colder temperatures, left the guerrillas far more vulnerable to thermal detection.

Yet Angus knew Lantu's success rested on more than the weather. The Shellhead admiral had already crushed the Resistance on Scotia, and now he was doing the same thing on Hibernia. He'd get to Aberdeen soon enough.

The first bad sign had been forced-labor logging parties assigned to clear fire zones around the Shellhead bases. Then they'd moved on, chopping away under their guards' weapons to cut wide lanes along the frontiers of the OZs. Angus hadn't worried at first; it was a tremendous task, and the Shellheads had little heavy equipment to spare for it. But then the shipments of defoliant arrived from Thebes, and the vertols swept back and forth along the frontiers, killing back the leaves.

The lanes could still be crossed, but at greater peril and a higher cost. About one in nine of his teams was being caught, and that was a casualty rate he could not long endure.

But that was only the first sign. The second was a redeployment of reaction forces to cover larger sectors—an arrangement the cleared lanes made workable. He'd wondered what Lantu meant to do with the troops he'd freed up, but only till the admiral transferred them all to Scotia, doubling his troop strength on that continent, and opened a general offensive. With the additional vertols and troops, extra scan sats, and defoliated kill zones, he'd pushed the Scotians hard, picking off their base camps one by one. Perhaps a quarter of them had escaped to Aberdeen; the rest were gone. Angus hoped some had managed to go to ground, but their casualties had been wicked.

And now, with the onset of winter, his own Base One had been spotted and destroyed. The SAM teams had cost the Shellheads some aircraft, and casualties had been mercifully light, but he'd lost a tremendous quantity of priceless equipment. Another strike had taken out Base Three, but his spotter network had spied that force on its way in. Most of his equipment and all his people had gotten away that time.

But he couldn't last forever. In the beginning, it had been the Shellheads who'd had to be lucky every time to stop him; now it was his turn. Lantu's relentless, precise attacks made the most of his material superiority, and Angus had learned the admiral was not inclined to do things by halves.

"Scratch one guerrilla camp, First Admiral," Colonel Fraymak crossed to the map and stuck a pin into the Hibernian mountains. "Strike recon says we got thirty percent of their on-site personnel and most of their equipment. Prisoner interrogation says we may have gotten Claiborne."

"Ah?" Lantu rubbed his cranial carapace. Duncan Claiborne was the Angus MacRory of Hibernia. If Fraymak's attack had, indeed, killed him, the Hibernian guerrillas would be in serious disarray.

"Yes, sir." Fraymak laid his helmet aside and frowned at the map, running a finger across the mountains. "Can we move the scan sats down this way? They didn't manage to burn all their records before we got to them, and there are indications of something fairly important down here."

"I suppose we could." Lantu moved to stand beside him. "Or there's a destroyer temporarily in orbit; I could swing her down to cover it."

"In that case, I think we can give you another camp this week, First Admiral. Maybe even wind up the Hibernian operation by the end of the month."

"Outstanding." Lantu tried to sound as if he really meant it, and the stubbornly professional side of him did. There was a grim satisfaction in the way his successes discredited Huark's bloody excuse for a strategy, but there was a deadness in his soul. As if none of it really mattered anymore.

He'd begun avoiding Manak. He knew it hurt the old man, but the fleet chaplain knew him too well. Manak's own faith might be hardening into a desperate conviction capable of ignoring the reality of impending defeat, yet he could hardly fail to spot the admiral's steady spiritual rot.

Not for the first time, Lantu cursed the stubborn streak in his own soul, for there was such a thing as too much integrity. If he could only have left well enough alone, he might not face these agonizing doubts. Might not have to worry that *he* might fall prey to the Inquisition.

Yet he was what he was, and he could no more have stopped himself than he could let his fleet die at Redwing. He'd been careful enough no one suspected—he hoped—but he'd delved deeply into the New Hebridan libraries and data base. He'd compared the Federation's version of history to that of the Church and found . . . divergences. Inconsistencies.

Lies.

And try as he might, he could not convince himself it was the humans who'd lied to him.

Caitrin's face was worn as she tossed another branch onto the fire. Then she leaned back against the cave wall, and Angus tightened his arm around her, trying to comfort without revealing his own anxiety. She would never admit exhaustion or fear, but he felt them sapping her inner strength like poison, and his hand brushed her ribs, then darted away from the slight swelling of her belly.

It was too much, he thought bitterly. A guerrilla war and pregnancy were just too much, and he cursed himself as the cause of it.

"Stop that." She caught his wrist and pressed his hand to the small bulge of their child. "I had a little something to do with it, too."

"Aye, but—"

"No 'buts'! It wouldn't have happened if I'd remembered my implant was running out—and if I weren't such a stubborn bitch, I'd have had it aborted."

Angus's arm tightened, and she pressed her face into his shoulder in silent apology. He would have understood an abortion—he'd spent seven years off-planet—but New Hebridans were colonials, not Innerworlders. Babies were precious to them in a way that went beyond logic, yet he knew Caitrin's decision went even deeper. She was determined to keep their child because it was part of *him*, and if the Shellheads caught up with him, she wanted that bit of him to remember and love.

He made himself loosen his embrace as Tulloch scooted into the cave.

"All under cover," he said tiredly, and Angus nodded.

"We mun make better time tomorrow."

"Aye." Tulloch glanced at Caitrin from the corner of one eye, then shook himself. "Weel, I'm off tae set the sentries."

He vanished, and Angus frowned into the fire.

"I've been thinkin'," he said slowly. " 'Tis but a matter o' time— and no sae much of it—afore the Shellies move back tae Aberdeen, Katie."

"I know," she said tiredly.

"Weel, then, 'twould be as well tae set up fall-backs now."

"Where?"

"Doon south. The weather's no sae cold, and we'd have better cover."

"That makes sense."

"Aye, sae I ken. But 'twill need one of us tae see tae it."

He felt her stiffen and stared steadfastly into the flames, refusing to meet her eyes. She started to speak, then stopped, and he knew she knew. If he sent her south, away from their current operational area, she'd have to cross an arm of the Zone, but the chance of interception was minute. And he might keep her safe . . . for a time, at least.

"How far south?" she finally asked tightly.

"A gae lang way—doon aboot New Gurock, I'm thinkin'."

"I see." He felt her inner struggle, her own stubborn strength rebelling against being sent to comparative safety. Had it been another woman and another child, she would have agreed instantly; that, too, was a factor in her thinking. And, he knew, she was thinking of him. Thinking of his need to see her as safe as he could make her.

"All right." Her voice was dull when she spoke at last. "I'll go."

❖   ❖   ❖

Lantu flipped the last chip into his "Out" basket with a sigh of relief. Rain beat on the window, but the office's warmth enfolded him, and he stretched his arms hugely, rotating his double-jointed elbows.

"Lantu?"

He looked up quickly as Hanat closed the door behind her. Her face was anxious, and the use of his name warned him.

"Yes?"

"One of the flagged names has come up." She wrung her hands in an uncharacteristic gesture, and Lantu lowered his own hands to his desk and sat very still.

"Where?"

"Checkpoint Forty-One. Routine papers check and the Warden's stamp was wrong. At least—" she tried to look as if she felt it were a good thing "—it wasn't a Warden post."

"True." He studied his interlaced fingers. "Which name was it?"

"MacDougall," Hanat said softly. Lantu flinched, then gathered himself and met her eyes.

"Use my personal code to lock the report and have her brought here."

"Lantu—"

"Just do it, Hanat!" His voice was far harsher than he'd intended, and he smiled repentantly. "Just do it," he repeated more gently, and she nodded miserably and left.

"Nay, Angus!" Sean Bulloch shook him fiercely. "We cannae lose ye both, mon! Are ye gone clean daft?!"

"Stand out o' my way, Sean Bulloch," Angus said coldly.

"Sean's right, Angus." Tulloch MacAndrew was almost pleading. "And Katie'd no want ye tae do it, lad. Ye know that!"

"I'll no say it again. Stand out o' my way, the lot of ye!" Angus reached for his grenade launcher before he could make himself stop, and his dark eyes glared at his friends.

"Would ye do it fer anyone else, then, Angus MacRory?" Sean asked very softly, and Angus met his gaze squarely.

"Nay. But 'tis no anyone else, now is it?"

Sean held his eyes a moment, then his own gaze fell and he shook his head slowly and released Angus's shoulders.

"Then there's nowt more tae sae," Angus said quietly.

"But what d'ye think ye're gang tae do fer her?" Tulloch asked. "If the Shellies ken who she is, she's likely dead, mon!"

"I think ye're wrong. If they ken sae much, they ken I'll come fer her. Lantu's nae fool, Tulloch. He'll use her tae get at me."

"Which is nae less than he's done already!"

"As may be, I've nae choice."

"Then I'll no let ye gae alone." Angus glared, but his beetle-browed lieutenant glared right back. "D'ye think ye're the only one tae love her, ye bloody fool? If ye're mad enow tae gae, there's many o' us mad enow t' gae wi' ye."

"I'll no let any—"

"And how are ye tae stop us?" Tulloch asked scornfully. "If ye're daft enow tae try, we'll only follow. Better tae take a few lads willin', like."

Angus glowered wrathfully, but he saw the determination in Tulloch's eyes. When he looked to Sean the same stubbornness looked back, and his shoulders slumped.

"Weel enow," he sighed, "but nae more than ten men, Tulloch!"

CHAPTER TWENTY-THREE

An Admiral Heretical

Caitrin MacDougall sat on the low bed, braced against the wall, eyes closed, and fought despair. The Wardens had changed their travel permit stamps only two days ago, but she was Angus's chief intelligence officer. She should have *known;* she hadn't, and though she'd managed to wound three of the guards, she hadn't made them kill her, either.

That was what terrified her, for the way she'd been whisked away, the crisp commands for the guards to forget they'd ever seen her, the curiosity in her "escort's" amber eyes, filled her with dread. The Shellheads had learned the value of intelligence since Lantu displaced Colonel Huark, and the way she'd been treated told her they knew who she was. *What* she was . . . and what might be forced from her. Her death might have broken Angus's heart; her survival might kill him.

One hand pressed the swell of the new life within her, and a single tear crept down her swollen cheek.

Lantu had adjusted his uniform with care. It might be silly to worry over appearances, but he was about to meet an enemy he respected deeply. And, he reminded himself, one who might get him killed.

He walked down the hall slowly, arms crossed behind him, thankful he'd ordered the prisoner's injuries treated despite the risk of discovery. He was still uncertain whether professionalism or compassion had prompted him, but the doctor's report was the one hopeful thing he had.

He unfolded an arm to return the guards' salutes. The Fleet Marines, part of his personal security force, gave no sign of their thoughts as he knocked lightly, then opened the door and stepped through it.

The bedroom had been converted into a cell in haste, and the adhesive sealing the plastic bars across the window had dripped down over the sill in polymer icicles. There'd been no time to replace the Theban furniture, but if it was far too low for his prisoner's convenience, at least she was alive.

She'd gathered herself to confront him, warned by his knock, and dark green eyes met his steadily. Her face was calm, but he saw a tear's wet track on the cheek a rifle butt had split. She sat unmoving, hands folded, yet he wasn't fooled by her apparent docility. He out-massed her, despite her half-meter height advantage, but she'd wounded three trained soldiers—one mortally—with no more than her concealed combat knife.

"Good afternoon, Corporal MacDougall," he said finally. "I am Lantu, First Admiral of the Sword of Holy Terra." Her eyes glowed with a feral light at his name, and she'd already tried to make them kill her. Would the chance to take the People's military commander with her make her try again? Part of him almost wished she would.

"Since I know who you are, you must realize I also know you possess information I need. I do not, however, intend to force that information from you." He snorted softly, amused despite himself by the disbelief on her face, but she didn't even blink.

"The Wardens don't know I have you"—*I hope!*—"and I don't plan to tell them. Yours is one of several names I had flagged to be brought directly to me if captured, and you are *my* prisoner."

"Why?" She spoke for the first time, almost startling him.

"I'm not really certain," he admitted. "Curiosity, in part, but I have . . . other reasons. As you know, I've released other guerrillas"— her eyes narrowed as he avoided the word "terrorists"—"with messages to Sergeant MacRory. If I can keep certain others from learning of your capture or who you truly are, I hope to release you in the same way."

"Why?" she repeated.

"I—" Lantu stopped, unable to confess his doubts to a human. Instead, he only shrugged and returned her steady gaze. "In the meantime, is there anything else you need? Do you require additional medical attention?"

"No." He nodded and turned for the door, but her icy voice turned him back. "I expected better of you, First Admiral. Peaceforcers understand the 'good cop-bad cop' technique as well as you do."

He was briefly puzzled, but then he understood and laughed harshly. "You misunderstand, Corporal MacDougall. By the People's standards, I'm a *very* 'bad cop' just now. I won't bother you with why—you wouldn't believe me anyway—but one thing I will tell you. For the moment, you are completely safe, not simply from me, but from the Wardens and the Inquisition itself."

She glared at him in patent disbelief, and he shrugged.

"You re pregnant," he said gently. "Among the People, that's a very holy state, one not even the Inquisition would dare imperil."

"Why? I'm an 'infidel,' and I don't plan to change," she said coldly.

"Perhaps not, but your child has had no opportunity to choose, has it?" he asked quietly. "No. Even if your identity slips, you, personally, are safe for now. But—" he met her eyes "—that doesn't mean Colonel Huark wouldn't use you to lure Sergeant MacRory into a trap. So, please, Corporal MacDougall, pretend you believe I'm truly concerned for your safety and do nothing to draw attention to yourself."

The GEV whined down a security lane well inside the OZ, searchlights probing the dark. It was the fourth lane so far, but Angus didn't even curse. He merely lay in the chill mud, waiting, with every spark of human hope—or fear—frozen into stony purpose.

His hard eyes narrowed as a wheeled vehicle appeared, trailing the GEV with a quietly humming engine . . . without lights. It grumbled softly past, its commander's bony head and bulky night optics protruding from the hatch, and he lay still for another ten minutes by his watch before he beckoned to Tulloch.

Eleven armed men slid deeper into the Zone like a grim band of ghosts.

"The fleet chaplain is coming to see you," Hanat said as Lantu returned from a late-night inspection. He paused, eyelids flickering, then nodded and continued towards his inner office, tossing his holstered machine-pistol onto the desk to unlatch his body armor and hang it up.

Hanat followed him, eyes wide.

"Don't you understand?" she said urgently. "He's coming *here.*"

"I understand."

"But—Does he *know*, Lantu?"

"Hush, Hanat." He cupped her head in his hands and stroked her cranial carapace gently. "If he knows, he knows."

"Oh, Lantu!" Tears gleamed, and he produced a handkerchief to dry them. "Why did you do it? *Why?*"

"*I* had to." Her wet eyes flashed angrily, and she began a sharp retort, but he silenced her with a caress. "Forgive me if you can, Hanat. I had no right to involve you."

"Idiot!" she said sharply. "As if I didn't—"

She broke off as an admittance chime rang softly. Her hands rose, gripping his caressing fingers tightly, then she straightened proudly— a small, slim figure with suddenly calm eyes—and went to answer it.

✧   ✧   ✧

Angus glanced down at the inertial guidance unit's LED, checking its coordinates against the annotated City Engineer's map from the local civilian intelligence cell, and touched a ladder.

"We're here," he whispered to Tulloch, and MacAndrew nodded, his face shadowed in the sepulchral glow of his slitted torch beam. The rest of their team was a vague blur in the darkness of the service tunnel.

"Aye, but I'd feel better tae ken just where *she* is."

"The lad wi' the map said they'd fetched her here. And—" Angus grinned hungrily "—there's one Shellie bastard will tell me where tae find her, admiral or no . . . afore I kill him."

"Holiness." Lantu felt a flush of relief as the fleet chaplain closed the inner office door on his four-man bodyguard. If Manak had come for the reason Hanat feared . . . "What brings you here at this hour?"

"Forgive me." Manak sat heavily, his eyes dark. "I'm sorry to bother you so late, but I had to see you."

"I'm at your disposal, Holiness."

"Thank you, my son. But this—" Manak stopped and gestured vaguely.

"What's happened, Holiness?" Lantu asked gently.

"The infidels have driven the Sword from Sandhurst," Manak said wretchedly, and the admiral sat bolt upright. "They'll attack here within the week—possibly within days."

"Holy Terra!" Lantu whispered.

"You don't know the worst yet. Jahanak will defend neither New New Hebrides nor Alfred! The coward means to fall clear back to Lorelei before he stands! Can you believe it?"

Lantu stroked the gun belt on his desk. "Yes, I believe it. Nor does it make him a coward. If he's been driven from Sandhurst, his losses must have been heavy, and there are no real fortifications here or in Alfred. He needs the support of the Lorelei warp point forts." He nodded. "Holiness, if I were in command, I would do the same."

"I see." Manak fingered his ring, then sighed deeply. "Well, if this is Holy Terra's will, we can but bend before it. Yet it leaves us with grave decisions of our own, my son."

Lantu nodded silently, his mind racing. He'd tried to blunt the Inquisition's excesses, but when the humans returned to New Hebrides and learned what had been done to its people, their fury would be terrible. It was unlikely they would recognize his efforts for what they'd been, but his own fate bothered him less than what it would mean for the People. If—

"We must insure the infidels do not defile this planet yet again."

The fleet chaplain's fervent words wrenched Lantu's attention back to him.

"Holiness, Colonel Fraymak and I will do our best, but against an entire fleet we can accomplish little."

"I know that, my son, but the infidels shall not have this planet!" Manak's harsh voice glittered with a strange fire. "This was the Messenger's destination. If no other world is saved from apostasy, this one must be!"

"But—"

"I know how to do it, my son." Manak overrode Lantu in a spate of words. "I want you to distribute our nuclear demolition charges. Mine every city, every village, every farmstead! Then let them land. Do you see? We'll *let* them land, then trigger the mines! In one stroke, we will return our souls to Holy Terra, save this world from defilement, and smite Her foes!"

Shock stabbed the admiral, and he groped frantically for an argument.

"Holiness, we don't *have* that many mines."

"Then use all we have! And Jahanak hasn't run yet, Satan-Khan take him! I still have some authority—I'll make him send us more!"

Lantu stared at him, transfixed by the febrile glitter in his eyes, and horror tightened his throat. He'd sensed his old mentor's growing desperation, but *this*—! He searched those fiery eyes for some shadow of the fleet chaplain he knew and loved . . . and saw only madness.

"Holiness," he whispered, "think before you do this."

"I have, my son." Manak leaned forward eagerly. "Holy Terra has shown me the way. Even if we catch none of the infidel Marines in our trap, this world will be lifeless—useless to them!"

"That . . . isn't what I meant," Lantu said carefully. "Do you remember Redwing? When we fell back to save the Fleet?"

"Of course," Manak said impatiently.

"Then think why we did it, Holiness. We fell back to *save* the Fleet, to save our People—Holy Terra's People—from useless death. If you do this thing, what will the infidels do to Thebes in retaliation?"

"Do? To *Thebes*?" Manak laughed incredulously. "My son, the infidels will never reach Thebes! Holy Terra will prevent them."

Sweet Terra, the old man actually believed that. He'd *made* himself believe it, and in the making he'd become one more casualty of the jihad, wrapped in the death shroud of his Faith and ready to take this world—and his own—into death with him!

"Holiness, you can't do this. The cost to the People will—"

"Silence!" Manak's ringed hand slapped Lantu's desk like a pistol. "How *dare* you dispute with me?! Has Holy Terra shown *you* Her mind?!"

"But, Holiness, we—"

"Be silent, I say! I have heard the apostasy of others, the whispers of defeatism! I will not hear more!"

"You must, Holiness. Please, you *must* face the truth."

"Dear Terra!" Manak stared at the admiral. "You, Lantu? You would betray me? Betray the *Faith*?! Yes," he whispered, eyes suddenly huge. "You would. Terra forgive me, Father Shamar warned me, and I would not hear him! But deep in my heart, I knew. Perhaps I *always* knew."

"Listen to me." Lantu stood behind the desk, and Manak shrank from him in horror, signing the Circle of Terra as if against a demon. Lantu's heart spasmed, but he dared not retreat. "Whatever you think now, you *taught* me to serve the People, and because you did, I can't let you do this thing! Not to these people and never—*never*—to our own People and world!"

"Stay back!" Manak jerked out of his chair and scuttled back. "Come no closer, heretic!"

"Holiness!" Lantu recoiled from the thick hate in Manak's voice.

"My eyes are clear now!" Manak cried wildly. "Get thee behind me, Satan-Khan! I cast thee out! I pronounce thee twice-damned, heretic and apostate, and condemn thy disbelief to the Fire of Hell!"

Lantu gasped, hands raised against the words of excommunication, and a dagger turned in his heart. Despite everything, he was a son of the Church, raised in the Faith—raised by the same loving hand which now cast him into the darkness.

But the darkness did not claim him, and he lowered his hands. He stared into the twisted hate of the only father he had ever known, and the stubborn duty and integrity that father had taught him filled him still.

"I can't let you do this, Holiness. I *won't* let you."

"*Heretic!*" Manak screamed, and tore at the pistol at his side.

Grief and terror filled Lantu—terrible grief that they could come to this and an equally terrible fear. Not for his life, for he would gladly have died before seeing such hate in Manak's eyes, but for something far worse. For the madness which filled his father and would destroy their People if it was not stopped.

Fists hammered at his office door as Manak's bodyguards reacted to the fleet chaplain's scream, but the stout door defied them, and the holster flap came free. The old prelate clawed at the pistol butt, and Lantu felt his own body move like a stranger's. His hand flashed out, darting to the gun belt on his desk, closing on the pistol grip.

"Die, heretic! *Die*—and I curse the day I called you son!"

Manak's pistol jerked free, its safety clicked off . . .

. . . and Lantu cut him down in a chattering blast of flame.

✧   ✧   ✧

"*Jaysus!*"

Tulloch MacAndrew recoiled from the service hatch he'd been about to open as the thunder of gunfire crashed through it. The first, sudden burst was answered by another, and another and another!

"Mother o' God!" Davey MacIver whispered. "What i' thunder—?"

"I dinnae ken," Angus said, jacking a round into the chamber of his own weapon, "but 'tis now or naer, lads. Are ye wi' me still?"

"Aye," Tulloch rasped, and drove a bull-like shoulder into the hatch.

The access panel burst open, and Tulloch slammed through it, spinning to his right as he went. A single guard raced towards him down a dimly-lit hall, and his rifle chattered. The guard crashed to the floor, and Angus and MacIver led the others through the hatch and to their left, towards the thundering firefight, while Tulloch followed, moving backwards, swinging his muzzle to cover the hall behind them.

More bursts of fire ripped back and forth ahead of them, and then a Shellhead leapt out an open door. He wore the green of a regular with the episcopal-purple collar tabs of the Fleet Chaplain's Office, and he jerked up his machine-pistol as he saw the humans.

He never got off a shot. Angus's burst spun him like a marionette, and the guerrilla charged through the door, straight into Hell's own foyer.

The outer office was a smoky chaos, littered with spent cartridge cases. A Shellhead lay bleeding on the carpet, and two more sheltered behind overturned furniture, firing not towards the humans but towards the *inner* office! One of them looked up and shouted as Angus skidded through the door, but he and MacIver laced the room with fire. Fresh bullet holes spalled the walls, and the guards' uniforms rippled as the slugs hurled them down.

Angus's ears rang as the thunder stopped and he heard the distant wail of alarms, but confusion held him motionless. What in God's name—?!

A soft sound brought his rifle back up, and his finger tightened as a figure appeared in the inner doorway. He stopped himself just in time, for the Shellhead's smoking pistol pointed unthreateningly at the floor. He moved as if in a nightmare, but his amber eyes saw the chevrons on Angus's collar.

"MacRory," he said dully. "I should have guessed you'd come."

"Drap it, Shellie!" Angus grated, and the Shellhead looked down, as if surprised to see he still held a weapon. His hand opened, and it thumped the carpet. Another sound brought MacIver's rifle around, but he, too, held his fire as a Shellhead woman rose from the floor behind a desk. She raced to the Shellhead in the doorway—a tiny figure, slender as an elf—and embraced him.

"Easy, Hanat," he soothed. "I'm . . . all right."

"I hate tae mention it," Tulloch said tightly, "but there's a hull damned Shellie army aboot th' place, Angus!"

"Wait!" Angus advanced on the Thebans, and his rifle muzzle pressed the male's chest above the woman's head. "Ye know me, Shellie, but I dinnae know *you.*"

"First Admiral Lantu, at your service." It came out with a ghost of bitter humor.

"Ah!" Angus thought frantically. He'd planned a quiet intrusion, but all the gunfire had trashed that. They were in a deathtrap, yet the senior Shellhead military commander would make a useful hostage. Maybe even useful enough to get them out alive.

"Intae the office, Shellie!" he snapped, and waved his men after him.

"Back agin the wall!" he commanded, still covering the Thebans with his rifle, and the other guerrillas spread out for cover on either side of the door. Another body lay on the floor in the bloody robes of a fleet chaplain, and Lantu's face twisted as he glanced at it, but he drew himself erect.

"What do you hope to achieve?" he asked almost calmly.

"I think ye ken," Angus said softly, and the admiral nodded. "Sae where is she?"

"I can take you to her," Lantu replied.

"And nae doot clap us oop i' the same cell!" someone muttered.

"No—" Lantu began, but Tulloch cut him off with a savage gesture, and Angus's face tightened as he heard feet pounding down the corridor at last. He tried to think how best to play the single card he held, but before he could open his mouth, the Shellhead woman darted out the door with dazzling speed, short legs flashing. Rory MacSwain raised his weapon with a snarl, but Tulloch struck it down. It was as well, Angus thought. Lantu's eyes had glared with sudden madness when Rory moved, and Angus knew—somehow—that if Rory had fired the admiral would have attacked them all with his bare hands.

Which got them no closer to—

His thoughts broke off as he heard the woman's raised voice.

"Oh, thank Terra you're here!" she cried. "*Terrorists!* They killed the fleet chaplain and kidnapped the admiral! They went that way— down the east corridor! Hurry! Hurry, *please!*"

Startled shouts answered, and the feet raced off while the guerrillas gawked at one another. But their confusion grew even greater when the tiny Theban walked calmly back into the office.

"There. That was the ready guard force. You've got ten minutes before anyone else gets here from the barracks."

"What have you *done*, Hanat?" Lantu demanded fiercely. "What do you think will happen when they realize you lied to them?!"

"Nothing," Hanat said calmly. "I'm only a foolish woman. If you're gone when they return, they'll be ready enough to believe I simply confused my directions. And you've got to go. You know that now."

"I can't," Lantu argued. "My duty—"

"Oh, stop it!" She caught his arm in two small hands and shook him. It was like a terrier shaking a mastiff, but none of the guerrillas laughed. They didn't even move. They were still trying to grasp what was happening.

"It's *over*! Can't you see that? Even the fleet chaplain guessed—and what will Shamar and Huark do without him to protect you? You can't do your 'duty' if you're dead, so go, Lantu! Just go!"

"With *them*?" Lantu demanded, waving at the guerrillas.

"Yes! Even with them!" She whirled on Angus, and he stepped back in surprise as she glared up at his towering centimeters. "You must have some plan to get out. He'll take you to the one you want—he's kept her safe for you—if you only take him out of here. *Please!*"

Angus stared at the two Thebans, trying to comprehend. It was insane, but the wee Shellie actually seemed to make sense. And whatever else he'd done, Lantu had always kept his word to the Resistance.

"Aye," he said grudgingly. "We're gang oot th' way we came in, and if ye take us tae Katie—and if we're no kilt gettin' tae her—we'll take ye wi' us, Admiral. Ye'll be a prisoner, maybe, but alive. Ye've my word fer that."

"I—" Lantu broke off, staring back and forth between the tall human and Hanat's desperate face. Manak's body caught at his eyes, but he refused to look, and he was tired. So tired and so sick at heart. He bent his head at last, closing his inner lids in grief and pain.

"All right," he sighed. "I'll take you to her, Sergeant MacRory."

CHAPTER TWENTY-FOUR

"It's what I tried to stop!"

Second Admiral Jahanak sat on *Arbela*'s bridge once more, watching his repeater display confirm his worst fears. He'd hurt the infidels badly in Sandhurst, but not badly enough to stop them short of Lorelei. And they were being more circumspect this time; each carrier through the warp point was accompanied by a matching superdreadnought or battleship. If he'd cared to trade blows—which he emphatically did *not*—they had the firepower to deal with anything he could throw at them. But after the hammering his battle-cruisers and escorts had taken from those Terra-damned invisible carriers in Sandhurst, he was in no shape to contest their entry. With the newly revealed range of their heavy missiles to support their fighter strikes, any action beyond energy-weapons range would be both suicidal and pointless. It was going to require a full-scale, point-blank warp point ambush, with all the mines, fortresses, and capital ships he could muster, to stop them.

"Pass the order, Captain Yurah," he said quietly, ignoring the empty chair in which Fleet Chaplain Hinam should have sat. Hinam hadn't been able to contest his decision to retreat without a fight—he knew too much about what the second admiral would face in such an attempt—but neither had he been able to stomach the thought of further flight. With Fleet Chaplain Manak's death at terrorist hands, he'd found an out he could embrace in good conscience and departed for the planet with all the Marines Jahanak had been able to spare to join Warden Colonel Huark's hopeless defense.

And so Jahanak's surviving mobile units departed the system. Other than the necessary pickets, they wouldn't even slow down in Alfred. Of course, there wasn't much there now to slow down for. . . .

The thought worried Jahanak a bit, not that he intended to mention it to anyone. After all, Holy Terra would triumph in the end. No issues would ever arise concerning the People's sometimes harsh but always necessary acts on the occupied planets—planets they were endeavoring to bring back into the light against the will of the hopelessly-lost human souls that inhabited them.

Still . . . Jahanak also never mentioned to anyone his private hope that that dunderhead Huark would have the prudence to destroy his records.

"So that's the last of them, Admiral," Tsuchevsky reported. The Theban ships had moved beyond the scout's scanner range, and any pursuit was pointless. "They've left the planet's orbital defenses—and presumably their ground forces there—behind to surrender or die."

"And we know they will not surrender." Kthaara's statement held none of Tsuchevsky's distaste—it was entirely matter-of-fact. "Shall we prepare a fighter strike, Admiral?"

Antonov studied the display himself, watching Admiral Avram's small carriers—escort carriers, the Fleet was calling them—deploy with Berenson's surviving light carriers behind the protective shield of his cruisers and battle-cruisers. Thank God, he thought, that Avram had held Danzig. It gave him an unexpected and invaluable secure forward base, and, after Sandhurst, those small carriers were worth their weight in any precious metal someone might care to name. Commodore Hazelwood's brilliantly improvised design made it abundantly clear his talents had been utterly wasted in Fortress Command, and the Danzig yards had made shorter work of repairs to Berenson's damaged units under his direction than Antonov would have believed possible. Certainly he'd put them back into service long before the fleet train's mobile repair ships could have.

He shook himself and glanced at Kthaara. "No. We lost enough pilots in Sandhurst. We'll stand off at extreme SBM range and bombard the fortresses into submission or into rubble." He had to smile at the Orion's expression. "Oh, yes, Kthaara, I know: they won't submit. But I'm hoping that afterwards, when we're orbiting unopposed in their sky, the ground forces will come to their senses." His tone hardened. "They must know by now that they're losing the war, and even religious maniacs may not be immune to despair when they're abandoned by, and utterly isolated from, their own people. At least," he finished, "it's worth a try."

"Why?" the Orion asked with disarmingly frank curiosity.

The guerrillas had been excited all day, though none of them had explained why. Now they were gathered in the cold mountain night, staring upward. The Theban who once had been a first admiral shambled almost incuriously out of the deep cave to join them, and a small pocket of silence moved about him with his guards.

As MacRory had promised, his life had been spared, though there'd been moments when he'd wondered if *any* of them would reach the mountains alive. He had no idea whether Fraymak had been searching for him to rescue or arrest him, yet it had been a novel experience to find himself on the receiving end of the relentless procedures he himself had set up.

But only intellectually so, for he hadn't felt a thing. After the terror of fighting for his life and the breathless tension of leading his captors to MacDougall's hidden cell, there'd been . . . nothing. A dead, numb nothing like the endless night between the stars.

His memories of their escape were time-frozen snapshots against a strange, featureless backdrop. He remembered the ferocity with which MacRory had embraced MacDougall, and even in his state of shock, he'd been faintly amused by MacRory's laconic explanations. Yet it had seemed no more important than his own incurious surprise over the service tunnels under his HQ. It was odd that he'd never even considered them when he made his security arrangements, but no doubt just as well. And at least the close quarters had slowed his captors to a pace his shorter legs could match.

It was different once they reached open country. He'd done his best, but he'd heard the one named MacSwain arguing that they should either cut his throat or abandon him. He'd squatted against a tree, panting, unmoved by either possibility. Yet MacRory had refused sharply, and MacDougall had supported him. So had MacAndrew. It hadn't seemed important, and Lantu had felt vaguely surprised when they all started off once more. After all, MacSwain was right. He was slowing them, and he was the enemy.

There was another memory of lying in cold mud beside MacDougall while the others dealt with a patrol. He'd considered shouting a warning, but he hadn't. Not because MacDougall's knife pressed against his throat, but because he simply had no volition left. There'd been more Thebans than guerrillas, but MacRory's men had swarmed over them with knives, and he'd heard only one strangled scream.

There were other memories. Searching vertols black against the dawn. Whining GEV fans just short of the Zone's frontier. Cold rain and steep trails. At one point, MacAndrew had snatched him up without warning and half-thrown him across a clearing as another recon flight thundered overhead.

But like the three days since they'd reached the main camp, it was all a dream, a nightmare from which he longed to wake, with no reality.

Reality was an agony of emptiness. Reality was gnawing guilt, sick self-hate, and a dull, red fury against a Church which had lied. Five generations of the People had believed a monstrous lie that had launched them at the throats of an innocent race like ravening beasts. And he, too, had dedicated his life to it. It had stained their hands—stained *his* hands—with the blood of almost a million innocents on this single world, and dark, bottomless guilt possessed him. How many billions of the People would that lie kill as it had killed Manak? How many more millions of humans had it already killed on other worlds?

He was caught, trapped between guilt that longed to return to the security of the lie, fleeing the deadly truth, and rage that demanded he turn on those who'd told it, rending them for their deceit.

Now he bit off a groan as he watched brilliant pinpricks boil against the stars, like chinks in the gates of Hell. The human fleet had arrived to kill the scanty orbital forts . . . soon their Marines would land to learn the truth.

He sat and watched the silent savagery, despising himself for his cowardice. He should strike back against those who had lied, if only to atone for his own acts. But when the rest of humanity learned what had happened here, they would repay New Hebrides' deaths a thousandfold . . . and if Lantu couldn't blame them, he couldn't help them do it, either. Whatever he'd done, whatever his beliefs had been, he'd held them honestly, and so had the People. How could he help destroy them for that?

New New Hebrides had the cloud-swirling blue loveliness of almost all life-bearing worlds in the flag bridge view screens.

The light orbital weapons platforms had perished as expected, unable even to strike back at the infidels who smote them with the horrible mutual annihilation of positive and negative matter from beyond their own range. And now Second Fleet, TFN, deployed into the skies of the defenseless planet in search of someone from whom its surrender could be demanded.

Their search ended in an unexpected way.

"Admiral," Tsuchevsky reported from beside the com station, "we're receiving a tight-beam, voice-only laser transmission from the surface, in plain language—and it's not the Thebans. It's someone claiming to be a Sergeant MacRory of the planetary Peaceforce, representing some kind of guerrilla force down there. Winnie is running a check of the personnel records from data base to . . . ah!" He nodded as Trevayne gave a thumbs-up from behind her own computer terminal. "So there *is* such a person. And he is using standard Peaceforce equipment. Shall we respond, sir?"

Antonov nodded decisively and stepped forward. "This is Fleet

Admiral Antonov, Terran Federation Navy. Is this Sergeant MacRory of the New New Hebrides Peaceforce?"

"It is that," was the reply, in a burr that could saw boards. "An' 'tis a sight fer sore eyes ye are in our skies, Admiral! But I mun waste nae time, fer the Shellies—sorry, the Thebans—will be tryin' tae—"

"Excuse me, Sergeant," Antonov's basso cut in impatiently. "I had understood this transmission was in plain language."

"An' so it is!" MacRory sounded a bit miffed. "Och, mon, dinna fash yersel' . . ."

Antonov turned to Tsuchevsky with a scowl. "What language do they speak on New New Hebrides, anyway? And why can't he use Standard English?"

Winnifred Trevayne smothered a laugh, then remembered herself and sniffed primly. "Actually, Admiral, I'm afraid that *is* English—of a sort. If you'll permit me. . . ." She introduced herself to MacRory and then took over the com link, which resumed after a faint murmur from the receiver that sounded like "Rooskies an' Sassenach! Aye, weel. . . ."

The conversation continued for several minutes before she finally turned back to Antonov with a troubled expression. "The Theban commander on the planet is a Colonel Huark, sir. I've already keyed in the coordinates of his headquarters. But as for trying to persuade him to surrender . . . well, some of what Sergeant MacRory's been telling me about what the Thebans have been doing on this planet is, quite frankly, hard to believe. . . ."

Huark's was the first living Theban face any of them had seen, and the hot yellow eyes that glared from the view screen made it very different from the dead ones.

He'd accepted the transmission curtly in the name of Fleet Chaplain Hinam and listened stonily to the demand for unconditional surrender. His only visible reaction had been a hardening of his glare when Kthaara entered the pickup's field. Now Antonov finished, and a heartbeat of dead silence passed before Huark spoke.

"I have consented to hear you, infidel, only that I might see for myself the depths of apostasy to which your fallen and eternally-damned race has sunk. But I did not expect even you to be so lost to the very memory of righteousness as to come against the faithful in the company of the Satan-Khan's own unclean spawn!" A strong shudder went through him, and his curt, hard voice frayed, rising gradually to a shriek.

"This world, the destination of the Messenger himself in bygone days, will not be delivered to you to be profaned by you who consort with demons and worship false gods! You may bombard us from space, slaughtering your fellow infidels . . . but on the day the first of your Marines sets foot on this planet's surface, the mines we have planted in every city and town will purge it with cleansing nuclear fire! You may slay us, infidel, for we are but mortal, but Holy Terra's children will never be conquered! You will inherit only a worthless radioactive waste, and may you follow this Terra-forsaken world down into the torment and damnation of the eternal flame!"

Antonov leaned forward, massive shoulders hunched and beard bristling. "Colonel Huark, listen well. We humans have learned from our own history that threats to hostages cannot be allowed to prevent the taking of necessary actions—and that any actual harm to those hostages must be avenged! Not only you, personally, but your race as a whole will be held responsible for any acts of genocide against the populace of New New Hebrides. If you don't care about your own life, consider the life of your home world when we reach it!"

Huark started to speak, then laughed—a high, tremulous laugh, edged with the thin quaver of insanity, that had no humor in it—and cut the connection abruptly.

Antonov leaned back with a sigh. "Well," he rumbled softly, "they laugh. Odd coincidence. . . ." He shook himself. "Commodore Tsuchevsky, I think we'd better get back in contact with Sergeant MacRory. This time, try for a visual."

Angus MacRory nodded slowly. "Aye, Admiral. Nae doot aboot it. Yon Huark's nae mair sane than any Rigelian. If he's the means, he'll do it." The red-gold-haired woman beside him in the view screen also nodded.

Antonov was adjusting to the New Hebridan version of English, but he was devoutly (if unwontedly tactfully) grateful for Caitrin MacDougall's presence. Between her educated Standard English and Winnifred Trevayne's occasional, polite interpretation, communication flowed fairly smoothly. Now he rubbed his beard slowly and looked glum.

"I was afraid you'd say that, Sergeant, given what we've learned about the Thebans. But I don't suppose I need to tell you and Corporal MacDougall about *that*."

"No, Admiral, you don't," Caitrin agreed grimly. "The question is, what will you do now?"

"Do, Corporal MacDougall?" Antonov shrugged. "My duty, of course. Which is to bring this war to a conclusion as quickly as possible. All other considerations must be secondary to this objective." The two New Hebridans noticed a slight thickening of his accent. Clearly he was troubled. Just as clearly, he would do whatever he felt to be necessary. The rising crescendo of terrorist outrages at the beginning of the twenty-first century had cured humanity of the twentieth's weird belief that terrorism's victims must be somehow to blame for it. Antonov wouldn't feel guilt over atrocities committed by his enemies. Which was not to say he looked forward to them; simply that he would never let the threat of them stop him.

"However," he continued, "while I cannot delegate responsibility, there is no reason I cannot ask advice. And I am asking yours now. Specifically, I'm asking you for an alternative to invasion. I'm prepared to listen to any suggestion that will enable me to prevent even greater mass murder on this planet."

"We understand, Admiral," Caitrin replied as they nodded in unison, "and thank you. We'll confer with our comrades . . . and with someone else."

"We mun talk," Angus said, and Lantu looked up from the fire with remote amber eyes.

"What about?" he asked from the drifting darkness of his mind.

"Aboot that bastard Huark's plans tae nuke the bloody planet!"

"*What?!*" Lantu jerked to his feet, his detachment shattered.

"He's gang tae nuke the cities and camps," Angus said coldly. "D'ye mean fer me tae think ye naer thought of it yer ainself?"

"It's what I tried to *stop!*"

"Is it, now?" Angus eyed him sharply, then sank down on another rock, waving Lantu back onto his own. "I almost believe ye, Shellie."

"I *do* believe him." Caitrin materialized out of the cavern's dimness, and Lantu looked up at her, wondering if he should feel gratitude.

"It's the truth." His eyes hardened as horror banished apathy. "Tell me exactly what he said he'd do."

Angus sat silently, letting Caitrin describe their conversation with Admiral Antonov while he watched Lantu. For the first time since his capture (if that was the word) the Shellhead seemed alive, his questions sharp and incisive, and Angus realized he was finally seeing the admiral who'd almost broken the Resistance.

"Huark's a fool," Lantu said at last, folding his arms behind him and pacing agitatedly. "The sort of blind, bigoted fanatic who'd actually do it."

"Sae I ken. But what's tae be done? They've started killin' in the camps again, and he's no likely tae stop if the Corps *doesn't* land."

"They've resumed camp executions?" Lantu's spray of facial scales stood out darkly as he stared at Angus.

"Aye. They started the day after ye . . . disappeared. 'Tis that makes me think ye re tellin' the truth, Shel—Admiral."

Under other circumstances, Angus's sudden change in address might have amused Lantu. Now he scarcely noticed.

"I think you'll have to invade anyway, Sergeant MacRory."

"And have him nuke the planet? Are ye daft?!"

"No, and you and Corporal MacDougall should understand if anyone can. You escaped from the Inquisition." Lantu didn't even flinch as Angus's eyes narrowed dangerously. "I know what you must have endured, but it means you've heard first-hand what the Church teaches."

"Aye," Angus said shortly.

"It's a lie." Lantu's voice was flat. "I know that now, but Huark and Shamar don't, and you can't leave defeated people who *believe* in the jihad in control of this planet! They've killed almost a million people when they thought they were winning—do you think they're going to stop *now*?"

"Sae it's die slow or die fast, is it?" Angus asked wearily.

"No! It can't end that way! Not after—" Lantu shook his head. "I won't let them do that," he grated.

"And how d'ye mean tae stop 'em?"

"I may know a way—if you trust me enough."

Antonov cut the connection, blanking out the images of MacRory, MacDougall, and . . . the other. He swung about and faced the officers seated at the table. They all looked as nonplused as he felt. They'd all hoped for, and expected, a resistance movement to welcome them when they arrived as liberators—but a Theban defector hadn't been part of the picture.

Especially not the Theban who commanded their fleet until Redwing, he thought grimly. *The Theban who directed the massacre of the "Peace Fleet."* He'd been certain the Thebans had gotten a new commander after Redwing; the old commander was the last individual he'd ever expected to meet, much less to find himself allied with.

"Well, ladies and gentlemen," he growled, "we've heard the guerrillas'—or, rather, Admiral Lantu's—plan. Comments?"

"I don't like it, sir," Aram Shahinian said with the bluntness that was, as far as anyone knew, the only way the Marine general knew how to communicate. "We're being asked to send down a force of my Raiders, lightly equipped to minimize the risk of detection, and put them in this Shellhead's"—the New Hebridan term had caught on quickly—"hands." He almost visibly dug in his heels, and a hundred generations of stubborn Armenian mountaineers looked out through his dark-brown eyes. "I don't like it," he repeated.

"And I," Kthaara put in, through his translator for the benefit of those not conversant with the Tongue of Tongues, "most emphatically do not like being asked to trust a Theban."

"But what's the alternative?" Tsuchevsky asked. "The guerrillas know Huark better than we do. They seem convinced he'll carry out his threat if we invade, and if we bombard, we'll merely be slaughtering the planet's population ourselves. We may as well let Huark do it for us! This plan involves risks—but does anyone have another idea that offers a chance of retaking the planet without civilian megadeaths?"

Winnifred Trevayne looked anguished. "We've already neutralized their space capability," she began with uncharacteristic hesitancy. "So Huark could pose no threat to our rear. We could simply proceed on to Alfred now. . . ."

"No." Antonov cut her off with a chopping motion. "I will not leave the problem for someone else to have to deal with later. And I will not leave this planet in the hands of a nihilist like Huark, to continue his butchery until someone with balls finally makes the decision I should have made!" He looked around the table, and at Kthaara in particular. "I don't trust this Lantu either—but Sergeant MacRory and Corporal MacDougall *do* seem to. And that they trust any Theban, after what they and their people have been through, must mean something!

"General Shahinian," he continued after a moment's pause, "your objections are noted. But we will proceed along the lines proposed by the New Hebridan Resistance. This decision is my responsibility alone. You will hold your full landing force in readiness to seize all cities and re-education camps as soon as the raiding party reports success—or to do what seems indicated if it does not."

"Aye, aye, sir." Shahinian knew Antonov well enough to know the discussion was closed. "I have an officer in mind to command the landing party—a very good man."

"Yes," Antonov nodded, "I think I know who you mean. See to it, General. And," he added with a slight smile, "we're going to have to do something about Sergeant MacRory, so have your personnel office prepare the paperwork. It won't do to have a sergeant in command of the liberation of an entire planet!" He looked around. "Does anyone have anything further?"

"Yes, Admiral." Kthaara spoke very formally, looking Antonov in the eye. The translator continued to translate, but this was between the two of them. "I request to be assigned to the landing party." He raised a clawed, forestalling hand. "No fighter operations will be involved, so I will be superfluous in my staff position. And since, as General Shaahiiniaaaan has pointed out, powered combat armor is contraindicated for this mission, my"—(deadpan)—"physical peculiarities will present no problem."

Antonov returned his *vilkshatha* brother's level stare. He knew Kthaara would never trust any of Khardanish'zarthan's killers, none of whom he'd yet had the opportunity to avenge himself upon in the traditional way of whetted steel.

And, Antonov knew, any act of betrayal by Lantu would be the Theban's last act.

"Request granted, Commander," he said quietly.

Angus stood in the windy dark, praying the Raiders had plotted their jump properly, for LZ markers were out of the question. Their window would be brief, and if any surviving scan sat detected anything . . .

Streaks of light blazed suddenly high above. The big assault shuttles burned down on a steep approach, charging into the narrow drop window with dangerous speed, and he held his breath. The plunging streaks leveled out, dimmed, and swept overhead, then charged upwards once more and vanished.

He waited, alone with the wind, then stiffened as a star was blotted briefly away. Then another and another. Patches of night fell silently, then thudded down with muffled grunts and curses, and he grinned, recalling night drops from his own time in the Corps, as he switched on his light wand. It glowed like a dim beacon, and a bulky shape padded noiselessly up to him.

"Sergeant MacRory?" a crisp Old Terran voice demanded, and he nodded. "Major M'boto, Twelfth Raider Battalion."

"Welcome tae New Hebrides," Angus said simply, and held out his hand.

The cavern was crowded by five hundred Terran Marines and two hundred guerrillas, their mismatched clothing more worn than ever beside the Marines' mottled battledress. The chameleon-like reactive camouflage was all but invisible, darkening and lightening as the firelight flickered, but weapons gleamed in the semi-dark as they were passed out, and soft sounds of approval echoed as the guerrillas examined the gifts their visitors had brought.

Major M'boto sat on an ammunition canister with Angus, facing Lantu, and the first admiral felt acutely vulnerable. The sudden influx of armed, purposeful humans had been chilling, even if he'd set it in motion himself, but not as chilling as the silent, cold-eyed Orion standing at the major's shoulder. His clawed hand gripped the dirk at his side, and even now Lantu had to fight a shiver of dread at facing one of the Satan-Khan's own.

"So," M'boto's black face was impassive, "you're First Admiral Lantu."

"I am," Lantu replied levelly. M'boto's black beret bore the Terran Marines' crossed starship and rifle, and Lantu wondered how many of the major's friends had been killed by ships under his command.

"All right, we're here. My orders are to place myself under Sergeant—excuse me, Brevet Colonel MacRory's orders. I understand *he* trusts you. For the moment, that's good enough for me."

"Thank you, Major." M'boto shrugged and turned to Angus.

"In that case, Colonel, suppose you brief me."

"Aye." Angus shook off a brief bemusement at learning of his sudden elevation and beckoned to Caitrin. "Fetch yer maps, Katie," he said.

Lantu crouched under a wet bush, no longer a sleepwalker stumbling in his captors' wake, and thanked whatever he might someday find to believe in that the guerrillas he'd faced had been so few and lightly-armed.

The seven hundred humans with him were all but invisible. The Marines had brought camouflage coveralls for everyone, but even without them, they would have been ghosts. The Raiders were better than he'd believed possible, yet the guerrillas were better still; they knew their world intimately and slipped through its leafless winter forests like shadows.

More than that, he'd learned the difference between the obsolescent weapons which had equipped the New Hebrides Peaceforce and first-line Terran equipment. Two Theban vertols had ventured too close during their night's march, but Major M'boto had whispered a command and both had died in glaring flashes under the Raiders' hyper-velocity missiles—five-kilo metal rods which were actually miniature deep-space missile drive coils. The HVMs had struck their targets at ten percent of light-speed.

He'd felt a brief, terrible guilt as those aircraft disintegrated, but he'd made himself shake it off. Far more of the People would pay with their lives for the Faith's lies before it ended.

Now Angus MacRory slithered quietly over to him with the major, and Lantu tried to ignore the silent presence of the Orion who came with them. Kthaara'zarthan had never been out of easy reach, and he was coldly certain of the reason.

"Huark's favorite HQ," he murmured. "We've made good time."

"I can see why he feels secure here." M'boto made certain his glasses' scan systems were inactive, then raised them and cursed softly.

A wide barricade of razor-wire fringed the inner edge of a cleared hundred-meter kill-zone, and heavily sandbagged weapon towers rose at regular intervals. The entire base was cofferdammed by thick earthen blast walls, and there were twelve hundred black-clad Wardens inside the wire and minefields, supported by two platoons of GEVs. Lantu eyed the vehicles bitterly, remembering his fruitless efforts to pry them loose from the Wardens. "How deep did you say those bunkers are?"

"About forty meters for the command bunkers, Major."

"Um." M'boto lowered his glasses and glanced at Angus. "The outer works are no sweat, Colonel. The HVMs'll rip hell out of them, and the blast will take out most of the open emplacements and personnel, but forty meters is too deep for them." He sighed. "I'm afraid we'll have to do it Admiral Lantu's way."

"Aye," Angus agreed, and settled down to await the dark while M'boto and Lantu briefed their squad leaders.

Warden Colonel Huark sat in his bunker, staring at the small touchpad linked to the switchboard, and his fingers twitched as he thought of the mass death awaiting his touch. There had been no further word from the infidel admiral. Did that mean he would force the colonel's hand?

Huark stroked the touchpad gently and almost hoped it did.

" 'Tis time," Angus said softly, and Lantu nodded convulsively. The Orion beside him muttered something to M'boto in the yowling speech of his people, but the major only shrugged and extended a weapon to Lantu.

He took the proffered pistol. It was heavy, yet it didn't seem to weight his hand properly. Dull plastic gleamed as he opened his uniform tunic and shoved it inside.

"You'll know when it's time," he said, and Angus nodded and thrust out a hand.

"Take care," he admonished. "Yer no sae bad a boggit."

"Thank you." Lantu squeezed the guerrilla's calloused, too-wide hand. Then he slipped away into the night.

Warden Private Katanak snatched at his rifle as something moved in the darkness. He started to squeeze the trigger, then made himself stop.

"Sergeant Gohal! Look!"

The sergeant reached for his pistol, then relaxed as a stocky, short-legged shape staggered from the forest into the glare of the perimeter floods.

"Call the lieutenant, Katanak. That's one of ours."

Lantu tried not to show his tension as he stumbled up to the gate. His hunched shoulders were eloquent with weariness, and the artful damage his human allies had wreaked on his uniform should help. But nothing would help if Huark had learned the truth about his "kidnapping."

"Who are—" The arrogant young lieutenant at the gate broke off and stared. "Holy Mother Terra!" he whispered. "*First Admiral Lantu?!*"

"Yes," Lantu gasped. "For Terra's sake, let me in!"

"B-b-but, First Admiral! We—I mean, how—?"

"Are you going to stand there and blither all night?" Lantu snarled. "Satan-Khan! I didn't escape from a bunch of murdering terrorists and sneak across a hundred kilometers of hostile territory for *that!*"

"Forgive me, sir!" The lieutenant's sharp salute was a tremendous relief. "We thought you were dead, sir! Open the gate, Sergeant!"

The gate swung, and Lantu stepped inside past the metal detector. The weapon inside his tunic seemed to scorch him, but there was no alloy in it.

"Thank you, Lieutenant." He injected relief into his thanks, but kept his voice tense and harried. "Now take me to the CP. Those Terra-cursed terrorists are planning—Never mind. Just get me to the colonel now!"

"Yes, sir!" The lieutenant snapped back to attention, then turned to lead the first admiral rapidly across the compound.

"He's in," M'boto murmured. "I hope he's been straight with us."

Angus only grunted, but Kthaara hissed something unintelligible—and unprintable—in the darkness.

Lantu let his feet drag down the steep bunker steps, playing his role of exhausted escapee. The guards by the main blast door looked up boredly as the lieutenant hurried over, then whipped around to stare at Lantu under the subterranean lights. One of them—a captain—crossed to him quickly.

"First Admiral! We thought you were—"

"The lieutenant told me, Captain," Lantu said tiredly, feeling his heart race, "but I'm alive, thank Terra. And I must see the colonel at once."

"I don't—" The captain paused under Lantu's suddenly icy eyes. "I'll tell him, sir."

"Thank you, Captain," Lantu said frigidly. The officer disappeared, and seconds were dragging eternities until he returned.

"The colonel will admit you, First Admiral."

Lantu grunted, ignoring the insulting phrasing, and followed the captain into the bunker's heart. The smell of concrete and earth enveloped him as his guide led him swiftly to Huark's staff section.

"Sweet Terra, it *is* you." Huark sounded a bit surly—apparently he'd been less than crushed by his succession to command.

"First Admiral!" Another voice spoke, and he turned quickly, eyes widening as Colonel Fraymak held out his hand. Lines of weariness and worry smoothed on the colonel's face, and Lantu tried to smile as a spasm of bitter regret wracked him. Why in the name of whatever was truly holy had *Fraymak* had to be here?

"Colonel. Colonel Huark. Thank Terra I reached you! I have vital information about the terrorists' plans."

He made himself ignore Fraymak's flicker of surprise at his choice of words.

"Indeed?" Huark leaned forward eagerly. "What information?"

"I think it would be better if I shared it with you in private," Lantu said, and Huark's eyes narrowed. Then he nodded.

"Everybody out," he said curtly, and his staff filed out. Lantu watched them go, willing Fraymak to accompany them yet unable to suggest it. Huark's eyes swiveled to his rival and he started to speak, but then he stopped, and Lantu's heart sank. Of course the Warden wouldn't risk his ire by ordering his most trusted subordinate to leave.

"All right, First Admiral," Huark said as the inner blast door closed behind his staff. "What is it?"

"The terrorists are planning a major attack," Lantu said, stepping back and casually engaging the blast door's security lock. "I stole one of their maps," he went on, reaching into his tunic, "and—"

His hand came out of his tunic with a bark of thunder.

"Now!" Major M'boto said harshly as a cluster of Wardens suddenly surged towards the HQ entrance. If Lantu had failed, three million human beings were about to die.

Colonel Huark lurched back, shocked eyes wide. Blood ran from his mouth as it opened. More frothed at his nostrils, and then he oozed down the wall in a smear of red.

Lantu ignored him. He was on auto-pilot, locked into the essential task he must accomplish, and his weapon barked again. The touchpad on Huark's desk shattered, and the main com switchboard spat sparks as he fired into it again and again, braced for the thunder of Fraymak's pistol. But when he whirled to face the colonel at last, his weapon was still holstered and he held his hand carefully away from it.

"F-First Admiral—?"

"I'm sorry, Fraymak. I couldn't let him do it."

Fists battered at the locked blast door as Fraymak stared at him. "*Terra!*" he whispered. "You didn't *escape*, you—"

"That's right," Lantu said softly, and the world exploded overhead.

HVMs scored the night with fire, and gun towers vomited concussive flame. Blast and fragments scythed through exposed flesh like canister, sweeping the life from open gun pits as assault charge rockets snaked through the wire and mortar bombs thundered across the motor pool. Shocked Wardens roused in the perimeter bunkers and streams of tracer began to hose the night, but the HVM launchers had retargeted and fresh blasts of fury killed the guns. Flames roared from broken GEVs, and the mortars shifted aim, deluging the shredded perimeter wire in visual and thermal smoke.

"CIC confirms explosions on Target One, sir." Major Janet Toomepuu looked up from her com station aboard TFNS *Mangus Coloradas*, hovering above Huark's HQ in geosynchronous orbit, to meet General Shahinian's eyes. "No sign of nuclear explosions anywhere on the planet."

"Does Scanning report any signs of large-scale troop movements?"

Toomepuu relayed the question to the big assault transport's combat information center.

"No, sir," she said, and Shahinian nodded.

"Land the landing force," he said, and the assault shuttles of the First and Second Raider Divisions, Terran Federation Marine Corps, stooped like vengeful falcons upon re-education camps and Theban military bases scattered across the face of New New Hebrides.

Huark's stunned Wardens staggered from their bunkered barracks, rushing to man their positions, but the enemy was already upon them. Half-seen wraiths swept out of the smoke behind a hurricane of grenades and small arms fire, and the defenders died screaming as human assault teams charged through the bedlam towards assigned targets.

Angus hurdled a dead Warden, and his grenade launcher slammed on full auto as a Shellhead squad erupted from a personnel bunker. Fists of fire hurled them back, and he reloaded without breaking stride. Return fire spat out of the darkness, and he cursed as Davey MacIver went down at his side.

The HQ bunker entrance loomed before him, and a machine-gun swung its flaming muzzle towards him, but a Raider dropped a grenade into the gun pit. Another Raider seemed to trip in mid-air as his head blew apart, and the high-pitched scream of Clan Zarthan's war cry split the madness as Kthaara emptied a full magazine into the bunker slit from which the fire had come. A Warden popped up out of the HQ bunker, gaping at the carnage, and Angus pumped an AP grenade into his chest. The Shellhead flew apart, and Angus dodged aside as a Marine sergeant and his flamer squad inundated the steep passage in a torrent of fire. Screams of agony answered, and then he and Tulloch MacAndrew were racing down the shallow, smoldering steps, leaping over seared bodies and bits of bodies, with the Marines and Kthaara'zarthan on their heels.

A rifle chattered ahead of them, and Angus threw himself head-long

down the stairs, grenade launcher barking. Three Marines went down
before the bursting grenades silenced the enemy, and Angus tobogganed
down the stairs on his belly, firing timed-rate as he went. The reek of
explosives and burned flesh choked him, but he hit the bottom and
rolled up onto his knees.

Tulloch charged through the open blast door. Dead Thebans littered the bloody floor, but interior partitions sheltered live ones. The
lights went out, muzzle flashes shredded the darkness, and Tulloch
upended a map table for cover as he fired back savagely. A thunderous explosion roared deep inside the bunker, and Angus cringed as
he crawled to Tulloch's side under the whining ricochets, reloading
and bouncing grenades off the roof and over the head-high partitions.

The defensive fire slackened, and Kthaara bounded forward, the
Marine sergeant cursing like a maniac as he tried to keep pace. Their
weapons swept the bunker, and Angus followed them, slipping and
sliding in a film of blood. There was a fresh bellow of automatic fire,
and then, impossibly, only sobs and moans and one terrible, high-
pitched, endless keen of agony that faded at last into merciful silence.

Angus straightened from his combat crouch, turning in a quick,
wary circle to search out possible threats. There were none, and he
stepped quickly into the short passage to Huark's offices.

"First Admiral?" he called, listening to the faint thunder still bouncing down the bunker steps from above, and a voice answered.

"Here, Colonel MacRory! Come ahead slowly, please."

Angus eased down the passage, flinching as the scattered, surviving emergency lights clicked on. A haze of gunsmoke hovered above
at least a dozen Shellhead bodies, all faced away from the main bunker
towards the sagging armored door a blastpack had blown half off its
hinges.

But it hadn't gone down entirely, and he squirmed past it, then
jerked his launcher up as he saw the Theban colonel, smoke still
pluming from the muzzle of his machine-pistol. Lantu sat on the floor,
holding one arm while blood flowed through his fingers, and his face
was pale, but he shook his head quickly as Angus's launcher rose.

"Don't shoot, Colonel!" Angus and the Theban both looked at him
sharply, and the admiral laughed a bit wildly, then hissed in pain. "I
meant you, Colonel MacRory. It seems I had an ally after all. Colonel MacRory, meet Colonel Fraymak."

CHAPTER TWENTY-FIVE

A Gathering Fury

"I spoke to Admiral Al-Sana at BuPers about you, Andy," Howard Anderson said.

"You did, sir?" Ensign Mallory looked at him in some surprise.

"Yes. You'll be a full lieutenant next week, and he's promised you a transfer to BuShips or Second Fleet—your choice."

"*Transfer?*"

"Personally," Anderson said, peering out the ground car window, "I think you'd probably learn more with Admiral Timoshenko, but if you go to Second Fleet, you should arrive in time for the Theban invasion, and combat duty always looks good on a young officer's record, so—"

"Just a minute, sir." Young Ensign Mallory had matured considerably, and he broke in on his boss without the flustered bashfulness he once had shown. "If it's all the same to you, I'd prefer to finish the war with you."

"I'm sorry, Andy," Anderson turned to him with genuine regret, "but it just isn't possible."

"Why not? When you get back from Old Terra and—"

"I'm not coming back," Anderson said gently. "I'm resigning."

"You're resigning *now*? When everything's finally coming together?" Mallory looked and sounded shocked.

"As you say, everything is coming together. The production and building schedules are all in place, the new weapons are a complete success—" Anderson shrugged. "Admiral Timoshenko can manage just fine without me."

"But it's not fair, sir! You're the one who kicked ass to make it work, and some damned money-gouging industrialist'll grab the credit!"

"Andy, do you think I really *need* the credit?" Mallory blushed and shook his head. "Good." Anderson reached over and squeezed the young officer's knee. "In the meantime, there's something I have to do on Old Terra, and I can't do it as a member of the Cabinet."

Mallory glanced at him sharply as the car braked beside the shuttle pad. Then his brow smoothed and he nodded.

"I understand, sir. I should have guessed." He got out and held the door. Anderson climbed out and thrust out his hand, and Mallory took it in a firm clasp. "Good luck, sir."

"And to you, Lieutenant—if you'll forgive me for being a bit premature. I'll expect to hear good things about you."

"I'll try to make certain you do, sir."

Anderson nodded, gave his aide's hand a last squeeze, and climbed the shuttle steps without a backward glance.

Federation Hall had changed.

Anderson stood in an antechamber alcove, and the faces about him were grim. He wasn't surprised, for every newscast screamed the same story. The classified reports had leaked even before he reached Old Terra, and though he couldn't prove it, he recognized the hand behind the timing. It seemed unlikely the war could last much longer, the next elections were only eight months away, and the LibProgs were looking to the ballot box. Pericles Waldeck wanted to lead his party into them with a resounding flourish to head off any embarrassing discussion of just who had gotten the Federation into this mess, and the "bloody shirt" was always a sure vote getter.

Anderson snorted contemptuously and stepped out into the crowd, nodding absent replies to innumerable greetings as he headed for the Chamber. He was reasonably certain Sakanami hadn't been a party to the leaks. Not because he put cold-blooded political maneuvers past the president, but because Sakanami couldn't possibly want to further complicate the closing stages of the war, and one thing was certain—the news coverage was going to complicate things in a major way.

Anderson couldn't blame the public for its outrage. Of six and a half million people on New New Hebrides, nine hundred and eighty thousand had died during the Theban occupation. The same percentage of deaths would have cost Old Terra one and two-thirds billion lives, and the newsies had been quick to play up that statistic. It wasn't as if they'd died in combat, either; the vast majority had been systematically slaughtered by the Theban Inquisition.

Humanity's anger and hatred were a hurricane, and it would grow worse shortly. Second Fleet had not yet moved into Alfred . . . but

Anderson had read the abstracts from the New New Hebrides occupation's records.

He shivered and settled into his seat, cursing the weariness which had become his constant companion. Age was catching up with him remorselessly, undercutting his strength and endurance when he knew he would need them badly. Ugly undercurrents floated through the Assembly, whispers about "proper punishment" for the "Theban butchers," and Anderson had heard such whispers before. Some of his darkest nightmares took him back to the close of ISW-3, when the Federation had agreed to the Khanate's proposals to reduce the central worlds of the Rigelian Protectorate to cinders. There had seemed to be no choice, for the Rigelians had not been sane by human or Orion standards. The Protectorate had never learned to surrender, and invasion would have cost billions of casualties. Almost worse, occupation garrisons would have been required for generations. Yet when the smoke finally cleared and the Federation realized it had been party not simply to the murder of a world, or even several worlds, but of an *entire race* . . .

He shook off the remembered chill and gripped his cane firmly as he waited for Chantal Duval to call the Chamber to order. Pericles Waldeck might be willing to condemn a race to extinction out of spleen and political ambition, but Howard Anderson was an old, old man.

He would not go to his Maker with the blood of yet another species on his hands.

The sight of New New Hebrides dwindling in the cabin's view port was lost on Ivan Antonov as he sat at his computer station, studying the final reports of the cleanup operation and stroking his beard thoughtfully.

A chime sounded, and he pressed the admittance stud. The hatch hissed open to admit Tsuchevsky and Kthaara.

"A final transmission from the planet, Admiral," Tsuchevsky reported. "The last of the high-ranking Wardens have been taken into custody and are awaiting trial with the surviving leaders of the Inquisition."

"Yes," Antonov acknowledged with a sour expression. "Trial for murder under the laws of New New Hebrides, I'm glad to say. I've never been comfortable with the idea of 'war crimes trials.'"

"So you mentioned." Kthaara's tone held vast disinterest in the legalisms with which humans saw fit to surround the shooting of Thebans. "Something from your history about the winners in one of your wars putting the losers on trial at . . ." He tried, but his vocal apparatus wasn't quite up to "Nürnberg."

Antonov grunted. "Those Fascists were such a bad lot it was hard for anyone to argue convincingly against putting them on trial. But when you start shooting soldiers for following orders to commit 'crimes against humanity,' the question arises: how does the soldier know what constitutes such a crime? How does he know which orders he's required to disobey? Answer: the victors will tell him after they've won the war!" He barked laughter. "So might makes right—which is what the Fascists had been saying all along!"

"I will never understand why Humans persist in trying to apply ethical principles to *chofaki*," Kthaara said with mild exasperation. "They can never be amenable to such notions. Honor, even as an unattainable ideal, is beyond their comprehension. Faced with a threat to your existence from such as they, you should simply kill them, not pass judgment on them! And if you insist on clouding the issue with irrelevant moralism, you find it growing even cloudier when dealing with an alien species. Especially," he continued complacently, "given your people's inexperience at direct dealings with aliens. Something else I will never understand is your 'Non-Intercourse Edict of 2097.'"

"The only nonhumans we'd discovered up to that time were primitives," Tsuchevsky explained. "Our own history had taught us that cultural assimilation across too great a technological gap doesn't work; the less advanced society is destroyed, and the more advanced one is left saddled with a dependent, self-pitying minority. Rather than repeat old mistakes, we decided to leave those races alone to work out their own destinies. Your race does have more experience in interacting with a variety of aliens—although," he couldn't resist adding, "historically, that interaction has been known to take the form of 'demonstration' nuclear strikes on low-tech planets."

"Well," Kthaara huffed with a defensiveness he wouldn't have felt a year earlier, "those bad old days are, of course, far behind us. And I will concede that this entire war would never have occurred if Saaan-Juusss had been more punctilious about observing the letter of the Edict. Still, there is something to be said for the insights our history gives us. Especially," he added pointedly, "now."

He referred, Antonov knew, to the two "guests" who occupied a nearby, heavily guarded stateroom. Lantu and Colonel Fraymak were in an ambiguous position; never having committed any of the crimes for which the Theban Wardens stood accused (even the Resistance admitted that they'd ordered no wanton murders or "reprisals" and had fought as clean a war as any guerrilla war can be), they hadn't been left to stand trial. So they, along with Sergeant—no, Colonel—MacRory, had departed with the Fleet. Kthaara had made no secret of his feelings about the two Thebans' presence, but everyone else seemed inclined to give some weight to Lantu's role in the relatively bloodless liberation of New New Hebrides.

But that, Antonov thought grimly, was all too likely to change.

An iron sense of duty had made him transmit to his superiors the findings culled from the records of New New Hebrides' Theban occupiers. But no one in the Second Fleet save himself, Winnifred Trevayne, and a few of her most trusted people knew what awaited them in the Alfred System. Not yet.

He really must, he decided, double the guard on the Thebans' quarters just before the warp transit.

It wouldn't have been as bad, Antonov reflected, gazing at the image of New Boston in the main view screen, if it hadn't come immediately after the euphoria of finding their entry into Alfred unopposed. Now, of course, they knew why that had been. The static from the communicators told them why, even before the images of radioactive pits that had been towns began to appear on the secondary view screens. There was nothing here to defend.

Kthaara was the first on the flag bridge to say it. "You knew," he stated, a flat declarative.

Antonov nodded. "New Boston has—*had*—only a little over a million people. The Thebans had no interest in trying to convert so small a population—not after the total failure of their 're-education' campaign on New New Hebrides. They just exterminated it as expeditiously as possible." His voice was at its deepest. "We will, of course, leave an occupation force to search for survivors; even a small human planetary population is hard to completely extirpate, short of rendering the planet uninhabitable." His voice trailed off. Then, suddenly, he sighed.

"A few very highly placed people on Old Terra already know. After this, it will be impossible to keep it from the public. The politicians and the media"—he made swear words of both—"will be like pigs in shit. It will be very hard, even for Howard Anderson, to argue successfully against reprisals in kind."

"*Minisharhuaak*, Ivaaan Nikolaaaaivychhh!" Kthaara exploded, causing heads to snap around. (The Orion oath was a frightful one, and he had never publicly addressed Antonov save as "Admiral.") "Anyone would think you actually feel *sympathy* for these treacherous fanatics!"

Antonov turned slowly and met the Orion's glare. And Kthaara, gazing across an abyss of biology and culture into the eyes of his *vilkshatha* brother, could for an instant glimpse something of what lay behind those eyes: a long, weary history of tyranny and suffering, culminating in a grandiose mistake that had yielded a century-long harvest of sorrow.

"I do," the admiral said quietly. Then he smiled, a smile that banished none of the sadness from his eyes. "And so should you, Kthaara

Kornazhovich! Remember, you're a Russian now. We Russians know about gods that failed."

Like ripples from a pebble dropped into water, silence spread outward from the two of them to envelop the entire flag bridge.

"We will end this war," Antonov resumed in a louder, harsher voice. "We will end it in the right way—the only way. We will proceed to Lorelei and then to Thebes, and we will smash the Theban Church's ability to do to any other human planet what they've done to this one. We will do whatever we must to accomplish this objective. But as long as I am in command, we will *not* act as fanatics ourselves! We owe the Thebans nothing—but we owe it to our own history to behave as though we've learned something from it!"

"Commodore Tsuchevsky, have Communications ready a courier drone and summon the rest of the supply ships. We will have use for the SBMHAWKs."

" . . . completes my report, Second Admiral."

Second Admiral Jahanak leaned back in his chair in *Alois Saint-Just*'s briefing room, rubbing his cranial carapace.

"Thank you, Captain Yurah." Jahanak's thanks covered much more than the usual morning brief, for Yurah had come a long way from the distrustful days immediately after Lantu's "relief," and Jahanak had learned to rely upon him as heavily as Lantu himself must have. The flag captain wasn't brilliant, but he was a complete professional, and though he knew exactly how grave the situation was, he managed to avoid despair. Even better, he did it without the fatalistic insistence that Holy Terra would work a miracle to save Her children which had forced Jahanak to relieve more than one subordinate. Faith was all very well, but not when it divorced a naval officer from reality.

The second admiral studied the holo sphere and the glowing lights of his units clustered about the New Alfred warp point. He was confident the inevitable attack must come from there, for the infidels had moved too far from Parsifal to worry about that warp point, at least for now. It would take them weeks to redeploy that far, and they wouldn't care to uncover either New New Hebrides or Danzig once more. Especially, he thought, not now that they knew what had happened on New Boston.

But if—*when*—they attacked, his defenses would give them pause, he told himself grimly. Eleven superdreadnoughts hovered in laser range of the warp point, supported by fifteen battleships. He would have been happier with more superdreadnoughts, but then, any admiral always wanted more than he had, and if the infidels would only hold off another few weeks he'd be able to deploy another four of them fresh from the repair yards.

He would also feel happier with more battle-cruisers. His missile-armed *Ronins* had lost heavily in QR-107, Parsifal, and Sandhurst. Worse, a dozen of them—plus half that many beam-armed *Manzikerts*—remained in yard hands, with lower repair priority than battleships and superdreadnoughts. On the other hand, he had four infidel battle-cruisers, refitted for Holy Terra's service, and three of his eleven superdreadnoughts were infidel-built, as well. Losses in lighter units had been even worse proportionally, but the yards were turning out replacement cruisers and destroyers with production-line efficiency. It was the capital ships with their longer building times that truly worried him, which was why deploying his battle-line so far forward made him nervous.

Yet the infidels' advantage at extended ranges, despite the range limitations of their new lasers, ruled out any other deployment. Large-scale production of the long-ranged force beam had been assigned low priority because of faith in the Sword's initial laser advantage, and a belated acceptance of the absolute necessity of rushing Holy Terra's own fighters into service precluded any immediate changes. Jahanak couldn't argue with that—except, he amended sourly, for the fact that the fighter decision had been so long delayed—but it meant he had to get in close, under the infidels' missiles and force beams, and stay there. And that meant a forward defense in Lorelei.

Yet if he had to fight well forward, at least he had the massive fortresses and minefields to aid him. The individual OWPs might be less powerful than those of The Line, but there were dozens of them, surrounded by clouds of the lethal hunter-killer satellites, and his reports had inspired Archbishop Ganhada's Ministry of Production to provide some of them with lavish armaments of the new primary beams. If the infidel battle-line came through first to clear a path for the carriers, his own capital ships and laser-armed fortresses would be waiting to savage them at minimum range. If the infidel admiral was foolish enough to commit his carriers first, the primary-armed forts would riddle their fighter bays before they could launch . . . assuming they survived mines and laser fire long enough to *try* to launch.

Not that he expected them to survive that long, for First Fleet was poised at hair-trigger readiness. Indeed, a full quarter of his units were actually at general quarters at any given instant. It cost something in additional wear on the equipment, but it meant the infidels weren't going to catch him napping. No matter when they came through, at least twenty-five percent of his force would be prepared to concentrate instantly on their vastly outnumbered initial assault groups.

"Very well, Captain Yurah," he said finally, "I believe we're as well prepared as we can hope to be."

"Yes, sir," Yurah agreed, but he also continued in a carefully neutral voice. "Has there been any more discussion of the carriers, Second Admiral?"

Jahanak hid a smile. For a bluff, unimaginative spacer, Yurah had a way of coming to the heart of things.

"No, Captain, there has not," he said, and saw a wry glint in Yurah's eyes. Over the past months, the flag captain had developed an unexpected sensitivity to the reality beneath Jahanak's outward acceptance of the Synod's pronouncements. It wasn't something he would care for many people to develop, but it certainly made working with Yurah simpler.

"The Synod," he continued in that same, dry tone, "has determined that our careful and thorough preparations—plus, of course, the favor of Holy Terra—make our victory inevitable. As such, they see no need to commit the limited number of carriers we currently possess and every reason to prevent the infidels from guessing that we have them."

"In other words," Yurah said, "they're staying in Thebes."

"They're staying in Thebes. From whence, of course, they will be available to surprise the infidels when we launch our counter-attack."

"Of course, sir," Captain Yurah said.

Antonov stared at the briefing room's tactical display a moment longer, then swung around to face the two whom he'd asked to remain after the final staff conference.

"Well, Admiral Berenson, Admiral Avram," he addressed the strikingly contrasted pair, "are you both clear on all aspects of the plan? I realize your duties elsewhere in this system prevented either of you from being present very much during its formulation."

There were other concerns, which he left unvoiced. Hannah Avram was a newcomer to his command team, and Berenson . . . well, it couldn't hurt to make sure of Berenson's full support. And, finally, they were both fighters who were being required not to fight until the coming battle's final stages. But they both nodded.

"We understand, Admiral," Berenson said. "The carriers will enter Lorelei in the last wave, to deal with any surviving Theban units." His eyes met Antonov's squarely, and Hannah sensed a rapport between them at odds with the stories she'd heard since linking with Second Fleet. There might be little liking there, but there was a growing— if grudging—mutual respect.

"Good." Antonov turned back to the display and the glowing dots representing his poised fleet: the serried ranks of superdreadnoughts in the first attack wave, the other battle-line units in the second, the carriers and their escorts in the third. But his somber gaze rested longest on the clouds of tiny, pinprick lights hovering nearest the warp point.

Screaming alarms harried the warriors of Holy Terra to their stations, and Second Admiral Jahanak dropped into his command chair, panting from his run to the bridge.

"Report, Captain Yurah?" he snapped.

"Coming in now, sir," Yurah said crisply. Then he raised his head with a puzzled expression. "Look at Battle Three, Second Admiral."

Jahanak glanced at the auxiliary display, and his own eyes narrowed. *Something* was coming through the warp point, all right, but *what?* He'd never seen such a horde of simultaneous transits, and dozens of the tiny vessels were vanishing in the dreadful explosions of interpenetration.

Yet that was only a tithe of them, and his blood began to chill as more and more popped into existence. Had the infidels devised a warp-capable strikefighter? No, the things were far larger than fighters, but they were far too *small* for warships.

The first arrivals had gone to an insanely agile evasion pattern, eluding the fire of his ready duty units, and they were so fast even Lorelei's massive minefields were killing only a handful of them. But whatever they were, they were hardly big enough to be a serious threat . . . weren't they?

Specially shielded navigating computers recovered, and the Terran Navy's SBMHAWKs danced madly among the fireballs where less fortunate pods had destroyed one another, whipped into squirming evasion of hostile fire while their launchers stabilized.

Ivan Antonov's decision to withhold the SBMHAWK had yielded more than the advantage of surprise. It had also bought Admiral Timoshenko and BuShips time—time to refine their targeting systems, time to improve their original evasion programs, and, most importantly of all, time to put the new system into true mass production. Now dispassionate scanners aboard the lethal little robot spacecraft compared the plethora of energy signatures before them to targeting criteria stored in their electronic brains. Decisions were made, priorities were established, and targeting systems locked.

Jahanak gasped, half-rising in horror, as the dodging light dots suddenly spawned. *Missiles!* Those were *missile* carriers—and now their deadly cargo was free in Lorelei space!

He forced himself back into his chair, clutching its arms in iron fingers as a tornado of missile traces erupted across his display. He fought to keep his shock from showing, but nausea wracked him as Tracking began projecting the missiles' targets. This was no random attack. Scores of missiles—*hundreds* of them—sped unerringly for his fortresses, and more were launching behind them.

"Evasive action!" he snapped, and watched his surprised mobile units lurch into motion. It was a pitiable response to the scale of the disaster engulfing them, but it was all that they could do.

He met Yurah's eyes. The flag captain said nothing, for there was nothing to say . . . and no point in trying to.

The fortresses suffered first.

Trios of missiles slashed out from individual pods, joined by the fire of their brethren in a single salvo of inconceivable density. No point defense system yet constructed had ever contemplated such a tidal wave of fire. The tracking ability to handle it simply didn't exist, and the forts' active defenses collapsed in electronic hysteria. Some fire control computers, faced with too many threat sources to prioritize, lapsed into the cybernetic equivalent of a sulk and refused to engage *any* of them. Not that it made much difference; even if every system had functioned perfectly, they would have been hopelessly saturated.

Fireballs pounded shuddering shields with antimatter fists, and those shields went down. Armor puffed into vapor as more missiles screamed in, and more. *More!* Structural members snapped, weapon systems and their crews vanished as if they had never been, and Second Admiral Jahanak's hands were deathlocked on his command chair's arms as he watched his fortresses die.

The majority of Second Fleet's SBMHAWKs had been targeted on the OWPs for a simple reason: Antonov's planners knew where to find them. They could be positive those targets would lie within acquisition range, but they'd been unable to make the same assumption about mobile units. Logic said the enemy must mount a crustal defense, but logic, as the TFN knew, was often no more than a way of going wrong with confidence, and so they had opted to assign sufficient of their weapons to guarantee the destruction of the forts.

They'd succeeded. Only a handful survived the thunder of the pod-launched SBMs, and that handful were shattered wrecks, broken and bleeding, without the power to affect the coming battle.

But that left the mobile units . . . and the SBMHAWKs which remained after the OWPs' deaths had been assured.

"There they go, Admiral," Tsuchevsky said unnecessarily.

Antonov grunted, eyes never leaving the flag bridge's master tactical display. The last SBMHAWK carrier pods of the initial bombardment moved into the warp point and vanished from the tidy universe of Einstein and Hawking, only to instantaneously re-emerge into it in the system of Lorelei, whose stellar ember of an M3 primary was invisible from Alfred, and where they would encounter . . . no one could say. There was every reason to assume the missiles had devastated the Theban fortresses as planned, but there was no way to be sure until living flesh committed itself to that warp transit.

And even as Antonov watched, the lead superdreadnoughts of the first wave moved up behind the departing SBMHAWKs. A half-dozen of those monster ships had been refitted with additional point defense armament for mine-sweeping purposes, which meant, of course, that something of their offensive armament had been given up in exchange. They could defend themselves well against missiles and mines, but their ability to fight back against whatever was left at the other end of the warp line was limited—especially at energy-weapons range, where the Thebans were always strongest. Behind the expressionless mask of his features, Antonov silently saluted those crews.

Angus MacRory stared down into the guarded briefing room's display as Second Fleet's first units disappeared into the warp point. He felt numb, wrapped around a taut, shuddery vacuum in his gut, and his own reaction surprised him. But only for a moment. It was knowing those ships' crews *knew* they were going to be pounded, and that they could only take it, that tied his insides in knots.

He raised his eyes to the two people seated across the table from him. Unlike Second Fleet's personnel, Angus had seen enough Shellheads to be able to read their alien expressions. Not perfectly, and not easily, but well enough to see the pain in Colonel Fraymak's eyes and sense the tormented clash of guilty loyalty with treason born of knowledge and integrity behind them. The colonel's face was the face of a being in torment, but the admiral's was the face of a being in Hell.

Angus shivered at the emptiness in Lantu's eyes, at the slack facial muscles and the four-fingered hands clasped tight about his agony. He shivered . . . and then he looked back at the display, for watching the light dots vanishing into the teeth of the Thebans' defenses was less heart-wrenching than watching Admiral Lantu's despair.

Jahanak clenched his teeth as still more missiles launched—not at the forts this time but at his warships. An involuntary groan went up from his staff as the superdreadnoughts *Eloise Abernathy*, *Carlotta Garcia*, and Yurah's old command, *Hildebrandt Jackson*, died, and the second admiral whipped around to glare at them.

"Silence!" The word cracked like a whip, wrenching their attention from the hideous displays to his blazing yellow eyes, and his voice was fierce. "We are the Sword of Holy Terra, not a pack of sniveling children! Attend to your duties!"

His officers jerked back to their instruments, and he returned his eyes to the display, grateful for the way his fury had cleared his own mind. He watched missiles shatter the battleships *Cotton Mather*, *Confucius*, *Freidrich Nietzsche*, and *Torquemada* while *Saint-Just* shuddered and lurched to hits of her own. None of his battle-line was unhurt—even his battle-cruisers were being targeted—and the missile storm was doing more than kill personnel and internal weapons. It was also irradiating his external ordnance, burning its on-board systems into uselessness before he had targets to fire it at. The infidel battle-line could not be far behind this hellish bombardment, and when it came through his shattered fleet could never stop it.

"Execute Plan Samson, Captain Yurah," he said flatly, and felt his words ripple across the bridge. No one had really believed Plan Samson would be required. Their defenses had been too strong, their tactical advantage too great—until they met the fury of the SBMHAWK.

The superdreadnoughts leading the first wave moved ponderously up to the warp point and began to vanish from Antonov's tactical display. The burly admiral watched them go with an odd calm— almost a sense of completion. His fleet was committed now, and he should soon get some definite word on what must be a maelstrom in Lorelei. Almost as soon, he would be entering that maelstrom himself. *Gosainthan* was among the capital ships of the second wave; she wouldn't transit in its lead group, but transit she would. Howard Anderson had ridden his flagship into the Battles of Aklumar and Ophiuchi Junction, and Ivan Antonov would do no less this day. TFN commanders accompanied those they commanded into battle. Always. This was no written regulation that could be evaded— it was a tradition that never could be.

The first Terran superdreadnoughts emerged into Lorelei on the SBMHAWKs' heels, and First Fleet of the Sword of Holy Terra lunged to meet them. The avalanche of missiles had stunned the defenders, but these were foes they could recognize . . . and kill.

The superdreadnought *Saint Helens* led the Terran attack into a holocaust of x-ray lasers. She survived transit by approximately twenty-three seconds, then died in a boil of spectacular fury as a direct hit ripped her magazines open. Modern missiles and nuclear warheads were among the most inert, safest to handle weapons ever devised; antimatter warheads were not, and their prodigious power made magazine hits even more lethal than they had been in the days of chemical explosives. Now the Theban fire smashed the containment field on one—or two, or possibly three—of *Saint Helens'* warheads, and her own weapons became her executioners.

Her sister ship *Yerupaja* survived her by a few seconds—long enough to lock her main batteries and her full load of external ordnance on the wounded Theban superdreadnought *Commander Wu Hsin*. The two ships died almost in the same instant, and then the savagery became total.

"More Omega drones, Admiral," Tsuchevsky reported quickly. "Their targeting data is already being downloaded to the remaining SBMHAWKs."

Antonov nodded absently. The data transfer was totally automated: computers talking to each other at rates beyond the comprehension of their human masters while he watched the second wave's leading elements approach the warp point.

"You may commit the reserve pods when you are ready, Commodore Tsuchevsky," he said formally.

Second Admiral Jahanak bared his teeth as his ships charged forward through their own minefields. He'd planned on a close action, but not on one as close as this. Yet with his fortresses gone, he had no choice. Before it died, First Fleet must hurt the enemy as terribly as possible to buy time for the defenders of his home world, and all the careful calculation which had guided his career no longer mattered.

The remaining SBMHAWKs flashed through the warp point, emerging amid the fiery incandescence of dying starships. There weren't many of them, but the ships who led the assault had lived long enough to give them very precise targeting data indeed!

Jahanak cursed as two more superdreadnoughts exploded. The battleships *Jonathan Edwards* and *Ali* followed, but it seemed the infidels' supply of their newest hell weapon had its limits, and First Fleet was in amid the wreckage of the first wave of attackers when the second started through.

X-ray lasers snarled at ranges as low as fifty kilometers—ranges at which it was literally impossible to miss—and hetlasers and force beams smashed back with equal fury. Ships flared and died like sparks from some monster forge, and the superdreadnought *Pobeda*, command bridge demolished by a direct hit, stumbled from the clear zone about the warp point into the impossibly dense Theban minefields and a hundred explosions tore her apart.

Missile fire from the lighter Theban ships—those the SBMHAWKs hadn't targeted—ripped at the attackers' shields, smashing them flat, and scores of *samurai* infantry sleds sped through the carnage.

Hard on their heels came the ships of the Ramming Fleet.

The roar of explosions and the scream of rent metal filled the passageway as the hull-breaching charge ripped through *Dhaulagiri*'s skin. The Marines flattened against the bulkhead in the combat zoots that kept them alive this close to the blast, flinching instinctively from the shock and flying debris, then swung back around even as the Theban boarders appeared, spectral in the smoke. In an instant, the passageway became a hell of explosions, plasma bolts, and hyper-velocity metal in which no unarmored life could have survived even momentarily.

The Shellheads hadn't been able to develop powered armor, Lieutenant Amleto Escalante thought as he blasted one of them down. But they'd produced vac suits with as much armor as Theban muscles could carry, and these boarders were harder to kill than those he'd faced at Redwing. Still, the zoots gave the Marines an overwhelming advantage. Trouble was, an inner corner of his mind reflected dourly, there were so goddamned *many* infantry sleds this time. The improved tracking and computer projections that had placed his unit at the boarders' point of entry had also told them there would be other points of entry. And *Dhaulagiri*'s Marines couldn't be everywhere. Some of the boarding parties would meet unarmored, lightly-armed Navy personnel. Escalante couldn't let himself think about that.

He soon had to.

"Heads up, Third Platoon!" It was Major Oels, commanding the superdreadnought's Marines from her station in Central Damage Control. It wasn't the sort of CP the Book had contemplated before the war, but damage control's holographic schematics gave her the best possible information on a battle like this one.

"Intruders have broken through in Sector 7D." The voice rattled in his earphone. "They're moving around behind you. Watch your six!"

They must know the layout of our ships from the ones they've captured, Escalante had time to reflect before the first Thebans appeared in the passageway intersection behind his position, armed with the shoulder-fired rocket launchers they'd learned to use against zooted Marines. He barked an order, and his odd-numbered troopers turned to face the new threat as the even numbers finished off the first boarders. It was too late for Corporal Kim . . . a rocket took her from behind, and the front of her zoot blasted outward in a shower of wreckage and guts, spraying Escalante's visor with gore.

"*Escalante, if you puke, your rosy pink ass is mine, sweetheart!*" The lieutenant blinked, head suddenly clear. Now what the hell was Sergeant

Grogan, his OCS drill instructor, doing here? But, no, that hadn't been the battle circuit. . . . Half blind and wishing the zoot's gauntlets were any good for wiping, he sent a plasma discharge roaring down the passage towards the Thebans.

What a cluster-fuck, a part of him managed to mutter from some deep inner shelter in the midst of horror.

More and more capital ships emerged from the warp point, battleships fleshing out the superdreadnoughts, and their fire began to tell. Second Fleet paid a terrible price, but its fleet organization was intact, and the Theban squadrons had been harrowed and riven by the preliminary bombardment. Too many beam-armed ships had died; too many datalinks had been shattered. Their surviving ships fought as individuals against the finely meshed fire of Terran squadrons, and two of them died for every Terran they could kill.

Battle-cruisers and heavy cruisers of the Ramming Fleet charged headlong to meet the enemy, and shields and drive fields glared and died in deadly spasms of radiation, but the tide was turning.

The universe stabilized in the flag bridge's main view screen as *Gosainthan* emerged from warp transit into another kind of chaos. Reports poured in faster than living minds, or even cybernetic ones, could absorb them. Antonov sat in his command chair, an immovable boulder of calm amid the electrical storm of tense activity as highly-trained personnel fought to impose some semblance of order.

"Summarize, Commodore Tsuchevsky," he ordered quietly.

"We're mopping up their conventional ships, sir." Tsuchevsky gestured at the read-outs of confirmed kills and observed damage. His brow was beaded with sweat as tension and excitement warred with decorum. "Our losses have been heavy—the first wave is practically all gone, and their ramming ships have been pressing home attacks on the earlier groups of this wave. Many ships report multiple boardings."

"It would seem we need all the firepower at our disposal, Commodore," the admiral rumbled. He touched a stud on his armrest communicator. "Captain Chen, *Gosainthan* will advance and engage the enemy."

"Aye, aye, sir," the flag captain acknowledged. He paused. "Plotting reports that we've already been targeted by at least one enemy ramming ship."

"Fight your ship, Captain," Antonov replied, and leaned back, expressionless. The reactionless drive rose from a soft, subliminal thunder felt through feet and skin to something that snarled with fury, and TFNS *Gosainthan* accelerated into the hell of Lorelei.

✧   ✧   ✧

Jahanak ran his eyes over the status boards one last time and felt almost calm. His fleet was done. More and more infidel ships emerged behind their dying sisters, joining their weaponry to the attack, slaughtering his lighter units. He watched a destroyer division lunge forward in a massed suicide run on an infidel superdreadnought, but they were too small to break through and defensive fire blew them into wreckage.

Only three of his mangled superdreadnoughts survived. At the moment, his light units' ramming attacks were forcing the infidels to ignore his capital ships while they defended themselves, but it was a matter of minutes—possibly only seconds—before that changed.

"Captain Yurah."

"Yes, Second Admiral?"

Jahanak looked into his flag captain's eyes and saw no fear in them. He nodded and drew his own machine-pistol, checking the magazine.

"Send the hands to boarding stations, Captain," he said calmly. "We will advance and ram the enemy."

"Aye, sir," Yurah said, and Second Admiral Jahanak of the Sword of Holy Terra closed his vac suit's visor as his dying flagship charged to meet her foes.

The damage control teams were finishing up and leaving, and the stench of burning was lessening on the bridge. Antonov didn't notice as he absorbed the tale told by the read-outs. Amazing, he reflected, how recently he'd thought of Parsifal as an appalling exercise in mass destruction. His standards in such matters had now changed. Would they change again when he entered the Thebes System?

Essentially, the entire Theban mobile fleet had been annihilated— but at what a cost! Of the twenty-four superdreadnoughts he'd taken into Lorelei, sixteen had been totally destroyed, and most of the survivors, including *Gosainthan*, were damaged in varying degrees. In fact, the flagship had gotten off very lightly compared to some. Only six of the fourteen battleships were total write-offs, but damage to some of the survivors was extensive. And personnel casualties were even heavier than might have been projected from the ship losses— Terran computer projections didn't have vicious boarding attacks by religious fanatics factored into them.

Winnie's precious Duke of Wellington should have been *here*, he thought grimly.

Thank God it had all been over by the time the carriers arrived in the third wave. They were unscathed, and even now Berenson and Avram were leading them in pursuit of the handful of Theban light units that had escaped. But unbloodied strikefighters or not, Second

Fleet would need months to repair its damages, absorb all the new capital ship construction Galloway's World could send and, perhaps most importantly, replenish its stock of SBMHAWKs.

The armrest communicator chimed for attention and Antonov touched the stud, bringing his small com screen alive with a puzzled-looking Pavel Tsuchevsky.

"Admiral," the chief of staff began, "I've been talking to our guests. Admiral Lantu"—by common consent, the Theban still received the title—"has requested permission to speak to you on a matter of utmost urgency."

Antonov scowled. He wasn't really in any mood to talk to the Theban. But—"Put him on, Commodore."

Tsuchevsky stepped aside, and Lantu entered the pickup. Expressions were always difficult to read on alien faces, but Antonov had more practice than most. And he knew haunted eyes when he saw them.

"Admiral Antonov," the slightly odd intonation the Theban palate gave Standard English was more pronounced than usual, and Lantu's voice quivered about the edges, "as you know, I observed the battle with Colonel MacRory. I'm as appalled as you must be by this carnage, and—"

"Get to the point, Admiral," Antonov snapped. He wasn't particularly pleased with himself for his outburst, but he *really* wasn't in the mood for some sort of apology from the Theban. But Lantu surprised him. He drew himself up to his full height (it should have been comical in a Theban, but in Lantu's case it somehow wasn't) and spoke without his previous awkwardness.

"I shall, sir. This slaughter has removed my last doubts: my people must—and will—be defeated. But the kind of suicidal defiance we've all just witnessed is going to be repeated in Thebes. It has to be, only it will be worse—*far* worse—in defense of our home system. If your victory takes too long, or costs too much—well, Colonel MacRory's told me about the debate over reprisals among your political leaders. I can't say it surprises me, and I know the Church *deserves* to perish. But my race doesn't, Admiral Antonov . . . and it will, unless this war can be brought to a quick end." He took a deep breath. "I therefore have no alternative but to place all my knowledge of our home defenses at your disposal."

For a long moment, Antonov and Lantu met each other's eyes squarely. Finally, the massive human spoke.

"I am . . . very interested, Admiral Lantu. I will meet with you, Commodore Tsuchevsky, and my intelligence officer in my quarters in five minutes," He cut the connection, stood, and moved towards the intraship car.

He would be a priceless intelligence asset, he reflected. *But how far can I trust him? How liberated is he, really, from a lifetime's indoctrination?*

There was no way to know—yet. But it was just as well Kthaara was off with the fighter squadrons, a good few astronomical units away!

CHAPTER TWENTY-SIX

"Buy me some time."

Ivan Antonov sat in his quarters, staring sightlessly through the armorplast view port at the glowing ember of Lorelei. His broad shoulders were squared, but the hands in his lap were very still and his mind worked with a strange, icy calm.

There had been few data bases to capture in Lorelei, but the fragments Winnie Trevayne's teams had so far recovered confirmed every word Lantu had said, and the thought of what that meant for his fleet was terrifying.

He stood and leaned against the bulkhead, searching the velvet blackness for a way to evade what he knew must be, but there was no answer. There would be none. The price Second Fleet had paid for Lorelei would pale into insignificance beside the price of Thebes.

He paced slowly, hands folded behind him, massive head bent forward. The far end of Charon's Ferry was a closed warp point. Unlike an open warp point, the gravity tides of a closed point were negligible. Even something as small as a deep-space mine could sit almost directly atop one, and the minefields the Thebans had erected to defend their system beggared anything Ivan Antonov had ever dreamed of facing.

And behind the mines were the fortresses. Not OWPs, but asteroid fortresses—gargantuan constructs, massively armed, impossibly shielded, and fitted with enough point defense to degrade even SBMHAWK bombardments. Dozens of them guarded that warp point. Enough SBMHAWKs could deal even with them, but he didn't have enough. He wouldn't have enough for months, and if Howard Anderson's letters from Old Terra were correct, he didn't have months.

A soft tone asked admittance, and he turned and opened the hatch, watching impassively as Kthaara'zarthan entered his cabin. The midnight-black Orion looked more like Death incarnate than ever, and Antonov studied his slit-pupilled eyes as Kthaara sat at a gesture.

"Well?" the human asked quietly.

"I have studied the intelligence analysis," Kthaara replied equally quietly. "I still do not share your concern for the Thebans, Ivaaan Nikolaaaaivychhh, for the *Zheeerlikou'valkhannaieee* do not think that way, but you and your warriors are Human. You cannot fight with honor if you act contrary to your honor. I accept that. But, clan brother, I do not see how such defenses may be broken in the time you say you have."

"Nor do I," Antonov rumbled, "but I have to find one. And there's only one person who may be able to find it for me."

"It goes against all I know and feel," Kthaara growled, and his ears flattened. "Thebans are *chofaki*, and you ask me to trust the very *chofak* who murdered my *khanhaku*."

"Kthaara Kornazhovich," Antonov said very softly, "the Orions are a warrior race. Has no Orion ever acted dishonorably believing he acted with honor?"

Kthaara was silent for a long, long moment, and then his ears twitched unwilling assent.

"I believe in Admiral Lantu's honor," Antonov said simply. "He did his duty as he understood it—as he had been *taught* to understand it—just as I have and just as you have. And when he discovered the truth, he had the courage to act against the honor he had been taught." The admiral turned back to his view port, and his deep, rumbling voice was low. "I don't know if *I* could have done that, Kthaara. To turn my back on all I was ever taught, to reject the faith in which I was reared, simply because my own integrity told me it was wrong?" He shook his head. "Lantu is no *chofak*."

"You ask too much of me." Kthaara's claws kneaded the arms of his chair. "I cannot admit that while my *khanhaku* lies unavenged."

"Then I won't ask you to. But will you at least sit in on my conversations with him? Will you listen to what he says? I've never admitted helplessness, and I'm not quite prepared to do so now . . . but I feel very, very close to it. Help me find an answer. Even—" Antonov turned from the port and met Kthaara's eyes once more "—from Lantu."

Two very different pairs of eyes locked for a brief eternity, and then Kthaara's ears twitched assent once more.

"I just don't know, Admiral Antonov." Lantu ran a four-fingered hand over his cranial carapace, staring down into the holo tank at the defensive schematic he and Winnifred Trevayne had constructed.

"I helped design those defenses to stop any threat I could envision—I never expected *I'd* be trying to break through them!"

"I understand, Admiral." Antonov raised his own eyes from the display. "We can break them, but it will take time, and our losses will be heavy. Commodore Tsuchevsky and I have studied the projections at length. Against these defenses, we anticipate virtually one hundred percent losses among our first four assault groups, losses of at least eighty percent in the next three, and perhaps forty percent for the remainder of the fleet. We simply do not have sufficient units to sustain such casualties and carry through to victory. We can build them . . . but it will take over a year."

Lantu shivered at the unspoken warning in the human's tone. A year. A year for Thebes to build additional ships and strengthen its defenses still further. A year for humanity's entirely understandable thirst for vengeance to harden into a fixed policy. And when that policy collided with the casualties Second Fleet would suffer . . .

"It's the mines," he muttered, wheeling abruptly from the tank. He folded his arms behind him, frowning at the deck. "The mines. You could deal with the fortresses with enough SBMHAWKs."

"True." Antonov watched the Theban pace. He could almost feel the intensity of Lantu's thoughts, and when he glanced at Kthaara he saw the glimmer of what might someday become sympathy in the Orion's eyes. "If it were an open warp point—if we had even the smallest space to deploy free of mine attack—" He stopped himself with a Slavic shrug.

"I know." Lantu paced faster on his stumpy legs, then stopped dead. His head came up, eyes unfocused, and then he whirled back to the display, and amber fire flickered in his stare.

"If you could break through the mines, Admiral Antonov," he asked slowly, "how long would it take you to prepare your assault?"

"Three months for repairs and to absorb and train new construction already *en route* from Galloway's World," Antonov rumbled, watching the Theban alertly. "But it will take at least a month longer for sufficient new SBMHAWKs to reach us. I would estimate four months. Commodore?"

He glanced at Tsuchevsky, and the chief of staff nodded. He was watching Lantu just as closely as his admiral.

"I see." Lantu rocked on his broad feet, nodding to himself. Then he looked up into Antonov's gaze. "In that case, Admiral Antonov, I think I've found a way to get you into the system."

Ivan Antonov sat before the pickup, recording his message, and his eyes were intent.

"I trust him, Howard," he rumbled. "I have to. No one who meant to betray us would have given us the data he has, and certainly he wouldn't have come up with an idea like this. It's not one we could afford to use often, but it's brilliant—and so simple I don't understand why *we* never thought of it.

"I know you're no longer Minister of War Production, but I need you to send me every tramp freighter you can find. Get them here as quickly as you can, even if you have to tow them on tractors between warp points. They don't have to be much—just big enough to be warp-capable. With them and enough SBMHAWKs, I am confident of our ability to break into Thebes.

"I recognize the stakes, and I will do my best, but even with the freighters and SBMHAWKs, Second Fleet will require at least four months to prepare the assault. It simply is not humanly possible to do it more quickly, and you must restrain the Assembly while we do. I don't know how—I'm no politician, thank God—but you have to."

He stared into the pickup, and his broad, powerful face was granite.

"Buy me some time, Howard. Do it any way you can, but buy me some time!"

Caitrin MacDougall walked slowly down the hall, wondering how her mother had survived five pregnancies. Her own was well advanced, and she hated what it was doing to her figure almost as much as she loved feeling the unborn infant stir. Knowing a new life was taking form within her was worth every backache, every swollen ankle, every moment of totally unanticipated yet seemingly inescapable morning sickness . . . but that didn't mean she liked those other things.

"Hello, Caitrin," a wistful voice greeted her as the door at the end of the hall opened.

"Hi, Hanat."

Hanat held the old-fashioned door for her, and Caitrin sank gratefully into an over-stuffed chair. It was going to be hell to climb out of, but she chose to enjoy its comfort rather than think about that.

The slender Theban woman sat in a chair sized to her tiny stature, like a child sitting at Caitrin's feet, but Caitrin no longer felt like a kindergarten teacher. She'd come to know—and like—Hanat, and though Hanat tried to hide it, Caitrin knew how it hurt to spend her time under virtual house arrest. Yet there was no choice, for Hanat had been Lantu's personal secretary. Her fellow Thebans would have torn her limb from limb—literally—for his "treason," and she would have fared equally badly at the hands of any number of New Hebridans. Virtually every family had deaths to mourn, and the population as a whole had yet to learn how Lantu had fought to reduce the death toll. Even many of those who knew didn't really believe it. And so, in superb if bitter irony, Hanat's only true friend on New Hebrides was not merely a human but the Resistance's second in command!

"How are you, Caitrin?" Hanat asked, folding her hands in her lap with the calm dignity which was like a physical extension of her personality.

"Fine . . . I think. This little monster"—Caitrin rubbed her swollen abdomen gently—"has excellent potential as a soccer star, judging by last night's antics. But aside from that, I'm doing fine."

"Good." Hanat's inner lids lowered, and her voice was soft. "I envy you."

Caitrin nibbled on an index finger, studying the top of Hanat's cranial carapace as she bowed over her hands.

"I got a message chip from Angus last night," she said after a moment. "A long one, for him. I think there were at least ten complete sentences." Hanat laughed, and Caitrin grinned. She loved the sound of Hanat's laughter. It was very human and yet utterly alien, a silver sound totally in keeping with the Theban's elfin appearance.

"He says the admiral is fine. In fact"—Hanat looked up quickly—"he and Colonel Fraymak are working with Admiral Antonov's planning staff."

"Oh, dear," Hanat said softly, folded hands twisting about one another in distress.

"Hanat." Caitrin leaned forward, capturing one of the slender hands despite a half-hearted attempt to escape. "You know he has to."

"Yes." Hanat looked down at the five-fingered hand clasping hers. "But I know what it's costing him, too."

"Just tell me if it's none of my business," Caitrin said gently, "but why don't you ever write him?"

"Because he hasn't written me. It's not seemly for a Theban woman to write a man who hasn't written her."

"Somehow I don't see you as overly burdened by tradition, Hanat."

"I suppose not." Hanat laughed again, sadly, at Caitrin's wry tone. "But he hasn't written on purpose . . . that's why I can't write him."

"Why not? If I'd waited for Angus to say something, we'd've died of old age! Of course, he's not exactly the verbal type, but the principle's the same."

"No, it isn't." Hanat's voice was so soft Caitrin had to strain to hear her. "Lantu loves me—I know he does, and he knows I know—but he won't admit it. Because—" she looked up, and tears spilled slowly down her cheeks "—he doesn't think he's coming back to me, Caitrin. He thinks he's going to die. Perhaps he even *wants* to. That's why I envy you and Angus so."

Caitrin bit her lip, staring into that tear-streaked alien face. Then she opened her arms . . . and Hanat burrowed into them and wept convulsively.

" . . . outrage, Madam Speaker! This wanton bloodshed—this *slaughter* wreaked against helpless civilians—sets the Thebans beyond the pale! Fanaticism must not be allowed to cloak butchery with any semblance of excuse."

Yevgeny Owens paused, and a soft rumble of agreement filled in the space. It was strongest from the LibProgs, Anderson noted—not surprisingly, since Owens was Waldeck's handpicked hatchet man— but a disturbing amount of it came from Erika Van Smitt's Liberal Democrats. And, he admitted unhappily, from his own Conservatives. He made himself sit still, folded hands resting on the head of his cane, and waited.

"Madam Speaker," Owens resumed more quietly, "this isn't the first time humanity has met racial insanity, nor the first time we've paid a price for meeting it. I remind this Assembly that few political leaders of the time could believe the truth about the Rigelians, either. We are told the Thebans have committed these unspeakable atrocities—have resorted to torture, to the murder of parents in order to steal and 'convert' their children, to the cold-blooded execution of entire towns and villages as 'reprisals' against men and women fighting only to protect their world and people—in the name of religion. Of a *religion*, Madam Speaker, which deifies the very planet upon which we stand. And, we are told, that religion was concocted by humans in direct violation of the Edict of 2097.

"Perhaps it was, but what rational species could have accepted such a preposterous proposition? What rational species capable of interstellar travel, with all the knowledge of the universe that implies, could truly believe such arrant nonsense?"

Owens paused again, and this time there was only silence.

"I do not accept humanity's responsibility for this insanity," he finally continued, very softly. "We cannot hold ourselves accountable for the madness of another species, and only a species which is mad could wage 'holy war' against the race which first gave them the blessings of technology in the name of some half-baked agglomeration of pseudo-religious maunderings. But even if humanity is responsible for the unintentional creation of this menace, for providing a race of interstellar sociopaths with the weapons of modern warfare and mass destruction, that does not change the situation we now face. Indeed, if such is the case, are we not confronted by an added dimension of obligation? If our species has, in any way, however unintentionally, helped create the crisis we face, it becomes *our* responsibility to face and accept whatever its final resolution demands of us.

"Madam Speaker, Ladies and Gentlemen of the Assembly, this matter cannot be settled on the basis of what we would like to be true. It can be resolved only on the basis of what *is* true, and the Thebans have proven their irrationality. Events on New New Hebrides and New Boston have proven their murderousness. The most recent Battle of Lorelei has proven their fanaticism. And when a murderous fanatic actively seeks martyrdom, when he is not merely willing but *eager* to die for his cause, then the only defense is to help him find the death he seeks."

The silence was icy as Owens paused a final time, and his eyes swept the Assembly's members from the huge screen behind the Speaker's podium.

"And, Madam Speaker," he finished quietly, "what is true of an individual is a hundred times more true of an entire race of fanatics armed with starships and nuclear weapons. Not merely our own safety but that of the Galaxy itself requires that we override the Prohibition of 2249, and I now move that we so do."

He sat, and Anderson ground his teeth. Owens believed what he'd said; that was what made him so damnably convincing . . . and why Waldeck had chosen him to lead the LibProgs on this issue.

Anderson drew a deep breath and pressed his call key.

"The Chair recognizes President Emeritus Howard Anderson," Chantal Duval said, and he started to rise as his image replaced Owens', then changed his mind. His legs' aching unsteadiness was growing worse, and it made him look feeble at a time when he must show no sign of weakness, allow no suggestion that he spoke from senility rather than clear-minded logic.

"Madam Speaker, Ladies and Gentlemen of the Assembly." He was pleased his voice still sounded strong, at least. "Mister Owens argues that the Thebans are mad. He argues, in effect, that humanity simply provided a vehicle through which that madness might express itself—that if it were not for 'the Faith of Holy Terra' they would have found some other madness to spur their actions. And he argues most cogently that we cannot make decisions on the basis of what we wish were true but only on the basis of what *is* true."

He paused for just a moment, then shook his head.

"He is, of course, correct." A shiver of surprise ran through the Assembly at his admission. "The worst mistake any governing body can possibly make is to allow hopes and expectations to twist its perception of reality. But, ladies and gentlemen, I must tell you that I have already seen *this* governing body do precisely that. Not simply once, but many times."

Feet shifted in a soft susurration of sound, and he smiled thinly.

"Oh, yes, ladies and gentlemen. I am an old man—a very old

man, whom some of you call 'senile'—who has watched the Terran Federation grow and change for over a century. Over a *century*, ladies and gentlemen. I've served it as a naval officer, as president, and now as a member of this Assembly, and I have seen it prove the heights to which all the best in humanity may aspire. I have seen the Federation resist aggression. I've seen it suffer terrible losses and fight through to victory. I have seen it extend the values we hold dear to its member worlds and forge the community of Man across the stars.

"But I have also seen terrible, terrible mistakes. Mistakes made in this very chamber, with the highest of purposes and the most noble of intentions. Mistakes made by good and compassionate people as often as by those less good and more unscrupulous." Across the chamber from him, Pericles Waldeck stiffened angrily, but his face was expressionless.

"Ladies and gentlemen, in 2246 this Assembly made one of those terrible mistakes. It made it for the highest of moral reasons—and for the most base. It elected to endorse the decision embodied in Grand Fleet Headquarters Directive Eighteen, authorizing genocidal attacks on the civilian populations of the Rigelian Protectorate."

The silence was absolute as his wise old eyes swept the chamber.

"We had no choice," Anderson said softly. "That was what we told ourselves. The Rigelians were insane, we said. There were too many worlds of them, and they fought too fanatically. Every Rigelian regarded himself or herself as an expendable asset, and no more honorable end existed for him or her than to die attempting to destroy any being who challenged the supremacy of the Rigelian race. Conquest was virtually impossible; occupation forces would of necessity have been insupportably huge. The casualties we'd already suffered—casualties thousands of times greater than those we have suffered in *this* war—would have been multiplied a thousand-fold again had we sought to invade those worlds . . . and in the end, we would have had to kill them all anyway.

"And so, ladies and gentlemen, the Terran Federation elected not to spend the lives of millions of humans and millions of our Orion and Ophiuchi and Gormish allies. The Federation elected instead to murder entire worlds with massive bombardments—bombardments very like that of New Boston—" spines stiffened at his quiet words "—because our only other option was to kill them one by one on the surfaces of those planets at the cost of too many of our own."

He paused once more, letting what he'd said sink in, then leaned closer to the pickup.

"All of those arguments were valid, but I was here—here in this very chamber, in the midst of the debate—and there was another argument, as well. One that was voiced only in whispers, only by implication, just as it is today. And that argument, ladies and gentlemen, was *vengeance*."

He hissed the last word, eyes locked on Owens' face across the floor, and saw the other man bite his lip.

"I do not say we could have avoided Directive Eighteen. I do not say that we *should* have avoided it. But I do say, as one who was there, that even if we could have avoided it we *would . . . not . . . have . . . done . . . so*." The slow, spaced words were cut from crystal shards of ice, and the old, blue eyes on the master display screen were colder yet.

"We had too many dead. Half a million Terrans at Medial Station. Eight and a half million at Tannerman. One and a third billion on Lassa's World, a billion more in Codalus. A billion Orions on Tol, another ninety million on Gozal'hira, eight hundred fifty thousand in Chilliwalt. Our military deaths alone were over two million, the Orions' were far worse, and we weren't gods, ladies and gentlemen. We wanted more than an end to the fighting and dying. We wanted *vengeance* . . . and we got it.

"Perhaps it was also justice, or at least inevitable. I would like to believe that. I *try* to believe that. But it was more than justice. Our Ophiuchi allies knew that even before we did it. They refused to participate in the bombardments, and for that refusal some of us called them 'moral cowards' . . . until the smoke cleared, and we knew it too.

"And so the same Assembly which authorized Directive Eighteen drafted the Anti-Genocide Prohibition of 2249. Not because it knew it had murdered an entire species when it need not have, but because it was *afraid* it had. Because it had acted in haste and hatred, and it could never know whether or not it might have acted differently. The Prohibition doesn't forbid genocidal attacks, ladies and gentlemen. It simply stipulates that any such future act must be authorized by a two-thirds majority of this Assembly. In a very real sense, the blood debt for our own actions is that the Legislative Assembly must forever more assume—specifically, unequivocally, and inescapably—the responsibility for acting in the same way yet again.

"I had hoped," he said very quietly, "to be dead before a second such decision faced this Assembly. Most of my colleagues of that time are. A few of us remain, and when we look out over this floor and hear what is said, we hear ourselves and the ghosts of our dead fellows. We *know* what those who call for vengeance feel and think, for we have felt and thought those same things.

"But Thebans, ladies and gentlemen, are not Rigelians. They now hold but a single habitable system. We are not speaking of billions of casualties from assaults on planet after planet. And whether they are mad or not, whether their madness would have found a vehicle without the interference of Alois Saint-Just and his fellow survivors or not, the 'religion' which drives them *did* come from humanity. Perhaps they *are* mad, but have humans not shown sufficient religious 'madness' of their own? How many millions have *we* killed for 'God' in our time? Have we learned from our own bloody past? And if we have, may not the 'mad' Theban race also be capable of learning with time?

"I don't know. But remember this, ladies and gentlemen—on New New Hebrides their Inquisition did not, to the best of our knowledge, kill a single child. Certainly children died in the invasion bombardments, and certainly children died on New Boston, but even when entire New New Hebridan villages were exterminated, the children were first removed. We may call this 'stealing children' if we will. We may call preserving children who know their parents have been slaughtered cruelty, or argue that they did it only to 'brainwash' them. But they spared their lives . . . and Rigelians would not have."

He paused yet again, then shook his head slowly.

"Ladies and gentlemen, I can't tell you we can safely spare the Theban race. I can't tell you that, because until we reach Thebes, we simply cannot know. But that, ladies and gentlemen, is the purpose of the Prohibition of 2249—to *force* us to wait, to compel us to discover the truth before we act. And so, with all due respect to Mister Owens, I must ask you to withhold your decision. Wait, ladies and gentlemen. Wait until Admiral Antonov secures control of the Theban System. Wait until we know, beyond a shadow of a doubt, that we have no choice and that we are *not* acting out of vengeance and hatred.

"I am an old man," he repeated softly, "but most of you are not. I have paid my price in guilt and nightmares; you haven't . . . yet. Perhaps, as I, you will have no choice, but don't, I beg you, rush to pay it. Wait. Wait just a little longer—if not for the Thebans, then for yourselves."

He cut the circuit and bowed his head over his folded hands, and utter silence hovered in the vast chamber. Then an attention bell chimed.

"The Chair," Chantal Duval said softly, "recognizes the Honorable Assemblyman for Fisk."

Yevgeny Owens stood. Anger still burned in his face and determination still stiffened his spine, but there were shadows of ghosts in his eyes, and his voice was very quiet when he spoke.

"Madam Chairman, I withdraw my motion pending the outcome of Admiral Antonov's attack on Thebes."

CHAPTER TWENTY-SEVEN

At All Costs

Ivan Antonov walked through the outer reaches of the Thebes System with light-second strides, and occasional asteroids whirled past him like insects. Not many—the Thebans had had generations to clear away a horizontal segment of the belt, as if it had been sliced across by a war-god's sword, and Antonov walked on a "floor" of artificially-arranged space rubble, while over his head there streamed a like "ceiling." Both held asteroids in a far higher density than anything in nature, but they were principally defined by the regularly spaced giant planetoids that had been forged into fortresses of unthinkable strength. Considerations of weapons' ranges and fields of fire had created that pattern, and the precision of its geometry was almost beautiful, like a decorative tracery worked in the dull silver of dim, reflected sunlight that would have been lovely . . . save for the mass death it held.

He turned his two-hundred-thousand-kilometer body on its heel and started back toward the warp point, deep in thought. He reached it in a few steps, and the universe wavered, then dissolved, returning him to the human scale of things, facing the small group of people standing against the outer wall of *Gosainthan*'s main holo tank.

Amazing how good these computer-enhanced simulations have gotten. Of course, this one was Winnie's pride and joy, painstakingly constructed with Lantu's help. He sometimes worried about the day when simulacra this good became commercially available—the sensation could become addictive. . . .

He shook off the thought and addressed his staff. "I have reviewed all aspects of our operational plan and can find no fault with it—except, of course, that it requires a force level that we don't have

244

entirely in place as yet. Still, the build-up is on schedule, and that will soon change."

"True, Admiral." Lantu crossed his arms behind him as he studied the holo display Antonov had just left and gave the softly buzzing hum of a Theban sigh. "Yet I remain somewhat concerned over the one completely uncertain variable. I wish I knew what the Ministry of Production's done about strikefighter development in light of Redwing. I suspect recent events have lent the project rather more urgency than my own earlier recommendations."

He paused, and his yellow eyes met Antonov's with an almost-twinkle, half-apologetic and half-rueful. The human admiral looked back impassively, but there might have been the ghost of an answering twinkle, the commiseration of one professional with a fellow hamstrung by inept, short-sighted superiors. Lantu turned back to the holo with a tiny shrug.

"Of course," he continued wryly, "I haven't exactly been privy to the Synod's decisions *since* Redwing, so I can only offer the truism that knowing a thing can be done is often half the battle in matters of R and D."

Winnifred Trevayne gave the somewhat annoying sniff that, in her, accompanied absolute certitude about her own conclusions. "I don't entirely share First Admiral Lantu's worries, sir. Permit me to reiterate my earlier line of reasoning.

"I don't think there can be any doubt that the Thebans have become well aware of the disadvantages imposed by their lack of fighters, but Lorelei's defenders obviously anticipated a desperate defensive action, as proved by their crustal defense and clearly pre-planned ramming attacks. This was natural, given Lorelei's crucial nature and the fact that the best they can possibly hope for against the Federation's mobilized industrial potential is a defensive war. Anyone prepared to expend *starships* in Kamikaze attacks would certainly have committed fighters to the defense of Lorelei *if they'd had them.*" She glanced at Berenson, who nodded; the intelligence officer had stated simple military sanity.

"We can therefore conclude," she resumed, all didacticism, "that three months ago, when we took Lorelei, the Thebans did not possess fighters—not, at least, in useful numbers. Given this fact, they cannot possibly have built enough of them, or produced sufficient pilots and launch platforms, to make a difference when our attack goes in next month."

She stopped and looked around triumphantly, as if challenging anyone to find a flaw in her argument.

"Your logic is impeccable, Commander," Lantu admitted. "But permit me to remind you of the great limitation of logic: your conclusion can be no better than your premises. And one of your premises disturbs me: the assumption that the Church does, indeed, consider itself on the defensive . . . or, at least, that it did at the time of the Battle of Lorelei."

They all stared at him, speechlessly wondering how the Synod could *not* so regard itself in the face of its disastrous strategic position. All but Antonov, who looked troubled.

Hannah Avram's feet rested inelegantly on the edge of the conference table as she watched the tactical simulation in the tank. It ended, and she grimaced. Dick had gotten her escort carriers up to sixteen units, and according to the tank, she'd just lost thirteen of them.

She rose to prowl *Haruna*'s briefing room, fists jammed into her tunic pockets. The problem was, it all depended on the assumptions she fed the computer. *If* the Thebans followed their own tactical doctrine, and *if* they didn't know about her tiny carriers, then Antonov's devious ploy should get her into Thebes unscathed. And *if* she got in unscathed *and* got beyond shipboard weapon range, her fighters should sting the Shellheads to death, since nothing they had could reach her. If she ran the problem with those assumptions, the computer usually killed no more than three ships. If she changed any one of them, losses climbed steeply. If she changed any two of them, her command was virtually annihilated.

She came to a stop, frowning down into the tank. Her ships were so small, so fragile, without the shields and armor of fleet carriers. In a way, that ought to help protect them—they shouldn't look like worthwhile targets until they launched—but if anyone did shoot at them, they would certainly die.

Yet she'd gone over Antonov's ops plan again and again, and she couldn't argue with any of its underlying assumptions. Based on what they knew and had observed, it was brilliant. The only thing that could really screw it up was for the Shellheads to surprise them with fighters of their own, and she had to agree with the logic of Commander Trevayne's analysis.

But some deeply-hidden uncertainty nagged at her. Worse, she knew it nagged at Antonov, whether he chose to acknowledge it or not.

"*Za vashe zdorovye!*"

Kthaara responded with a phonetic approximation of the Russian toast of which he was extremely proud, but Tsuchevsky mumbled his response, clearly preoccupied.

"What is the matter, Paaavaaaal Saaairgaaiaavychhh?" the Orion asked expansively. As always, his spirits had risen with the approach of decisive action. "Are you still worried by that Theban's misgivings?"

He gave the choked-off snarl that answered to a human's snort of impatience, tossed off his drink, reached for a refill, then offered the bottle to Tsuchevsky. "Come, Paasssha. Why are you fucking a *mairkazh?*"

It was the first time he'd essayed that particular transliteration, and Tsuchevsky sputtered into his vodka, spilling half of it to Kthaara's loud cry of anguish. But Antonov only allowed himself a brief smile. He hadn't shared the contents of Howard Anderson's latest message with the other two. There was no reason why they should have to share his own frustration at acting under politically-imposed time pressure. Besides, Kthaara wouldn't understand. To him, preparation for battle was an annoying necessity; he would never really be able to sympathize with a desire for more of it.

The admiral's slight smile vanished and he brooded down into his glass as he contemplated the machinations of that most loathsome of all human sub-species, the politico. There were, he conceded, occasional true statesmen in human history. Unfortunately, their rare appearances only made the lower orders of political life even more disgusting by contrast. Yevgeny Owens might have withdrawn his motion, but Pericles Waldeck had refused to accept defeat. He'd simply shifted to other, less-principled front men to keep the issue alive, and he was taking gradual toll of the anti-override mood (and, Antonov could tell, of Anderson's health). The attack could be postponed no longer. It would, as he'd just announced to his staff, commence in ninety-six hours.

Damn all politicians to hell! Antonov shook himself and tossed off his vodka. *Cheer up, Vanya! Things could be worse.*

The stupendous asteroid fortresses waited, three and a quarter light-hours from the binary star system's GO component. The distance-dimmed light of Thebes A woke spectral gleams from occasional surface domes and sensor arrays, but the fortresses' teeth were hidden at their iron hearts. It had been the work of decades to clear the cosmic rubble of the star's outermost asteroid belt away from the closed warp point, but the largest lumps of debris had been carefully saved when the rest went to the orbital smelters. The huge chunks of rock and metal, most as large or larger than Sol's Ceres or Epsilon Eridani's Mjolnir, had been bored and hollowed to receive their weapons and station-keeping drives, then towed by fleets of tugs to their new positions.

They floated within their own immense minefields, sullen with power, shielded and armored, fit to laugh at armadas. The Sword of Terra's final mobile units—destroyers and light cruisers, supported by a pitiful handful of superdreadnoughts and battle-cruisers, a scattering

of captured infidel carriers, and the converted freighter "barges"—
the Ministry of Production had cobbled up—hovered behind them,
beyond the projected range of the infidels' new weapons, but it was
the fortresses which mattered. The smallest of those titans was seven
times as powerful as the largest superdreadnought ever built; the
biggest was beyond comprehension, its strength graspable only
through abstract statistics. Once there'd been no doubt of their ability
to smash any attack, but that was before the infidels revealed their
warp-capable missiles.

Now construction ships labored furiously, modifying and refitting
frantically in light of Lorelei. They couldn't possibly finish all they
had to do, and too many of the new systems—the massed batteries
of point defense stations and hastily constructed hangar bays—were
surface installations, for there was no time to bury them deep, but
the engineers and fortress crews had attacked their duties with desperate energy, for the People stood at bay.

The last bastion of the Faith lay behind those forts, and the Holy
Messenger's own degenerate race hovered one bare transit away, poised
to break through in this dark hour and crush the Faith it had abandoned. Beside such horror as that, clean death in Holy Terra's cause
was to be embraced, not feared, for death meant less than nothing
when the fate of God Herself rested in their merely mortal hands.

Ivan Antonov's eyes watched the first-wave SBMHAWKs' cloud of
tiny lights reach the warp point, waver slightly on the display, and
vanish. Then they turned to the other precise clusters of matching
lights, each indicating yet another wave that waited, quiescent.

It was different this time. Each of those waves had not a class of
targets, but a single one.

He glanced across the flag bridge at Lantu, standing with Angus
MacRory. It hadn't been easy to retrieve the data to permit such precise
targeting. No conscious mind—least of all one whose primary concerns had lain in the realms of grand strategy—could hold such a
mass of technical minutiae, and adapting the techniques of hypnotic
retrieval to a hitherto-unknown race had been a heartbreaking labor.
And, of course, however willing he might be, Lantu's subconscious
couldn't yield up what it had never known—such as any last-minute
refitting the forts might have undergone. But what they now knew
should be enough. . . .

Lantu watched a smaller version of the same display through the
cloudy veil of his inner eyelids. He forced his face to remain impassive, and he was glad so few humans had yet learned to read Theban
body language.

The last of the first wave of lights vanished, and he closed his outer lids, as well, wishing he'd been able to stay away. Like Fraymak. The colonel had never questioned Lantu's decision, yet he hadn't been able to bring himself to watch the working out of its consequences. But Lantu couldn't *not* watch. He knew too much about what waited beyond that warp point, knew too many of the officers and men those missiles were about to kill. He had reached an agonizing point of balance, an acceptance of what he must do that had given him the strength to do it . . . but it was no armor against the nightmares. So now he watched the weapons he had forged for the death of the People's defenders, for to do otherwise would have been one betrayal more than he could make. Angus MacRory never said much; now he said nothing at all, but his hand squeezed Lantu's shoulder. He felt it through his shoulder carapace, but he didn't open his eyes. He only inhaled deeply and reached up to cover it with one four-fingered hand.

A wave of almost eager horror greeted the first infidel missile packs. Nerves tightened as the hell weapons blinked into existence and the defenders realized the climactic battle of the People's life was upon them, but at least it had come. At least there was no more waiting.

Captain Ithanad had the watch in Central Missile Defense aboard the command fortress *Saint Elmo* when the alarms began to shriek. His teams were already plotting the emerging weapons, and he swallowed sour fear as he saw the blossoming threat sources.

"All units, engage!" he barked through the alarms' howl.

Second Fleet's SBMHAWKs darted through the minefields virtually unscathed while the fortress crews rushed to battle stations and the first defensive fire reached out. Three squadrons of Theban fighters on standing combat patrol swooped into the mines after them, firing desperately, and a few—a very few—of the wildly dodging packs were killed. But not enough to make a difference. Targeting systems stabilized and locked, and hundreds of missiles leapt from their launchers.

Captain Ithanad paled.

The missile pods weren't spreading their fire. The infidels must have captured detailed data on Thebes, for every one of those missiles had selected the same target: *Saint Elmo*, the very heart and brain of the defenses!

Hundreds of SBMs streaked towards his fortress in a single, massive salvo, and Ithanad's lips moved in silent prayer. Many of them were going to miss; more than four hundred of them weren't.

✧   ✧   ✧

This time the SBMHAWK wasn't a total surprise, and *Saint Elmo* was no mere OWP. Her already powerful anti-missile defenses had been radically overhauled in the four-month delay Jahanak's stand had imposed upon Second Fleet, and not even that colossal salvo was enough to saturate her tracking ability. But it *was* enough to saturate her firepower.

Space burned with the glare of counter missiles. Laser clusters fired desperately. Multi-barreled auto-cannon spewed thousands upon thousands of shells, hurling solid clouds of metal into the paths of incoming weapons. Over two hundred SBMHAWKs died, enough to stop any previously conceivable missile attack cold . . . but almost two hundred got through.

Captain Ithanad clung to his command chair as the universe went mad. Safety straps—straps he'd never expected to need on a fortress *Saint Elmo*'s size—bruised his flesh savagely, and the thunder went on and on and on. . . .

Antimatter warheads wrapped *Saint Elmo* in a fiery shroud, and her surface boiled as her gargantuan shields went down. Fireballs crawled across her like demented suns, gouging, ripping, destroying. Her titanic mass resisted stubbornly, but nothing material could defy such fury.

The long, rolling concussion came for Captain Ithanad and his ratings and swept them into death.

The Sword of Holy Terra stared in horror at the sputtering, incandescent ruin. *Saint Elmo* wasn't—quite—dead. Perhaps five percent of her weapons remained. Which was a remarkable testimonial to the engineers who'd designed and built her, but not enough to make her an effective fighting unit.

And *Saint Elmo* had been their most powerful—and best protected—installation.

Tracking crews aboard the other fortresses bent over their displays, tight-faced and grim, waiting for the next hellish wave of pods.

"Second wave SBMHAWKs spotted for transit, Admiral," Tsuchevsky reported.

"Very well, Commodore." Antonov glanced at the chronometer. "You will launch in three hours fifty minutes."

"Aye, aye, sir." The chief of staff shivered as he turned back to his own displays, wondering what it must feel like to sit and wait for it on the far side of that warp point. He pictured the exquisite agony of tight-stretched nerves, the nausea and fear gnawing at the defenders' bellies, and decided he didn't really want to know.

He glanced at Admiral Lantu, hunched over the repeater display beside a tight-faced Angus MacRory, and turned quickly back to his instruments.

The alarms shrieked yet again, dragging Fifth Admiral Panhanal up out of his exhausted doze as the holo sphere filled with familiar horror. He didn't have to move to see it. He sat on the bridge of the superdreadnought *Charles P. Steadman*, just as he'd sat for almost a week now. He would have killed for a single night's undisturbed sleep or died for a bath, yet such luxuries had become dreams from another life. He stank, and his skin crawled under his vac suit, but he thrust the thought aside—again—and fought back curses as the fresh wave of missile pods spewed from the warp point.

He rubbed his eyes, trying to make himself think, for he was the Sword's senior officer since Fourth Admiral Wantar had died with Fleet Chaplain Urlad aboard *Masada*. That had been . . . yesterday? The day before?

It didn't matter. The devils in Lorelei had pounded his defenses for days, sending wave after wave of hell-spawned missiles through the warp point. They could have sent them all through at once, but they'd chosen to prolong their Terra-damned bombardment, staggering the waves, taunting the Sword with their technical superiority. Each attack was targeted upon a single, specific fortress, mocking the People with the totality of the data they must have captured. The shortest interval between waves had been less than fifteen minutes, the longest over nine hours, stretching the Sword's crews upon a rack of anticipation between the deadly precision of their blows.

He watched his units do their best to kill the pods . . . and fail. He'd brought his precious carriers to within forty light-seconds to maintain heavier fighter patrols, for the fortresses' exposed hangar decks had been ripped away by the crushing, endless bombardment. The fighters had gotten better at killing the pods . . . for a time. But their pilots were too green and fatigued to keep it up, and keeping them on standing patrol this way exhausted them further, yet even as their edge and reflexes eroded they remained his best defense.

The latest attack wave paused suddenly. He shut his eyes as the cloud of missiles slashed towards *Verdun*, the last of his fortresses, and behind his closed lids he saw the storm of defensive fire pouring forth to meet them. A soft sound—not really a moan, but dark with pain—rose from his bridge officers.

Panhanal opened his eyes and turned to the visual display as the terrible flashes died. Then he relaxed with a sigh. *Verdun* had been built into one of the smaller asteroids, and there was nothing left of her. Just nothing at all.

He leaned back, checking the status boards. Half a dozen of the once invincible forts remained, but all were broken and crippled, little more dangerous than as many superdreadnoughts. Indeed, *Vicksburg* and *Rorke's Drift* were less heavily armed than battle-cruisers. Forty years of labor had been wiped away in six hideous days, and Terra only knew how many thousands of his warriors had perished with them. Panhanal didn't know, and he never wanted to.

The infidels would come now that they'd killed the forts. But at least the minefields remained. He tried to cheer himself with that, for he knew what those mines would have done to any assault the People might have made. Yet the infidels had to know about the mines—the precision of their attacks proved they'd known exactly what they faced. And if they knew about them and still meant to attack, then they must think they knew a way to defeat them.

The thought ground at his battered morale, and he prayed his personnel felt less hopeless than he. Of course, the rest of the Sword didn't know Fleet Chaplain Sanak had excused himself briefly from *Steadman*'s flag bridge last night. Not for long. Just long enough to go to his cabin, put the muzzle of his machine-pistol in his mouth, and squeeze the trigger. Panhanal made himself look away from the empty chair beside his own.

"Stand by all units," he rasped.

"Aye, sir. Standing by," his flag captain replied in a hoarse, weary voice.

The neat files of light dots moving slowly toward the warp point in Antonov's display belied the motley nature of the ships they represented.

Against all reasonable expectation, the tramp freighter had reappeared in the interstellar age. The reactionless drive represented a healthy initial investment, but its operating expenses were small, as it required no reaction mass. And the nature of the warp lines meant any vessel that could get into deep space could travel between the stars, so there was a vast number of hulls to be commandeered. The real problem—and the cause of much of the delay—had been the need to equip them with minimal deception-mode ECM so that they could fill the role Lantu had in mind for them. And if they did that, then they were worth every millicredit of the compensation that had been paid to their owners.

Tsuchevsky cleared his throat softly, and Antonov saw the time had arrived. The chief of staff—and, even more so, Kthaara—had been fidgeting for hours, but Antonov had been adamant. The Thebans must have time to feel their exhaustion and despair, just enough for their tense readiness in the wake of the final SBMHAWK salvo to ease a bit.

Now he nodded, and Tsuchevsky began transmitting orders.

Admiral Panhanal's crews had relaxed. Or, no, they hadn't "relaxed" so much as sagged in dull-minded weariness when no immediate attack followed *Verdun*'s destruction. Panhanal knew they had, and even as he tried to goad and torment them into vigilance, his heart wept for them. Yet it was his job, and—

Two hundred superdreadnoughts erupted into the system of Thebes.

The admiral stared at his read-outs in stark, horrified disbelief as entire flotillas of capital ships warped into the teeth of his mines in a deadly, endless stream of insanely tight transits. Not possible! It wasn't *possible*! Not the Satan-Khan himself could have conjured such an armada!

"Launch all fighters!" he barked, and then the visual display exploded.

Despite himself Panhanal cringed away from its flaming fury. He peered at it through his inner eyelids, outer lids slitted against the incandescence, and a tiny part of his weary mind realized something was amiss. Wave after wave of ships appeared, dying in their dozens as the mines blew them apart, but they were dying too quickly. Too easily.

And then he understood. Those weren't superdreadnoughts—they were *drones*! They had to be. Fitted with ECM to suck the mines in if they were under manual control, perhaps, but not real superdreadnoughts, and his blood ran cold as he realized what he was seeing. The infidels weren't "sweeping" the mines; they were *absorbing* them!

He cursed aloud, pounding the padded arm of his chair. His mines were hurling themselves at worthless hulks, expending themselves, ripping the heart from his defenses, and there was nothing he could do about it!

The last freighter vanished into the nothingness of the warp point, and the lead group of the real assault's first wave—five superdreadnoughts converted for mine-sweeping—moved ponderously up. Antonov watched their lights advance, followed by those of the second group—three unconverted superdreadnoughts and three of Hannah Avram's escort carriers.

The lead group reached the warp point, and their lights wavered and went out.

The superdreadnought *Finsteraarhorn* blinked into reality, and the surviving Theban mines hurtled to meet her, but the tramp freighters' "assault" had done its job. Only a fraction of them remained, and *Finsteraarhorn*'s heavy point defense handled the attacking satellites with ease. More ships appeared behind her, and their external ordnance lashed out at the air-bleeding wrecks of the surviving fortresses.

Return fire spat back, x-ray lasers and sprint missiles hammering at pointblank range. The last mines expended themselves uselessly, lasers lacerated armor and hulls, shields went down under the hammer blows of missiles that got through the mine-sweepers' point defense, yet they survived.

Rear Admiral Hannah Avram exhaled in relief as TFNS *Mosquito* made transit behind the superdreadnought *Pike's Peak*. *Mosquito* had survived—and that meant the anti-mine plan had worked.

Her eyes narrowed as her stabilizing plot flickered back to life. The lead group of mine-sweepers streamed atmosphere from their wounded flanks, yet they were all still there, and TFNS *Rainier* followed on *Mosquito*'s heels. The light codes of Theban capital ships blazed, but they were hanging back, obviously afraid Antonov had reserved a "mousetrap" wave of SBMHAWKs as he had in Lorelei. A half-dozen forts were still in action—no, only five, she corrected herself as the avalanche of *Pike's Peak*'s external missiles struck home—and the Shellheads were following their doctrine. They'd never seen her escort carriers, and they weren't wasting so much as a missile on lowly "destroyers" while superdreadnoughts floated on their targeting screens. Now to get the hell out of range before they changed their minds.

"All right, Danny. Course is one-one-seven by two-eight-three. Let's move it!"

"Aye, aye, sir!" MaGuire acknowledged, and she heard him snapping maneuvering orders as the next group of superdreadnoughts and escort carriers made transit behind them. It looked like the dreaded battle was going to be far less terrible than anyone had predicted, especially if—

Her heart almost stopped as the first fighter missile exploded against *Rainier*'s shields.

Admiral Panhanal bared his teeth, bloodshot eyes flaring. The ready squadrons had clearly taken the infidels unaware—there hadn't even been any defensive fire as they closed!—and now *all* of his fighters were launching.

TFNS *Rainier* shuddered as her shields went down and fighter missiles spalled her drive field, and her fighter/missile defense officer stared at his read-outs in shock. Fighters! The Shellheads had *fighters*!

His fingers stabbed his console, reprogramming his defenses to engage fighters instead of missiles, but there was no time. More and more missiles pounded his ship, and the fighters closed on their heels with lasers. He fought to readjust to the end, panic suppressed by professionalism, and then he and his ship died.

"Launch all—*No!*" Hannah chopped off her own instinctive order as Battle Plot's full message registered. Theban fighters speckled the plot, not in tremendous numbers, but scores more were appearing at the edge of detection, *and every one of them was the bright green of a friendly unit!*

She swallowed a vicious curse of understanding. The Thebans had duplicated their captured Terran fighters' IFF as well as their power plants and weapons—and that meant there was no way to tell *her* fighters from theirs!

"Communications! Courier drone to the Flag—Priority One! 'Enemy strikefighters detected. Enemy fighter emission and IFF signatures identical, repeat, identical, to our own. Am withholding launch pending location of enemy launch platforms. Message ends.'"

"Aye, aye, sir!"

"Follow it up with an all-ships transmission to the rest of the task group as they make transit. 'Do not, repeat, not, launch fighters. Form on me at designated coordinates.' "

"Aye, aye, sir. Drone away."

"Tracking, back-plot that big strike. Get me a vector and do it now!"

"We're on it, sir." Commander Braunschweig's voice was tight but confident, and Hannah nodded. More and more Theban fighters crept over the rim of her display, and she looked up at her fighter operations officer.

"You've got maybe ten minutes to figure out how our people are going to keep things straight, Commodore Mitchell."

The message from *Mosquito*'s courier drone appeared simultaneously on Antonov's and Lantu's computer screens, and at effectively the same instant, their heads snapped up. Two pairs of eyes—molten yellow and arctic gray—met in shared horror. No words were necessary; it was their first moment of absolute mutual understanding.

"Commodore Tsuchevsky," Antonov's deep, rock-steady voice revealed how shaken he was only to those who knew him well. "Have communications pass a warning to assault groups that have not yet departed. And give me a priority link to Admiral Berenson."

TFNS *Mosquito* raced away from the besieged superdreadnoughts, followed by her sisters. It took long, endless minutes for all of them to make transit, and Hannah's face was bloodless as she watched the first massed Theban strike smash home. Only a handful of fighters came after her "destroyers," and she forced herself to fight back only with her point defense. Her own pilots would have been an incomparably better defense . . . but not enough better.

Her conscious mind was still catching up with her instinctive response, yet it told her she'd done the right thing. If she'd launched immediately, her fighters might have made a difference in the fleet defense role, but their effectiveness would have been badly compromised by the identification problems. Worse, they would have further complicated the capital ships' fighter-defense problems; the superdreadnoughts would have been forced to fire at *any* fighter, for they could never have sorted out their true enemies. But worst of all, it would have identified her carriers for what they were, and there was no question what the Thebans would have done. Her tiny, fragile ships represented a full third of Second Fleet's fighter strength. Antonov couldn't afford to spend them for no return.

She winced as another Terran superdreadnought blew apart. And a third. She could feel her crews' fury—fury directed at *her* as she ran away from their dying fellows—and she understood it perfectly.

Fifth Admiral Panhanal tasted his bridge crew's excitement. The Wings of Death were proving more effective than they'd dared hope. The infidels had smashed his fortresses and won a space clear of mines in which to deploy, but it wouldn't save them. His strikefighters swarmed about them like enraged *hansal*, striking savagely with missiles and then closing with lasers. They were as exhausted as any of his warriors, and their inexperience showed—their percentage of hits was far lower than the infidel pilots usually managed—but there were many of them. Indeed, if they could continue as well as they'd begun, they might yet hold the warp point for Holy Terra!

He glanced at a corner of his plot, watching the fleeing infidel destroyers, and his nostrils flared with contempt. Only three of his fighter squadrons had even fired at the cowards! If the rest of their cursed fleet proved as gutless . . .

"Well, Commodore?" Hannah asked harshly.

The last of the superdreadnoughts had made transit and the first battleships were coming through. The warp point was a boil of bleeding capital ships and fishtailing strikefighters lit by the flash and glare of fighter missiles, and her own ship was sixteen light-seconds from it. Her rearmost units were less than twelve light-seconds out, but it was far enough. It had to be.

"Sir, I'm sorry, but we can't guarantee our IDs." Mitchell met her eyes squarely. "We're resetting our transponders, which should give us at least a few minutes' grace, but they've got exactly the same equipment. There's no way we can keep them from shifting to match us."

"Understood. But we *can* differentiate for at least a few minutes?"

"Yes, sir," Mitchell said confidently.

"All right. Bobbi, do you have those carriers for me?"

"I think so, sir," Roberta Braunschweig said. "We've got what looks like three or four *Wolfhound*-class carriers—prizes, no doubt—and something else. If I had to guess, they're converted freighters like our barges back in Danzig, but the range is too great for positive IDs."

Hannah turned back to Mitchell. "I know we don't have time to set this up the way you'd like, but I want you to hit those carriers. Retain four strikegroups for task group defense. All the rest go." Her gaze locked with his. "Those carriers are 'all costs' targets, Commodore," she said softly.

TFNS *Baden* reeled under repeated, deafening impacts, and only the bridge crew's crash couches saved them. Most of them. The deck canted wildly for a mad instant before the artificial gravity reassumed control, and the bridge was filled with the smoke and actinic glare of electrical fires.

"Damage control to the bridge!" Captain Lars Nielsen's voice sounded strange through the roaring in his head. His stomach churned as he felt his ship's pain, heard her crying out in agony in the scream of damage alarms, and his hand locked on his quivering command chair's arm as if to share it. She was too old for this. Too old. Taken from the Reserve and refitted to face this horror instead of ending her days in the peace she'd earned.

Another salvo of missiles smashed at her, and drive rooms exploded under their fury. *Baden*'s speed dropped, and Nielsen knew she could never prevent the next squadron of fighters from maneuvering into her blind zone and administering the *coup de grace*.

He stared at his one still-functioning tactical display, eyes bitter as he recognized the amateurishness of the Theban pilots. They should have been easy meat for the fighters aboard the escort carriers—the carriers which had fled almost off the display's edge without even trying to launch.

God damn her. Nielsen was oddly calm as he looked around his ruined bridge and heard, as if from a great distance, the report of more incoming fighters. *God damn her to He—*

The universe turned to noise and flame and went out.

"Admiral Berenson is in position, sir," a haggard Pavel Tsuchevsky reported.

Antonov nodded. He felt like Tsuchevsky looked, but order had finally been re-established. The plan for an operation of this scale was a document almost the size of the annual Federation budget, and changing it at the last moment was like trying to deflect a planet. But the fleet carriers Berenson now commanded had been pulled out of their position in the very last assault groups, moved to the head of the line, and paired off with battle-cruisers. Antonov didn't really want to send them in at all—they would be in combat before their cloaking ECM could be engaged, possibly before their launch catapults could stabilize. But he had no choice. His vanguard was dying without fighter support. Still he hesitated—and, as if to remind him, yet another Omega drone sounded TFNS *Baden*'s death cry.

"Order Admiral Berenson to make transit as soon as possible," he told Tsuchevsky, all indecision gone.

"*Go!*"

Catapults roared with power aboard sixteen tiny ships, and one hundred and ninety-two strikefighters erupted from their hangars. Forty-eight of them formed quickly about their carriers, heavy with external gun packs to supplement their internal lasers. The others streaked away, charging for the Theban carriers just over a light-minute away.

Hannah Avram felt the whiplash recoil in *Mosquito*'s bones and made herself relax. One way or the other, right or wrong, she was committed.

It took Panhanal precious seconds to realize what had happened. His exhausted thoughts were slow despite the adrenalin rushing through him, and the escort carriers were far away and his plotting teams were concentrating on the carnage before them.

Then it registered. Those fleeing "destroyers" weren't destroyers; they were carriers, and they'd just launched against *his* fighter platforms!

He barked orders, cursing himself for underestimating the infidels. There had to have been some reason they'd sent such tiny ships through in their earliest assault groups, but he'd been too blind, too weary and bleary-minded, to realize it.

His own fighters split. Two thirds curved away, racing to engage the anti-carrier strike, and his initial panic eased slightly. They were closer, able to cut inside the attackers and intercept well short of their bases.

Half his remaining pilots streaked towards the infidel carriers themselves. He could see they'd held back at least some of their own fighters for cover, but they didn't have many, and his strike would vastly outnumber them.

His remaining fighters continued to assail the infidel capital ships, yet they clearly lacked the strength to stop battle-line units by themselves. On the other hand, his starships had yet to engage. If he could get in close, bottle the attackers up long enough for his own fighters to deal with theirs and then return . . .

"Shellhead fighters breaking off attack, sir!"

The scanner rating was very young, and Captain Lauren Ethridge didn't feel like reprimanding him for his elated outburst—nor the rest of *Popocatepetl*'s bridge crew for the brief cheer that followed it. They'd been engaged since the instant of their emergence, and the enemy fighters had made up in doggedness what they lacked in tactical polish. Then her scanners told her what Admiral Avram was up to.

Yes, she thought. *Let them have their elation. It won't last anyway.*

"Sir," the same scanner rating reported, this time in a quiet voice, "Theban battle-line units approaching at flank speed." He keyed in Plotting's analysis, and it appeared on the tactical screen. There was no doubt every surviving unit of the Theban battle fleet was coming straight at them.

Shit. Captain Ethridge began giving orders.

"On your toes, people." Captain Angela Martens' voice was that of a rider gentling a nervous horse. She watched the untidy horde racing to intercept her strike, and despite the odds, she smiled wolfishly. They were about to get reamed, and she knew it, but that clumsy gaggle told her a lot about the quality of the opposition. Whatever was about to happen to her people, what was going to happen to the Shellies was even worse.

"Stand by your IFF," she murmured, eyes intent on her display. The lead Thebans were almost upon her, and she felt herself tightening internally. "Stand . . . by . . . *Now!*"

There was a moment of instant consternation in the Theban ranks as their enemies' transponder codes suddenly changed. It should have helped them just as much as the Terrans, but they hadn't known it was coming. And they weren't prepared for the fact that a full half of the Terran fighters were configured for anti-fighter work, not an anti-shipping strike.

The Terran escort squadrons whipped up and around, slicing into them, a rapier in Martens' hand against the clumsy broadsword of her foes.

Fifty Theban fighters died in the first thirty seconds.

The dimly perceptible wrongness in space that was a warp point loomed in TFNS *Bearhound*'s main view screen. David Berenson glowered at it as if at an enemy.

"Ready for transit, Admiral," *Bearhound*'s captain reported. Berenson acknowledged, then swung around to his ops officer.

"Well, Akira, will it be ready in time? And, if it is, will it work?"

Commander Akira Mendoza's face was beaded with sweat, but he looked satisfied. "Sir, I think the answers are 'Yes' and 'Maybe.' The fighters' transponders should be reset by the time we reach the warp point." There was no way for him to know he and Kthaara had, in a few minutes' desperate improvisation, independently duplicated Mitchell's idea. "And it ought to work . . . I hope." He outlined the same dangers Mitchell had set forth for Hannah Avram, but his professional caution fooled no one. He was a former fighter pilot, with his full share of the breed's irrepressible cockiness. So was Berenson, but he was a little older. He nodded thoughtfully as Mendoza finished, then sighed deeply.

"It'll have to do, Akira. We're committed." He leaned back towards his armrest communicator. "Proceed, Captain Kyllonen. And have communications inform Admiral Antonov we are making transit."

Hannah sat uselessly on *Mosquito*'s bridge. It was all in Mitchell's hands now—his and his handful of defending pilots. She watched the AFHAWKs going out as the lightly-armed escort carriers fired, and then her own fighters swept out and up to engage the enemy.

The Theban pilots were tired, inexperienced, and armed for shipping strikes. Fighter missiles were useless against other fighters, and the few without missiles were armed with external laser packs—longer ranged than the Terrans' gun armament and ideal for repeated runs on starships but less effective in knife-range fighter combat. The defensive squadrons closed through the laser envelope without losing a single unit, and their superior skill began to tell. Both sides' craft were identical, but the Terrans knew far more about their capabilities.

Theban squadrons shattered as fighter after fighter blew apart, but there were scores of Theban fighters. Terran pilots began to die, and Hannah bit her lip as the roiling maelstrom of combat reached out to engulf her carriers. *At least they haven't managed to shift their transponders yet.*

It was her last clear thought before the madness was upon her.

Admiral Panhanal fought to keep track of the far-flung holocaust. It was too much for a single flag officer to coordinate, yet he had no choice but to try.

Charles P. Steadman lurched as she flushed her external racks and blew a wounded infidel battleship apart. *Steadman* had only three surviving sisters, but they were unhurt as they entered the fray, and

Panhanal snarled as their heavy initial blows went home. Yet infidel ships were still emerging from the warp point, the forts were gone, and his remaining warp point fighters had exhausted their missiles. They were paying with their lives as they closed to strafe with their lasers, but they were warriors of Holy Terra; the dwindling survivors bored in again and again and again.

Panhanal stole a glance at the repeater display tied into his carriers and blanched in disbelief. The escorting infidel fighters had cut their way clear through his interceptors and looped back, and space was littered with their victims. But his own squadrons had ignored their killers to close on the missile-armed infidels, and fireballs blazed in the enemy formation.

They were better than his pilots—more skilled, more deadly—but there weren't enough of them. A handful might break through to the carriers; no more would survive.

And the infidel carriers were dying. He bared his teeth, aware even through the fire of battle that he was drunk with fatigue, reduced to the level of some primeval, red-fanged ancestor. It didn't matter. He watched the first two carriers explode, and a roar from Tracking echoed his own exultation.

He turned back to the main engagement as *Steadman* closed to laser-range.

Mosquito staggered as missiles pounded her light shields flat. More missiles streaked in, and damage signals screamed as fighter lasers added their fury to the destruction.

Hannah's plot went out, and she looked up at a visual display just like the holo tank. Like the holo tank with a wrong assumption. Six of her ships were gone and more were going, but the Theban strike had shot its bolt.

And then she saw the trio of kamikazes screaming straight into the display's main pickup. A lone Terran fighter was on their tails, firing desperately, and one of the Thebans exploded. Then a second.

They weren't going to stop the third, Hannah thought distantly.

The range fell, and the last battle-line of the Sword of Terra engaged the infidels toe-to-toe. The Theban battleship *Lao-tze* blew up, and the Terran superdreadnought *Foraker* followed. *Charles P. Steadman* shouldered through the melee, rocking under the fire raining upon her and smashing back savagely.

Angela Martens whipped her fighter up, wrenching it around in a full-power turn, then cut power. The Theban on her tail charged past before he could react, and her fire tore him apart. She red-lined the drive, vision graying despite her heroic life support, and nailed yet another on what amounted to blind, trained instinct. Her number two cartwheeled away in wreckage, and Lieutenant Haynes closed on her wing to replace him. They dropped into a two-element formation, trying to find the rest of the squadron in the madness and killing as they went.

The bleeding remnants of Hannah Avram's strike lined up on the Theban carriers, and if more were left than Admiral Panhanal would have believed possible, there still weren't enough. Lieutenant Commander Saboski was strike leader now—the fourth since they'd launched—and he made a snap decision. They couldn't nail them all, but the barges were too slow and weak to escape Admiral Berenson's strikegroups if the big carriers got in.

"Designate the *Wolfhounds*! he snapped, and the command fighter's tactical officer punched buttons and brought the single-seat fighters sweeping around behind it. The strike exploded into a dozen smaller formations, converging on their targets from every possible direction.

Bearhound emerged from the disorientation of warp transit, and the humans aboard her could do little but sweat while her catapults stabilized and her scanners fought to sort out the chaos that was the Battle of Thebes.

Almost simultaneously, Primary Flight Control announced launch readiness and Plotting reported the location and vector of Hannah Avram's escort carriers. Berenson's orders crackled, and *Bearhound* lurched to the recoil of a full deck launch even as she turned directly away from the escort carriers with her escort, TFNS *Parang*. He stared at his plot, watching *Bearhound*'s sister ships fight around in her wake as they made transit, following their flagship through the insanity.

"ECM coming up!" Mendoza snapped, and the admiral grunted. They couldn't get into cloak this close to the enemy, but deception-mode ECM might help. He stared into his display and prayed it would.

"Fighters, Fifth Admiral!"

Panhanal looked up at the cry, and his heart was ice as fresh infidel fighters raced vengefully up the tails of his shattered squadrons and the stroboscopic viciousness of the nightmare visual display redoubled.

The infidel carriers vanished as the data codes of battle-cruisers replaced them. There was a moment of consternation in his tracking sections—only an instant, but long enough for the leading infidels to turn and run while the computers grappled with the deception. Yet warp transit's destabilizing effect on their ECM systems had had its way, and the electronic brains had kept track of them. The data codes flickered back, and the admiral bared his teeth.

"Ignore the battle-cruisers—go for the carriers!"

"Aye, Fifth Admiral!"

Captain Rene Dejardin had heard Winnifred Trevayne's briefings, yet he hadn't really believed it. It wasn't that he doubted her professional competence, but rather that he simply couldn't accept the notion that a race could travel in space, control thermonuclear fusion, and still be religious fanatics of the sort one read about in history books. It was too great an affront to his sense of the rightness of things.

Now, as he tried desperately to fight his carrier clear of the warp point after launching his fighters, he believed.

The Theban superdreadnought bearing down on *Bulldog* showed on visual—*without magnification.* The latest range read-out was something else Dejardin couldn't really believe. Five hundred kilometers wasn't even knife-range—it was the range of claws and teeth. At such a range, *Bulldog's* speed and maneuverability advantage meant nothing. There was no evading the colossus on the view screen. And there was no fighting it—a fleet carrier was armed for self-defense against missiles and fighters; her ship-to-ship armament was little more than a sop to tradition. And the superdreadnought's indifference to the frantic attacks of *Bulldog's* escorting battle-cruiser removed his last doubts as to the zealotry of the beings that crewed her.

Steadman's massed batteries of x-ray lasers fired as one, knifing through *Bulldog's* shields at a range which allowed for no attenuation, and mere metal meant nothing in that storm of invisible energy.

But even as *Bulldog* died, her sisters *Rottweiler, Direhound,* and *Malamute* emerged and began to launch their broods.

The wreckage of the anti-carrier strike fell back, fighting to reform, and Captain Martens cut her way through to them. The Thebans broke off, desperate to kill their attackers yet forced to retreat to rearm. They had to use the barges; none of the carriers remained.

Thirty-one of the one hundred forty-four attacking fighters escaped.

Hannah Avram dragged herself back to awareness and pain, to the sliminess of blood flowing from her nostrils and lungs filled with slivered glass, and knew someone had sealed her helmet barely in time.

She pawed at her shockframe. Her eyes weren't working very well—they, too, were full of blood—and she couldn't seem to find the release, and her foggy brain reported that her left arm wasn't working, either. In fact, nothing on her left side was. Someone loomed beside her, and she blinked, fighting to see. The vac suit bore a captain's insignia. Danny, she thought muzzily. It must be Danny.

A hand urged her back. Another found the med panel on her suit pack, and anesthetic washed her back into the darkness.

TFNS *Gosainthan* emerged into reality at the head of Second Fleet's last five superdreadnoughts. Ivan Antonov remained expressionless as he waited for communications to establish contact with Berenson. Preliminary reports allowed him to breathe again as he studied the plot while Tsuchevsky collated the flood of data. The Theban fighters still on the warp point were a broken, bewildered force, he saw grimly, vanishing with inexorable certainty as Berenson's pilots pursued them to destruction.

Gosainthan's heading suddenly altered, and he glanced at his tactical read-outs as Captain Chen took his ship and her squadron to meet the surviving Theban superdreadnoughts. The admiral nodded absently. Yes . . . things could, indeed, be worse.

"The Wings are rearming, sir. They'll begin launching again in seven minutes."

Admiral Panhanal grunted approval, but deep inside he knew it was too late. Those cursed small carriers had diverted him, sucking his fighters off the warp point just in time for the fleet carriers to erupt into his face. Five of the newcomers had been destroyed, others damaged, but they'd gotten most of their fighters off first. And enough survived to rearm every infidel fighter in the system.

He'd lost. He'd failed Holy Terra, and he stared with burning, hate-filled eyes at the fleeing fleet carriers and the battle-cruisers guarding their flanks. He was so focused on them he never saw the trio of emerging infidel superdreadnoughts that locked their targeting systems on *Charles P. Steadman*'s broken hull.

For the first time in far too many hours, David Berenson had little enough to do—acknowledge the occasional report of another Theban straggler destroyed, keep Antonov apprised of the pursuit's progress— that he could sit on *Bearhound*'s flag bridge and look about him at the system that had been their goal for so long.

Astern lay the asteroid belt, with its awesomely regular cleared zone, where Antonov had wiped out the last of the Theban battle-line. *Must tell Commander Trevayne how accurate her holo simulation turned out to be,* he thought with a wry smile. Ahead gleamed the system's primary stellar component, a G0 star slightly brighter and hotter than Sol, whose fourth planet had been dubbed Thebes by that extraordinary son-of-a-bitch Alois Saint-Just. The red-dwarf stellar companion, nearing periastron but still over nine hundred light-minutes away, was visible only as a dim, ruddy star.

"Another report, Admiral." Mendoza was going on adrenalin and stim pills, but Berenson hadn't the heart to order him to get some rest. "A confirmed kill on the last fighter barge."

Berenson nodded, and a small sigh escaped him. The destruction of the remaining Theban mobile forces had been total. The TFN now owned Theban space. The beings who ran the planet that lay ahead now had no hope at all and would surely surrender. Wouldn't they?

CHAPTER TWENTY-EIGHT

A World at Bay

Fire wracked the skies of Thebes as the planet's orbital fortresses died.

Ivan Antonov had no intention of allowing those fortresses to figure in whatever action he finally took—or was required by his political masters to take—with respect to the planet. Nor did he have any intention of bringing his surviving capital ships within range of the weapons mounted by those forts and the planet they circled. Even assuming that the planetary defenses had not been strengthened since Lantu's fall from grace (and Antonov cherished no such fatuous assumption), Thebes was best thought of as a fortress itself—a world-sized fortress with gigatonnes of rock to armor it and oceans to cool the excess heat produced by its titanic batteries of weapons.

So Second Fleet stood off and smashed at the orbital forts with SBMs. Fighters also swooped in, their salvos of smaller missiles coordinated with the SBMs to saturate the Theban defenses. They took some losses from AFHAWKs, but the forts had no fighters with which to oppose them. The drifting wreckage to which Second Fleet had reduced the enormous Theban orbital shipyards would build no more, and all of Thebes' limited number of pilots had been committed to the captured carriers and barges . . . and died with them.

Everyone made a great production of stressing that point to Winnifred Trevayne: the Shellheads' fighter strength *had* been limited after all. It didn't help. She might sometimes fall into anguished indecision when lives were *immediately* at stake—her well-hidden but painfully intense empathy, Antonov had often reflected, would have made her hopeless as a line officer—but in the ideal realm of logic, with the actual killing still remote enough to admit of abstraction, her conclusions were almost always flawless. It was a weakness, and a strength, of which she was fully cognizant. Yet this time a misassessment of a mentality utterly foreign to her own had led her to a conclusion as inaccurate as it was logical. No one blamed her for the lives which had been lost . . . no one but herself.

It worried Antonov a little. Irritating as her certainty could sometimes be, she would be no use to him or anyone else if she lost confidence in her professional judgment. So it was with some relief that he granted her uncharacteristically diffident request for a meeting with him, Tsuchevsky, and Lantu.

"Admiral," she began, still more subdued than usual but with professional enthusiasm gradually gaining the upper hand, "as you may recall, the captured data base that gave us our first insights into Theban motivations contained statements suggesting that the flagship of the old colonization fleet had survived to the present day, and serves as the headquarters and central temple—the 'Vatican,' if you will—of the Church of Holy Terra."

"I seem to remember something of the sort, Commander. But it didn't seem very important at the time."

"No, sir, it didn't. That was one reason I didn't emphasize it; another was that I wasn't really sure, then, although it seemed a fairly short inference. But now Admiral Lantu has confirmed that that ship, TFS *Starwalker*, does indeed still rest where it made its emergency landing. It will never move under its own power again, but its computers are still functional." She paused, and Antonov gestured for her to continue. He wasn't sure where she was going, but she was clearly onto something, and she seemed more alive than she had since the battle.

"You may also recall that in the course of analyzing that data base, I sent back from QR-107 to Redwing for the records of the original colonization expeditions in this region. What I got was very complete—the old Bureau of Colonization clearly believed in recording *everything*. Including—" she leaned forward, all primness dissolving in a rush of excitement "—the access codes for *Starwalker*'s computers!"

Suddenly, Antonov understood.

"Let me be absolutely clear, Commander. Are you telling me it may be possible to access those computers from space?"

"But, Admiral," Tsuchevsky cut in, "surely the Thebans have changed the codes over all these generations. And even if they haven't . . . is such remote access really possible?"

"It wouldn't be possible if *Starwalker* were a warship, or even a modern colony ship, Commodore," Trevayne admitted, answering his second question first, "but BuCol built her class—and their

computers—before we ever ran into the Orions, back when humanity believed the Galaxy was a safe place." She made a slight moue
at Tsuchevsky's snort, dark eyes twinkling for the first time in much
too long.

"I know. But because they believed that, they were more concerned
with efficiency than security, and her computers don't have the security programming imperatives and hardware ours do. In fact, they were
designed for remote access by other BuCol ships and base facilities. And
as for the Thebans changing the codes . . . my technical people tell me
it would be extremely difficult. We're talking about a combined hardware *and* software problem, which would require almost total reprogramming. Assuming"—her eyes glowed—"that they'd ever even
considered the possibility of its being necessary!"

"Even if it were possible," Lantu said slowly, "the Church won't have
done it." He gave a brief Theban smile as they turned to him. "Everything about that ship is sacred; even the damage she suffered before
setting down has been preserved unrepaired. The successive prophets
have locked all the data pertaining to the Messenger's—to Saint-Just's—
lifetime, but if they tried to change it in any way the entire Synod would
rise up in revolt."

"So," Antonov mused in an even deeper voice, "we can steal all that
data. . . ."

"Or wipe it," Tsuchevsky stated bluntly.

Antonov almost smiled at the looks on Trevayne's and Lantu's faces.
He was learning to read Theban expressions—and Lantu was clearly
still capable of being shocked by sufficiently gross sacrilege against
a faith in which he no longer believed. And as for Winnie . . . Antonov
had a shrewd notion of what was going on behind that suddenly
stricken face.

Tsuchevsky saw it, too.

"Well," he said a bit defensively, "consider what a body blow it would
be to Theban morale. Not to mention the confusion caused by the
loss of all the information they may've added to those data bases more
recently."

"No," Antonov said quietly. "I will not permit any attempt to wipe
the data. Its historical value is simply too great. And the morale effect
might be the opposite of what you suppose, Pavel Sergeyevich—sheer
outrage might make them fight even harder." He turned to Trevayne.
"Commander, you will coordinate with Operations and prepare a
detailed plan for covertly accessing *Starwalker*'s computers."

"Aye, aye, sir." Her dark eyes glowed. "Now we'll *know*—not merely
be able to infer—what *really* happened on Thebes!"

And confirm that your analysis was right all along. This time Antonov
did allow himself a small smile.

✧   ✧   ✧

Father Trudan groaned, rubbing his cranial carapace and wishing the lights weren't quite so bright. He hated the late-night shift, and never more than now. Panic hung over Thebes like a vile miasma, creeping even into *Starwalker*'s sacred precincts, yet at this moment the priest was almost too tired to care. His own gnawing worry ate at his reserves of strength, and the Synod's insatiable demands for data searches robbed him of sleep he needed desperately, despite his nightmares.

He lowered his hands, cracking his knuckles loudly, and his expression was grim. Terra only knew what they hoped to find. They'd been back through every word the First Prophet had ever written, searching frantically for some bit of Holy Writ to answer their need. Indeed, he suspected they'd delved even deeper, into the locked files left by the Messenger himself, but he couldn't be certain. Only Synod members, and not many even of them, had access to *those* records, and—

Trudan's thoughts broke off, and he frowned at his panel. He'd never seen that particular prompt before. In fact—he rubbed his muzzle, cudgeling his weary brain—he didn't even know what it meant. How peculiar!

The prompt blinked a moment, then burned solid green, and bemusement became alarm. He was one of the Synod's senior computer techs; if *he* didn't know what it meant, it must be one of the functions restricted to Synod members. But what in Terra's name did it do? And why was it doing it *now*?

He checked his board, assuring himself none of the other computer stations were manned, and disquiet turned rapidly to fear. He scrabbled for the phone and punched in Archbishop Kirsal's number.

"Your Grace? Father Trudan. I realize it's late, but something strange is happening on my board." He listened, then shook his head. "No, Your Grace, I don't know what it is." He listened again and nodded sharply. "Yes, Your Grace. I definitely think you'd better come see it for yourself."

He hung up, staring at his panel, and the mysterious prompt continued to blaze. He watched it, praying the archbishop would hurry and wondering what "RMT ACC ENG" meant.

First Admiral Lantu looked physically ill. His eyes were haunted, and his short, strong body hunched as he rested his feet on the stool before his human-size chair. Now he looked into Ivan Antonov's bedrock face as Winnifred Trevayne stopped speaking, and the pain in his alien expression stirred a matching sympathy in the burly admiral. He knew, as a Russian, too well how "history" could be manipulated to serve the needs of a ruling clique.

"I must agree with Commander Trevayne," Lantu said quietly. He drew a deep breath. "The First Prophet was either mad...or a tyrant who seized his chance. This"—his four-fingered hand gestured to his own copy of the report—"is no mere 'error'; it's a complete and utter fabrication."

Antonov grunted agreement and looked back down at the matching folder before him. Alois Saint-Just's soul must be writhing in Hell over what had been wrought in his name, and in a way, he almost hoped it was. Whatever the man's original intent, he'd contributed directly to the creation of a monster almost beyond belief.

"So." His deep voice was a soft, sad rumble as he touched the printed hardcopy. "You and Commander Trevayne are both convinced Saint-Just never mentioned religion at all."

"Of course he didn't," Lantu said harshly. "His own journal entries show he never claimed Terra was divine. He emphasized the desperation of the Federation's plight again and again, but every word he said made it perfectly clear Terrans were mortal beings, despite the superiority of their science." The Theban gave a short, bitter bark of laughter. "No wonder Sumash's fellow 'disciples' were horrified when he proclaimed Terra's divinity! They knew the truth as well as he did—*damn* his soul to *Hell!*"

His voice was raw with agony and hate, and more than one set of eyes turned away from his distress. Kthaara'zarthan's did not. They rested enigmatically on his anguished face, and they were very still.

"The First Admiral is correct, sir," Trevayne said softly. "We can never know why Sumash did it, but he knowingly set about the construction of an entirely falsified religious edifice only after the last Terran died. There is absolutely no hint of divinity in any of the records predating Saint-Just's death, yet the fusion of so many different elements of Terran history into 'the Faith of Holy Terra' couldn't have been accidental. Someone clearly researched the historical sections of *Starwalker's* data base to concoct it, and that someone could only have been Sumash. He'd eliminated all other access to the records...and anyone who might have disputed his version of what they held."

"But the Synod *must* know!" Lantu protested. "They have access to the forbidden sections. They have to know it's all a lie! They—" Angus MacRory's big hand squeezed his shoulder, and he bit off his outburst with visible effort.

"They do," Trevayne confirmed, "but not all of them. Only the current Prophet and those he designates have access to the original documentation. Those designations are made not on the basis of seniority but on the basis of who he trusts, and there's substantial evidence that on the occasions when his trust has been misplaced, the weak link has been quietly eliminated. I've analyzed the security lists. Eleven prelates have died of unspecified 'natural causes' within one week of gaining access."

Lantu was silent, but his teeth ground as he remembered Manak's death. The old man hadn't known. He must have known the Church edited the information it transmitted to its flock, but there'd been too much integrity in his soul for him to have lived such a lie. And that very integrity—that unshakable faith in the lie—had killed him.

"But why didn't they just wipe the original evidence?" David Berenson wondered aloud. "No matter how tight their security, they must have known there was a chance it would leak."

"Human history, Admiral Berenson," Antonov said flintily, "abounds with megalomaniacs who chose to preserve information they suppressed. I see no reason to assume a megalomaniacal Theban should act any more rationally."

"In a sense, they probably had no choice," Trevayne suggested. "Not after the first generation or so, anyway. This is the seminal holy writ, Admiral Berenson, the most sacred of all their texts. Even if no one's allowed to read it, their programmers know it's there—and they might know if it had been destroyed. If it were, and the news got out, it would do incalculable damage."

"Which suggests at least one interesting possibility," Tsuchevsky mused.

"It wouldn't work, Commodore," Lantu rasped. Tsuchevsky raised an eyebrow, and the first admiral shrugged. "I assume you're referring to the possibility of using the truth to discredit the Synod?" Tsuchevsky nodded. "Then I'm afraid you underestimate the problem. All of you are 'infidels' in the eyes of the Church and so of the entire Theban race—and I, of course, would be an even more detestable heretic. They know they can't win, yet they're still digging in to fight to the death. If we tell such 'faith-filled' people the truth, it will be seen only as clumsy propaganda inspired by the Satan-Khan. The sole effect would be to fill the People with an even greater hatred for us all as defilers of the Faith."

"Then you see no hope of convincing Thebes to accept the truth and surrender," Antonov said flatly.

"None," Lantu replied even more flatly. He rubbed his face with both hands, and his hopeless voice was inexpressibly bitter. "My entire race is prepared—almost eager—to die for a lie."

The medical shuttle hatch opened. It was summer on New Danzig, a day of dramatic clouds pierced by sunlight, and the moist scent of approaching rain blew over the attendants guiding the litter down the ramp.

The woman in it stared up at the clouds, brown eyes hazy, lying as still as the dead. As still as the many dead from this planet she had left behind her, she thought through the drugs which filled her system. Tears gleamed, and she tried to brush them away with her right hand. She couldn't use her left hand; she no longer had a left arm.

Her right arm stirred, clumsy and weak, and one of her attendants pressed it gently back and bent over her to dry them. She tried to thank him, but speech was almost impossible.

Hannah Avram closed her eyes and told herself she was lucky. She'd been a fool not to seal her helmet when the fighters came in, and she'd paid for it. The agony in her lungs before Danny drugged her unconscious had told her it had been close, but it had been closer than she'd known. She owed MaGuire her life, yet not even his speed had been enough. A fragment of her right lung remained; the left was entirely ruined. Only the respirator unit oxygenating her blood kept her alive.

A warm grip closed on her remaining hand, and she opened her eyes once more and blinked at Commodore Richard Hazelwood. His face was so drawn and worried she felt a twinge of bittersweet amusement. The medship's staff had gotten her stabilized, but they'd decided to leave the actual lung replacement to a fully-equipped dirtside hospital, and he'd apparently thought she was in even worse shape than she was.

Her litter moved around the base of the shuttle pad, and she twitched at a sudden roar. She stared up at Hazelwood, lips shaping the question she had too little breath to ask, and he said something to the medics. They hesitated a moment, then shrugged, and one of them bent over the end of the self-propelled unit. She touched a button and the litter rose at an angle, lifting Hannah until she could see.

She stared in disbelief. Hundreds of cheering people—thousands!—crowded the safety line about the pad, and the thunder of their voices battered her. There were Fleet personnel out there, but most were civilians. Civilians—cheering for the stupid bitch who'd gotten so many of their sons and daughters killed!

The sea of faces blurred and shimmered, and Dick was beaming like a fool and making it a thousand times worse. She tugged at his hand and forced her remaining fragment of lung to suck in air despite the pain as he bent.

"Wrong," she gasped. The word came out faint and thready, propelled by far too little breath, and she shook her head savagely. "Wrong. I . . . lost your . . . ships!" she panted, but his free hand covered her mouth.

"Hush, Hannah." His voice was gentle through the cheering that went on and on and on, and her mind twisted in anguish. Didn't he *understand?* She'd lost twelve of her carriers—*twelve* of them! "They know that—but you won the battle. *Their* people won it. They didn't die for nothing, and you're the one who made that possible."

She could no longer see through her tears, and her attendants lowered her back to the horizontal, moving her toward the waiting ambulance vertol, but she refused to let go of his hand. He walked beside her, and when her lips moved again he bent back over her once more.

"Something . . . I never . . . told you," she got out, "when I . . . took com—"

His hand hushed her once more, and she blinked away enough tears to see his face. His own eyes glistened, and he shook his head.

"You mean the fact that you were only frocked to commodore?" he asked, and her eyes widened.

"You . . . know?"

He climbed into the vertol beside her, still holding her hand. The hatch closed, cutting off the surf-roar of voices, and he smiled down at her.

"Hannah, I always knew," he said softly.

The Legislative Assembly sat in dreadful silence. President Sakanami had come to the floor to make his report in person, and every eye stared at him in horror as he stood at Chantal Duval's podium. Second Fleet's losses had been so terrible even the announcement that Ivan Antonov now controlled Theban space seemed almost meaningless.

Howard Anderson hunched in his chair, cursing the weakness which had become perpetual, and tried not to weep. Better than any of these politicians, he knew—knew bone-deep, in his very marrow—what Second Fleet had paid. He had commanded in too many battles, seen too many splendid ships die. He closed his eyes, reliving another terrible day in the Lorelei System. The day he'd cut the line of communication of an Orion fleet which had driven deep into Terran space during ISW-2, sealing a third of the Khanate's battle-line in a pocket it could not escape. Ships had died that day, too—including the superdreadnought *Gorbachev*, the flagship of his dearest friend . . . and his only son's command.

Oh, yes, he knew what Second Fleet had paid.

" . . . and so," Sakanami was saying heavily, "there is no indication of a Theban willingness to yield. Admiral Antonov has summoned the 'Prophet' to surrender, and been rebuffed. He has even threatened to disclose the contents of *Starwalker*'s secret records, but the Prophet rejects his threat. Apparently they realized those records had been accessed, for they have already begun a campaign to prepare their people for 'falsehoods and lies which may be spread by the Satan-Khan's slaves.' "

A grim, ominous rumble filled the chamber, and Anderson's hands tightened on his cane. Sakanami was being as noninflammatory as he could, but the hatred Waldeck's LibProgs had stoked for months hung in the air, thick enough to taste. However dispassionately the president might report, his every word only fed its poisonous strength.

"At present," Sakanami continued, "Admiral Antonov has invested the planet from beyond capital missile range. The planetary defenses, however, are so powerful that the collateral damage from any bombardment which might destroy them would render Thebes . . . uninhabitable."

He drew a deep breath in the silence.

"That concludes my report, Madam Speaker," he said, and sat.

An attention bell chimed.

"The Chair recognizes the Honorable Assemblyman for Christophon," Chantal Duval said quietly, and Pericles Waldeck appeared on the huge screen.

"Madam Chairman, Ladies and Gentlemen of the Assembly," the deep voice was harsh, "our course is plain. We have made every effort to spare the Theban race. We have suffered thousands of casualties in fighting our way into their system. Their position is hopeless, and they know it. Worse, their own leaders know their so-called 'religion' is, in fact, a lie! Yet they refuse to surrender, and we cannot" —must not—leave madmen such as they have proven themselves to be the power ever to threaten us again."

He paused, and Anderson heard the Assembly's hatred in its silence.

"There has been much debate in this chamber over the Prohibition of 2249," he resumed grimly. "Some have striven mightily to spare the Thebans from the consequences of their crimes against the civilized Galaxy. They are an immature race, it has been said. Their atrocities stem from a religious fervor they might outgrow with time. Whatever their crimes, they have been *sincere* in their beliefs. And now, ladies and gentlemen, now we see that it is no such thing. Now we see that their leadership has known from the outset that their 'jihad' was born in falsehood. Now we know their fanaticism, however real, has been forged by a cold and calculating conspiracy into a tool for interstellar conquest—not in the name of a 'god' but in the name of *ambition*.

"Ladies and Gentlemen of the Assembly, it is time to do what we know in our hearts we must! They themselves have forced our hand, for if their space industry has been destroyed, their planetary industry has not. We know they must now have sensor data on the strategic bombardment missile. With that data, it is only a matter of time before they develop that weapon themselves. Every day we hesitate increases the chance of that dire event, and when it comes to pass, ladies and gentlemen, when those massive defense centers are able to return fire with thousands upon thousands of launchers, the cost of crushing them will be inconceivable."

He paused again, and his voice went cold and flat.

"If this mad-dog regime is not destroyed, such battles as Second Fleet has fought may be forced upon us again and again and again. There cannot be—*must not be*—any compromise with that threat. A landing attempt against such powerful defenses would incur unthinkable casualties, and the bombardment required to cover it would effectively destroy the planet anyway. Invasion and occupation are not tenable options, but at this moment in time Second Fleet can bombard the planet from beyond the range of any weapon they possess. We must act *now*, while that advantage still exists, for we have no choice.

"Ladies and Gentlemen of the Assembly, I move for an immediate vote to override the Prohibition of 2249, and to direct Admiral Antonov to execute a saturation bombardment of the Theban surface!"

The delicate balance for which Anderson had fought, the tenuous restraint he had nursed so long, crumbled in a roar of furious seconds it took Chantal Duval ten minutes to calm, and Howard Anderson's heart was chill within him.

"Ladies and Gentlemen of the Assembly," the Speaker said when silence had finally been restored, "it has been moved and seconded that this Assembly override the Prohibition of 2249 and direct Admiral Antonov to bombard the planet of Thebes." She paused for a heartbeat to let the words soak in. "Is there any debate?" she asked softly.

Anderson prayed someone would speak, but not a single voice protested, and he cursed the fate which had let him live this long. Yet the stubborn will which had driven him for a century and a half drove him still, and he pressed the button.

"The Chair," Duval said, "recognizes President Emeritus Howard Anderson."

Anderson tried to rise, but his legs betrayed him, and he heard a soft ripple of dismay as a lictor appeared magically at his elbow to catch his frail body and ease him back into his chair. For once, the "grand old man of the Federation" felt no anger. He was beyond that, and he sat for a moment, gathering his slender store of strength as the same lictor adjusted his pick-up so that he need not stand.

Silence hovered endlessly until, at last, he began to speak.

"Ladies and gentlemen." His strong old voice had frayed in the past half year, quivering about the edges as he forced it to serve his will.

"Ladies and gentlemen, I know what you are feeling at this moment.

The Federation has poured out its treasure and the lives of its military protectors to defeat the Thebans. Civilians have died in their millions. The price we have paid is horrible beyond any mortal valuation, and now, as Mister Waldeck says, we have come to the final decision point."

He paused, hoping the assembly would think it was for emphasis without recognizing his dizziness and fatigue. He was so tired. All he wanted was to rest, to pass this burden to another. But there was no one else. There was only one sick, tired old man who had seen too much killing, too many deaths.

"Ladies and gentlemen, I can't tell you he's wrong about the current Theban regime, for the truth is that it is every bit as fanatical, every bit as corrupt, as he would have you think. Not all of it, but enough. More than enough, for the portion which is those things controls the Church of Holy Terra and, through it, every Theban on their planet.

"Yet they control them through *lies*, ladies and gentlemen." Flecks of the old sapphire fire kindled in his eyes, and his wasted frame quivered with his desperate need to make them understand. "The mass of the Theban people *do* believe in 'Holy Terra,' and it is through that belief that the Prophet and his inner clique—a clique which is only a fraction of their entire Synod—drive and manipulate them. The people of Thebes haven't rejected surrender; their religious leader— their *dictator*—has rejected it in their name!"

He leaned into the pick-up, braced on his cane, and his lined face was cold. His strength slipped through his fingers, and he no longer sought to husband it. He poured it out like water, spending it like fire.

"Ladies and Gentlemen of the Assembly," his voice lashed out with the old power, "the human race does not murder people who have been duped and lied to! The Terran Federation does not murder entire worlds because a handful of madmen hold their populations in thrall!"

He struggled to his feet, shaking off the anxious lictor, glaring not into the pick-up but across the chamber at Pericles Waldeck as he threw all diplomatic fiction to the winds.

"Whatever the Thebans may be, *we* are neither mad nor fools, and this Assembly will be *no one's* dupe! We will remember who we are, and what this Federation stands for! If we do not extend justice to our foes, then we are no better than those foes, and the genocide of an entire race because of the twisted ambition of a handful of insane leaders is *not justice*. It is a crime more heinous than any the Thebans have committed. It is an abomination, an atrocity on a cosmic scale, and I will not see murder done in the name of my people!"

His knees began to crumble, but his voice cracked like a whip.

"Ladies and Gentlemen of the Assembly, Pericles Waldeck would have you stain your hands with the blood of an entire species. He may drape his despicable deed in the cloak of justice and the mantle of necessity, but that makes it no less vile." His vision began to blur, but he peered through the strange mist, watching fury crawl across Waldeck's strong, hating features, and hurled his own hate to meet it.

"Ladies and gentlemen, one man, more than any other, wrought this disaster. One man led his party into dispatching the Peace Fleet to Lorelei. One man crafted the secret orders which placed Victor Aurelli—*not Admiral Li*—in command of that fleet's dispositions!"

The fury on Waldeck's face became something beyond fury, deeper than hatred, as a chorus of astonished shouts went up. The younger man rose, glaring madly across the floor, and the lictor pressed the emergency button on his harness. He tried to force Anderson back into his seat, and a white-coated medic was running across the floor, but the wasted old man clung to the edge of his console and his voice thundered across the tumult.

"*One man*, ladies and gentlemen! And now that *same* one man calls on *you* to cover his stupidity! He calls upon you to destroy a planet not to save the Galaxy, not to preserve the lives of Second Fleet's personnel, but out of *ambition*! Out of his need to silence criticism for political gain! He—"

The thundering words stopped suddenly, and the fiery blue eyes widened. A trembling old hand rose, gripping the lictor's shoulder, and Howard Anderson swayed. A thousand delegates were on their feet, staring in horror at the Federation's greatest living hero, and his voice was a dying thread.

"Please," he gasped. "*Please.* Don't let him. *Stop* him." The old man sagged as the racing medic vaulted another delegate's console, scrabbling in his belt-pouch medkit as he came.

"I beg you," Howard Anderson whispered. "You're better than the Prophet—better than *him*. Don't let him make us murderers again!"

And he crumpled like a broken toy.

CHAPTER TWENTY-NINE

The Final Option

"Good Lord!" Winnifred Trevayne blinked at the technical read-outs on the screen. "What in heaven's name *is* that?"

Admiral Lantu was silent—he'd said very little for days—but Colonel Fraymak snorted at her other elbow. The colonel had read *Starwalker*'s records for himself, and the stance he'd taken largely out of respect for Lantu had been transformed by an outrage all his own as he threw himself wholeheartedly into collaboration with his "captors."

"That, Commander," he said now, "is an *Archangel*-class strategic armored unit."

"The hell you say," General Shahinian grunted. "That's a modification of an old Mark Seven CBU." Trevayne looked blank. "Continental bombardment unit," Shahinian amplified, then frowned. "Wonder where they got the specs? Unless . . ." He grunted again and nodded. "Probably from *Ericsson*. I think I remember reading something about BuCol giving colonial industrial units military downloads after ISW-1 broke out." He made a rude sound. "Can you see some bunch of farmers wasting time and resources on something that size?" He shook his head. "Just the sort of useless hardware some fat-headed bureaucrat would've forgotten to delete."

"I've never seen anything like it," Trevayne said.

"You wouldn't, outside a museum, and it's too damned *big* for a museum. That's why we scrapped the last one back in—oh, 2230, I think. Takes over a dozen shuttles to transport one, then you've got to assemble the thing inside a spacehead. If you need that kind of firepower, it's quicker and simpler to supply it from space."

"When you *can*, sir," Colonel Fraymak pointed out respectfully.

"When you *can't*, Colonel," Shahinian said frostily, "you've got no damned business poking your nose in in the first place!"

Trevayne nodded absently, keying notes into her memo pad. That monstrosity would laugh at a megatonne-range warhead, and that made it a sort of ultimate area denial system, assuming you planned to use the real estate it was guarding.

She sighed as she finished her notes and punched for the next display. The data they'd pirated from *Starwalker* was invaluable—the Synod had stored its most sensitive defense information in the old ship's computers—but the more of it she saw, the more hopeless she felt.

Thebes was the best textbook example she'd ever seen of the sort of target Marines should *never* be used against. The planet was one vast military base, garrisoned by over forty million troops with the heaviest weapons she'd ever seen. And while those weapons might be technical antiques, Marines were essentially assault troops. The armored units they could transport to the surface, however modern, were pygmies beside monsters like that CBU. Even worse, their assault shuttles would take thirty to forty percent casualties. Fleet and Marine doctrine stressed punching a hole in the defenses first, but not even Orions had ever fortified an inhabited planet *this* heavily. There was a fifty percent overlap in the PDCs' coverage zones. The suppressive fire to cover an assault into that kind of defense would sterilize a continent.

She glanced guiltily at the sealed hatch to the admiral's private briefing room. In all the years she'd known and served Ivan Antonov, she had never seen him so . . . elementally enraged. It had gone beyond thunder and lightning to a cold, deadly silence, and her inability to find the answer he needed flayed her soul. But, damn it—she turned back to the display in despair—there *wasn't* an answer this time!

Antonov swiveled his chair slowly to face his staff, and his eyes were glacial. The doctors said Howard Anderson would live . . . probably . . . for a few more years, but the massive stroke had left half his body paralyzed. His century and more of service to the Federation was over, and the thought of that dauntless spirit chained in a broken, crippled body—

He chopped the thought off like an amputated limb. There was no time to think of the price his oldest friend had paid. No time to contemplate getting his own massive hands on that *svolochy*, that scum, Waldeck for just a few, brief moments. No time even to take bleak comfort in the ruin of Waldeck's political career and the rampant disorder of the LibProgs as the truth about the Peace Fleet massacre came out.

It was not, Antonov reminded himself bitterly, the first time fighting men and women had been betrayed to their deaths by the political swine they served. Nor would it be the last time the *vlasti* responsible escaped the firing squad they so amply deserved. That wouldn't be *civilized*, after all. For one moment he let himself dwell on the fate the *Zheeerlikou'valkhannaieee* reserved for such *chofaki*, then snorted bitterly. No wonder he liked Orions!

But in the meantime . . .

"I have received final clarification from Admiral Brandenburg," he rumbled. "The Assembly has opted to seek 'expert guidance' in determining policy towards Thebes." Those bleak, cold eyes swept his advisors. "Before voting to override the Prohibition of 2249, they wish my recommendation. I have been informed that they will act in whatever fashion I deem most prudent."

Winnifred Trevayne inhaled sharply; the others were silent, but he saw it in their faces. Especially in Kthaara's. The Orion had been unwontedly diplomatic over the Peace Fleet revelations and the Assembly's confusion, but now his contempt bared ivory fangs. And with good reason, Antonov thought. Whatever his decision, the politicos had managed in time-honored fashion to clear their own skirts with a pious appeal to "expert military opinion." What a shame they so seldom bothered to seek it *before* they created such a bitched-up shitball!

"With that in mind," he continued, "I need whatever insight any of you may offer. Commodore Tsuchevsky?"

"Sir," the chief of staff said somberly, "I don't have any. We're still examining the data—we know more about the enemy's defenses than any other staff in military history—but the only solution we can see is a massive application of firepower. There are no blind spots to exploit, no gaps. We can blow a hole in them from beyond their own range, but doing so will have essentially the same effect as applying Directive Eighteen. And—" he paused, visibly steeling himself "—much as I hate to admit it, Waldeck had a point. It's only a matter of time before the Thebans' planet-side industry produces their own SBMs and we lose even that advantage."

"I will not accept that." Antonov's voice was quietly fierce, the verbal pyrotechnics planed away by steely determination, and he turned his gaze upon Lantu. The first admiral looked shrunken and old in his over-large chair. The fire had leached out of his amber eyes, and his hands trembled visibly as he looked back up at Antonov from a pit of despair.

"You must." His voice was bitter. "Commodore Tsuchevsky is correct."

"No," Antonov said flatly. "There is an answer. There is no such thing as a perfect defense—not when the attacker has data this complete and the services of the enemy's best and most senior commander."

"Best commander?" Lantu repeated dully. He shook his head. "No, Admiral. You have the services of a fool. A pathetic simpleton who was asinine enough to think his people deserved to survive." He stared down at his hands, and his voice fell to a whisper. "I have become the greatest traitor in Theban history, betrayed all I ever believed, sacrificed my honor, conspired to kill thousands whom I trained and once commanded—all for a race so stupid it allowed five generations of charlatans to lead it to its death." His hands twisted in his lap.

"Do what you must, Admiral Antonov. Perhaps a handful of the People will live to curse me as I deserve."

The humans in the room were silenced by his agony, but Kthaara'zarthan leaned forward, eyes fixed on Lantu's face, and gestured to his interpreter.

"I would like to tell you a story, Admiral Laaantu," he said quietly, and Lantu looked up in astonishment sufficient to penetrate even his despair as, for the first time ever, Kthaara spoke directly to him.

"Centuries ago, on Old Valkha, there was a *khanhar*—a war leader. His name was Cranaa'tolnatha, and his clan was sworn to the service of Clan Kirhaar. Cranaa was a great warrior, one who had never known defeat in war or on the square of honor, and his clan was *linkar'a ia' Kirhaar*, Shield-Bearer to Clan Kirhaar. Clan Tolnatha stood at Clan Kirhaar's right hand in battle, and Cranaa was Clan Kirhaar's *shartok khanhar*, first fang of all its warriors, as well as those of Clan Tolnatha.

"But the *Khanhaku'a'Kirhaar* was without honor, for he betrayed his allies and made himself *chofak*. None of his warriors knew it, for he hid his treachery, yet he spied on those who thought themselves his *farshatok*, selling their secrets to their enemies. And when those enemies moved against them, he called Cranaa aside and ordered him to hold back the warriors of Clan Tolnatha while he himself commanded Clan Kirhaar's. Clan Tolnatha was to lie hidden, he told Cranaa, saved until the last moment to strike the enemy's rear when their allies—including Clan Kirhaar—feigned flight."

He paused, and Lantu stared at him, muzzle wrinkled as he tried to understand.

"Now, Cranaa had no reason to think his *khanhaku's* orders were a lie, but he was a skilled warrior, and when he considered them they made no sense. His forces would be too far distant to intervene as ordered, for by the time messengers reached him and he advanced, the feigned flight would have carried the battle beyond his reach. And as he studied his *khanhaku's* commands, he realized that a 'feigned flight' was no part of their allies' plans. The battle was to be fought in a mountain pass, and if they yielded the pass they would be driven back against a river and destroyed.

"All but Clan Kirhaar," Kthaara said softly, "for they formed the reserve. They would be first across the river's only bridge, and it was they who had been charged with mining that bridge so that it might be blown up to prevent pursuit. And when Cranaa realized those things, he knew his *khanhaku* had betrayed him and all his allies. Clan Tolnatha would advance but arrive too late, and it would be destroyed in isolation. Clan Kirhaar would fall back, and his *khanhaku* would order the bridge destroyed 'to hold the enemy,' and thus deliver his allies to their foes. And when the battle was over, there would be none alive to know how his *khanhaku* had betrayed them.

"But Cranaa had sworn *hirikolus* to his *khanhaku*, and to break that oath is unthinkable. He who does so is worse than *chofak*—he is *dirguasha*, outcast and outlawed, stripped of clan, cut off from his clan fathers and mothers as the prey of any who wish to slay him. There is no greater punishment for the *Zheeerlikou'valkhannaieee*. Before we suffer it, we will die at our own hand.

"Yet if he obeyed, Cranaa's clan would die, and its allies, and the traitor would wax wealthy and powerful upon their blood. And so Cranaa did not obey. He broke his oath of *hirikolus*—broke it not with proof he could show another, but on the truth he knew without proof. He refused to lead his clan into battle as he was commanded, but chose his own position and his own time to attack, and so won the battle and saved his clan.

"And in doing so, he made himself *dirguasha*. He could not prove his *khanhaku's* treachery, though few doubted it. Yet even had he been able to do so, it would not have saved him, for he had thrown away his honor. He was cast out by his own litter mates, outlawed by the allies he had saved, deprived of his very name and driven into the waste without food, or shelter, or weapons. A lesser warrior would have slain himself, but to do so would be to admit he had lied and cleanse his *khanhaku's* name, so Cranaa grubbed for food, and shivered in the cold, and starved, and made his very life a curse upon his *khanhaku's* honor. And so, when he was sick and alone, too weak to defend himself, his traitor *khanhaku* sent assassins, and they slew him like an animal, dragging him to death with ropes, denying him even the right to die facing them upon his feet.

"Thus Cranaa'tolnatha died, alone and despised, and his bones were gnawed and scattered by *zhakleish*. Yet all these centuries later, the *Zheeerlikou'valkhannaieee* honor his courage ... and not even Clan Kirhaar recalls his *khanhaku's* name, for they have stricken it in shame. He was a traitor, Admiral Laaantu—but our warriors pray to Hiranow'khanark that we, too, may find the courage to be such traitors if we must."

There was utter silence in the briefing room as Lantu stared deep into Kthaara'zarthan's slit-pupilled eyes, and the others almost held their breath, for something was changing in his own eyes. They narrowed, and an amber light flickered in their depths—a bright, intent light, divorced from despair.

"There might," First Admiral Lantu said softly, "be a way, after all."

It was, Ivan Antonov thought, an insane plan.

He stared out the view port of his quarters, trying to convince himself it might work, trying not to think about the cost if it failed.

He turned from the port, pacing back and forth across his cramped cabin, wrestling with his fears. It was to risk all upon a single throw of the dice, yet hadn't he done precisely that at Redwing? Hadn't he done it again on New New Hebrides?

Of course he had, but then he'd had no choice. Here he had an option, one which he knew would work without risking a single Terran life. What possible logic could justify sending three full divisions of Marines to almost certain death when that was true?

But it wasn't true. He wheeled abruptly, staring back out at the silent stars. He could save sixty thousand Terran lives . . . but only by taking six *billion* Theban ones.

He drew a deep breath and nodded once.

"This, ladies and gentlemen," Winnifred Trevayne said, "is Planetary Defense Center Saint-Just on the Island of Arawk. It is, without doubt, the most powerful single fortification on the entire planet—and your objective."

The staff of the Third Corps, TMC, looked at the holographic schematic for one horrified moment, raised their eyes to her in total disbelief, then turned as one to stare at their commander. General Shahinian looked back silently, and more than one hard-bitten officer paled at the confirmation in his expression. Their gazes swiveled back to Commander Trevayne, and she moved in front of the holo and folded her hands behind her, masking her own dismay in crisp, decisive words.

"PDC Saint-Just is the central planetary command and control facility and the Prophet's personal HQ. The primary works are buried under two hundred meters of rock in Arawk's Turnol Mountains and protected by concentric rings of ground defenses forty kilometers deep. We believe that at least two and possibly four strikefighter squadrons based on Saint-Just have been held back to intercept incoming assault shuttles, but Second Fleet's fighter strength should be more than sufficient to cover you against their attack. Of greater concern are the aircraft also based inside Saint-Just's perimeter. Under the circumstances, it will be impossible for us to insert our own aircraft to engage them, nor can we neutralize them with a pre-attack bombardment. Any attempt to do so would only alert the defenders, and the ancillary damage would make the actual penetration of the facility even more difficult."

"*Penetration?*" That was too much, and Brigadier Shimon Johnson, Third Corps' ops officer, wheeled back to his CO in pure, unadulterated horror.

"Penetration." Shahinian's confirmation sounded like broken glass, and he gestured to Trevayne, who sat in unmistakable relief. The general's shoulder-boards of stars glittered as he stood in her place.

"We're going inside." There was dead silence. "This fortress contains the only Shellheads who *know* their religion is a lie. These are the people who refuse to surrender—the ones using our unwillingness to destroy their entire species against us. They're terrorists, holding their own race hostage while they sit under the most powerful defensive umbrella on the planet. If we can take *them* out, we may be able to find someone sane to negotiate a surrender with. By the same token, our ability to neutralize their most powerful defensive position should prove tremendously demoralizing to the Thebans as a whole. Finally, Arawk's island location limits the overlap in its neighboring PDCs' coverage to less than fifty percent. Destruction of Saint-Just's ground-to-space weapons will open a hole—a small one, I know, but a hole nonetheless—through which future assaults can be made without resorting to saturation bombardments."

"But, sir," Second Division's CO, Lieutenant General Sharon Manning, said quietly, "there won't be enough of us left to *make* any future assaults."

"I believe that may be a somewhat pessimistic estimate, General," Shahinian replied. "And, in any case, the decision has already been made."

Manning started to say something more, then cut herself off at her superior's bleak expression. Aram Shahinian had come up through the ranks; he knew precisely what he was sending his troops into. She closed her own mouth and sat back, black face grim, and Shahinian gestured to Trevayne once more.

She began punching buttons to manipulate the holo image and highlight features as she itemized Saint-Just's defensive capabilities, and the Marines went absolutely expressionless as battery after battery of weapons glowed crimson. Missile launchers, massed point defense stations that doubled as shuttle-killers, buried aircraft and strikefighter hangars, mutually supporting auto-cannon and artillery pillboxes, mortar pits, minefields, entanglements, subterranean barracks and armored vehicle parks. . . . It wasn't a fortress; it was one enormous weapon, designed to drown any attacker in his own blood.

Trevayne displayed the last weapon system and turned to the iron-faced officers. Most of these people knew her well, some were close friends, and they stared at her with hating faces. It wasn't her fault, and they saw the anguish in her own eyes, but they couldn't help it.

"General Shahinian will brief you on his general tactical objectives," she made herself say levelly, "but we do have one priceless advantage: Admiral Lantu is intimately familiar with Saint-Just and the network of secret tunnels radiating from the PDC. These serve two purposes: to provide an access route safe from radioactive contamination following any bombardment, and to evacuate the Prophet and Synod in the event Saint-Just is seriously threatened. We intend to use one of these tunnels to insert a small, picked force under cover of the main attack."

No one spoke, but she could hear them thinking very loudly indeed. *Secret passages? Only a Navy puke could come up with something that stupid!*

"These routes rely primarily on concealment for their security," she went on, "with computer-commanded antipersonnel weaponry. Although they're shown in the *Starwalker* data base, the majority of Saint-Just's garrison knows nothing about them, and access is controlled entirely by security-locked computers. Admiral Lantu knows the access codes, and even though they were included in the data we extracted from *Starwalker*, there is no reason for the Synod to alter them, as there is a retinal-scan feature built into the security systems. No human eyes could activate them, but Admiral Lantu's retinal patterns are on the authorized list, and the Thebans, with no knowledge that he's come over to us, have no reason to delete them. They certainly haven't deleted them from any of the other security lists we recovered from *Starwalker*.

"We hope to accomplish two objectives via this penetration. Colonel Fraymak will lead one element of the assault party directly to Saint-Just's primary command center, where our Raiders will eliminate the PDC's command staff, central computers, and com net. A second element, led by Admiral Lantu, will be charged with the seizure and deactivation—" she paused and drew a deep breath "—of the two-hundred-megatonne suicide charge under the base."

In the utter silence that followed, it was with some relief that Trevayne acknowledged the raised hand in the back row.

"Question, Commander," came the drawl. "What do we do *after* lunch?"

✧   ✧   ✧

Ivan Antonov stood in *Gosainthan*'s boat bay and watched First Admiral Lantu and Colonel Fraymak exchange a few final words with General Shahinian before departing for the transport *Black Kettle*. There was no longer any distrust in the Marine's expression as he bent slightly to listen to the two Thebans, out there was pain . . . and envy. Shahinian was about to commit three of his four divisions to an attack which would gut them, even if everything went perfectly, and he could not accompany them. He would remain on his command ship, *Mangos Coloradas*, coordinating an elaborate deception maneuver with his staff, while General Manning took his troops in on the ground.

The conversation ended, and Lantu and Fraymak crossed to Antonov. Their hands rose in Theban salute, and he returned it, feeling Kthaara's bitter disappointment at his side. The two Thebans had to accompany the assault, despite their inability to wear combat zoots; Kthaara did not, and his skill in fighter operations might be invaluable to Shahinian if, in fact, the Thebans had managed to secrete more fighters than they knew.

"Good luck, Admiral, Colonel." Antonov clasped their backward, too-narrow hands firmly. The colonel looked tense, anxious, and just a bit frightened even now of the sacrilege he proposed to commit; Lantu looked completely calm, and somehow that worried Antonov more than Fraymak's tension.

"Thank you, Admiral Antonov." Lantu looked deep into the human's eyes. "And thank you for running such risks to save my people."

The burly admiral made an uncomfortable gesture, and the Theban swallowed anything else he might have been about to say. He turned towards the waiting cutter, but an arm covered in night-black fur reached out and stopped him. He twitched in surprise and looked down at the clawed hand on his forearm, then looked up at Kthaara'zarthan.

The Orion's interpreter wasn't present. Antonov or Tsuchevsky could easily have translated for him, but Kthaara said nothing. He simply reached to his harness, and steel rasped as he drew his *defargo*. The bay lights gleamed on the honor dirk's razored edge as he nicked his own wrist. Crimson blood glittered amid sable fur as he gave the weapon a strange little flick, tossing it up to catch it by the guard and extend its hilt to the Theban.

Lantu stared at it for a moment, then reached out. He held it while Kthaara unhooked its scabbard one-handedly from his harness and extended it in turn. And then, though Antonov knew he could not possibly have been told of the significance of the act, the Theban raised his own wrist. The unbloodied edge of the blade snicked, drawing Theban blood to match that of the *Zheeerlikou'valkhannaieee* already on it, and Kthaara'zarthan's eyes glowed. He drew a small square of silky fabric from a belt pouch and wiped the blade reverently, then watched as Lantu sheathed it and affixed it to his own belt.

Antonov wondered how many others present recognized the formal renunciation of *vilknarma*—and why he himself felt no shock. He only watched as his *vilkshatha* brother extended his right arm, gripping Lantu's too-long arm in a *farshatok's* clasp, and then stepped back beside him.

Lantu's eyes were unnaturally bright, and his hand caressed the *defargo* at his side. Then he drew himself up, nodded once, sharply, and followed Colonel Fraymak into the cutter.

CHAPTER THIRTY

Vengeance Is Mine

First Marshal Sekah stood in PDC Saint-Just's central command and frowned at the holo sphere. He was a son of the Church, prepared to die for Holy Terra, but the thought of all the deaths which would accompany his sickened him. *Yet better that than defilement,* he told himself fiercely. *Better death of the body than of the soul.*

Still, the infidels' quiescence had puzzled him. They'd destroyed his orbital works over a month ago, yet made no move against the planet itself. Was it possible they simply didn't know what to do with it? He grinned mirthlessly, recalling the utter lack of fortification on the captured infidel worlds and the infidel tactical manuals' insistence on keeping combat out in space "where it belonged." As if Holy Terra's People should fear to live or die with their defenders! But even such as they must realize the People would never yield, so why delay? They had the range to slay Thebes from a position of safety—surely they couldn't be so foolish as to think the Prophet might change his mind and surrender to the Satan-Khan as they had!

Now he watched the shifting patterns in the sphere and shivered. It seemed whatever had caused them to delay obtained no longer. Formations of infidel starships were sweeping into position, close to the edge of the capital missile envelope yet tauntingly beyond it, and Sekah's mind heard sirens howling in every city across the planet. Not that it would do any good.

"Summon the Prophet," he said quietly to an aide.

"All units in preliminary positions, Admiral," Tsuchevsky reported, and Antonov nodded his massive head.

"Get me *Mangus Coloradas.*" Aram Shahinian looked out of the com screen at him, and Antonov gave him a thin, cold smile. "The Fleet is at your disposal, General," he said simply.

"Aye, aye, sir." Shahinian saluted, the screen blanked, and Antonov leaned back in his command chair and crossed his legs. He'd just become a passenger in his own fleet.

"Firing sequence locked in." TFNS *Dhaulagiri*'s gunnery officer acknowledged the report and watched her chronometer tick steadily down. Somebody down there was about to take an awful pasting—if not quite as bad as the one he probably expected.

Lantu looked up as a towering zoot paused beside him, then smiled in faint surprise as Angus MacRory grinned.

"I hadn't realized you were coming, Colonel."

"An' where else should I be? Ye're still my prisoner, in a manner o' speakin'."

"And you're coming along to make certain I don't escape. I see."

"Actually, First Admiral," Major M'boto said from Lantu's other side, "Colonel MacRory's in command. He'll be leading the element which accompanies you."

"Indeed? And why wasn't that mentioned to me sooner?"

"We weren't certain the colonel would complete his zoot training in time." M'boto's teeth flashed in his ebon face. "That was before he shaved almost two weeks off the old record."

First Marshal Sekah folded his arms behind him as the first infidel missiles launched, then looked up as the Prophet and his entourage arrived.

"Your Holiness." He unlocked his arms and genuflected, but something about the Prophet's eyes—a bright, hard glitter too deep in their depths—bothered him. He brushed the thought aside. Even Holy Terra's Prophet might be excused a bit of tension at a moment like this.

The First Marshal returned his attention to the sphere and frowned. The infidels still appeared to be trying to limit collateral damage—perhaps they hoped despair might yet seduce the People into apostasy and surrender? No matter. What mattered was that they were flinging their missiles at the isolated PDCs crowning the northern ice cap. Well, that suited Sekah. He was in no hurry to see the People's women and children die, and those fortresses were eminently well equipped to look after themselves.

Immensely armored PDC silo covers flicked open and then closed, and the atmosphere above Thebes' pole blazed with kilotonne-range counter-missiles. The SBMs were intercepted in scores, but statistically a few had to get through, and fireballs marched across the sullen PDCs, vaporizing rock and ice, shaking the ice-crusted continental mass with their fury.

Shock waves quivered through flesh and bone, but the grim-faced Theban defenders watched their read-outs with slowly mounting hope. They were stopping more missiles than the most optimistic had projected, and those that got through were doing less damage than they'd feared. The megatonnes of concrete, rock, and steel armoring their weapons glowed and fused, yet the infidels seemed to have no deep-earth penetrators, and surface bursts lacked the power to punch through and disembowel the forts.

The atmospheric radiation count mounted ominously, yet it, too, was lower than they'd feared. The infidels were employing only nuclear warheads, without the antimatter explosions the defenders had dreaded.

First Marshal Sekah scanned the PDCs' reports and bared his teeth. They were hurting him, and even these lower radiation levels meant terrible contamination, but no fleet could match a planet's magazine capacity. Even if Theban missiles were too short-ranged to strike back, the infidels would have to do far better than they were to breach *those* defenses before they exhausted their ammunition.

General Aram Shahinian watched his own read-outs, glancing occasionally at the visual display and the glaring inferno blasting ice into hellish steam. His eyes were calm, his expression set. His worst fear was that someone down there would run an analysis and realize Second Fleet was deliberately throwing lighter salvos than it might have for the express purpose of *helping* their point defense, but there was nothing he could do about it if they did.

He glanced at his chronometer and keyed his com button.

"Execute phase two," he said.

"They're moving, First Marshal."

Sekah grunted and rubbed his cranial carapace. The infidels' fire had slackened, suggesting exhaustion of their longer-ranged missiles, and their ships were closing to the edge of the capital missile zone to maintain the engagement. Their ECM was far better than his, and they could dodge; his PDCs couldn't, but he would take any shot he could get. His weapons might be less accurate, but he had far more launchers than they.

"Infidel fighters launching," Tracking reported, and he chuckled mirthlessly.

"First Marshal?" He looked up at the Prophet's quiet voice.

"Strikefighters don't worry me, Your Holiness," he explained. "Their missile loads are meaningless beside what the infidels are already firing, and fighters themselves are useless in atmosphere. The infidels can't be certain we're not hoarding fighters they don't know about, so they're deploying a combat patrol to cover their ships." He bared his teeth again. "It won't help against what they *should* be worried about."

A huge, soft hand squeezed Lantu as *Black Kettle* launched her assault shuttles. He sealed his helmet, then realized just how pointless that reflex was. If anything hit a vessel as small as this one, its occupants would never know a thing about it.

He smothered a half-hysterical giggle at the thought. What in the name of whatever was truly holy was he doing here? He was an admiral, not a Marine! He glanced up at the face behind Angus MacRory's command zoot's armored visor, and Angus's set, tense expression made him feel oddly better.

Ivan Antonov's eyes gleamed coldly as he wondered what the Thebans made of the numbers. Over twelve hundred small spacecraft were jockeying into the positions Kthaara and Shahinian's staff had worked out with agonizing precision over the past two weeks, but only three hundred were truly fighters. The other nine hundred were the slightly modified assault shuttles of three Marine Raider divisions, each fitted with a fighter's transponder. Now if the enemy would only concentrate on killing starships and ignore any little anomalies their scanners might detect . . .

Sekah felt an edge of surprise. That was several times the People's best estimate of their fighter strength. Why hadn't they used more in their warp point attack, if they had so many? He shrugged the thought away. It scarcely mattered now, and he had more urgent concerns. The first infidel ships entered the range of the polar PDCs, and he nodded to his exec.

Stomachs clenched aboard the capital units of Second Fleet as hundreds of capital missiles lunged at them.

XO-mounted EDMs sped out to interpose their false drive fields between the enemy and their mother ships. Point defense crews tracked incoming warheads with professional calm while heat-lightning tension crackled through their nerves. Counter missiles raced outward. Laser clusters and auto-cannon slewed rapidly, and brilliant balls of flame began to pock the vacuum, reaching across the light-seconds towards the ships of Terra.

Gosainthan lurched as the first Theban missile eluded her defenses. Another got through. And another. But it was only a handful, Antonov told himself. A tiny fraction of that incredible storm of fire. His flagship's shields shrugged the damage aside—for now—and he tightened his shockframe.

Sekah smiled as the first infidel shields began to fail. It wasn't much—yet. But if the fools would only stay there a little longer . . .

"You will observe, Your Holiness," he said, "that we are spreading our fire widely at the moment. This confronts the infidels with smaller salvos and enhances the effectiveness of their point defense, but it also allows us time to further refine our tracking data while forcing them to expend their EDMs. After a few more salvos, we will have reduced their ability to deceive our missiles and greatly improved our fire control solutions." He smiled wickedly. "Which is when our PDCs will suddenly switch their firing patterns to concentrate on a handful of targets with everything they have."

The Prophet smiled in understanding, and Sekah glanced at the holo sphere once more. The infidel fighters were spreading out, clumping on the sunward side. They were almost directly overhead, and Saint-Just's fire control officer asked for permission to engage with AFHAWKs.

"A little longer, Colonel. They're still closing; let them get all the way to the edge of atmosphere if they want to, then go to rapid fire."

Aram Shahinian checked his read-outs once more, and a drop of sweat trickled down his forehead. The Shellheads were playing it smart, whittling away Second Fleet's EDMs. If someone down there was keeping count, they'd know the capital ships were running dangerously low. Any minute now, they were going to change their targeting, and his brain screamed to rush the attack wave so he could get the fleet the hell out of it.

He made himself wait. Every second they didn't open up with AFHAWKs let his shuttles creep a little closer and meant a fraction of a percent more were going to get through. If the Shellies ran him out of EDMs first, the fleet was just going to have to take it.

He punched another com stud. "General Manning?"

"Aye, sir." Sharon Manning's taut voice was barely a shade higher than usual. There was, Shahinian reflected, a hefty pool awaiting someone the first time Sharon's voice actually broke.

"I doubt they're going to ignore you much longer, General. You are cleared to go when the first AFHAWK launches."

"Now, Your Holiness," Sekah murmured.

✧   ✧   ✧

TFNS *Viper* bucked in agony as the first massed salvo saturated her point defense. The battleship writhed as brutal explosions killed her shields, ripped at her drive field, and gouged deep into her hull. Atmosphere gushed out despite slamming blast doors, and another salvo pounded her weakening defenses. A direct hit wiped away her bridge. Another smashed main missile defense, and her point defense faltered as it dropped into local control.

Viper's exec wiped blood from his forehead and cursed as he stared at the displays in after control.

"Condition Omega!" he snapped. "Abandon ship! All hands, abandon ship!"

His command crew jerked their feet in close to their chairs as escape pods slammed closed about them. Explosive charges blasted them out of their ship, but the exec clung to his console just a moment longer, repeating his bail-out command until he was certain everyone had heard.

He waited one moment too long.

Ivan Antonov's jaw tightened as *Viper* blew apart. It was the only change in his rock-hard expression.

Sharon Manning's dark face was expressionless, but she couldn't believe they'd gotten this close. Of course, no one had ever been insane enough to try such a maneuver before. Guile and deception were all very well, but a good, heavy bombardment beat hell out of either of them.

She checked her systems again. Dear God, they were less than two hundred klicks out of atmosphere! Didn't anybody down there have a *brain?* Even a Marine knew fighters avoided atmospheres like the plague!

She fought her impatience, trying to ignore the capital ships blazing behind her, and almost prayed someone would open fire on her.

"Very well, Colonel," Sekah said, smiling as Saint-Just's tactical officer almost danced with impatience. He could hardly believe the targets the infidel strikefighters were giving them, either, but it passed belief they would come still closer. "You may engage."

Another battleship exploded. The superdreadnoughts, with their greater external ordnance capacity, still had EDMs; the battlewagons did not.

"Order the battleships to open the range," Shahinian said. He hated to do it—but not as much as he hated watching them die.

"Aye, aye, sir." Janet Toomepuu passed his order, then stiffened.

She started to speak, but Shahinian already saw it in his own display.

"Assault wave—*go!*" General Manning barked as the first AFHAWK exploded. More followed it, hundreds more, and the real fighters on the edges of her formation took the brunt. The Shellheads were firing clusters of the damned things at each target, bracketing its potential evasion maneuvers with merciless precision. A pilot might evade the first, even the second, but number three or number four was waiting for him when he did.

Yet they didn't have to take it for long. Nine hundred assault shuttles suddenly screamed forward—not away from the planet, but *towards* it—even as Kthaara'zarthan's fighters played his final trick. A thousand close attack missiles punched out, aimed not at the planet but at a point just beyond its atmosphere. The heavy warheads exploded as one in an intolerable flash of plasma . . . and an incredible pulse of radiation.

Three divisions of Terran Marine assault craft attacked out of the blinding fury of an artificial "sun."

First Marshal Sekah whipped around to the holo sphere in disbelief. *What in the name of Holy Terra—?!* No amount of EMP could burn out his hardened sensors, but they'd never been intended to confront *that* massive a dose! For one priceless moment they were blind, and in that moment nine hundred assault shuttles slammed into atmosphere at reckless speed, shrieking downward like homesick meteors to close on a single island in the sunlit Sea of Arawk.

"*It worked, by God!*"

Aram Shahinian actually flinched from the high-pitched soprano scream, and then, despite everything, his face creased in an enormous grin. Sharon must have forgotten her mike was open—and someone had just come into a tidy little sum, indeed.

Lantu tried to tell himself this was a foolish moment to worry about his dignity, but he felt like an utter idiot as Angus snatched him up bodily. The admiral's armored vac suit didn't have a repulsor unit, and that meant—

He gasped as the shuttle rolled and its entire side opened. A corona of superheated air ripped past, lethally beautiful on the far side of a mono-permeable field of force. He stared at it in fascination, then closed his eyes in terror as MacRory gathered him to his chest in massively armored arms and hit his jump gear. A savage foot kicked Lantu in the belly, a fierce stab of heat clawed at him through the protection of

MacRory's repulsor field, and then the two of them were falling through ten thousand meters of empty air.

"Sweet Terra, it was a trick." Sekah whispered as his scanners came back up. "They're not after the polar PDCs—they're after *Saint-Just!*"

The Prophet eyed him blankly, clearly not understanding, and Sekah seized his arm. He almost shook him before his staggering brain realized who he'd grabbed, but he turned the Prophet towards the sphere and pointed.

"Those aren't fighters, Your Holiness! They're assault shuttles! The infidels are landing Marines right on top of Saint-Just—and they're already inside our engagement range!"

The Prophet paled in understanding, staggering back a half pace as the first marshal released him and whirled to his staff. He began barking orders, and alarms screamed throughout the vast subterranean base.

Marine Raiders plummeted like lethal, ungainly hawks, and the totally surprised defenses of PDC Saint-Just roused to meet them. Stunned crews flung themselves at their targeting scopes as close-range missile launchers and cannon muzzles slewed crazily, but there wasn't enough time. Not enough to sort out target signatures as small as single repulsor fields. Not enough to track and lock. A few defensive emplacements got lucky, and almost a thousand Marines died before they grounded, but they came in fast and dirty. Getting down quickly was more important than a precise landing pattern, and they overrode their automatics ruthlessly, screaming down at velocities which would have seen any one of them busted back to doolie if they'd tried it in training.

Another few hundred died or broke limbs, despite their zoots, at the speed they hit, but three Raider divisions were down, and their total casualties were barely five percent of what a conventional assault into those defenses would have cost them.

Sharon Manning slammed into the ground, cursing as two bones broke in her right foot, but her zoot was in one piece and she hit her rally signal even as she reached for her own heavy flechette launcher.

This ain't no place for a general, she told herself as a totally astonished Shellhead sentry emptied his magazine at her and she blew him into bloody rags, *but it beats hell out of being dead!*

"Get them back—now!" Aram Shahinian snapped, and Second Fleet's capital ships hurled themselves towards the limits of capital missile range.

✧   ✧   ✧

First Marshal Sekah cursed horribly, despite the Prophet's presence, as the infidel fleet retreated. It was all a *trick*—and he'd fallen for it!

More and more surface defense positions went into action, but the infidel assault shuttles had already made their drops. Heavy weapons and ammunition canisters still plummeted behind the Raiders, but the shuttles were streaking away, hugging the sea to stay below his heavy weapons, and he snarled in frustration at their speed. The cursed things were too fast for his aircraft to catch—and they were armed. One squadron of high performance jets managed to cut the angle and intercept, but it took everything they had in full afterburner, and they got one shuttle—*one!*—before the rest of the infidel formation blotted them from the heavens.

But those shuttles were still dead if Saint-Just held. They might run rings around atmospheric craft, but they couldn't get *out* of atmosphere without braving his defensive umbrella. Yet if they *did* manage to take Saint-Just, they'd have a gap. A narrow one, but wide enough for more assaults to break through and nibble away at his ground bases. . . .

But *why?* Why run the insane risk of coming in on the ground? They could have opened the same hole from space without putting thousands of people on the planet, cut off with no retreat if their assault failed! It made no sense, unless . . .

The Prophet! They knew where he was, and they were after the Prophet himself!

He crossed quickly to the Prophet's side, bending close to murmur into his ear.

"Your Holiness, I believe the infidels know you're here. They hope to capture or kill you with this insane assault! I urge you to evacuate immediately. Allow us to deal with them before you return."

"Evacuate?!" The Prophet stared at him. "Don't be preposterous, First Marshal! This is the strongest fortress on Thebes. They'll never take it with a few thousand infantry!"

Sekah stared at him, longing to argue, but the Prophet had spoken—and this was, indeed, Thebes' strongest fortress. But was it strong enough? If the infidels had known exactly where to strike, might the Satan-Khan also have told them *how* to strike?

His spine stiffened, and he returned to his staff with a grim expression. Satan-Khan or no, the infidels would get to the Prophet only over his own dead body.

A Theban bunker vaporized as the HVM struck, and Sharon Manning popped her jump gear, hurling herself into the glowing crater.

Her staff—what of it had managed to join her—tumbled into it about her, zoots ignoring the fiery heat. A heavy weapons section materialized out of the chaos, setting up to cover the hole, and Manning grunted. It wasn't much of a CP, but it didn't look like anyone could range on them—except for that damned mortar pit. She barked an order, and three Raiders swarmed out to deal with it.

They did, but only one of them came back.

Lantu grunted in anguish as they hit the ground and MacRory's unyielding armor bruised him viciously through his armored vac suit. But he was intact, more or less, and Angus set him instantly on his feet. More Raiders filtered out of the forest about them, zoots slimed with tree sap and broken greenery, but not a single weapon fired on them. They were over two hundred kilometers from the inferno raging atop Saint-Just, and Lantu swayed dizzily as he found his bearings. Major M'boto came bounding up in the effortless leaps of his jump gear, carrying Fraymak like a child.

"That way." Lantu raised an arm and pointed. "We're still about ten kilometers east of—*ullpppp!*"

He cut off in chagrin as Angus snatched him up again and the entire battalion went streaking off along the mountainside.

Ivan Antonov watched his display, clamping his jaw and wishing his scan sections could show him what was happening. But the range was simply too great. He could only watch the relayed data from *Mangus Coloradas* and pray.

He looked up as someone stopped beside his chair.

"Well, Kthaara," he said quietly, "your little trick worked."

"Indeed," the Orion replied softly, flexing his claws as he, too, stared at the display. One hand touched the empty spot where his *defargo* had hung, and he seemed to relax slightly.

Sekah sat before his console, taking personal command of Saint-Just's defense, and sweat rimmed his cranial carapace. Those weren't mortals—they were demons! He'd never dreamed of infantry weapons like the ones they were using against him, and that powered armor—! No wonder the Fleet's boarding attacks had been so persistently thwarted after the first few months!

But demons or not, his interlacing fields of fire were killing them. Not in hundreds as they should have, but still in dozens and scores.

His orders rolled out, diverting troops from unthreatened sectors to back up his fixed positions as the infidels blew them apart. They were coming in from the west, carving a wedge-shaped salient into Saint-Just's defenses, and they were through the outer ring and into the second in far too many places. But the deeper they came, the more they exposed their flanks.

A battalion commander led his men scuttling through the personnel tunnels and launched them into the rear of an infidel company advancing up a deep ravine.

"Your six! Watch your s—!" Major Oels' voice died suddenly, and Lieutenant Escalante spun to the rear. A screaming wave of Shellhead infantry rolled over Delta Company like a tsunami, rocket and grenade launchers flaming. A dozen Raiders went down in an instant, and then the rest of the company was on them. A tornado of flechettes and plasma bolts piled the attackers in heaps, but eight more Delta troopers went with them.

Escalante panted, turning in circles, flechette launcher ready, but there were no live Shellheads left. Then someone touched his arm, and he damned near screamed. He whirled to face Sergeant Major Abbot, and the sergeant's grim expression crushed his scathing rebuke stillborn.

"Skipper just bought it, Lieutenant," Abbot said harshly, and Escalante noticed the blood splashed all over his zoot. "Captain Sigourny, too."

Escalante stared at him in horror. Third Battalion had been spread all over the island in the drop. Murphy only knew where the other three companies were, and Delta had already lost Lieutenant Gardener and Lieutenant Matuchek. Dear God, that meant . . .

The big sergeant nodded grimly.

"Looks like you're it, sir."

Lantu hung onto his breakfast grimly as branches lashed at his armored body. The drunken swoops wouldn't have been so bad if he, like MacRory, had known when they were coming. The colonel's jump gear was a marvel, but it was like being trapped in a demented, sideways elevator, and just clutching his inertial guidance unit was—

"Stop!" he shouted, and five hundred Terran Marines slammed to a halt as one. He was too preoccupied to be impressed. "Put me down, Colonel!"

Angus deposited him gently on the forested mountainside, and the admiral peered about, wishing it hadn't been winter the one time he'd seen this spot with his own eyes. All these damned leaves and branches. . . .

"There." He pointed, and the Terrans craned their necks at the creeper-grown hillock. It didn't look like a heavy weapons emplacement—until they checked their zoot scan systems.

"'Twould seem yer on yer ain, Admiral," Angus said, but Lantu was already scrambling up the slope.

General Manning nodded thanks without even looking up from her portable map display as Sergeant Young slapped a fresh power cell into her zoot. This was her third CP, if such it could be called, since landing, and she was amazed they'd gotten this far. The tangled mountainsides made beacon fixes hellishly difficult, but it looked like they were into the fourth defensive ring. She grinned humorlessly. Only four more to go, and then they'd hit the *hard* stuff.

Amleto Escalante couldn't believe it. Here the Shellheads went and bored these nice, big tunnels so they could shuttle infantry back and forth, and they didn't even bother to cover them with sensors!

Not that he had any intention of complaining.

His lead squad was a hundred meters ahead of him, probing cautiously. He could have wished for more spacious quarters—in fact, his skin crawled at the thought of wallowing around in here like a bunch of troglodytes—but if there wasn't enough room to use jump gear there was still enough for them to move two abreast. He only had sixty troopers left, but he had a sneaking suspicion Delta Company was deeper into the defenses than anyone else. Now if he only knew what he was doing. . . .

"Two branches, Lieutenant," Abbot reported. "One east, one west."

Escalante flipped a mental coin.

"We go east," he muttered back.

Lantu's heart hammered as he approached the entrance. He carried only captured Theban equipment, and the Terrans had stopped beyond the scanner zone, but if they'd guessed wrong about his retinal prints . . .

He drew a deep breath as no automated weapon system tore him apart. As long as nothing fired, no alarm had been tripped—now it was up to him to keep it that way, and he removed his helmet with clumsy fingers.

A push of a button opened an armored panel, and he leaned forward, presenting his eyes and wincing as brilliant light flashed into them. He held his breath, staring into the light, then exhaled convulsively as the blinding illumination turned to muted green. He cleared his throat.

"Alpha-Zulu-Delta-Four-Niner-One," he recited carefully, and then his mouth twisted. "Great is the Prophet."

Something grated, and a vast portal yawned. He stepped through quickly, reaching for a blinking panel of lights on the tunnel wall, stabbing buttons viciously. There was a moment of hesitation, and then he grinned savagely as the entire panel went blank.

First Marshal Sekah muttered to himself as reports flooded in. The infidels were cutting still deeper, but their rate of advance was slowing. He cursed himself for not having seeded the outer rings with nuclear mines. The infidels were bunching up, and sacrificing a few thousand of his own troops would have been a paltry price for taking them out. He'd already tried air strikes, but their damned kinetic missile launchers had an impossible range. None of the nuclear strike aircraft from his other bases had lived to get close enough, and Saint-Just's own air fields were closed by heavy fire.

But even without nuclear weapons, he was grinding them down. It was only a matter of time, he thought, and tried not to think about the Satan-Khan's malign influence.

The first twenty Raiders crowded into the lead monorail car as Lantu clambered into its control chair. He'd been more than half afraid to summon the vehicles lest he trigger someone's suspicions, but they needed the speed. And the system was fully automated. With so much else to worry about, he doubted anyone had the spare attention to monitor it.

"Ready?" He looked back at MacRory, and Angus nodded sharply. The first admiral breathed a silent prayer to Whoever might really be listening, and five hundred Terran Marines—and two traitorous Thebans—went streaking into the heart of PDC Saint-Just at two hundred kilometers per hour.

"Oh, *shit!*"

Escalante hugged the wall in reflex action as the sudden roar of combat rolled down the tunnel. He punched an armored fist into the stone, then jerked back up and bounded forward. Sergeant Major Abbot grabbed for him, missed, and went streaking after him, cursing all wet-nosed officers who didn't have the sense Mithra gave a Rigelian.

"Sweet Terra!"

Sekah jerked as fresh alarms shrieked, and his eyes turned in horror to the illuminated schematic of Saint-Just's personnel tunnels. A crimson light glared—*and it was inside the final defensive perimeter!*

Escalante rounded a bend into a huge, brilliantly lit cavern just as his point finished off the last astonished Shellhead missile tech. He looked around him in disbelief, staring at the sequoia-sized trunks of capital missile launchers. Sweet Jesus—they were inside *the main base!*

"Sar'major Abbot!"

"Aye, sir!" Abbot appeared almost as if he'd been chasing him, and Escalante pointed across the cavern.

"Cover that tunnel! Mine it and drop it. Then I want blastpacks on that hatch over there—move it, Sar'major!"

"Aye, aye, sir!" Abbot barked. Mithra! Maybe this idiot knew what he was doing after all!

"Brigadier Ho is pinned down, sir."

Sharon Manning grimaced and tried to think. Ho's brigade was her point now, and he'd been shot to hell. She stared at her map display, scrolling through the terrain and thanking God Commander Trevayne had managed to get them such detailed maps. Now where—?

It had to be coming from that bunker complex. And that meant . . .

"Hook Fourth Brigade around to the north." A burst of rifle fire battered her zoot, and she curled around, automatically protecting the display board without even looking up. The cough of a flechette launcher from behind her silenced the fire, but she hardly noticed. "While the Fourth moves up," she went on without a break, "get Second Battalion of the Nineteenth out on their flank. Tell them to watch out for rocket fire from—"

She went on snapping orders, and tried not to think of how many of her people were already dead.

A company of Theban infantry pounded down the tunnel to Missile Bay Sixty-Four, unable to believe their orders. There was no way— *no way*—infidels could be *inside* Saint-Just! It *had* to be a mistake!

The captain at their head raced around a turn and sighed in relief as he saw the closed hatch. *False alarm,* he thought, waving for his troops to slow their headlong pace. *If it weren't, that hatch—*

Fifty kilos of high explosive turned the hatch into shrieking shrapnel and killed him where he stood.

Escalante started to wave his troopers forward, then stopped dead. Fuck! Maybe Sergeant Grogan had been right about what lieutenants used for brains! Here he was deep inside the enemy position, and he hadn't even bothered to tell anyone about it! But none of their coms would punch through this much rock, so . . .

His eye lit on Private Lutwell. Something big and nasty had wrecked the exoskeleton of her zoot's right arm, and the useless limb was clipped to her side while she managed her flechette launcher with an awkward left hand.

"Lutwell!"

"Sir?"

"Shag ass back down that tunnel. Tell 'em we're inside and that I'm advancing, sealing branch corridors with demo charges to cover my flanks."

"But, sir, I—"

"Don't fucking argue!" Escalante snarled "*Do* it, Trooper, or I'll have your guts for breakfast!"

Lutwell popped into the tunnel like a scalded rabbit, and Escalante swung back to his front. He paused for just an instant as he saw the grin on Abbot's face, and then his people were moving forward once more.

The monorail braked in a dimly-lit tunnel, and the battalion spilled out, looming like chlorophyll-daubed trolls in the semi-dark. Lantu scuttled out behind Angus as Fraymak pelted up with M'boto.

"That shaft, Fraymak." Lantu pointed. "Remember the security point just before Tunnel Fourteen." Fraymak nodded. He could handle the standard security systems on the way, but his retinal patterns couldn't access the classified security point; he and M'boto would have to blow their way through.

"Remember," Lantu said, "give us ten minutes—at least *ten* minutes—before you blow it."

"Yes, sir." Fraymak saluted, then held out his hand. Lantu took it. "Good luck, sir."

"And to you." The admiral squeezed the armored gauntlet and stepped back. "This way, Colonel MacRory," he said. Angus scooped him up once more, and the battalion vanished into the darkness down two different shafts.

"Your Holiness," Sekah's face was pale, "the infidels are inside our inner ring."

The Prophet inhaled sharply and raised one hand to grip the sphere of Holy Terra hanging on his chest. Sekah swallowed and cursed himself viciously. He didn't know how they'd gotten so deep, but he should have stopped them. It was his *job* to stop them—and he'd failed.

"I don't know how big a force it is," he continued flatly. "It may be only a patrol—but it may be the lead elements of an entire regiment. I've diverted reinforcements, but it will take them fifteen minutes to get there." He drew a ragged breath. "Your Holiness, I implore you to evacuate. You can escape to safety in one of the nearby towns until we've dealt with the threat or . . . or—" He broke off, and the Prophet's eyes narrowed. But then he smoothed his expression and touched Sekah's shoulder carapace gently.

"As you say, my son. Doubtless you will fight better without us to worry over, anyway." He raised his hand and signed Holy Terra's circle. "The blessings of Holy Terra be upon you, First Marshal. She will give you victory, and I shall return to see your triumph."

"Thank you, Your Holiness." Sekah's eyes glowed with gratitude, and the Prophet turned away. He beckoned to Archbishop Kirsal, and the prelate leaned close as they hurried from the control center.

"That fool will never hold," the Prophet murmured.

"Agreed," Kirsal returned equally quietly.

"We'll swing by my chambers. The suicide charge will cover our absence long enough to escape the island."

Private Sinead Lutwell stuck her head out of the tunnel—and jerked back as a blast of powered flechettes blew rock dust over her.

"*Hold your fire, you dip-shit, motherless bastard!*" she screamed, and the trooper who'd fired reared back in astonishment. She squirmed forward on her belly and glared up into the business end of a flechette launcher that was lowered with a sheepish grin.

"Delta Company's *what?*" This time General Manning did look up from her display, and her jaw dropped at her aide's asinine grin.

She bent back to the display unit, punching buttons madly, and an unholy smile lit her own face. She didn't know who the hell Lieutenant Escalante was, but he was damned well going to be *Captain* Escalante by sunset!

"Contact Fifth Brigade!" Fifth Brigade was Fourth Division's reserve, and this was just why The Book insisted on reserves. "I want at least a regiment—two, if they've got 'em loose—up that tunnel yesterday!"

"Aye, *aye*, sir!"

Lantu gestured abruptly, and Angus set him down as the final security panel came into sight. The admiral scuttled over and presented his eye, then pressed a careful sequence of buttons. The panel flashed bright for an instant until he punched two more and it went dead. A hatch slid wide.

Lantu stepped through, looked both ways down the tunnel, then waved, and two hundred and fifty Raiders filed out as quietly as their zoots would permit. He started down the passage, but an armored hand stopped him.

"Wait," Angus said quietly, and held him motionless until twenty Raiders had put their zooted bodies between him and anyone they might meet.

✧   ✧   ✧

Escalante swore as the auto-cannon blew his point man into mangled gruel, then ducked as grenade launchers coughed. Echoing thunder rolled over him like a fist, and his dwindling force moved forward once more, slipping in bits of entrails and less mentionable things which had once been a Shellhead gun crew.

Colonel Fraymak checked his watch, then nodded to Major M'boto. Four blastpacks went off as one, blowing the armored hatch clear across Tunnel Fourteen, and four zooted troopers followed before it bounced. Two spun in each direction, hosing the passage with fire, and a dozen hapless technicians died before they realized what the concussion was.

Angus MacRory stopped, and Lantu pushed his way quickly through the Terrans. This circular chamber was the meeting point of all the escape routes, and Marines were already spreading out to cover all twelve of them. Lantu ignored them as he hurried past the elevators from above toward the coffin-shaped steel box against one wall. He stripped off his gauntlets—this one required fingerprints and retinal prints alike—and bent over it.

First Marshal Sekah whirled as a fist of thunder battered its way through the command center hatch. What—?

Major M'boto swore savagely as a flail of rocket fire smashed down the tunnel. They'd gotten in clean only to run into what sounded like a fucking regiment! What the hell were they doing running around this deep inside—?

He glanced at a mangled Theban body and froze, then grabbed the corpse, jerking it up to see better. His eyes widened as he saw the episcopal purple collar tabs and the golden sphere of Terra. God, no wonder they were taking such heavy fire! They'd just collided with the Prophet's personal guard!

More rockets streaked in, but his people were hugging the walls for cover and pouring back an inferno all their own. He eased forward behind them, keeping himself between the incoming and Colonel Fraymak.

The Prophet stepped into his personal chambers, ignoring the priceless artwork and tapestries. He crossed to a utilitarian computer station and brought the system on line with flying fingers, then frowned in concentration as he slowly and carefully keyed the complex code he needed.

✧   ✧   ✧

Lantu threw back the cover of the bomb and stepped quickly aside as Angus reached in past him. His armored fist closed on the junction box the admiral had described in the planning stages. Exoskeletal "muscles" jerked.

The Prophet punched the last key and stood back with a smile—a smile that turned into a frozen rictus as a scarlet light code flashed. He bent forward once more, pounding the keyboard in a frenzy.
Nothing happened.
He wheeled with a venomous curse, wondering what freak of damage had disabled the arming circuit. Well, no matter! He could set the charge by hand as they went by it.

M'boto's Raiders inched forward, driving the Prophet's Guard before them. It wasn't easy. The fanatical Thebans contested every meter, and casualties were mounting. Even zoots couldn't bull through such close quarters against people who could hardly wait to die as long as they took you with them.

Colonel Ezra Montoya led his regiment down the tunnel as quickly as they could move. To think a grass-green little first lieutenant had stumbled onto something like this and known what to do with it when he did! It only proved, the colonel told himself firmly, that there really was a God.

First Marshal Sekah coughed as smoke drifted down the tunnel. The Guard were fighting like heroes, but the bellow of combat was coming closer. He turned his back on the hatch, trying to decide from his displays where the other infidel penetration had gotten to.
He didn't know, but *this* one couldn't be them . . . could it? Yet how could *two* infidel forces have pierced Saint-Just's heart?
No matter. He had to deal with the one he knew about, and he snapped fresh orders. Two battalions which had been feeling their way towards the other penetration wheeled and converged upon the Guard.

M'boto crouched with Fraymak behind a shattered blast door. But for the Prophet's Guard, they'd already have been inside the command center, but the bastards had slowed them just long enough to get help, and reinforcements were springing up like ragweed.
He looked at the colonel, and Fraymak's eyes were bitter. They weren't going to break through, but if they stayed where they were, someone was going to take them in the rear, and then—
The two officers froze as a roar of weapons erupted behind them.

✧　　✧　　✧

Sekah bared his teeth at the report. The infidels had gotten within two hundred meters of his CP, but they were done for now. He had them trapped between the surviving Guard, reinforced by a fresh battalion, and a second battalion coming in behind them. Powered armor or not, they could never survive that concentration of firepower.

Amleto Escalante had never been so tired, so scared, or so alive. They'd moved the better part of a klick in the last ten minutes without seeing a soul, and he was just as happy. His people were out of demo charges, and their flanks were hanging wide open with no way to seal the side passages, but so what? They should all be dead already, right? And the deeper they got before they had to fort up, the better.

He looked around at his remaining thirty troopers and saw the same "what the hell" grins looking back at him. He waved them forward.

Major M'boto squirmed around and headed down tunnel, then stopped as he saw his rear-guard falling back toward him. Whatever was coming must be nasty, and he reached out and grabbed the nearest demolition man.

"Charges!" he snapped. "There, there, and there. When the last of our people come by, blow the whole fucking thing in their faces!"

"Aye, aye, sir!"

M'boto headed back up front. That took care of the back door. Unfortunately, it also meant the only way out was forward.

The Prophet shoved past Kirsal into the elevator and waited impatiently for the others. They crowded the large car uncomfortably, but his thoughts were on other things as he punched the "down" button.

Lantu sat on the disarmed bomb, holding his Theban-made assault rifle across his lap. Terra, he was tired! He realized what he'd thought and grinned, but he was really too weary to think up a fresh oath. He watched Angus deploying one company to hold the tunnels while the other headed back to link up with M'boto before a pincer up the elevator shafts opened a second avenue to the control center.

He inhaled deeply and marveled at the sheer, sensual joy of doing so. He'd never expected to be alive this long—hadn't, he finally admitted, *wanted* to be alive—but he was. And it felt remarkably good.

He grinned again and reached for his armored gauntlets, then froze as a light blinked above the elevator doors.

Escalante's tiny force stiffened as they heard the thunder ahead of them, and the lieutenant grinned fiercely.

"Well, Sar'major, sounds like some more of our people've dropped by."

"Can't hardly be anything else, Skipper," Abbot agreed with an answering grin.

"Let's go crash the party."

Sekah cringed as a fresh explosion sent rock dust eddying into the command center. Frantic voices in his headphones told him the infidels had dropped the tunnel roof on the rear battalion's lead platoon, but his people between them and the control room were still holding. Barely.

He punched commands into his console, looking desperately for troops to divert to the fire fight. If he could just bring in a few more—

Something made him look up, and he gawked in horror at the troll which had suddenly appeared in the unguarded hatch across the control room.

He was still lunging to his feet and clawing for his machine-pistol when Lieutenant Amleto Escalante, TFMC, blew him into bloody meat.

The Prophet swore with satisfaction as the elevator came to a halt. The doors slid open, and he stepped out, already turning towards the bomb.

The last thing he ever saw was the muzzle flash of First Admiral Lantu's assault rifle.

General Manning limped slowly along the tunnel, unable even now to believe they'd done it. Casualty reports were still coming in, and they sounded bad. So far, she had at least nine thousand confirmed dead—fifteen percent of her total force—plus God only knew how many wounded, and she knew damned well they were going to find lots more of both.

But for the moment she pushed the thought aside and opened the visor of her bullet-spalled combat zoot. Even the smoke inside PDC Saint-Just smelled better than *she* did after nineteen hours of combat.

She was on her last set of power cells, like almost all of her people, but the destruction of the command center had been decisive. The defenders' coordination had vanished, and when Montoya brought an entire regiment right into the middle of their position, the Shellheads had nowhere to go but Hell.

Which, she thought grimly, was precisely where most of them had gone.

She stepped over a heap of Theban bodies into what had been the command center, and her eyebrows rose as she saw both of their

Theban allies. Incredible. She'd never expected any of that forlorn hope
to survive.

People saluted, and she returned their salutes wearily. MacRory, she
saw—and what asshole ever let a sergeant with his potential slip away
without re-upping?—and M'boto. And somebody else.

"General," MacRory said, " 'tis a fine thing tae see ye."

"And you, Colonel." She nodded to Colonel Fraymak and Admiral Lantu, filing away the latter's strange, deeply satisfied expression
for later consideration, then turned her attention to the young man
sitting on the computer console between MacRory and M'boto. A big,
grim-faced sergeant hovered protectively behind him, and he was no
longer wearing his zoot—for obvious reasons, given the blood-soaked
splints on his left leg and arm. There were more bandages strapped
around his torso, and his face was pasty gray. Nasty, Manning thought,
but all the bits and pieces still seemed to be attached. That was all
the medics really needed these days.

"And who might this be?" she asked, for the youngster had lost his
shirt in the first-aid process, and she saw no rank insignia.

"Och, 'tis the lad who saved M'boto's arse!" MacRory grinned, and
M'boto nodded firmly. "Lieutenant Escalante, General."

"I'm afraid you're wrong, Colonel," Manning said. The injured young
officer looked up at her in more confusion than pain-killers alone
could explain, and she held out her right hand. He extended his own
automatically, and she clasped it firmly, ignoring the baffled expressions all around her.

"This, gentlemen," she announced, "is *Captain* Escalante, the newest
recipient of the Golden Lion of Terra."

It was really too bad, she always thought later, that she hadn't had
a camera with her.

CHAPTER THIRTY-ONE

The Terms of Terra

Ivan Antonov glowered at the recorded image on his screen and tuned out the long, impassioned diatribe. Sooner or later the Theban would run down and get to the heart of his reply. And, unless the Theban race truly was insane, Antonov knew what that reply would be. Of course, he was beginning to wonder if, with the exception of a few individuals like Lantu and Fraymak, there might not be something to the theory of racial insanity.

PDC Saint-Just had cost less than he'd feared, if far more than he would find easy to live with, and if there were any justice in the universe its loss would have finished the Church of Holy Terra. But no. The surviving Synod had gotten together, canonized its dead Prophet, anointed a new Prophet in his stead, and announced its determination to pursue the jihad even unto martyrdom.

Personally, Antonov was about ready to oblige the *svolochy*.

Vanya, Vanya that's the nasty side of you talking! And so it was, but if he could contrive to hang just the Synod, perhaps the rest of the population might learn from example?

Of course, the best way to encourage fanaticism was to provide it with fresh martyr-fodder, yet he couldn't quite suppress the wistful temptation. It was really too bad he couldn't even voice it aloud, but he shuddered to think how Kthaara would react after all his lectures. And it didn't help his mood to find the Synod reacting to the truth about the First Prophet exactly as Lantu had predicted. The new Prophet stubbornly insisted that if infidels could extract data from *Starwalker*'s computers they could also *insert* data, and his fire-and-brimstone denunciation of monsters vile enough to defile sacred scripture had brought Antonov to the point of apoplexy. And the worst of it—the absolute worst—was that the old bastard actually *believed* the *polneyshaya* he was spouting. They'd gotten rid of a clique of self-serving, lying charlatans only to replace it with a crop of true believers!

Religious fervor! The only thing it's good for is turning brains to oatmeal! And if there's one thing in this galaxy worse than Terran *politicians, it's* theocratic *politicians!*

The Prophet's latest fulmination reached its peroration, and Antonov's eyes sharpened as the Theban who had once been Archbishop Ganhad of the Ministry of Production glared at him.

"And so, infidel," the Prophet said bitterly, "we have no choice but to hear your words. Yet be warned! Your accursed master the Satan-Khan will not pervert our Faith as he has your own! The true People of Holy Terra will never abandon their Holy Mother, and the day shall come when you and all of your apostate race will pay the price for your sins against Her! We—"

Antonov grunted and killed the message before the old fart got himself back up to speed. That was all he really needed to know—now he could let Winnie wade through the rest of this drivel and summarize any unlikely tidbits of importance. He felt a tiny qualm of conscience at passing the task to her, but rank, after all, had its privileges.

Thank God.

"Actually," Lantu said, "I must confess to a bit of hope."

The first admiral's almost whimsical smile was a far cry from the tortured expression he'd worn before his personal extermination of the Prophet and his entourage, and Antonov envied him. Kthaara'zarthan envied him even more, but he was content. His *defargo* had been present if he couldn't be, and he'd almost purred as he made Lantu relive every moment of the encounter. The bared-fang grin of total approval he'd bestowed on his one-time mortal enemy had surprised even Antonov; the rest of Second Fleet's senior officers were still in shock. And when Tsuchevsky had caught the Orion initiating the Theban into the pleasures of vodka—!

"You must?" Antonov asked, suppressing yet another ignoble urge to twit his *vilkshatha* brother.

"Indeed. Aside from his religious fervor, Ganhad is no fool. Once you get past his ranting and raving, it looks as if he recognizes the reality of his helplessness, and unlike his predecessor, he truly cares about the People. That should make some sort of settlement possible."

Antonov grunted and turned his glass in his hands. Delighted as he was by Pericles Waldeck's fall from power, the chaos on Old Terra had dumped yet another pile of manure in his lap. President Sakanami's administration had been devastated by Howard's Assembly revelations. One or two LibProgs were actually muttering about impeachment in the apparent hope of saving themselves by poleaxing their own party's president, and his cabinet was a shambles. Of all the pre-war ministers, only Hamid O'Rourke remained. Waldeck and Sakanami had gone behind his back to transmit Aurelli's pre-Lorelei orders via the minister for foreign affairs, and his work since the Peace Fleet massacre, especially as Howard's ally within the cabinet, had won widespread approval. There was even—Antonov grinned at the thought—talk of running him for president. One thing was certain; no one would be renominating Sakanami Hideoshi!

Meanwhile, however, the confusion left the foreign affairs ministry a total, demoralized wreck, too busy defending the careers of its survivors and fending off Assembly "fact-finding" committees to worry about diplomacy. And since he'd done so well fighting the war, the politicos had decided to let Ivan Antonov *end* the war. After everything else they'd saddled him with in the last two and a half years, the *vlasti* had decided to make him a peace envoy!

"No, really." Lantu's improbably long arm stretched out to refill his own vodka glass. "You're not going to get him to accept unconditional surrender, and if you show a single sign of weakness or wavering he may be able to convince himself 'Holy Terra' is intervening on his side and turn stubborn, but otherwise I think he'll accept the terms you actually plan to offer."

"The terms *you* plan to offer," Antonov corrected for, in a sense, that was no more than literal truth. Lantu's personal familiarity with the Synod's members had guided the careful crafting of a package both sides might be able to live with, though the prelates' reaction, had any of them suspected who the infidels' advisor was, scarcely bore thinking on.

Lantu gave him a small, Theban smile and shrugged.

"Actually, Admiral, I believe the first admiral is correct." Winnifred Trevayne's diffidence couldn't quite hide her delight. She was in her element analyzing the Theban responses—which, Antonov reflected, probably said something unhealthy about her intellect. "The new Prophet will undoubtedly rant and rave, but he has no realistic option. He knows that. If he didn't, he wouldn't have agreed even to meet with you, and I think he's afraid you're going to demand something far worse. No doubt he's screwed himself up to accept martyrdom rather than that something worse, and when you start turning the screws, he's going to be certain that's what's coming. Which means that when you offer him the rest of the terms Admiral Lantu's suggested they'll seem so much better than his expectations he'll jump at them." She smiled slightly. "In fact, he'll probably think you're a fool for letting him off so lightly."

"You do great things for my self-esteem, Commander," Antonov growled, but his eyes gleamed appreciatively.

"Well, sir, it's not really that different from a military operation, is it?" she replied. "We don't care what they think of us. We only have to worry about what they do."

The Prophet of Holy Terra's nostrils flared as he entered the conference room. His stiff face was expressionless, but his eyes flitted about as if he expected the Satan-Khan himself to materialize in a puff of smoke. Antonov rose on the far side of the table, flanked by his staff and senior officers (with the conspicuous exception of his special deputy for fighter operations) as the Prophet's delegation of bishops and archbishops followed him. Their yellow eyes flared with contempt for the heretics before them, but contempt was a frail shield for the terror which lurked behind it.

Antonov waited as they took their waiting chairs stiffly, then sank into his own chair, followed a fraction of a second later by his subordinates. He faced the Prophet across the table and cleared his throat.

"This is only a preliminary meeting," he rumbled, "and there will be no discussion. You may debate among yourselves at your leisure; I do not intend to do so."

The Prophet stiffened even further, but Antonov's flinty eyes stopped him before he spoke. They held the Theban's gaze unwaveringly, and the Prophet closed his lips firmly.

"I will say only this," Antonov resumed when he was certain the other had yielded. "Were we indeed the 'infidels' you term us, your planet would be dead. You have no weapon which can prevent us from destroying your species. We have not done so solely because we *choose* not to do so. Our continued restraint is contingent upon your ability to convince us that we can allow you to live without endangering ourselves or our allies, and the only way in which you can convince us is to accept the terms I am about to announce."

Two pairs of eyes locked anew, and Antonov felt a stir of satisfaction at the desperation in the Prophet's. Lantu and Winnie were right. The Theban was terrified of what he was about to hear, yet knew he had no choice but to hear it.

"First," he said coldly, "Thebes shall disarm, totally and completely. All planetary defense centers will be razed. All heavy planetary combat equipment will be destroyed. No armed starships will be permitted."

He watched the dismay in the Thebans' faces and continued unflinchingly.

"Second, the Terran Federation Navy shall maintain asteroidal forts and OWPs, in strength sufficient to satisfy its own security determinations, within the Thebes System. These fortifications will command a radius of ten light-minutes from the system's warp point.

"Third, the Federation government shall retain possession of the planetary defense center on the Island of Arawk and shall maintain there a garrison of up to one Terran Marine division plus support troops. A spaceport facility shall be built within the enclave so established and shall be under the exclusive control of the Terran Federation."

Dismay became horror at the thought of an infidel presence actually profaning the surface of Thebes, and he paused, letting their revulsion work upon them. As Lantu had predicted, they were clearly gathering their courage to reject the still worse demands to come, and he cleared his throat.

"Fourth," he said quietly, "there shall be no general occupation of Thebes." The Prophet's eyes widened in astonishment, but Antonov maintained his stony expression. "The Terran presence on Thebes beyond the Arawk enclave shall be limited to inspection parties whose sole purpose shall be to determine that the conditions of the peace settlement are fully observed. Said inspections shall have complete, unlimited access to any point on Thebes, but Theban inspectors shall be free to accompany our own.

"Fifth, any Theban citizen who desires to emigrate shall have the right to do so. If the Theban government chooses not to support such emigration, the Terran Federation will do so through its facilities on Arawk Island.

"Sixth, the Terran Federation shall be free to present its interpretation of the history of Terra to the Theban people via electronic media." Breath hissed across the table at the thought of such spiritual contamination, but he continued unhurriedly. "We are aware that you reject the truthfulness of your own computer files. We do not share your doubts as to their veracity, but the Terran Federation will declare that the events described in that data occurred on the planet of Thebes and, as such, constitute a portion of the history of Thebes, and not of Terra. We will, therefore, undertake to make no reference to any events which occurred within the Theban System prior to the present war."

The Prophet sank back, his eyes more astonished than ever. Surely the agents of the Satan-Khan couldn't resist the opportunity to attack the very foundations of the Faith! Antonov noted his expression, and this time he permitted himself a thin smile.

"Seventh, the government of Thebes shall have sole and unchallenged control over its own immigration policy, with the exception of movements within the Arawk enclave."

More of the Synod gawked at him. No general occupation? No use of the locked files against them? Not even an insistence on infiltrating agents of heresy in the guise of "tourists"?!

"Eighth, the Terran Federation, which honors a tradition of freedom of conscience and guarantees a legal right to freedom of religion, shall neither forcibly suppress the Faith of Holy Terra on Thebes, nor restrict the right of Theban missionaries to move freely among Federation planets and their populations."

The Thebans verged on a state of shock. Had they been even a little less experienced in the Synod's political infighting, jaws would have hung slackly.

"Ninth, although Thebes will be permitted no armed starships, a Theban merchant marine may be established if the people of Thebes so desire, with the sole restriction that all starships departing the Thebes System shall do so subject to boarding by Federation inspectors from the fortifications to be maintained therein. Said inspections shall be limited to a determination that the inspected vessels are indeed unarmed. Theban trade shall not be restricted in any way, and Thebes shall be free to trade with the Federation should it so desire.

"Tenth, in light of the fact that Thebes will be allowed no military forces, the Terran Federation shall guarantee the security of the System of Thebes against external enemies.

"Eleventh, Thebes shall not be required to pay indemnities or reparations to any star nation. *However*"—Antonov's voice hardened—"the government of Thebes *shall* be required to acknowledge, formally and for the record, that the attack by its armed forces on the Tenth Destroyer Squadron, Khanate of Orion Space Navy, was made without provocation under the guise of an offer to parley. And the government of Thebes shall further acknowledge that this attack was made on the express orders of the then Prophet."

Ivan Antonov leaned forward and spoke very quietly.

"Twelfth, Theban personnel responsible for atrocities on planets of the Terran Federation shall be held personally accountable by the Federation."

He met the Prophet's eyes coldly.

"I do not care why this war was launched, Prophet, but there will be no question, now or ever, of who fired the first shot and under what circumstances, nor will we permit criminals to escape punishment. The Federation will return its Theban prisoners of war as rapidly as possible, but individuals who, while in occupation of Terran-populated worlds, committed acts which constitute criminal offenses under the laws of those worlds, will be tried and, if convicted, sentenced by Terran courts. We did not attack you. We have suffered far higher civilian casualties than you. Our legal system will deal with those who have committed atrocities against our people."

He held the Theban's gaze unwaveringly, his face carved from granite, and it was the Prophet's eyes which wavered.

"The terms I have just enunciated are those of the Terran Federation. They are not negotiable. You have one standard week to accept or reject them. If you choose not to accept them by the end of that time, my forces will move against Thebes in whatever strength I deem appropriate."

He rose, his staff standing behind him, and his voice was frozen helium.

"This meeting is adjourned."

CHAPTER THIRTY-TWO

Khimhok za'Fanak

This time Francis Mulrooney felt no surprise when the *khol-okhanzir's* herald led him into the guarded apartment, yet tension more than compensated for its absence. The aged Orion on the dais seemed not even to have moved in the thirty-two standard months since their last meeting, and his bright eyes watched the Terran ambassador's approach.

Mulrooney stopped and bowed, then straightened. Liharnow'-hirtalkin's hand rose. It held the formal parchment document, signed by the Prophet of Holy Terra and sealed with the sigil of his faith.

"I have received your message and your document, Ambassador," the *Khan'a'khanaaeee* said. "Your Admiral Aantaahnaav is to be commended upon his understanding of the *Zheeerlikou'valkhannaieee* and the demands of our code of honor." The Khan's ears twitched. "Perhaps he had also some small assistance from Kthaara'aantaahnaav," he added dryly, and Mulrooney felt an icicle of relief at his tone. Then Liharnow's ears straightened more seriously, and he sat fully erect.

"Neither the *Zheeerlikou'valkhannaieee* nor the Federation read the original events in Lorelei aright, Ambassador. Had we done so, much suffering on the part of your people might have been averted. Yet even after the truth was known, the Federation honored its responsibilities. This"—he twitched the parchment—"shall be placed among the state records of my people and of my clan to serve the *Zheeerlikou'valkhannaieee* forever as an example of a *khimhok's* fidelity. We have received *shirnowkashaik* from the oath-breakers who slew our warriors, and in the name of the *Zheeerlikou'valkhannaieee* I now renounce all reparations. There has been *khiinarma. I am*

316

content, and I declare before Hiranow'khanark and my clan fathers that the Federation is *khimhok za'fanak.*"

Despite decades of diplomatic experience, Mulrooney exhaled a tremendous sigh of relief and bent his head with profound gratitude.

"In the name of my people, I thank you, *Hia'khan,*" he said softly.

"Your thanks are welcomed, but they are not necessary," the khan replied just as softly. "The *Zheeerlikou'valkhannaieee* themselves could not have more honorably acquitted themselves. There will be no more talk of *chofaki* among my fangs. You are not *Zheeerlikou'valkhannaieee,* yet we learned to respect your warriors' courage as allies against the Rigelians; now their honor makes the differences between us seem as nothing. And that, Ambassador, is what truly matters to us all."

Mulrooney bowed once more, touching his fist to his chest in silence, and the Khan rose with fragile, aged grace. The Terran's eyes widened as the *Khan'a'khanaaeee* stepped down from his dais and performed an unthinkable act. He extended his hand and touched an alien ambassador.

"It is time to present this *shirnowkashaik* to my fangs," Liharnow said, leaning upon the human's arm for support, "and I would have you present when they receive it." He smiled a wry, fang-hidden smile as the Terran moved with exquisite care, supporting his weight as if it were the most important task in the Galaxy. "For today, you shall be Fraaanciiis'muuulroooneeee, a *hirikrinzi* of the *Zheeerlikou'valkhannaieee,* and not the Ambassador of the Terran Federation, for ambassadors are not required between warriors who have bled for one another's honor."

All the other farewells were over—but for one—and for now Antonov and Kthaara had the small lounge in Old Terra's Orbit Port Nineteen to themselves. They stood side by side, human and Orion silhouetted against the transparent bulkhead as they gazed at the breathtaking blue curve of the world they had left only hours before.

Kthaara had accompanied Antonov back to the home world that was, in part, now his. He had wanted to see it . . . and he had stoically endured the ceremonies in which humanity loaded him down with decorations and promoted him to captain, a rank he would now hold for life. And now he awaited the liner that would take him on the long voyage back to *Valkha'zeeranda* to become again a small claw of the Khan and resume the life he would never again see through quite the same eyes.

He finally broke the companionable silence. "Well," he said mischievously, "has the new Sky Marshal settled into his duties?"

Antonov snorted explosively. "They couldn't give me more rank," he rumbled, "so they created a new rank. And they've decided they need a clearly defined military commander in chief . . . especially now that they won't have Howard Anderson to tickle their tummies and wipe their butts for them! Of course," he smiled thinly, "they don't *really* believe they'll ever need the position—or the military—again. Every war is always the last war!" His smile grew even thinner. "Well, the politicians may *think* they've put me in a gilded dust bin, but until I finally take Pavel Sergeyevich's advice and retire to Novaya Rodina, those *vlasti* aren't going to forget I'm here! I'm going to use the position to make sure the Navy is ready when it's needed again—as it will be!" He sighed deeply. "There is much we can learn from the Orions, Kthaara . . . such as seeing the universe as it is."

"There is much the *Zheeerlikou'valkhannaieee* can learn from your race, as well," Kthaara replied quietly. "And before you depart for Novaya Rodina—where I expect you will be terribly frustrated, since a young colony cannot afford a surplus of politicians for you to growl about!—I plan to hold you to your promise to visit *Valkha'zeeranda* and meet the other members of your clan." He grew serious. "You are right, of course. Dangers which we cannot foresee will threaten our two races in the future. But whatever happens, the Federation will always have a friendly voice in the councils of the *Khan'a'khanaaeee.* Clan Zarthan is now linked to your people by bonds of blood, for we are *vilkshatha.*" He gave a carnivore's smile in which Antonov could recognize sadness. "My ship departs soon, so let us say our farewells now . . . Vanya."

He had never heard anyone call Antonov that (in fact, the mind boggled at the thought), but he'd looked up the familiar form of Ivan and practiced until he could produce a sound very close to it. Now he waited expectantly . . . and saw an expression he'd never seen on his friend's muscular face. He even—incredibly—saw one droplet of that saline solution Human eyes produced for any number of oddly contradictory reasons.

"You know," Antonov said finally, "no one has called me that since Lydochka . . ." He couldn't continue.

"You never speak of your wife. Why is that?"

Antonov tried to explain, yet could not. In the decades since Lydia Alekseyevna Antonova had died with her infant daughter in a freak, senseless traffic accident, her widower had gradually become the elemental force, without a personal life, the Navy now knew as Ivan the Terrible . . . but there were some pains even Ivan the Terrible could not endure explaining—even to himself.

Now he gave one of the broad grins only those who knew him well were ever allowed to see. "Never mind. Farewell, Kthaara," he said, and took the Orion in a bear hug that would have squeezed the wind from a weaker being.

"Well, isn't this cozy!"

Howard Anderson's powered wheelchair hummed into the lounge. The right corner of his mouth drooped, and his right hand was a useless claw in his lap, but the old blue eyes were bright, and if his speech was slurred it was no less pungent than of yore.

"My ship leaves soon, and I only just gave my nursemaid the slip. And unlike some people—" he gestured at the remains of the bar "—I'm about to dry up and blow away! So for God's sake pour before the doctors catch up with me, Ivan! Two bourbons—right, Kthaara?"

"Actually, Admiral Aandersaahn, I believe I will have vodka." Anderson's eyebrows rose, but worse was yet to come. Kthaara tossed off his drink with what sounded awfully like an attempt at a Russian toast, then addressed Antonov. "Oh, yes, Ivaan Nikolaaayevicch, that reminds me. Thank you for the translations—and I hope you can manage to send more." He turned to Anderson. "Although I admit to some trouble with the names—a problem, I understand, not entirely unknown even among Humans—I find I have acquired a taste for Russian literature. Indeed," he continued with the enthusiasm of the neophyte, "I regard it as a unique ornament of your race's cultural heritage. Do you not agree, Admiral Aandersaahn?"

Anderson turned, horrified, to face Antonov's beaming countenance. "You Red bastard!" he gasped. "You've corrupted him!"

Old Terra receded in Anderson's cabin view port, and the left side of his mouth twitched in a tiny smile as he contemplated the chaos he was leaving behind on that world. Just over a year of Sakanami Hideoshi's presidency remained, and if he was very lucky he might be able to fix a traffic fine before leaving office; he certainly wasn't going to achieve any more than that. Anderson was a little sorry for him, but only a little. The man had done a workman-like job of actually fighting the war, but if he'd done his duty properly, there never would have *been* a war. If he was as astute a politician as Anderson thought, he knew that only his resignation might let him end on a note of dignity.

Nothing, on the other hand, was going to save Pericles Waldeck from history—or his fellows. He was guilty of two crimes too terrible for political pardon: he'd lied to the Assembly and provoked a war . . . and he'd been caught at it. That was a source of unalloyed satisfaction to Howard Anderson. The LibProgs would recover—probably by denouncing Waldeck and Sakanami more vociferously than anyone else—and the Corporate Worlds' political power would continue to grow, but he'd taken them down a peg. He'd slowed them, and the planet of Christophon would require decades to regain the prestige it had lost.

Yet the fates of politicos, however satisfying, were as nothing beside his pride in the Terran Federation and its Navy. With all its warts—and God knew they were legion—humanity had risen to its responsibilities once more. He wouldn't be here to see its next great challenge, but as long as there were Ivan Antonovs, Angus MacRorys, Caitrin MacDougalls, Andy Mallorys, Hannah Avrams, and, yes, Hamid O'Rourkes, the human race would be in good hands.

And for now, he had one last task to perform.

He looked down at the document folder in his lap, and his left hand stroked the embossed starships and planet and moon of the Terran Federation Navy on its cover. He had promised Chien-lu he would visit Hang-chow, and so he would—to deliver personally to Chien-lu's son the official verdict of the Court of Inquiry on the Battle of Lorelei.

His fingers stilled on the folder and he leaned back against his cushions to watch the stars.

Hannah Avram walked slowly out into the sunlight and brushed back her hair with her right hand. She was becoming accustomed to her robotic arm, but even under her therapists' tyranny, it would be months yet before she trusted its fingers for any delicate task. She stood leaning against the hospital balcony's rail, reveling in the sheer joy of breathing as her grafted lungs filled with New Danzig's autumn air. The ghosts of her dead had retreated, especially after the crushing defeat the New Danzig electorate had handed Josef Wyszynski and his entire Tokarov-backed slate of candidates.

The door opened behind her, and she turned as Dick Hazelwood joined her on the balcony. He, too, wore an admiral's uniform, and he squeezed her right shoulder gently, then leaned on the rail beside her, staring out over the city of Gdansk.

"It's official," he said quietly. "Admiral Timoshenko wants me for The Yard."

"Good. You deserve it."

"Maybe, but . . ." His voice trailed off and he turned to frown at her. She met his gaze innocently, and his frown deepened. "Damn it, Hannah," he sighed finally, "I know it's a great opportunity—better than I ever thought I'd see—but I don't want to leave New Danzig."

"Why not?"

"You *know* why," he said uncomfortably, looking back out over the city.

"I do?"

"Yes, you do!" He wheeled back to her with a glare. "Damn it, woman, are you going to make me say it? All right, then, I love you and I don't want to leave you behind! There! Are you satisfied now?"

She met his eyes levelly, and her lips slowly blossomed in a smile.

"Do you know, I think I am," she murmured, reaching up to touch the side of his face. "But I'm not going to be in therapy here forever, you know. In fact—" her smile turned wicked "—they're transferring me to Galloway's World to finish my convalescence before I take over Sky Watch there."

Lantu—no longer First Admiral Lantu, but simply Lantu—stood with his arm about his wife and watched Sean David Andrew Tulloch Angus MacDougall MacRory scuttle across the floor towards his mother. The infant's speed astounded Lantu, for Theban children were much slower than that before they learned to walk. And, he thought with a small smile, he would have expected the sheer weight of his name to slow him down considerably!

The commander in chief of the New New Hebrides Peaceforce stood beside Caitrin, craggy face beaming as he watched his son, and he chuckled as Caitrin scooped him up.

"Och, Katie! 'Tis a gae good thing he takes after yer side o' the family, lass!"

"Oh, I don't know." Caitrin ruffled the boy's red-gold hair, cooing to him enthusiastically, then smiled wickedly at her husband. "He's got your eyes—and I haven't heard him say a word yet, either!"

Angus grinned hugely, and Lantu laughed out loud. He and Hanat crossed to their hosts, Hanat moving a bit more slowly and carefully than was her wont. Her slender figure had altered drastically in the last two months, for Theban gestation periods were short and multiple births were the norm, but her smile was absolutely stunning.

Angus waved them into Theban-style chairs on the shady verandah, and the four of them sat, looking out through the green-gold shadow of the towering banner oaks at the sparkling ocean of New Hebrides.

"Sae, then, Lantu," Angus said, breaking the companionable silence at last. "Is it an official New Hebridan ye are the noo?"

"Yes." Lantu leaned further back, still holding Hanat's hand. "The Synod knows about Fraymak and me, and we've both been anathematized and excommunicated." He grimaced. "It hurts—not because either of us cares about their religious claptrap but because we can never go home again."

"Ah, but hame is where yer loved, lad," Angus said gently, and Caitrin nodded beside him. " 'Tis no what I expected when I was scheming how t' kill ye, ye ken, but 'tis true enow fer that."

"I know," Lantu looked over at his hosts and smiled with a trace of sadness, "and I imagine the Synod's been a bit surprised by how many of our people refused repatriation. I suspect they're going to be even more surprised by what happens to their religion once younger generations start comparing humanity's version of Terran history to theirs, too. Fraymak and I may even get a decent mention in Theban history books, someday."

"Aye t' that," Angus agreed, holding his friend's eyes warmly. "Any race needs a Cranaa'tolnatha of its ain," he said softly.

In Death Ground

In difficult ground, press on;
In encircled ground, devise stratagems;
In death ground, fight.

Sun Tzu,
The Art of War,
circa 400 B.C.

BOOK ONE

Before the Thunder

The cruiser floated against the unmoving starfield with every active system down. Only its passive sensors were powered, listening, watching—probing the endless dark. It hovered like a drifting shark, hidden in the vastness as in some bottomless bed of kelp, and no smallest, faintest emission betrayed its presence.

"So, Ursula! Is the circus ready?"

Commodore Lloyd Braun grinned at his flagship's captain. Despite requests, HQ had decided Survey Flotilla 27 was too small for its CO to require a staff, so Commander Elswick had found herself acting as his chief of staff as well as his flag captain. She hadn't known that was going to happen when her ship was first assigned to Braun, but she had the self-confidence that came with being very good at her job, and now she cocked an eyebrow back at him.

"It is if the ringmaster is, Sir," she said, and he chuckled.

"In that case, what say we get this show on the road? Outward and onward for the glory of the Federation and all that."

"Of course, Sir." Elswick glanced at her com officer. "Inform Captain Cheltwyn we're about to make transit, Allen."

"Aye, aye, Sir."

"As for you, Stu," Elswick continued, turning to her astrogator, "let's move out."

"Aye, aye, Sir." The astrogator nodded to his helmsman. "Bring us on vector, Chief Malthus, but take it easy till I get a feel for the surge."

The helmsman acknowledged the order, and Commodore Braun sipped coffee with studied nonchalance as the plot's icons blinked to reflect his command's shift to full readiness. The fact that Captain

Alex Cheltwyn, commanding Light Carrier Division 73 from the light cruiser *Bremerton,* was Battle Fleet, not Survey Command, had bothered Braun at first. The captain's seniority had made him Braun's second-in-command, and while Braun knew too much about the sorts of trouble exploration ships had stumbled into over the centuries to share the cheerful contempt many Survey officers exuded for the "gunslingers" the Admiralty insisted on assigning to even routine missions, he really would have preferred Ursula Elswick or Roddy Chirac of the *Ute* in Cheltwyn's slot. Both of them were Survey veterans, specialists like Braun himself, with whom he'd felt an immediate rapport.

Yet any reservations about Cheltwyn had faded quickly. Alex wasn't Survey, but he *was* sharp, and, despite Braun's seniority, he was also a far better tactician. Of course, a Battle Fleet officer *ought* to be a better warrior than someone who'd spent his entire career in Survey, but Alex had gone to some lengths to pretend he didn't know he was. Braun wouldn't have minded if he hadn't bothered, but that didn't keep the commodore from appreciating his tact. And, truth to tell, Braun was delighted to have someone with Cheltwyn's competence commanding the warships escorting his six exploration cruisers. Traditionally, Survey crews found boredom a far greater threat than hostile aliens, but it was comforting to know help—and especially *competent* help—was available at need.

The commodore blinked back from his thoughts as TFNS *Argive* edged into the fringes of a featureless dot in space, visible only to her sensors, and her plotting officer studied his readouts.

"Grav eddies building," Lieutenant Channing reported. "Right on the profile for a Type Eight. Estimate transit in twenty-five seconds."

Braun sipped more coffee and nodded. Survey Command had known the warp point was a Type Eight ever since the old *Arapaho* first plotted it during the Indra System's initial survey forty years back, but Survey considered itself a *corps d'elite.* Channing was simply doing his job as he always did—with utter competence—and the fact that he might be using that competence to hide a certain nervousness was beside the point . . . mostly.

Braun chuckled at the thought. He'd literally lost count of the first transits he'd made, yet that didn't keep *him* from feeling a bit of— Well, call it nervous anticipation. R&D had promised delivery of warp-capable robotic probes for years now, but Braun would believe in them when he saw them. Until he did, the only way to discover what lay beyond a warp point remained what it had always been: to send a ship through to see . . . which could sometimes be a bit rough on the ship in question. The vast majority of first transits turned out to be purest routine, but there was always a chance they wouldn't, and everyone had heard stories of ships that emerged from transit too close to a star—or perhaps a black hole—and were never heard of again. That was one reason some Survey officers wanted to rewrite SOP to use pinnaces for first transits instead of starships. Unlike most small craft, pinnaces were big and tough enough to make transit on their own, yet they required only six-man crews, and the logic of risking just half a dozen lives instead of the three hundred men and women who crewed a *Hun*-class cruiser like *Argive* was persuasive.

Yet HQ had so far rejected the notion. Survey Command lost more ships to accidents in *normal* space than on exploration duties. Statistically speaking, a man had a better chance of being struck by lightning on dirt-side liberty than of being killed on a first transit, and that, coupled with the enormous difference in capability between a forty-thousand-tonne cruiser like *Argive* and a pinnace, was more than enough to explain HQ's resistance to changing its operational doctrine.

A pinnace had no shields, no weapons, and no ECM. Because a *Hun*-class CL *did* have shields, it could survive a transit which would dump a pinnace within fatal proximity to a star. It could also defend itself if it turned out unfriendly individuals awaited it—something which might have happened rarely but, as Commander Cheltwyn's presence reflected, could never be entirely ruled out. And while its emissions signature was detectable over a far greater range than a pinnace's, it also mounted third-generation ECM. Unless someone was looking exactly the right way to spot it in the instant it made transit, it could disappear into cloak, which no pinnace could, and, last but not least, its sensor suite had enormously more reach than any small craft could boast. All in all, Braun had to come down on HQ's side. Things that could eat a "light" cruiser the size of many heavy cruisers were far rarer than things that could eat a pinnace.

"Transit—now!" Channing reported, and Braun's stomach heaved, just as it always did, as the surge of warp transit wrenched at his inner ear. He saw other people try to hide matching grimaces of discomfort, and his mouth quirked in familiar amusement. He'd met a few people over the years who claimed transit didn't bother them at all, and he made it a firm policy never to lend such mendacious souls money.

But that was only a passing thought, for his attention was on his display. For all his deliberate disinterest, this was the real reason he'd fought for Survey duty straight out of the Academy. Survey attracted those with incurable wanderlust, the sort who simply *had* to know what lay beyond the next hill, and the first look at a new star system—the knowledge that his were among the very first human eyes ever to see it—still filled the commodore with a childlike wonder and delight.

"Primary's an M9," Channing reported, yet not even that announcement could quench Braun's sense of accomplishment. A red dwarf meant the possibility of finding a "useful" habitable planet was virtually nonexistent, but that didn't make the *system* useless. Many an unpopulated star system had proved an immensely valuable warp junction, and—

"Sir, our emergence point's a Type Fourteen!" Channing said suddenly, and Braun twitched upright in his command chair.

"Confirm!" he said sharply, but it was only a reflex. Officers like Channing didn't make that sort of mistake, and his mind kicked into high gear as Plotting double-checked the data.

"Confirmed, Commodore. Definitely a Type Fourteen."

"Prep and launch the drone, Captain Elswick. Then go to Condition Baker, standard spiral." Braun made himself sit back once more, laying his forearms on the arms of his chair, and pushed the sharpness out of his voice. No need to get excited just because it was a closed warp point, he told himself firmly. They weren't all *that* uncommon.

"Aye, aye, Sir. Communications, launch the drone. Tactical, take us into cloak at Condition Baker and confirm!"

Braun frowned at his plot as *Argive* expelled a warp-capable courier drone to alert Cheltwyn and the rest of the flotilla then began to move once more, sweeping outward in a standard survey spiral, hidden by her ECM while passive sensors peered into the endless dark. A subtly different tension gripped her bridge crew, and Braun's frown deepened as he ran through his mission brief once more.

There'd been little pressure to survey the Indra System's unexplored warp point for forty years for two reasons. First, there'd been no human population within five transits of it until the first outposts went in in Merriweather and Erebor, so Survey had seen no pressing need to explore further. That, as Braun well knew, reflected budgetary constraints as much as anything else. The Corporate World-dominated Federal government was much more inclined to fund Survey's operations to maintain nav beacons and update charts for heavily traveled areas than to "waste" money on "speculative missions" in underpopulated regions of the Fringe.

But the second reason no one had attached any urgency to exploring Indra's single unsurveyed warp point was that nothing had ever come *out* of it. The nonappearance of anyone else's surveying starships had seemed to indicate there was no star-traveling species—and so no external threat to the Federation's security—on its other side.

But that comfortable assumption had just become inoperable. "Closed" warp points were far less common than "open" ones—or, at least, astrographers had traditionally assumed they were. It was hard to be positive, since the only way to locate a closed point was to come through it from an *open* one at the far end of the link, and the latest models suggested closed points might in fact occur much more frequently than previously assumed. Indeed, the more recent math predicted that the conditions which created such warp points in the first place would tend to put closed points at *both* ends of a link.

If true, there could be hundreds of undetectable warp lines threaded all through explored space, but what mattered just now was that the discovery that Indra's open warp point connected to a closed one here automatically upgraded SF 27's mission status. If no one could even *find* the thing, the fact that no one had come through it meant nothing, so the possibility of meeting another advanced species increased exponentially. Star-traveling races were rare. So far humanity had encountered barely half a dozen of them, but some of those encounters had been traumatic, and Survey Command's operational doctrine had been established as far back as the First Interstellar War. The first responsibility of any Survey ship was to report the existence of such a race before attempting to make contact, and the second was to see to it that no potentially hostile species learned *anything* about the Federation's astrography until formal contact—and the newcomers' bona fides—had been established. The best way to accomplish both those ends was to be sure no newly encountered race even knew the survey force was present until it had been observed at length, which was the reason the *Hun*-class mounted cloaking ECM.

"We've completed the initial sweep, Commodore." Braun looked up as Channing swiveled his own bridge chair to face him. "No artificial emissions detected."

"Thank you." Braun leaned back once more and crossed his legs, rubbing his chin as he glanced at Commander Elswick. "It looks like we're in clean," he said, and she nodded.

"Yes, Sir. The question is whether or not there's anyone out there to notice anything anyway."

"True. True." Braun pursed his lips, then shrugged. "You know the odds against that, but we'll play this strictly by The Book. Continue your spiral but hold your drive to no more than half power and maintain Condition Baker."

"Of course, Sir."

Elswick returned her attention to her own console, and Braun settled himself in his chair. It was going to be a longer watch than he'd anticipated.

"Well, that seems to be that, Sir," Commander Elswick observed.

"Um." Braun nodded slowly, his eyes still on the rough holo chart.

The system they'd assigned the temporary name of Alpha One was thoroughly unprepossessing, with only eight planets, the innermost a gas giant seven light-minutes from its dim primary. *Argive* had been in-system for over six days now without detecting anything but lifeless worlds and what *might* be a second warp point just over three light-hours from the star. There'd certainly been none of the clutter star-traveling civilizations tended to leave lying about, like nav buoys or com relays. On the other hand, any star system was an enormous haystack. Scores of starships could be hidden in this one, and as long as they radiated no betraying emissions, they'd all be effectively invisible. *Argive* by herself had far too little sensor range to sweep such a huge volume for covert targets—assuming there were, in fact, any to be found—and Braun was eager to get on with the system survey which was his proper task.

The question was how he did so. SOP required him to bring his escorts through to cover the Survey cruisers, but Cheltwyn's "gunslingers" had no cloaking ECM. If Braun brought them up, the flotilla's presence would be obvious to any hidden watcher. The cloaked *Huns* might not be detectable, but the carriers and their screen would be, even under tight emissions control.

He snorted mentally at his own thoughts. If Ursula's scanner crews hadn't spotted anything, odds were there was nothing *to* spot, despite the volume to be searched, for *Argive* had a far better chance of detecting anyone else than they had of detecting *her*. Even the best sensors had an omnidirectional range of little more than seventy-two light-minutes against something as small as a starship's drive field, and given that their entry warp point had been a closed one five light-hours from the primary, no one could even have known where it was in order to keep a sensor watch on it. Not even the most eagle-eyed watcher could have detected their actual arrival, and they'd gone into cloak immediately, so for anyone to be out there and unseen, they'd have to be hiding just as hard as *Argive* was, and that was ridiculous. Why should anyone hide in his own stellar backyard, particularly when he thought the backyard in question held no unexplored warp points? It would take something more severe than mere paranoia to inspire that sort of behavior!

"All right, Ursula," he said finally. "Call Alex forward. We'll hold the gunslingers on the warp point under tight em-con and turn the rest of the squadron loose in cloak."

"Yes, Sir." *Argive*'s captain seemed to hesitate a moment, her eyes on Braun's face, and the commodore quirked an eyebrow.

"Something on your mind?"

"I was thinking about asking *you* that, Sir. I've got the feeling you're not entirely comfortable about something."

"Not comfortable?" Braun frowned at the holo, then shook his head. "I'm not uncomfortable. This isn't my first closed warp point—just the first one when I've been the fellow in command. I suppose I'm finally beginning to understand why the old fuddy-duddies I used to serve under seemed to take so long to get off the pot. But—" he shoved himself up with a grin "—that's why they pay me the big money, isn't it? Go ahead and get the drone off to Alex."

CHAPTER ONE

The Fate of the *Argive*

The drifting cruiser had missed Argive's arrival, but it stirred at last as a cluster of energy sources appeared where they had no right to be. Passive sensors reoriented on the betraying signatures of unknown starships, and a trickle of power sent it sliding closer to them, silent as the vacuum about it, a darker shadow in a lightless room. The newcomers were obviously practicing strict emissions control, but they were not cloaked, and the signatures of their standby drive fields betrayed them. The watching cruiser hovered, counting them, prying at their emissions to learn their secrets, and a com laser deployed. It adjusted itself with finicky precision, aligning its emitter on another patch of space—one as empty to any sensor as that which held the cruiser itself—and a burst transmission flicked across the light-hours.

There was no acknowledgment, but the watching cruiser had expected none. It had discharged the first part of its own function by sounding the warning; now it set about the second part of its duties, maintaining its stealthy watch upon the intruders . . . and waiting.

"Everything in order at your end, Alex?" Commodore Braun asked the face on his com screen.

"Yes, Sir. *Kersaint's* got the backdoor, and the rest of the flotilla's ready when you are."

"Good." Braun nodded in satisfaction. Detaching the single destroyer to cover the Indra warp point was almost certainly unnecessary, but standing orders were firm. *Kersaint* was the insurance policy. If anything nasty transpired, the destroyer would be clear of it, able to fire out courier drones to alert the rest of the Federation, whatever happened to the rest of SF 27.

333

Not that anything was likely to happen. They'd spent almost four months sweeping Alpha One without turning up a single sign of intelligent life. The survey had taken much longer than usual due to Condition Baker's requirement that the Survey cruisers remain permanently cloaked, and Braun knew his personnel were even more eager than usual to check out the two outbound warp points they'd plotted. If neither of *them* led to closed points, the flotilla could revert to normal operations and put all this stealthy creeping about behind it.

"Very well, then, Alex. We'll check back with you shortly."

"We'll be here, Sir," Cheltwyn agreed, and Braun waved a casual salute to the screen and glanced at Elswick.

"Once more into the breach, dear comrades."

"Yes, Sir. You have the con, Stu."

"I have the con, aye," the astrogator confirmed, and TFNS *Argive* crept forward into yet another warp point.

A dozen ships waited, hidden in cloak and spread to intercept any vessel bound in-system from the warp point, but the picket cruisers' reports had revealed a problem: many of the intruders were faster than any of the waiting defenders. The defenders couldn't overtake them in a stern chase, nor could the pickets send warning when the intruders made transit. The alien ships were clustered about the warp point, certain to spot any courier drone which might be sent through, and that would warn them to flee. The defenders thus found themselves forced to guess about the enemy's current maneuvers and plans, but they knew he was surveying. That meant he was bound to come through eventually, and so the ambush had been set. If the intruders were obliging enough to send their entire force through the warp point and into point-blank range, there would be no need to pursue . . . and if they declined to do so, perhaps they could be induced to change their plans,

The transit was a rough one, but Braun shook off his disorientation and nausea as *Argive*'s temporarily addled electronics sorted themselves out and Channing checked his readouts.

"System primary is a G0," the lieutenant reported.

Braun's display restabilized, and he grimaced. A starship's initial heading upon emergence from an unsurveyed warp point was impossible to predict. Grav surge could—and did—spit a ship out on any vector, and until a point had been thoroughly plotted, no astrogator could adjust for it. Of course, that seldom mattered much. Since he didn't know anything about what lay at an unplotted warp point's terminus, one vector was as good as another.

In this instance, however, the system's central star lay almost directly astern. The warp point was well above the ecliptic, giving *Argive*'s sensors an excellent look "down" at it, but her course took her steadily away from the primary, and Braun had just opened his mouth to order Commander Elswick to bring her ship about when Channing's senior petty officer spoke up.

"Emergence point is a Type Six," she announced, and Braun exhaled in satisfaction. A Type Six was open, so perhaps they could forget all this cloaked sneaking about and—

"I'm getting artificial emissions!" Channing snapped suddenly, and Braun whipped his command chair around to face Plotting.

"What sort?" he demanded.

"Clear across the spectrum, Sir." Channing's voice was flatter, but it was the clipped, hard flatness of professionalism, not calmness. "Looks like navigation beacons further in-system, but I'm also getting radar and radio."

"I'm showing unknown drive fields in-system," the tac officer said in the same clipped tones.

"How many?"

"Lots of them, Sir," Tactical said grimly. "Over a hundred, at least."

"Jesus," someone whispered, and Braun felt his own face tighten.

"Condition Able, Captain Elswick!"

"Condition Able, aye." Elswick nodded sharply to the tac officer, and the shrill, atonal wail of *Argive*'s General Quarters alarm whooped. Despite her size, the specialized equipment of her calling put a severe squeeze on the Survey cruiser's armament. She had barely half the broadside of Battle Fleet's *Bulwark*-class heavy cruisers, but her weapons crews closed up with gratifying speed as the alarm screamed at them.

"Update the drone. Append a full sensor readout and launch," Braun ordered through the disciplined chaos. *Argive*'s speed was so low the range to the warp point had opened to little more than a thousand kilometers, and the courier drone's drive was no more than a brief flicker across the plot as it streaked away at 60,000 KPS. The commodore watched it go, then turned his eyes back to the fresh icons appearing on the large-scale master plot as Plotting and Tactical worked with frantic haste to update it.

"Commodore, I've got something strange here." Channing sounded as if he could hardly believe his own sensors, and Braun raised his eyebrows at him. "Sir, this system has at least three planets in the liquid water zone. I've only got good reads on two of them from here, but— Sir, I'm picking up massive energy signatures from both of them."

"*How* massive?"

"I can't be certain from this far out—" Channing began, but the commodore chopped a hand at him.

"Give me your best guess, Lieutenant."

"Sir, I've never seen anything like it. *Both* of them look bigger than Old Terra herself."

Braun stared at him in disbelief. Humanity's home world was, by any measure, the most heavily industrialized planet in known space. Not even New Valkha came close.

"I'm sorry, Sir," Channing said defensively, "but—"

"Don't sweat it." Braun shook himself and managed a crooked smile. "Just be sure the stand-by drone gets a continuous update of your findings."

"Aye, aye, Sir." Channing sounded relieved by the mundaneness of the order, and Braun turned to Commander Elswick.

"Let's not get in too deep, Ursula. Come to zero-five-zero. We'll sweep the perimeter for a while and see if we can get a better feel before we move further in-system."

"They've found *what?*"

Captain Alex Cheltwyn looked at his communications officer in disbelief, then yanked his eyes down to the display at his elbow as the drone completed its download and a new star system appeared. Detail was sadly lacking from the preliminary data, but bright, scarlet icons glowed balefully in its depths, and his nostrils flared as he studied them.

Commodore Braun held the ultimate responsibility, but he was on the far side of the warp point. It was up to Cheltwyn to decide what to do with the rest of the flotilla, not just the escort, and his brain shifted into high gear.

Even *Argive*'s preliminary info suggested the presence of a massive, highly advanced culture, and, unlike the link to Indra, both of this line's warp points were open—so why hadn't they seen any sign of these people on *this* side? There might not be any habitable worlds, but why weren't Alpha One's warp points even buoyed? It was possible its only other open point led to an equally useless cul-de-sac, which might explain the absence of navigation buoys, but Cheltwyn couldn't afford to assume that. Yet if that wasn't the case, then the absence of *any* spaceborne artifacts could only represent a deliberate decision on someone's part. Either that, or—

"Com, raise *Ute*. Advise Commander Chirac of *Argive*'s report and instruct him to stand by to fall back on the Indra warp point with the rest of the *Huns*. Then get off a transmission to *Kersaint*. Download the full report and instruct Commander Hausman to relay to Sarasota."

"Aye, aye, Sir."

"Allison, bring us to Condition Able and have Commander Mangkudilaga arm *San Jacinto*'s squadrons for a shipping strike. We'll use *Sha*'s for fighter defense if we need them."

"Yes, Sir." His exec turned to her terminal and began inputting orders, and Cheltwyn stared back down into his plot and gnawed his lower lip. Something didn't add up here, and a worm of acid burned in the pit of his belly.

The fact that the intruder had emerged from an unexplored warp point headed out-system wasn't surprising, but it hadn't changed course to head in-system. Like all its other electronic systems, its cloaking ECM had fluctuated as it made transit, and the watching sensors had spotted it easily. With that head start and helped by its low speed, they tracked it with relative ease despite its cloak, but its heading took it directly away from the ships deployed to catch it. Worse, it had not summoned its fellows forward, and its sensors must be amassing more system data with every passing second. Minutes trickled past while the intruder continued to move away from them, and then, at last, six superdreadnoughts and six battle-cruisers turned to pursue.

"Sir? I think you'd better take a look at this."

"At what?" Commander Salvatore Hausman looked up with a frown. Captain Cheltwyn's electrifying transmission had come in three hours ago, and Hausman had been deep in discussion of its implications with his executive officer.

"This, Sir." The tac officer tapped his display, and Hausman stepped closer to look over his shoulder. A vague blur of light flickered in the plot, and Hausman's frown deepened.

"What is that, Ismail?"

"Skipper, that's either a sensor ghost . . . or an active cloaking system at about thirty-six light-seconds."

"A *cloaking system*?" Hausman stiffened, eyes suddenly wide, and the tac officer nodded grimly. "How long has it been there?"

"Just turned up, Skip. If it is somebody in cloak, he's closing in very slowly. I make it about fifteen hundred KPS."

Hausman grunted as if he'd been punched in the belly, and his mind raced. It *couldn't* be a cloaked starship . . . could it? The very idea was insane, but Ismail Kantor wasn't the sort to make that kind of mistake.

The commander turned away and pounded his fists gently together. *Kersaint* was four and a half light-hours from the rest of the flotilla, and that meant Hausman was on his own. If that *was* a cloaked ship, it could only mean the people whose existence Commodore Braun had just discovered already knew the flotilla was here. But if they knew and hadn't even attempted to make contact, and now they were trying to sneak in close—

"Stay on it, Ismail," he said. "Don't go active, but get Missile Defense on-line. I want an intercept solution cycling ten minutes ago."

"Aye, aye, Sir."

"Com!" Hausman wheeled to his communications officer. "Record for transmission to Captain Cheltwyn."

"Recording," the com officer replied instantly, and Hausman faced the pickup.

"'Sir, Tactical has just detected what may be—I repeat, *may be*— a cloaked starship closing my position from—'" he glanced at his repeater display "'—zero-niner-two one-zero-three at approximately fifteen hundred KPS. I will initiate no hostile action, but if attacked, I will defend myself. Please advise me soonest of your intentions and desires.' Got that?"

"Yes, Sir."

"Send it Priority One," Hausman said grimly, and settled back in his chair as the light-speed burst transmission sped across the vacuum. His warning would take over four hours to reach its destination. Any reply would take another four hours to reach him, and, he thought grimly, if that signature *was* a cloaked ship, that would be at least six hours too long.

The picketing cruiser eased closer to the unsuspecting enemy ship that sat motionless on the warp point. Its active sensors and targeting systems remained on standby, but its missiles were ready, and its mission was simple.

Commander Elswick and Braun stood side by side, staring into the master plot, and *Argive's* captain shook her head as still more icons appeared. The range was for too great for detailed resolution, but Braun had decided to chance deploying a pair of recon drones. It was a risk, since the drones couldn't cloak, but their drive fields were weak. The chance that someone might notice them was remote, yet they extended *Argive's* sensor reach over a light-hour further in-system, and what they reported was incredible.

The system swarmed with activity. Drive fields tentatively IDed as freighters moved back and forth between its huge asteroid belt and the inner planets, and the RDs had long-range readings on the mammoth orbital constructs those freighters apparently served. Braun had once spent twenty months in the Sol System on a routine cartography update, and the spaceborne activity of *this* system dwarfed anything he'd seen there. He pinched the bridge of his nose, then looked up as Lieutenant Channing appeared beside him.

"Commodore, you're not going to believe this," the lieutenant said quietly, "but I've just gotten a look at the third orbital shell. It's not another habitable planet—it's *two* of them."

"Twin planets?"

"Yes, Sir. They're both around one-point-two standard masses, orbiting about a common center." The lieutenant shook his head. "That makes four of them, Sir. *Four* in one system."

"Lord." Braun shook his own head, trying to imagine the sort of industrial base a star system with four massively populated planets could support. Survey Command had come across quite a few twin planets in its explorations, but he couldn't remember a single system with *this* much habitable real estate. Which raised an interesting question.

"This is a big system, Ursula," he mused. "If you were these people, wouldn't you feel a certain need to make sure nothing nasty happened to it?"

"Sir?" Elswick frowned, and he plucked at his lower lip.

"They've got four inhabited planets. From all the energy they're radiating, each of them must have a population in the billions, assuming our own tech base is any sort of meterstick. Shouldn't a nodal system like this have better security than we've seen?"

"But we don't *know* what sort of security they have, Sir," Elswick pointed out. "We're assuming all these drives—" her finger stabbed at the plot "—are freighters because there's no reason they should be anything else, but we're still way too far out to get any kind of look at what they may have in the inner system. I'll bet their inhabited worlds have orbital fortifications, and we didn't see any sign of them on the far side of the warp point. To me, that suggests they figure Alpha One's a cul-de-sac." She shrugged. "If the system's useless, there's no point maintaining fortifications or a standing picket to watch its warp point. For all we know, the points that *do* lead somewhere are crawling with OWPs and patrols."

"Maybe." Braun peered into the plot for another long moment, then turned back to his command chair. "Maybe," he repeated, shaking his head as he sat, "but I don't buy it. If Sol had more than one warp point, don't you think Battle Fleet would at least picket the second one, even if we 'knew' it didn't lead anywhere? Think about it. We know closed warp points exist—don't you think these people must know it, as well?"

"Well, yes, Sir. . . ."

"And if they know about them, why aren't they even remotely concerned? We've been sneaking around in their space for over ten hours now. If we were so inclined, we could sneak right back out and whistle up the entire Home Fleet."

"What are you getting at, Sir?" Elswick asked slowly.

"I don't know," Braun admitted. "It just doesn't make sense to me." He frowned for another moment, then shrugged. "Well, whoever these people are, it's time to leave. I don't want to sound paranoid, but I'd feel a lot more confident making a first contact with someone this big if at least half of Home Fleet *was* handy."

"Paranoia can be a survival tool, Sir," Elswick observed, and Braun snorted in agreement.

"Turn us around, Captain. Let's get out of here."

The pursuing starships had drawn their dispersed units into closer company, but they'd been unable to overhaul the intruder. It was just as fast as they, and its course had persisted in carrying it away from them, but now it had come about, and they slowed.

The intruder's new course would carry it directly back to its entry warp point, and, coupled with its failure to summon its consorts to join it, that was an ominous sign. It must have obtained sufficient data for its purposes. Now it was falling back to join the others, and the enemy's unwillingness to thrust all of its ships into an ambush was unacceptable.

The guardian starships halted, then the superdreadnoughts came to a new heading, bound for the invaders' entry warp point at their maximum speed while the battle-cruisers waited.

Lloyd Braun made himself sit quietly, radiating calm. It was hard. He was even more aware of the gnawing tension than *Argive*'s crew was, for the ultimate responsibility was his. That was true of any commanding officer, but at a moment like this—

The sudden, shocking howl of an alarm jerked his eyes down to his display, and his face went white. Six drive fields had blinked into existence, appearing out of nowhere, directly ahead of *Argive,* and he swallowed an incredulous, frightened oath as their field strength registered.

"Six unknowns," Channing said in the flat, sing-song half chant of someone relying on training to keep him functioning in the face of shock. "Frequency unknown. I show battle-cruiser-range masses. Bearing zero-zero-three, zero-one-zero. Range one-six light-seconds and closing."

"Wide-band emissions from unknowns!" Tactical weighed in. "Radar and laser. Battle Comp calls them targeting systems!"

"Com, initiate first contact protocols!" Braun snapped, but deep inside he knew the effort was futile. Those ships had appeared too suddenly, and they were too close, barely five light-seconds outside standard missile range and already well inside the capital missile envelope. Watching *Argive*—even stalking her—from cloak might have been no more than a sensible precaution, but uncloaking this abruptly and lighting her up with tracking systems without even attempting to communicate first was something else, and he looked at Elswick.

"Bring in the Omega circuit for continuous drone update, but do not launch."

"Aye, aye, Sir." Elswick jerked her chin at her com officer, passing on the order, but her attention was focused on Tactical. The rest of the flotilla was Braun's responsibility; the survival of her ship and crew was hers.

"Any response to our hail?" the commodore asked tautly.

"None, Sir." The com officer's voice was flat, and Braun's jaw tightened as fresh light codes flashed beside the red-ringed dots of the unknown battle-cruisers. There were no Erlicher emissions to indicate readied force beams or primaries, but the energy signatures of activated missile launchers were unmistakable. Instinct urged him to launch the drone now, for his overriding responsibility was to get his data out, but the drone launch would almost certainly be construed as a hostile act. Unlikely as it might be that the newcomers' intentions were pacific, there was no way he could *know* they weren't until and unless those battle-cruisers fired.

"Sir, there's something odd about their drive fields," Tactical said, and Braun and Elswick both looked at him as he tapped keys at his console. "They're too unfamiliar to be certain, but I think those may be commercial drives," he said finally, and Braun frowned.

Commercial drives? Why would anyone put civilian drives into *battle-cruisers*? Commercial engines were more durable, more energy efficient, and required smaller engineering staffs than the units most warships mounted. Unlike military drives, they could also could be run at full power indefinitely, but they paid for that by being twice as massive, and their maximum speed was barely two-thirds as great. Freighter designers loved their durability and cost efficiency, but only a few special-purpose warships—like *Argive* herself, who spent most of her time moving slowly along surveying—could afford the mass penalty . . . or accept a lower combat speed.

But whether or not commercial-engined BCs made sense, it might give *Argive* a minute chance of survival, for it meant the alien vessels were no faster than *she* was.

"Still no response, Com?"

"None, Sir," the communications officer replied, and Braun nodded grimly.

"Go to evasive action, Captain."

"Aye, aye, Sir. Helm, come about one-eight-zero degrees!"

Braun stared into his display, watching the battle-cruisers as *Argive* swung directly away from them. Her efforts to avoid them might be taken as the final proof her intentions were hostile, but he dared not let that much firepower into any closer range. *Argive* carried only standard missiles, but those ships were big enough to mount capital launchers. If they did, they were already well within their own range, and if they were inclined to—

"Missile separation!" Tactical snapped suddenly. "I have multiple missile separations! Time to impact . . . twenty-two seconds!"

"Stand by point defense," Ursula Elswick said harshly.

The battle-cruisers flushed their external ordnance racks, and forty-eight capital missiles screamed through space at .6 c, closing on the single alien ship like vengeful sharks.

Counter missiles raced to meet the incoming fire, but *Argive* was an exploration ship. Her defenses were far too light to survive that weight of fire, and Commodore Braun's jaw clenched.

"Launch the drone!"

The cruiser's ready courier drone blasted from its box launcher, streaking towards the warp point, and it seemed to take the enemy by surprise. None of them even tried to engage it as it flashed past them on a diametrically opposed vector, and Braun tried to take some bleak satisfaction from that, but he couldn't look away from the incoming fire.

Fireball intercepts began to spall the space between his flagship and her enemies. Each savage flash was one less missile for the close-in defenses to handle, but too few were dying. Thirty missiles broke through the counter-missile zone, and laser clusters swiveled and spat like coherent light cobras. More missiles died, but the rest kept coming, and then *Argive* lurched like a wind-sick galleon as the first warhead exploded against her shields. The explosions went on and on, battering the ship like the fists of a furious giant, and Braun clung to the arms of his command chair with fingers of iron until the terrible concussions ended.

"Seven hits, Skipper," Tactical reported. "All standard nukes."

"Damage?" Elswick snapped back.

"We've lost ninety percent of our shields and we've got some shock damage, but that's it." The tac officer sounded as if he couldn't believe his own report, and Braun didn't blame him. That many battle-cruisers should have torn *Argive* to bits—not that he intended to complain!

He sat tense and still, waiting for the next salvo. There wasn't one, and he felt his muscles slowly unlock as he tried to figure out why. He punched a query into his plot with steady fingers that felt as if they were shaking like castanets, and his eyes narrowed. That salvo density was too low, unless. . . .

"Those were all from their external racks."

He hadn't realized he'd spoken aloud, but Elswick's head snapped around to face him, and he shrugged. "If they'd fired from internal launchers as well, there'd have been at least twenty or thirty more birds. So maybe they don't *have* any internal capital launchers."

"Maybe," she agreed. "I'm certainly not going to complain if they don't, anyway!"

"Me either," Braun replied, but something nagged at the back of his brain. He shoved himself back in his chair, mind racing while Engineering labored with trained haste to put the ship's shields back on-line, and his frown deepened. He tapped more commands into his display and watched the entire encounter replay in accelerated time, starting from the moment the battle-cruisers uncloaked, and suddenly he stiffened. Dear God, had they—?

"Captain Elswick!"

"Yes, Sir?"

"I think they've suckered us. They *wanted* us to survive their first salvo!"

"I beg your pardon?" Elswick's eyes widened at his preposterous statement, and he shook his head sharply.

"They should have scored more than seven hits with that many birds. And why did they uncloak when they did? With luck, they could have closed the range another four light-seconds before we picked them up. We would've been almost into standard missile range if they'd waited. They couldn't have counted on that, but why *concede* that big an advantage?"

"But, Sir, why would—?"

"Because they *did* have pickets in Alpha One," Braun said flatly. "They've known we were there the whole time."

Dead silence filled the bridge. Every officer's eyes clung to the crimson-on-crimson light dots pursuing their ship, and the sick, hollow voids in their bellies mirrored Braun's.

"Commercial drives," Elswick said, and the soft words were a bitter, venomous curse.

"Exactly." Braun's fist clenched on the arm of his command chair, but he made himself speak levelly. "This wasn't an accident, Ursula. Not a failed communications attempt. They were stalking us from the get-go. But if *all* their ships have commercial drives and they did have pickets watching us, they must have realized the carriers and their escorts can outrun them. *That's* why they let us see them early—and why their targeting was so poor when they finally fired."

His eyes met those of *Argive*'s captain, cold and bleak as death.

"We're bait, Ursula."

Six superdreadnoughts bored through space. A courier drone flashed almost directly through their formation, easily within engagement range, and they let it pass without a shot.

✧   ✧   ✧

"Courier drone coming through, Sir!"

Alex Cheltwyn looked up from the memo board in his lap, then rose and crossed to the com officers station to look over her shoulder as she queried the drone's memory. She tapped keys for a few moments, then jerked upright in her chair.

"*Argive* is under attack, Sir!" she exclaimed, and an icy fist squeezed Cheltwyn's heart.

"Download the tac data to Plotting!" he barked, and spun towards *Bremerton*'s master plot. The data flashed, and he flinched as he saw the battle-cruisers appear from cloak. He stood tautly, watching the plot, and someone gasped behind him as the angry light dots of capital missiles suddenly speckled the display. The drone had launched before impact, and he had no way to know how much damage that salvo had inflicted, but it looked bad.

Lightning thoughts flickered through his brain as the ambush played itself out before him, and his lips drew back in a snarl. The bastards had ambushed *Argive,* but they must not have counted on the rest of the flotilla's presence. Six BCs could tear any survey cruiser apart . . . but five *more* cruisers, especially with two light carriers in support, could more than return the favor,

"Communications! Transmit the drone download to *Kersaint.* Instruct Commander Hausman to make immediate transit to Indra and relay the data to Sarasota."

"Aye, aye, Sir," the com officer responded, and he wheeled to his exec.

"We're going through, Allison. *Callahan* will lead, then the carriers. The rest of the *Huns* will bring up the rear."

"Yes, Sir." The exec bent over her console, punching in orders, and Cheltwyn made himself return to his chair while Survey Flotilla 27 erupted into furious action.

The picket cruisers noted the courier drone's arrival, and, unlike Alexander Cheltwyn, they'd known it would be coming. Even before Bremerton's *com officer queried its memory, a com laser had already sent another message burst streaking across the system.*

TFNS *Callahan* raced through the warp point. Commander Chirac of the *Ute* had already worked up the sensor data from *Argive*'s initial drone, and his rough calculations of the warp point's stresses made *Callahan*'s transit far less violent than *Argive*'s had been. It was still more than rough enough, but none of the destroyer's crew had time to waste on nausea. Their sensors were already sweeping the space about the warp point for any sign of the enemy.

There was none, and *Callahan*'s skipper fired his own drone back to announce the all-clear.

The oncoming superdreadnoughts picked up the first alien ship's drive signature. The enemy had reacted more swiftly than expected, and the capital ships were still beyond effective engagement range. But they had no desire to engage until all the enemy vessels were into the system, anyway, and they altered course slightly, curling still further away from the system primary on a vector which would take them to the warp point well after the last enemy ship made transit. With the aliens' only avenue of retreat sealed, they would have no choice but to come to the superdreadnoughts on the defenders' terms, and speed would avail them nothing then.

Bremerton made transit, with *San Jacinto* and *Sha* on her heels, and Cheltwyn breathed a sigh of relief as the *Hun*-class cruisers followed them through. He'd been half afraid he was heading into an ambush, but the enemy had screwed up. They must have assumed *Argive* was operating solo, or they never would have let the rest of the flotilla into the system unopposed.

"Instruct Commander Chirac to launch recon drones," he said. "I want a light-hour shell up and maintained. Then tell Commander Mangkudilaga to hold his launch for my command."

"Aye, aye, Sir."

He shoved himself firmly back in his comfortable chair. There was no point advertising his full capabilities any sooner than he had to. It was remotely possible the opposition didn't have fighters—after all, the Thebans hadn't had any sixty-odd years ago. Even if it did, his own would prove far more effective if the bad guys didn't know he had them until they—

"Sir, we're picking up a loop transmission from *Argive*!"

"On my display!" Cheltwyn snapped, and looked down as Commodore Braun's grim face appeared on the screen beside his knee. The time display in the corner of the screen was a half-hour old, and the captain shivered at the thought that the man behind that face might well already be dead, but then that thought vanished as Braun spoke.

"Alex, if you receive this, turn around and get out of here," the commodore said harshly. "We've been mouse-trapped. These people have commercial—repeat, *commercial*—drives, and they're using *Argive* as bait. They were waiting for us, and they're probably waiting for *you*. If you're not already engaged, you will be shortly, so get the hell out. That's a direct order." Braun paused for a moment, then forced a bleak smile. "Good luck, Alex. Get my people home."

The screen blanked, then lit once more, replaying the same message, and Alex Cheltwyn's blood turned to ice. He stared at the display, willing the transmission to change, to say something else, but it simply repeated, and he closed his eyes tight.

Braun might be wrong, and if he was—and if he was still alive—Cheltwyn's ships were *Argive*'s only hope. But he might *not* be wrong . . . and as the captain's brain ran back over the data from the drone download he felt sickly certain the commodore wasn't. And if he wasn't, there were only two possible reasons his own command wasn't already under attack. Either the enemy hadn't gotten to the warp point yet . . . or else he was waiting for Cheltwyn to move still further in-system before he sprang the trap.

Every instinct cried out to ignore Braun's order, to go to his commodore's rescue, but the cold, pitiless light of his intellect said something else, and he drew a deep breath.

"Bring us about, Allison," he said, and his iron-hard voice was a stranger's.

The cruiser which had crept stealthily closer to TFNS Kersaint *for so many hours received the transmission from its sister. The enemy had advanced into the trap; now it was time to destroy the only vessel which might get word of the ambush out.*

"Skipper, I'm picking up a transmission of some sort."

"What d'you mean, 'of some sort'?" Salvatore Hausman's nerves had wound tighter and tighter as he watched the light blur on his plot. It hovered on the very edge of the standard missile envelope now, and the agonizing wait turned his voice harsh. "Is it from Captain Cheltwyn?"

"No, Sir. I can't—" *Kersaint*'s com officer shook her head. "It doesn't seem to be *saying* anything, Skipper. It's just some sort of electronic noise."

"Noise?" Hausman repeated sharply.

"Yes, Sir. It's almost like it's just a carrier. If it's got any content, my computers can't recognize it."

"Source?"

"I can't say for certain, but the bearing's about right to be from Captain Cheltwyn."

"Skipper, that bogey's moving again!" Lieutenant Kantor's crisp voice pulled Hausman's attention away from the com officer, and he darted another look at his display. The light blur *was* moving, and whoever was in command over there had to know he was at the edge of certain detection, cloaked or not, so why . . . ?

The transmission. It had to be the transmission, and if the bogey was still coming in rather than revealing its presence and attempting to communicate—

The picket cruiser slid still closer, and then, suddenly, the alien starship which had seemed so oblivious to its presence reacted. Targeting systems lashed out, locked on, and before the picket could respond, the alien opened fire.

"There he is, Skip!" Ismail Kantor snapped as his first salvo exploded. The range was long, but his passive sensors had been given over five hours to plot the bogey's movements. His targeting solution took full advantage of that data, and his external racks and internal launchers sent a dozen missiles streaking straight for it. Nine of his birds got through, and cloaking ECM was useless against active sensors at such short range. Light codes danced and flickered in the fire control display, and then the bogey glowed with the red-circled white dot of a hostile cruiser.

"She's a CL," Kantor reported as his second salvo went out, and Hausman bared his teeth. A light cruiser was thirty percent larger than his destroyer, but cramming cloaking ECM into something that small ate deep into weapons volume. Unless the bastard had some sort of weapons technology the Federation had never heard of, he and *Kersaint* were evenly matched.

Answering fire spat back, and Hausman's vicious smile grew broader as its weight confirmed his guess.

"Launch the drone!" he barked, and his com officer sent a courier drone streaking through the warp point for the Sarasota fleet base. Whatever happened here, the Federation would know *something* had happened . . . and the Terran Federation Navy would do something about it. The corner of one eye watched the drone disappear, but his attention was on the enemy's light dot.

"Come to zero-niner-zero, zero-zero-three! Let's close the range on this bastard!"

The shocked picket cruiser writhed under the attack. The fire's accuracy proved its target had seen it coming, known it was there, and the sheer number of missiles was a dismaying surprise. The first, stunning salvo ripped away its shields, breached its hull in dozens of places, and irradiated its external missiles into useless junk. The wounded ship belched wreckage and air as the alien vessel sprang into motion, speeding straight for it, but it made no attempt to flee. Instead, it accelerated to meet its foe.

Two missile-armed starships charged straight towards one another, their launchers in continuous rapid fire. *Kersaint* was handicapped by the TFN practice of carrying no antimatter warheads in peace-time lest a fluctuating containment field blow a ship apart. The enemy cruiser was under no such constraint, but at least it seemed to mount only first-generation AMs, not the vastly more destructive second-generation weapons. The range flashed downward, and both ships staggered as hits got through, but *Kersaint*'s initial salvo had given her a crushing advantage, and she exploited it savagely. A dozen more of her missiles scored direct hits, lacerating her enemy, in return for only three hits of her own, but the enemy cruiser didn't even try to break off. It came straight for her, and both ships went to sprint-mode fire as the range fell to five light-seconds. The missiles shrieked in at such high velocities point defense could no longer stop them, and Salvatore Hausman snarled as his ship staggered again and again. But he was winning. He could take the bastard, and then . . .

His eyes flared suddenly wide as the enemy cruiser altered course once more. It was only a small alteration, but—

"Hard a starboard!" he shouted. "*Hard a—*" A savage fireball glared in the soundless depths of space as two starships met head-on at a closing velocity of .17 *c.*

The superdreadnoughts were still at extreme missile range when the aliens suddenly stopped advancing. They paused for just an instant, then reversed course, darting back the way they'd come, and the range was too great to stop them.

But it wasn't great enough to let them escape totally unscathed. The superdreadnoughts twitched as they expelled a lethal cloud of external ordnance. A hurricane of fire sizzled towards the enemy, and even as they fired, one of the superdreadnoughts activated a com laser. If there were no mice to be trapped, there was no longer any need to preserve the cheese, and a message flashed out to other cloaked ships.

A fresh alarm sounded, and Commodore Lloyd Braun looked down into his plot. More icons spangled it—dozens of them strewn across *Argive*'s bow in lethal clusters of crimson. He watched identification codes blink beside them, and his mouth tightened. Not with surprise. Not even with fear. He'd known this was coming, and all he felt was a strange, singing emptiness as the proof appeared.

"I make it ten superdreadnoughts and at least twenty battle-cruisers, Sir," Commander Elswick said softly, and he nodded.

"Do you think Captain Cheltwyn got out, Sir?" she asked quietly.

"I don't know, Ursula. I hope so. And he's good. Maybe he did." The commodore looked down into his plot, and his eyes flicked to the six battle-cruisers still clinging to his heels. He gazed at them for a long, silent moment, then drew a deep breath.

"Somehow I don't feel much like surrendering," he said almost calmly. He looked up and caught Elswick's eye, and the commander nodded. "All right, then. We can't do much against those big bastards in front, but those fellows behind us have been chasing us long enough. Perhaps it's time we let them catch us."

Ursula Elswick simply nodded, then raised her voice. "Allen, launch the Omega drones. Then purge the computers."

"Aye, aye, Sir," the com officer said quietly, and Elswick looked at her astrogator.

"Bring us about, Stu," she said. "We're going down their throats."

CHAPTER TWO

Storm Wind Rising

Alex Cheltwyn sat stiff and still as his display's lurid damage codes confirmed Commodore Braun's worst suspicions. His shell of recon drones had still been racing outward when the first salvos roared in, and only the extreme range and command datalink had saved his ships from destruction. His RDs had gotten one good look at the enemy vessels, despite their cloak, before *Bremerton* fell back to Alpha One. No wonder the initial salvos had been so heavy . . . and thank *God* they'd concentrated on his escorting warships!

Survey ships were intended to *evade* enemies, but Battle Fleet units were designed to survive the crucible of combat, and *Bremerton's* battlegroup command net fused all the escorts into a single, multiship entity. Their offensive fire functioned in fine-meshed coordination . . . and so did their active defenses. The *Huns* were forced to rely solely on their own on-board point defense, but the escorts were able to bring the antimissile firepower of every ship in the net to bear on fire directed against *any* of them. The Survey ships had taken heavy damage, despite the relatively light fire targeted on them, but his escorts had survived virtually unscathed. Not, he reflected bitterly, that there hadn't been enough wrack and ruin to go around this bloody day.

The gunslingers had covered the Survey ships' retreat, waiting until all the *Huns* had made transit back into Alpha One before they followed. All Cheltwyn had been able to do was grit his teeth and take it while he ran, for none of his shipboard weapons, could even engage the enemy. His only long-range offensive power was his light carriers' strikegroups, but thirty-six fighters couldn't possibly have taken out six SDs, and he dared not linger in missile-range of capital ships

350

to recover them, anyway. Launching them would have sentenced all of their flight crews to death, and so he'd done nothing but run, and he'd never felt so useless in his entire life.

TFNS *Ute,* the last Survey ship through, had taken a dreadful pounding before she could transit, but worse was waiting when Cheltwyn returned to Alpha One and discovered what had happened to the other Survey ships he was "protecting." *Cheyenne* had led the retreat . . . and run straight into the totally unexpected fire of two light cruisers. The effects of warp transit had put her defenses far below par, and the cloaked CLs' first salvos had come scorching in before she even knew they were there. Their fire had smashed her into an air-streaming hulk and killed two-thirds of her crew, and her sister *Sudanese* had taken almost as many hits before anyone else could assist her. *Myrmidon* and *Tutu* had at least managed to find the attackers, and, in combination with *Callahan,* their broadsides had been enough to destroy them, but not before *Callahan* had been pounded even harder than *Sudanese.*

Now he sat waiting, hands clenched in ivory-knuckled fists, while his com section worked frantically to sort out the bad news, and the bile of failure burned in his throat. *Argive* and all her people were gone. If they weren't dead already, they would be soon, and his soul would never forgive him for abandoning her. Now he had four more savagely wounded ships—ships he was supposed to protect—and it had been left to the exploration specialists, not their Battle Fleet escorts, to engage the enemy. He knew it wasn't his fault. Neither he nor Commodore Braun had been given any reason to suspect what was coming, and, under the circumstances, the survival of *any* of SF 27's units was near miraculous. He *knew* that . . . and none of it did a thing to reduce his crushing sense of guilt.

"Sir?" He looked up as Commander Nauhan appeared beside him. "*Cheyenne's* a write-off, Skipper," she said. "She's lost all power—can't even blow her fusion plant to scuttle. We think we've gotten every-one off who's still alive, but—"

She shrugged helplessly, and Cheltwyn nodded in bitter understand-ing. With the cruiser's power down, dozens of people could be trapped in her ruined compartments, and there was no time for systematic rescue efforts.

"*Tutu* and *Ute?*" he asked harshly.

"Yard jobs, both of them." Nauhan met his gaze unflinchingly, and he saw the echo of his own pain in her brown eyes. "*Tutu's* lost her ECM, and *Callahan's* drive damage is even worse than theirs is. None of them can make more than half speed, Sir."

"*Damn,*" Cheltwyn whispered. Then he shook himself. Those SDs had to be coming in pursuit, and he had no time for the luxury of grief. "All right, Isis. Tell Chirac, Sergetov, and Ellis to set their scuttling charges and abandon. We'll take them aboard *Bremerton* and the carriers for now and redistribute later."

"Commander Sergetov is dead, Sir," Nauhan said quietly. "Lieutenant Hashimoto's assumed command."

"*Hashimoto?*" Cheltwyn stared at her. Arthur Hashimoto was *Tutu's* assistant engineer, *ninth* in the chain of command. Dear God in heaven, how heavy had her casualties *been*?

"I don't care who's in command!" he snapped, and knew his harsh voice gave him the lie even as he spoke. "Just get them aboard!"

"Yes, Sir." Nauhan's reply was carefully expressionless, and he clenched his jaw.

"*Bremerton* will stand by *Cheyenne*. As soon as we've got all the survivors transferred, we'll destroy the wreck by fire."

"Yes, Sir. Understood."

"All right." Cheltwyn shoved back in his chair and made himself think. With *Argive, Tutu, Cheyenne,* and *Ute* gone, there were only two survey ships left: *Myrmidon* and *Sudanese.* They were thirty percent slower than the escorts, but if the murderous bastards beyond that warp point did, indeed, mount commercial drives, they were still a third again faster than the pursuing superdreadnoughts. Adding them to the battlegroup net would slow his warships, but he could still stay away from the enemy if he could get out of range in the first place, and neither of them could hope to survive on their own if they *didn't* get out of range. Besides, he thought bleakly, with *Kersaint* detached and *Callahan* abandoned, he had two nice, empty slots to put them in.

"Get *Sudanese* and *Myrmidon* plugged into the net," he said heavily, and Nauhan nodded.

"Yes, Sir."

Cheltwyn nodded back, then turned to his tactical officer. "What do we know, Fritz?" he demanded.

"Not much, Skipper," Lieutenant Commander Szno admitted. "From the little data I have, it looked like the Commodore was right. They do seem to mount commercial engines, thank God. That's about all I can say with any assurance. I can make a few guesses based on the pattern of the engagement, but guesses are *all* they'll be."

"Call 'em any damned thing you like, but trot them out fast." Cheltwyn's mouth twitched in a bleak parody of a smile, and Szno tugged on an earlobe.

"I'd say we've got the tech edge, Skip. They were firing in three-ship groups, which probably means they don't have command datalink, and that *should* give us the advantage in any missile engagement. Or—" his smile was as bleak as his CO's "—it would if three superdreadnoughts didn't mount more internal launchers than our entire battlegroup."

"Understood. Is that the only reason you think we've got better tech?"

"No, Sir. This is more speculative, but sensors confirm they used only standard nukes and first-generation antimatter warheads."

Cheltwyn cocked his head with a frown, then nodded. "All right," he said. "I think you're onto something there. Anything else?"

"Not really, Sir, and I'm afraid to assume a bigger edge. Just because we developed systems in a given pattern doesn't mean they've done the same thing. Remember the X-ray laser. The Thebans' general tech base was well behind ours, but we'd never even thought of that one. These people may have surprises of their own."

"Point taken," Cheltwyn grunted, and turned his head as Nauhan reappeared.

"We've gotten everyone we could find off *Cheyenne,* Sir, and *Myrmidon* and *Sudanese* are tied into the net. We should have the last personnel off *Callahan, Tutu* and *Ute* in another ten minutes; the small craft are docking with them now."

"Then get us underway. The boats are fast enough to overtake us, and I want as much distance as possible between us and this warp point before the bad guys come through."

"Aye, aye, Sir." Nauhan nodded to *Bremerton*'s astrogator and the tattered survivors of Survey Flotilla 27 and its escorts began to move.

"Do you have lock on *Cheyenne,* Fritz?"

"Aye, Skipper." Szno sounded unhappy, and Cheltwyn didn't blame him. No one liked to destroy one of his own, but they couldn't let that hulk's data or technology fall into enemy hands.

"Destroy her," he said harshly, and the tac officer pressed the firing key. There was no drive field to interdict, and the Survey cruiser's shattered wreck vanished in a sun-bright boil as a single warhead took her dead amidships. Cheltwyn watched the visual display as *Cheyenne* died, and his bitter eyes matched the hellish glare of her pyre. Then he made himself look away as Nauhan finished passing his orders to the small craft evacuating the other three ships. He beckoned to her and rose from his own chair to glower into the main plot.

"We'll try to run without engaging them, Isis. Fritz thinks we've got a tech advantage, but it's not enough to let us go toe-to-toe with capital ships."

"Yes, Sir."

"Have Mangkudilaga rearm his birds. Shipping strikes against that much firepower would be suicide, and we'll need them for a combat space patrol if they bring up carriers of their own."

"Yes, Sir. Should we launch *Sha*'s group now? They're already configured for intercepts."

Cheltwyn shook his head. "No. We should have enough warning to get the CSP off from standby before anyone can hit us, and I want maximum endurance on their life support when we do launch."

"Understood, Sir."

"All right. Once you've passed those instructions, get a fresh RD shell deployed. We don't have enough of them, so use them to sweep a sixty-degree cone along our line of advance. We'll just have to take our chances on the flanks."

"We could cover that with the recon fighters—" Nauhan began, then shook her head. "No. We'll need every bird we've got for self-defense."

"Exactly," Cheltwyn agreed. "Besides—" he gave another bleak smile "—I want to keep the fact that we've got them our little secret for as long as possible. It's unlikely these people don't have fighters of their own, but if they think *we* don't, they may come in fat and happy, and we need every edge we can get."

"Yes, Sir."

"As soon as we've gotten all that done," the captain went on, "run everything we got from Commodore Braun's drone and every sensor reading Tactical and Plotting got on the actual engagement through the computers. Add *Callahan*'s download from what happened here and put Battle Comp on it. See if they can improve on Fritz's guesstimate of their capabilities, then download the results and all the raw data to two courier drones. Send one to *Kersaint* so Hausman knows what's going on, and send the other straight to Sarasota."

"Yes, Sir." Nauhan gazed into the plot for a moment, then raised her eyes to her CO's.

"What does Sarasota have available, Sir?" she asked softly, and Cheltwyn sighed.

"Not enough," he admitted in an even lower voice. "Admiral Villiers is on maneuvers in K-45, but he's only got a light task group. The next closest force is Admiral Murakuma's, and she's clear up beyond Romulus. She'll need time to get here . . . and her heaviest unit's a battleship." He turned to face his exec squarely. "These people have one hell of an industrial base just in this one system. If they come after us, we're going to lose a lot of systems before we can get enough Fleet units in here to stop them, Isis."

Nauhan opened her mouth, then closed it, nodded, and walked towards the com section. Cheltwyn watched her go, and his thoughts were grimmer even than his face, for he knew what she hadn't said. There were only five thousand colonists in the Golan System, but there were eight million in Merriweather, another thirty million in Justin, over a hundred million in Sarasota, and more than a *billion* in the five inhabited systems of the Remus Cluster, and Alex Cheltwyn and the Terran Federation Navy were oath bound to protect them all.

He knew that. It was the highest calling he could imagine—the reason he'd first put on Navy black and silver and sworn himself to the Federation's service—and he knew the men and women of the Fleet would honor that oath or die trying.

But he also knew that unless the TFN had one hell of a technological advantage, this time it was a promise they couldn't keep.

CHAPTER THREE

The Stuff of Dreams

No one had ever really been able to account for the existence of warp points, least of all the humans who'd blundered onto the one in Sol's outer system by accident. Centuries ago, the great Orion astrophysicist Feemannow'hhisril predicted the presence of Khanae's warp points, but only by inference from their effect on that system's bodies; his work begged the question of causation. Everyone agreed they must in some way be related to the still-imperfectly-understood phenomenon of gravity, which shapes space—that much was clear from the grav surge that made them directly detectable. So the most popular theory held they must result from interruptions in a galactically vast pattern of gravitational interrelationships. Fortunately for this theory, most warp points occurred in association with the gravity wells of stars. Unfortunately for it, some didn't.

Starless warp nexi were as depressing for starfarers as they were frustrating for theorists. For it was only here that humans—or members of any other known species, for that matter—ever experienced the reality of the interstellar abysses they normally bypassed. Here, with no nearby sun to give a reference point, finite minds must confront infinity, and the bottomless void could swallow the soul of anyone who stared into it too long.

Rear Admiral Anthony Villiers knew the void well, for he'd spent a goodly percentage of his life in space. He knew it was just as well that most of TF 58's personnel never needed to look beyond the bulkheads of their ships. The terror that could overtake even strong minds—the sensation of lostness, of awakening from a dream of cozy ordinariness into a horrifyingly incomprehensible reality—was a problem that had been outweighed in the TFN's estimation by the security advantages of conducting maneuvers in a starless nexus like K-45. Villiers wasn't altogether convinced.

But now he stood, ramrod-straight as usual, and stared into the flag bridge's view screen. None of the task force's other ships were visible, of course; even if they'd been close enough, what light was there for them to reflect? There was only an emptiness that mirrored what he felt inside as he listened to his chief of staff announce the unthinkable.

" . . . and so Com was able to finish copying the message before the last of the drones transited to Justin," Captain Santos reported, plowing doggedly ahead despite the Admiral's lack of response. Could *nothing* take the starch out of that stiffness? "Captain Cheltwyn concludes his report to HQ by stating that he'll soon be transiting to Indra but doesn't intend to halt there. He'll proceed directly to Golan and assume a defensive posture. He requests that all available reinforcements—"

"Quite," Villiers cut in abruptly, turning on his heel to face Santos. "We will discontinue the maneuvers forthwith. All elements of the task force will proceed immediately to Golan at maximum speed, Commodore." In some segments of the TFN, the shipboard courtesy "promotion" of anyone holding the rank of captain, reserving the sacrosanct title for the skipper, was considered passé. Villiers upheld it with the same rigor he brought to the enforcement of the most traditional possible interpretation of uniform regulations. This surprised no one, least of all his staff, who now stood uncomfortably under the gaze of those pale blue eyes.

"But, Admiral," Santos said hesitantly, "we've received no orders to—"

"We scarcely need them, Commodore," Villiers clipped in that version of Standard English which, coming from that little island of Old Terra which had birthed the language, held a certain prestige-conferring rightness everyone else in the Federation recognized even as they resented it. "As the nearest force, we are not only authorized but required to respond to Captain Cheltwyn's request for reinforcements. Standing Order 347-A admits of no ambiguity in this matter."

Santos' brown face remained impassive, but Commander Frankel, the operations officer, hadn't been with Villiers long. He turned his head a few degrees toward Commander Takeda, the supply officer, and muttered, "Oh, yeah. The Orglon Scenario."

The lips under Villiers' micrometrically trimmed mustache thinned even more than was their wont, and he gave Frankel a glare beneath which the ops officer wilted. "I believe, Commander, that we can all identify the standing order in question without recourse to sensationalistic labels which the popular media have dredged up from cheap science fiction." Everyone tried to be as inconspicuous as possible, for Frankel had disturbed a particularly rampant bee in Villiers' bonnet. The real problem, of course, was that the "cheap science fiction" had been produced by a fellow TFN officer—not that Villiers would have willingly accorded Captain Marcus LeBlanc any such status. The maverick intelligence officer would have been anathema to Villiers even had he not used his spare time to write a novel almost as notable for its iconoclasm about the upper Fleet echelons as for its hetero-doxy concerning potential alien threats. Still, LeBlanc's "Orglon Empire" had filled what seemed to be a widespread need after two generations of peace. Plausible menaces were hard to come by these days.

Santos came to Frankel's rescue by changing the subject. "You said 'maximum speed,' Sir. Did you mean that literally?"

"What, pray tell, might lead you to suspect I did not?" Villiers asked in a deceptively mild tone.

"But, Sir, if we run the drives flat out over that long a period, we're likely—

"I am quite aware of the implications, Commodore." Villiers' cold gaze swept over the staff before he resumed in fractionally less gla-cial tones. "If there is any truth to Captain Cheltwyn's report—and I cannot believe he would be guilty of hysterical exaggeration—the urgency of this matter cannot be overstated. Both time and firepower are of the essence, and the task force *will* proceed at maximum. See to it, Commodore." Without another word, he turned away from the array of eyes with their varying degrees of resentment and gave his attention to the tactical display.

Presently the little colored dots that represented three battleships, seven battle-cruisers, four light carriers, three heavy cruisers, two light cruisers and three destroyers began to curve around into courses that would take them to the warp point leading to Erebor and thence to Golan. He stole a glance at the view screen, where the stars were precessing as TFNS *Rattlesnake* altered heading.

It sometimes occurred to Villiers to imagine how one of the pio-neering astronauts of four centuries ago would have reacted to the sight of spacecraft performing this kind of maneuver. Depending on tem-perament, the astronaut would probably have sought out either psy-chiatric counseling or the nearest bar. For in those days, reaction drives had been—and, the physics of the day had confidently asserted, would always be—the only way to get around in space. Todays reactionless drives slipped through a then-unsuspected loophole in the law of con-servation of momentum, although they didn't really cancel inertia. Rather, a modern ship wrapped itself in a drive field which could best be described as an inertial sump, although the term caused the spe-cialists to wince. Thus it had become possible to cheat Newton even before the discovery of warp points had made it possible to cheat Einstein.

But, like anything else, the drives could go wrong. . . . Villiers glanced back at the tac display and noted the tight formation as the task force accelerated to the maximum 25,000 KPS its battleships could maintain. Of course, how long it could continue to move at eight percent of light-speed was anyone's guess. Military engines allowed a higher tactical speed than any commercial engine could produce—the maximum speed of a battleship or SD with a commercial drive would be almost 10,000 KPS slower—but their higher power levels made them more failure prone. Running them at such high output for the entire voyage to Golan could have catastrophic effects, however good his engineers, and he knew it as well as Santos. Yet he'd spoken no more than the truth to the captain—indeed, rather less than the truth. His command was too weak to defeat the forces Cheltwyn had reported in a deep-space battle. His only real chance was to fight delaying actions until help reached him, and he could not afford to give up a single warp point without a fight. He could only hope the mysterious unknowns—the Orglons, some annoying imp whispered at the back of his mind—would continue surveying Indra until he reached Golan, and even at these ruinous power levels, the odds that he would arrive in time were low.

None of which mattered in the least as far as his responsibilities were concerned. For now, he wouldn't let himself think about it— or about the civilians at the Golan outpost, more civilians than he could possibly evacuate even if he packed them in like the cargo of some ancient slave ship. . . .

He stood at the notoriously misnamed position of parade rest, gazing into the view screen and thinking thoughts that none of the men and women on the flag bridge would have guessed. For he was thinking of the sixty years that had passed since the Theban War, and wondering if anyone ever recognized a golden age before it was over.

"Excuse me, Admiral."

Villiers looked up from the paperwork on his terminal as Captain Santos entered his briefing room.

"Yes?"

"I've just receipted a message from *Naginata,* Sir. Commander Plevetskaya's engineers have reported a serious harmonic in her Number Two Drive Room."

"How serious?"

"Bad enough they had to shut it down, Sir. Plevetskaya's got enough reserve speed to hold station for the moment, but her people report signs of collateral damage in Drive One. She's requested time to conduct diagnostics, but she needs to shut down Drive One to do it, so, with your permission, I'll instruct the task force to slow to let her—"

"Out of the question, Commodore. I will depart from my usual practice and repeat myself: all elements of the task force are to proceed at maximum speed for Golan."

Santos opened his mouth, then closed it with a click, nodded sharply, and withdrew. The hatch hissed shut behind him, and Villiers gazed at it for a long, silent second. Task Force 58 was barely halfway to Erebor, and he would be fortunate indeed if *Naginata* was the only ship which had to drop out of formation, yet he dared not slow. It was a cruel trade-off. If he maintained speed, he lost ships he might need desperately, but if he slowed down he lost something even more precious: time.

Perhaps that's why these buggers put commercial drives into their warships in the first place, he thought. *No Terran designer would accept such a tactical inferiority, but look at the* strategic *advantage it gives them. Their superdreadnoughts can actually move fifty percent faster than ours over any sort of long voyage.*

He gazed at the hatch for another endless moment, then sighed. *Well, I can't change what I have—and I suspect I shall be happy enough to have it once the shooting starts!*

He snorted a mirthless chuckle and returned his attention to his terminal.

As soon as possible after the task force's arrival in the Golan system, Villiers had the man he was relieving piped aboard *Rattlesnake*.

Ordinarily, Captain Cheltwyn knew, his haggardness would have drawn at least an unspoken rebuke from the admiral, whose standards of punctilio sometimes provoked muttered speculations about time travelers from the Victorian era. But Villiers greeted him with his very best attempt at warmth . . . not that it really mattered to Alex Cheltwyn at that moment. He'd seen most of his command die and then waited in this system, praying that reinforcements arrived before the attack that would obliterate his three effective ships with contemptuous ease. He could still function, but he would never again be young.

Now he sat facing Villiers and his staff in *Rattlesnake*'s outrageously spacious—or so it seemed to a man accustomed to ships of heavy cruiser size or smaller—briefing room. The staffers' eyes told him they'd hoped for some sort of reprieve from him, some silver lining to the pall his courier drones had cast over their universe, and he felt an altogether irrational guilt because he had none to give.

His eyes sought the briefing room's view screen. Nothing could be seen save the star-blazing firmament. Golan B, this system's class-M secondary sun, lurked two hundred and fifty light-minutes away with its sterile brood of planets, not even visible as a ruby star. Golan A, the system primary, would have gleamed with a Sol-like yellow light calculated to awake memories imprinted in Cheltwyn's genes, but it was in the wrong direction. So for lack of an alternative, his eyes wandered back to the troubled faces around the table.

Villiers, however, remained unruffled. Cheltwyn had never met the admiral, but so far he'd seen nothing to contradict his reputation as a man who would never enjoy widespread affection but who had a certain martinet style.

"Now, then, ladies and gentlemen," the admiral rapped, reasserting control of a meeting that had threatened to drift into despondent aimlessness, "first things first. Commodore Santos, have the pinnaces completed transit to Indra?"

"They have, Sir."

"Excellent." It had been one of Villiers' first priorities on arrival. Cheltwyn could fully understand why, after having waited in this system while an enemy of unknown but certainly overwhelming strength prowled on the far side of a warp point. He'd had to live with it; none of his surviving ships could be left behind in Indra, and none of them carried warp-capable pinnaces. Villiers' capital ships did, and he'd dispatched three of them at once. They would lurk in the outer reaches of the Indra System, probing stealthily inward toward the fire of Indra's sun to observe the enigmatic foe. They didn't carry courier drones, of course; they were little bigger than courier drones themselves. But they would always leave at least one of their number near the warp point, poised to dash through with word of any onrushing attack.

It was, Cheltwyn reflected, a classic problem. He who would defend a warp point knew exactly where his opponent must come from; but he normally could not know *when* the attack would come, and—contrary to the assumptions of journalists and politicians—no military organization can remain permanently at maximum alert. But Villiers' opponents hadn't yet settled into Indra and, indeed, probably hadn't yet surveyed the warp point that led to Golan, a fact he meant to exploit for all it was worth. He might face overwhelming numbers, but he would not be taken by surprise.

"Excellent," the admiral repeated, absently tapping the edge of the table with a light-pencil that he contrived to wield like an ivory-and-gold baton. "Now, as to our deployment, I know of nothing to invalidate the tactical conclusions which we reached en route, and of which I believe Commodore Cheltwyn has been apprised." He lifted one inquisitory eyebrow, and Cheltwyn nodded in confirmation. "Well, then, it's clear enough that a light battle-line such as ours can't hope to go toe-to-toe, as it were, with an opponent who can bring to bear the kind of tonnage Commodore Cheltwyn observed . . . especially in light of our lack of antimatter ordinance—"

"And," Frankel muttered, in tones just low enough to be arguably short of insubordination, "in light of the fact that we haven't got *Naginata*."

Cheltwyn sucked in a breath and braced himself for an explosion. But none occurred, and he came to the realization that he was the only one who was shocked. Clearly, the ops officer had tapped into a deep pool of resentment. Even Santos' glare at his immediate subordinate seemed motivated more by outrage at violated proprieties than by any fundamental disagreement.

Villiers didn't allow the silence to stretch. "Commander Plevetskaya has personally assured me that she anticipates no great delay in solving her engineering problems since being left behind," he said mildly. "So *Naginata* should be rejoining us in short order. In the meantime, we will follow our preplanned operational dispositions. Our carrier group, including *Sha* and *San Jacinto*—" he inclined his head in Cheltwyn's direction "—will deploy so as to be able to cover the warp point. Our battle-line will hold back and offer long-range missile support." He turned toward Cheltwyn again. "Our fighters should come as an unpleasant surprise to an opponent who apparently lacks any knowledge of them—and still lacks it, thanks to Commodore Cheltwyn's courageous act in forbearing to reveal his fighter capability." Cheltwyn felt a glow of satisfaction at praise from a man to whom praise clearly did not come naturally.

"At the same time," Villiers continued, "this deployment will also minimize the enemy's opportunity to use boarding tactics like those of the Thebans. Admittedly, none of Commodore Cheltwyn's observations suggest that they employ any such tactics. Nevertheless, we want no surprises along these lines. We're ill-equipped to face boarders in the absence of our Marines."

Heads nodded around the table. After transiting from Erebor to this system, Villiers had first proceeded to Golan A II—a life-bearing planet, but no great prize from the standpoint of human habitability—and landed all his ships' Marine detachments there before proceeding on to rendezvous with Cheltwyn's survivors. The publicly announced reason had been to help the outpost's administration maintain order in event of panic. The real reason was known to everyone in the briefing room, but Villiers' next words brought it home to them anew, and Cheltwyn felt his depression come flooding back.

"This leads us to the matter of contingency planning for the evacuation of Golan A II," the admiral stated inexorably. "The chief engineer has prepared an estimate of how many civilians we can accommodate with the Marine berthing spaces freed up and by going to emergency life-support procedures. It is, of course, nothing like the outpost's entire population. But, on a positive note, it is a figure which we can realistically hope to embark in a short period of time, especially given the fact that the Marines are already planet-side and won't have to be debarked simultaneously." Villiers paused reflectively, evidencing no reaction to, ór even awareness of, the seeming drop in the briefing room's temperature. Then he resumed with his customary briskness.

"The problem, of course, is one of choosing which civilians can be evacuated and which will remain. After studying the chief engineer's report and the local demographic data, I have decided that first priority will be given to children of age twelve and under, and second priority to pregnant women. We should be able—barely—to accommodate all members of these two categories."

Santos spoke impassively, breaking the silence. "One possible problem, Admiral. The separation of the members of these . . . categories from their families may cause difficulties. It could result in disruptions which we can ill afford, since any such evacuation will, by its nature, be subject to a tight schedule—if," he added, almost defiantly, "it takes place at all."

"A valid concern, Commodore. Before his disembarkation at Golan A II, I spoke privately to Major Kemal. He is fully aware of such potential problems, and is prepared to take whatever measures are necessary to assure the successful evacuation of those we are able to evacuate. He," Villiers continued, laying a slight stress on the pronoun, "is under no illusions as to our inability to save all the civilian population here, nor as to our duty to save those we can." He ran his cold eyes around the table, forcing each of them to meet his gaze. And some of them thought of that which he left unsaid: the fact that if they were forced out of Golan they'd be in the same position all over again in Erebor . . . except that this system held five thousand civilians and that one held over fifty. . . .

The chime of his bedside communicator, and the whooping of klaxons through the structure of the ship, awakened Villiers. He tried to speak, but had to swallow before he could address the machine. "Yes?"

"Admiral," came the voice of *Rattlesnake*'s captain, "the pinnaces have transited back from Indra, broadcasting the alert. As per your standing orders, I've sounded general quarters."

"Quite right, Captain. I'll be on the flag bridge directly."

Odd, he thought as he swung out of his bunk. He should have been fighting a black tide of despair, because he'd awakened into his ultimate nightmare: the attack had come before any reinforcements had reached him. But he found he preferred that nightmare, even though there was no awakening from it, to the one from which the communicator had roused him—the one in which all the dying women and children had worn the faces of his wife and daughter.

CHAPTER FOUR

"What else would you have me do?"

Explosions and all other manifestations of violence, however cataclysmic, produce no noise in the vacuum of space. So there was nothing incongruous or eerie about the silence in which the events at the warp point linking Golan with Indra were transpiring. What *was* eerie was the silence on *Rattlesnake*'s flag bridge, where Anthony Villiers and his staff stood with shock-marbled faces and watched Ragnarok unfold.

The returning pinnaces had warned them of what to expect. But those dryly factual reports hadn't prepared them for the reality of a dozen mountainous superdreadnoughts emerging one after another from the warp point, intruding their brutal masses into the metrical frame of local space/time like malignant tumors.

Nevertheless, there had been enough warning for the six carriers, positioned to cover the warp point, to launch their full complements of fighters before the first of the mysterious hostiles materialized. And the invaders' vectors were randomized, as was inevitable on emergence from an unsurveyed warp point. So it was under optimum conditions that the fighters, laden with external FR1 close attack missiles, swooped down on those mammoth ships out of hell.

Sending them in against such odds with weapons as short-ranged as the FR1 had been a grim decision, yet there was little choice. The longer-ranged FM2 would have allowed them to attack from beyond the effective close-in envelope of most antifighter weapons, but an entire squadron could mount only twelve FM2s, and that throw weight was too little to saturate a superdreadnought's point defense. One or two would probably get through, but even if TF 58 had had antimatter warheads, the FM2 couldn't mount one. They needed the greater damage the heavy warhead of an FR1 could deliver, and the close-attack weapon moved at such high velocities as to be impossible for point defense to intercept. Villiers' pilots would pay a high price to get into range in the first place, but once they did, they would also inflict far, far greater damage.

Fortunately, it soon became apparent that Cheltwyn—now aboard *Ska* commanding the carriers—was right. No opponent with experience of fighters would have made so little effort to avoid letting those tiny craft slip into the blind zones that starships' space-distorting reactionless drives created directly aft of themselves . . . a conclusion reinforced by the ineffectual quality of the enemy's point defense fire. So almost all of the carriers' hundred and eight fighters survived to send their FR1s racing ahead, overloaded little drives piling acceleration atop the fighters' own vectors and suicide-compelled cybernetic brains seeking self-immolation.

It took seconds for the light of the explosions to reach Villiers' battle-line, hanging back at extreme missile range. The people on the flag bridge watched, faces bathed in the glare of nuclear warheads and the strings of secondary explosions that erupted as shields went down and bare metal sundered. They watched in silence as the readouts told a tale of devastation beyond their peacetime-conditioned imaginations—all of them but one. For Villiers, though appalled as any, forced himself to analyze the readouts beyond the raw totals of vaporized tonnage.

"Commodore Santos," he said after a moment. The chief of staff started, for the clipped voice had been almost like a gunshot in the hush. "If you will note, certain patterns appear to be emerging in the data."

"Patterns, Sir?" Santos moved to join the admiral while the others looked on. "You mean the enemy's apparent unfamiliarity with fighters?"

"Yes; Commodore Cheltwyn certainly stands confirmed on that point. But I'm thinking now of the response to our own missile fire." The battleships and battle-cruisers had been supporting the fighters with missile fire, not very effective at this range. "Or, rather, the lack of any such response after the initial release of their external ordinance. This, combined with the volume of energy-weapon fire the fighters have reported—ineffectual fire, unsurprisingly given that ship-to-ship weapons aren't intended for an antifighter role—point to only one conclusion."

"You mean, Sir . . . ?"

"Precisely. Those superdreadnoughts are pure energy-weapon platforms, with no integral missile armament. So the enemy's possession of antimatter warheads is, at present, academic." Villiers' sharply chiseled features wore an annoyed expression. "Pity. We could have positioned ourselves at a more effective missile range from the warp point. But that's water over the dam, isn't it? At present, the fighters are retiring to rearm, and the enemy is still coming. We must engage them more closely at once. Captain Kruger," he spoke in the direction of a com pickup, addressing *Rattlesnake*'s captain. A series of orders was passed, and the battle-line began to advance.

"Sir," Santos spoke up, "superdreadnought-sized enemy units are still emerging from the warp point. Some of them, in the later waves, are bound to mount missile launchers. And they *do* have antimatter warheads. . . ."

"True enough, Commodore. But I call your attention to another pattern in the data. Please note these recurring figures in the fighters' reports of the volume of fire they encountered."

Santos studied the columns of figures, while others, including Frankel, peered over his shoulders. Slowly, the chief of staff's frown smoothed itself out into understanding.

"Admiral, unless I'm misreading the data, those—" he caught himself before using a colorfully obscene term "—hostiles really *don't* have command datalink!"

"Exactly so, Commodore; Commodore Cheltwyn would appear to have been correct about that, as well. And, given that advantage in fire control technology, I am prepared to risk a missile duel with an antimatter-armed opponent—even without *Naginata*." The battle-cruiser had limped into Golan only four hours before the attack had begun, and was still toiling across the system at a speed not even Commander Plevetskaya's frantic determination could improve. "And now, ladies and gentlemen, I suggest that we let Captain Kruger fight her ship and concentrate on trying to discern further clues as to the enemy's capabilities and intentions."

Santos' "Aye, aye, Sir" was echoed by a rumble of agreement from the staff, including an unexpectedly emphatic contribution from Frankel.

Villiers' battle-line—so puny in tonnage compared to the procession of enemy SDs that continued to emerge into Golan space—closed to effective missile range, and the space-wracking release of energies escalated to a level that space itself seemed insufficient to contain.

It soon became apparent the enemy's fire control was, indeed, a generation behind the TFN's. Only half as many of those dark ships could link into a single entity for targeting purposes. Perhaps even more importantly, that applied to defensive fire as well as missile salvos, for after the first dozen superdreadnoughts had come others that *did* mount missile launchers, in the numbers possible only to hulls of such size.

And they *did* have antimatter warheads for those missiles. But only occasionally could such a missile get through the lattice of defensive lasers from as many as six Terran ships. The few that did were enough to savage the battleships *Aigle* and *Culloden* and obliterate the heavy cruiser *Emanuele Filberto* and the destroyers *Lancer* and *Suleiman*—nothing less than a capital ship could withstand more than a very few hits from the fires of antimatter annihilation. But time and again six of Villiers' ships sent the entire output of their launchers to converge on a single target as though actuated by a single will. Their warheads, though limited to essentially the same merely nuclear energies that had seared Hiroshima and Bombay so long ago, would ignite simultaneously in a cluster of fireballs that grew, touched and blended together in a single glare of destruction that revealed an expanding cloud of gas and glowing debris when it faded. And Villiers, maintaining a mask of cold aloofness amid the whoops and shouts of triumph on the flag bridge, allowed himself for the barest instant to hope.

But *still* those ships came. There were no more superdreadnoughts after the twenty-fourth of those Brobdingnagian vessels had emerged—to their deaths, in nine cases. But battle-cruisers followed, one after another with nightmarish repetition, and they were armed with missiles—full magazines of missiles. Villiers studied the dwindling totals of his own ships' depletable munitions with a concentration broken only by the report that the destroyer *Danton* had died. That brief, cruel moment of near-euphoria that had slipped past his defenses only made it worse.

The admiral drew himself up, armored in formality, and turned to Santos. "Commodore, it is now time to implement our contingency plan for evacuating this system. Have Com raise Commodore Cheltwyn for me."

The chief of staff, his brown face speaking silently for all of them, gave an order. Villiers looked into the face of Alex Cheltwyn, and past it at the tightly controlled excitement on *Sha*'s bridge as the light carrier prepared to send her rearmed fighters back into the struggle.

"Commodore Cheltwyn," he began without preamble, "it has become necessary for us to break off engagement. Our speed advantage should enable us to reach Golan-A II before the enemy. But if he presses the pursuit, he will arrive there in time to prevent completion of our evacuation plan. It is therefore imperative that the fighters cover our withdrawal, delaying the enemy's advance. Can you do it?"

"We'll try, Sir."

"Remember, your carriers are too valuable to be risked within missile range of the enemy. You're to avoid letting them close with you, while harrying them with fighter strikes."

"Understood, Admiral. We'll do our best."

"I'm sure you will, Commodore. You know, of course that much depends on it." Villiers made no direct mention of the civilians on Golan A II, nor did he need to.

The battle-cruisers slid through space, pulling ahead of the ponderous superdreadnoughts. But not as far ahead as they might have, for the inexplicable little attack craft persisted in their stinging, irritating attacks, which had to be dealt with. The seemingly impossible performance data of their tormentors was not really a matter of interest, except on the level of tactical utility. Analysis would, of course, be left to Higher Authority. And, aside from minor tactical adjustments, no deviation from course was thinkable, for the main enemy force had broken off, fleeing towards the electro-neutrino spoor which betrayed a habitable world. Those battleships must not be allowed to escape . . . and if they were foolish enough to stand in defense of that world, so much the better.

At the outpost's longitude, Golan A was setting in a red glow all too suggestive of blood.

"No! Lydochka!" Ludmilla Igorevna Borisovna strained between the arms of two Marines and cried out to her daughter. Two-year-old Lydia Sergeyevna, blond hair whipping in the wind around a face congested with terror, screamed back as she was borne away across the space-field, and Ludmilla struggled harder, heedless of her husband's efforts to restrain her.

Then a shadow fell across them and, from the height afforded by powered combat armor, a face looked down—a swarthy face with a hawklike nose and slitted dark eyes. The tribes of humanity had been united under the Federation since the days before they had ventured off Old Terra into interstellar space, and ethnic distinctions meant nothing anymore. Of course. And yet . . . too many times, men with faces like that had ridden out of the steppes, looking on the Slavic tillers of the soil simply as another herd to be thinned.

But this man wore the insignia of a major of TFN Marines. And he looked down at them with a compassion that shone through his sternness.

"I'm sorry, Mr. and Mrs. Borisov," Major Mohammed Kemal said, "but the admiral's orders are clear. Children and pregnant women take priority. I must insist that you cooperate."

"*Chernozhopi!*" Ludmilla spat. Kemal blinked in incomprehension of the word—literally, "black ass"—that the Russians had used for his sort of people from time immemorial. She was about to say more, but a hand grasped her shoulder from behind as Irma Sanchez, maneuvering her swollen belly through the crowd, moved up from her place next in line.

"Let them take her, Ludmilla," she said urgently. "She'll be safe—I'll look after her, I promise. And you'll rejoin her. You heard the major's announcement earlier: the Navy will pick up everyone else before they leave this system. They *have* to—don't they, Major?"

"Of course, Ma'am," Kemal stated emphatically.

"You hear that, 'Milla?" Sergei Ilyich Borisov tried his clumsy best to be soothing. "Everything will be all right, you'll see. Now let's go."

Ludmilla stared fixedly ahead, but the blond head had vanished in the crowd just as the screams had been swallowed tracelessly by the general din, and she was denied a final look. "Lydochka," she whispered before letting her husband lead her away.

"Thank you, Ma'am," Kemal said quietly.

"Don't thank me, you motherless bastard," Irma Sanchez spoke dispassionately. "I did it for them, not to make it easier for you to carry out your goddamned orders. And the fact that those orders are *right* doesn't make you any less a liar." Head aloft, she marched out across the field towards the waiting shuttle without a backwards look.

Kemal stared after her, and everything that went into his makeup prevented him from shouting after her, as he wished to, *What else would you have me do?*

The last of the light carriers sailed out of the warp point into the sky of Erebor and Anthony Villiers allowed himself an inaudible sigh of relief. Less than a third of the fighters those ships had once carried were still aboard them—the others remained in the Golan System, either as impalpable clouds of infra-debris or as derelict hulks, now lifeless or soon to be, that had been beyond the hope of recovery as the task force fled Golan. But all six of the carriers had survived. And they'd done their job of delaying the enemy's advance. Villiers couldn't actually hear the weeping and moaning of the children and pregnant women crowded into *Rattlesnake*'s bowels, but he imagined he could.

It had been a near thing. The mysterious foe had come inexorably on, slowing to fight off their attackers but never allowing themselves to be swayed from their course, as though held by some wizard's geas to advance by the most direct route toward the nearest concentration of human life. Villiers had almost stopped trying to imagine what manner of beings crewed those silent engines of destruction, and he'd ceased reprimanding people who used the word "Orglons," for he had no better theory to offer.

Captain Marcus LeBlanc, wearing his novelist's hat, had tapped into a nightmare which had receded nearly to the vanishing point in the years of peace. He'd conjured the ultimate enemy, an alien empire that had been expanding for millennia through one warp point after another, growing like a melanoma in the body of the galaxy. His Orglons represented the obscene end-product of the unrestricted cyborging on which humankind had turned its back after some bad experiences in the twenty-first century: flesh and metal, neurons and silicon, blended into a soulless amalgam created long ago by a race that no longer knew or cared what its own original organic form might have been—if, indeed, that race could still be said to exist at all, after having merged its identity into that of its machines. Villiers had scoffed, but now, with the memory of those relentless attackers fresh in his mind, he wasn't so sure.

On impulse, he turned to the intelligence officer. "Commander Santorelli, you know Marcus LeBlanc, don't you?"

Lieutenant Commander Francesca Santorelli looked up from her terminal, surprised. "Why, yes, Admiral. I met him on my first deployment. He was chief intelligence officer aboard—"

"Well, Commander," Villiers went on, as though he'd barely heard her, "when you're preparing your summaries for the courier drones, I suggest you keep him, and the sorts of things he'd want to know, in mind. You see, I have a feeling he's going to be called in on this."

He turned away to face the tactical display and watched his task force—with its empty missile magazines and its two-thirds empty fighter bays and its refugee-crammed berthing spaces—deploy to meet the possibility he tried not to let himself think about: an immediate enemy advance through the warp point whose location they must know about, since they'd been within scanner range to observe his ships vanishing into it. No, he couldn't think about that just now— nor about the fifty-three thousand colonists on Erebor A II. For if those silent ships emerged from conquered Golan, laden with death, he'd have precisely one option: immediate withdrawal, without even thinking about trying to evacuate the colonists.

"Well," Commodore Augustino Reichman breathed as the disorientation of transit subsided and the sunless sky of Warp Nexus K-45 took shape in the view screen, "just one more transit and we'll be in Erebor. And Admiral Villiers knows we're coming, so he must have gotten the colony set up for rapid evacuation. *This* time there'll be no civilians left behind." Not on *my* watch, he didn't add.

"No, Sir," echoed Captain Yu. Most of the flag captain's attention was on the tactical display, as one after another of Task Group 58.1's superdreadnought-sized *Flower*-class transports and *Dull Knife*-class assault transports, emerged with their six escorting light cruisers. The task group had been hastily assembled with the single objective of getting Erebor's colonists out of harm's way, for that system's puzzling reprieve couldn't last forever. Yu couldn't help thinking about it.

"I wonder why whoever-they-are have delayed so long, Sir? I mean, it's been almost a month."

"Who's to say, Wang? Maybe we're the first opponent they've ever met who's ahead of them technologically. From his report, Admiral Villiers must have given them a good shaking-up before he had to evacuate Golan."

There was a silence at the mention of Golan. Yu broke it diffidently. "Too bad about those civilians. What do you suppose . . . ?"

"Oh, I'm sure most of them're still all right." Reichman's voice was just a shade too hearty. "The enemy—whoever in God's name the enemy *is*—will want to keep them alive for forced labor, and maybe for their hostage value. Only makes sense, doesn't it?" He made a dismissive gesture. "Anyway, we can't let ourselves worry about that now. Our job is to make sure the same thing doesn't happen in Erebor on a larger scale."

"Yes, Sir," Yu agreed. "Believe me, I'm not complaining about the time the enemy's given us! And I imagine Admiral Villiers isn't either."

"You can be sure of that." Warships and ammunition colliers, faster than Reichman's lumbering transports, had already reached Erebor in the maximum numbers Fleet had been able to scrape up. "He's been heavily reinforced—especially since Admiral Teller should've gotten there by now. And he's been replenished with antimatter warheads, so if the enemy still think they've got a monopoly on those, they're in for a rude awakening! And, judging from that courier drone we passed in the Sarasota System, Admiral Murakuma's task force should be on the way. . . ."

Those pre-space denizens of Old Terra who bequeathed Rear Admiral Vanessa Murakuma her married surname would have been shocked to know they had, for she was unmistakably *gaijin*. Generations of the 0.78 *g* gravitation and UV-poor sunlight of Truman's World had produced a fairness of skin that was rare indeed among Old Terra's grandchildren after so many centuries of racial blending. Her green eyes and the slenderness that made her seem taller than her hundred sixty-eight centimeters mingled with waist-length, flame-red hair to give her the look of one of the ancient *Sidhe* from the misty island whence Truman's World's original settlers had come. She also seemed too young to be an admiral, but that was an illusion conferred by the antigerone treatments the Federation supplied to its colonists. In odd contrast to the strong chin that redeemed her face from delicacy, she had dimples which appeared, to her annoyance, in moments of amusement.

They were not in evidence now.

"Did you get in my last addendum to the report, Leroy?" She paused in her pacing to glance again at the blip that represented the receding courier drone.

"Affirmative, Sir. I double-checked with Communications." Captain Leroy Mackenna, her chief of staff, wondered why the admiral was so antsy about her urgent request that Marcus LeBlanc be assigned to her staff. Of course, there *was* the rumor that she and the intelligence community's slightly aging *enfant terrible* had once— But even the juiciest versions of that rumor agreed that it had been a long time ago. Surely it couldn't be the reason. . . .

The admiral seemed to read his thoughts in that disquieting way she had, for her lips curved in a smile too slight to conjure even the ghost of a dimple. "I need his insights, Leroy. He's the only one who's done any thinking lately on the subject of unprecedented alien threats, however little some people—" (of course she couldn't name names, least of all that of Admiral Anthony Villiers) "—think of his speculations . . . or the way he went public with them."

Mackenna grinned. "Don't worry, Sir. There was plenty of time to amend the report before we fired it off."

She acknowledged with a distracted smile and resumed her pacing. TFNS *Cobra*'s flag bridge was maintained at the TFN's statutory one standard Terran gee, but Murakuma, for all her light-world upbringing, paced with a determined stride for which the flag bridge seemed too confining. She was thinking of the unknowable that lay ahead . . . and of the courier drones that had already proceeded up the communications chain, and how far their reverberations must have reached by now. Indeed, they must have reached Old Terra itself by now. . . .

"But *surely* the Fleet could have *tried* to *communicate* with them! After all, *anyone* who can build spaceships must be *rational,* and *all* rational beings *must* want peace. . . ."

Sky Marshal Hannah Avram thought beautiful thoughts and tried to tune the whiny voice out. She didn't even waste the mental effort it would have required to wonder if the Honorable Legislative Assemblywoman had forgotten the genocidal Rigelians and the fanatical Thebans, both of which races had been all too capable of building spaceships and neither of which had subscribed to the philosophy the Honorable Legislative Assemblywoman, with a parochialism fit to shame a medieval peasant, assumed must be universal. She'd long ago given up hoping for anything better from Bettina Wister of Nova Terra and the rest of her mush-minded ilk. It wasn't that they were *incapable* of rational thought—Wister, for example, was a past mistress at servicing her constituents and managing the bureaucratic political machine which assured her continual reelection to the Legislative

Assembly. They were simply too lazy, ignorant and self-absorbed to look beyond their own rice bowls, and attempting to hold them to a higher standard was pointless. Better to just let this Naval Oversight Committee meeting meander to its conclusion and try to catch up on her sleep.

But the nasal platitudes wouldn't go away. "And besides," Wister bleated on, "as *all* civilized beings recognize, violence *never* settles *anything....*"

All at once, Avram decided she'd had enough. Carried beyond a certain point, stupidity was personalty offensive to her. "Tell that to the Confederate States of America and the National Socialist German Workers' Party, Assemblywoman Wister," she cut in. "If, that is, you can find them."

Wister looked blank—the liberal-Progressive Party that ruled Nova Terra had long since reduced the teaching of history to an elective. Obviously Wister had never so elected, and she had no idea what Avram was talking about. But some others in the committee room failed to altogether smother their laughter, and no one reprimanded the Sky Marshal. Hannah Avram could get away with quite a lot by trading on her record; her fame from the Theban War stood second only to that of Ivan Antonov, now rusticating in retirement on Novaya Rodina. Avram chuckled inwardly at the memory of some of the things Ivan the Terrible had said out loud in this place. Wister would be hiding under the table if *he* were here! The thought encouraged her to exploit the pause she'd created.

"I invite the committee to recall Captain Cheltwyn's report: Commodore Braun implemented full com protocols despite the unarguable fact that the aliens had deliberately lured him into a trap. In fact, such protocols are automatic in first-contact situations—and cover the entire spectrum of possible frequencies. But, by definition, it takes two to communicate. At no time have these unknowns evinced any response other than automatic, unreasoning, and lethal hostility. Under the circumstances, the on-scene commanders have behaved in the only manner possible, and I stand squarely behind their actions." Her eyes scanned the entire committee, finally settling on the chairman.

Agamemnon Waldeck of New Detroit peered back at her from between rolls of fat. He had the features that typified his clan of Corporate World magnates, almost obscured in his case by blubber. "All very well, Sky Marshal," he rumbled. "But what about Admiral Villiers' loss of Golan? Shouldn't he have been able to hold a warp point against an anticipated attack?"

"Yes!" Wister honked. "We should set up a ... a special subcommittee to investigate the Military Establishment's *inexcusable* failure to defend our citizens. Mister Chairman, the people have a right to know the facts behind this, and no coverup can be permitted to—"

Avram's attention didn't stray from Waldeck's porcine little eyes. Wister was merely contemptible, but the chairman rated a certain respect as a villain. He knew perfectly well that Howard Anderson himself couldn't have held Golan; he was just pandering to the electorate's need to believe that any bad news from the front could only be the result of uniformed incompetence. So when she spoke, addressing him directly and ignoring Wister, she didn't even bother to mention the impossible circumstances and overwhelming odds Villiers had faced.

"Aren't we forgetting something, Mister Chairman?" Her voice was of normal volume, but something in it cut Wister off in mid-vaporing. "Aren't we forgetting the time lapse involved?"

"I'm afraid I don't quite follow you. . . ."

"Then permit me to spell it out. Only *twelve standard Terran days* elapsed between the attack on Survey Flotilla 27 and the fall of Golan. In other words, what invaded Golan—two dozen super-dreadnoughts, for starters—was this enemy's idea of a *quick-reaction force.*"

Waldeck's normally florid face paled. "You mean . . . ?"

Avram nodded. "Yes, Mister Chairman. We have to ask ourselves what we'll be facing when the enemy has *mobilized.*" She let the silence stretch before adding, "In fact, for all we know, Admiral Villiers may already be facing it."

"Transit completed, Sir," Captain Yu reported as the sky of Erebor settled into focus.

Commodore Reichman nodded complacently. "Good crossing time for these tubs, Wang. Shape a course for planet A II—but, of course, check in with Admiral Villiers at once."

"Aye, aye, Sir. Admiral Villiers has a picket just off this warp point; should only be a short time delay in hailing her and receiving acknowledgment."

While Yu turned aside and spoke to his com officer, Reichman studied the system display. Erebor A's Type K orange companion-sun was fifty light-minutes away—this wasn't a very widely-separated binary, and it was lucky to have planets. Equally lucky was that a system so young—component A was a Type F—had given birth to life. In fact, it had done so twice, though component B's heavy, dense-atmosphered second planet was no place for humans. The little orange secondary sun was ignorable, as was the system's third warp point, leading to the cul-de-sac system of Seldon, for the outpost there had already been evacuated. His goal lay ahead . . . the white glare of Erebor A, moving into the center of the view screen. . . .

"Commodore." Yu's voice brought him abruptly out of his musings. "We've contacted the picket. And . . . and, Sir, there's already a battle going on here."

CHAPTER FIVE

Buying Time

Admiral Villiers had gotten his first surprise when the enemy emerged into Erebor.

He'd been sitting on *Rattlesnake*'s flag bridge. The flagship had happened to be among the third of his units that were currently at GQ; there'd be no pinnaces to warn of an attack this time, and TF 58 had been on rotating general quarters for a Terran month. So there'd been a full bridge crew on hand as he'd studied the tactical display and wished for the thousandth time for the minelayer support he'd repeatedly and urgently requested. With fields of mines—actually cheap homing missiles with only a "dash" capability—covering the warp point, he would have slept a lot better lately. As it was, he had to struggle to keep haggardness from encroaching on his almost dandyish norm.

Still, he couldn't complain about the support Fleet had managed to push through to Erebor. His task force was now up to seventeen battleships and battle-cruisers, ten light carriers, and eighteen cruisers and destroyers. An impressive augmentation of his strength by any standard except the one that mattered: the numbers and tonnage he knew he would have to face.

So he and Rear Admiral Jackson Teller, who'd arrived in Erebor a week ago, had settled on a variation on the delaying tactics he'd used at Golan. Once again, the carriers with their escorting battle-cruisers and lighter units were positioned to cover the warp point with their fighters, which now numbered one hundred and forty-nine—not full complements for his ten *Shokaku*-class light carriers, but still better than what he'd had in Golan. And better armed, for the antimatter munitions he'd received had included the far more lethal FRAM variant of the FR1. After they'd inflicted the maximum possible destruction on the leading attack waves, Villiers would advance with his battle-line to extreme missile range. It was a terrifying gamble, for he would be facing superdreadnought-sized leviathans, and analysis of the sensor data from Golan had told him things he didn't want to know about their armament. Some could hurl equivalents of the TFN's capital missiles, superior to any of his in range and destructive capability; others mounted capital-ship force beam projectors that could reach out to missile ranges with wrenching, disrupting tractor beams that oscillated between positive and negative attraction in microsecond bursts. But Villiers, relying on his superior fire-control technology, would duel with his mammoth opponents until his magazines were empty, then use his superior speed and the harassment value of his fighters to beat a fighting retreat across the system to Erebor A II—which, he devoutly hoped, would stand empty, its colonists already evacuated by Commodore Reichman's transports, which ought to be arriving any time now. . . .

With the thought came, unbidden, the memory of his address to the Golan refugees just before their departure to what he still dared hope was the safety of the Sarasota System. He hadn't wanted to do it—he never felt comfortable dealing with civilians. But his officers' eyes had told him clearly enough what they thought of his avoidance of the massed human misery in the lower decks, and when the transports had come he'd said a few words to the children and pregnant women who were being taken off his hands. He'd wanted to be reassuring but knew beyond any possibility of self-deception that he hadn't been. As he forced himself to remember the scene, his recollections narrowed to a single face, a face in which Castillian blended with Aztec. The pregnant young woman had stood holding a blond, blue-eyed toddler that couldn't possibly have been her own, and her face had worn an expression Villiers could not forget. . . .

It was in his mind's eye at the instant the alarm klaxon sounded.

He thrust that face out of his mind, along with the leaden thought, *Reichman's not here yet,* and stood up with the briskness of invincible habit. He turned to face Santos . . . and the expression on the chief of staff's face stopped him with his mouth half open.

"Sir," Santos said with the kind of impassivity that set off alarm bells in anyone who knew him, "I think you'd better have a look at the readouts from the pickets."

Villiers did so. At first, what he was seeing didn't even register. When it did, his immediate thought was, *Instrument malfunction.* But a lifetime's mental discipline didn't let that denial reflex survive for even an instant. He knew that what he was seeing was an accurate report of what was happening at the warp point that led to Golan and hell.

The forces that roil in the maelstrom of a warp point have never been fully understood, but their *effects* are understood all too well. In that vortex of the unknowable, conservation of momentum loses its meaning, which means there can be no such thing as "formation flying" through a warp point. Ever since the dawn of interstellar flight, the first principle of safety—indeed, of sanity—had been that ships transited one at a time. Simultaneously transiting ships could emerge in any sort of relationship to each other—including that of *occupying the same space*. This, of course, was impossible . . . and people who commit impossibilities tend to come to *very* bad ends. Villiers, like every naval officer, took the principle so completely for granted that for that first split second his mind simply rejected what the sensors and his eyes had reported.

Light cruiser-sized ships—*thirty-six* of them—materializing simultaneously in that Type One warp point. Of course, not all of them *remained* material for very long. . . .

"Eight hostiles interpenetrated on emergence, Sir," Santos reported in a monotone. He didn't waste words describing what had happened to those eight ships. Villiers scanned the readouts of the energy releases involved, and wondered what those four explosions—what an inadequate word!—had done to the communications and sensor capabilities of the other twenty-eight hostiles.

"They must be robots," Frankel breathed. At any other time, Villiers would have slapped him down for uttering rot. The early computer age's forecasts of artificial intelligence, like those of direct neural interfacing, had proven overoptimistic to the point of giddiness. Time and again, autonomous robotic combat units had lasted precisely as long as it had taken them to come up against opposition directed by a trained and motivated sentient brain. Villiers, like the rest of the military, had long since written off as chimerical the dream—nightmare?—of eliminating the human (or equivalent) element from war. But surely no living beings could have crewed those ships!

He forced himself to concentrate on studying the overall tactical picture while resisting the temptation to fire off signals that would only distract people who had their orders and knew their jobs. And they were doing those jobs as well as could be expected, considering the stunning surprise that had been heaped atop the fatigue of a month spent alternating between general quarters and mere "alert" status. The fighters of the combat space patrol swooped in and launched as the invaders tried to bend their randomized vectors into some kind of organized formation. Ships as small as light cruisers had no business trying to absorb the fury of antimatter warheads; one after another, they died in that hellish glare . . . but not without taking toll, for the foe had learned from what had happened in Golan. The antifighter fire, while still far short of TFN standards, had improved significantly enough for the difference to fairly leap out of the raw data. More fighters were dying than even Villiers' worst-case estimates had allowed for at this stage of the battle. Before the last of the invasion's vanguard had been destroyed, the surviving fighters had exhausted their missiles—and much of the task force was still struggling to come to full readiness. The admiral gazed at the columns of figures and the swarming lights in the master plot's holo tank, and saw his plan lying in ruins.

The CSP's survivors had just turned to return to their carriers to rearm and the other carriers were not yet prepared to launch when the first superdreadnought emerged from the warp point. It was alone—evidently not even this enemy could afford to treat those huge ships as expendable, and there were no more lunatic simultaneous transits—and Villiers turned to Santos and proceeded to exceed even his usual capacity for studied understatement.

"We appear, Commodore, to be faced with an unanticipated gap in our fighter coverage of the warp point. We must therefore make adjustments to our plan. The battle-line will advance."

The Assault Fleet had done its work. As the superdreadnought oriented itself, its sky-sweeping sensors revealed that the anticipated little attack craft had exhausted their armament in reducing the light cruisers of the initial transit to the handful that survived, and were now withdrawing to their tenders. The enemy battle-line—the same sort of ships as before, little more than two-thirds as massive as a superdreadnought, but more of them this time, as was to be expected—was closing to within standard missile range.

It would be necessary to induce them to narrow the range even more.

Villiers' outward impassivity, so habitual as to be unconscious, was now a dike holding back a rising flood of despair.

His battle-line's finely orchestrated salvos of antimatter missiles had done fearful damage to the oncoming superdreadnoughts. But those implacable behemoths continued to come, and come, and come . . . and each of them mounted massed arrays of point defense that made it a difficult target even without the ability to coordinate its antimissile fire with that of its fellows. And these enemies were of the class that mounted capital force beams. Those weapons' destructiveness was attenuated at this range, but there were a lot of them, and Villiers' battleships began to take damage that felt like a rending and tearing at his own guts.

After an interval that seemed far longer than it was, the reserve carriers finally began to launch their fighters. A small cheer arose on the flag bridge at the news, and Santos cursed the young jackasses under his breath and braced himself for thunderbolts from the admiral's station. A full heartbeat passed before he realized that they hadn't come.

Suddenly concerned, the chief of staff turned and stared at the admiral, who hadn't moved. Concern growing, he stepped over to Villiers' side. "Sir . . . ?"

Villiers turned his command chair to face him. For a shocking instant Santos saw behind that face, saw the full depths of the hell in which the admiral's soul now dwelt. And he spoke as he'd never thought he'd live to speak to Anthony Villiers.

"It's not going to be enough, is it, Sir?"

A tiny smile caused Villiers' mustache to twitch upward. "No, it isn't, Raoul." At any other time, the use of his first name would have sent Santos into shock. Now, like so much else, it didn't seem to matter very much. "The fighters will do a lot of damage. But I think I'm learning how these . . . beings think. They send in what they *know* will be an overwhelming force and accept whatever losses it takes to secure the objective. They sent two dozen superdreadnoughts into Golan and we gave them a good fight—so they'll send in at least two or three times that here. They'll just keep coming and coming. . . ." He shook his head slowly. "Our options have narrowed to withdrawing now or . . ." His voice trailed to a halt, and Santos wondered what he was thinking. "Of course," Villiers resumed, "the decision would be an easy one if only Commodore Reichman had gotten here—"

"Sir!" The cry from the com station seemed to shatter a glass case around Villiers and Santos. "The picket at the K-45 warp point reports that Commodore Reichman's ships have begun to enter the system!"

Once again there was a muted cheer. Villiers and Santos stood apart from it. But then Villiers stood up straight. He seemed to slough off his despairing indecision, but Santos, eyeing him narrowly, saw that only the indecision was gone; the despair was still there.

"Well," the admiral spoke with a ghastly caricature of his old briskness, "that settles that, eh? Have Com raise Admiral Teller."

"Sir, you don't have to do this!"

Rear Admiral Jackson Teller forced himself to sit through the delay as his blurted appeal sped across the light-seconds to *Rattlesnake* and back again. All he could do was stare at the com screen, at the face of the man who'd just condemned himself to death.

Finally, the reply came. "My mind is made up, Admiral Teller. The weight of point defense those SDs mount individually is canceling out our fire-control advantage—especially in light of the fact that our datalinked point defense is useless against their capital force beams. So I am resolved to take point defense out of the equation entirely by taking the battleships in to ranges where their missiles can be used in sprint mode."

"Sir . . . they've already put a dozen superdreadnoughts into this system, and there's no sign they've stopped coming. You can't stop them!" Ordinarily, he wouldn't have dreamed of saying that to Anthony Villiers, but times had ceased to be ordinary.

"Of course not, Admiral Teller." Villiers' time-lagged response came in a shockingly mild-tone. "With the forces we have available, the idea of stopping them cannot enter our tactical calculations, can it? My objective is to inflict the maximum possible damage on them—hopefully enough to make them pause in their advance. Your responsibility—" (*After succeeding to overall command,* he did not add) "—will be to gain Commodore Reichman enough time to complete the evacuation of planet A II. And now," he concluded, "I'll sign off. Good luck, Admiral."

"Good luck, Sir." Teller barely had time to make the meaningless noise before the screen went dark. Then he turned to the tactical display's swarming points of light. The green ones representing Villiers' battleships were crawling towards the purple circle that denoted the Golan warp point, still expelling the red dots of enemy superdreadnoughts in a kind of horrid ejaculation.

"Admiral." Francesca Santorelli interrupted his thoughts. The intelligence officer had been here aboard the command battle-cruiser *Sorcerer* when the attack had begun and was now an ad hoc addition to Teller's staff. "These latest superdreadnoughts to emerge are a new class, judging from some subtle differences in their energy signatures."

"A 'new class,' Commander?" Teller queried, preoccupied.

"Yes, Sir. The first dozen belonged to one of the classes we encountered at Golan—what we've seen of their weapons mix confirmed our initial identification. But these coming now are . . . something else."

"Give those conclusions to the computer, Commander. I want this different class tagged so they show up in the plot."

"Aye, aye, Sir." Presently, thin red circles appeared around the newly arriving dots. And as Villiers' battle-line closed in, Teller began to notice something. The survivors of the earlier superdreadnought waves continued to target the battleships with their force beams. But from the haloed newcomers, no fire came.

Worried, Teller turned to a small screen flanking his command chair's shock frame. It showed the exterior view from a pickup on Villiers' flagship. As usual, not much could be seen of space combat, such were the distances across which it was waged. But the coming clash of capital ships, at what passed for point-blank range, promised to be more visually stimulating than most. Here and there were the flashes of detonating warheads as Villiers' missiles smashed at their targets in uninterceptable sprint mode. Lasers were, of course, invisible in vacuum, as force beams were anywhere. Glancing at the tac display, Teller saw that the battling heavyweights were passing very close indeed now. In fact, the dots of *Rattlesnake* and a hostile were almost brushing against each other on the plot. He looked back to his private screen and thought, with a faint prickling of the neck, that the stupendous enemy ship would be visible were there light from a nearby sun for it to reflect. . . . There! Maybe that was it, occluding a tiny segment of the dense star-fields. . . .

Almost too swiftly for Teller to catch, what looked like coherent lightning flashed from the enemy ship to a point just to the left of the pickup, not far away on *Rattlesnake*'s hull. As Teller bunked his dazzled eyes, the universe as revealed by the pickup shook and lurched violently and then went out.

Teller's stunned silence lasted less than a heartbeat. "Com!" he roared. "Raise *Rattlesnake* at once!"

"No can do, Sir," came the com officers harried voice. "They must have taken a serious bit—their communications array is out."

"Keep trying." Teller whirled on Santorelli. "What in God's name *was* that thing?"

"Unknown, Sir." The intelligence officer sounded as shaken as Teller imagined he himself did. "It happened too fast for any kind of analysis. But . . . we're getting reports from some of the other battleships, and some of them are downloading some meaningful data." She studied that data while Teller watched with horror as one after another of the green dots in the tac display began to flicker and then vanish.

"Sir," Santorelli reported after a time, "we've got enough readouts now—that weapon has a hellacious emissions signature—for some tentative conclusions. What we're looking at seems to project a bolt of plasma contained in an electromagnetic bottle."

"But that's crazy!" blurted Teller's own staff spook. Lieutenant Tranh's feelings about being shouldered aside by a visiting lieutenant commander made him even more argumentative than the theory itself would have. "That mag bottle couldn't hold together for more than an infinitesimal amount of time after leaving its generator."

" 'Infinitesimal' might be a little strong, Lieutenant," Santorelli retorted. "But in essence you're right. Still, the fact that it's near light-speed makes it workable as a short-range weapon. And within that range . . . it must be almost like a directional fusion bomb."

"Couldn't point defense disrupt the mag bottle?" Tranh asked in a more subdued tone.

"In theory, yes. But it would be like shooting at a missile in sprint mode. Easier to detect, granted—but also even faster, hence even less

tracking time. In fact—" Santorelli fell silent, staring at the tac display. Teller followed her gaze and saw the flickering green dot that
represented *Rattlesnake*—and all the friends she must have aboard
her—had vanished.

"I think you're in command now, Sir," she whispered.

Teller tore his eyes away from the holo tank and its tale of disaster and addressed the com officer levelly. "Com, I want you to patch
me through to all the carriers, and all the presently deployed fighters you can reach. Tell the carrier skippers to put me on intercom."

"Aye, aye, Sir." It didn't take long, and Teller only had a moment
to gather his thoughts as he watched the three battleships still able
to do so swing away in an attempt to escape. The ringed scarlet sigils
of enemy superdreadnoughts moved in pursuit, as still more of the
behemoths continued to emerge from the warp point, and emerge,
and emerge. . . .

"Ready, Sir," Com reported.

"This is Admiral Teller speaking. Since Admiral Villiers is unable
to communicate—" (*True, as far as it goes,* some ghastly voice gibed
inside him) "—I am assuming command of the task force. I will be
blunt with you. Our objective—the *only* objective we can allow ourselves to even contemplate achieving—is to delay the enemy as long
as possible. Every minute we can buy for Commodore Reichman
means hundreds of civilian lives. I intend to press home fighter strikes
to the limits of our ability while holding the carriers just outside capital
missile range on a vector designed to draw the enemy away from planet
A II." He paused for breath, then started to say more . . . but what
more do you say to pilots you've just declared a forlorn hope and
carrier crews you've just declared bait? "That is all," he finished.

*The Fleet completed its destruction of the enemy battle-line and shook
down on its new vector. The small attack craft were no surprise this time,
and the Fleet had learned much from its previous encounter with them.
It knew they must come to it—and that it lacked the speed to overtake
the mother ships from which they operated. The Fleet could not reach
their bases, and so it made no attempt to. It would kill the attack craft
as they closed, accepting its own losses to wear them away. And in the
meantime, the plethora of com signals and powerful energy sources
clustered around the life-bearing planet ahead of the Fleet whispered that
a better target than ships it could not kill awaited it.*

Flight after flight of fighters struck, returned to rearm, and struck
again. They soon learned the enemy's plasma weapon was deadly to
fighters, yet they couldn't stay beyond its limited range. The enemy
capital ships carried too much point defense for FM2s to penetrate;

that left them the sole option of flying into the throats of those hell-weapons in order to strike home with the FRAMs *no* point defense had time to stop.

And they did it. Over and over, they did it.

Teller watched from *Sorcerer's* flag bridge, and nausea warred with pride as he saw those splendid young people spend themselves, trading their lives for whatever damage they could do to an enemy they couldn't even visualize, an enemy that seemed but a faceless essence of elemental, inexplicable malevolence. Their losses sickened him, as did the fact that they'd been unable to prevent the destruction of the last of the battleships. Villiers' gallant gesture had sunk without trace in a bottomless pit of futility. But what sickened him most was the fact that the invaders refused to be sucked into pursuing his carriers and battle-cruisers. Like monstrous insects drawn to light, they made their implacable way sunward towards the warmth that might shelter life.

"Their course is gradually pulling them away from us, Sir," Santorelli observed.

"I see it is," Teller growled, then ordered himself not to take it out on the intelligence officer. "We'll have to follow them; otherwise the range will widen to the point where we won't be able to conduct fighter strikes. But we'll stay out of missile range. . . ." He seemed to reach a decision, and turned to face his ops officer. "Commander DeLauria, I want a general order sent out to all carriers. The fighters are to spread out their attacks."

"Spread them out, Sir?"

"Right. Instead of concentrating on one ship and pounding it to pieces, I want to hit as many as possible, inflict just enough damage to slow them down." He smiled faintly. "I know it goes against the fighter jocks' training and temperament—they want to go for the kill. But it's as I told them earlier: our job is to buy time."

"They'll understand, Sir." DeLauria was a former fighter jock herself. Orders began to go out.

Teller couldn't keep his eyes off the serene blue-marbled loveliness of Erebor A II that curved below him, even though he knew it was a lie. The truth was in the screens that showed the endless lines of refugees moving slowly towards the shuttles. At least they were orderly. Too orderly. Even the children seemed subdued as they shuffled along clutching favorite toys. Their faces showed little more bewilderment than their parents'.

Teller shared their feelings. He could hardly have felt a greater sense of unreality if the screens had shown sacrificial victims being led towards a blood-drenched altar, or Jews being herded into gas chambers disguised as showers. Things like this weren't supposed to happen anymore.

The truth was also in the com screen that showed Augustino Reichman's face. The full-fleshed commodore was generally an embodiment of good-living solidity. Now his haggardness brought home to Teller what was happening in a way the anonymous thousands in the screens could not.

"Jackson, I've *got* to have more time! I can get them all off this planet—I have the berthing capacity." Reichman took a deep breath. "Sorry; I know your people have already done all that was humanly possible to slow them down. But . . . look, maybe we could speed things up if I could get more people down to the planet. I've got volunteers lined up!"

Teller shook his head slowly. His idea for slowing the enemy advance had worked—and as he contemplated the eighty-five percent of his fighters he'd lost, he couldn't bring himself to feel the least stir of self-satisfaction. But the two hundred-plus pilots who'd flown those one hundred and twenty-seven fighters had bought more time with their lives than he'd dared hope, forcing the enemy fleet to slow its pace to that of its cripples. Teller's battle-cruisers and carriers had swept around them in a wide arc just outside missile range and proceeded to this planet, where Reichman now had sixty-six percent of the colonists aboard his transports, or else in shuttles en route to orbit or ready to lift off.

But still the enemy came on. They came slowly, but they came. And Teller, with four battle-cruisers, ten nearly-empty light carriers, and thirteen light combatants (including Reichman's) faced a situation materialized from sheer nightmare.

Jackson Teller had never thought of himself as a particularly brave man. Indeed, he'd often wrestled with doubts about the adequacy of his courage. So he'd long ago forced himself to face all the likely ways in which he might be called on to sacrifice his life on the altar of duty. For he was, above all else, a conscientious man, and he needed to know he would be able to call on something to serve in place of whatever quality people meant when they spoke of "dash." He'd confronted all his demons, and felt he'd stared them down.

Now he realized how inadequate his efforts to imagine demons had been. For the decision he must now make rendered the hazarding of his own life almost banal by comparison.

He shook his head again. "No, Augustino. I've got only twenty-three fighters left, and almost no munitions. And as soon as these . . . creatures realize an evacuation's underway, they'll send their undamaged superdreadnoughts ahead at full speed—they must know I can't even put up a pretense of fighting them. And slow as they are, they're as fast as your transports. So if you don't get a head start on them, *nobody* will be saved." He took a deep breath. "We have to depart for K-45 as soon as we can recover the shuttles now en route or on the ground—and the ones on the ground have to lift at once."

Reichman's round face paled. "No, by God! A third of the colony's still down there! We can't—"

It seemed to Teller that someone else spoke, in a voice other than his. "You will abort the evacuation *now*, Commodore, and prepare for immediate departure from this system. That is a direct order, which you may have in writing if you wish."

For a full heartbeat, Reichman seemed about to say the unsayable. But the moment passed. "That won't be necessary, Admiral," he said expressionlessly.

Teller turned away, for he didn't want to look at Reichman's face any longer. And he *definitely* didn't want to be looking at the view screens when the crowds on the planet's surface heard the announcement that no more passengers would be accepted.

"Commander DeLauria—"

"Yes, Admiral?"

"Get with Com and Engineering. As we proceed to the K-45 warp point, I want to lay a chain of com buoys. I also want you to patch me through to whoever's in charge on the ground down there." Teller wasn't looking at DeLauria. He seemed to be listening to the low, ugly roar over the pickup audio—the refugees must have heard the announcement. "You see," he continued quietly, "I want the ground stations to keep broadcasting as long as they can. I want them to report everything they can possibly tell us about whoever or whatever is doing this."

CHAPTER SIX

Slow Them Down

"Attention on deck!"

Vanessa Murakuma's green eyes swept her collected flag officers and squadron commanders like fire control lasers as she entered TFNS *Cobra*'s main briefing room with Leroy Mackenna, Ling Tian and Marcus LeBlanc on her heels. The dark-complexioned captain had never bothered to do anything about his receding hairline—not even Murakuma had ever figured out whether he was simply too busy to bother with such inconsequentials or whether his baldness was its own affectation—but the neatly trimmed beard he'd grown in compensation was an expression-shielding asset for any intelligence officer. *Especially today,* she thought, as she studied her senior officers' faces. Most were grim and strained, but her own was composed, almost serene. No one had to know how hard it was for her to keep it that way.

She crossed to the head of the table and took her seat while her three staffers stood behind the chairs to her right and left.

"Be seated, ladies and gentlemen." Her soprano was as calm as her face, and a quiet rustle filled the briefing room as her subordinates sat. She tipped back her chair and laid one fine-boned hand on the tabletop. None of them had yet seen the official reports from Erebor, but their faces said they'd heard the rumors, and she drew a deep mental breath.

"I'll come straight to the point," she said. "The enemy—whoever and whatever they are—have taken Erebor." Someone inhaled at the confirmation. "We anticipated that. What we did *not* anticipate was the destruction of Admiral Villiers' entire battle-line." A sort of electric shock ran around the table, and she continued in that same, quiet voice. "Captain LeBlanc and Commander Ling will bring you up to speed on our best current information in a moment, but I want each of you to understand what this means."

She paused a moment, as if to let them brace themselves, then continued flatly.

"The Federal government has activated the mutual assistance clauses of our treaties with the Orions and Ophiuchi Association. Both of our treaty partners have promised assistance and begun redeploying their own units, but neither they nor any substantial numbers of our own units can reach us for many weeks. In short, we're it . . . and we're out of time.

"As you know, our original orders were that, while Admiral Villiers screened the approaches, we were to hold station here in Sarasota to assemble our entire assigned order of battle before advancing. That's no longer possible. We must advance now—immediately—to K-45 to cover the evacuation of Merriweather. All indications are that it will be at least another two months—possibly three—before we can be sufficiently reinforced to think about actually stopping the enemy. What we *can*, and must, do is slow him down. Sky Marshal Avram's instructions are unequivocal: we *must* buy time to evacuate as much of the Merriweather and Justin populations as we can, yet we must do so without suffering crippling losses of our own. We're all there is, ladies and gentlemen, and you all know how hard it's been to scrape up even this many ships. If we allow ourselves to be destroyed, the reinforcements currently en route will, in all probability, be too little to stop the enemy short of Romulus or even Belkassa, and it will be at least *another* two months before follow-on units can reinforce *them*. Which means—" she turned her head, sweeping them all with cold, still eyes "—that if it becomes a choice between heavy Fleet losses or abandoning populated worlds, we will have no choice but to withdraw."

An almost-sound of protest swept the table, but those dark jade eyes froze it back into stillness. Every officer in that compartment knew the TFN tradition: the Fleet died before it abandoned civilians. That wasn't policy; it was a matter of duty, honor, and pride . . . but they also knew she was right. That wouldn't save them from the poisonous guilt they would feel, but they knew she was right.

"Very well, then." She let her chair slip forward, laid both hands on the table, and looked at her ops officer. "Commander Ling?"

"Yes, Sir." Ling was the most junior officer present, but her dark eyes met those of the assembled admirals, commodores and captains levelly as she brought her terminal on-line.

"We have a reasonably complete report from Admiral Teller," she began. "Most of his carrier group and its escorts survived, but his strikegroups took catastrophic losses. Of the one hundred and forty-nine fighters with which he began the engagement, twenty-three survived."

Rear Admiral Waldeck, Murakuma's second-in-command, flinched visibly, but Ling continued in her most clinical voice.

"The good news, such as it is, is that the enemy still has not employed fighters, SBMs, SBMHAWK missile pods, or second-generation antimatter warheads. Coupled with our more sophisticated datalink, we continue to hold an overwhelming advantage in long-range actions. With anything approaching equality of forces, we should be able to stop these people cold. As it is, we estimate the tonnage loss is as much as four-to-one in our favor, and they still keep coming. Captain LeBlanc—" she nodded at the intelligence officer "—will address this point, but my own concern is with the immediate operational consequences rather than the enemy's motives."

Her eyes dipped to her terminal screen, then rose once more.

"The bad news is that the enemy *has* demonstrated both a new tactic and a previously unknown weapon which, in combination, brought about the destruction of Admiral Villiers' battle-line. Without SBMHAWKs, he seems to have adopted another approach to assaulting a warp point: a simultaneous transit. Captain LeBlanc and I are still analyzing the record, but it appears the enemy has built an entire fleet component of cruiser-sized vessels expressly to mount mass transits to clear his battle-line's way. Obviously, his losses from interpenetration will be considerable, but it allows him to introduce a massive amount of firepower quickly.

"No one in TF 58 anticipated such a tactic. When it was actually employed, Admiral Villiers felt he had no option but to close . . . at which point he discovered the existence of the enemy's new weapon system. For want of a better name, we're currently calling it a 'plasma gun.' Our tech people don't yet know how the enemy projects a containment field to hold it together, but they estimate that it must be quite short-ranged compared to conventional energy weapons. Unfortunately, it's also extremely powerful, and from the numbers of plasma guns a single SD apparently mounts, it must be considerably less massive than our own energy weapons. We're trying to formulate doctrine for dealing with it, but it combines the nastier features of a sprint-mode missile and an energy weapon: high accuracy over its range, massive destructiveness, and a velocity too great for effective point defense engagement. At the moment, the only real advice we can give is to stay out of its envelope."

She paused and flicked her eyes over her terminal once more, then looked back up.

"I've prepared a download of Admiral Teller's data for you and your staffs. My assistants and I are continuing our own analysis of it. By the time we arrive in K-45, we should be prepared to discuss it in much greater detail, but any additional input will be most appreciated."

She sat back, and Murakuma looked to her left.

"Captain LeBlanc?"

"Yes, Sir." The newly arrived intelligence officer produced a crooked smile. "What we seem to have here, ladies and gentlemen, is something out of a bad novel." One or two officers actually surprised themselves with barks of laughter. Even Murakuma smiled briefly, but then LeBlanc leaned forward, and there was no humor at all in his deep-set brown eyes. "Even with this new plasma weapon, our technological advantages are surely as evident to the enemy as they are to us. As Commander Ling just pointed out, the loss ratio is overwhelmingly in our favor and seems likely to remain so, yet the enemy continues to throw superdreadnoughts at us, and now he's added this assault fleet component. All humor aside, I never actually expected to run into the Orglon Empire, but that seems to be exactly what's happening. To date, we haven't been able to examine any enemy wreckage or databases to get any idea of his psychology, so all we can do is make inferences from his tactics, and those inferences aren't good."

The briefing room was deathly still, and he cocked his chair back slightly.

"First, and of the greatest immediate concern, he's far less sensitive to losses than we are. I submit that no Terran admiral would continue to advance this aggressively after suffering such heavy—and one-sided—casualties. Quite aside from morale damage, the cost in terms of lost hardware would make it unthinkable. I suppose we might postulate that this sort of behavior reflects how close we are to what must be one of their most important star systems, if not their home system itself. If Sol were under threat, no doubt Home Fleet would be willing to accept mammoth losses to push the enemy back, and it's possible these people are driving so hard to build defensive depth before we can bring up our main strength. Tempting as that explanation may be, however, I do not believe it to be correct. Or, to be more accurate, the second salient point about their operations convinces me it's not the *entire* answer."

"Second point, Captain?" Waldeck asked quietly.

"Yes, Sir. These people never even attempted to communicate with Commodore Braun before opening fire. Not even the Rigelians began a full-fledged war against the Federation without at least attempting to evaluate us first; these people simply started shooting. By our own standards, or those of any other race we've previously encountered, that sort of reaction is insane, which suggests the xenologists are going to have a hard time figuring out what makes them tick. Obviously, an inability to understand what motivates them will make it extremely difficult to project their probable actions, but it's very tempting—so far, at least—to assume that this violent aggressiveness, more even than our proximity to a nodal system, underlies their strategy to date.

"Perhaps even more to the point, we have this assault fleet component. Think about that for a moment. As Admiral Murakuma herself pointed out to me years ago, no reasonable race would sacrifice hundreds of capital ships in headlong assaults on a succession of defended warp points. Against warp points they *knew* were critical to their opponent, yes; perhaps they *would* do that if it was the only way to break through. But simple mathematics would make that unthinkable as a *routine* tactic. It takes us the better part of two standard years to build an SD. Completely ignoring the question of training a capital ship's crew, no one can afford to expend that big a chunk of industrial output without a good reason.

"*These* people, however, seem to have found an approach they think *is* cost-effective. There's no way to prove it—yet—but Commander Ling's initial analysis agrees with mine: the ships they used for that simultaneous transit were purpose built. Whatever we *don't* know about our enemies' psychology, we've been given very convincing evidence that they're willing to accept massive losses in light units—which can be replaced in a much shorter time frame—to clear the way for their heavies. To me, at least, this suggests we can expect to see suicide tactics on the Rigelian or Theban model, and I advise all of you to be on the lookout for them.

"Finally, I'd like to return to the losses in capital ships which they *have* so far accepted . . . which suggest we have to assume an industrial base *at least* as large as our own." Someone made a sound of disagreement, and LeBlanc smiled grimly. "I realize we're accustomed to considering the Federation's industrial capacity as unmatched in the galaxy. To date, we've had every reason to think just that, but could *we* expend so many SDs to capture what are obviously colonies, not core systems? Let me stress once more that, however ferocious he may be, the enemy still has to build the starships he's using up. More, he has to realize we're still redeploying to meet him—that we may have a much greater strength to throw at him than he's seen yet. In similar circumstances, *our* response would be to use probing forces we could afford to lose. We certainly wouldn't cut our mobile forces to the bone in offensive operations that left us unable to meet counterattacks. While we dare not assume our own idea of logic governs these people, I find it very difficult to believe we're *that* different. And if we aren't, their losses to date must represent an *acceptable* loss rate.

Which, in turn, suggests they have enormous reserves of capital ships, and for that to be true, they have to have an industrial base capable of building them in the first place."

LeBlanc shrugged, and more than one of the grim faces around the table paled. The enemy's insensitivity to losses had been a tactical concern, but the Federation's status as the most productive civilization in galactic history was so fundamentally accepted—by nonhumans, as well as humans—that few of them had gotten around to considering what LeBlanc had just said. It simply wasn't possible for anyone to outproduce them . . . was it?

Murakuma let them live with the implications for a few moments, then cleared her throat.

"We can't know if Captain LeBlanc is correct, but the consequences of overestimating an enemy are certainly less likely to be fatal than those of underestimating him. And whether he's correct or not, *our* concern has to be slowing these people down until the rest of Battle Fleet can respond."

Several people nodded, and she smiled a thin, cold smile.

"Very well, then. Since we do seem to possess the technological edge at the moment, I suggest we decide how best to use it. Commander Ling's current analysis of the Erebor action is available on your terminals. Please take fifteen or twenty minutes to peruse it. After that—" her smile was colder and thinner than ever "—the floor will be open for suggestions."

Vanessa Murakuma sat in her palatial day cabin and watched a display with empty green eyes. K-45 was no more than an empty spot where three warp lines met, and the massed ships of Task Force 59, Terran Federation Navy, held station on TFNS *Cobra* as she floated in that emptiness. It was a powerful force—twelve battleships, twenty battle-cruisers, and twelve light carriers, plus escorts—and she supposed she should be excited to have it under her flag. Yet she felt no elation. She'd fought all her life to exercise an authority just like this one, and now, as she faced the hideous decisions that authority was about to force upon her, all she felt was a sick, gnawing need to pass it to someone—*anyone*—else.

She killed the display, blanking away the light dots of the thousands of human beings waiting to live or die at her orders, and her face twisted as her eye fell on the innocent-looking data chip on her desk. She stared at it, bile churning in the back of her throat, then drew a deep breath and made herself look away as her cabin's entry chime sounded.

She squared her shoulders, forcing the sick despair from her expression, and pressed the admittance stud. The hatch slid open, and the officers she'd asked to join her walked through it. Rear Admiral Teller led the way, followed by Demosthenes Waldeck, Leroy Mackenna and Marcus LeBlanc. The four of them sat in the comfortable chairs facing her desk at her gesture, and she made herself pick up the data chip.

"Thank you for coming, gentlemen." Her flat voice sounded overcontrolled even to her, but it was the only one she had. "I assume you've all viewed the visual records from Erebor?"

Heads nodded, and she felt a stab of sympathy for Teller's haunted eyes. It wasn't his fault. He'd gotten everyone he possibly could out, yet it made no difference to his bitter self-loathing, and Murakuma understood only too well. Just as she knew it would make no difference to her own when the time came. She studied his face for a moment, then cleared her throat.

"Before we continue, Admiral Teller, I'd like to thank you for your efforts in Erebor." Dull surprise flickered in the junior admiral's eyes, and she faced him directly. "I can only imagine what you're feeling, Jackson," she said quietly. "I'm very much afraid that will change shortly, and I'll be honest with you—with all of you—" she let her eyes sweep over the others "—and admit that terrifies me. It terrifies *all* of us now," her hand tightened on the data chip, "but we can't admit that. We have to put it away somewhere deep inside and pretend it isn't there, because if we don't, if we let it show and affect our personnel or, even worse, paralyze us ..."

She shook her head. The others looked back without speaking, but Waldeck nodded curtly. Demosthenes Waldeck came from one of the most powerful of the Corporate World dynasties which ruled the Federation, and many of Murakuma's fellow Fringers, including her own chief of staff, were prepared to hate him for that. Despite the Federation military's long-standing tradition of political neutrality, the festering hatred between the Fringe, which produced an ever growing percentage of the Fleet's total manpower, and the Corporate Worlds had spilled over into the Navy, and that saddened Murakuma. She understood it, and watching the Corporate World politicos' cynical manipulation of political power disgusted her, yet she felt something precious and irreplaceable slipping away from the Fleet. It was like virginity, she thought sadly. That sense of something special and almost holy—of being a fellowship of arms whose dedication to protect and preserve placed it above political factionalism and pettiness—could never be regained once it was lost.

Even worse, it sowed distrust, and that was something the human race simply could not afford. She and Leroy Mackenna had come as close to a shouting match over that as they ever had, for Mackenna was from Shilo, whose economy had been devastated fifty years back for daring to defy a major Corporate World shipping line.

The Liberal-Progressive Party had enacted special legislation to "clarify" the dispute between the system government and Trans-Stellar Shipping, and Mackenna's family was one of the many who'd been paupered by its provisions. Expecting him ever to forgive the Corporate Worlds for that was not only unreasonable but wrong, yet Murakuma had no option but to insist that he put it aside in his new position.

Especially, she thought, *in this case.* For all the Waldeck clan's immense power, it was also one of those confusing families whose members sometimes refused to fit neat stereotypes, and Demosthenes' branch had a habit of producing outstanding naval officers. His grandmother, Minerva Waldeck, "the mother of Terran carrier ops," had been a heroine of ISW-3, one of the greatest officers ever to wear the TFN's black and silver. Murakuma had known Demosthenes for years, and none knew better than she that he was cut from the same cloth as his grandmother. Even Mackenna was coming to accept that, almost against his will, and after Teller's, Waldeck's face was the grimmest in her cabin. The massive Waldeck jaw clenched tight, and his eyes were shadowed, but his deep, measured voice was level when he spoke.

"You're right, Sir. We *can't* allow this to paralyze us . . . but with all due respect, it has to affect our planning. I realize we can't afford to take heavy losses, but we're talking about millions of lives. We've *got* to slow these bastards down enough to get as many out as we possibly can."

Mackenna's strong-nosed black face wore a strange expression as he looked at the admiral. Under other circumstances Murakuma would have been pleased to see Leroy realize Demosthenes was as determined to save Fringers as he would have been to save Corporate Worlders, but there was no room in her for pleasure this day.

"Agreed," she replied, "and that's why I'm so grateful to Jackson. If he hadn't preserved his command, we'd have only four carriers, not twelve. And if he hadn't laid the comsat chain from Erebor, we wouldn't know what was happening to the people we didn't get out." She looked back to Teller, and her voice was soft. "I realize pulling out of Erebor was a hard decision. I know it's going to haunt you, and I know a lot of second-guessers who weren't there and didn't have to make the call will suggest all sorts of clever ways you could have avoided it. I happen to believe you did exactly the right thing, and I've so advised Sky Marshal Avram."

"Thank you." Teller's tenor was low and hoarse. She heard the genuine gratitude in it, but she also heard the strain, and his hands trembled visibly before he gripped them together in his lap. "If I'd had even a few more fighters left . . . or maybe if they hadn't been bringing up still more SDs . . ." His voice trailed off, and his nostrils flared as he inhaled deeply.

"You did the right thing," she said again, stressing the measured words, then leaned back with a sigh and dropped the chip on her desk. "Nonetheless, Demosthenes is also correct. We know what the stakes are now."

All of them nodded this time, and Murakuma shuddered as her mind insisted on replaying the chip yet again. Some of the Erebor ground stations had survived long enough to transmit footage of the enemy's landings and . . . activities via Teller's chain of comsats. They'd seen the enemy now, and she'd felt a shiver of pure, atavistic horror at her first sight of them. They looked, she thought, like some obscene alloy of spider and starfish—eight-limbed, hairy monstrosities that moved with a hideous, flowing, tarantula-like gait. Humanity had encountered other life forms at least as strange to human eyes, but none of them had ever awakened such a sense of instant, instinctive hatred as these creatures did. It was as if they resonated somehow with humankind's darkest phobias, and their behavior on Erebor only validated that hatred.

The xenologists had dubbed them "Arachnids," and the current best guess was that they were carnivores. It was only a guess, but whether they were pure meat-eaters or not was beside the point. The Federation would never know who'd been behind the camera which transmitted the horrifying footage, for the transmission had ended with terrifying abruptness as one of the aliens loomed suddenly before the lens, but humanity owed whoever it had been a debt beyond any price, for he'd caught them feeding. Without that footage, mankind would not have known that *these* aliens regarded humans as a food source.

Vomit rose in her throat once more, and she wondered if the government would dare release the imagery. A part of her hoped it would be forever sealed, but she knew better. Sooner or later it would be released, or leaked, or stolen, and every living human would know what she knew now. For all their long, segmented, spiderlike legs, the aliens massed no more than half again as much as humans . . . and they preferred their food living. That made *children* just the right size for—

Vanessa Murakuma clenched her fist and thrust the memories violently aside, then made herself look at Mackenna and LeBlanc.

"I've just received a response to our dispatch to Sarasota," she said as normally as she could. "They agree with our assessment. In order to evacuate the maximum possible numbers from Merriweather and Justin we'll have to use Sarasota as the collection point. We simply don't have enough lift capacity to take them any further back, and even stopping at Sarasota we're never going to get everyone out."

"How soon can they get additional transports to us, Sir?" Mackenna asked quietly.

"Not soon enough." Murakuma's voice was flat, and she pinched the bridge of her nose. "What Reichman has now is everything in the sector. Even for a hop as short as the one to the Sarasota Fleet Base, we simply don't have enough personnel lift. Admiral Eusebio has authorized me—" she smiled bleakly "—to use my discretion in utilizing what we do have most effectively."

LeBlanc made a harsh, disgusted sound, but Murakuma shook her head.

"I don't blame him. I'm the commander on the spot, and making decisions like that comes with the job."

"With all due respect," Waldeck began hotly, "you've got enough on your shoulders fighting the damned battle without having to accept resp—"

"I said I don't blame him, Demosthenes," Murakuma said flatly. He closed his mouth with a snap, and she smiled more naturally and squared her shoulders.

"At least knowing what we now do simplifies our priorities, gentlemen. Leroy, I want you and Tian to get with Commodore Reichman and his staff as soon as his transports return from Sarasota. We have to establish hard guidelines on who we evacuate and in what order. We'll begin with minor children and pregnant women. Whenever possible in two-parent families, I want one parent included, as well. After that, we go with second parents and the elderly."

"The elderly, Sir?" Mackenna asked with a careful lack of expression, and Murakuma smiled bitterly. She knew what he wasn't saying—and what someone else most assuredly would. The elderly, after all, had already lived full lives and had less to contribute to the war effort. She loathed the people who could make that argument, but they existed . . . and whatever she decided would be wrong in their eyes. How would it feel, she wondered mordantly, when they started calling *her* a monster—and a coward—for "saving herself" by "abandoning civilians to their fate"?

"The elderly," she repeated, trying—and failing—to hide her pain. "We owe them that . . . and their age will make them more of a liability for the people we can't get out."

"A 'liability' in what way, Sir?" LeBlanc asked.

"There are no noncombatants in this war, Marcus." Murakuma's voice went harsh. "Admiral Eusebio is stripping Sarasota of infantry weapons and sending them up with Reichman. He'll drop them off at Justin, and while Leroy and Tian are conferring with the Commodore on ship movements, *you,* Marcus, are going to be working with General Servais on deployment plans for Marine garrisons on Justin, Harrison and Clements."

"*Garrisons?*" Waldeck looked at her in disbelief, and she raised an eyebrow. The other admiral hesitated for a moment, then gripped the nettle. "Sir—Vanessa—if we can't keep the enemy from taking the system, how can we possibly justify sending in *ground* troops? Once the enemy controls the high orbitals, they'll be in a deathtrap!"

" '*We*' aren't justifying it; *I* am," Murakuma said flatly. "Everyone else on those planets will already be in a deathtrap unless we can somehow fight our way back in. We can't fool ourselves here, Demosthenes. These . . . *creatures* don't distinguish between military personnel and civilians. Anyone we leave behind won't just be killed—they're going to be *eaten,* and I will *not* simply abandon them. We may not be able to save them, but we can at least give them the weapons and advisers to make the bastards *pay* for them!"

Flaming green eyes pinned her subordinates in their chairs, and her voice was a sliver of soprano ice.

"This war is going to be for *survival,* worse than ISW-3 ever was. We've grown out of the habit of thinking that way, but *this*—" she slammed the heel of her hand on the data chip "—says we'd damned well better remember how. And, gentlemen, starting right here—right now—we are going to teach these fucking monsters humans don't come cheap!"

CHAPTER SEVEN

To Face the Hurricane

"The Admiral is on the bridge."

Officers looked up, but Murakuma's wave sent them back to their tasks as she crossed to her command chair, settled into it, and fiddled with her plot's contrast controls. She adjusted it to her satisfaction, then looked up and beckoned to Commander Ling, and the ops officer gathered up her memo pad and crossed to her side.

"Good afternoon, Admiral." The commander was ten centimeters shorter than Murakuma, but she was also a native of Old Terra—one of the very few native Terrans, relatively speaking, in TF 59—and for all her petite slenderness, she looked almost stocky beside the taller admiral.

"Tian," Murakuma acknowledged, then pointed at the memo pad. "Did you and Admiral Teller reach the same conclusions I did?"

"Yes, Sir." Ling set the pad on Murakuma's console and switched it on. Its tiny holo unit projected its display before the admiral, and Ling highlighted a block of characters in amber. "You were right," she said. "*Akagi, Bunker Hill, Cabot, Emperor* and *Kuznetzov* didn't want to admit it, but analysis of their operations indicates pilot fatigue's become a definite problem for them."

"Not surprising," Murakuma murmured, studying the numbers. Sarasota had been able to make good the enormous hardware losses of Jackson Teller's strikegroups by sending forward every reserve fighter in inventory, but Admiral Eusebio had been unable to replace their dead flight crews. It was a hellish choice, for Sarasota depended heavily on fighters for its own defense, and Eusebio *could*, in fact, have brought Teller's groups back up to strength . . . but only by sending up enough pilots to critically reduce his own capabilities. As it was, the Fleet Base's

399

squadrons were at barely sixty percent strength, and he refused to deplete them still further.

Murakuma couldn't fault him for that. What had happened in Erebor was grim proof of the sort of casualties TF 59 might suffer, and if that happened, Eusebio's fighters were all he'd have. But understanding made her own problems no less pressing, and she frowned at the uncaring numbers.

Teller's staff had done its best to redistribute its available pilots, but fighter squadrons were intricately meshed organisms whose members worked together almost as much by instinct as order. Breaking them up or introducing newcomers, however well trained, degraded effectiveness until the replacements had time to settle in, and no one knew how much time they had. They knew only that TF 59 would be heavily outnumbered when the time came, and the Federation's apparent monopoly on the strike-fighter made those fighter groups pearls beyond price. They *had* to be as efficient and deadly as possible, so Teller, with her approval, had left the groups of the four newly arrived carriers untouched, and mixed and matched to rebuild those of the Erebor survivors as best he could.

They had sufficient personnel to operate all their fighters, but fighter ops were the most physically demanding duty the TFN offered. They were also among the most dangerous, as Vanessa Murakuma knew only too well, for Lieutenant Tadeoshi Murakuma had died on routine ops exactly three days after their second daughter was born. But it was the fatigue factor which worried her now. A carrier normally carried twice as many crews as fighters, so it could rotate its personnel, but the groups of the five carriers Ling had listed were at barely forty-two percent strength, and most were scratch-built out of bits and pieces from Sarasota after the complete replacement squadrons had been distributed to other ships. The strain of shaking down as combat-capable entities while simultaneously pulling their weight in TF 59's routine patrols showed, and pilot fatigue was rising rapidly towards unacceptable levels.

"All right," she said finally. "I want those groups stood down for at least forty-eight hours—have Admiral Teller redistribute patrol assignments to adjust. Once they've had a couple of days to recuperate, he can reintegrate them, but I want his primary emphasis to be on getting them shaken down, not scouting duties. After all—" she smiled thinly "—we know where the enemy will be coming from."

"Yes, Sir." Ling tapped a note into the memo pad, and Murakuma crossed her legs.

"The minelayers completed their operations on schedule?"

"Yes, Sir." Ling's reply was as calm as ever, and Murakuma surprised herself with a brief chuckle. She'd been an ops officer herself, and

Tian's unflagging courtesy couldn't fool her. The commander didn't have to say "of course" for Murakuma to hear it.

Ling arched a graceful eyebrow, but Murakuma only shook her head. Bad enough that she was fretting over routine details without admitting she *knew* she was.

"That's all for now, Tian," was all she said, and smiled fondly at the commander's back as Ling returned to her station. Then her smile faded, and she steepled her fingers under her chin as she gazed back down at her icon-frosted plot.

Classic warp point defense doctrine was to hit the enemy as he made transit in the old wet-navy equivalent of catching him as he emerged one ship at a time from a narrow strait. Sixty years ago, before the Theban War, the defender's advantage had been so crushing the mere thought of a full-scale warp point assault could turn any admiral gray, but the pendulum had shifted in the attacker's favor with the SBMHAWK. The warp-capable missile pods were expensive, both to build and in terms of freighter lift, but enough of them could gut any close-in defense . . . as Ivan Antonov had proved almost exactly fifty-nine years before at the Fourth Battle of Lorelei.

But this enemy didn't seem to have SBMHAWKs, which made a close defense far more appealing—or would have, without his assault fleet. Murakuma couldn't afford to expose her lighter battle-line to a mass simultaneous transit that was almost certain to enjoy the advantage of surprise, however briefly. Even light cruisers could tear battleships apart if enough of them caught the capital ships when they weren't at battle stations.

Yet she did have one huge advantage Villiers had been denied in Erebor. The minelayers had emplaced every antimatter mine and laser buoy Sarasota could scrape up around the enemy's entry warp point. There weren't as many as Murakuma could have wished, and neither mines nor buoys could be placed directly atop an open warp point, since the grav tides of an open point would suck in and destroy anything that small. But they could be placed *around* the point, and Ling's patient report confirmed that hundreds of them had been.

No doubt most of the single-shot buoys would expend themselves on the simultaneous transit rather than its betters, but the mines behind them should at least pen the big boys up until they could be cleared. It was tempting to hold her full force—or at least the ones armed with strategic bombardment missiles—in range to batter them while they fought to break through the mines, but the enemy would have an enormous advantage in launchers, and the fact that he hadn't used the extended range SBMs yet didn't *prove* he didn't have them. Worse, Sarasota's R&D staff still couldn't give her a definitive estimate on the range of those damned plasma guns. She dared not assume their envelope was as tight as R&D *thought* it was, and even if it was, they knew the enemy had the capital force beam. Add capital missiles from his missile-heavy SDs, and sheer volume of fire would quickly cripple her lighter battleships if she met him head on.

No, she told herself again. A conventional defense was out of the question. She had to concede the warp point—bleed them on it, yes, but let them have it—and make it a running fight in deep space, where her speed and tech advantages could be exploited to the maximum. If she'd had any chance at all of stopping them dead, she would have accepted the losses of a close defense to do it, but she didn't. All she could do was mount a fighting retreat that inflicted the maximum attrition . . . and pray the people trapped in Merriweather when she finally withdrew wouldn't haunt her dreams with the horror she knew they would.

"All right, Marcus. Give me the bad news."

Captain LeBlanc sighed. His recliner was cocked back at a comfortable angle, one hand held a tall, iced drink, and he'd kicked his boots off—something he never would have done if anyone else were present—but his eyes belied his relaxed posture.

"It's not good, Vanessa," he admitted. "Commodore Reichman's working wonders, but it's going to take at least six more round trips to get everyone out."

"What if we detached our destroyers?" She leaned forward in her own chair, left hand squeezing the fingers of her right. "The *Johnstons* are too small to be really combat effective, and—"

"Vanessa." LeBlanc interrupted her more firmly than a captain should interrupt an admiral, and she looked up from her hands. "It wouldn't matter," he said. "They don't have enough life support to make any difference. Even if you let Reichman have all seven of them, they couldn't squeeze more than two thousand people aboard."

"But—" Murakuma chopped herself off, then sighed and rubbed her face with her palms. "You're right." Her hands muffled her voice, but he heard the pain in it. "I'm dithering, aren't I?"

"In a word," he said gently, "yes. God knows I don't blame you, but would giving up those ships really save enough colonists to justify dropping them from your order of battle?"

"No," she said. "It's just knowing what those fucking Bugs are going to do. . . ."

She broke off with a shudder she would have let no other member of her staff see, and his mouth tightened. Forty years had passed since the demands of their service careers terminated their Academy affair. He didn't know if anyone suspected they'd once been lovers, and it wouldn't have mattered to him if they had, but at this moment a tiny, ignoble part of him wished he knew Vanessa less well. She needed *someone* with whom to share her inner strain, and, in many ways, he was honored to be that someone. Yet in at least one way he was just like any of her other officers; his own desperate fear needed the rocklike strength she radiated in public, and knowing how savagely her responsibilities were wounding her frightened him. She looked so delicate—"bird-boned," his mother had called her the time she came home with him for a visit. He knew better than most that appearances could be deceiving, but how in God's name could the determination to meet something like *this* be packed into such a frail-looking package?

"They aren't really insects, you know," he said as lightly as he could. "I know it's tempting to reach for a Terran analogue. Even the xenologists did that when they tagged them as 'Arachnids,' but if you start ascribing insect behavior to them—"

"They're bugs," she said flatly. His eyes flicked back up to her face in surprise at the cold, vicious hatred in her voice. "They're not Orions, not even Tangri. They're filthy, vile, crawling *bugs,* and we are by God going to *exterminate* them like the vermin they are."

"Vanessa, I—" he began, but she cut him off with a bark of laughter.

"Don't worry. I'm not losing it yet, Marcus. But I mean it. There won't be any treaties after *this* war—not once the Assembly sees the Erebor footage. We're going to dust off General Directive Eighteen, and we're going to wipe these monsters from the face of the universe."

Her cold, flat, absolute certainty sent a shudder through LeBlanc. Intellectually, he knew she was almost certainly right, and his own emotions agreed with her, but hearing so much icy, distilled hatred from Vanessa frightened him, and he cleared his throat.

"I never thought you would 'lose it.' I only wish it hadn't landed on you."

"If not on me, then on someone else," she said more normally, and shrugged and reached for her own drink. "Whoever else it was would still—"

The sudden, raucous scream of *Cobra*'s GQ alarm ripped across her voice. She jerked as if she'd just grabbed one end of a live wire, then whirled to her com terminal.

"Status!" she barked even before the officer of the watch's image solidified on the screen.

"Tsushima." The stress-flattened word was harsh, and her face tightened. "Simultaneous transit, Sir. Plotting makes it—" the woman on the screen paused to consult her plot "—fifty-plus bandits in a single wave."

"Understood. Activate Plan Able."

"Yes, Sir!"

Murakuma released the key and spun away from the terminal, already unsealing her tunic. Her vac suit closet had opened automatically when the alarm went, and she bounded across the carpeted cabin towards it.

"Marcus—"

"Already gone." She darted a glance at him and felt a hysterical urge to giggle as he snatched up his boots and headed for the cabin hatch in sock feet. "See you on Flag Bridge."

The hatch closed behind him before she could reply, and she reached for her suit, eyes automatically checking the tell-tales even as her mind reached out to the horde of starships coming to kill her.

Sixty light cruisers erupted into normal space in a single massive wave. Twelve vanished in sprawling boils of plasma as they interpenetrated, and more died under the laser buoys' fury. The bomb pumped lasers consumed themselves in the instant they fired, stabbing immensely powerful beams straight through electromagnetic shields to shatter armor and hull members, but their programming spread their fire among all the cruisers. They inflicted crippling damage, yet only a handful of intruders actually perished.

The wounded, air-streaming survivors paused, searching for enemies, but no one was in range to attack them. They hesitated a moment longer, and then—one-by-one—headed away from the warp point . . . and straight into the waiting mines. Savage explosions pocked space as the hunter-killer satellites lunged at them in eye-tearing flares of detonating antimatter, yet they accomplished their goal.

Vanessa Murakuma's pitiless face was stone as she watched the last enemy cruiser die.

"They're going to break clear of the mines sooner than anticipated," Mackenna said, and she nodded. It didn't really matter, given the battle plan she'd evolved, but it was fresh proof of the terrifying difference between the beings who'd crewed those ships and humans. Even allowing for the mines' antimatter warheads, the fields hadn't been *that* heavy. Sarasota hadn't had enough to stop capital ships, but these people— these *Bugs*—hadn't even tried to sweep them normally. What kind of psychology could see the deliberate self-destruction of ships they could have saved, if only for future use, as a reasonable alternative to minor damage to minesweeping capital ships?

"It doesn't matter," she said aloud, and looked up from the master plot. "How long since we sent Commodore Reichman the alert message?"

"Ten minutes, Sir."

"Um." Murakuma cocked her head and considered K-45's geometry.

The warp point to Erebor lay "below" the two leading to Merriweather and Justin, distributed like the points of a right triangle. The distance from the Erebor point to Justin was only five-and-a-half light-hours—sixty-five hours' transit time for her battleships—but the line from Merriweather to Justin formed the triangle's hypotenuse, and Reichman's transports were in Merriweather. Her alert would reach him in seven hours, but his transports were slow; they'd need fifteen hours just to get back to K-45, then another eighty to reach the Justin warp point. She wasn't worried about their being intercepted in deep space—they were as fast as anything the enemy had, and all they needed to do was stay beyond missile range—but even if Reichman pulled out the instant her warning reached him, he'd still need a minimum of a hundred and two hours to escape to Justin.

That defined how long she *had* to hold the enemy's attention. She had to lead those superdreadnoughts outside their detection range of Reichman and away from the Justin warp point for at least five standard days, keeping them in play until she was certain the transports were clear, before she could fall back herself. Of course, the Bugs were so slow they'd take a hundred hours to reach the warp point even on a least-time course, but she dared not cut things that close. If anything delayed Reichman in Merriweather and the Bugs reached his exit point first, he and all the evacuees packed aboard his ships would be hopelessly trapped.

"Anything on their battle-line's composition?"

"Plotting's on it now," Ling replied. "So far, they make it forty-two superdreadnoughts, but they're still coming through. We think the lead element were either *Augers* or *Acids,* but we're seeing at least some *Archers* in the follow-on waves."

"Any sign of the *Avalanches* yet?"

"No, Sir, but we're still not sure we can distinguish them from the *Augers.*"

Murakuma nodded, walked slowly to her command chair, and racked her helmet on its side while she thought. They wouldn't know anything about the enemy's technology until they managed to stop the bastards and examine their wreckage, but they'd assigned tentative reporting names, based on observed armament, to some of his classes. The *Augers, Acids* and *Avalanches* mounted almost pure energy armaments. Analysis suggested the *Augers* had heavy primary beam outfits, and the *Acids* carried those damned plasma guns, but it was the *Avalanche-* and *Archer-class* ships which worried her. The *Archers* were pure missile platforms, with massive capital missile batteries, while the *Avalanches* mounted equally heavy capital force beam armaments.

The *Augers* were potentially deadly, since no known defense could stop a primary beam. If they had capital primaries, which hadn't been confirmed but seemed likely, they'd have an effective range of almost nine light-seconds, and they'd punch straight through anything they hit. But they'd also be slow-firing, and the ships which mounted them were forty percent slower than her slowest unit. The only way they'd get into range of her would be if she *let* them.

No, it was the *Avalanches* and, especially, the *Archers* she had to sweat, and she looked up at Mackenna.

"We'll go with Tsushima Six, Leroy." Her calm voice gave no indication of the tension twisting in her belly, and the chief of staff nodded with matching control.

"Aye, aye, Sir. Tsushima Six."

"Have Admiral Waldeck com me as soon as he has everything in motion."

"Yes, Sir."

Mackenna turned to begin passing orders, and Vanessa Murakuma watched her repeater plot as her ships deployed.

The Fleet moved out through the minefield gap, advancing on the light dots of the enemy at five percent of light-speed. The Fleet knew nothing about this warp junction's astrography. Its ships were slower than its enemies, and by now it knew about many of the enemy's technological advantages, but that didn't matter. It had the firepower to crush him, and for all his superior speed, he had only two choices: engage it or abandon the nexus without a fight.

The oncoming superdreadnoughts would settle for either.

"All right, Demosthenes," Vanessa Murakuma said quietly to the face on her plot. "Let's do this right the first time."

"Agreed." Her battle-line commander bared his teeth. "Husac is coming up on her firing position now."

"Good." Murakuma nodded to the pickup, then turned back to her plot and made herself keep her mouth shut as TF 59 executed Tsushima Six.

She'd split her force into two task groups—59.1 under Jackson Teller, who commanded her carriers and their screen from the battle-cruiser *Sorcerer*, and 59.2, the battleline units, under Waldeck in the battleship *Pit Viper*. Delegating authority had always been hard for her, and it was even harder when so much depended on the execution of *her* battle plan, yet she had no choice. She might hold overall command, but it was Jackson's and Demosthenes' job to execute her plan while she monitored and adjusted for anything that went wrong, and if she yielded to her penchant for back seat driving it would only make them think she questioned their competence.

Rear Admiral Jennifer Husac's two battlegroups of *Dunkerque*-class battle-cruisers were TF 59's rearmost units, trailing astern of the battle-line as it fell steadily back before the advancing superdreadnoughts, leading them away from the Justin warp point. The *Dunkerques* were smaller and more lightly protected than battleships, but they were Murakuma's long-range snipers, with heavy capital missile batteries, and despite their smaller size, their superior datalink meant they could actually throw heavier salvos than the missile-armed SDs. Plotting's analysis was tentative, but it suggested that the opposing *Archers* outnumbered them by at least fifty percent. That was an awesome edge in launchers, but she didn't expect Husac to take out the enemy all alone. Hurt him, yes. That much she expected, but Husac's real purpose was to positively identify the missile ships by drawing their return fire.

"All right," she said quietly as the range from the *Dunkerques* to the enemy fell. "Let's see what these bastards have."

"Coming into extreme range . . . now," Commander Trang said.

"Stand by." Jennifer Husac watched her display intently as TFNS *Endymion*'s tactical officer made his tense announcement.

"Good luck, Sir," Trang added, and Husac's lips quirked in a humorless smile. Trang wanted to open fire *now*, as soon as his internal launchers had the range, and she didn't blame him. Her twelve ships were a preposterously frail force against seventy-plus superdreadnoughts, and any intellectual awareness of superior technology ran a poor second to visceral awareness of the odds. On the other hand, the enemy had yet to demonstrate any equivalent of the missiles she was about to fire at him. Only a handful of the Terran ships he'd yet engaged had carried strategic bombardment missiles, and none had really had the chance to use them as doctrine dictated, but Husac was about to change that. Each SBM ate up twenty-five percent more magazine space than a regular capital missile, so Terran ships never carried pure loads of them and Sarasota had had too few in stores to provide Husac's ships with full load-outs, but she intended to make best use of the ones she had. Their poorer ECM made them easier point defense targets than capital missiles, but they had a full five light-seconds more range, and Trang wanted to use it all. But one of Husac's objectives was to confirm whether or not the enemy had the weapon, which meant she had to make sure she was well within its envelope. Besides, every light-second she closed gave *her* birds a better chance of scoring.

"Eighteen light-seconds," Trang said. More endless seconds crept away as the two forces continued to close. "Seventeen . . . we're in range for the external birds, Sir."

"Let the range fall to sixteen light-seconds," Husac said softly.

✧   ✧   ✧

Murakuma chewed her lower lip. It was hard to believe the Bugs
didn't have the SBM, yet Husac was three full light-seconds inside
its range, and not a shot had been fired. If the Bugs *didn't* have
the weapon now, it shouldn't take someone with their evident tech
capability long to develop it once it was used on them, but in the
meantime . . .

"Sixteen light-seconds," Trang said flatly, and Husac nodded.
"Hold us at this range, Helm," she said, then—"Engage the enemy,
Commander Trang!"

Twelve battle-cruisers sent a hundred and sixty-four missiles slashing
through space as both battlegroups flushed their external racks and
opened up with their internal launchers as well. Not a single shot
replied, and Jennifer Husac's eyes glowed with hellish delight. *That
answers one question; if the bad guys had them, they'd sure as hell use
them now!*

Her eyes blazed still brighter as the massive opening salvos roared
down on just two SDs, and countermissiles began to explode. The
bastards' early-generation datalink left each of those ships on its own
against the incoming fire, but no single ship could stop *those* salvos,
and a snarl ran around *Endymion*'s flag bridge as they struck. The
fireballs were eye-watering even at this range, but Husac refused to
look away, and when the glare died, both of her targets had vanished.

"Two down," someone said, and the admiral nodded.

"Let's add to that," she said grimly. "Make them count as long as
they last, Commander."

*The Fleet ground steadily onward, despite the missiles battering it
from beyond its own range. The enemy battle-cruisers' first salvos had
exhausted their external ordnance, and the follow-on broadsides were
thirty percent lighter, but they continued their deliberate pounding in
overpowering waves of thunder that smashed through all active defenses
by sheer weight of numbers. Shields flared and died, shattered armor
fumed away in vapor, skeins of atmosphere trailed behind, and some
ships fell out of formation with damaged drives. They could have fallen
back—no enemy was in range to prevent them—but each wounded
leviathan simply kept coming. No ship could stand more than three
of those devastating salvos, but each targeted ship made the enemy
expend those missiles upon it.*

"SBMs are running dry, Sir," Trang said tautly. "We've got two more
salvos, then we're down to CMs."

"Confirmed kills?" Husac demanded.

"We make it eight with . . . two more badly damaged. We *think* they were all *Archers*, but our ID criteria are pretty tentative. Until they return fire, we can't positively identify them."

"Understood." Husac watched the last two SBM salvos roar from her internal launchers. The enemy continued to advance, accepting the slaughter she'd wreaked on him without flinching, and a primitive corner of her mind gibbered that *nothing* should wade into such fire when it couldn't even shoot back. It was like fighting the insensate violence of a hurricane, not living, thinking beings, and that primitive part of her whispered they *were* an unstoppable force of nature. But it was only a tiny part, and she bared her teeth. "All right, Li-Dong. Phase Two."

"Admiral Husac's exhausted her SBMs," Demosthenes Waldeck announced from Murakuma's com screen. "She's closing to capital missile range now."

"Understood." Murakuma turned to Ling Tian. "Warn Plotting. They'll be returning fire shortly, and I want every one of those *Archers* fingerprinted the instant it opens up."

The battle-cruisers began to close once more. They were entering the Fleet's reach now, and targeting systems watched them come.

"Fifteen light-seconds," Trang reported. "Coming into— Missile launch! Multiple hostile launches! One hundred twenty plus inbound. Impact in two-seven seconds from—mark!"

"Return fire!" Husac snapped, and locked her command chair shock frame as the enemy's missiles scorched towards her.

The bastards had taken a page from her own book and concentrated all their fire on a single target. They obviously couldn't tell her *Thetis*-class command ships from the *Dunkerques*, or perhaps they didn't realize there was any difference to look for. If they didn't have command datalink, then they had no way to know only a single ship in each battlegroup mounted the master systems that tied them together. Yet what they knew or didn't know made no difference to TFNS *Goeben*, and she watched the ship go to violent evasive action.

But unlike Husac's targets, *Goeben* wasn't alone against the storm. *Endymion's* datanet wove a deadly, fine-meshed net of warheads and spitting lasers, ripping the incoming missiles apart, and the enemy's cruder command and control systems split his fire into smaller salvos that couldn't saturate the battlegroup's defenses.

Point defense stopped ninety-five percent of the incoming fire short of *Goeben*, yet simple probability theory said at least *some* birds had to get through, and the battle-cruiser heaved as they wiped away her shields and tore at her armor. Husac's fists clenched as damage reports chattered over the net, and her face was grim. They'd done well to stop that many incoming, but well or not, another exchange like that would blow the ship apart . . . and she had only twelve ships.

"Hit the bastards!" she snarled, and *Endymion* bucked as she threw fresh fury at her foes.

"*Goeben*'s been hit hard, Sir," Commander Ling said, and Murakuma nodded curtly. Battle-cruisers were too light to face SDs, however superior their datalink, but she had no choice. The *Dunkerques* and *Thetises* were the only CM-armed ships she had; they *had* to engage the *Archers*—and be engaged in return—if only to identify the missile ships for her.

"IDs on the *Archers?*" Her voice was flat, and Ling nodded.

"Tracking is confident, Sir. Two more salvos and we'll have them nailed."

The superdreadnoughts shuddered under the battle-cruisers' fire, but the odds were evening. Even with the enemy's heavier salvos and more destructive warheads, he needed three salvos to guarantee a kill, but the Fleet's projections indicated that each battle-cruiser could survive no more than two like the last one.

Another superdreadnought vanished in an expanding ball of fire, but the enemy had an iron lock on *Goeben*, and this time the other SDs flushed their external racks in support. The battlegroup's point defense performed brilliantly, but three more missiles got through. Men and women died as concussion and flame and radiation came for them, atmosphere streamed from breached plating, and Jennifer Husac's voice was harsh.

"Get her out of it, Li-Dong!"

Orders flashed over the net, and *Goeben* turned away. She'd lost an engine room, but she was still twice as fast as the oncoming superdreadnoughts. She swung away from them, fleeing their fire, and their targeting systems shifted to her sisters.

"*Goeben*'s breaking off," Waldeck said. "Looks like they're shifting to *Nevada,* but Husac took out another of them first."

"Understood." Murakuma watched the wounded battle-cruiser accelerate clear of the Bugs' envelope, but even as a part of her cheered the ship's survival, another cursed bitterly. If only she had a few missile SDs of her own! The battle-cruisers were fighting magnificently, but their superior systems were overmatched by their opponents' sheer toughness. The *Archers* were still dying, yet *Goeben*'s withdrawal diluted the weight of her battlegroup's next salvo—and the effectiveness of its point defense—by a sixth.

"Instruct Admiral Teller to launch his strike," she said.

"Launch!"

Twelve light carriers twitched as mass-drivers hurled fighters through their drive fields and into space. Two hundred and sixteen small, deadly craft, heavy with external ordnance, curved up and away at .2 *c*, shaking down into formation, turning for the enemy, and Commander Anson Olivera watched the continuous tactical update spill across his command fighter's display. Admiral Husac was taking a fearful pounding—her own battlegroup was down to only three ships and falling back behind its consorts—but only five confirmed and one possible *Archer* remained.

"Target designation." His strain-flattened voice was clipped as he tapped keys on his console. "Paired group strikes. Commander Renquist has *Archer* One. Slattery takes Two, Sung takes Three, and Takagumi and Marker take Four and Five. We'll take the last two strikegroups in to clean up the survivors ourselves. Confirm input."

"My board confirms," his tac officer called back, and Olivera switched to the central net. Sweat beaded his hewn-granite face, but he made his words come out even, almost jovial.

"Go get 'em, boys and girls. Last one back to the barn buys the beer."

The fighters swept past Husac's battered battle-cruisers. The *Dunkerques*' magazines were down to thirty percent, and her own group had been gutted. All its ships survived, but *Goeben, Nevada, Barham,* and *Jean Bart* had been driven out of action with heavy damage. Yet the enemy's concentration on only one of her battlegroups was the first real mistake he'd made; he'd crippled one of them, but the second was untouched.

"Pass tactical command to Commodore Suchien." Her voice was vicious with mingled loss and satisfaction as she watched the fighters. "Tell him the force advantage is about to shift."

Targeting priorities changed as the small, fleet craft hurtled into the Fleet's midst. They were fast and agile, squirming in wild evasion maneuvers even as they lined up on their targets, but a hurricane of close-in fire met them. One died, then another. Two more. A fifth. Dozens of fireballs glared as point defense lasers or force beams or missiles ripped into them, but still they came on, charging into the teeth of their own destruction. They tore into the missile SDs like demons, spitting deadly quartets of short-ranged missiles, and scores of antimatter warheads erupted against shuddering shields and the alloy they protected.

Banshee howls of triumph erupted from the speakers as Teller's flagship relayed his strikegroups' voice telemetry to *Cobra*. Those howls and the fireballs that spawned them were thirty seconds old by the time Vanessa Murakuma heard and saw them, and she clenched her jaw as all too many jubilant shouts chopped off in sudden silence. Of the two-hundred-plus fighters she'd committed, only a hundred and seventy fell back on their carriers, but they'd done their job. All remaining *Archers* and two suspected *Avalanches* were gone, and despite the anguish of her own losses, her brain ticked smoothly, efficiently within its protective cocoon of professionalism.

So far she'd lost only four badly damaged battle-cruisers and fifty-two fighters to kill sixty light cruisers and seventeen superdreadnoughts. That outmassed her entire task force, but the bastards were still coming, and a shudder very like the one Jennifer Husac had felt coursed through her. How in God's name could *anything* keep coming after a pounding like that?

But they *were* coming . . . and they had fifty-eight SDs left.

The surviving battle-cruisers, unopposed now by any capital missile, closed to the very edge of the standard missile envelope, battering their enemies, but their magazines had to be almost dry, and she might well need them even more later. She looked at her link to *Pit Viper*.

"Have Husac fall back to the colliers and reammunition, Demosthenes."

"Yes, Sir."

"Once she's clear, move the battle-line into extreme missile range. It's *our* turn to have a go at the bastards."

"Aye, aye, Sir." Waldeck's voice was taut, but there was savage satisfaction in it, as well, and Murakuma nodded with a grim smile.

All right, you fuckers, she thought coldly. *We've pulled your missile ships' teeth. Try bringing your goddamned energy armaments into range now!*

Rear Admiral Vanessa Murakuma crossed her legs and leaned back in her command chair as twelve battleships of the Terran Federation Navy advanced against their overpowering foe.

CHAPTER EIGHT

Options and Obligations

Major General Xavier Servais looked up as Colonel Mondesi entered the compartment. The colonel's great-great-grandparents had migrated from the island of Haiti to the Fringe World of Christophe, and his face was the color of obsidian . . . and utterly expressionless. Which, Servais thought as he stood behind his desk, meant Mondesi had already heard about his orders.

"Colonel." Servais offered his hand, and the younger man clasped it firmly. "Sit, please." Servais gestured at a chair and waited until Mondesi obeyed his polite command before he reseated himself. He pulled a pipe from his pocket and took his time stuffing it. It was an archaic affectation, but he sometimes found it a useful bit of stage dressing, and he used the delay to study Mondesi.

He liked what he saw. The colonel had posted a superb record in the specialized world of the Marines' Raiders, and despite whatever he'd already heard, he returned the general's measuring gaze levelly. That argued for more than his fair share of intestinal fortitude . . . and he was going to need all of that he had.

"I wanted to see you to discuss a special operation, Colonel," Servais said once he had his lit pipe drawing. "We're calling the overall plan Redemption, and you've been tapped to command one component of it: Operation Citadel. The good news, such as it is, is that you're being breveted to brigadier for the op, but I won't sugarcoat things. The odds of your living long enough to have the rank confirmed aren't good."

He paused for Mondesi's reaction, but the colonel simply nodded and said, "May I ask what this operation will consist of, Sir?"

"You may." Servais leaned back, caressing the polished bowl of his pipe with one hand. "Now that the enemy—the 'Bugs,' as Admiral Murakuma calls them—have K-45, it's only a matter of time until they hit Justin. The Fleet hurt them badly, but they got in their own licks, and the Admiral's staff estimates we have no more than three weeks before they resume the advance."

Raphael Mondesi nodded again. Most space battles were both violent and brief. When fleets threw antimatter warheads at one another, it seldom took long for the weaker side to be annihilated or run, but the Battle of K-45 had been different.

TF 59 had done what it set out to do and mauled the enemy brutally, but at a price. With the *Archers* eliminated, TG 59.2's battleships' superior datalink had let them hold their own, but their mixed missile and force beam batteries had compelled them to come into range of the enemy's *Avalanche*-class SDs. They'd learned the hard way that the *Acids* did, in fact, mount missile launchers to back their plasma batteries, but their salvos had been too light to break through Murakuma's point defense, and the only Bug energy weapon with the range to reach her had been the *Avalanches'* force beams. She'd taken a pounding from those beams, but she'd ignored the *Acids* and coordinated the fire of her battle-line's shipboard weapons with strikes by carefully hoarded fighters to pick off as many *Avalanches* as possible, then broken off. But this time it hadn't been to withdraw. She'd disengaged just long enough to carry out emergency repairs to her own ships, then resumed the action.

No one had ever seen a battle like it. For five full *days,* Vanessa Murakuma had played matador, smashing away at her overwhelming opponents with ever dwindling numbers, drawing them ever further from her exit warp point. She'd battered ship after ship into wreckage, and as each mangled hulk fell out of formation, her surviving fighters pounced upon it and finished it off. She and Demosthenes Waldeck had reorganized their battlegroups on the fly—mixing and matching as damage drove individual units out of action, pulling out ships with empty magazines to race back to the colliers and reammunition. Damage control crews had labored till they dropped, fighting the mounting tide of crippled systems, and not a single unit of her own battle-line had escaped unhurt. When she finally disengaged for good, she'd lost eighty percent of her fighters, a battleship, three battle-cruisers, two heavy cruisers, and five destroyers, with eight more capital ships—including the battleships *Conquistador* and *Héros*—so damaged they'd barely been able to limp back to Sarasota. But she'd destroyed fifty-three superdreadnoughts first.

It was, by any measure, the most one-sided victory in naval history . . . and it hadn't changed a thing, for yet another wave of Bug capital ships had entered K-45 even as Murakuma disengaged. Her superior speed had let her break contact, preventing the Bugs from tracking her to her exit warp point, so they'd have to find it the hard way, but when they did . . .

"I understand, Sir," the colonel said. "May I assume Citadel has something to do with what happens when they do arrive?"

"You may." Servais' voice was much grimmer than before. "In the absence of direct divine intervention, they're going to push us out of Justin. We managed to evacuate eighty-five percent of the Merriweather colonists . . . but that left over a million behind. And while the transit time from Justin A to Sarasota is less than twenty percent that from Merriweather to Sarasota, there are four times as many people in the system, and we've got, at best, a month. That means we're going to have to leave at least nine million more people behind. Admiral Murakuma feels—and I agree—that we cannot simply write those people off, and that's where you come in."

He pinched the bridge of his nose, then sighed.

"I don't like last-man battles," he said, "but that's exactly what this war's going to demand. We can't negotiate civilian surrenders, because we don't have the least idea how to communicate with these Bugs. And, judging by the Erebor transmissions, there's no point trying to figure it out. They see us as food sources, Colonel. All we can do is give them the worst case of bellyache they ever had, and civilians don't have the training or the firepower for that."

"But Marines do," Mondesi said.

"Marines do," Servais confirmed. Their eyes met for a long, silent moment, and then the colonel nodded once again.

"What's the plan, Sir?" he asked quietly.

"We'll concentrate on evacuating Justin A." Servais activated a holo display of the Justin Binary System above his desk. "Justin and Harrison"—the third and fourth planets of Component A flashed as he named them—"have much larger populations than Clements"— Justin B II lit in turn—"and with the Sarasota warp point associated with Justin A, the transit time is seventy hours shorter. Admiral Murakuma's already instructed Clements to shut down all emissions and go bush. There are less than a million people on the entire planet, scattered around in very small settlements, so they may be able to conceal their presence from anything but a very close scan.

"But we can't do that for Justin A, so Admiral Eusebio's sent up every rifle, mortar and HVM he can find. Your job, Colonel, is to distribute those weapons to the civilians of Justin and Harrison. I've already contacted General Merman, the system Peaceforce CO, and we're organizing quicky classes to bring his people up to speed on frontline equipment. We're also combing out our Marine contingents, and I estimate we can give you the equivalent of a light division."

Servais paused, looking into Mondesi's steady eyes, and raised one hand, palm uppermost.

"Even with the Peaceforcers to back you, a light division could never stand off an invasion, Colonel, but that isn't your job. The Navy's going to reinforce as quickly as possible, and it's our intention to retake Justin at the earliest possible moment. I wish I could tell you how soon that will be. I can't. All I can tell you is that it's *your* job to organize and lead a guerrilla resistance for as long as you can—hopefully until we *can* retake the system. In the meantime, Admiral Murakuma's staff is organizing a plan for Redemption, a raid to be launched in the event the Bugs offer us an opportunity to mount it. They will designate refuge areas, landing zones from which we will attempt to lift out anyone we can if we're able to fight our way back in even temporarily, but don't count on that happening."

The grim-voiced general held the colonel's gaze and spoke very quietly.

"I have never before sent an officer into a situation in which I *expected* him to die, Colonel Mondesi. In this case, however, I have no choice but to do precisely that. Admiral Murakuma truly thinks she may be able to relieve you. I believe she'll make every humanly possible effort to do just that . . . but I expect her to fail. Which means you and all your people will be on your own. I won't insult you or them by pretending otherwise to stiffen your morale. I will simply remind you that you are Marines and that you will be defending nine million civilians."

Servais stood and held out a data chip to the officer he'd just condemned to death.

"Your official orders and full data on Justin and Harrison are on the chip. Under the circumstances, the least I can do is give you complete freedom in planning your own operations. Anything my staff or I can do to assist you is yours for the asking."

"Yes, Sir." Mondesi slipped the chip into his pocket. "We'll remember we're Marines, General," he said.

"I never doubted it, Colonel." Servais extended his hand once more, and Mondesi gripped it as firmly as he had when he first entered the compartment. "God bless, Colonel," the general said very quietly, and Mondesi nodded, released his hand, and walked through the hatch.

Captain Andrew Foote Prescott of the battle-cruiser *Daikyu* came to attention as the delicate, red-haired woman by the holo tank straightened and turned to face him. Her black-and-silver uniform set off her coloring with a perfection any HD producer would have killed for, and she stood tall and straight, but there were lines of strain on her oval face.

"Captain Prescott." Prescott was of only average height and build, yet he found himself taking the hand she extended gingerly, as if he feared a firm grip would shatter the fragile bones. The skin around her weary eyes crinkled, and a faint smile dimpled her cheeks, as if she was used to the reaction, but she squeezed hard.

"Admiral," he said, and found himself smiling back. For all her fatigue and obvious strain, this woman still radiated an indefinable serenity and a very definable aura of command.

"Thank you for coming so promptly," she said, and gestured at the tank. "Have a look."

He quirked an eyebrow, then stepped closer to the tank. It held a small-scale display of the Justin System, centered on the F8 furnace of Justin A. Justin B, its G0 companion, lay the better part of five light-hours distant, barely visible at the edge of the tank, but what caught his eye were five crimson dots scattered about the Justin B asteroid belt at its closest approach to Justin A. He gazed at them for a moment, then looked inquiringly at his admiral.

"Those are—or shortly will be—the locations of hidden supply ships, Captain. Yours."

"Mine, Sir?"

"Yours," she repeated. She pointed at a chair and folded her hands behind her to consider him as he slid into it and laid his cap on the table.

The Prescott family had served the Fleet well. It ought to have, for naval service was bred into its bone and blood. A Prescott had served Prince Rupert of Bohemia aboard the *Royal James* at the Four Days Battle. Others had died on the decks of the brig *Lawrence* in the Battle of Lake Erie and the *Cumberland* at Hampton Roads, and yet another had sailed into Manila Bay aboard the cruiser *Olympia*. His grandson had flown from the deck of the carrier *Yorktown* at the Battle of Midway, and when the Federated Government of Earth merged the old national militaries, the Prescotts had taken their tradition into the Federation's Navy. Murakuma was only the third member of her family to don naval uniform, but this man's naval lineage stretched back for over six standard centuries. That was one reason she'd chosen him, and she could almost feel his ancestors' silent presence at his shoulder as he looked calmly back at her.

"I intend to hold this system if at all possible, Captain," she said finally. "I think I have a chance to do so, but it isn't a good one. Whatever we do to these creatures, they simply keep on coming, and without reinforcements—"

She shrugged, and Prescott nodded. This woman had just won one of the greatest naval victories in history. Some officers in her position would have hidden their fears for the future behind pride in the past, but Vanessa Murakuma didn't, and her composure—and frankness to a relatively junior captain—impressed him.

"Because it seems likely we will, in fact, fail to hold Justin," she went on, "it is incumbent upon me to plan for the worst. That's where you come in."

She took one hand from behind her back to gesture at the holo tank.

"We're going to leave a lot of civilians behind, and the decision to withdraw will be mine. I, Captain Prescott, will personally sentence nine million human beings to death." He opened his mouth to dispute her cruel self-accusation, but she shook her head. "No, Captain. I realize I'll have no choice, and my orders from the Admiralty are clear. The Justinians must be considered expendable, and I am specifically forbidden to risk the destruction of my command to save them. But I also intend to move heaven and hell to get as many of them out as possible. Perhaps it's only a sop to my conscience or a whimsical gesture, but I will not sacrifice a single human being I can save to these monsters, whatever my orders!"

Prescott stiffened in his chair as bared steel clashed behind her serenity, and her exhausted eyes flickered with a hard, dangerous light.

"I want you to understand something, Captain Prescott," she said softly. "What I intend to do could be construed as a violation of my own orders from Sky Marshal Avram. I cannot order you to accept the responsibility I'm about to ask you to shoulder. I can only ask you to volunteer, and if you do so, your chance to succeed—or survive—will be slight."

"What, precisely, do you want me to volunteer *for*, Sir?" Prescott asked in a level voice.

"I'm asking you to accept an extremely hazardous assignment." She folded both hands behind her once more and looked into his eyes. "Your ship's a *Broadsword* class, with cloaking ECM. If and when we're forced to withdraw, I want to detach *Daikyu* as part of a scouting force which will remain in Justin to observe the enemy."

"To what purpose, Admiral?" Prescott asked after a moment.

"It will be some time before Battle Fleet can reinforce us sufficiently to take the offensive. It is remotely possible, however, that before that time comes, the chance to raid Justin from Sarasota will arise. My staff is currently planing for just such an operation under the codename 'Redemption,' but we've come up against one problem again and again. For an inferior force to raid a superior one, it *must* have accurate information on its enemies' strength and deployments."

"I see." Prescott looked down at his cap for a moment, stroking its braided visor with a forefinger, then looked back up at his admiral. "I can think of several difficulties, Sir," he said calmly, "but I'm sure we can figure out a way around most of them if we put our minds to it."

CHAPTER NINE

They Just Keep Coming

It was late as Vanessa Murakuma prowled Flag Bridge. She ought to be in bed. Her wakefulness and inability to sit still only advertised her edginess and might well shake her subordinates' nerve, but she couldn't help it. It was harder each day to project the composure and certainty her personnel needed, and her ignorance of the Bugs' activities only made it worse.

She wheeled back to the master plot and glowered into it. Each of the twenty-two days since the Battle of K-45 had added its weight to her millstone tension, yet each had also been a priceless treasure. Sarasota had done wonders with the ships she'd sent back to it, and a few desperately needed reinforcements had arrived, as well, headed by five fleet carriers and three *Matterhorn* missile SDs, but she was grimly certain the Bugs had been reinforced even more heavily.

Certain, yet unable to confirm it. She'd tried sneaking pinnaces through to K-45, but the cost had been too high. Over eighty percent had been picked off before they could reverse course and escape. Volunteers continued to come forward, but there was no possible way to justify sacrificing them, particularly when she knew the enemy was heavily equipped with cloaking ECM. Enough of her people were going to die when the Bugs finally attacked; she wouldn't send them to their deaths in efforts to spy on an enemy who could hide so much of his strength, anyway.

Perhaps another admiral could have done it. Perhaps it would even have been justified in the cold, brutal math of war. She couldn't, yet the strain of waiting in ignorance twisted her nerves, and her nights were haunted by nightmares whose existence she dared admit to no one, even Marcus, though she suspected *Cobra*'s chief surgeon guessed.

He hadn't argued when she finally went to him to demand something to help her sleep, at any rate.

It wasn't her fault. She knew that, and she'd tried to accept that lack of options absolved her from guilt. But she'd learned more about herself in the last three months than in all her previous sixty-seven years, and there was a flaw at her core. The very one, she knew now, which had sent her into uniform in the first place: responsibility. It was her *job* to protect civilians, to stand between them and their enemies. To die, if that was the only way to save them. Most of them never spared the Navy a thought in peacetime. Of those who did, many complained bitterly about funds the Fleet diverted from other expenditures, but that changed nothing. It was her job to keep them safe enough they could afford to feel that way about her, and she'd never fully realized how deep her sense of responsibility cut until she'd been forced to abandon millions of them to horrible death. Now she did, and she wondered, in the night while she waited for the nightmares to come, how many more worlds she could abandon before she broke.

She gazed down into the plot for endless minutes, searching for an answer. But no answer came, and, at last, she drew a deep breath, turned, and walked from the flag bridge to her cabin.

The light cruisers of the Assault fleet formed up. It had taken the survey ships less time than usual to locate the warp point—the enemy's attempts to use small craft as spies had helped—but the staggering losses the fleet had so far suffered had delayed its timetable. Yet it was ready now, and its ships floated silently in space, ready to resume the advance at last.

The alarm's wail yanked her from her sleep, and she jerked upright even as one hand reached automatically for the inhaler. She fumbled it to her face, then squeezed the button and gasped as a fiery pinwheel exploded in her brain. The stimulant was as brutal as the surgeon had warned it would be, but it smashed the drugged fog from her mind, and she shook herself fiercely.

She tossed the inhaler aside and activated her bedside com.

"Talk to me!"

"They're coming through, Sir." It was Leroy Mackenna's grim voice, and she wondered what he was doing on Flag Bridge at this hour. Was he having as much trouble sleeping as she?

"Strength?" she demanded, shoving the blankets aside.

"Only their light cruisers so far," Mackenna said tensely. "Plotting makes it seventy-five-plus of them. I expect we'll see the big suckers shortly, Sir."

"Understood. On my way." She cut the com circuit and climbed into her vac suit, wincing in pain as she made the plumbing connections with ruthless haste. There was a preternatural sharpness to her thoughts—a gift, no doubt, from the stim—yet even with that edge (if edge it was), she couldn't understand the Bugs' tactics. Surely K-45 had taught them she wouldn't risk a point-blank defense! And if none of her ships lay within the cruisers' engagement envelope, taking losses from interpenetration was pointless.

She snatched up her helmet and headed for the hatch at a run. Maybe the bastards were simply slaves to The Book. Despite herself, her lips quirked as she pictured a Bug admiral with The Book open in front of him, eye-stalks cocked as he ran the tip of a tentacle down the type, but the smile vanished quickly. That many light cruisers might indicate a commensurate increase in capital ships, and there was nothing at all humorous about that.

Ninety cruisers made transit. Seventy-one survived the experience, and their sensors scanned the space about the warp point while courier drones raced back to confirm transit. There were none of the mines that had cost their fellows so dear in the last battle, and they moved outward, englobing the warp point at one light-second's range.

Mackenna and Ling Tian were bent over the master plot when Murakuma stepped onto Flag Bridge, and Demosthenes Waldeck looked down from a bulkhead com screen. Jackson Teller's face filled another screen, and Rear Admiral John Ludendorff, who'd arrived with the *Borzoi-* and *Kodiak*-class fleet carriers, occupied another from the bridge of TFNS *Polar Bear*. Although senior to Teller, Ludendorff had readily agreed to serve as the junior admiral's exec rather than shake up TF 59's command team.

Mackenna started to speak as Murakuma strode quickly to the plot, but her raised hand stopped him long enough for her eyes to devour the icons. The Bug CLs had spread out about the warp point, and a long, lethal line of superdreadnoughts had begun to flow through in their wake.

"Is Admiral Kuzak ready?" she asked him then.

"Yes, Sir. She's standing by for your order."

"Good." Murakuma watched the display a moment longer, then nodded. "Tell her to do it," she said flatly.

"Yes, Sir," Ling Tian replied, and Murakuma racked her helmet on the side of her command chair and watched her repeater plot as she seated herself.

Her ships' icons blinked from the amber of standby to the flashing brilliance of General Quarters, and the ready fighters spat from her carriers' catapults, but her eyes dropped to the light codes representing the five OWPs which had orbited Justin A III until she'd demanded enough *Turbine*-class fleet tugs to move them to within ten light-seconds of the warp point. *Turbines* were more powerful than civilian tugs, able to give the "immobile" OWPs a velocity equal to any Bug ship's. Just as importantly, they mounted light shields, point defense . . . and datalink. They could be brought inside the OWPs' datanets, and their skippers had orders to keep their ponderous charges between them and the enemy. In effect, Murakuma had turned the forts into a mobile support force, and her lips skinned back at the thought. Each of those OWPs was the size of a superdreadnought, and none of its hundred and eighty thousand tonnes were devoted to the engines an SD required. Four were pure missile platforms—with standard missiles, not capital launchers, unfortunately—and the fifth was the command base, with a pure energy armament to support its master datalink and deep space control systems. Its heterodyne lasers were powerful weapons, but she doubted she was going to get much use out of them. Which didn't bother her. Given the unorthodox strategy she'd evolved, the command base was about to prove worth its weight in any precious substance someone cared to name, and each standard base had the offensive missile power of an entire battlegroup of *Belleisle*-class battleships. She'd had to break them into two battlegroups and use Admiral Kuzak's *Cottonmouth* as the second group's command ship, but they'd be able to throw an awesome number of missiles once they engaged.

For the moment, however, her attention was on the command OWP. She'd exhausted her supply of mines in K-45, but someone up the logistics pipeline had scraped up something even better for this fight. One hundred small buoys floated in a thin shell, six light-seconds from the warp point. There were so few of them, and they were so widely dispersed, the Bugs might not have picked them up at all. Even if they had, they'd probably assumed they were laser buoys—a threat, but an acceptable one. Only they weren't laser buoys; they were independently deployed primary beam platforms, and the command base had just ordered them to engage.

Four seconds passed while the order sped to the nearest buoys, then another twenty while they waited until their more distant brothers received the command base's targeting setup and confirmed their readiness to the master buoys. And then, in one terrible instant, one hundred primary beams stabbed out in a single, deadly salvo.

The lead superdreadnoughts staggered as unstoppable stilettos stabbed through shields and armor with contemptuous ease, and the SDs—safely outside the enemy's range—had made no effort to take evasive action. Over seventy primaries scored direct hits on the ten lead ships. The narrow-focus weapons punched tiny holes, little more than five centimeters across, but they punched those holes through anything . . . *including magazines.*

The beams ripped into the stored warheads. Containment fields ruptured, matter met antimatter, and a deadly chain reaction tore through every warhead aboard the targeted ships.

"*Yes!*"

Leroy Mackenna's exultant hiss filled *Cobra's* flag bridge as fireballs glared on the warp point, and Murakuma's fist slammed down on her command chair's armrest. She'd hoped to hurt the bastards, but her most optimistic prediction had fallen short of this! Ten clear kills—*ten!*—in the opening salvo! By God, she might be able to stop them after all!

"Ready, Jackson?" she asked, looking up at Teller's com screen.

"Ready, Sir!" The carrier admiral's fierce exultation matched her own, and she nodded.

"Send them in," she said, and glanced at Waldeck. "Engage the enemy, Admiral Waldeck."

For just a moment, even the Bugs seemed paralyzed by the destruction visited upon their battle-line's van. Then the first Terran missile salvos began to rip into them even as their sensors detected the closing signatures of two hundred and sixty strikefighters, and the globe of light cruisers moved closer to the warp point to screen the emerging line of superdreadnoughts.

"Jesus! *Look* at that bastard!"

Commander Olivera nodded grimly. He was the backup strike commander this time, and that gave him too much leisure to observe the light cruiser Lieutenant (JG) Carlton Hathaway had centered on his display. The damned thing must mount nothing *but* point defense, because it was putting out three times the defensive fire of a *Belleisle*-class BB, and that was bad. Very bad.

"How many of them do you see?" he asked tautly.

"I make it at least fifteen, Skip—probably more. What the hell is that thing?"

"How the fuck do *I* know?" Olivera demanded harshly, then shrugged. "Hell, maybe it's a minesweeper—if it matters!" He glanced at Lieutenant Malachi, his command fighter's pilot. "I hope you're feeling agile, Jane."

"As a weasel, Skip." Malachi was the quintessential fighter jock; her voice only got calmer as the tension rose, and Olivera managed a tight smile, then looked back at the tac officer.

"Punch up the alternate command net, Carl."

Hathaway nodded in grim understanding. Gloved fingers danced across his panel, and Olivera bent over his own, setting up a running download from the strike leader in case he had to take over.

"We've got a new light cruiser class, Sir!" Ling Tian's voice was clipped, but sudden worry burned in its depths. "It appears to be an antimissile ship or minesweeper. Whatever it is, it's got at least fifty percent more point defense than a *Dunedin!*"

Something inside Murakuma flinched. The *Dunedin*-class escort light cruisers were antimissile platforms designed to bolster the defenses of light carrier or battle-line battlegroups. CLEs were fragile compared to a capital ship but mounted enormously powerful point defense for their size, which made them extremely efficient at killing missiles . . . or fighters.

"Switch the *Matterhorns* and OWPs to them!"

"Aye, aye, Sir."

Murakuma bit her lip as Ling's acknowledgment came back to her. She hated taking her bases and handful of superdreadnoughts off the Bug heavies, yet those CLEs would wreak havoc among her fighters, and the OWPs and *Matterhorns* were her best chance to take them out. The bases had the sheer volume of fire to saturate their defenses and the penetration aids of the *Matterhorns'* capital missiles might just let them sneak through, and it wouldn't take many hits with second-generation AM warheads to blow a light cruiser apart.

She bit her lip harder. Should she recall the strike, wait until she'd had a chance to whittle away at this unanticipated threat? The casualties her strikegroups were about to take said yes, but if she pulled back now she lost her best—possibly her only—chance to actually *stop* the bastards. The warp point was a holocaust of exploding warheads, ripping at the incoming capital ships. She'd already killed ten, and half a dozen more were bleeding air. If she could just hit them hard enough, savage them terribly enough, surely even Bugs would break off!

Her long-dead husband's face flickered before her, and she closed her eyes, fighting Tadeoshi aside while options and costs and possibilities cascaded through her brain. Even if she pulled them back now, they might take equally heavy losses later, she told herself. If she backed off on the strike, let the capital ships make transit in strength, the defensive fire would be almost as terrible even if every CLE were blown apart. But the decisive factor, the one she simply could not ignore, was timing, the possibility of getting the fighters in quickly enough, in sufficient strength, to stop the enemy dead and save nine million civilians.

She opened her eyes once more and watched the fighter icons streaking towards the holocaust and said nothing.

"It's gonna be a rough ride, Skipper," Hathaway said flatly, and Olivera nodded. Whatever their designed purpose, the Bug cruisers' defenses made them missile sponges. They were soaking up enormous volumes of fire . . . and diverting TF 59's fire from the Bug battle-line when its transit-destabilized units were at their most vulnerable.

"Entering their envelope in fifteen seconds." The tac officers voice was flatter than ever, and Olivera felt his guts tighten.

The fighters slammed into the Bugs' defensive globe, and Vanessa Murakuma's face went white as every light cruiser opened fire simultaneously. The CLEs were the most effective, but the class Ops had codenamed *Carbine* was almost as bad. They didn't have the AFHAWK, thank God, but they didn't really need the specialized antifighter missile—not when they had enough sprint-mode standard missiles to go around. The Bug cruisers had to be extremely austere designs, she thought almost calmly, without the support systems Terran designers included as a matter of course. If they were regarded as expendable throwaways, that actually made sense . . . and it also meant the tonnage they *didn't* use for self-protection could be diverted to offensive purposes. The *Carbines'* missile broadsides were twice as heavy as a TFN light cruiser's, and she watched in horror as they ripped into her fighters.

"Coming up on our final turn, Skip!" Hathaway's voice was jagged with tension, and nausea swirled in Olivera's belly as Malachi went to full power and evasive action and a savage fist crushed him back in his couch. No one had ever figured out how to build a fighter inertial compensator with the efficiency of a starship's or even a larger small craft's. Fighters were the smallest, fastest, most agile deep-space craft ever designed, and the engineers had been forced to accept some fundamental compromises to offset the acceleration effects which would otherwise have turned any human passenger into gruel. In effect, a fighter's inertial sump was shallower than that of anything else in space. It worked . . . but it didn't work as *well* as those of larger units, and that was what made fighter ops so physically punishing when they went to full power.

Malachi took them into the teeth of the enemy's fire at .2 *c,* and Olivera felt another, colder nausea twist his gut as fighters began to die.

I *should have called them back.* The icy thought burned in Vanessa Murakuma's brain as dozens of Terran fighters exploded. *I should have called them* back!

But she hadn't, and her hands locked on her command chair's armrests like talons as her bleeding squadrons continued to close.

"Captain Brigatta's gone!" Hathaway barked, and Olivera nodded.

"Rampart Strike, this is Rampart Two," he said over the net while the giant's fist crushed him back and antiacceleration drugs fought his body's abuse. "Maintain profile. We're going in."

Half the fighters were already dead when the survivors broke through the cruisers, and more died as they charged across the final light-seconds towards their targets. Clumsy, waddling superdreadnoughts tried to turn aside even as their own weapons lashed at their attackers, but this was what Rampart Strike had come for. It would not be denied, and broken bits of squadrons bucked and bounced through the curdled space in the SDs' wakes. The warp point was a mad confusion of fishtailing fighters and swerving capital ships; Bug jammers overpowered squadron datanets; light cruisers turned to follow them into the madness, point defense firing furiously while the Terran missiles it was ignoring roared in to kill them; and even as Rampart Strike closed, fresh superdreadnoughts continued to make transit into the maelstrom. No computer could have sorted it all out, but that no longer mattered. Rampart Strike's survivors swerved into the blind spots of their victims, and Olivera knew there would be too few left for a second strike like this. They had to get close—so close not a shot missed, for it was the only pass they were going to get.

"Visual range!" he barked over the net. "*Visual range launch!*"

"Holy Mary, Mother of God, blessed art thou among women ..." Carlton Hathaway whispered as an enemy superdreadnought loomed on his targeting screen. The range was less than a hundred thousand kilometers, and it flashed downward like lightning with the fighter's overtake velocity as Malachi lined up. The tac officer's hand rested on the control panel built into the armrest of his flight couch, and the ball of one gloved thumb reached for the big, red button.

" ... pray for us sinners at—"

The SD appeared suddenly on his visual display, and his thumb jabbed.

"*Birds away!*" he screamed, and threw up into his helmet as Jane Malachi redlined her drive in a vicious hairpin turn. Four antimatter-armed close attack missiles blasted from the fighter, roaring down on the SD, and eight more missiles followed them in from the only other two survivors of Olivera's original squadron.

All twelve scored direct hits. There was no wreckage.

✧　　✧　　✧

Vanessa Murakuma's bleak, frozen eyes watched the fragments of Jackson Teller's fighters fall back to their carriers. They'd killed sixteen SDs, and Plotting estimated that they'd inflicted heavy damage on six more, but they'd paid for it with almost seventy percent of their number, and it was her fault.

She stared into her own soul, loathing what she saw, then made herself accept it and set it aside. There would be time to face her dead later.

She drew a deep breath and looked back into her plot. They'd put the next best thing to thirty superdreadnoughts out of action, but that many more were already in-system, and more were making transit as she watched. It was unbelievable. Whatever she did, however many she killed, however brutally she smashed them, they just kept *coming*, and with her fighter strength decisively blunted, she couldn't stop them. Perhaps she couldn't have stopped them anyway. Perhaps her hope of doing that had never been anything more than a hope, no more than a desperate need to believe she could do it. But whatever it had once been, it was only one more failure now.

She inhaled again, nostrils flaring, then looked up at Ling Tian and Leroy Mackenna.

"Go to Charlie Seven," she said, and her own calm, even voice as she ordered her task force to begin its long retreat astonished her.

"Yes, Sir," Mackenna said softly, and she looked at Teller's ashen face on the com screen.

"Consolidate your squadrons, Jackson. I'll give you as much time to reorganize as I can."

"Yes, Sir." There wasn't a trace of condemnation in his voice, and she wanted to scream at him. But she stopped herself. Somehow she stopped herself.

"Once you've consolidated, detach any carrier without at least two squadrons on board," she said flatly. "Send them back to Justin and Harrison to evacuate every civilian you can pack aboard. You're authorized to redline your environmental systems."

"Yes, Sir," Teller said once more, and Murakuma nodded. She leaned back in her command chair, watching the ravaged light dots flashing back towards their carriers, and her mouth twisted.

At least she'd just made sure they'd have lots of spare life support for the civilians, she thought bitterly.

CHAPTER TEN

"We *can't* wait!"

One inescapable consequence of the physics of the reactionless drive was that the instant a drive field went down, any velocity it had imparted went with it. The energy shedding process as the immense forces concentrated in the surface of the field's "bubble" dissipated was spectacular but harmless, and the ability to decelerate virtually instantaneously from .1 *c* to whatever a starship's relative motion had been at the moment the drive was engaged could be invaluable. There were, however, circumstances under which the velocity loss required some inventiveness.

And this, Andrew Prescott thought sardonically, watching *Daikyu's* master display with what he hoped was an air of calm confidence, *is one of them.*

The battle-cruiser slid stealthily through the system's outer reaches, creeping along (for her) at barely 15,000 KPS under cover of her ECM while passive sensors probed the vacuum like a cat's quivering whiskers. Her course carried her directly towards the Justin-Sarasota warp point, but that invisible dot lay two billion kilometers ahead, and she had no intention of approaching it any more closely than she must. While a coward would never have let himself be "volunteered" for his present mission, Andrew Prescott was no fool. He was confident he could spot and evade any enemies which weren't cloaked, but even though his scanners hadn't found any, the presence of cloaked Bug pickets was a certainty, and logic suggested there were more of them than there were of him.

He looked around the bridge once more, and his mouth quirked at the duty watch's tense body language. The last three weeks had been nerve-wracking for his subordinates, but those same weeks had held another, even deeper strain for him. The others were concerned primarily only with surviving; he was responsible for the success of his mission, as well.

His half-smile vanished at the thought, for if *his* ship had evaded all enemies, her consort *Longsword* hadn't. He couldn't be certain, but he suspected Captain Daulton had gotten too close to the warp point—either to probe it or in an effort to get a courier drone to Sarasota—five days ago. Whatever his intention, *Longsword* had been detected, ambushed and destroyed with all hands. *Daikyu* had been just close enough to catch the omnidirectional Code Omega which confirmed her destruction, and Andrew Prescott was determined the Bugs would not get his ship, as well. *Daikyu* had a job to do, and to do it, she must survive.

But she also had to know what was going on and—trickier still— whether or not what she knew was important enough to report. Just securing the data was hard enough, as his present elaborate maneuvers illustrated, but it was easier than deciding when that data was vital enough to risk passing it on. He'd made up his mind at the outset not to make any reports that *weren't* vital, and *Longsword*'s destruction reconfirmed his determination, for there was no way the Bugs could miss a transiting courier drone. Even assuming they didn't manage to backtrack it to *Daikyu,* its mere existence would tell them *Longsword* hadn't been the only spy left to watch them, and their efforts to find *Daikyu* would redouble if they knew positively that she was there to be found. Worse, it might cause them to rethink whatever deployment had inspired him to send the drone in the first place, and unless he was in a position to see any changes they made—*and* report them to Sarasota—those changes could turn his original message into a trap.

The same considerations applied to recon drones. An RD was a low-signature object, with every built-in stealth feature the TFN could devise, but even the stealthiest drone's drive field could be spotted under the wrong circumstances, especially at close quarters, and he needed to get his RD right on top of the warp point. Redemption couldn't be risked on questionable data; he had to reduce the uncertainty factor to the absolute minimum. The problem was to somehow get the damned thing to point-blank range *without* using its drive, and he and Fred Kasuga, his exec, had wracked their brains to find a way. The actual suggestion had been Kasuga's, but like everything else, the final responsibility for its success—or failure—was Andrew Foote Prescott's.

He grimaced at the familiar thought, then sighed. There were times he wished he'd told Murakuma to hand the stinking job to some other captain, but *someone* had to do it, and he'd accepted it because it had to be done. And, he admitted privately, because deep down inside he was convinced *he* could do it better than anyone else.

Well, Mister Wonderful, if you're so hot it's about time you prove it, he thought, and glanced at his astrogator.

"On profile?" he asked quietly.

"Yes, Sir. Coming up on release point in—" Lieutenant Commander Belliard glanced at the countdown ticking away in a corner of his display "—eight minutes."

"Good." Prescott looked at his tac officer. "Status on the bird, Jill?"

"Just completed the final diagnostic, Skipper." Lieutenant Commander Cesiaño popped a chip out of her console, loaded it into a message board, and handed it to him, and he glanced over it. Every system checked—as he'd expected from Cesiaño—and he handed it back with a nod.

"Outstanding. Now if everything works, we may even get away with it."

The tac officer grinned, and he smiled back at her as he felt the rest of the bridge crew respond to his wry tone. *Funny how even really bright people can be amused by stupid jokes,* he thought, and settled into his command chair to watch the final minutes limp into eternity.

"Stand by for release," Cesiaño said finally, and Prescott tipped his chair back and steepled his hands across his flat belly. All he could really do at a moment like this was try even harder to radiate confidence, and—

"Drone away!" Cesiaño said, and Prescott's eyes narrowed. The RD's low-signature materials made it all but invisible even to *Daikyu*'s sensors, and it radiated no active emissions at all. Even its drive was down—indeed, Cesiaño's missile crews had physically disabled it, just in case—and it stopped dead as it penetrated *Daikyu*'s drive field. But a readied tractor jerked it instantly back into motion. It couldn't accelerate without a drive of its own, but the tractor tugged it bodily along, imparting the momentum of *Daikyu*'s velocity. It couldn't maneuver or change course, but it also offered no betraying energy source to warn anyone it was coming, and its present heading would take it directly past the Sarasota warp point in almost exactly thirty-six hours at a range of less than fifteen light-seconds. And in the meantime . . .

"Execute breakaway," he said.

"Aye, aye, Sir," Belliard responded. "Executing now."

Cesiaño cut the tractor, and *Daikyu* looped up and away from the drone. The range opened gradually, and Prescott inhaled in satisfaction as it vanished from even *Daikyu*'s ken four minutes later. It was unlikely in the extreme that anyone would see it coming, but that left the trickiest parts still to accomplish. First, *Daikyu* had to up her speed (and consequent chance of detection) enough to circle round the warp point to catch the drone at the appointed rendezvous on the far side, and then—

And then, Andrew Prescott told himself, *I have to decide if the result of the exercise is worth breaking silence to inform Sarasota.* He grimaced again and looked at the chronometer. Three days. The time, he knew, was not going to pass quickly.

"They're coming over us! *They're coming over us!*"

An explosion roared over the link, and the voice in Acting Major Frieda Jaëger's earbug went from a tenor shout to a soprano scream. The link brought the terrible concussion right into her command vehicle with her, slamming her head aside in involuntary reflex as her mind pictured the carnage with masochistic clarity, and her hands fisted. Somehow the transmitter at the other end had survived the explosion, and she heard the scream collapse into a horrible, high-pitched, endless sound of agony before her com officer could cut the circuit.

Jaëger drew a deep breath and shook herself. Lieutenant Furness wasn't the first to die since the Bugs came to Justin. *He won't be the last, either,* her mind said grimly, but he'd blown hell out of the Bug point before they called in the heavy stuff on him.

She dropped her eyes to the map display. So far, the Bugs didn't seem to have sorted the recon satellites out of all the other orbital junk, but Colonel—*No, Brigadier Mondesi,* she corrected herself—wasn't taking chances. A sneaky opponent might opt for planting scanners around the satellites to track their whisker laser transmissions to whatever was receiving them, so Mondesi had them reporting to widely dispersed (and unmanned) remote ground stations, and aside from short-range tactical traffic, all transmissions were compressed into burst transmissions and then bounced off anything *but* one of the recon or surviving comsats. Transmission quality might suffer, but there was almost always some handy piece of space junk, manmade or natural, to get the message through, and the tight beams were virtually undetectable.

Which was good, because hiding things like Jaëger's Asp command vehicle from an enemy who controlled the high orbitals was hard enough without radiating "Oh kill me now!" emission signatures. In fact, she would have preferred to command her "battalion" of Marines, Peaceforcers, and civilians from her battle armor and a hole in the ground that gave the Bugs nothing at all to spot. Unfortunately, she had too many civilians and Peaceforcers and too few armored Raiders to make that practical. Worse, her force was spread so thin and so widely dispersed that she needed all the command and control capability she could get, and in that respect an Asp was vastly superior to anything even a Raider "zoot" could provide.

For what it was worth.

She glared at the display as the Asp's computers turned Furness's position from green to crimson. The Bugs' operational doctrine sucked, and they didn't appear to have any equivalent of the Corps' zoots, but the bastards were incredibly fast and strong even without it. The intelligence pukes' best guess was that they came from a high-grav world, though none of the planets *Argive* had reported had been massive enough to account for it. That was an unsettling thought. Jaëger had seen the population estimates Intelligence had formed based on Commodore Braun's report, and if that many Bugs lived in a star system that didn't even contain their home world—

Jaëger snarled at her own wandering thoughts. *Fatigue. I've got to find a way to get at least some shut-eye, or my brain's going to go straight to mush. But how the hell am I supposed to do that when the bastards keep coming this way?*

She forced her mind back to the present. Wherever their home world was, the Bugs' strength let them carry weapons almost as heavy as a zooted Raider's, and they could scuttle through even close terrain with dreadful, flowing speed. Man for man (though applying the term "man" to a Bug, however obliquely, made Jaëger gag mentally), they were far better armed than most of her non-Marines, and much faster. Without zoots or vehicles, it was desperately difficult for any of the Justin Defense Force's units to disengage and break contact. Worse, these bastards were perfectly willing to launch frontal assaults and accept incredible losses to get in among her positions, and once they did, their firepower made them hideously effective killers.

But that same attack mentality could be used against them. For all their individual firepower, they were only sparsely equipped with support weapons, and Mondesi's Marines had quickly taught their hodgepodge of police and civilians to show them targets in order to suck them into prepared fire sacks. If they took the bait, the support squads lurking in ambush could inflict massive casualties, and their own aggressiveness kept them coming when any Terran unit would have broken off, which only increased the body count. The defenders had managed to destroy more than one attack force down to the last Bug—*which,* she thought grimly, *seems to be the only way to guarantee breaking contact.* Furness, unfortunately, hadn't, and she'd been unable to reinforce in time to save his platoon. Not, at any rate, without committing her zoots or handful of remaining assault skimmers, and she had to be extremely careful how she moved those. The energy they radiated moving at speed was painfully visible from orbit, and the defenders had learned the hard way that the Bugs were perfectly willing to nuke any juicy target they saw.

But at least Furness had drawn the attack onto his own unit, and its fight to the death had diverted the Bugs from the refugee camp long enough for its occupants to scatter into the hills. Some would be caught by the clumsy helicopters which seemed to be the Bugs' only tactical aircraft, but the Bugs had learned—also the hard way—what happened to any chopper that encountered a Marine with an HVM. The man-portable hyper velocity missile moved at ten percent of light-speed, giving them energy-weapon accuracy over any tactical range, and the kinetic energy released when they struck their target was far worse than merely devastating.

"Have Blocker One-One move down the valley to here," Jaëger said, and dropped an icon into the display. "Blocker One-Five and Back-Up Zero-Four can cover them from overwatch here and here." Two more icons appeared atop hills flanking the valley. "Inform Lieutenant Harpe that his mission is to *delay* the Bugs. He's buying time for the refugees to get clear, not trying to wipe the bastards out, so tell him I'm going to rip him a new asshole if he forgets it."

"Yes, Sir." Her com officer bent over his own panel, inputting the orders and instructing his systems to compress them for burst transmission and consult the Asp's orbital catalogs for suitable bodies to bounce the signals off. Jaëger left the ex-Peaceforcer to the task and looked over her shoulder at Master Sergeant Helen McNeil. The sturdy, auburn-haired Raider had been bumped to acting sergeant-major of Jaëger's makeshift battalion, and the look in her eyes matched the one in her CO's. Harpe was a hotshot who was almost as good as he thought he was, and he'd already pulled off two successful ambushes. Jaëger and McNeil both knew he was just aching to make it three and that they couldn't afford the losses they'd take if he screwed it up. That was why Jaëger hated to use him at all, but his were also the only troops close enough to turn the trick, and Jaëger had lost too many civilians already. She would *not* lose a single additional life she could save—even if it meant putting Harpe into the line.

Brigadier Raphael Mondesi watched his own display as Major Jaëger's overstretched battalion fought desperately to hold the Bugs, and his face was ebon iron. His HQ's camouflage would have made even a Marine instructor smile in approval, and all his communications went by secure, undetectable land line to one of eight remote transmission sites . . . which only made him feel even more guilty. It was an irrational guilt—the Justin Defense Force's CO *had* to have a secure command center—but that didn't make it any easier to live with. Whatever his collar insignia said, he still felt like a colonel, and a colonel's place was with his regiment.

"What's close enough to support Jaëger?" he asked harshly.

"Nothing." His executive officer's voice was just as harsh, and Mondesi looked up quickly. He opened his mouth to dispute the single, flat negative, then closed it with a snap. General Simon Merman was a cop, not a Marine, but he'd learned a lot in the last two terrible weeks, and half Jaëger's troops were his Peaceforcers. If anything had been in position to support the major, he would have moved heaven and earth to get it there.

"Damn." The Marine sighed, and his ramrod-straight spine sagged just a bit.

"At least they're still scatter-gunning us," Merman said.

Mondesi nodded. He'd hoped his SigInt sections might manage to at least track the Bugs' tactical traffic, but as the Navy had discovered against their starships, Bugs didn't seem to *say* anything to one another. The signal intelligence types had picked up lots of transmissions—the Bugs seemed to rely primarily upon easily intercepted omnidirectional radio—but none of those transmissions carried anything his people could even identify as communications. They had to be carrying *something*, but the most painstaking analysis couldn't *find* anything!

It was maddening—and dangerous. If they'd even been able to tell which transmissions were addressed to military units, Mondesi's people would have been in a far better position to estimate what the Bugs were up to; as it was, he could only guess in the dark. The Bugs had landed troops in and around all the larger cities and slaughtered every human they found (or, worse, collected them for later consumption), and they had sizable forces in the field, yet there seemed no discernable pattern to their operations there. More than half Mondesi's hastily camouflaged refugee camps weren't even threatened; others had been hit in overwhelming force and wiped out to the last man, woman, and child, but it was almost as if they attacked only those targets they happened to stumble across, and his total inability to predict their intentions made it all but impossible to adjust his own deployments to meet them. But at least Merman was right, and the brigadier tried to feel grateful. The Bugs' attacks might be virtually random so far as he could tell, but they *had* left the majority of his camps unhit. Unfortunately . . .

"They may be 'scatter-gunning' us, Simon," he said, "but look at this." He punched a command into the holo unit, and patches of scarlet flashed. Each formed a rough wedge, reaching out from the invaders' main concentrations in no apparent pattern—certainly none were angled to meet one another—but three aimed almost arrow-straight at a trio of small, green shuttle icons.

"See?" the Marine asked quietly.

Merman stared at the holo for a long, silent moment, then inhaled sharply.

"Shit," he said, and Mondesi nodded again.

"Exactly. In about—" he glanced at the estimate his ops officer had put together that morning "—twelve more days, they're going to reach three of our alpha sites."

"Can we adjust?" Merman asked tightly.

"Some. But we placed the original camps in relation to the planned evac sites. If we start moving large bodies of refugees around, the Bugs are almost certain to spot at least some of them. If they do, they'll attack in force . . . but if we *don't* move them, they won't be able to reach any of the other evac sites in time to be picked up without one hell of a lot more notice than the Fleet's going to be able to give us."

"Which means?" Merman was a policeman, but his tone said he already knew what Mondesi was going to tell him. Unfortunately, he was right.

"Which means," the Marine said heavily, "that if the Navy doesn't launch Redemption within the next ten days, we'll have only two choices. Move the refugees anyway and hope at least some survive to reach a backup site, or leave them where they are. And if we do that, at least twelve thousand people we *might* have been able to get out won't have any place to get out *to*."

Andrew Prescott sat in his command chair once more. The last three days had been more nerve-wracking than usual, for there were even more Bug scouts swarming about the warp point than he'd feared, and their courses carried them further out from it than he'd anticipated. At one point, he'd actually had to shut down everything—including *Daikyu's* drive field—and imitate a drifting hunk of rock, and his forehead had been a solid sheet of sweat as the prowling light cruiser passed within less than eight thousand kilometers of his ship. If it had seen her and popped off a broadside while her drive was down, a single hit would have vaporized his command.

As it happened, it *hadn't* spotted *Daikyu*, but the delay had put them twelve hours behind schedule to collect the RD. Given the fact that they knew its exact course, that *shouldn't* pose any problem, but the damned thing would be so hard to spot on passive, even for the people who'd launched it, that he couldn't help sweating every minute until it was safely back aboard, and—

"Contact." He sat up straight as Lieutenant Commander Cesiaño's quiet announcement broke the stillness. "Zero-zero-two by zero-zero-five. It's definitely the drone, Skipper."

"*Very* good, Jill," Prescott said, equally quietly, then looked at his exec. "Nudge us a little closer, Fred. I want the weakest tractor we can generate to pull it in."

"Aye, aye, Sir." Kasuga nodded to Belliard, and *Daikyu* moved to match vectors with her offspring. It took another fifteen minutes of slow, careful maneuvering, and then Cesiaño stabbed the drone with a tractor.

"Got it, Skip!" she announced, and a quiet rustle of approval ran around the bridge.

"Well executed, everyone," Prescott said sincerely as Belliard altered course without orders and took the ship away from the rendezvous point on the prearranged vector. The captain watched his plot a moment longer, then rose, crossed to Cesiaño's station, and frowned as data began to scroll across the bottom of her display. Most of her screen was occupied by a map of the warp point's immediate environs, which showed the dense clouds of mines he'd expected. But something else had been added, and he leaned over her shoulder to tap the sphere of small red dots which represented individual starships just outside the minefields.

"Are those what I think they are?" he asked, and Cesiaño nodded.

"Definitely those CAs we saw earlier, Skipper."

"Um." Prescott rubbed his chin. They'd spotted a bevy of commercial-drive, heavy-cruiser-sized vessels moving across the system at a suspiciously low speed, even for Bugs, two weeks earlier, and he'd decided to risk coming in close for a better look. They already knew the Bugs used military drives, not civilian ones, in the light cruisers of their "Assault Fleet," probably because the less massive military units let them devote more mass to weapons in units which were, after all, designed to be expended in action.

The fact that the mystery CAs used commercial engines had thus suggested they, at least, weren't intended for the assault role. While low top speeds wouldn't be much of a problem for a simultaneous transit—they wouldn't have far to go—such slow units could hope neither to catch an enemy nor to run away from one under normal combat conditions. That suggested they were another specialized unit, and their present deployment certainly appeared to confirm his original guess as to what their purpose was.

Makes sense, too, he thought grudgingly as he watched still more data appear. *We haven't used SBMHAWKs yet, so they may not know we can send missiles through a warp point, but they have to know we could use our own Assault Fleet. These suckers may be tactically slow, but fitting them with commercial engines gives them a decent strategic speed, and that lets them build 'em back home, then send them forward under their own power and save the time we spend putting OWPs together in forward systems. They're smaller than most forts, but enough should still do the trick, and if* all *they have are weapons and defenses . . .*

He shook free of his thoughts and looked back up at Cesiaño.

"Any sign of heavy units in close to the point?"

"No, Sir," the tac officer replied, and her tone mirrored the cold satisfaction of her eyes as she looked up at her CO. "In fact—"

She tapped a function key, and Prescott smiled a shark's smile as he watched her display. The drone had caught a cluster of over thirty superdreadnoughts falling back from the warp point once the cruiser sphere was in place,

"Looks like these fellows—" Cesiaño tapped her display "—are pulling back to join the rest of their battle-line."

"So it does," Prescott murmured. He patted her shoulder and walked slowly back to his chair while his mind raced. It appeared the Bugs had at least one thing in common with humans: *they* couldn't remain at general quarters indefinitely, either, and they'd been rotating their battle-line units on the warp point ever since taking the system. As one group of units reached the end of its GQ endurance, it fell back to over two light-minutes, well outside the weapons envelope of any attacker, and another replaced it. It was a reasonable move to protect their capital ships from surprise attack, but if they'd turned responsibility for the close-in defenses over to the CAs . . .

He settled into the chair, tipped it back, and rested his heels on his repeater plot as he thought. Before detaching his ship, Murakuma had brought him up to speed on her anticipated reinforcement schedule. Assuming it had been met, she wouldn't have received much in the way of additional ships yet, but she *should* have received at least the first wave of SBMHAWKs. If she had, and if the second-generation AMBAMs had also arrived, the Bugs' shift in deployments might just offer her a chance to mount Redemption after all.

Unfortunately, she didn't know that, and if he used a courier drone to tell her, the Bugs would know he had. Would they revert to their original dispositions and back up the CAs with capital ships once more? *He* certainly would, but the Navy had already learned that human-style logic could be no more than a way to screw up with confidence where Bugs were concerned.

He pursed his lips as he considered another point. If Murakuma's munitions *hadn't* arrived, she'd be unable to do anything with his data even if it got through to her, in which case he'd have risked warning the Bugs to change their strategy (and, incidentally, risked *Daikyu's* own detection and destruction, as well) for nothing.

It was tempting to wait, but Brigadier Mondesi was still getting transmissions out from Justin A III. The brigadier didn't know where they went after they hit the stealthed comsats, and since setting out to deploy the RD, Prescott had been unable to tap his own end of the satellite chain which brought the transmissions back from the support freighters in Justin-B, but the Marine CO's reports made grim reading. If Redemption wasn't launched within the next week to ten days, there wouldn't be much of anyone left to rescue.

Captain Andrew Prescott scowled as he faced the decision he had to make, then sighed, sat up straight, and looked at his com officer.

" . . . so that's the situation, ladies and gentlemen," Leroy Mackenna said.

Marcus LeBlanc sat quietly, showing no sign of his own worry, as Mackenna and Ling Tian finished their presentation to the task group and battlegroup COs. Murakuma nodded to them, and they put the holo of the Justin A System on hold and resumed their seats. She gazed at the display, then looked around at her assembled flag officers.

"Captain Prescott's done an outstanding job," she said. "Now it's up to us to do ours."

A sort of ripple ran through the admirals and commodores. Jackson Teller, John Ludendorff, and Demosthenes Waldeck, as her senior officers, looked at one another, and then Waldeck cleared his throat.

"Should we assume from your statement that you intend to launch Operation Redemption on the basis of this information, Sir?" he asked carefully.

"I do," she said flatly.

Waldeck might have winced, but he said nothing. Neither did Ludendorff, but Teller leaned forward to make eye contact with Task Force 59's CO.

"I appreciate your desire to get as many people out as possible, Sir," he said quietly, "but I must point out that we haven't received a single additional starship, while Captain Prescott's report clearly indicates the Bugs have been heavily reinforced."

"I realize that." Murakuma laid her fine-boned hands on the table and squared her frail-looking shoulders. "We have, however, repaired our damages and received the munitions we were promised, and your strikegroups have been brought back up to strength."

More than one officer quailed before her soprano voice's icy tonelessness, yet Jackson Teller was made of sterner stuff. He was junior to both Waldeck and Ludendorff, whatever the table of organization might say, but it was his fighter crews who'd suffered the heaviest proportionate casualties in the last two engagements.

"I realize we can blow our way into the system," he said in that same, quiet voice. "I also realize their decision to pull their battle-line back should give us the chance to use our speed and range advantages to full effect in deep space. But if they close the point behind us, we'll still have to come to them to fight our way back out. And while my strikegroups are *officially* back up to strength, less than ten percent of my squadrons can really be considered combat ready. Most are still shaking down replacements. If I commit them to close action, they'll take catastrophic losses."

He'd been careful not to say "again," but something inside Vanessa Murakuma winced anyway, and then Waldeck spoke up.

"Admiral Teller's made a valid point, Sir, and there's another one. We'll have twelve more superdreadnoughts and six additional fleet carriers within five days. With those reinforcements, we'd be in a much stronger position to—"

"I realize that." Waldeck's eyebrows rose, for it wasn't like Murakuma to break in on one of her subordinates and her voice was flint. "I *also* realize, however, that we don't have the luxury of waiting. As Captain Prescott pointed out, the mere fact the Bugs know he's reported to us may cause them to alter their dispositions, in which case even the reinforcements you've mentioned would find it extremely costly to break into the system. Either we attack now—immediately—or we give up what may be the only chance we'll ever have to mount Redemption, and the people dying in Justin even as we sit here are *civilians* we—*I*—had no option but to leave behind."

She glared around the table—as if, LeBlanc thought uneasily, the briefing room were filled with Bugs, not her own officers. There was a dangerous, brittle quality to her, one he'd never seen before, and he felt a sudden chill. He understood her argument, yet there was something more behind it. A personal something that pursued her like the Furies' whips, and he wondered suddenly if she'd somehow slipped over the edge without his noticing. He started to open his mouth, then changed his mind. Anything he said was unlikely to change her decision; that much was painfully obvious, whatever was going on in her head. And if she *was* starting to lose it (and God knew she had a right to!), he couldn't afford to antagonize her into seeing *him* as an enemy.

"The question of whether or not we attack is not debatable," she said in that same frozen scalpel of a soprano. "We *can't* wait, whatever the arguments in favor of doing so. The task force will attack within the next twelve hours, so I suggest we all turn our attention to our ops plan."

She hadn't raised her voice, but Waldeck and Teller closed their mouths and sat back without another word. She ran those flinty eyes around the conference table one more time, then sat back in her own chair with the harsh ghost of a smile.

"Good," she said softly. "In that case, Admiral Waldeck, we'll start with the battle-line."

CHAPTER ELEVEN

Recall

"Of course we *all* agree that the visuals—assuming they can be relied upon—are *horrifying*. But at the same time, there must be some *rational* basis for their actions, some *misunderstanding* that could *surely* have been avoided if it hadn't been for the Military Establishment's vested interest in having an enemy to justify its own existence. . . ."

Hannah Avram smiled grimly as she listened to Bettina Wister's strident bleating from across the presidential reception room and watched the embarrassed maneuvers of people trying to get away from her. The evidence of what the Bugs—the term was rapidly achieving universal use—did to occupied planets' inhabitants had discredited Wister's viewpoint in all but the most hopelessly blinkered of eyes. But she was still a member of the Naval Oversight Committee, and it had been impossible to avoid inviting her to this reception for the newly arrived Orion representatives to the Grand Allied Joint Chiefs of Staff.

The formal speechifying had ended earlier, and at least that had been done on a higher level than Wister's—or even Prime Minister Quilvio's. President DaCunha had spoken for the Federation, for his office still remained its visible embodiment. Despite all the unnatural acts that had been performed on the Constitution, it was only proper that mankind's highest elected official speak for humanity on such an occasion as the reactivation of the Grand Alliance that had crushed the Rigelians. The other parties had responded with every evidence of good grace. Privately, they might take a "better thee than me" attitude towards humanity's current troubles, but they'd learned from experience that such troubles were best squelched as early as possible.

Avram's grin widened as she watched Agamemnon Waldeck succeed in disengaging himself from Wister's diminishing audience. He might be a son-of-a-bitch, but he and his Corporate World fellows could be counted on to support the military, which kept the Federation's commerce safe from the Tangri, renegade Orions and other predatory types. It was a persistent fissure in their alliance with the Heart Worlds—which had been too rich and too safe for too long—and their one patch of common ground with the despised Fringers.

She sipped her white wine—something stronger might have helped her get through this reception, but with advancing age she found alcohol did less and less for her—and felt depression close in as it always did when she contemplated the political dislocations of the Federation that held her loyalty. The human race had expanded outward in three waves, punctuated by wars. First the Heart Worlds had received Federation-subsidized colonies, ethnically balanced to the nicety mandated by twenty-first-century notions. Then, in light of the expense of the wars with the Orions, expansion had shifted to the private sector under the auspices of megacorporations which farsightedly seized the "choke point" systems with multiple warp nexi, the gateways to the universe beyond. Then, after the Third Interstellar War had made Federation and Khanate allies and removed the Rigelian threat, the impetus for colonization had been provided by ethnic, national, cultural and other groups seeking to preserve identities they saw vanishing tracelessly into cosmopolitan sameness. The result was a vast number of newly settled worlds with small—albeit fast-growing—populations.

The Corporate World magnates were incapable of seeing the Federation as anything more than one of their own tame planetary governments writ large—an engine for maximizing profit. Avram despised the game they played, but she couldn't deny the skill with which they played it. They'd amended the Constitution into a parliamentary cabinet system, reducing the President—still elected by direct Federation-wide popular vote, ever more difficult even with modern communications and data processing—to a figurehead. Besides, for all their power, the Corporate Worlds alone could deliver too little of the popular vote to control the election of the presidency. On the other hand, the Prime Minister who held the real power had to command the support of a majority of the Legislative Assembly, which the Corporate Worlds effectively controlled by virtue of their own single-mindedness and dense individual populations, the Heart Worlds' disunity and philosophical confusion, and the Reapportionment of 2340. The reapportionment plan had been bitterly resisted by the Fringe Worlds for a very simple reason: Corporate World populations

averaged close to 1.75 billion, while the average Fringe World was
fortunate to have a total population of thirty to forty million. The
Constitution guaranteed every Federated World at least one representative in the Legislative Assembly, but the Reapportionment had pushed
the qualifying population base for each additional representative up
to ten million. A particularly populous Fringe World thus might boast
five or six representatives, while a planet like Galloway's World was
entitled to over two *hundred*. Given the centralized cooperation of
the Corporate Worlds' Liberal-Progressive Party, that kind of concentrated Legislative bloc gave politicos like Agamemnon Waldeck enormous power . . . and they knew it.

They see themselves as the lords of creation, Avram thought, looking across the room at Waldeck, conversing with a knot of his cro-
nies. *The hell of it is, they're right*. Morosely, she raised her left
arm—the prosthetic one, legacy of the Theban War (at times she found
herself forgetting which was which)—and took another sip of Cha-
blis.

She became aware of motion beside her and turned with a smile
of greeting. The senior Orion representative to the Grand Allied Joint
Chiefs of Staff evidently didn't share her aversion to booze. Nor did
most members of his species, which alcohol affected in much the same
way it did homo sapiens. Indeed, the Khanate had become a major
importer of bourbon. In that respect, Kthaara'zarthan was atypical;
his glass held straight vodka, and Avram had observed him sprinkle
a pinch of pepper into it, something she'd never seen on Old Terra
west of Minsk or east of Vladivostok.

"Lord Talphon," she greeted him formally. "I hope you're enjoying yourself." Uncontrollably, a chuckle bubbled up. Kthaara raised
one tufted ear, signifying inquiry. "Oh, I was just recalling the response
a great playwright of ours, George Bernard Shaw, made to precisely
that question, under similar circumstances: 'That, madam, is the *only*
thing I am enjoying.'"

Kthaara emitted the deep purring cough of Orion laughter. Aside
from rare individuals with *extremely* flexible vocal apparatus, the two
species couldn't produce the sounds of each others' languages, but they
could learn to understand them. That understanding represented a
triumph over the gulf that yawned between completely alien evolutions. As always, Avram had to remind herself that the human char-
acterization of Orions as "felinoid" was worse than simplistic. The
resemblance was purely coincidental; a Terran lizard, or oak tree, was
more closely related to Terran cats than was the urbane being who
stood before her, unconsciously smoothing out his spectacular whiskers.
His pelt was the midnight-black of the oldest Orion noble families,
now acquiring a silvery frosting that indicated advancing age to those

who knew what to look for. *Well,* she reflected, *none of us are getting any younger.* She'd met Kthaara late in the Theban War, when he'd been serving under Ivan Antonov in his quest for vengeance against his cousin's murderers. The Orions lacked humanity's antigerone treatments, and despite their century-and-a-half natural life spans . . .

"Ah, yes," Kthaara broke in on her thoughts. "I remember Zhaaaw. A classic example of the way literary brilliance can coexist with political imbecility." He gave a teeth-hidden carnivore's grin. "And speaking of the latter, how do you manage to put up with her sort?" He indicated Wister. "Or perhaps the question I am really asking is *why* you put up with them."

"Well, Lord Talphon, some humans tend to believe that the further removed a political philosophy is from reality, the more morally pure it must be."

"Why?" Kthaara's perplexity was manifest. "I know you better, Sky Marshal"—the title he really used was "First Fang"—"than to think you yourself believe anything of the kind."

"You're quite right. But I'm trying to explain the biases of the civilization which initially gave form to the Federation. That civilization's dominant religion—which I myself don't subscribe to, by the way—was heavily influenced in its formative years by a philosophy called Gnosticism, which held that the world as reported by the senses was inherently corrupt and deceptive. Given that assumption, the only reliable source of knowledge was correct doctrine, and the attitude lingers on in secularized form. Demonstrated unworkability in the real world merely proves a belief system's 'higher truth' in the eyes of its true believers."

Kthaara's ears twitched in the slow movement that conveyed incredulity as he listened to her explanation. "I shall never understand your species, First Fang." He sighed.

"Just as well, Lord Talphon." Avram grinned. "We'll never understand ourselves either!"

They sipped their respective drinks for a few moments in a silence which wasn't destined to last, for the Ophiuchi and Gorm representatives to the Joint Chiefs approached.

"Ah, Ssssky Marssshallll," Admiral Thaarzhaan said, "I sssee the ssseniorrr memmmbers of our ressspective partnersssshipsss are deep in dissscussion. Sssurely a good ommmen forrr the smmmooth ffffunctioning of the Grrrannnd Alliannnce, is it nottt?"

Fleet Speaker Noraku, the Gorm representative, was the tallest person in the room (when he stood fully upright), but Thaarzhaan came in second by a safe margin. Terra's traditional Ophiuchi allies were no more "birds" than her old enemies and recent allies the Orions were "cats." The number of forms a viable tool-making animal could take, while numerous, were finite, however, and coincidences were bound to occur in a galaxy of four hundred billion suns . . . especially in the vanishingly rare cases where a species specialized in two different things—in the case of the Ophiuchi, flying and tool using.

Still, Avram sometimes caught herself being surprised that Thaarzhaan didn't exhibit a certain . . . well, *apprehension* in Kthaara's presence. She shouldn't have, of course. Orions might be felinoid carnivores and Ophiuchi might be among the galaxy's more pacific races—now—but Thaarzhaan and his people were hardly oversized canaries. They had evolved from raptors which, like the Orions themselves (or, for that matter, humans), had stood at the top of their planet's food chain, and the tall, down-covered, hollow-boned Ophiuchi retained the massive, crested heads and wickedly hooked beaks of their ancestors. *And,* she reflected, *the fact that they're the only known race that make even better fighter pilots than the Tabbies doesn't hurt.*

That predilection for fighter ops was also one of many reasons the Ophiuchi Association Defense Command was so prized by its Terran allies. The Association had been a Terran treaty partner ever since ISW-2, when they'd allied against the Khanate, and over the centuries the Ophiuchi had proven utterly reliable. Less militant even than humans, far less Orions, they were determined, gallant and pragmatic when military action became unavoidable. Perhaps *especially* pragmatic. The Association had exhausted its open warp points. Faced with an inescapable physical limit on interstellar expansion and physically uncomfortable with population densities humans or Tabbies found acceptable, the Ophiuchi had stabilized their planetary populations at relatively sparse levels which limited the size of the navy they could build or maintain, but their technology was among the galaxy's best and their units routinely exercised as integral parts of TFN formations. Any Terran admiral regarded their carrier strike-groups as pearls beyond price, yet the almost emaciated-looking Ophiuchi projected an undeniable appearance of frailty.

The Gorm, on the other hand, could hold their own physically with just about anyone, Avram thought as she watched Fleet Speaker Noraku advance with the almost prancing gait allowed by Terra's low gravity. His facial features were unsettlingly humanlike (aside from the triple eyelids and extremely broad nose), but there was no chance of confusing the Gorm with any Terran evolutionary branch. Descendants of hexapods, the grayish, armor-hided beings generally moved on their rearmost pair of limbs alone, as Noraku was doing now; but the middle limbs with their dual-purpose "handfeet" could be used as a second pair of legs if greater speed was desired. Or if the ceiling were lower.

Heavy-grav life forms tended to be either very small or very large, and the Gorm inclined toward the latter. Noraku stood just under three meters in height when fully erect, and he was not a particularly tall member of his race.

That size was one reason the Gorm, unlike the Ophiuchi, made extremely *poor* fighter pilots. Squeezing that much body mass into a strikefighter was hard enough, and their hexapedal body form only made it worse. Gorm "chairs" were more like saddle-like couches, supporting their length to just above their mid-body shoulders, which left them poorly adapted to the *g* forces a fighter's "shallow" inertial sump couldn't fully damp. There *were* some Gorm fighter jocks, but by and large, they preferred to leave such duties to their Orion fellow-citizens.

She was relieved to note that the Fleet Speaker seemed to be breathing normally. Native to a 2.68 *g* planet whose partial pressures of the standard atmospheric gasses would have killed an unprotected human, and wishing to avoid the nuisance of the full helmets his race normally used to equalize pressures, Noraku had volunteered to help field test an experimental implanted respirator during his extended stay on Nova Terra, where the Joint Chiefs were expected to establish themselves.

Avram was never quite sure how to characterize the Gorm's relationship to the Orions. The Gorm were a subject race . . . sort of. But though they were subjects of the Khan, the Empire of Gormus was an autonomous, self-governing entity within the Khanate, whose dominance by the Orion race and culture was undeniable and undenied. There were several reasons for that. One was the way their outnumbered navy had come within a hair of kicking the Tabbies' butts in the Gorm-Khanate War of 2227-2229, which had earned them tremendous respect from the Orions. Another was their heavy-grav origins, for the Gorm had spread throughout the Khanate's vast sphere to colonize planets whose atmospheres would have been lethal to the Tabbies, and people who could turn worlds like that into revenue-generating propositions were far too valuable *not* to be granted special status.

They were also as unlike the Tabbies philosophically as they were physically, yet they got along remarkably well with the prickly Whisker-Twisters. They might make poor fighter pilots, but they were just as pragmatic as the Ophiuchi and even more stubborn than Terrans. They were almost too logical to make good analysts (as far as Avram knew, no Gorm in recorded history had *ever* played a hunch), and their lack of any formal system of permanent naval or military ranks sometimes confused their imperial partners . . . or, for that matter, anyone else. Noraku's own title of "Fleet Speaker" was as close as any Gorm would ever come to "Chief of Staff," yet it was only a temporary, acting rank. For purposes of getting along with other navies they assigned their personnel equivalent seniorities, but the fact of the matter was that not even the Tabbies truly understood how the consensual Gorm picked their military officers. No doubt *minisorchi*, the mysterious Gormish telepathic ability, played a part, but whatever the process, a Gorm who commanded a superdreadnought this week might have moved over to head the tactical section of a battle-cruiser next week. Such instability would have made a shambles of any human chain of command, yet it worked for the Gorm. Precisely *how* it worked was something Avram had never understood, but no one could doubt its efficacy. The Gorm Space Navy's tacticians were among the best in the business, and the high tactical speed of their starships made them especially valuable to the KON by providing it with the fastest battle-line in the galaxy.

Nevertheless, Avram often wondered how they had managed—or been allowed—to retain their distinctive character, free from any foredoomed attempt to culturally assimilate them. And she was intellectually honest enough to doubt that humans could have managed matters so sensibly in either race's position.

She shook free of her bleak thoughts and addressed herself to Thaarzhaan's question. "Of course, Admiral, even as it is encouraging that associates of the Federation and the Khanate such as yourself and Fleet Speaker Noraku work together in such obvious harmony." All three aliens gave their races' equivalent of sonorous nods. Avram hated being put in the position of arbiter—it was inevitable, inasmuch as the Federation was the galaxy's acknowledged first power, but she was still uncomfortable with it. At least she wouldn't have to deal with it much longer. "Of course, my own connection with the Grand Allied Joint Chiefs of Staff will be indirect."

"Ah, yes," came Noraku's basso profundissimo. Unlike Thaarzhaan, whose beak gave his consonants an odd, drawn out sibilance, the fleet speaker's vocal apparatus could manage Standard English almost as well as a human's. Which, Avram reflected, was a vast relief, since it would obviate the need for yet another echelon of interpreters at their working meetings.

"We're still awaiting the arrival of our Human member," Noraku continued, and glanced at Kthaara. Everyone knew Lord Talphon's appointment to represent him on the new allied military command had been widely seen as an earnest of the Khan's commitment to fulfilling his treaty obligations. And it was an appointment that all but mandated who the Terran representative must be. . . .

Assuming, Avram reflected, *that he accepts the job.*

Aloud, she was all smooth assurance. "Even as we speak, Fleet Speaker, a liaison officer has been sent to brief him and arrange his journey to Nova Terra."

✧   ✧   ✧

Skimmers were no longer strictly military and emergency vehicles, for steady improvements in the low-powered version of the reactionless space drive had brought them within reach of the private sector. But on a relatively young and not-too-affluent Fringe World like Novaya Rodina, it was only official business that brought one of the vehicles swooping soundlessly across the sky.

Captain Midori Kozlov gazed through the transparency at that sky, whose tinge of orange she doubted she could ever have become used to. She knew all about the harmless airborne microorganisms that caused it, but it still seemed wrong. Her eyes strayed downwards to the plains, where endless fields evidenced a degree of agricultural inefficiency that she, child of the resolutely rationalized culture of Epsilon Eridani, found even harder to get used to than the sky's color. But that was fine with the colonists. Their grandparents had come here to preserve a bit of Russia, or of what Russia had once been, or might have been, or *should* have been, and no vision of Russia, however idealized, could ever include much in the way of efficiency.

All of which ruminations, Kozlov realized, merely served the purpose of distracting her from thinking about her mission here. Her belly annoyed her by tightening, and she felt an odd envy of her prespace ancestors. *They* hadn't had to worry about meeting their legends in the flesh, for in those days people generally hadn't lived long enough to *become* legends before they were decently dead.

The skimmer went feet-wet over the Ozero Kerensky—Novaya Rodina was a world-continent with landlocked seas, not a world-ocean with island-continents like most Earth-like planets. The waters sped beneath the skimmer for what seemed a short time as Kozlov tried to organize her thoughts. Then a coastline backed by low, villa-dotted hills appeared ahead and swiftly grew. The skimmer homed unerringly on a particular *dacha* and settled onto a landing area outside a gate in a low outer wall.

Kozlov thanked the pilot and emerged into the summer warmth, smoothing nonexistent imperfections out of her black-and-silver uniform. She looked around at the landscape, which she'd heard was about as similar as you could get on this planet to a peninsula of Old Terra called the Crimea. The smell of roses suffused the air; the man she'd come to visit had occupied his retirement with developing a subspecies that would grow in these latitudes of Novaya Rodina. She stood before the gate and let its security sensors scan a face that reflected more ethnic strains than just the Japanese and Russian that her name suggested.

"Identify yourself, please," the gate finally requested.

She cleared her throat and spoke with the clarity and distinctness that were advisable when addressing robots. "Captain Midori Kozlov to see the Sky Marshal." Though the *dacha* owner's permanent rank was that of Admiral of the Fleet, he was entitled to be addressed for life by the title he'd held at the time of his retirement. "I believe I'm expected."

A moment passed in silence, just long enough for the entirely human bass rumble to be startling. "For God's sake, don't call me by that damned title! Come on in. My secretary will meet you."

The gate swung silently open. In the absence of further instructions, Kozlov followed a graveled walkway around the left side of the *dacha*. A man stood waiting—*not* the man she'd come to see. This man looked late-middle-aged (she'd have to see him move before deciding whether his apparent age was natural or the result of antigerone treatments) and contrived to wear his entirely civilian clothes like a uniform. Kozlov recalled what she'd been told of a very senior enlisted man who'd followed his admiral into retirement, and the sense of walking into a historical novel—which had been growing on her for some time—intensified.

"Good afternoon, Captain," the secretary said in faintly accented Standard English. "Please follow me."

They were rounding the rambling *dacha* when a man came stumping around a corner—a white-bearded man whose massive solidity made him seem shorter than he was. He wore an anachronistic-looking smock and carried gardening tools in his big, grimy hands . . . and Kozlov felt her body, acting for her without orders, come to the position of attention.

Ivan Nikolayevich Antonov glared at her from under shaggy white eyebrows. That glare gave her an instant to take in more of his appearance. He was certainly in good shape for a man of one hundred and forty-five standard Terran years. But, she recalled, he'd committed himself by contract at a relatively early age to emigrate after retirement, and thus obtained access to the antigerone treatments long before he would have gotten them anyway by special act of the Legislative Assembly as victor of the Theban War. The Federation had a long-standing policy of encouraging colonization by providing colonists with the anti-aging technology that was available on the inner worlds only to those who somehow obligated society to them. And in a sudden flash of insight she wondered if the willingness of Heart Worlds like her own native Odin to be passive accomplices in the Corporate Worlds' political sodomizing of the Fringe Worlds might have less to do with all the well-known rationalizations than with simple, elemental, unadmitted envy.

Antonov's bass broke in on her uncomfortable thoughts. "Thank you, Kostya," he addressed the secretary in what Kozlov suspected was his very best attempt at a mild tone. "Please excuse us."

"*Da*, Nikolayevich," the man responded. Memories of grandfather Kozlov, combined with her orientation briefings, enabled her to recognize the "affection" and "respectful affection" modes of address in that exchange. The latter was old-fashioned, very uncommon, and *not* an automatic prerogative of superior military rank. But then Kostya was gone and the living legend turned his glare on her again.

"Well, I agreed to see you, so I suppose I have to be civil, even to a headquarters *zalyotnik*." She knew that the idiom—literally, "butterfly"—wasn't exactly a flattering one. "So come inside and have a drink, Captain Kozlova."

She recalled the conversation she'd had with Hannah Avram just before departure, and the Sky Marshal's advice on how she must respond at this point. So she took a deep breath and commanded her voice to steadiness and her eyes to a level gaze. "Excuse me, Sir, but that's 'Captain *Kozlov*.' My Russian ancestors—I'm only one-eighth Russian, by the way—emigrated to Epsilon Eridani in the early twenty-second century. It's been generations since the family used the Russian language or Russian naming conventions, including feminine forms of surnames."

For a moment, Antonov's brows drew together and almost met, and Kozlov was reminded of fissionable material reaching critical mass. But she wouldn't let herself flinch. Then, all of a sudden, the bearlike former Sky Marshal expelled a bark of laughter, rather like a volcano venting its force harmlessly. The chuckles that followed were like seismic aftershocks.

"Well, that's the first time since the Theban War, when Angelique Timoshenko . . ." Antonov shook his head and chuckled again. "I see you don't frighten easily, Captain. That's good. Maybe you're not a complete butterfly after all. Let's get that drink."

It was early in the day for her, but she quoted platitudes about Rome and the Romans to herself. "Very well, Sky Marshal."

"I thought I told you not to call me that!" Antonov's scowl was back as he led the way into the glass-walled loggia that faced the sea. "I'm Ivan Nikolayevich." He stomped over to the bar. "Vodka?"

She detested the stuff, but—"Certainly, Sk . . . Ivan Nikolayevich."

"Better," Antonov rumbled as he brought the drinks and waved her towards a leather-bound armchair. He then settled into the chair's mate and raised his glass. "*Za vashe zdorovye*." He tossed back his vodka with a rapidity that made Kozlov's stomach lurch at the mere sight of it.

"So," he said after a moment, "you come from Hannah Avram. How is she?"

"She's well, Sir. Although, of course, the situation now—"

"Yes, yes; I've been following it." He reached for the vodka bottle and refilled his glass. He scowled at Kozlov's glass, at which she'd been sipping. "*Ty chto mumu yebyosh?*" he growled. Then he suddenly seemed to remember himself, and the broad muscular face wore an incongruous expression of embarrassment. "Er, it means 'Drink up,'" he explained. Then he intensified his scowl as though to make up for his lapse. "Well, this new war is Hannah's problem. She was fool enough to accept that damned 'Sky Marshal' title they dreamed up for me after the Theban War. By now she must have found out what it really means: having to deal day in and day out with those *tarakani* in the Legislative Assembly. Well, she can have it! I'm retired. You couldn't pay me enough to dive back into that cesspit! 'Reactivating my commission,' eh? Well, you can tell them I said to take my reactivated commission, complete with the stiffest shoulder boards they can find, and shove it up their—"

"Oh, I think you misunderstand about your reactivation, Sir." Antonov stopped and gave her the look of a man unused to being interrupted. She hurried on. "You're not being recalled as Sky Marshal. As you yourself pointed out, that's a special rank, invented for the military commander-in-chief of the Fleet. You'll be back on the active list under your permanent rank of Admiral of the Fleet, as the Terran member of the Grand Allied Joint Chiefs of Staff."

For a heartbeat of utter silence, Antonov seemed to expand slightly, as though building up to an explosion. "You mean," he said in a tone whose quietness wasn't even meant to be deceptive, "I'd be *subordinate* to Hannah Avram?"

"Well, Sir, that might be an oversimplification of the relationship. After all, you'd be functioning outside the normal TFN command structure, on the Joint Chiefs of which you . . ." Kozlov paused. She'd been about to say, "Of which you will undoubtedly be chairman," but she had a pretty good idea of how this man would react to anything that even smelled like flattery. So she fell back and regrouped. "On which you will be serving with Kthaara'zarthan, among others."

The air seemed to go out of Antonov. "What? You're telling me that Kthaara Kornazhovich is the Khan's representative on this Grand Allied boondoggle?"

"Yes, Ivan Nikolayevich. Your *vilkshatha* brother is on Old Terra even now." She smiled inwardly, for Hannah Avram had told her of the bastard Orion-Russian patronymic Antonov had bestowed on the Orion who'd admitted him to the oath of *vilkshatha* that made two warriors members of each others' families—the first non-Orion in history to be so admitted. It annoyed Kthaara almost as much as the even more bastardized diminutive "Kthaasha." Aloud, she continued in a neutral tone. "In fact, I spoke with Lord Talphon before my departure. He sends his best regards. Also, in connection with your reluctance to accept the reactivation of your commission, he asked me to memorize a certain Russian phrase and convey it to you." Her brow creased with puzzlement. "Oddly enough, it was the same one you translated a few minutes ago as 'Drink up.' But according to him, it means 'Why are you fucking a cow?' "

For an anxious moment, she thought Antonov was going to have a stroke. But then she saw that he was really struggling to contain a gargantuan guffaw. He finally released it as a kind of gasping cough. "Well, er . . . you see, that's the literal translation," he explained when he'd gotten his breath. "It can be used in any context to mean 'get a move on' or 'get the lead out.' " He shook his head and chuckled. "Old Kthaasha . . . ! Well, I suppose this wouldn't be the worst foolishness I've ever gone along with." He deployed his scowl again. "All right, maybe I'll do it . . . but on one condition. I want you on my staff."

Kozlov almost spilled her still half-full vodka glass. "Sir?"

"Yes. You've got ba—er, guts. I like that. I'll need an Intelligence officer—I'm not so old I can't read your insignia. And Winnie Trevayne is too damned senior now," he added, naming the Director of Naval Intelligence—who, Kozlov recalled, had been his staff spook in the Theban War. "Well?" he barked.

She tossed off the remainder of her vodka. It felt like an expanding sun going down her gullet. She hardly noticed until she tried to speak. "Ah . . . of course Sir, if . . . well, Sky Marshal Avram would have to approve my going on detached duty from her staff. . . ."

"Oh, Hannah will come around," Antonov rumbled. He reached out and refilled her glass. "And now, unless I'm mistaken, you have a classified briefing for me. All I know is the news any other old *muzhik* can get."

"Yes, Sir," she said, still wheezing a little and gazing with dismay at the refilled glass.

"Good." Antonov topped off his own glass and raised it. "*Nalivay!*"

CHAPTER TWELVE

What Price Redemption?

The heavy cruisers floated about the warp point. The time to resume the advance would come, yet the losses already suffered dictated that any new attack wait until more reinforcements reached this system. For now, the cruisers waited—forty-eight of them, screened by thousands of mines—rotating through their readiness cycles as they guarded against any threat.

Andrew Prescott swore with silent venom as another drive field appeared on his sensors. There were three now—light cruisers all, moving in a search pattern which could only mean they'd gotten a sniff of *Daikyu*. It couldn't have been a clean sensor hit, or they wouldn't still be searching, but they'd managed to pin down her rough location.

He made himself cross his legs and consider his options. *Daikyu* had the firepower to kill all three of those ships, but the Bugs probably *wanted* him to go after them, given how openly they were operating. For all he knew, a dozen cloaked battle-cruisers lurked just below his sensor horizon, waiting for their beaters to drive him into their sights— or for his own fire to reveal his position. One of his ancestors, a submarine commander back on Old Terra, had once been hunted for three days by a Japanese antisubmarine flotilla, and now he knew exactly how that long-dead Prescott must have felt.

But great-great-whatever-granddad got his ass *out of it,* he reminded himself. *All I have to do is be as good as he was.*

"Come to zero-three-zero, one-zero-five," he said quietly.

"Aye, Sir. Coming to zero-three-zero, one-zero-five," Daryl Belliard replied, and Prescott watched his display alter as Commander Kasuga stepped back from the master plot.

"We're too close to the warp point, Sir," Kasuga said too softly for anyone else to hear. Prescott nodded in curt agreement, but he refused to be driven any further from it. He'd used no less than five courier drones to alert Sarasota, and it was as well he had. Only two had gotten past the OWP CAs, and, as he'd known they must, they'd alerted the enemy to *Daikyu's* presence.

The Bugs' most obvious response had been to race for the drones' origin point to mount an intensive search, but he'd programmed the CDs' nav systems for delayed activation before dropping them, and he'd been over a light-minute clear when their drives came on-line. That had given him some margin to play with, yet it was essential he stay close enough to the warp point to spot any move to reinforce it. If that happened, he'd be forced to send fresh drones to Admiral Murakuma. That would almost certainly bring the Bugs straight in on him, yet Task Force 59 *had* to know if the situation changed.

He didn't know if the Bugs realized his intentions. If they did and threw up a shell of scouts well outside the warp point then simply swept inward, they were bound to get lucky eventually. In the meantime, his course turned *Daikyu's* stern—the most vulnerable aspect for any cloaked vessel—away from all known searchers. It wasn't much, but—

"Pods transiting the warp point!" Jill Cesiaño's abrupt, half-shouted announcement smashed through the tension, and Prescott whirled to face her. "Dozens of them, Sir—hundreds!"

The plot flashed as clouds of diamond-bright icons exploded from the warp point, and Prescott throttled a whoop of delight as he recognized the SBMHAWKs.

One moment all was serene; the next, a horde of tiny, robotic spacecraft burst into being. Some vanished in the star-bright boils of interpenetration, but only a small percentage, and the waiting cruisers had no idea what they were. They were too small for warships, yet they must represent some threat, and the ready-duty cruisers began tracking. But there were too many pods; they saturated the defenders' fire control, and less than ten more had been destroyed before the cruisers found out exactly what they were.

The Terran Navy had invented the Strategic Bombardment Missile, Homing All the Way Killer pod for the Theban War, but the latest-generation SBMHAWK was deadlier than anything dreamed of during that war. It carried more missiles, its guidance and tracking systems were more accurate, and each warhead was vastly more destructive. Now scores of them adjusted their attitudes as sensors located their targets. Passionless computers ignored the fire beginning to destroy their fellows while they considered targeting criteria and ordered their launch queues.

And then they fired.

The CAs' designers had never contemplated the volume of fire which screamed in upon them. Each ship was the target not of dozens but of scores of second-generation antimatter warheads. Point defense might stop the first three, or five, or seven, but the others got through, and no heavy cruiser could survive direct hits of such power.

One minute after launch, every cruiser had been wiped from the face of the universe, and even as they died, superdreadnoughts and battle-cruisers made transit on the pods' heels.

No mine could be emplaced directly atop an open warp point, and that gave TF 59's warships a small space in which to deploy. The surrounding mines confined them to the limited clear zone, but that was why the TFN had produced the Anti-Mine Ballistic Missile. The new, internally-launched AMBAMs were big, ugly mass hogs, eating up magazine space which might have been devoted to antiship missiles, but Vanessa Murakuma didn't care, and her green eyes flamed as her capital missile-armed ships began to launch.

The AMBAMs sped out—slow and clumsy by missile standards, but fast enough for their task—and deployed with ungainly precision, then belched spreading shoals of independently targeted antimatter warheads that coated her plot like diamond dust, invading the minefields. Then they exploded, and for just one instant, space flamed like a star's transplanted heart. The perfectly synchronized detonations merged into a torrent of heat and blast and radiation, and the mines caught in that riptide died. The sheer volume of space was too vast for many to suffer outright destruction, but their control systems were irradiated, blinded, burned into so much useless junk, and Murakuma smiled a shark's smile as her AMBAMs ripped a hole clean through the dense minefields and her starships charged into it.

The superdreadnoughts and battle-cruisers were over two light-minutes from the warp point. By the time their light-speed sensors reported the enemy's arrival, every defending cruiser was dead and the totally unexpected AMBAMs had blasted a path through the mines, but their crews knew what to do, and the entire vast force wheeled ponderously towards the invaders.

"Their battle-line's moving, Skipper. They're heading straight for Admiral Murakuma."

"Understood." Prescott watched his plot, forcing his face to remain calm, but exultation boiled behind his eyes. *Daikyu* had done it! They'd actually *done* it, and TF 59 was in clean!

"Picking up three battle-cruisers!" Cesiaño said abruptly, and Prescott's eyes narrowed. The bastards *had* been waiting for the CLs to drive him into their arms, but the fresh threat had changed their minds. They'd gone to full power, turning to race towards TF 59, and he bared his teeth.

"Bring us around behind them as they pass, Daryl," he said.

"Aye, aye, Sir!" Anticipation edged Belliard's acknowledgment, and Prescott turned that hungry smile on his tac officer.

"They're giving us a nice, clean shot into their blind spots, Jill. Let's make it count."

The trio of battle-cruisers sped towards the invaders. Despite reckless power settings, they were far beyond any range at which the oncoming starships' sensors could pierce their ECM. They could never hope to stop so much firepower, but if they got into a suitable ambush position, they could make the enemy pay heavily to kill them.

They continued on their course, their original mission forgotten in the face of this greater threat, and never noticed the silent, stealthy killer sliding in behind them.

"Firing . . . *now!*"

Jill Cesiaño closed the master key, and TFNS *Daikyu* went instantly to rapid fire. Her five standard launchers lacked the range and massive striking power of a *Dunkerque*'s capital missile batteries, but they fired far more rapidly, and she was in her targets' blind spots, hidden beyond the distortion their own drive fields created. They'd never guessed she was back there, and even if they had, point defense couldn't engage missiles it couldn't even see.

Prescott's fire streaked in with deadly accuracy, and he slammed a fist down on his chair arm as the warheads struck. *Just like stamping on a spider,* he thought with cold, savage hatred.

"Tracking reports antimatter detonations, Sir."

Murakuma blinked at Tian's announcement. Then her darting eyes found the explosions in her plot, and her brow furrowed for a moment before she nodded sharply.

"It's Prescott," she said. "It must be—whoever it is is shooting up at least three targets . . . and kicking the hell out of them, too," she added respectfully as one of the Bugs suddenly blew apart. "Warn the screen he's out there, Tian—we don't want any misunderstandings when he's done so well this far—then launch the RDs."

❖   ❖   ❖

Commander Olivera settled firmly into his couch as TFNS *Dalmatian* prepared for action. His command fighter shuddered as the tractors deposited it in the big fleet carrier's number three catapult, and he flicked his eyes over his panel while he tried to ignore how dry his mouth was.

He didn't know how he and his crew had survived K-45 and First Justin, and a fatalistic part of him accepted that he was living on borrowed time. But at least he had a better chance of hurting the bastards this time. Strikegroup 47's survivors had been transferred to *Dalmatian* as the core of her rebuilt attack group, and he had twice as many fighters under his direct command.

"Launch status Alpha," a voice said in his earbug.

"Alpha confirmed," he replied, and punched a button. "Computers cycling."

"Green board," PriFly responded. "Tac feed on-line. Give 'em hell, Commander."

"We've got them on the drones, Sir," Commander Ling reported. "Battle Comp's IDs match *Daikyu*'s figures for their main force, but we're missing several picket CLs."

"Cloaked," Mackenna said, and Murakuma nodded. No doubt some of those hidden light cruisers would try to duplicate Prescott's ambush, but it was unlikely they could penetrate her drone shell. If they did, that was why capital ships had escorts, and she turned her attention to the main Bug force. There were ninety-two superdreadnoughts, eighteen battle-cruisers, and over a hundred and twenty light cruisers over there—six times as many ships as she'd brought with her, and God only knew how vast the Bugs' tonnage advantage was. If *she'd* had that sort of edge, she would have been perfectly willing to let a faster, longer-ranged enemy stooge around the system however he chose. After all, if she moved directly to the warp point and sat on it, he'd be forced to engage on *her* terms, not his, when he tried to go home again.

But the Bugs weren't doing that, and she gave LeBlanc a fierce, satisfied smile. The intelligence officer returned it with interest, and her mind whirred with detached ferocity as she looked back at the display. They might not know how these monsters' strategic doctrine worked, but at least they seemed to follow predictable *tactical* patterns. They were charging after her at their best speed, precisely as they'd done in their earlier engagements. They'd still have a chance to intercept on her withdrawal, despite their lower speed, as long as they stayed between her and the warp point, but that was fine with her. In fact, it was exactly what she *wanted* them to do.

Still, it wouldn't do to give them too much time to consider other options. . . .

✧   ✧   ✧

"*Launch!*"

Dalmatian's catapults spat thirty-six heavily armed fighters into space, and Anson Olivera grunted as a familiar lead boot kicked him in the stomach. He grunted again as his bucking fighter rammed through the CV's drive field, but his eyes clung to his display.

The Bug CLEs which had wreaked such havoc in Justin, glared crimson within the enemy's formation, but there weren't many, and he bared his teeth in satisfaction. He didn't know how the Bugs could be stupid enough not to have brought more forward—unless their own lack of fighter experience kept them from realizing how effective they were?—but he didn't much care.

"I make it only eighteen *Cataphracts*, Carl. Do you confirm?"

"Affirmative, Skip." Lieutenant Hathaway sounded equally satisfied, and Olivera punched into the strikegroup command net.

"All right, people—listen up! We stay the hell away from the *Cataphracts* and leave the *Cleavers* and *Cannons* to Commander Yeung and Commander Abbot. *We* want the *Carbines*."

"Lucky us," someone muttered, and despite his tension, Olivera smiled. The intelligence pukes who'd coined the reporting names for the Bug cruisers had a sense of humor. The *Carbines* were missile ships, while the *Cleavers* carried pure primary armaments and the *Cannons* packed heavy plasma gun broadsides. Primaries were useless against targets as maneuverable as fighters, and plasma guns had too little reach to engage them beyond FRAM range, but if the Bugs had cooked up an equivalent of the TFN's AFHAWK anti-fighter missile, his people would take a pounding from the *Carbines*. Still, they hadn't shown anything like it yet. . . .

The first attack wave scorched towards its targets, and the cruisers obliged by forming a screen to intercept it short of their main force. Under normal circumstances, that was a smart move; given the plan Admiral Murakuma's staff had evolved, it was a recipe for disaster.

"Coming up on Initial Point," he murmured over the group net, and spared a glance for Jane Malachi. His pilot was completely focused on her controls, eyes glued to the red cursor of the initial point as she sped towards it and SG 47 held formation on her. Despite their losses and the short time they'd had to work up their replacements, the group was steady as a rock, and Olivera felt a fierce pride in his men and women.

"IP . . . *now!*" he snapped. The group whipped through a sharp turn, arrowing straight for its assigned targets while Bug tracking systems locked them up for the close-in defenses to slaughter, and he grinned savagely. *That's right*, he thought. *Keep your point defense configured to shoot us, you bastards. We've got a little surprise for you.*

"Launch in seventeen seconds," Hathaway said flatly. "Fifteen. Ten. Five. *Launch!*"

The command fighter shuddered as it launched its missiles from five light-seconds, and Olivera's eyes flamed with vengeful delight. The FM2 fighter missile had a lighter warhead than a FRAM, but it also had five times the range . . . and the Bugs had never seen it before. They'd expected the Terran squadrons to close to knife-range once more, and they'd configured their point defense to shoot at *fighters*, not missiles. His group's fire streaked in virtually unopposed, and if his warheads were lighter, enough of them would do the job just as well.

Leprous light boils spalled the Bug formation. Someone howled gleefully as the first light cruiser belched air and debris, and Olivera wanted to howl himself as four more followed. SG 47 sent seventy-two missiles into its targets, and most scored direct hits. None of the ships were dead, but all fell out of formation, crippled and lamed, and the Bugs' pursuit of Murakuma's starships left them behind. That was fifteen percent of their total *Carbines;* it looked as if the other groups had done even better against their targets; and TF 59 hadn't lost a single fighter!

"All right, people—back to the barn," Olivera said. "You did good; now let's come back and do better."

"The first strike nailed eighteen," Ling Tian reported. "The second wave's going in now."

Murakuma nodded. Light cruisers were trifling targets compared to superdreadnoughts, but she had no intention of throwing her fighters against an unshaken wall of fire again. First she would whittle away at their most vulnerable screening elements, taking the easy kills and blooding her green pilots. Every cruiser she killed would weaken the close-range defenses, and then . . .

"They're still pursuing, Sir," Mackenna said quietly, "but they're dividing their forces."

He used a light pencil to indicate the twenty-odd SDs and escorting fight cruisers splitting off from the main Bug formation. It left the main force more than enough firepower to deal with TF 59—assuming it could catch the Terrans—but the second force was dropping back to cover Murakuma's most probable vector for a return to the warp point. Despite their slower speed, the two formations could "herd" her further and further from her only way back to Sarasota if they tried, but that was fine with her.

"As long as they keep concentrating on us," she murmured softly, and watched the first fighter strike race back towards its carriers to rearm.

❖   ❖   ❖

Formations shifted as the infernally fast little attack craft poured missiles into the light cruisers. The escorts drew in closer to the capital ships, seeking to shelter under the umbrella of the battle-line's fire, for however expendable they were, there was no point in spending them for no return. Yet the move was little help. The attack craft couldn't throw dense enough salvos to overwhelm a superdreadnought's point defense, but they didn't try to. They ignored the bigger ships to continue pounding the cruisers, and only the Cataphracts *had sufficient missile defenses to stave off their fire. At last the surviving cruisers actually moved inside the battle-line's globe, concealing themselves from the enemy, but only thirty-one of them lived long enough to hide.*

"Well, we're done shooting fish in a barrel." Mackenna grimaced as the last light cruiser vanished into the midst of the Bug formation, and Murakuma nodded.

"Distance from the warp point?"

"Just over twelve light-minutes for Bug Two," Ling Tian replied. "Bug One is at fifteen light-minutes; we're at seventeen."

Murakuma nodded again and glanced into the com screen linking her to TFNS *Pit Viper*. Demosthenes Waldeck looked back at her, and she raised one hand.

"Execute Able Three," she said.

TF 59 slowed, letting the range close, and fresh fighter strikes went in as the *Matterhorn* superdreadnoughts and *Dunkerque* battle-cruisers began to fire. The *Dunkerques* carried almost pure SBM loads, keeping their lighter shields and weaker point defense beyond the range of any return fire, but the *Matterhorns* carried the smaller, shorter-ranged capital missiles, for they had the strength to stand up to counterfire and they could cram far more CMs into their magazines. The fireballs of heavier warheads began to blaze, this time concentrating on the Bugs' similarly armed *Archers,* but the starships' salvos were carefully timed to coincide with the fighter strikes. The incoming missiles forced the Bugs to split their point defense between them and the fighters, weakening the antifighter barrage as the Terran squadrons streaked in to point-blank range at last.

Despite the covering fire, they took losses this time. Almost five percent of the attacking fighters were killed short of launch, but those who made it rippled salvos of FRAMs, and powerful warheads pounded the enemy brutally. More starships fell out of formation, and they were no longer light cruisers. The Bug battle-line trailed air-bleeding wrecks in its wake, and Murakuma nodded to Commander Ling.

"Alert Mondesi and launch the drones."

"Sir! Sir!"

Raphael Mondesi swore and snatched for a towel as the young Peaceforce lieutenant charged into the head, waving a message board in one hand, and skidded to a halt.

"What?" Mondesi asked sharply, killing the water with one irritated hand while the other tried awkwardly to whip the towel about his waist. He was not amused, but Lieutenant Jeffers seemed unaware of that as she thrust the message board at him.

"It's Redemption, Sir! *They're mounting Redemption!*"

Mondesi forgot all about showers and jerked the board from her hand. He darted a lightning glance over the display, then threw the board back to her, knotted the towel in place, and ran barefoot for his command center.

"Drone coming through, Sir."

Commodore Reichman looked up quickly, and the light cruiser *Ashigara*'s com officer pressed her earbug more firmly against her ear as she listened to the downloaded message.

"Execute Redemption!" she announced, and Reichman nodded to his ops officer.

"You heard the admiral, Al."

"Yes, *Sir!*" Commander Alvin Lopez grinned as hugely as if he were headed for one of his beloved jai alai games rather than an excellent chance of getting himself killed and began transmitting orders to Task Group 59.3's thirteen *Dull Knife* transports and the three CVLs and nine light cruisers of their escort.

Frieda Jaëger jerked as a hand pounded her shoulder. She blinked sleep-crusted eyes and reached instinctively for her com console as adrenaline flooded her exhausted body, but she wasn't in her Asp. She was in her bedroll under it, and she reached up to catch Sergeant Major McNeil's wrist before the noncom could pound her again.

"What the *hell*—" she began sharply, but McNeil broke in on her.

"Redemption, Sir! We just got the alert—Admiral Murakuma's launching Redemption!"

Jaëger rolled out from under the Asp, irritation forgotten. She stared at McNeil for a fleeting moment, then bounded to her feet.

"ETA?" she snapped.

"Two hours," the sergeant replied, and Jaëger winced. She'd known warning would be short, but the original plan hadn't counted on having a Bug division less than forty klicks from the Edward Mountain evacuation site. The refugees immediately behind her battered battalion were well concealed, but she had to start them moving within ninety minutes if they were going to be on-site when the shuttles arrived. Yet the Bugs were almost certain to spot them the instant she put them in motion. Worse, their movement towards the LZ would point the Bugs at *that*, as well.

"Any orders from HQ?"

"Your discretion, Sir," McNeil said grimly, and Jaëger mouthed a silent curse. She couldn't fault HQ's decision—she *was* the senior officer on the spot—but the crushing responsibility for five thousand civilian lives slammed down on her like a boulder.

She stared into the moonlit night and rubbed her hands up and down her thighs as she tried to balance imperatives and possibilities. She *had* to get those people moving, but what was left of her battalion could only hold the Bugs off so long. . . .

"Seventy minutes," she said abruptly, and turned to face McNeil. "Find Captain El-Hamna. Have him pass the order to stand to. As soon as the civilians start moving, all hell is going to come down on us. We'll go with Stonewall."

"Aye, Sir!" McNeil dashed off into the darkness, and Jaëger bent to pick up her uniform jacket, wishing she hadn't given up her own zoot to help equip her small mobile reserve.

She had a feeling she was going to need it.

Commodore Reichman's task group scorched through the warp point at its best speed. The big, vulnerable transports slowed it, but the main Bug units were too far away to intercept, and he stared fixedly at his plot, hoping they stayed that way. The *Dull Knifes* were big enough to read as battleships to any hostile sensors, and if the Bugs thought they really *were* battleships, they might well wheel to go after them.

But it didn't look like they were going to. His CVLs launched recon fighters to sweep ahead while recon drones covered the flanks, and the battle between Murakuma's main body and its pursuers redoubled in intensity as she pounded them harder than ever. It was her job to draw the enemy onto her own force, luring him away from the transports, and she was paying a price to do it. Scanner resolution was poor at this range, but her superdreadnoughts were taking a beating, and now her handful of shorter-ranged battleships were closing to support them.

The sudden appearance of still more invaders surprised the Fleet. The new force was less numerous than the first, but it contained twice as many battleships. Added to the force already engaged, it might have had a decisive effect, yet it was running away from the engagement. The Fleet's doctrine offered no explanation for its purpose, but if those ships wished to abandon their consorts to destruction, that was acceptable.

❖　　❖　　❖

"Got something, Skip. Looks like a cloaked *Barfly*."

Commander Alice Depogue, CO of the light carrier *Amir,* glanced at her plot and nodded.

"Got it, Frank," she told her exec, and studied the data relayed from the recon fighter. It certainly looked like one of the cloak-capable picket cruisers, and it seemed to be maneuvering to ambush TG 59.3. *Gutsy move,* she conceded silently, *but stupid.* The TFN had amassed enough data to know the *Barflies* were easy meat for fighter strikes, and she bared her teeth.

"Have the recon birds stay clear. If they don't know we've seen them, keep it that way."

"Aye, Skip." *Amir's* com officer nodded, and Depogue looked at her fighter ops officer.

"Pass the word to Commander Sinkman, Etienne. Full group launch—I want that bastard killed in a single pass."

Reichman watched *Amir's* strikegroup blow the lone cruiser to vapor and nodded in approval as the victorious squadrons wheeled quickly back to rearm while the recon fighters continued their search for prey. But there was tension under his satisfaction. The smaller of the two Bug forces was dropping back. It was still closer to Murakuma than to him, but it might not *stay* that way, and he had only fifty-four fighters of his own. If the bastards came in on him . . .

He twitched his shoulders. There was nothing he could do but wait and see, and he was already closing on the planet. The Bugs had placed a dozen missile platforms around it—not to engage attacking starships, but to support their ground troops with orbital strikes—and he had to kill them before they spotted the evacuation sites, whatever the risk to TG 59.3.

"Instruct *Akagi* to launch her strike," he said harshly, and a full third of his limited fighter strength went scorching off towards the distant sapphire on his visual display.

"Holy shi—!"

The expletive in Major Jaëger's earbug chopped off with sickening suddenness as whoever had started to utter it died. Her camouflaged Asp sat in the saddle of a steep ridge, and the night below her was hideous with explosions and small arms fire. The Bugs were coming in on her even harder than she'd feared, and her support squads were running short of ammo. Here and there Bug thrusts had gotten into her positions, and deadly firefights raged as her people fought frantically to beat them back again.

She wrenched her eyes to the display, and her fists clenched on her console. Her main line was buckled, but it was holding. Barely, perhaps, and at hideous cost, but holding. Yet while it held, a Bug pincer was sweeping out around her flank. No doubt it meant to curl into her rear and smash her, but one of the refugee columns lay squarely in its path. She bit her lip so hard she tasted blood as she thought of the five hundred terrified men, women and children struggling through the darkness, and her voice was harsh.

"McNeil!"

"Aye, Sir!"

"Tell Lieutenant Harpe—"

"Harpe's dead, Skipper," the zooted sergeant interrupted, and Jaëger cursed.

"All right. Get over there and take command. There's a Bug thrust coming around Captain Thaler's flank. Hit them at the river and hold their asses."

"Aye, aye, Sir!"

McNeil vanished in a whine of exoskeletal "muscles," and Jaëger stared after her for a moment. They both knew what the sergeant was going into, and she suddenly wished she'd taken time to say goodbye.

"They're pounding Jaëger hardest," Simon Merman said, "but they're going after the Lake Anderson site almost as hard."

"I know." Mondesi stared at the display, fingers drumming on the edge of his console, then nodded grimly. "Send Major Ashman to support Lake Anderson," he said harshly.

"But Jaëger—" Merman began, but Mondesi cut him off.

"Jaëger's gone, Simon." Loss and helpless rage filled his grating voice. "She's too weak, and we can't get there in time. If we try to reinforce both sites, we'll only lose them both."

"But we're talking about five *thousand* civilians!" Merman protested in raw anguish, and Mondesi closed his eyes.

"I know," he repeated, "but we can't reinforce failure. If we try, we lose *ten* thousand." He stared into the plot, unwilling to meet Merman's eyes. The blur of combat chatter muttered from the com section behind him, and the Peaceforcer barely heard his final words. "Jaëger's on her own, God help her," Brigadier Raphael Mondesi said softly.

The second enemy force launched attack craft at the planet, blotting away the fire support stations, and the smaller of the defending forces reacted at last. It curved away from the main engagement, swinging back towards the planet as the threat to its own ground forces finally registered. If those battleships wanted to, they could sterilize the planet with a saturation bombardment, paying the trifling price of their own noncombatants to wipe out every warrior on its surface. That could not be permitted, but the enemy was foolishly reluctant to sacrifice his starships in combat. A threat in sufficient strength might deflect him from his mission, and the massive superdreadnoughts forged ahead at their best speed to present that threat.

"They're coming in on us, Sir."

Reichman looked at Tactical's display. Twenty-three SDs and the tattered remnants of forty CLs bore down on his rear, and he studied the time estimates closely. The Bugs were slower than he. He could break off and evade them with ease, but if he continued with his mission, they'd be able to range on him within forty-five minutes of the time he entered orbit. He bit his lip for a moment, then punched a com stud.

"General Servais?"

"Yes, Commodore?"

"The enemy is diverting a heavy force after us. That means our window just got a lot narrower, but I think we've swept the area between us and the planet clear of Bug starships, and the little we're getting from planet-side sounds like Mount Edward and Lake Anderson are under heavy pressure. I recommend you launch your shuttles now, Sir."

"Agreed." The confirmation came back immediately, and the assault shuttles of four fresh battalions of Terran Marine Raiders, every man and woman of them a volunteer, spat from the transports *Hasdrubal, Insula* and *Viracocha.* They raced for the planet, stark naked if the fighters had missed a single Bug cruiser, and Reichman watched them go, then looked at his ops officer.

"Turn the escorts around," he said quietly. "We've got to buy the transports some time."

"We can't hold 'em, Skipper!" Helen McNeil's voice burned in Jaëger's earbug, and the major's face was beaten iron as the thunder of combat came to her over the link. Her main position had been breached frontally in two places, and the force battering McNeil's hopelessly outnumbered Raiders was less than five klicks from the refugee column.

"We're down to fifteen zoots," McNeil continued, "and—"

"Buy me some more time, Helen!" Jaëger heard the desperation in her own voice and hated herself for asking the impossible.

"We're trying, Skip, but—"

McNeil's link went dead, and Jaëger's heart twisted in anguish. It was all coming apart. Her entire position couldn't hold fifteen more minutes. Even now, less than half her people could possibly disengage, and if she didn't start pulling back now—

"Edward Mountain, Edward Mountain. This is General Servais. I have two Raider battalions twenty minutes out. Send drop coordinates. Edward Mountain, Edward Mountain, I say again. Two battalions with shuttle air support twenty minutes out. Send coordinates now."

Jaëger twitched as the totally unexpected voice rattled her earbug. For just an instant, hope flared, but then it died. Her people couldn't hold twenty more minutes if God Himself ordered it. She could fall back, but with Bugs already in among her positions, the chances of disengaging were minute. And even if she pulled it off, she would have abandoned five hundred civilians, and she couldn't do that. She simply couldn't. Even if she could, it was unlikely she could stand again anywhere short of the evacuation site itself, and air support or no, if Servais' raiders had to drop into a landing zone under direct enemy fire—

Her nostrils flared, and she closed her eyes. Then she opened them once more, and they were very still as she punched the transmit button.

"This is Edward Mountain. Your LZ is the evacuation site, General."

"We can reinfor—" Servais began, but she shook her head, almost as if he could see her.

"I say again, your landing zone is the evac site," she said flatly, and switched frequencies.

"Lieutenant Haldane."

"Aye, Sir!"

Weapons thundered in the valley below as the commander of her last four surviving assault skimmers replied. Jaëger watched the holocaust grinding up the slope towards her and knew Haldane expected her to send him into it in a desperate bid to hold the enemy while she disengaged. But that wasn't what she intended. A fighting withdrawal wouldn't work, yet there was still one way she might manage to divert the Bugs from the evac site.

"We've lost our right flank," she said almost conversationally, "and the Bugs are closing on Reitner's refugee column at Alpha-Six. Get over there. Hit the bastards with everything you've got and open a hole for him, then cover him to the evac site. Understood?"

There was a moment of silence, and then Haldane cleared his throat.

"Understood, Sir, but . . . what about the battalion?"

"Just get Reitner's people out, Jeff," Jaëger said softly. She tapped one last frequency change into her console, patching into the all-channels com net of her dying battalion, and stood. She shimmied into the access trunk of the Asp's turret, settled herself in the fighting chair, and placed her hands on the grips of the single multi-barreled autocannon which was the lightly armored vehicle's sole offensive weapon, then keyed her boom mike.

"All units, this is Jaëger," she said. "Fresh forces are dropping on the LZ in—" she glanced at her chrono "—seventeen minutes. It's up to us to make sure there's an LZ for them to land on, and that means sucking the enemy away from it. Attack. I repeat, attack. Break into the bastards. Make them worry about *us,* not advancing . . . and God bless."

She closed down the com and looked at the small screen that held her driver's face.

"Let's go, Sandy," she said quietly, and the Asp lurched downslope into the inferno.

CHAPTER THIRTEEN

"You *know* I can't tell him that!"

Alpha Centauri A was at midmorning height, and its yellow light streamed at a forty-five degree angle through the conference room's tall windows. Alpha Centauri B, the orange companion star, was too far away in its highly eccentric orbit to complicate the day-night dichotomy. And the late-M type third component was, as always, invisible without the aid of powerful telescopes. Midori Kozlov recalled that component C—distinctly second-rate even as red dwarfs went—had been discovered in the twentieth century and dubbed "Proxima Centauri" because it had possessed the one lonely distinction of being Old Terra's closest stellar neighbor. (Except, of course, for Sol, which didn't count.) Nobody had thought of it for generations, least of all the inhabitants of Nova Terra and Eden, the twin planets that occupied Alpha Centauri A's second orbit and constituted humanity's oldest, richest and most populous extrasolar colony.

Gazing around at the austere, understated elegance of the chamber, Kozlov thought it had been good of Nova Terra's planetary government to provide these facilities, for there was certainly nothing so nice in the TFN reservation. The footage from Erebor had shocked the mush-minds who governed this planet into an awareness of which universe they were living in. They'd doubtless recover from their temporary attack of common sense, but for the present they were cooperating with the military in exemplary fashion. And right now, like everyone else, they were euphoric over the news of Operation Redemption. Murakuma had lost a battleship, three battlecruisers and six lighter units, but she'd inflicted the customary disproportionate losses and snatched 48,000 civilians from the teeth, or whatever, of the Bugs.

Like all the staffers, Kozlov sat with her back to the chamber's walls, well back from the oval table—well back, but readily available at call. They didn't have long to wait before the Grand Allied Joint Chiefs of Staff began to file in and take their places at the table, where only they might sit. Ivan Antonov stationed himself before the chair directly in front of her, while his three colleagues moved to their specially designed chair equivalents. Last to enter was Hannah Avram, who moved to a chair midway along one side of the table.

"Please be seated, ladies and gentlemen," the Sky Marshal said. The form of address was automatic, even though all four of the Joint Chiefs were males of their respective species. And, Kozlov reflected, at least it was a nice gesture from the standpoint of the females among the spear-carriers lining the walls. Avram waited a couple of heartbeats after everyone was settled before resuming.

"On behalf of the Terran Federation Navy, I formally declare this meeting convened. I am gratified that the work of establishing Allied Grand Fleet Headquarters is going smoothly, and that everyone concerned came so readily to agreement that the Alpha Centauri System was the logical location for it—"

"Especially considering the alternative," a mischievous voice whispered into Kozlov's left ear. She turned a slantwise glare on the speaker, but Ensign Kevin Sanders' blue eyes lost none of their twinkle and his grin made his sharp features look even more foxlike than usual. The fresh-caught snotty must have attracted somebody's attention at the Academy, for he'd gone directly to work—albeit in a very junior capacity—for the Sky Marshal's staff spook. And although he was a little too irrepressible for Kozlov's tastes, she'd taken him along to Antonov's staff. These days, with so much to deduce about the Bugs from so little data, a capacity for original thought covered a multitude of sins.

And, she reminded herself, he was right. It would have been out of the question to headquarter Allied Grand Fleet in the Solar System, where it would have looked entirely too much like a Federation agency for alien sensibilities. Alpha Centauri might be only one warp transit from Sol (and an insignificant four-and-a-third light-years in realspace, though nobody but astronomers thought in those terms anymore), but that one warp transit placed it at a symbolically important remove from the Federation government's seat on Old Terra.

Still, the choice made military as well as political sense. In addition to being an economic powerhouse, Alpha Centauri possessed no less than eight warp points—one of which connected with Sol's solitary one. This system had been humanity's gateway to the galaxy, and from the security standpoint its location deep in the heart of the Federation was unbeatable. Where could the Grand Alliance's top brass be any safer than here?

She dragged her attention back to Hannah Avram's words, for the Sky Marshal had begun getting down to practicalities. "As you're all aware, my status as convening officer of this initial meeting is simply a formality, consequent upon my position as commanding officer of the 'host navy.' Rest assured that the Terran Federation Navy intends to function as a coequal member of the Grand Alliance, under the overall operational direction of the Joint Chiefs of Staff—that is, of this body. As soon as you have organized yourselves, I will revert to my regular duties as commander of a component navy of the Allied Grand Fleet. I therefore open the floor to nominations for chairman of the Grand Allied Joint Chiefs of Staff."

Less than a human heartbeat passed before Fleet Speaker Noraku rose to his full height. Kozlov was prepared to entertain the possibility that he'd never considered the psychological advantage that height conferred. His ability to form the sounds of Standard English unaided also helped.

"I submit," came the almost subliminal bass, "that there is only one possible choice: the only living being who has exercised fleet command in a large-scale war, and led his star nation's forces to total victory in that war. The being whose campaigns have set the standard for our profession since before many in this room were born. The being, moreover, who represents the star nation actually under attack. I refer, of course, to Admiral of the Fleet Ivan Antonov, TFN. I nominate him for chairman of the Grand Allied Joint Chiefs of Staff."

An affirmative murmur ran around the room, and Kozlov commanded herself not to grin as matters took their prearranged course, played out for the benefit of the news media. Kthaara, as Antonov's *vilkshatha* brother, could hardly nominate him. Neither could Thaarzhaan; as representative of a Federation ally which was clearly a junior partner but was resolved to maintain its independence, he was unsuitable from all standpoints. That left Noraku.

Kthaara rose as the Gorm resumed his seat. "I second the nomination." All of the Joint Chiefs understood the Tongue of Tongues, and interpreters translated for those staffers who didn't—or would have done so if any translation had been necessary.

"The nomination is made and seconded," Hannah Avram spoke formally. "The floor is open for discussion."

Thaarzhaan unfolded himself from the uncomfortable-looking framework "chair" his race favored. "Sssssky Marshhhhhhal, I move thattttt the sssssselection be by acccccclamation."

"The motion is made and seconded," Avram said after Noraku's rumbled second had ceased reverberating. Then she smiled and seemed to relax from her formality. "There appears to be no need for further discussion. Admiral Antonov, I'll ask you to assume the chair."

"*Davai glaz nalyom!* Let's put one in the eye!" Antonov sighed deeply as he settled into his armchair and loosened the collar of his uniform.

Hannah Avram grinned crookedly at him. "Not bad enough you should steal my staff intelligence officer, Ivan Nikolayevich; you also have to be a bad influence on me, as usual. Oh, well. *Le chaim!*" She raised her vodka glass. Then her mood darkened even before it reached her lips. "A good toast these days, no? Life—our kind of life, anyway—seems to be getting scarcer."

"Ah, don't be so gloomy Hannah—you're not even Russian." He tossed off his vodka. "*Ty chto mumu yebyosh?*"

She drank a moderate sip and grinned again. "I may not be Russian, you old reprobate, but my ancestors lived there a long time ago . . . and I know a few phrases of the language, including that one."

"Oh." Antonov took on a philosophical look. "Amazing the number of people I meet whose ancestors *left* Russia at some time or other. I wonder why that is?"

"Think about it," she suggested archly.

They both chuckled, then sat in companionable silence for a time. Alpha Centauri B was visible tonight, a superlatively bright orange star, and it shone through the broad window of Antonov's office, banishing most other stars even though the night was clear and moonless. Of course, *all* nights of this hemisphere of Nova Terra were moonless; the giant "moon" Eden hung perpetually over the antipodes of this planet, whose rotation it had long ago halted. The inhabitants of *that* hemisphere's island chains—mountaintops, really, that were all the ocean's fixed tidal bulge had left above water—had the permanent spectacle of an Earth-like planet filling a good portion of their sky. They could never make sense of the expression "once in a blue moon."

No question about it, Nova Terra was a lovely place. If it had a fault, it was the inconvenient day-night cycle as the twin planets revolved around their common center of mass in slightly over sixty-one standard hours. Avram's stay here hadn't lasted long enough for her to adjust to it. But at least, she thought, recalling a five-and-a-half-centuries-old quotation about "an equality of dissatisfaction," it was an adjustment that all four of the Alliance's member-races, coming from worlds with more typical diurnal periods, had to make.

Antonov finally broke the silence. "So, Hannah. How is your charming family?"

"Fine—I think." Avram's tone carried a carefully metered edge of genuine bitterness. "Dick is back out at Galloway's Star, up to his hip pockets in that slime pit. God knows I'd like to see more of him, but we *need* someone riding herd on those . . . those—"

Words failed her, and she bit her lip for a moment. Her husband had attained senior flag rank himself, but in BuShips, not one of the combat arms. Unlike her, he'd been able to retire with a clear conscience almost twenty years ago and become a highly sought after defense consultant. His relationship to Sky Marshal Avram would have barred him from any lobbying employment, but it was the military itself, not the contractors, who valued his expertise, and that was exactly why he'd been sent to Galloway's Star. The Corporate World industrialists of Galloway's World had a nasty reputation for intentional cost overruns and generally inventive bookkeeping, and it was Dick's job to keep them honest.

A task, she reflected, *not unlike that of a gentleman named Hercules and a certain stable. Or Sisyphus, perhaps.* She gave herself a mental shake.

"At any rate, he's fine, even if we're both feeling sorry for ourselves over the separation, and at least most of the kids had the sense to avoid service careers. Josh is the only one with any real aptitude for it, and he just made captain." She grinned. "At the risk of sounding prejudiced, I think the young sprout may actually be ready for it— not that I intend to tell *him* that!"

"Hannah, Hannah!" Antonov gave another seismic chuckle. "*You've* certainly changed from the young commodore—*arguably* a commodore, at least—who came to report to me after Second Fleet relieved Danzig."

Six decades rolled away, and Avram recalled every step she'd taken through the superdreadnought's passages as she'd marched to meet Ivan the Terrible and face the consequences of her own actions. It had not been a cheerful exercise for an officer who'd used Federation Marines to seize dictatorial control of an entire star system on the basis of a more than questionable legal opinion. But she'd survived the meeting, and her memory continued marching, through the subsequent battles that had cost part of her body and all that remained of her youth to the long years of peacetime service and the political infighting that was so much more exhausting than combat ops. She gave her head a shake, stirring hair that was now iron-gray. "Yes, I've changed, all right: less young—and less slender! Antigerone treatments aren't magic, you know."

"No, no, it's more than that. You've grown up in a lot of ways, Hannah. You've become . . . not 'cynical' or 'world-weary,' nobody will ever be able to call you that. Your ideals, the things that make up your essence as a person, are unchanged. But you've seen more of the ways life can frustrate those ideals, and still not lost them. Those who *do* lose them become less than they were. You've become more."

For a moment, Avram felt something akin to embarrassment, for there couldn't be many to whom Antonov spoke in this way. Then, in the wake of a score of generations of ancestors, she took refuge in levity. "Hey, dealing with politicians this many years would do it to anybody! You of all people ought to know that."

"Ha! Did I ever tell you how glad I was when you became Sky Marshal? I had to laugh at the thought of those *svolochy* wetting their pants every time they looked at you and remembered how you dealt with your *local* politicians in the Danzig system."

"Oh, come on, Ivan Nikolayevich! The circumstances there were extraordinary. Unique, even. And I had legal precedents for my actions."

"*Da, da.* I know. Your legal officer must have been a *pyzdobol*—a real piss-artist. And your little coup was upheld in the end. Still . . ." He chuckled again, with pure pleasure. "Nothing improves a politician's character like fear."

"You're incorrigible!"

"So Howard Anderson used to tell me," Antonov acknowledged. "For some reason, he felt I lacked sufficient respect for properly constituted civilian authority."

Avram emitted a fairly ladylike snort. "Where do you suppose he ever got *that* idea?" Abruptly, her mood darkened again. "Speaking of politicians, I've been unable to prevent some uniformed ones from accompanying Admiral Murakuma's reinforcements."

Antonov scowled. "That's always the way, isn't it? There are always a certain number of *zalyotniki* who make careers out of being somebody's eyes and ears in the Fleet." Then his scowl smoothed itself out into a look of something resembling fatalism. "Well, at least we *are* getting reinforcements to Sarasota finally."

"Personally," Avram said bleakly, "I'm even more pleased we've gotten all those piled-up refugees *out* of Sarasota. They're far enough back now they may actually be safe, and we're starting to make progress on evacuating Sarasota itself."

"*Da.* And the first Ophiuchi elements should be arriving there soon, with the Orions and Gorm not far behind. By the time we're ready to upgrade Murakuma's task force to a full fleet, it won't just be an organizational fiction."

"And that leads to another political problem," Avram said grimly. "Certain highly placed people think this new Fifth Fleet ought to be commanded by an officer of 'appropriate seniority' rather than a mere rear admiral. They're bringing pressure on me to replace Murakuma."

"What?" Antonov shook his head ponderously. "*Eto polneyshaya yerunda.* That's rubbish. They must know what Murakuma's accomplished. She's destroyed over ninety superdreadnoughts outright, and intelligence estimates she's sent another fifty-odd to the repair yards. God alone knows the losses she's inflicted in the lighter ship classes. And, more importantly, it's because of her we've gotten the time to bring her forces up to fleet level. She won that time for us with her raid into Justin. Aside from the civilians she got out, she must have rocked the Bugs back on whatever they use in place of heels, and made a shambles of their timetable for the next offensive against Sarasota." He shook his head again, this time with a chuckle. "I remember her—not too well, I'm sorry to say—from her days on the faculty at the War College. She must be quite a lady, Hannah. Maybe I've been a little too hasty with some of the things I've said about the younger generation of officers."

"Unfortunately, some people don't see it that way. Like Agamemnon Waldeck." Avram paused, slightly apprehensive. So far, Antonov had taken all this very quietly—suspiciously so, in fact. She waited for him to erupt with full-throated fury at the mention of the Naval Oversight Committee's chairman. But no volcanic activity came, and she pressed on. "He thinks the Justin raid was reckless. For that reason, as well as her lack of seniority, he wants her replaced. He even has a replacement in mind: Vice Admiral Mukerji." She hurried on, hoping to forestall a reaction she expected would cause permanent hearing loss. "Yes, yes, I *know* about Mukerji. He's like . . . well, I can't even come up with a comparison. But one of my more history-minded staffers mentioned somebody named Marshal Bazain. . . ."

"That's actually an insult to Bazain," Antonov remarked with a mildness far more startling than the expected eardrum-bruising roar would have been. "Other names occur to me. General Elphinstone, for one."

Avram was beginning to be alarmed. It was all very well to joke about the limitations of the antigerone treatments. But was the Grim Reaper finally catching up with Antonov? Could he be—God forbid—*mellowing?*

"Well," she challenged, "what do you suggest I do? Given Waldeck's position, I can hardly ignore him."

"No, you can't. But it's a situation you'll have to handle, Hannah. I and my colleagues are responsible for overall strategic direction of the war, but TFN personnel assignments are a matter for the TFN. And, if you really want my advice, that's what you should tell Assemblyman Waldeck: that this is a military decision, best handled within the legally appointed chain of command." Avram's concern mounted, but Antonov continued in the same mild tones. "Of course, there are a few other steps you can take. First, you can light a fire under the board and get Murakuma promoted to vice admiral—it should have been done already, and it will dispose of the argument that she lacks seniority. Second, you can tell Legislative Assemblyman Waldeck that, while the Grand Allied Joint Chiefs of Staff have no intention of meddling in a purely internal TFN matter, you've been assured by the chairman of that body that Terra's allies have full confidence in Admiral Murakuma and would view with concern a change of command at such a crucial juncture. And, third and finally ..." He suddenly grinned, and his high cheekbones squeezed his eyes into slits through which the twinkle was barely visible. "You can tell Legislative Assemblyman Waldeck to fuck himself—if he can find the place to do it, in all that blubber."

Avram had just raised her vodka glass to her lips. Now she spluttered a good portion of the contents onto her lap. "Well," she gasped when she'd gotten her coughing fit under control, "you certainly had me going, you ... you ..." Once again, if for very different reasons, words failed her. "Damn it, Ivan Nikolayevich, you *know* I can't tell him that!"

"Pity. But the important thing is that you keep Murakuma in command of Fifth Fleet." Antonov's eyes took on a distant look. "Believe it or not, Hannah, there have been one or two politicians in human history who weren't total wastes of space. One of them— an American, of all things—was once urged to dismiss a general who'd run up a hefty casualty list. He replied, 'I can't spare this man; he fights.'" Then the grin was back. "You know, I believe I'd like to renew my acquaintance with Admiral Murakuma. And I have a feeling that Kthaara Kornazhovich would like to meet her. I wonder ... yes. After things are running themselves here, I think he and I need to conduct an inspection tour to get a feel for conditions at the front. Don't you?"

CHAPTER FOURTEEN

"This time we *hold*!"

Vice Admiral Vanessa Murakuma stood once more on her flag deck and studied the master plot. *Cobra* floated over five light-minutes from the Justin warp point, surrounded by the mobile units of her newly renamed Fifth Fleet, and she folded her hands behind her as she considered their precise formations of icons.

The promised heavy units had arrived . . . fortunately. Everyone else was euphoric over the success of Operation Redemption, but as one of Murakuma's favorite pre-space statesmen had once observed, "Wars are not won by retreats," and the cost in destroyed and damaged ships—especially the light cruisers screening Reichman's transports—had been excruciating. For all the damage she'd inflicted in return, she was privately certain that if the Bugs had kept coming she would have lost Sarasota, as well.

The thought sent a chill through her, and she closed her eyes. The transports had lifted out every civilian who'd lived to reach an evacuation site, yet she'd not only lost over eight thousand Marines and God alone knew how many Peaceforcers and civilian volunteers but reduced TF 59 to near impotence to save them. In the cold math of a war against a seemingly limitless foe, that had to be counted a questionable bargain, especially when it had left Sarasota so exposed.

She'd confidently expected Sky Marshal Avram to relieve her, and a part of her desperately wished Avram had. None of her staff—except, perhaps, for Marcus—seemed to realize how little she had left inside. Even Mackenna thought she should be delighted by her successful rescue mission, yet proud as she was of her personnel, forty-eight thousand was such a tiny number beside the millions she *hadn't* gotten out. They haunted her dreams, wearing the faces of people she'd known and cared for, and the knowledge that over a hundred million more of them waited behind Fifth Fleet's frail shield weighed upon her soul like a neutron star.

I can't survive another retreat, she thought numbly. *I just* can't. *I have to stop them this time. I tell everyone it's because I'm sure I can do it, but it's a lie. Not confidence—desperation. Dear God, I am so tired of death! And if they knew the truth, if they guessed all my "confidence" and "determination" are no more than a need to evade more guilt even if it kills us all. . . .*

She drew a deep breath and reopened her eyes, staring at the icons once more, seeing the ships beyond them, and her hands fisted behind her. She was stronger than she'd ever been, with a solid core of sixteen superdreadnoughts, nine battleships, twenty-five battle-cruisers, eleven fleet carriers, and seven CVLs, plus their escorts, the five fortresses of Sarasota Sky Watch and the enormous, heavily-armed orbital Fleet Base, and over six hundred fighters. She had minefields, laser buoys, primary buoys, and SBMHAWKs. It was a massive force, as powerful—given the advances in weaponry—as any Terran admiral had ever commanded, yet she cringed whenever she thought of the Bug squadrons she knew were massing against her. By Marcus and Tian's most conservative estimate, the Bugs' losses to date were half again the TFN's *entire* pre-war battle-line, yet each attack force so far had been bigger and more powerful than the last. What *conceivable* kind of navy could absorb that loss rate and keep *coming* like this?

She wasn't fighting a navy. She was fighting an elemental force, something forged in the bowels of Hell to smash anything in its path, and she was afraid. So afraid. Not of dying—death would be welcome beside abandoning still more civilians—but by the hideous conviction that she faced Juggernaut . . . that she would both die *and* fail the civilians she was sworn to save.

She knew she would, but it was knowledge she hid behind the confidence she showed her subordinates, for it was her duty to lie to them and lead them all to death in her hopeless cause.

She heard a sound and drew a deep breath, then turned as Demosthenes Waldeck, Jackson Teller, and John Ludendorff arrived for their conference. Leroy Mackenna, Ling Tian, and Marcus LeBlanc stood behind them, along with her subordinates' chiefs of staff, and she bared her teeth in a cold, confident smile as she checked the bulkhead time display.

"Right on time, I see," she said. Her smile grew broader as they nodded back, and she raised one slender hand to gesture at the briefing room hatch. "In that case, ladies and gentlemen, let's get to it. We've got some Bug ass to kick."

✧   ✧   ✧

Marcus LeBlanc sat in his quarters, fingers occasionally flicking his keypad, but even as his eyes scanned the neat blocks of characters, his mind was less on the ops plan before him than on the woman who'd created it. He came to the end of a section, sighed, and sat back, rubbing his face with both hands, and wrestled with his dilemma.

Vanessa was losing it. He knew she was . . . he simply didn't know what to do about it. No one else seemed to realize the ragged thread by which her stability hung, but they didn't know her as well as he did. Even Mackenna and Waldeck—that ill-assorted pair who worked so closely with her—were blinded by the magnificent job she'd done so far. They knew her pain cut far deeper than she let them see, but like everyone else, they were mesmerized by the losses she'd inflicted on the enemy. By any meterstick, no admiral in history—not just human history, but *anyone's*—had ever wreaked such one-sided havoc on a foe. Their own losses, however savage, paled to insignificance beside the enemy tonnage Vanessa had smashed into glowing wreckage.

Yet none of those other officers were in command, and none of them—except, perhaps, Jackson Teller—could truly understand the crushing psychic wounds her authority had inflicted upon her. But LeBlanc did. He'd seen them growing deeper for weeks, for he was the only one with whom she'd dared drop her mask, and there was so pathetically little he could do. He could only be there, listen, share her pain, try to find some way—*any* way—to ease it. Old feelings he'd thought had transmuted into simple friendship long ago complicated his efforts, yet this was no time to think about such things, especially when it was his job to remain her clearheaded analyst, and so he'd shoved them back down, pretended they didn't exist. But he'd known about her pain.

He saw the ghost of every butchered civilian in her green eyes, felt the despair in her soul, and he knew she was a woman with her back to the wall. One who couldn't—not wouldn't, but literally *could not*—abandon still more people to death. That was the true reason she'd made no contingency plans for a withdrawal this time; because another retreat, however desperately the military situation demanded it, simply was not an option for her.

For *her*, Vanessa Murakuma the woman, not Vice Admiral Murakuma.

He rubbed his face harder, wondering yet again if he should speak to Waldeck. It would be a personal betrayal of someone he'd once loved—*still* loved, if he was honest with himself, or perhaps loved again—but it was also his duty. If Fifth Fleet fought to its own destruction, the Federation would lose not only Sarasota but the entire

Romulus Cluster. Surely his responsibility to prevent that outweighed his loyalty to Vanessa!

But—

The door chime sounded, and he lowered his hands and pressed the admittance button, then snapped to his feet in surprise as Vanessa stepped through the hatch.

"Good evening, Marcus." Her eyes flickered to the ops plan on his display, then back to his face, and she smiled. There was no humor in that smile, and he wondered uneasily what his own expression might have betrayed before he got it back under control.

"Hello, Vanessa," he replied after a moment, and watched her sink into a chair, cross her legs, and clasp her hands on her raised knee while she surveyed him.

"To what do I owe the honor?" He tried to make his voice light and knew he'd failed when her lips quirked again.

"To the fact that you think I'm losing my grip," she said softly, and he winced.

"Vanessa, I—"

A raised hand stopped him in mid-protest, then rejoined its companion on her knee.

"Don't." She sat deeper in the chair, jade eyes dark. "I didn't want to discuss this with anyone, especially you, but you've been watching me too closely. You know, don't you?"

"Know what?" he asked as neutrally as possible.

"Please, Marcus. We've known each other too long for lies."

He winced again at her voice's quiet, infinite weariness, then bowed his head to stare down at his own hands. He longed to pretend he didn't know what she meant, but she was right. They *had* known each other too long, and so he nodded slowly, without looking up at her.

"Why haven't you said anything?"

"Because—" He stopped and inhaled deeply, then shrugged. "I don't know why, really. I'm your intelligence officer. I know what will happen if we lose Fifth Fleet, and this—" he looked up at last and gestured at his display "—is a very good way to do just that if we don't hold them. Vanessa, it's my *duty* to point that out, but—" He shrugged again.

"I thought so," she said so softly he hardly heard her, and stared deep into his eyes for a long, still moment. Then she leaned back, crossing her arms below her breasts, and smiled with a dreadful, aching whimsy.

"Poor Marcus," she murmured. "You know I'm losing my grip, and the officer in you needs to tell someone, but the man in you . . ." She shook her head sadly. "You're a good man, Marcus LeBlanc. Too good to be caught in a disaster like this. But, then, I suppose a lot of good people are caught in it with us, aren't they?"

"Vanessa, please," he leaned towards her, extending one hand.

"You've done a brilliant job. God knows, if anyone in this universe has a right to lose her grip you're her, and I don't want—*God,* how I don't want!—to dump anything else on you. But we both know you're right. You can't take much more of this. You *know* you can't."

"What do you want me to do?" she asked in a bleak, terrible voice. "Request my own relief? Dump the responsibility on Demosthenes? Go back to the rear and say, 'Well, you gave it your best shot, Vanessa. Now let someone else shoulder the guilt'?"

He flinched, then shook his head.

"You're not God. None of this is *your* fault, and, intellectually, you know that. But this battle plan . . ." He shook his head again. "Vanessa, you *can't* stake an entire star cluster's survival on holding them here, not if they keep coming like they have."

"Oh yes I can," she said, and he heard the ring of steel in her deadly-soft voice. "This time we *hold*. Not the Bugs, not the devil, not God Himself, is pushing me out of Sarasota. No more retreats. No more slaughtered children. No more parents who die knowing the Fleet abandoned them. Not this time, Marcus!"

"But—"

"No." She cut him off again, more sharply, and a dangerous fire flickered in her eyes. "I know the risk, but there's a point where 'military logic' becomes irrelevant, and that point is right here, right now. There are a hundred *million* humans in this system, and I won't let these fucking monsters have it while I have a single starship or fighter to throw at them!"

She paused, glaring at him, then drew a deep breath and made her voice calm.

"Oh, you're right—if I dig in to hold to the last ship, I can lose it all, but have you really considered what happens if I *don't* dig in? How many systems can we write off out of 'military necessity' without devastating not only our own morale but our allies', as well? The first Ophiuchi units are only two weeks out, with the first Orions right behind them. We're stronger than we've ever been, reinforcements are on their way, and Remus is right behind us. If we lose that system, we lose the entire cluster, and this is the last place we can stand short of it. If we don't fight to the last ship *here*, what does that say to the *next* CO . . . or the civilians of the next system on the Bugs' list? They just keep coming, Marcus—not like a navy, but like some pestilence or forest fire. You've seen how desperate our people are. You know why they *have* to regard Redemption as a major victory. If they don't, they have to admit it's hopeless, and if we ever admit that, what happens to our will to fight? No." She shook her head sharply. "We have to stop these monsters somewhere, whatever it costs, and that somewhere is here. This time, we *hold*!"

LeBlanc sat back, staring at her while madness edged her voice, and knew, with absolute certainty, that she'd made her decision for all the wrong reasons. All her arguments, however logical, were no more than afterthoughts to her own bleeding need to die before she fell back again. Yet that didn't necessarily make them *wrong*, and he wondered, suddenly, how many of history's great stands had been fought by people who simply couldn't make themselves do anything else. Leonidas and the Three Hundred, Maccabeus and Masada, Zizka and his war wagons, Castle Saint Elmo and the Siege of Malta, Hougemont and La Haye-Sainte, Travis and Bowie, Gordon and Khartoum, Leningrad, the Warsaw Ghetto, First Tannerman, Second Redwing— the list went on and on, and if all too many of those desperate stands had ended in death and defeat, a handful had not. And even the ones which *had* weren't always in vain. . . .

" 'They shall not pass,' " he murmured. Murakuma blinked at him, and he smiled sadly. "From another war, Vanessa. From another war." He cocked his head, and a faint edge of true amusement edged his smile's sadness. "Sometimes it takes a madman—or woman—doesn't it?"

"Am I mad?" she asked with almost childlike wonder, and he shook his head.

"Maybe you are, but your secret's safe with me." Her shoulders twitched with relief, and he smiled again. "Go fight your battle, Vanessa. And, do you know, I think you may be right. We may just hold this time after all."

CHAPTER FIFTEEN

In Good Company

Losses to date, though much higher than projected, were acceptable in light of the systems captured and the size of the Reserve, and the enemy was either far weaker or else so sensitive to losses he was unwilling to press attacks home. Only his technological advantages made him dangerous, and those advantages would not last. Already the first new weapons had reached the Fleet, and the serried ranks of waiting superdreadnoughts would be far more dangerous. No doubt many would still die—probably far more than they killed. But there were far more of them . . . and this time the Fleet knew how to force the enemy to stand and fight.

One moment all was calm in the Sarasota System; in the next a lightning bolt of starships erupted from the warp point. But this wasn't *quite* a simultaneous transit—the Bugs spent all of thirty seconds sending their ships through, which reduced the kills from interpenetration.

Reduced, but did not eliminate, and as alarms wailed and men and women rushed to battle stations, searing explosions announced Juggernaut's arrival as laser buoys and primary platforms added their fury to the blazing cauldron pent within the minefields. Over sixty cruisers were blown apart and a score more were reduced to wrecks, but that left seventy, and Vanessa Murakuma's eyes flicked to the tactical sidebar scrolling down her plot.

Unlike Second Justin, the Bugs had brought along a solid phalanx of those damnable *Cataphracts*. More, they'd held them back, phasing their transits to decrease their losses. It was hard to be certain from this range, but it looked like at least thirty of them had survived. That promised agonizing losses for her fighter jocks, yet the Bugs' failure to send their light units crashing into the mines was almost more ominous.

Assault Fleet had accomplished its mission to secure the warp point. It was unfortunate the enemy had once more declined to deploy within reach of its weapons, but aside from the mines and energy buoys, its cruisers were beyond his range, as well. Courier drones returned to Justin, announcing success, and the superdreadnoughts and their escorts began to make transit.

"Here come the big boys," Mackenna murmured.

Capital ships came steadily, deliberately, through the warp point, like some nightmare pre-space freight train, and Murakuma's belly tightened. Forty. Fifty. Sixty. They kept on coming, flowing into existence in an endless stream of alloy, shields and weapons, and she fought the urge to lick her lips. Every instinct screamed to hit them *now,* but she couldn't contest the warp point without crippling her own fleet too early. She had to let them in, give them room to deploy, and pray her speed and range advantages were enough to stop them once she had.

If you can *stop them,* her mind whispered mercilessly. *If they haven't learned enough, adapted enough. If they haven't figured out some way to offset your advantages. If—*

She strangled the whisper and checked her display again.

The computers were losing track—with so many ships packed into so small a volume mutual interference made it impossible to generate an accurate drive field count—but Plotting estimated there were already ninety-plus Bug SDs in the system, and Fifth Fleet's total order of battle was only a hundred and seventeen ships, twenty percent of them tugs or antimissile escorts without a single offensive weapon. The odds were even more daunting than she'd feared, and she toyed with the seal of her vac suit.

Transit was complete, and the superdreadnoughts and battle-cruisers settled into precise formation while the cruisers advanced into the waiting mines. Pre-war doctrine had assigned that task to the CLEs, but those ships had proven too valuable against the enemy's small attack craft, and two-thirds of them were held back while the remainder, with their more vulnerable consorts, moved forward. Those consorts were easy targets for the hunter-killers, for they lacked the CLEs' point defense batteries, but that had been anticipated. They might kill relatively few mines before they died, but they would draw them down upon themselves, tricking them into wasting themselves on what were, after all, expendable units.

✧　　✧　　✧

"Damn. I expected the mines to do better," Mackenna muttered, and Murakuma shrugged.

"They're still scoring a lot of kills."

"Yes, Sir, but only on cruisers. We're not getting any big boys at all."

"I'll take what I can get." Murakuma's voice was so flat Mackenna looked up in surprise. She was staring too intently into her plot to notice, and he glanced at LeBlanc. The intelligence officer was watching her closely, and the chief of staff felt a sudden stab of worry. Something about the admiral's fixed, unyielding glare and LeBlanc's anxious eyes made him wonder if he'd missed something. LeBlanc knew the admiral far better than he, and if *he* looked so worried—

"They've cleared a lane." Ling Tian's quiet announcement snapped Mackenna's attention back to his own display. "Plotting makes their losses close to ninety cruisers, but they're in, and it looks like they're heading directly for the planet."

"The SBMHAWKs?" Murakuma asked without looking up.

"They've receipted their programming, Sir."

"Good." Murakuma brooded at her plot a moment longer while her thoughts whirled. SBMHAWK replacements hadn't fully replaced Redemption's expenditures, but she'd placed the ninety she had near the warp point. She'd hoped the Bugs would lose more heavily to the mines, but she'd been convinced they'd settle for clearing a single lane. Given the way they "swept" mines, they had little choice; their assault units might be expendable, yet their numbers were finite. Not even Bugs could throw away enough cruisers to clear multiple lanes.

But a single lane would give the SBMHAWKs their best chance. They wouldn't engage as the Bugs passed through it inbound, for there were too many starships out there. The pods relied on saturating an enemy's point defense, and the sheer numbers of targets would spread their fire too thin. But if Operation Thermopylae worked, the Bugs would be in a situation they hadn't faced yet. Despite their losses, they'd taken their objective in every previous battle; if they *couldn't* take this one, even they might withdraw. And if they did, the SBMHAWKs would be waiting on the flanks of the cleared lane. With far fewer targets to spread themselves among, a totally unexpected ambush in what was supposedly a safe zone . . .

A small, savage smile curled Vanessa Murakuma's lips. Something hot and primitive with vicious hate boiled within her, and she embraced it.

"Demosthenes," she glanced at her second-in-command's com image, "are you and John ready?"

"As we can be," Waldeck replied from TFNS *Amazonas*' flag deck.

"All right. We'll go with Thermopylae Four, Jackson." Her eyes flicked to her carrier commander. "Roll them out."

Anson Olivera wished Strikegroup 47 hadn't done *quite* so well last time, and he remembered his favorite instructor from his days at Brisbane. "Old pilots," the grizzled veteran had said, "got that way by never flying with anyone braver than them and *never* letting the brass know how good they really were." Given that Commander Hidachi had earned so much fruit salad it wouldn't all fit on his tunic, Ensign Olivera had figured it was just a line old sweats used to impress newbies. Now he understood. If the brass decided you were really, really good, guess who got dropped into all the deepest crap?

He grimaced and settled himself in his couch. His was the command fighter for the entire first strike, twenty-five full-strength squadrons, and at least he wasn't required to close with the *Cataphracts*. Not yet, anyway.

"All right people," he murmured. "Stay loose. We've got plenty of time to work on them."

No one replied, but he hadn't expected them to, and he punched up his master display as Jane Malachi led Fifth Fleet's first thrust towards the enemy.

Tracking systems locked on, but this time the Fleet knew about the small attack craft's longer-ranged weapons. Only the CLEs configured their fire control for close engagement, for they had point defense and to spare to both kill enemies and stop missiles. All other units reserved their point defense solely for missile intercepts and waited while the attack swept in.

"They're holding course for the planet," Ling Tian reported, and Murakuma nodded. She'd been afraid of that. These creatures clearly made detailed plans, then stuck to them come Hell or high water, and they'd let themselves be pulled after her faster warships in every previous engagement. But that didn't mean they couldn't learn, and they weren't letting themselves be diverted this time. If she wanted to stop them, *she* had to come to *them,* and that meant, sooner or later, that she was going to have to enter *their* engagement envelope.

Maybe I will, she conceded, *but I can sure as hell* bleed *the bastards first.*

She raised her eyes to John Ludendorff's screen. The neatly bearded rear admiral commanded her two least orthodox battlegroups, and he already knew what she was going to say.

"Once the fighters have worked on them for a bit, it's going to be up to your OWPs to open the ball, John. Watch your ammo. If these bastards keep coming for the planet, you may be able to break off and rearm." *Unlike First Justin, where they just kept right on chasing us.* "If they're willing to give us the chance, *I'm* willing to take it."

"Understood, Sir," Ludendorff replied, and she nodded and looked back at her plot. His task group's superdreadnought flagship and six OWPs with their individual tugs moved steadily forward through her formation, settling down on the edge closest to the Bugs, as the fighters streaked towards their targets.

"Here we go, people! Make 'em count!"

Olivera smiled thinly. The bastards must know what was coming this time, but that wasn't going to help them, because none of Olivera's chicks were ever going to enter their range . . . unless, of course, they'd managed to develop the AFHAWK since the last time.

They hadn't. Each squadron volleyed its missiles in a single, synchronized salvo. Not all of their missiles caught their wildly evading targets at this range, and many of those which might have were killed by point defense. But Olivera's attack plan had allowed for that, and he concentrated his entire assault on a mere five targets. He didn't kill all of them, but the two survivors fell astern, streaming debris and atmosphere, and he grinned viciously.

"Good job, troops! We do this good a few more times, and there won't be any of 'em left by supper! Now back to the barn. Let's see what Captain Janowski's strike can do."

Squadron commanders acknowledged and wheeled for their hangar bays, but Olivera knew his blithering optimism hadn't fooled anyone. They were taking the easy kills, clearing the way to the ships they really wanted, but sooner or later they had to go in after the *Cataphracts*, and they'd need FRAMs to get through their point defense.

There were going to be empty bunks in Flight Country tonight . . . lots of them.

Wave after wave of Vanessa Murakuma's fighters launched from just beyond the Bugs' range. It was like watching army ants gnaw at the hide of an elephant or rhino, each taking one more tiny bite without ever threatening its vitals. But every ship killed was one less threat when her battle-line had to close, and even if it hadn't been, the hatred in her soul exulted as she pictured thousands of Bugs withering in flame.

Die, you bastards! The venomous thought crackled in the back of her brain as still another cruiser died. *Goddamn you to Hell,* die!

The range of the enemy's weapons made efforts to withdraw the more vulnerable cruisers deep within the main formation useless. It was impossible to spread the formation far enough to force him into its defensive envelope, but that had been accepted when the plan was devised.

Besides, it wasn't as if those ships were important.

"We've nailed most of the regular CLs and CAs, Sir," Jackson Teller reported. "My evaluation people make it about fifty ships. That leaves the *Cataphracts*. From here on, we'll have to go in after them."

"We'll see if we can't help you out a bit first, Jackson." Murakuma looked at Waldeck and Ludendorff. "Gentlemen, our fighter jocks would appreciate a little assistance."

Five huge, ungainly Type Five OWPs, never intended for mobile warfare, dropped further back in Fifth Fleet's formation, accompanied by their superdreadnought flagship. *Mekong* would probably draw the most fire, but her presence was necessary; only one of the forts carried a datalink master installation, and it was vital that their tugs be brought under their point defense umbrella. But unlike First Justin, four of *these* forts mounted capital missile launchers—a *lot* of launchers: twice as many as a *Matterhorn*-class SD and six times as many as a *Mount Hood*. The command base mounted a primarily energy armament, but the sixth was a pure antimissile/antifighter platform, and that base was tucked into the "battlegroup" closest to the enemy.

The fortress crews knew their jobs, and Plotting had worked overtime to give them precise data. They knew the Bugs had thirty-six of their *Archer* missile superdreadnoughts, and they opened a heavy, deliberate SBM bombardment from beyond capital missile range. Jennifer Husac's ten *Dunkerques* joined them, pouring in their own SBMs, and *Archers* began to die. Not quickly or easily, for they were tough, but steadily.

Murakuma watched them die and bit her lower lip. They were going, but she *still* didn't have enough SBMs to fill her magazines with the longer-ranged missiles. What her ships had now were all they had for the entire battle; once they were gone, it would all be up to the capital missiles, and the Bugs *could* match *their* range.

Husac's BCs exhausted their SBMs and turned to race for the ammunition colliers. The fortresses, with their larger magazine space, didn't. They still had plenty of CMs left, and it was time to start using them.

Ludendorff let the range fall still further and shifted his targeting. The first answering fire spat back from the surviving *Archers*, and Murakuma watched it come. She hated to take her fire off those ships, but she *had* to hammer those CLEs back for her fighters, and capital missiles were the hardest birds to stop. At least some of them would get through even a *Cataphract*'s point defense, especially with salvoes that dense, and—

Four *Cataphracts* died in the opening salvo, but then the first Bug capital missiles arrived, and Vanessa Murakuma went white as one of them got through against a fort. The single hit smashed a twelfth of the OWP's shields flat, and she heard Ling Tian suck in air.

"That was a second-generation warhead, Sir!" The ops officer tried to hide her own shock, but Murakuma knew Ling was as dismayed as she was. God, those bastards were quick off the mark if they'd already figured out how to put AAMs into production!

"Forget the cruisers, John!" she snapped. "Kill as many *Archers* as you can—the fighters are just going to have to deal with the *Cataphracts* themselves."

"Aye, Sir." Ludendorff's voice was grim, for he, too, understood what those warheads meant. Powerful as his forts were, they couldn't stand up to many AAMs—and their tugs could stand even less. Murakuma's plan to kill the escorts so her fighters could go after the Bug missile platforms had just gone out the airlock; she had to nail those *Archers* as quickly as possible.

"Permission to support?" Waldeck asked tautly, and she didn't hesitate. His SDs could stand less damage than the forts, but they carried another eighty launchers.

"Granted," she snapped, and Waldeck's battle-line sped towards the enemy. She was putting it in far sooner than she'd planned, but she had no choice.

The missile ships shuddered under the enemy's pounding, but at last he had to come within their reach, and they poured back fire. Their individual salvoes were lighter, but there were a great many of them, and the new warheads performed exactly as predicted.

Anson Olivera stood in his squadron's ready room, watching dry-mouthed as the ops plan came apart. None of Admiral Ludendorff's forts had been destroyed yet, and the Bugs seemed not to realize that killing the tugs would immobilize them, but the sheer weight of fire was awesome. Point defense intercepted hundreds of missiles, but some got through, and three of the forts had already lost their shields. They'd killed five more *Archers,* but now each hit ripped into their armor. They weren't knocking down shields now; they were killing people and weapons.

A tone beeped, and he turned to the com screen. "Saddle up, Commander," TFNS *Dalmatian*'s captain said grimly. "You're going in."

❖   ❖   ❖

A fort exploded as something reached its magazines, and Murakuma bit her lip so hard she tasted blood. Ludendorff's *Mekong* was shields-down, as well, and she wanted desperately to order him back, but she couldn't. She needed that ship where it was, holding its net up, and—

TFNS *Mekong* blew apart. There were no life pods. There was barely even time for her automatic transmitter to begin her Omega transmission. One instant she was there; the next she was an expanding cloud of plasma, and her datanet went with her.

"Get them out!" Murakuma barked, but it was too late. Stripped of their interlinked antimissile defenses, not even Type Five OWPs could stand that battering. Missiles ripped down on targets now totally reliant on their own, individual defenses, and she watched sickly as two tugs and a fort exploded. Life pods littered the display, proving at least some of their people had gotten out in time, but *Mekong*'s entire battlegroup died within two minutes of its command ship, and Vanessa Murakuma closed her eyes in agony.

"Shall I order the other battlegroup to withdraw?" Ling Tian asked quietly, and instinct screamed to say yes, but Murakuma shook her head.

"No," she said flatly. "They went for *Mekong* because they could pick her out. Unless they get the command fort by sheer coincidence, they can't knock her net down."

She didn't look up from her plot, but she felt her flag bridge crew's eyes on her, and her soul cringed from what she might have seen in them had she looked.

Fifth Fleet's fighters launched. The big fleet carriers held back a small reserve, but every other fighter went. SG 47 led the wave, and Olivera watched his tactical feed from *Dalmatian* as seven hundred and fifty fighters screamed towards the enemy. Only fourteen *Archers* remained in action, though three more had fallen astern, yet the Bugs had wiped out over half the OWPs, and the battle-line had taken a battering of its own. As Olivera watched, TFNS *Borah* pulled out of line, limping away with half her launchers out of action, and two more superdreadnoughts bled atmosphere. The remaining *Archers* were hurting, too—they *had* to be—but Bugs didn't break off. They went right on firing until they died, and they were hurting Fifth Fleet badly.

But not for much longer, Olivera told himself grimly. He and his people were going to take savage losses, but they had the strength to kill the bastards, and—

He blinked as a sudden cascade of tiny lights speckled his display. What in God's name—?

✦　　✦　　✦

"Sir! The Bugs have just launched small craft!"

"*Small craft?*" Murakuma stared at Ling Tian in surprise, then looked at LeBlanc.

"Yes, Sir. We've got over two hundred *cutters* coming at us." Ling sounded as confused as Murakuma felt, but LeBlanc's face tightened in instant, instinctive understanding.

"Kamikazes," he said flatly. Murakuma looked at him blankly for a moment, then paled. If those cutters were loaded with antimatter—

"Divert your strike, Jackson!" she snapped, wheeling to Teller's com screen.

"But, Sir, the *Archers*—"

"Get the cutters! We think they're kamikazes!"

"Kami—Dear God!" Teller whirled to his own com officer, and Murakuma slammed a fist down on her command chair's arm. The Bugs could not have launched at a worse time. She *needed* those fighters to take the pressure off Demosthenes, and it was terribly tempting to send them on in. After all, her ships were designed to kill fighters; their defenses ought to have a field day against *cutters*! But she didn't know how much antimatter could be crammed aboard. They didn't have much cargo capacity, but they wouldn't *need* a lot, either.

Olivera's jaw clenched as *Dalmatian* changed his mission. *Kamikazes?* No one had used them since ISW-3! But they should have guessed the *Bugs* would, and he started snapping orders.

The small craft fanned out, spreading far and wide. If they could get through to their targets, well and good, but it would be almost as satisfactory if they simply diverted the enemy's more capable attack craft. And that was precisely what they were doing.

The battle-lines' fire grew more vicious as the wounded survivors smashed one another in an orgy of mutual destruction, and Murakuma knew the exchange was in the Bugs' favor. If they destroyed Waldeck's missile-armed SDs, even at the cost of every one of their *Archers*, they won the round, for aside from Husac's battle-cruisers, they were the *only* heavy missile ships she had.

The massive fighter strike had dissipated in wild confusion as its squadrons raced after the suspected kamikazes, and she swallowed a curse as she checked the large scale plot of the entire system. The Bugs were driving straight for Sarasota. They hadn't reached it yet, but they would.

"*Korab, Kerintji* and *Toubkal* are Code Omega, Sir. *Borah* and *Apo* have disengaged successfully, but they're out of it. Only one missile fort is still in action."

"Understood. The Bugs?"

"Seven *Archers* left, Sir. They're all damaged; we don't know how badly."

"Admiral Husac?"

"Rearmed and returning. ETA seventeen minutes."

Murakuma nodded and looked back up at Waldeck's com screen. "Pull the SDs back. We'll have to let Husac handle them."

"Agreed." Waldeck's voice was as bitter as her own thoughts.

"Can what's left of John's command get free?"

"I think so. They don't have much firepower left anyway."

"Then pull them out. We might as well save *somebody*," she said harshly.

"Sir, it's not your fault," Waldeck said quietly. "No one could have—"

"Just pull them out, Admiral," Vanessa Murakuma said flatly, and turned away.

The battle raged on. The Fleet's missile ships were gone, but the enemy had suffered heavily. All his missile superdreadnoughts and five of his battle-cruisers had been driven out of action or destroyed. Neither side now possessed an extended-range missile capability, but the Fleet retained a solid core of forty-eight superdreadnoughts, screened by twelve battle-cruisers . . . and if the enemy wanted to engage them, he would have to come into their range.

Murakuma paced savagely about her briefing room. The Bugs had been reduced to a bare third of their initial strength over the last seventy-nine hours, but that third was still coming. Her fighters had hunted down all but four of the cutters, and those four had been easily picked off by her starships' defenses, but the huge fireballs as they died confirmed Marcus' suspicion. Only heavy loads of antimatter could account for them, yet knowing she'd been right to divert her fighters made her feel no less a murderer. She'd left her missile-armed battle-line to fight unsupported, and it had been battered into uselessness, and the fact that it had done the same to the Bugs' missile ships was scant comfort, given how damned many *other* SDs they had left.

She took another turn around the compartment, like an exhausted, goaded animal. She'd battered the Bugs viciously, slashing in with coordinated fighter strikes and pounces by her short-ranged missile ships, but they were still *coming*, and—

The admittance chime sounded, and she whirled towards the hatch. For one moment, her lips drew back in a snarl, but then she closed her eyes and drew a deep, shuddering breath.

"Enter," she said flatly, and Marcus LeBlanc stepped into the briefing room.

The intelligence officer looked worn and worried, but unlike her, he'd actually managed a few hours' sleep, and she wanted to curse him for the concern in his eyes. Concern for her.

"Well?" she said sharply.

"I—" LeBlanc shrugged. "Tear my head off if you want, but someone has to say it. You need rest."

Murakuma opened her mouth to flay him, but then she made herself stop and turned her back, fists clenching as she stared at the holo display above the conference table.

The planet Sarasota hung there, and her exhausted, bloodshot eyes clung to the huge Fleet Base in orbit around it. That base was as heavily armed as twenty superdreadnoughts. Against any rational foe, she would have backed it to handle every battered capital ship still headed for it, but if even a single Bug superdreadnought managed to penetrate its defenses and ram, it would die.

"I *don't* need rest," she grated. "The stims are holding."

"Like hell," LeBlanc said. "Damn it, Vanessa, you're killing yourself!"

"Why not?" Hysteria edged her jagged laugh. "That's what I'm best at, killing people."

"It's not your fault! Damn it to hell, you're not *God!*"

"This discussion is closed." She wheeled back to him, and he recoiled from her raw fury.

"No it isn't." He tried to keep his voice calm and rational. "Someone has to say it, and none of the rest of your staff will—"

"I said it's closed! Or do you need a little brig time to remind you what a direct order is?!"

He opened his mouth again, then closed it. She truly meant it, he realized shakenly.

"All right," he said finally, his tone leached of all emotion. "But whether you're willing to rest or not, you have to make a decision. You've done a hell of a job, but they're still coming, and for all we know, there's a hundred more SDs right behind them."

"There aren't," she said flatly. "If there were, they'd already have called them forward."

"Why?" he shot back. "Because *we* would?" He barked a laugh. "The one thing I can tell you for absolute certain is that these things sure as *hell* don't think like we do! Maybe they're expending this entire force just to grind us up so they can send in a reserve for the kill!"

"No." She shook her head so violently she had to catch herself on a chair as her exhausted body staggered. "No, this is it. All they have. And they're not taking this system away from me."

"It's over, Vanessa," he said softly. "No one could have done more, but it's over."

"No it isn't." She shoved herself back upright and glared at him. "But—"

"*It isn't over!*" He stepped back involuntarily as she shouted at him, and then she stormed past him onto the flag deck. He followed quickly, mind racing for some argument, *any* argument, that might get through to whatever rationality remained under her exhausted desperation.

"Get me Admiral Teller," she told her com officer, and turned to the screen as Teller's face appeared. "How many fighters do we have left?" she asked without preamble.

"About two hundred, plus the Fleet Base's group. Call it three hundred."

"Call the base's fighters forward. We'll stage them through your bays."

"That will leave the planet without any fighter cover," Teller began, "and—"

"I know that. Just do it—now."

Teller's eyes widened. She saw them dart over her shoulder, as if seeking someone else, and deliberately stepped between him and LeBlanc. The movement wasn't lost on the other admiral, and after a moment, he nodded.

"Yes, Sir," he said quietly. "May I ask what I'll do with them once they arrive."

"You may." Murakuma punched a stud, bringing Demosthenes Waldeck's worn face up on another screen, and faced them both. "Demosthenes, we're calling in the base's fighters. Once they've arrived and our own groups have had time to reorganize, activate Leonidas."

Waldeck's face stiffened, and, for just an instant, she felt the protest hovering behind his eyes. Leonidas was the last-ditch option, a headlong attack into the enemy. It had been devised as a contingency plan, one to be activated only after the Bugs had been decisively weakened, and she recognized his desperate concern for his battered battle-line. His remaining ships were heavily out-massed by the surviving Bug superdreadnoughts, and Leonidas would commit them to a fight to the death within the enemy's weapons envelope.

"Sir, are you certain about this?" he asked quietly.

"I am. I know they outmass us, but they're hurting, too. And they don't have any fighters. You'll coordinate with Jackson and we'll go in together, fighters in tight. We'll hold them there till we're into energy range, then throw them in the bastards' faces."

It was a council of desperation, and she knew her subordinates knew it, but Waldeck said nothing for a moment. And then, to her exhausted astonishment, he nodded slowly.

"It might just work," he said, and Leroy Mackenna looked up from his console in disbelief as the Corporate Worlder nodded again.

"It better," Teller said grimly. "We won't have anything left to try again if it *doesn't*."

"Sir, have you considered waiting just a little longer?" Ling Tian asked hesitantly. "We're still wearing them down, and—"

"And they're wearing *us* down," Murakuma cut her off. "The odds aren't going to get any better, and we can't let things that use starships for projectiles get close enough to ram the base."

"We won't be in any shape to stop a follow-up attack, Sir," Waldeck cautioned, but his tone was that of a man considering all options, not a protest.

"We'll worry about that then," Murakuma said flatly. "Now let's get moving."

" . . . and that's the plan," Anson Olivera told Fifth Fleet's three surviving strikegroup COs. Given the plan he'd just briefed them on, he didn't expect to survive much longer . . . and neither did they. It was against the fighter jock's code to ever sound less than breezily confident, however tough the mission profile, but all four of them were having trouble pulling it off this time.

"That's *it*?" Lieutenant Commander Beachman asked. "We just go right down their throats with the battle-line and shoot anything that moves?"

"That's it," Olivera confirmed, and managed a thin smile as the other three stared at him. "The battle-line will be shooting the whole way in, so how can we predict which targets'll be left for us? There's no way to set this one up neatly. We'll be tied into the Flag for the approach, and Admiral Murakuma's staff will try to give us targeting updates, but no one can guarantee that."

"Jesus," Beachman muttered, shaking her head. " 'Go shoot a superdreadnought—*any* superdreadnought.' They never put *that* one in the Brisbane syllabus! We're going to have all kinds of targeting conflicts. What if we screw up and mob three or four of them and let the others by us? We're going to lose command and control the instant we mix it up with these bastards. What are our squadrons supposed to do if we can't even tell them who to go after?"

"I asked Admiral Murakuma more or less the same question," Olivera agreed.

"And she said?" Commander Liracelli asked.

"She paraphrased an ancient wet-navy order." The others looked at him blankly, and he actually felt himself smile. "She said, 'Something must be left to chance. No pilot can do very wrong if he fires on the enemy.' "

"Sounds like the prelude to the biggest cluster-fuck in history," Beachman grumbled. "Who the hell ever gave an idiot order like that?"

"Horatio Nelson," Olivera told her. "And if it worked at Trafalgar, it might even work here."

Vanessa Murakuma looked up as a shadow fell over her console, and her mouth tightened. Marcus LeBlanc looked at her for a long silent moment, and she hunched an impatient shoulder.

"We're going in in ten minutes," she said. "If something's on your mind, say it quick."

"I was just thinking about the fellow you named this operation after," he said quietly.

"Leonidas? What about him? Or—" her eyes hardened dangerously "—is that a not so subtle reference to what happened to *him*?"

"I suppose it was," LeBlanc said in that same, quiet voice, "but not the way you're thinking." He saw the surprise in her exhausted eyes, and under it he saw the grim death grip she'd fastened on herself. The absolute, total determination—the *fanaticism*, for that was the only word which truly fitted now. He looked down at her for a moment longer, and then he squeezed her shoulder gently, oblivious to all the flag bridge's watching eyes.

"'Go, stranger, and to the listening Spartans tell, that here, obedient to their laws, we fell,'" he quoted softly. "Whatever happens, you're in good company." He squeezed her shoulder again. "God bless, Vanessa."

"And you, Marcus." She smiled, and somehow that gentle smile looked completely right on her exhausted, warrior's face. Then she nodded at his console. "Take your station, Captain."

"Aye, aye, Sir." LeBlanc slid into his couch, and as he adjusted his shock frame, he heard Vanessa Murakuma's voice—a voice that had somehow shed its exhaustion and uncertainty and fear.

"All units, this is the Flag. The Fleet will advance!"

CHAPTER SIXTEEN

"We're going back."

The Orion cutter drifted through the monopermeable force field into TFNS *Cobra*'s boat bay, and Vanessa Murakuma watched it settle to the deck, then nodded to the lieutenant who headed the side party.

" *'Ten-shun!*" The side party snapped to attention as the cutter's hatch opened into the squeal of bosun's pipes, and Murakuma offered up a silent prayer that someone had warned her guest, for Orion hearing was far more acute than Terran. She had no idea how a bosun's pipe might sound to a Tabby, but she suspected it didn't sound *good*.

If it didn't, the tall, tan-furred being who stepped from the cutter gave no sign of it. Fifty-Sixth Fang of the Khan Anaasa'zolaath, Khanate of Orion Navy, was well into his seventh decade, but there was little silver in his pelt. His jeweled metal harness flashed with what seemed barbaric splendor, but the furred Tabbies, who went unclothed in normal environments, invested all the effort humans expended on tailors on their metalsmiths, and by Orion standards, Anaasa's harness was downright modest.

The Orion came to his race's version of attention and touched his right hand first to his *defargo* honor dirk and then to his chest in salute until the pipes stopped wailing, then spoke. It sounded like an angry, basso-profundo tomcat to Murakuma, but the translator listening in over the boat bay intercom whispered through her earbug.

"He asks permission to come aboard, Sir."

"Permission granted," Murakuma said clearly, and the big Tabby smiled the polite, teeth-hidden smile of his carnivorous race and yowled something else.

"He says thank you, Sir."

Anaasa stepped forward, extending his right hand in the human

496

gesture of welcome, and she took it. She'd tried for years to acquire at least enough mastery of Orion to understand it—as Anaasa had obviously mastered Standard English, given his lack of any earbug—but her tone deafness had defeated her. But it hadn't kept her from learning all she could about Orion culture, and Anaasa's smile broadened as she squeezed his right hand, then raised her left, fingers clawed, and slapped her nails lightly against the side of his face. His own hand came up, needle-sharp (and still highly functional) claws bared, and brushed her own cheek with equal care. Once that exchange had been quite different, with each warrior slashing his claws in with all the speed he could and stopping at the last possible instant. It had been a tremendous loss of face to draw blood, but an even greater one to flinch from the strike, and the Tabbies had lost more than one high-ranking officer to the duels clumsy greetings had inspired. That was why Liharnow the Great had insisted his warriors adjust to more civilized ways a hundred and fifty Standard Years ago.

"In the name of my government and people, Fang Anaasa," she said clearly, "I welcome you to Sarasota. The speed with which your Khan has met his treaty obligations does honor to him, who sent you, and to you, who have come."

"Honor comes to he who acts with honor," Anaasa yowled back through her translator. "When *farshatok* call, their war brothers must answer, for if my claws guard not your back, whose claws shall guard mine?"

Murakuma bowed, then gestured politely for Anaasa to accompany her to the intraship car. The Tabby padded gracefully along at her side, silent in the open-toed sandals his people wore in place of the TFN's boots, and his shoulder-wide whiskers quivered with interest as his bright eyes compared *Cobra* and her company to his own battle-cruiser flagship. The two of them stepped into the car together, and Murakuma felt as if an enormous weight had been partly lifted—not completely, but partly—from her shoulders as she pressed the button.

The rest of Fifth Fleet's senior officers and their staffs rose as Murakuma and Anaasa entered the briefing room. There were more of them now, and she felt a pang as she looked at the woman beside Demosthenes Waldeck. Rear Admiral Carlotta Segram was a fine officer, but she'd stepped into John Ludendorff's slot, and every time Murakuma looked at her she saw an expanding cloud of gas she should have withdrawn sooner.

She gave herself a savage mental shake, banishing the image, and walked to the head of the table with Anaasa. It was fortunate that the Tabby was junior to Demosthenes Waldeck but senior to every other Allied officer present, for his five fleet carriers, eight battle-cruisers, and five heavy cruisers were the largest Allied contingent yet to reach Sarasota. More, the Khanate of Orion was the Federation's only true peer as a Galactic Power, and his rank made him the natural commander for her third task force—which was good, since TF 53 would consist entirely of *his* ships. In a way, she would have preferred to integrate his units into her other two task forces, but the Tabbies' datalink wouldn't interface with the TFN's.

The same was not true, fortunately, of Rear Admiral Saakhaanaa's Ophiuchi ships, for the Ophiuchi Association Defense Command's units were specifically designed to fight in joint TFN-OADC battlegroups, and Murakuma glanced at Saakhaanaa as she and Anaasa seated them-selves. The Ophiuchi and his staff were the tallest people in the briefing room, but they probably weighed no more than Ling Tian. Murakuma guessed they *did* outmass her own low-grav-adapted body, though it couldn't have been by much.

She finished seating herself and smiled as she watched Anaasa and Saakhaanaa project matching airs of physical comfort neither felt. Orions preferred a damper, more humid—and warmer—climate, while Ophiuchi preferred drier worlds. Orion atmospheric pressures also ran well above Terran norms, while the Ophiuchi preferred lower-grav worlds with proportionately lighter pressures. Ophiuchi could survive aboard Orion ships, and vice-versa, but neither could have functioned efficiently there, whereas humans could adapt to either. And, as this widely assorted gathering demonstrated, both allied races could adapt to Terran conditions. In a way, she mused, that summed up what made her own species so successful. Both Ophiuchi and Orions did some things better than humans, but Man remained the known galaxy's ultimate generalist.

"Thank you all for coming," she said, and knew her alien allies recognized the stark, simple honesty of her gratitude. "With your help and the fortifications being emplaced on the Justin warp point, I now feel confident of holding Sarasota against any fresh offensive. Indeed, we may be in a position to take the battle to the enemy at last."

A small stir ran around the table, and she flicked a sidelong glance at Marcus LeBlanc. Only he, Mackenna and Ling Tian had known she intended to say that, and she knew he retained strong reservations. The tension between them had eased, but he was still unconvinced she truly had herself back together. *And,* she admitted, *he may have a point. But all I can do is the best I can do.*

She returned her attention to her assembled officers.

"Since you've just joined us, Fang Anaasa, I felt we should begin with a complete briefing. I realize you've seen our reports to GHQ, but the Centauri System's far enough back there's bound to be some com lag. More to the point, this will give you a chance to ask any questions which may have occurred to you en route. Please feel free— as should all of you—" she added, eyes sweeping over the other officers "—to stop us at any time for clarification or expansion. It's essential that we develop a firm, shared appreciation of the situation, and I welcome any input from a perspective other than my own."

She paused until Anaasa and Saakhaanaa indicated assent, then gestured to LeBlanc.

"Captain LeBlanc, my intelligence officer, and Commander Ling, my operations officer, have prepared a brief for us. Captain LeBlanc will begin with what we have so far learned, deduced, and guessed about the enemy, after which Commander Ling will update us on our own strength and deployments. Captain LeBlanc?"

"Yes, Sir." The captain activated a holo unit, and the image of a charging Bug warrior, captured on a Marine's zoot scanners and firing on the run, appeared above the table. Murakuma felt Anaasa tense beside her and heard a faint hiss as he bared his fangs in instant, instinctive challenge. *Interesting. He seems to react to it exactly the way* humans *do. And so did Saakhaanaa, the first time* he *saw the imagery. I wonder how much of that stems from what they know about the Bugs' actions and how much of it is just plain instinct?*

"This, ladies and gentlemen, is an Arachnid," LeBlanc began in his most clinical tones, and Murakuma leaned back in her chair to listen.

"I still think you're pressing too hard." LeBlanc's voice was carefully professional, and Murakuma felt the effort with which he strained all personal feeling from it. It was hard on both of them, and she wondered if she'd been right to request him in the first place. He was undoubtedly the best man to have at the sharp end of this particular intelligence stick, but was he the right intelligence officer for *her*? They meant too much to one another for either to listen to the other with total, detached professionalism, and it was a source of tension which wore upon them both.

"I realize that," she said, and looked at the others she'd invited to this small, private meeting. LeBlanc and Mackenna were the only staffers present, but Waldeck, Teller and Anaasa, as her task force commanders, and Saakhaanaa, as Fifth Fleet's senior Ophiuchi, sat in chairs designed for their respective species. Saakhaanaa nibbled on a *sharkü* stick, crunching the dried, jerky-like delicacy quietly, and Anaasa nursed a flagon of *chermaak*, the spicy, slightly alcoholic beverage his race used instead of coffee and beer alike, while Demosthenes—in what was undoubtedly the most bizarre habit of all—puffed on a black briar pipe. At least he'd been careful to place himself directly under a ventilator and as far from Anaasa's sensitive nose as possible!

"I realize that," she repeated, keeping her own voice neutral, "but perhaps we *need* a little pressing. So far, they've lost almost two hundred SDs, and even *they* have to run out of capital ships eventually. But how can we know if they have unless we at least probe for information?"

Saakhaanaa cocked his head in an Ophiuchi gesture of agreement, but his eyes narrowed. That indication of curiosity was one of the few expressions his race and humanity shared, and she wondered if he wondered why she was arguing with a mere intelligence officer. The TFN didn't usually do that, and he knew it. Anaasa, on the other hand, seemed completely at ease. Well, it wasn't unheard of for even a junior member of an Orion commander's staff to argue violently with him. It must make staff meetings lively, but the Khanate's size was proof it worked.

"I agree their losses are catastrophic by the standard of any other race we've ever met," LeBlanc conceded. "At the same time, they appear almost totally insensitive to casualties. The way they didn't even attempt to break off here in Sarasota is the clearest possible indication of that. And because they are, I must stress again my belief that they must have an enormous reserve strength. We, on the other hand, while substantially reinforced, *also* suffered heavy losses, and we're unlikely to see any additional large reinforcements for another two or three months. If we lose still more ships and the enemy *isn't* running out of superdreadnoughts—"

He shrugged, and Murakuma nodded, hiding her wince at the words "heavy losses." Leonidas had stopped the Bugs, but the cost had been as dreadful as she'd feared. By the end, Fifth Fleet had lost seven hundred fighters, three out of five OWPs (with the others so shattered Fortress Command had written them off rather than rebuild them), eight superdreadnoughts, twelve battle-cruisers, and over thirty percent of its screen. Demosthenes' surviving battle-line had been battered into near impotence, and only Teller's carriers—with a bare hundred fighters embarked—had escaped undamaged.

She'd known, as she surveyed her shattered command, that Marcus had been right. If the Bugs had put in a second attack—even a weak one—they would have rolled right over what was left of Fifth Fleet. *But they* didn't, *and that's the point. If they'd had them to put in, they* would *have.*

"Captain LeBlanc has a point," Mackenna said diffidently. "With the new mines and energy buoys—not to mention the OWPs—we've got a mighty strong stopper in the bottle. If we move into Justin, we expose ourselves to heavy starship losses we can't really afford, but if we wait another sixty days, enough additional heavy stuff will arrive to mean we *can* accept losses."

"And while we wait," Murakuma said very quietly, "anyone left in Justin is being eaten."

Mackenna winced, and LeBlanc shut his mouth firmly as he heard the echo of her desperate guilt, but Anaasa looked up from his *chermaak*.

"You raise an important point, Ahhhdmiraahl," he said while her earbug translated. "We are warriors. It is our function to protect and defend civilians, whatever race those civilians may belong to, against such menaces as the Baahgs."

"Exactly!" Murakuma looked at Waldeck and raised an eyebrow. "Demosthenes?"

"Of course it is," the Corporate Worlder said simply. "Captain LeBlanc and Commander Mackenna have both raised valid arguments, but the bottom line is that if we have the firepower to take the battle to the Bugs, we clearly have to do just that. *If* we have the firepower."

"And do we?" Murakuma challenged.

"I don't know," Waldeck said frankly. "Captain LeBlanc's right about the implications of their willingness to take losses, but you have an equally valid point in their failure to try Sarasota a second time when they have to know how close they came the first time. Certainly no Terran—or Orion or Ophiuchi—" he added with a courteous nod to the two aliens "would give an opponent any longer to fort up than he had to when he knew he'd had him on the ropes before. Under the circumstances," he tilted his head back for a moment, then shrugged, "I'd have to come down on your side of the analysis. But, as you say, the only way to *know* is to go look."

"Admiral Saakhaanaa?" Murakuma asked.

"I am forrrced to agree withhh Admiral Waldeckk," the Ophiuchi said. "Ifff we can take the warrr to the Buggsss, we mussst do ssso."

It was odd, Murakuma thought, that different as all their vocal apparatuses were, all of them could manage a form of "Bug" that was at least recognizable.

"In that case, I think we can consider the decision made," she said, and met LeBlanc's eyes with a hint of challenge. "Leroy, please inform Tian that Operation Salamis is a go. Gentlemen, we're going back to Justin!"

CHAPTER SEVENTEEN

"I saw what I wanted to."

Captain Anson Olivera frowned at the reports on his terminal. His new promotion should have taken him out of a cockpit. Normally, a fighter jock had to move onto something more "important" than squadron or even strikegroup command to advance beyond commander, but the Navy had decided to take a page from the Tabbies' book. The Orions—arguably the best (and certainly the most enthusiastic) strikefighter practitioners—were far less rigid in their personnel career tracks, and it wasn't uncommon for an Orion pilot to reach the rank of small claw or even claw—roughly equivalent to a TFN commodore—while still drawing flight pay. Indeed, the present Lord Talphon had made it all the way to small fang before they pried him out of a cockpit, though that was a special case.

Olivera grimaced. It irked him to admit it, but the Tabbies were better than Terrans at fighter ops. For that matter, they were better even than the Ophiuchi. Their equipment wasn't—in fact, it wasn't as good—and their individual pilots were less capable than Ophiuchi. But unlike the TFN, the KON was uncompromisingly carrier oriented. The Federation Navy was a "balanced" fleet in which the battle-line and carrier forces were coequals. That had proven a lifesaver on occasions when carriers accidentally strayed into range of enemy capital ships, and carriers were ill-suited to things like warp point assaults. They were meant to stay away from hostile starships while their fighter "main batteries" went out and killed the enemy, not to mix it up with capital ships, minefields, or energy buoys. That sort of silly operation was the purview of the battle-line.

The Tabbies didn't see things that way. For them, the only truly honorable form of combat was between *individuals,* which had made

502

the fighter a gift from the gods for them. Unlike the TFN, the KON relegated the battle-line to a purely supporting function except in warp point assaults. The fighter was *the* decisive weapon for the Khan's fangs, one they'd learned to wield with more *élan* and skill than any other navy in space, and Olivera suspected the seniority their active-duty pilots could attain was a major part of the reason.

Admiral Murakuma seemed to agree. She and Admiral Teller had reorganized their carriers on a distinctly Orion pattern, and that was why Olivera and what was left of SG 47 had moved to the carrier *Orca*, flagship of Carrier Division 503. Admiral Teller had opted to retain the battle-cruiser *Sorcerer* as his flagship, but Admiral Rendova, his second-in-command, flew her lights in *Orca*, and she'd wanted Olivera where he was handy, because Ms. Olivera's little boy Anson had just become the TFN's first *farshathkhanaak*. The Orion term translated roughly as "lord of the war fist"—a somewhat poetic way to describe an entire task force's or fleet's senior pilot. Except in purely administrative matters, Olivera's group and squadron COs reported to *him*, not the skippers of whatever carrier they happened to fly from. He would not only lead them in combat but represent them at the highest levels, and unnatural as it seemed, he had almost as much clout on the ops end as Admiral Teller did.

Which was all very well, but didn't change how expensive those ops were proving. Fighter jocks always had lower combat life expectancies than battle-line personnel, but the glitz and glamor of the deadly little strikefighters kept attracting the hot dogs—like, Olivera admitted, himself—anyway. And from a cold-blooded viewpoint, it made sense. A fighter squadron consisted of only thirty or forty people, including alternate flight crews, and fighters were cheap compared to starships. Any group CO sweated blood to bring all his people back every time, but fighters were fragile, ultimately expendable weapons, and the people who flew them knew it.

Oh, yeah, we know *it,* Olivera thought grimly, *but we've taken at least eighty percent losses in every battle to date except Redemption, and sooner or later these bastards are going to come up with their own AFHAWK. Nobody who's ever tried to penetrate their close-in defenses is dumb enough to think they're* stupid, *whatever their SOP looks like. They know how badly they need a long-ranged fighter killer, and once they develop it, we're going to get hurt even worse.*

He shook his head irritably. Of course they were getting hurt, but that was largely because of the odds they faced! Doctrine called for using numbers to saturate the enemy's defenses, and they hadn't been able to do that . . . yet. But Fifth Fleet now boasted the most powerful carrier component assembled in sixty years—since the First Battle of Thebes—and there were enough long-ranged heavy hitters in the battle-line to take a lot of pressure off them. He wasn't going to indulge in any foolish optimism, but—

He inhaled deeply, shook himself, and returned to his paperwork. One way or another, they'd learn how effective those changes were in about forty-seven more hours.

Vanessa Murakuma stood on *Cobra's* flag bridge, hands clasped behind her, and watched the master plot. Demosthenes and Jackson were exasperated with her for retaining her battleship flagship now that sufficient superdreadnoughts were available, and she understood their frustration. A battleship was a fragile place for a fleet commander to fly her lights, but *Cobra* had been her flagship for over two years. Her tactical and plotting departments were a smoothly functioning extension of her own staff, and she wasn't about to spend the time breaking in a new flagship in the midst of a campaign this furious.

Besides, we've taken less damage than any other capital ship in the fleet. Who was it who said "I'd rather be lucky than good"? Her mouth flickered in a small smile at the thought, but then the smile vanished and her eyes narrowed. It was time.

The Justin warp point's environs had changed drastically in the last two months. The huge Fleet Base had labored—was *still* laboring—to repair her damaged units, though the worst hurt ones had been sent further up the line. But while the Base's yard modules dealt with her warships, hordes of construction ships were busy assembling powerful, prefabricated OWPs drawn from Fortress Command's peacetime stockpiles. They'd put them together well away from the warp point and any pounce the Bugs might engineer, but now a solid shell of twenty had been towed into position. Another ten were almost ready, and still more were being thrown together at top speed. Coupled with the dense minefields and energy buoys which were finally available, they had the firepower to handle even one of the Bugs' simultaneous transits. Even if she couldn't retake Justin, it would no longer be necessary for her to concede the warp point.

But at this moment, her attention wasn't on the forts or minefields. It was on thirty-six tiny icons, each representing a single pinnace. A lot of the volunteers crewing those small craft were about to die, but she *had* to have some idea of the Bugs' deployment, and until the R&D types got off their asses and put the promised warp-capable recon drones into production, those pinnaces were the only way to get it. If she threw enough through in a single transit, the odds said at least one or two would get back with the data she needed.

She brooded over the plot, watching the clock tick down, and bit her lip, hating herself for what she had no option but to do. She and her staff had assembled ten different ops plans, each predicated on a different Bug deployment. Ten minutes after the surviving pinnaces returned and uploaded their data, one of those plans would go into effect.

Forty-eight heavy cruisers floated amid the minefields. There might have been more, but the enemy's last attack had proved he could destroy them any time he chose, and the Fleet had decided not to expose additional units. But that had not deprived the cruisers of a mission, and they waited to perform it.

A sudden shoal of small craft sped out of the warp point. A few interpenetrated, but most survived, and they swept outward while augmented sensor suites probed the warp point's environs. The mines ignored such small, agile targets, as did the laser buoys seeded among them, but the ready-duty cruisers opened fire instantly. Another half dozen pinnaces died, but the range was long, they were difficult targets, and the heavy cruisers were far too slow to pursue them. They could only engage any foolish enough to enter their envelope, and over half the pinnaces survived to dash back through the warp point to safety.

The cruisers watched them go. They had done their duty . . . and the trap was set.

Ling Tian waited patiently. She knew *Cobra's* Combat Information Center would upload the information as soon as all the pinnaces' reports had been collated, and she forced her face to remain serene while she waited.

Ah! Her display blinked, and a forest of light codes appeared. Her trained eyes skimmed them quickly, and she allowed a small smile to flaw her serenity.

"We've got the first run, Sir," she called. Admiral Murakuma walked towards her, and she went on speaking. "We make it forty-five to fifty of those OWP cruisers right on the warp point, with another, larger force just over one light-minute out. They seem to be in standby mode."

"Numbers?" Murakuma rested a hand on Ling's shoulder and bent over her display.

"Even with their sensors augmented, that's long range for pinnaces, but we've got a tentative count. It looks—" Ling punched a button and watched the sidebar change "—like forty-two SDs and forty-five to fifty CLs. We can't pick the *Cataphracts* out at this range."

"Any breakdown on the superdreadnoughts?"

"Negative. We can't tell an *Archer* from an *Avalanche* until they bring up their systems."

"True." Murakuma rubbed her lip, but her green eyes flamed. She'd been right—they *had* hurt the bastards badly. Only forty-two superdreadnoughts and *no* battle-cruisers . . . no *wonder* they hadn't put in a second attack on Sarasota! Fifth Fleet had only twenty-five SDs of its own, but she had eight battleships and almost fifty battle-cruisers to support them. Even without any fighters at all, *she* finally had the force advantage.

And I do *have fighters,* she thought viciously. *Over a thousand of them!*

She nodded sharply and turned to the screens linking her to her task force and battlegroup commanders. "It looks like their dispositions are tailor made for Salamis Four," she said crisply. "Demosthenes, we're transmitting the target profiles now. Update your birds; we'll go through on their heels, and I want to hit them before they can redeploy!"

The heavy cruisers which had been at standby brought their systems to full readiness. It would do no good in the long run, but if the enemy were cunning enough to send through more pinnaces as observers, he might wonder why they didn't even attempt to defend themselves.

Eighty SBMHAWKs flashed into Justin. The defenders poured fire into them, and killed nineteen before they could launch, but sixty-one *did* launch, and three hundred-plus SBMs roared down on the cruisers. Point defense stopped almost a quarter of them; the other two hundred and thirty reduced forty-three heavy cruisers to glowing wreckage.

The five Bug survivors were drifting, toothless hulks when the first Terran starships came through, but they hadn't been the warp points only defenders. Laser buoys attacked instantly, and the first three ships were ripped and torn. Massive armor blew apart, atmosphere fumed into space, and men and women died, but superdreadnoughts were tough. They survived, and they'd drawn all the buoys' onto themselves. Undamaged consorts moved past, already firing AMBAMs into the mines, and TFNS *Antifola*, *Erciyas* and *Hsinkao* turned to limp back into Sarasota while damage control and rescue teams fought to save trapped and wounded crewmates.

Their battle had lasted all of ninety seconds.

Murakuma set her teeth against the nausea of transit, then waited impatiently for her plot to steady. *There!*

She peered into it, and her eyes burned hotter. The Bug battle-line was only beginning to move in on the warp point, and all of Waldeck's TF 51 had already made transit. They were still bunched within the confines of the mine-free zone, but the AMBAMs were doing their job, and Demosthenes' lead battle-cruisers were already probing forward through the lanes. Battleships and superdreadnoughts moved in their wakes, and she bared her teeth as the Bugs suddenly stopped advancing. They hung there for a moment, and then they began to fall back. They fell *back*. They were retreating! For the first time in eight months, the bastards were *retreating*.

"We've got them," she whispered. "By God, this time we've *got* them!"

"The enemy appear to be withdrawing at maximum speed, Sir." Ling Tian couldn't have heard Murakuma's whisper, but her confirmation was perfectly timed, and the admiral heard her ops officer's own exultation behind the professionalism of her report.

"They can run, but they aren't fast enough to hide," Murakuma said flatly, and looked at Waldeck's com screen. "Go get them, Demosthenes! Jackson can follow at his best speed. With a little luck, he'll be ready to send in his first strike about the time your SBMs range on them."

"Aye, *aye*, Sir!" Waldeck's smile was almost as hungry as her own, and Fifth Fleet's battle-line went to maximum power as it thundered after its slower foes.

Jackson Teller prowled TFNS *Sorcerer*'s bridge deck like a caged Old Terran tiger while the rest of Fifth Fleet pursued the Bugs. He had even more reason than Waldeck to even the score. He *wanted* their asses, wanted to watch them die, wanted to be there personally when they paid for the civilians they'd butchered. And he *would* be there. It took time to pass thirty carriers and light carriers, seventeen battle-cruisers, and their escorts through a warp point, but his slowest unit was twice as fast as a Bug superdreadnought, and his fighters were even faster. He'd catch the bastards, and then he and Demosthenes would kill every fucking one of them.

His last unit made transit, and he turned to his com section as his task force started through the cleared lanes. Captain Olivera looked tense but eager on the small screen linked to the cockpit of his command fighter, and Teller bared his teeth as their eyes met.

"Launch your birds, Captain. Get the recon fighters out to cover the flanks, then take your strike forward. With any luck, we'll finish these things off in a single pass."

"Sir, that sounds good to me," Olivera agreed, and switched to his command net. "All units, we will launch in succession. Launch order Alpha One. I say again, Alpha One."

Acknowledgments came back, and then *Orca*'s catapult kicked him in the belly.

Teller watched the first fighters appear on his display. Under emergency conditions, he could have flushed full decks and put every fighter into space in a single launch, but there was always a risk of collision when carriers in close company did that. The congestion of the cleared lane through the mines only made that worse, and he had plenty of time, so—

"*Incoming fire!*" someone screamed. "Missiles in acquisition, bearing one-seven-three, zero-two-seven! Impact in seventeen seconds—*mark!*"

Teller wheeled to *Sorcerer*'s master plot, and his face went white. Dozens of missiles, scores—*hundreds!*—of them had just appeared out of nowhere. They must have been launched from cloak, and now they streaked in from dead astern—*straight out of his blind spot!*

"Expedite launch!" he shouted. "Get them off—*get them off!*"

His carrier commanders tried to obey, but the missiles were coming in too fast, and Teller's face went even whiter as he realized those were SBMs. The Bugs had *SBMs,* and that was why they hadn't been spotted. Because they'd been able to hide in cloak further from the warp point than anyone had suspected and still engage.

His *Dunedin*-class CLEs swung wildly to open their broadsides. If they could get around, acquire clear tracking data, his carriers could still engage the incoming fire with datalinked point defense. But there wasn't time for *that,* either. Just one of his four heavy carrier groups managed to acquire; the other three were defenseless as the missiles shrieked in, and only the accuracy penalties imposed by the extremely long range at which the Bugs had fired saved any of them.

Fireballs ripped through TF 52's heart. TFNS *Airedale* and *Beagle* blew apart, and four thousand men and women—and seventy-two priceless fighters—went with them. More ships staggered as the missiles screamed in, and *Coachdog, Dalmatian,* and the Ophiuchi carriers *Zirk-Bajaamna* and *Zirk-Kohara* died. And then a massive salvo roared down on *Sorcerer,* and she and her entire company—including Vice Admiral Jackson Teller, TFN—vanished in an incandescent cloud of gas.

"Dear God." Vanessa Murakuma's whisper hung in her own ears as the Bugs massacred her carriers. They were seventy light-seconds astern, far beyond any range at which she could intervene, and the frantic crackle of battle chatter washed over her as men and women fought for survival. Three of the *Dunedins,* still maneuvering hard in an effort to get their point defense into action, strayed into the minefield and were blown apart, but at least some of her ships were managing to defend themselves against the last few salvoes.

"A decoy." She turned her head, green eyes shocked, and saw savage comprehension on LeBlanc's face. "Those fucking CAs were *decoys*—Judas goats! They *wanted* us to blow our way in over them. They *deliberately* sacrificed fifty cruisers for *bait!*"

Horror crackled in his voice, and a detached corner of Murakuma's brain realized why. He'd stressed the Bugs' willingness to take losses over and over, like some stuck recording. If anyone in Fifth Fleet had grasped that point, it was he . . . yet the minds of beings who could condemn fifty starships and their crews to death simply to lure an opponent into ambush were too fundamentally inhuman, in every sense of the word, for even Marcus to have seen this coming.

And I didn't either. I saw what I wanted to see. I saw them running, and I saw a chance to kill them, and I took it, and, oh, dear God, how many of my own people have I just killed?

"Sir, the first force is turning back. They're coming in to engage!" Ling Tian, alone, seemed unaffected. She wasn't. She was simply doing her duty—burying herself in it to escape her own horror—but Murakuma wanted to spit curses at her. The admiral clenched her fists and shook herself savagely. Somehow she had to get her people out. She was an incompetent, little better than a murderer, but she was still in command, and she reached out to the terrible weight.

"Com, prepare to record for courier drones," Vanessa Murakuma said, and her soprano voice was calm, almost even.

The Fleet achieved only that single, devastating firing pass before the enemy managed to adjust formation. His lighter escorts swung around, tacking back and forth across his bleeding formation to clear their sensors, and despite his surprise, his point defense knocked down the follow-up salvoes with relative ease. But the fire had concentrated on the ships that carried his attack craft. Most were damaged, one was an immobile hulk, and ten had been destroyed outright. At least half the attack craft had been destroyed in their launch bays, and the Fleet charged forward, still cloaked. It would overrun the warp point and crush the cripples, then cut the rest of the enemy off from retreat.

Fifty-Sixth Fang of the Khan Anaasa'zolaath raged about his flag deck like a wounded *zeget*, and officers flinched aside as he swept down upon them, claws flicking in and out, in and out of their sheaths in a combat instinct he could not overcome. Sixty thousand years of instinct screamed to rush to his human commander's aid, but her own orders held him here, waiting. He understood her reasoning, and even in his fury a part of him felt enormous respect for her cool calculation, but every dragging minute tore at him like white-hot pincers.

"Sir, the pods—"

He wheeled with such a furious snarl Claw Renassaa recoiled. The fang's ears flattened with shame at his ops officer's response, and he fought himself back under control.

"Yes, Renassaa?" He made the words come out calmly, and the claw straightened.

"The pods have been programmed, Sir," he said, and Anaasa gave an approving ear flick.

"Good, Renassaa. Good." He rested a clawed hand lightly on the other's shoulder for a moment, then forced himself to walk slowly to his command chair. He settled himself in it and leaned back, for there was nothing else he could do.

The three worst damaged of Teller's surviving CVs were also closest to the warp point. They managed to turn and run, trailing atmosphere like blood. More missiles screamed in on them, but they vanished back to Sarasota before the warheads struck. TFNS *Lexington* was less fortunate, and the helplessly crippled light carrier vanished in another eye-tearing boil of fury.

The rest of TF 52's survivors were too far from the warp point; they could only run towards TF 51 at the best speed they could still manage. *Sorcerer* had died, but at least the rest of their command ships had escaped, and the nets were still up. As long as any member of any net could track the incoming fire, they could defend against it, and Admiral Ellen Rendova's *Orca* led them as they ran desperately for the doubtful cover of the trapped battle-line.

Damage reports flooded *Orca*'s command deck, and Rendova winced at the litany of disaster. Two-thirds of her fighters had been destroyed in their bays or were trapped aboard ships too damaged to launch them, and the Bugs had SBMs. Fifth Fleet's range advantage had been stripped away, and without her fighters to redress it—

"Got 'em, Sir!" She whirled to her ops officer. Commander Houston stared into a display tied to the recon fighters sweeping back along the incoming missiles' tracks for the enemy turn. She saw his shoulders tighten, and then he looked up at her. "Seventy of them, Sir," he said. "Twenty-four battle-cruisers and forty-six superdreadnoughts. Looks like only twelve are *Archers;* most of that first wave must have come from the others' XO racks."

"Position?" Rendova snapped.

"They'll reach the warp point in six minutes," Houston said flatly.

The force TF 51 had been pursuing had turned. It was sweeping back, and already its first SBMs crossed with Murakuma's. *At least we've still got better point defense,* she thought bitterly, but that was her only remaining advantage, and it wasn't going to be enough against so many launchers. She could still take the first group of Bugs, but they'd beat Waldeck's battle-line to scrap in the process, and then that second force would sweep up the pieces.

But only if I let them! she told herself fiercely, and looked up at Waldeck's com screen.

"Ready, Demosthenes?"

"Yes, Sir." The burly Corporate Worlder managed a grim smile. "I sure hope this works."

"It'll work—I just don't know how well." Murakuma made herself draw a deep breath, buttressing herself against guilt and despair while her flashing brain rechecked her desperate plan for flaws. She found none—but, then, the situation was too grim for complicated maneuvers.

"Very well, Demosthenes. It's up to you. Bring us about."

The enemy's battle-line reversed course, rushing back to succor its wounded companions, and that was the stupidest thing he had done yet. He was faster than the Fleet. He should have run for it, drawn out of range, tried to maneuver his way around *the defenders, instead.*

His new course was headed directly for the warp point, as if he thought he could blast his way through the waiting superdreadnoughts and battlecruisers, but he was wrong. Com lasers whispered across the gulf between the Fleet's separated battle-lines, and the second component slowed. It would move just past the warp point, maneuvering to stay between the enemy and his only way home, and wait until its fellows drove him into its tentacles.

Anson Olivera gathered his battered strikegroups astern of the carriers. He didn't know exactly what Admiral Murakuma planned, and the thought of leading his pilots into that much firepower turned his belly to lead, but he knew she had no choice, and his earlier thoughts about expendability jeered at him. If the destruction of every surviving fighter got even a single division of superdreadnoughts out of the trap, the exchange would be completely worthwhile . . . which wasn't much comfort for the human and Ophiuchi pilots about to sacrifice themselves.

The pursuing Bugs swept past the warp point and slowed. They came to a halt, backs to the warp point, targeting systems tracking his fighters, and he swallowed. He sat tense and still, waiting for the order, and a corner of his brain noted the courier drones flashing past him.

"Fang Anaasa!" Anaasa looked up at his com officer's shout. "The drones!" the officer said sharply, and Anaasa bared his fangs.

"*Go!*" Olivera's command crackled over the net, and two hundred fighters streaked straight down the Bugs' throat. Every one of those pilots knew—didn't think; *knew*—he or she was going to die. But they were doomed anyway, and they rammed their power through the emergency gate, for if they had to die, at least they could kill a few more enemies first.

Olivera's vision grayed as Malachi took them in at a velocity so far beyond design limits he couldn't believe the bird was holding together, and he bared his teeth—then jerked in surprise, despite the crushing power of the drive, at Carl Hathaway's shriek of delight.

"Beautiful! Oh, *beautiful!*" the tac officer screamed. "Look at 'em, Skip! *Look at those fucking Tabbies go!*"

One moment, the second Arachnid force had the situation completely under control; the next, an insane explosion of violence ripped into it as TF 53—the *Orion* task force the Bugs had never seen, never suspected had been held back—flashed through the warp point into its rear. No one in the galaxy was better at fighter ops than the KON, and Fang Anaasa's deck crews set a new all-Navy record for launch speeds. Two hundred and ten fresh fighters charged straight up the Bugs' blind spots as *their* missiles had charged up TF 52's, and they weren't alone, for the SBMHAWKs Murakuma hadn't used in her initial bombardment came with them. There'd been no need to use them to kill a mere fifty cruisers; now seventy fresh pods belched missiles into the astonished Bugs, and the fighters screamed in behind them, ripple-salvoing their FRAMs.

It was the most devastating fighter strike in history. Twenty Bug superdreadnoughts were blown apart in sixty shrieking seconds, and eighteen battle-cruisers went with them. Almost every surviving ship was damaged, many badly, and the Tabby pilots closed in, accepting brutal losses from the survivors' point defense to strafe with their onboard lasers. Less than forty seconds later, Anson Olivera's fighters came howling in from dead ahead, taking their own losses but slamming a fresh wave of FRAMs down the Bugs' throats.

The twin strike couldn't kill them all, but it hurt them, and the ships which had lured Murakuma into pursuing them had fallen too far astern of TF 51 to help them. Demosthenes Waldeck's battle-line flashed past TF 52's wounded carriers, and *Rendova's* ships reefed around in the hairpin turns of inertia-canceling drives to follow in their wake. But it was up to the heavies to clear the way, and Waldeck and Vanessa Murakuma took them straight into the Bugs' teeth as though *superdreadnoughts* were so many more fighters.

It was insane, a violation of every manual ever written . . . and the only path to salvation. Every one of Anaasa's carriers and battle-cruisers was within the Bugs' weapons envelope; if TF 51 *didn't* close, they would be annihilated, despite the shocking damage they'd inflicted, and Murakuma *had* to break through before the Bugs pursuing her could overhaul. The enemy knew it, too, and detached his faster cruisers in a desperate bid to assist their fellows on the warp point. But the cruisers had to get past TF 52, and Rendova launched her surviving escorts into them in a savage, short-ranged hammering match that kept them off Waldeck's back . . . at a price.

Yet furious as that fight was, it was a sideshow, and Murakuma sealed her helmet as TF 51 slammed into the Bugs. Launchers went to sprint-mode, spitting standard missiles and the heavier, far more destructive, CM-sized close assault missiles. Answering fire smashed back, and *Cobra* heaved as fists of flame hammered her shields flat. Force beams, primaries, plasma guns, hetlasers, and Ophiuchi particle beams snarled at ranges as low as eight hundred kilometers, and armor ripped like tissue. Damage alarms screamed, two of her superdreadnoughts blew apart, a Bug battle-cruiser rammed a Terran battleship head-on, two more battleships vanished in massive fireballs, and then something smashed into *Cobra* like the hammer of Thor. She felt her flagship heave, heard the scream of escaping air, saw Ling Tian torn in half by a flying axe that was once a bulkhead. And then something exploded into the side of her own command chair, and her universe vanished in an instant of agony too terrible to endure.

The last Bug superdreadnought blew up under the fire of three Terran superdreadnoughts and sixty fighters, and TF 51's survivors turned at bay. They faced the remaining enemy force, holding it off until the last damaged carrier made transit. Of the five hundred fighters which had actually launched, two hundred and six escaped aboard Anaasa's carriers and the only three unhurt Terran CVs, and then the rearguard retreated to Sarasota, still smashing sullenly at its foes.

Eight superdreadnoughts, seven battleships, fourteen battle-cruisers, eleven carriers, five heavy cruisers, and eighteen light cruisers remained behind forever.

"M-Marcus?" Vanessa Murakuma didn't recognize her own hoarse whisper, but Marcus LeBlanc bent over her instantly. She lay under crisp sheets, staring up at a pastel overhead, and she could feel nothing from the waist down.

"Hi," LeBlanc said softly.

"T-Tian?" she whispered, and he flinched. Then he shook his head gently, and she turned away in agony. Her tears blotted the pillow, but LeBlanc's gentle fingers cupped her chin, making her turn back to him.

"You got them out, Vanessa," he said quietly.

"But how many?" Her voice was stark and wounded, her green eyes dark, bottomless wells of pain, and he blinked his own eyes as tears stung.

"More than anyone else could have," he said. Her mouth twisted, and he bent lower over her. "Damn it, Vanessa, it's true! All right, they suckered you. Well, they suckered me, Waldeck, Teller, Anaasa—even Tian! *No one* could have seen that coming . . . and no one *else* could have gotten us out of it. Don't you *dare* think otherwise, or . . . or—"

"Or what?" She expected it to come out with savage bitterness, but to her astonishment it came out soft, almost chiding.

"Or as soon as you're out of that bed, Sir, I'll put you over my knee, peel down those trousers, and whale the living shit out of you!" he told her fiercely, and a soft ghost of a laugh gurgled in her throat. Her eyes softened, and she raised an arm which felt far heavier than even a full standard gravity could account for to touch the side of his face.

"Oh, Marcus," she whispered. "I should have listened to you, love."

"Why? You thought I was arguing just because I was worried about *you* . . . and I was," he admitted. He sank into a chair and caught her hand as it started to fall, cradling it against his cheek. "I guess maybe that's why Regs frown on people who love each other in the same chain of command, isn't it?" he said gently.

"Maybe. But you were still right."

"It's my job to be right, and sometimes I manage it. But it's *your* job to win battles, not take counsel of your fears. Or mine." He smiled and stroked red hair back from her forehead.

"How bad is it?" she asked after a moment, gesturing at her lower body with her free hand, and he smiled again.

"It looks terrible," he said frankly, "but the doctors are delighted with themselves, and they say you should be up and around again within six or seven weeks. You'll have to take it easy for quite a while, but you're going to be fine, Vanessa. Really."

"Well, at least I'll have time to 'take it easy,' " she said with a trace of bitterness, and he raised an eyebrow. "Come on, Marcus! You *know* they're going to relieve me after *this* fuck-up!"

"You have a strange way of describing a battle in which you kicked the bad guys' ass, Admiral Murakuma," LeBlanc said, and she snorted her opinion of his judgment. "No, I mean it. The Bugs lost a hundred and thirty-nine ships. That's a better than two-to-one ratio in hulls, and the tonnage balance was even more decisive. Sky Marshal Avram is very pleased with you—and she's going to be even more pleased when she hears what happened yesterday."

"Yesterday?" Murakuma repeated blankly, and he nodded.

"The Bugs tried to bounce Sarasota. I guess they figured they'd hurt us badly enough to make it easy, and they brought up reinforcements. But Demosthenes and Leroy—and, Lord, how I *wish* you'd seen that pair working together!—got reorganized with Anaasa and put Leonidas Two into operation exactly as you'd planned it. They lost every cruiser and the first twenty-five SDs that tried to follow." His eyes blazed, and he stroked more hair from her forehead. "They broke off, Vanessa! You finally stopped the bastards so cold they *knew* they were licked!"

"You mean Demosthenes did," she whispered, but her own eyes glowed, and LeBlanc shook his head.

"Woman, you aren't allowed any more doubts. After all—" he grinned wickedly "—that's why *I'm* here, right?"

She laughed again, softly, and then he bent still closer and kissed her.

CHAPTER EIGHTEEN

"Welcome along, Sir."

The powered walker whined softly as Vanessa Murakuma "walked" from the intraship car into the boat bay. The muscle feedback-controlled walker was less responsive than the direct neural-feed prosthetics used to replace lost limbs, which made her progress more than a little clumsy, but she wasn't complaining. She didn't *want* permanent replacement parts, however efficient, and the surgeons promised her legs would be good as new in time. They were talking about six months, though she intended to make it in four, and this wasn't even the first time she'd had to use a walker, for her home world prepared its people poorly for the planets most humans lived on. She'd spent three years exercising her Truman-bred muscles before reporting to the Academy, but New Annapolis' 1.25 gravities had still been a hideous ordeal. The medical staff had insisted she stick with the walker for her first semester, and the aching cramps protesting a body weight sixty percent greater than the one she'd been bred to had made her perfectly willing to obey.

Now she maneuvered herself into position in TFNS *Euphrates'* boat bay and tried to suppress a pang of grief for her last flagship as another cutter docked. *Cobra* had been luckier than many of Fifth Fleet's ships, but she'd still taken a fearsome pounding. She'd only returned to service last week, and two-thirds of her tactical department were squeaky-new replacements for men and women who'd died in Justin. Murakuma no longer had a logical reason to oppose shifting her lights to one of the better-protected *Mekong*-class SDs—and, she admitted, she no longer wanted to. Seeing all those new faces in place of the ones she'd come to know so well . . .

She shook off the thought as a hatch opened and the side party's

516

two separate honor guards—one of Terran Marines, gorgeous in black-and-green dress uniform, and a second of even more gorgeously bejeweled Orion Marines—snapped to attention.

The first person through the hatch was a human. He was of little more than average height for his race, but despite the snow-white hair and beard, he radiated a sense of purposeful mass which made him seem much bigger. His Orion companion's night-black pelt was liberally threaded with silver, yet the Tabby carried himself with a springy predator's grace, only slightly stiffened by age. No one, however, would have described the human as "graceful." He certainly wasn't *clumsy*, but he moved with a burly, unstoppable momentum which dared any object to intrude into his path . . . and promised no quarter for anything foolish enough to accept the challenge.

"Grand Fleet, arriving!" the intercom announced through the twitter of the bosun's pipes, and *Euphrates'* captain nodded to the side party.

"Preeee-sent, *arms!*"

The barked command was in Standard English, since *Euphrates* was a human ship, but both Marine contingents snapped to their version of present arms with the simultaneous precision of careful practice. A corner of Murakuma's eye noted the perfection of the maneuver, yet her attention was focused on the two visitors as they saluted the Federation banner on the boat bay's forward bulkhead, then turned to salute Captain Decker as well.

"Permission to come aboard, Sir?"

"Permission granted, Sir," Jessica Decker said.

The visitors crossed the line on the deck, formally boarding the ship, and Murakuma's walker whined as she stepped forward and saluted.

"Admiral Antonov, Fang Kthaara. Welcome to Fifth Fleet."

"Thank you, Admiral Murakuma." Antonov's deep, bass rumble hadn't gotten any frailer since his retirement. She'd met him several times during her stint as a War College instructor, and she felt a bit odd addressing him as "Admiral," since he'd been Sky Marshal at the time.

"It's good to see you again," Antonov went on, and waved a hand at the tall Tabby. "I don't believe you've met Lord Talphon?"

"No, Sir." Murakuma turned to the Orion with a polite, tooth-hidden smile of greeting. Ninth Fang of the Khan Kthaara'zarthan, Lord Talphon and *Khanhaku'a'zarthan*, had been a pilot's pilot in a service where the fighter reigned supreme. He was also the ninth ranking active-duty officer in the Khan's service and almost as legendary—in TFN service, as well as the KON—as Antonov himself, and Murakuma's small, Orion-style bow of greeting was deeply respectful. "I've certainly heard a great deal about you, however, Sir.

I'm honored to meet you at last, and my carrier pilots have asked me to extend their invitation to a small party aboard *Orca*. I believe they want to offer you an, ah, traditional welcome to the Fleet."

The big Tabby's whiskers twitched as he gave her a small, answering bow of acceptance.

"I would be honored, Ahhhdmiraal," he yowled as her earbug translated, "although a warrior of my advanced years may find it somewhat difficult to do full justice to their invitation."

"Ha!" Antonov snorted derisively. "No doubt they'll offer you bourbon or some other anemic substitute!"

"No, Sir," Murakuma murmured. "Least Fang Anaasa has informed us Lord Talphon prefers vodka, and I understand a suitable supply has been laid in."

"*Khorosho!* Good! Perhaps we'll civilize our flight crews yet!"

"We'll certainly try, Sir," Murakuma agreed, then waved towards the intraship car. "In the meantime, I've asked the Fleet's senior officers to assemble in Briefing Room Three. If you and Fang Kthaara would care to accompany me—?"

"Of course, Admiral." Antonov nodded briskly to the side party and honor guards, and he and Kthaara adjusted their pace to that of Murakuma's walker as they crossed to the waiting car.

Murakuma steered the walker into her cabin and allowed herself to sigh with relief as the hatch closed behind her. She worked her way behind her desk, maneuvering carefully in quarters designed for people with two good legs, and parked at her terminal. That was the only word for it. Handy as her artificial suspension was, it was a pain to climb in and out of, but at least, she reminded herself with a weary grin as she brought up Fifth Fleet's current order of battle, it was also the right height to let her work at her desk without a chair.

Just as well, too. The way the paperwork keeps piling up, I'll be stuck here for hours. Don't think I'll complain, though. The problems I've got now beat the crap out of the ones I had two months ago!

She studied the order of battle with deeply grateful satisfaction, for despite the reaming her command had taken in Third Justin, she was stronger than ever before, and the trickle of reinforcements flowing down through the Romulus Cluster was about to become a torrent.

We did it, she thought almost wonderingly. *We actually did it. We held the bastards long enough for the Alliance to get organized . . . and now*—her face turned suddenly grimmer—*it's time to turn this thing around and kick their asses the hell out of Justin!*

She ran her eyes down the OB. Additional units had come up from every Allied navy: Terran, Ophiuchi, Orion—even the first Gorm ships.

She was particularly glad to see the latter, for the high tactical speed of Gorm starships made them especially valuable. More to the point, perhaps, the GSN had the furthest to come to reach Sarasota, and the arrival of its first units had been an enormous shot in the arm for Fifth Fleet's morale.

Not that their contribution was solely symbolic. Fifth Fleet now counted over a hundred and twenty starships, headed by eighty-one capital ships (including six GSN superdreadnoughts and five GSN battle-cruisers) and supported by nineteen fleet and eight light carriers. Its Task Force 54—commanded by the newly promoted Rear Admiral Reichman since his return to active duty—consisted of twenty-nine massive fortresses, with almost eight hundred fighters embarked, and still more forts were under construction. Fifth Fleet's mobile units could put over nine hundred more fighters, almost half of them Orion, into space, and for the first time, Vanessa Murakuma was absolutely confident of her ability to stop any Bug offensive cold.

But the point isn't to stop them, she reminded herself, green eyes momentarily bleak.

She studied the numbers a moment longer, then punched a combination into her com panel, and the screen lit almost instantly with the face of a painfully young female lieutenant.

"Intelligence, Lieutenant Abernathy," the young woman announced, then stiffened to a sort of seated attention as she recognized Fifth Fleet's CO. "How can I help you, Admiral?"

"Is Commodore LeBlanc there?"

"No, Sir. He's in CIC."

"Would you ask him to join me in my quarters? I'd like to see Captain Mackenna and Commander Cruciero, too. Please run them down for me and ask them to accompany him."

"Of course, Sir."

"Thank you." Murakuma cut the circuit and leaned back. Antonov's decision to inspect the front meant he and Lord Talphon would be looking over her shoulder, but both of them had earned reputations as aggressive, hard-hitting COs in the Theban War, and nothing indicated they'd changed since. She was confident she could convince them to authorize the operation . . . assuming she could convince her own staff she hadn't lost her mind.

"You want to do *what?*"

LeBlanc hadn't raised his voice. In fact, he sounded more resigned than incredulous, and Mackenna simply sat back in his chair with a sigh. Commander Ernesto Cruciero, Ling Tian's replacement as Murakuma's ops officer, was another matter. His hawk-nosed, dark face was well suited to concealing strong emotion, yet he couldn't quite hide his shock. He looked back and forth between his seniors for a moment, then cleared his throat.

"Excuse me, Sir," he said diffidently, "but we don't know a thing about what the Bugs are doing on the other side of the warp point, and we *do* know at least one of their major systems is far closer to Justin than we are to our own core systems. Given the fleets they've thrown at us so far, don't we have to assume they must have reinforced at least as strongly as *we* have?"

"Certainly," Murakuma agreed, and smiled thinly at the commanders expression. "I understand your point, Ernesto, but the transit times for our reinforcements—and theirs—aren't going to change. If we decide we can't risk action as long as they can reinforce faster than we can, we'll never take the offensive at all."

"No doubt, Sir," Mackenna put in, "but our first responsibility has to be keeping them out of Sarasota, not battering ourselves against *their* defenses."

"Agreed." Murakuma nodded, but there was no give in her expression. "That's why we have TF 54 and the minefields covering the warp point. The purpose of fixed defenses, however, is to *free up* mobile forces, not anchor them in place. With Admiral Reichman to mind the store, we can afford to take some chances with our striking force—and I remind you all that there are still Terran civilians trapped in Justin. If our first responsibility is to protect Sarasota, surely our next highest obligation is to save as many Justinians as we can."

Mackenna and Cruciero glanced at each other. There was no possible counter for that argument, but clearly they both remembered Fifth Fleet's last venture into Justin. Murakuma watched them for a moment, then looked at LeBlanc.

"Marcus?" Her tone was neutral, but she held his eyes, and, after a moment, he shrugged.

"Leroy and Ernesto both have valid points, but so do you. And while I agree that they've probably reinforced even more heavily than us, there's an element no one else has mentioned." He sounded like a man who didn't like the point he was about to make, but he made it unflinchingly. "We may have the technological edge, but we've already seen how quickly these things put both second-generation antimatter warheads and SBMs into production. Since they had neither when they started shooting ten months ago, the fact that they have them *now* indicates their R&D is quick off the mark. Which—" he looked at Cruciero "—means that the longer we wait, the more chance there is of losing our current advantages, and that would put pressure on us to hit them as quickly as possible even if they were only in a position to *match* the tonnage we can deploy."

"So you think we should attack?" Murakuma pressed.

"No—I only think we *have* to," he said unhappily. There was a moment of silence, and then Mackenna twitched his shoulders.

"Marcus is right, Sir," he said flatly. "I shouldn't have let myself overlook that aspect."

"But even if they *do* duplicate our systems, they still have to put them into production." Cruciero's tone was respectful but persistent, and Murakuma noted it with approval. She didn't know him well yet—Mackenna had selected him while she was still in hospital—but he'd already demonstrated his competence, and it took courage for a commander to argue against the united opinion of an admiral, a commodore, and a captain. That was good. The last thing she wanted was an ops officer who rolled over and played dead.

"Maybe so," Mackenna said now, "but we can't afford to mirror-image them. We know how long it takes *us* to introduce new hardware, but they may be faster. Worse, we don't know how far their R&D has to go, and we won't know they've closed the gap on us—if they do—until they get around to using any new systems against us. That means we have to hit them as hard as we can while we do hold the edge. And, as the Admiral says, we've got an obligation to take Justin back while at least some of its people are still alive."

Cruciero sat back, eyes hooded, then nodded, and Murakuma hid a sigh of relief. They'd come around more quickly than she'd expected, and she suddenly wondered why she'd thought they wouldn't. Was it a leftover from the terrible pressures of her retreat to Sarasota? Or was it because *she* knew how dreadfully Fifth Fleet could get hurt in Justin? Had she been projecting her own inner doubts onto her staffers?

She shook the thought aside and leaned towards them.

"All right, then. Marcus, I want you and Leroy to bring our appreciations and projections up to date. I know they're all tentative, but they're all we've got to work from. Once you've done that, I want the four of us to work out several rough ops plans. I don't need a lot of detail yet, but I want something tangible in hand before I sit down with the Allied COs. I don't expect anyone to question the necessity of the operation; I only want a clear, definite basis for discussion."

"With your task force commanders, or with Admiral Antonov?" LeBlanc asked with a slight smile, and Murakuma looked at him innocently.

"Why, Marcus! Whatever makes you think I'm concerned by the Admiral's presence in our midst?" Her subordinates chuckled, and she smiled back. "All right, gentlemen—go put it together. I want your preliminary efforts on my terminal by 0900 tomorrow morning."

"A most audacious plan, Admiral Murakuma."

Ivan Antonov's deep voice was thoughtful as he gazed at the holo

above the conference table. Ernesto Cruciero may have had his doubts
about Operation Navarino, but the half-dozen alternative ops plans
he'd put together were impressively aggressive and made maximum
use of the Alliance's tactical advantages. Now Antonov studied the
display, conscious of the eyes watching him with carefully hidden
tension . . . and of the youth behind those eyes. Even Murakuma was
less than half his age, and the near veneration of her younger staffers made him uncomfortable. That unquestioning sense of awaiting
the oracle's response was one of the reasons he'd retired in the first
place. The antigerone treatments, unlike flashy gadgetry such as
reactionless drives and faster-than-light travel, had changed the human
condition in a fundamental way—the first such change since convenient contraception had broken the immemorial link between repro-
duction and sexual jollies. Now, a species selected by evolution to get
out of the way of its adult children had the dubious blessing of living fossils like himself, as though Black Jack Pershing had lived on
to command Operation Desert Storm.

On the other hand, he reminded himself, *perhaps a Pershing who'd
kept himself technologically current wouldn't have been such a bad thing.
At least he'd have had the experience to know what happens when you
call a campaign off early!*

He shook the thought aside and used a light pencil to highlight
the transport echelon which the holo showed following in the wake
of Fifth Fleet's warships.

"I don't recall GHQ's having provided you this many Marines,
however," he rumbled mildly. "According to this, you're planning on
using a full corps—just over thee divisions."

"We are," Murakuma agreed, and nodded to Mackenna.

"We've checked the numbers, Admiral Antonov," he said confidently,
"and we can make them up if we strip the Fleet Base, comb out all
our shipboard Marine detachments, *and* combine Terran and Orion
Marines in composite regiments. We'll have some problems with equipment and doctrine compatibility, but General Mondesi and Least Claw
Thaaraan believe they can overcome the difficulties if we give them
a couple of weeks."

"I see." Antonov glanced at his *vilkshatha* brother, and Kthaara gave
a small ear flick of agreement. The admiral returned his eyes to the
holo, his face giving no hint of the thoughts behind it, and sat in
silence for another endless ninety seconds, then nodded slightly.

"Your plan seems sound, given what you know, Admiral Murakuma,"
he said slowly. "The problem, of course, is what you *don't* know, and
omniscience is possible only for the Almighty. You have sufficient
SBMHAWKs for the break in?"

"We believe so, Sir. Fang Anaasa's fleet train is bringing forward

Orion pods in some numbers. They won't link with ours, but we intend to split the targeting assignments. Our birds will go for one type of unit—probably the heavy cruisers, if they've deployed as before—and the Orions' will go for any superdreadnoughts sufficiently close to the warp point."

"And if there *are* no capital ships?"

"Then we'll simply have to send them through in two waves and hit them with successive salvos. Or, if we have sufficient TFN pods, we can hold the Orion SBMHAWKs in reserve to cover our retreat in the event we're pushed back."

"I see." Antonov cocked his chair back, still gazing at the holo, then shrugged. "Fifth Fleet is your command, Admiral. *I* never enjoyed having some rear echelon gasbag second guess *me*—" Kthaara gave a deep, purring chuckle, which Antonov ignored "—so I suppose I should grant you the same freedom I enjoyed."

"Then you approve the operation, Sir?"

"Fifth Fleet is your command," Antonov repeated, "and you enjoy my fullest confidence. I would appreciate the chance to review your final ops plan, but, yes, I approve the operation." He smiled suddenly. "I only wish I could see the politicians when *they* hear about it!"

"I knew we would hear about politicians eventually, Vaanyaa!" Kthaara laughed.

"Ha! If you'd had to put up with all the officious shit *I've* had to endure, you'd have a more respectful attitude, Kthaara Kornazhovich!" Antonov shot back. "Do you remember how the *pizdi* were all shitting their pants before Parsifal?"

"Those were the days, were they not?" the big Tabby yowled regretfully. "But we were younger then—and you! You were a *zeget* with a broken tooth!"

"And you weren't?" Antonov snorted, then shook his head. "But you're right. We've grown too old. At last I truly understand how Howard Anderson must have felt." He looked at Murakuma, and his deep voice was soft. "Remember this moment, Admiral. The most horrible lesson a commander ever learns is that people die following his orders. However good he is, however carefully he plans, however brilliantly he leads them, they die. I realize you've already learned that, yet at least you have this much: you risk your own life with them. You have not yet come to the point at which you must send them to their deaths from safety."

It was as if he and she were alone in the briefing room, and Vanessa Murakuma stared into the eyes of a legend—of the man still known as "Ivan the Terrible," who'd fed his ships into the meat grinders of Parsifal, the Fourth Battle of Lorelei, and the Battle of Thebes without a tremor. There was pain in those eyes, and a grief utterly at odds with the ruthless image of the legend, and she felt strangely moved that he would lift his mask, however briefly, to share it with her. To tell her, she suddenly realized, that she was not alone against her nightmares or the crushing weight of her responsibility, for they were nightmares and a weight he, too, had faced.

"You and Fang Kthaara aren't that old yet, Sir," she heard herself say equally softly, "and there's an extra command chair or two aboard *Euphrates*." She felt LeBlanc and Mackenna staring at her in horror, and she knew they were right to feel it, but it made no difference as she watched Ivan the Terrible sit straighter in his chair. His dark, deep-set eyes brightened, cored with a fire that hadn't touched them in decades, but he shook his head.

"Prime Minister Quilvio would have me shot at dawn," he rumbled, yet there was a yearning note in his voice, and Kthaara laughed suddenly.

"Oh, *shaarnulk* to the politicians! Or would you tell me you have begun to worry about the reactions of *droshokol mizoahaarlesh* at this late date?" The Orion turned his slit-pupilled eyes to Murakuma. "For myself, Ahhhdmiraal Murrrakuuuuma, I will take one of those chairs you have so kindly offered. Warriors should die in battle, not in bed!"

Murakuma smiled at him, but her attention was on Antonov, and the white-bearded fleet admiral glanced back at the holo, then at her face, and shrugged.

"Very well, Admiral Murakuma. Make that *two* command chairs."

"Of course, Sir." Murakuma beamed while her staff looked on in stunned disbelief, then reached across the table to extend one slender hand to the military commander-in-chief of the Grand Alliance. "Welcome along, Sir," she said, and he laughed as his huge hand enveloped hers.

CHAPTER NINETEEN

"I beg to report . . ."

Vanessa Murakuma stood in her walker, seeming frailer than ever with Ivan Antonov's massive presence on one side and Kthaara'-zarthan's sable menace on the other, and watched as CIC's interpretation of the scouting pinnaces' data coalesced on Cruciero's display. The pinnace losses had been even heavier than she'd feared, and she understood why when she saw what she'd sent them into, but she shoved that guilt into the back of her brain and bent to study the data.

"Well," she sighed, "it appears they *do* have normal OWPs to back those CAs."

"Yes, Sir," Cruciero agreed, but his tone was quite different. He touched a function key, and his hawklike face creased with predatory satisfaction as eighteen superdreadnought-sized vessels flashed on the plot. "They've got forts, Sir, but they aren't very smart about how they emplace them. These aren't warships—look at the energy readouts. They're construction ships."

"*Construction* ships?" Murakuma looked at the light codes glowing beside the flashing ships, and her eyes narrowed. "They're actually *assembling* forts right on top of a warp point?"

"Exactly, Sir," the ops officer gloated. "It looks like they've got the shields on-line, but not one of those forts even tried to pot a pinnace. They would have if their point defense was operable, and look here."

He entered another command, and a visual replaced the icon-studded schematic. One of the pinnaces had made a close pass on an OWP, and the fort was studded with leprous patches of naked girders. A clumsy construction ship hovered nearby, and the imagery had actually caught its tractors transferring a capital missile launcher from its own holds to the base for installation, and Vanessa Murakuma bared her teeth in a smile her Orion allies would have understood perfectly.

"By God, we caught them with their pants down," she murmured. *And thank God we did! If they'd had time to get those things on-line . . .*

She felt Antonov's presence, yet he'd made it clear this was her show. No doubt he would offer advice if she asked for it, but he had no intention of second-guessing her decisions, and she was grateful. She stood for a moment, thinking hard, then nodded sharply.

"All right, we'll go with Navarino Six. Our SBMHAWKs will take the cruisers and the forts—if their point defense isn't up, we shouldn't need many to take them out—and TF 53 will hold its pods in reserve. The construction ships can't be heavily armed, so we'll take them out with shipboard weapons. But be sure they're designated as primary targets. I don't want any of them getting away in the confusion."

"Yes, Sir. And their main force?"

"Ignore them. They're too far out for clean kills, and they might decide not to chase us if they have cripples."

"Yes, Sir."

"Set it up quickly, Ernesto," she told him, squeezing his shoulder to emphasize her urgency. "They know we're coming."

The Fleet raced to readiness as the last pinnace vanished back into the warp point. The enemy had chosen a bad moment. Even a few more days would have seen enough fortresses on-line to stop him; as it was, his missile pods could sweep them all away. The construction ships turned about, fleeing at their best, lumbering speed, and the massed superdreadnoughts of the picket force gathered their escorts close. They turned towards the warp point, but it was no part of their plan to enter the radius of the enemy's pods. Had the forts been ready they might have been able to kill enough pods before they could fire; as it was, they could but wait to strike the enemy when he presented himself, and at least they were present in overwhelming strength.

"Execute!" Ernesto Cruciero snapped, and the TFN's SBMHAWKs slammed through the warp point, locked their targeting systems . . . and fired.

The forts couldn't maneuver at all, and the slow-footed heavy cruisers were almost equally immobile. Point defense did its best, but only thirteen of the cruisers escaped destruction, and losses were even heavier among the fortresses.

Demosthenes Waldeck's TF 51 crashed through the warp point on the pods' heels, led by twenty Terran superdreadnoughts. The Bugs had seeded their minefields with laser buoys, but they had fewer of them than a Terran admiral would have employed, and none at all of the far more lethal primary buoys.

Unfortunately, Cruciero had been wrong about the OWPs. Or, more precisely, he hadn't been entirely correct, for five were fully operational. They'd been mauled and battered, but they were as big as the TFN's OWP-6s. Half-destroyed as they were, each of them retained the missile power of a *Matterhorn*-class SD, and they poured close assault missiles into TF 51's teeth. For all intents and purposes, the CAMs were sprint-mode capital missiles, virtually impossible for point defense to engage, and the stress of transit had reduced their targets' systems efficiency, as well. TFNS *Fuji San*, *Gunnbjørns* and *Grand Paradiso*, leading the Terran assault, blew apart under the pounding, but their consorts answered their deaths with massive, vengeful broadsides, and the forts were already badly damaged. That single, agonizing salvo was all they got off, and the Terran superdreadnoughts turned their missile batteries on the minefield even as their energy armaments massacred the frantically fleeing construction ships.

AMBAMs blew their lanes through the mines, and the rest of TF 51—and the Terran and Ophiuchi carriers of Vice Admiral Saakhaanaa's TF 52—formed up behind the battle-line.

The enemy had learned. He made no effort to lunge after the deep-space picket through the gaps his missiles had blown in the mines. Instead, he waited, bringing forward all of his units and launching his small attack craft to cover them. The small, fleet vessels fanned out, ignored by the hunter-killer satellites, but there were fewer of them this time. The last battle's ambush had killed many of the ships which carried them, and that was good. It meant they would be less able to swarm over the defending starships, and the enemy seemed to realize it as well, for they did not rush to the attack. Instead, they swept the space about the warp point, assuring themselves no additional units of the Fleet lurked in cloak to ambush them once more.

The Fleet hesitated, but then its light-speed sensors began to report. They identified only eight of the attack craft mother ships, and the laser buoys must have done better than projected, for many enemy superdreadnoughts streamed atmosphere in proof of heavy hull breaching. More than that, several had suffered drive damage, as well; their emissions were far weaker than usual, promising that they could be but little faster than the Fleet, and the picket force accelerated towards the warp point once more.

"They're coming in." Commander Cruciero's voice was grimmer. He was the one who'd first assumed none of the OWPs were fully operational, and Murakuma heard his sense of guilt. But she'd leapt to the same conclusion, and she rested a slender hand on his shoulder once more.

"Good," she said. "It looks like your little brainstorm is working, Ernesto."

The ops officer looked up at her, then smiled almost shyly and bobbed his head in thanks for her reminder, and she turned her walker to cross to the command chair. She parked beside it, reaching out to rest her right hand on the helmet racked on its side, and watched the master plot.

She and Cruciero had spent hours putting their surprise together, and she smiled thinly at the sensor readouts. Half her SDs had shut down anywhere from half to two-thirds of their shield generators and opened personnel locks to vent atmosphere. With their drive power reduced, they presented a chillingly realistic appearance of heavily damaged units, even to her, and her smile grew still thinner as she glanced at Saakhaanaa's carriers. All nine of his Terran CVs had their ECM in deception mode, and they showed on her plot as battle-cruisers, not carriers. Two could play the decoy game, she thought viciously, and glanced at her com officer.

"Are the drones ready?"

"Yes, Sir. All we need is the sensor data from Plotting."

"Good." The AMBAMs had completed their mine clearing duty, and Murakuma nodded to the com screens linking her to Demosthenes Waldeck and Saakhaanaa's command decks. "You know the plan, gentlemen," she said. "Now suck these bastards in and kick their asses."

The enemy moved at last, flowing through one of the cleared lanes towards the system's habitable planets. Clearly he intended a fight to the finish this time, for his wounded ships came with him rather than fleeing to safety, and that was good. Not only would it bring them out where the Fleet could reach them, but it indicated he was weaker than anticipated. From his previous tactics, he would have sent them back . . . unless they were all he had and he needed them here.

"They're splitting up, Sir," Cruciero reported. "Most are coming after us, but it looks like—Yes, Sir. They're peeling off a dozen SDs and their escorts to close the warp point."

"Good." Murakuma glanced at Antonov, and the burly admiral nodded in grim approval. The main Bug force retained a solid core of ninety-six superdreadnoughts and twenty-four battle-cruisers, but every little bit helped. Besides, it would make Anaasa happy.

"Composition of the detachment?"

"They look like *Acids,* with *Carbines* and *Cataphracts* attached to cover them."

"Makes sense, Sir," Mackenna observed quietly. "The *Acids*' plasma guns to kill anything that tries to get past them either way, with the cruisers to cover them against fighter strikes. The main force probably figures it's got the point defense to handle fighters without them."

"Then Admiral Saakhaanaa and Captain Olivera will just have to show them the error of their ways. Com, update the alert drones and get them off. I want them out of here before the enemy's close enough to see them past our drive signatures."

"Aye, aye, Sir. Update downloaded and locked. Launching—now."

Two courier drones separated from *Euphrates*. There was no need for more with no one to shoot at them as they vanished back through the warp point, and their emission signatures were lost in the background of Fifth Fleet's drive fields.

"Come to one-one-five, Demosthenes."

Fifth Fleet altered heading, curving away on a wider arc, and the main Bug force shifted its vector to cut a chord across it. The maneuver let it simultaneously make up distance and get behind Murakuma's ships, edging between them and any retreat while its detachment headed directly for the warp point as insurance. Thanks to her superdreadnoughts' "drive damage," the Bugs were actually a bit faster for a change. They were making the most of it, and she smiled thinly. The Alliance might still be unable to figure out what made the bastards tick, but it was nice to know they could be manipulated on a tactical level.

The enemy continued on course. No doubt he would eventually realize he could not defeat the Fleet's battle-line with so few attack craft to support his wounded ships. When he did, he would turn to flee as he always did, but the blocking force would hold him in play and the pursuit force would crush him against the warp point like a hammer.

The blocking units slid into position, and the pursuit force turned directly after him.

"Launch the execute drones!" Murakuma snapped, and hordes of courier drones—a torrent so vast the Bugs had no hope of stopping it—streamed through the warp point, and even as they launched, Admiral Saakhaanaa's cloaked carriers dropped their deception. Hundreds of additional fighters, the Terrans configured for antishipping strikes and the Ophiuchi as a combat space patrol, streamed from their bays, and as they went out, the superdreadnoughts which had been masquerading as cripples switched shields and drives to full power and stopped venting air.

TF 52's carriers accelerated away to keep clear of the battle, but

TF 51's battle-line turned back upon its enemies as the first jaw of Vanessa Murakuma's trap sprang . . . and then the *second* jaw struck.

The sudden wave of courier drones completely surprised the block-ing force. It opened fire as they flashed into their teeth, but only out of reflex, for the Fleet had only begun to consider what their purpose might have been when it found out.

These courier drones carried no message; their appearance *was* their message, and Fifty-Sixth Fang of the Khan Anaasa bared his fangs in predatory delight. He hadn't liked his secondary role as first explained, but he was too experienced a warrior to argue. After all, the humans' weapons and defensive technology were superior to his own, and system incompatibilities left his Orion and Gorm ships unable to integrate directly with their allies. And while he might dislike his own role, he admired the plan itself. It was more Orion than human in concept, for the TFN believed in simplicity. Small Claw LeBlanc had tried to explain "the demon Murphy" to Anaasa over most of a bottle of bourbon, and the fang had listened politely, but his own people preferred a more subtle approach which emphasized carefully timed converging strokes. If pressed, he would admit the human insistence on minimizing complexity had its own virtues, but he was an Orion, not a human, and the more he saw of Vanessa Murakuma, the more he liked her.

Now he yowled a terse order that sent seventy Orion SBMHAWK pods through the warp point, programmed with the targeting crite-ria Murakuma's first drones had provided, and six superdreadnoughts of the GSN led fourteen battle-cruisers through on their heels.

The guardian superdreadnoughts shuddered in agony as the pods spawned behind them. The enemy's missiles ignored the escort cruisers; instead, they concentrated on the capital ships and missile CLs, and a wave of antimatter fury crashed over them. All the targeted cruisers died, the superdreadnoughts were savagely mauled, and even as the Fleet reeled under the unexpected blow, fresh capital ships charged through the warp point at impossible speeds.

Class for class, Gorm warships were the fastest any navy had ever built. The Gorm world was a harsh place, with brutally high gravity and background radiation levels higher than those of any other known sentient race's home planet. That environment had produced the Gormish philosophy of *Synklomus*, which enshrined the responsibil-ity of every adult Gorm to protect all members of the *lomus,* or "household," from harm as his primary and overriding duty, but it had also produced a species which was incredibly tough. The Gorm were not only physically strong, with the blinding reaction speed their gravity well imposed; they also had a radiation tolerance no other species could match . . . and their starships took advantage of that tolerance.

The fundamental technology of the enhanced drive system was common knowledge, but few navies were willing to pay the price the "tuners" imposed. It was nice to be able to build a superdreadnought as fast as anyone else's battle-cruisers, yet the torrents of radiation the tuners produced were too much to expose one's personnel to. Unless, of course, those personnel were Gorm, who could endure far higher radiation levels than anyone else.

GSNS *Hazak* led her consorts through the warp point at a speed which would have had any Terran crew vomiting on the deck plates, and her capital missile launchers spat CAMs as she came. Only seven *Acids* had survived the SBMHAWK bombardment, and their battered defenses were no match for the massive fire of their undamaged foes. Only *Nirtanahr*, the third ship in Force Leader Darnash's battle-line took any hits in return, and her heavy shields shrugged the pair of missiles aside almost contemptuously.

None of the *Carbines* had survived, and the *Cataphracts* were suddenly helpless. They were minesweepers and antimissile ships, fearsome opponents for any fighter but without a single weapon capable of damaging a starship. They turned on their foes, trying to ram, but the Gorm and their escorting Orion battle-cruisers were too maneuverable. They evaded the kamikaze attacks, pouring energy fire into the cruisers while they dodged, and within four minutes, every unit of the blocking force had been destroyed without the loss of a single Allied unit.

It was a trap.

The blocking force was gone, and even as it died, torrents of small attack craft streaked from the "battle-cruisers" accompanying the enemy's "crippled" battle-line even as still more carrier starships emerged from the warp point behind the impossibly fast superdreadnoughts.

The Fleet came to an abrupt halt, and then, for the first time since the war had begun, it turned to flee. It had no option, for it could neither overtake its foes unless the enemy chose to be overtaken nor stand off such massive waves of attack craft. Its starships launched antimatter-loaded cutters in efforts to divert the attack craft, but this time the enemy refused to be diverted. Only a few attack craft swerved aside, engaging the cutters with lethal efficiency; the others bored straight in, and waves of additional craft came howling up from the warp point in support.

✧   ✧   ✧

Vanessa Murakuma watched with eyes of ice-cored jade as her fighters smashed into the Bugs. Dozens of them died, but they rammed their attack home, and the first strike was decisive. The Ophiuchi combat space patrol swarmed over the kamikaze small craft, piloted by the finest dogfighters in space, and the Terran and Orion pilots sent a tsunami of FRAMs into the superdreadnoughts. They didn't attempt to kill their targets; instead, they concentrated on battering down the shields and armor of the *Archer*-class missile ships, pounding each ship just hard enough to be *certain* they'd destroyed its fragile, first-generation datalink. They reduced the Bugs' entire missile component to individual units, incapable of synchronizing their fire, and then they broke off, their losses incredibly light compared to earlier engagements, while Waldeck's battle-line closed in from one side and Force Leader Darnash swept in from the other.

It wasn't totally one-sided. A few Bug missiles were bound to get through, despite the *Archers'* catastrophic damage, and they ignored the fire pouring in on them to concentrate everything they had on one or two Allied ships at a time, yet they were doomed. Waldeck and Darnash had an overwhelming advantage, and they used it ruthlessly. They smashed the *Archers* into wreckage, then pulled back beyond standard missile range, pounding the shorter-ranged survivors with utter impunity, and the Bugs broke. Enveloped by faster, longer-ranged enemies in deep space, they scattered in a desperate effort to save at least a few ships by forcing the Allied capital ships to choose which ones they would pursue and kill.

But that was what Saakhaanaa and Anaasa had been waiting for, and their rearmed, reorganized squadrons swept down on the Bugs as they fell out of mutual support range. Entire strikegroups drove in on single, isolated superdreadnoughts, taking their losses from the close-in defenses to streak in and blow them out of space. Once the Bugs broke, it *was* one-sided—a massacre—and Vanessa Murakuma watched with cold, hating eyes as, one by one, the Bug leviathans died under the stings of her deadly swarms of wasps.

It took less than two hours, and when those two hours ended, not a single enemy starship survived in the entire Justin System.

"All right, Demosthenes," she said then. "Secure the K-45 warp point. You can send a few pinnaces through for a look, but don't take any chances."

"Yes, Sir." The embers of battle still smoked in Waldeck's eyes, but he nodded soberly.

"Com," Murakuma looked over her shoulder, "inform General Mondesi that he can proceed against the planets."

"Aye, aye, sir." The communications officer dispatched another courier drone to the transports in Sarasota, and Murakuma's walker whined softly as she turned to face Ivan Antonov.

"Sir," she said very quietly and formally, "I beg to report that Fifth Fleet has regained control of the Justin System."

CHAPTER TWENTY

Ashes of Victory

"It's confirmed, Sir—they never even landed on Clements!"

"I'll be damned." Major General Raphael Mondesi, TFMC, Lion of Terra, Grand Solar Cross, shook his head. He'd never believed—never *let* himself believe—Admiral Murakuma's order to go bush would work, but the entire population of Justin B had eluded the Bugs. *It* wouldn't *have worked against humans,* he thought. *We're too damned curious. Someone would've landed, if only to see what was there. But the Bugs didn't. Interesting—and possibly useful. If they're that much less curious than we are, we may just be able to use it against them.*

He nodded, but he had little time to ponder the thought, for his assault force was closing on the planets of Justin A. After lengthy discussion, he and Least Claw Thaaraan, Fang Anaasa's senior Marine, had concluded they had no choice but to hit Justin and Harrison in succession. Neither liked it, and their troopers were going to be enormously outnumbered anyway, however they operated, but this time Mondesi had the assets to equalize the odds. His transports' assault shuttles would make mincemeat out of any Bug helicopter foolish enough to contest the air, and their escorting starships would be available for fire support. They could lay conventional precision-guided munitions in right on his own positions at need, and the Fleet Base had diverted enough of its capacity to build sufficient support weapons to arm the Allied contingents with Terran mortars, heavy grenade launchers and HVM.

He turned to the holo Fleet had already generated from radar and optical mapping, and his eyes were bleak. That detailed, space-eye look at the terrain was invaluable, but it also revealed what had happened to the planets he'd tried to defend.

534

What had been cities were wastelands churned by high explosives, incendiaries . . . even nukes. The humans of Justin and Harrison had known what would happen to them, and those who'd been unable to make it to the refugee camps had stood and fought with the ferocity of despair. Now their hopeless fight had ground to its ghastly conclusion, and the shattered ruins told him what he was going to find.

He glared at the glass-floored crater which had once been Justin's capital, and hate boiled at his core like lye. This deliberate mass slaughter of noncombatants said there not only would not but *could* not be any question of quarter or negotiated peace. As Admiral Murakuma had said so many months before, when this war ended, there would be only the victors and the dead, and so Raphael Mondesi embraced his hatred, for if a species must die, it would not be his.

The Terran transports slid into orbit, and grim battalions from three different races filed into their assault shuttles. The handful of Marines aboard the Gorm ships wouldn't be used—they lacked powered armor, and the planet would have been a hostile environment for them—but the Ophiuchi and Orions had provided the equivalent of two and a half more brigades of Raiders. The Tabbies' armor wasn't quite as good as the Federation's, but the Ophiuchi's was actually better. Even so, Mondesi was going to have to use a lot of people in regular battle dress. That was a losing proposition against Bugs, but he had a plan to reduce the odds, and as part of that plan, he'd picked spots for his spaceheads just beyond weapons range of the Bugs' main concentration. Now the shuttles swooped into atmosphere to land their troops and heavy lift shuttles brought in Terran assault skimmers, artillery, and air-defense batteries manned by drafted Navy technicians. And even as the troops dug in, the assault shuttles howled back aloft. Half were tasked to bring in the follow-up waves, but the other half were armed with external ordnance to provide air support.

In any peacetime exercise this size, Mondesi reflected, there would have been massive confusion, even without the need to cooperate with nonhuman allies. There'd simply been too little planning time for any other outcome. But there was very little muddle now, and draconian orders sorted out any that *did* arise ruthlessly. In less than three hours, each of his divisions had a two-brigade force down and dug in, ready for any Bug counterattack.

Not only ready, but praying for it. This time *they* had the firepower, and every Bug that died discovering that fact would be one less they'd have to hunt down later.

"What's the latest?" the general growled, settling into the padded chair aboard his Cobra divisional command vehicle. His ops officer dumped the data from her own panel to his display, and he bared his teeth as he saw Bug forces rolling towards his LZs. He'd hoped the compact target of the spaceheads—far enough apart to offer the temptation of crushing them in detail, yet so close they invited envelopment—would draw a massive response, and it had. Seven separate columns advanced with the obvious intention of launching simultaneous converging attacks. But first they had to get into position, and a lot of them weren't going to.

"Still nothing but those choppers?" he asked, checking his display sidebar.

"Not so far," Major Windhawk replied. "Orbital recon of their main facilities shows what could be atmospheric fast-movers at Alpha and Tango, but they're staying put. If they try to lift, the fire support ships will nail them from orbit."

"Good." Mondesi studied the display a few minutes longer, bringing up specific areas in high-order magnification for closer examination, then looked at his fire support officer.

"All right, Varnaatha. We'll start with Bravo and Charlie, then take out Golf."

"Yes, Generaaal." The Orion FSO punched keys, highlighting the designated Bug columns on her display. Mondesi had had a few doubts about accepting an Orion on his staff—not because he doubted the Tabbies' capabilities, but because of the language problem—but Daughter of the Khan Varnaatha'shilaas-ahn's sheer professionalism had won him over. Least Claw Thaaraan swore she was the best fire support officer in the Orion Atmospheric Combat Command—the equivalent of the Terran Marines—and an allied operation's command staff *had* to be integrated. Besides, Varnaatha was the Orion equivalent of a "Tabby specialist." She understood not only Standard English but the colloquialisms which baffled many Orions, and she never forgot Mondesi was a human. Despite a two-year intensive languages course, his command of Orion was much poorer than her ability with English, and she spoke slowly and distinctly to avoid any confusion.

She also, Mondesi suspected, chose the simplest possible way to express herself, but that was fine with him.

"Shall I utilize the support ships?" she asked now.

"No. We want the other columns to stay bunched until we get around to them, and they're likely to disperse if they figure out we've got starships to back up the shuttle strikes."

"Understood," she yowled, and he watched his display sidebar shift and flow as the computers projected the results of her instructions to the shuttles. He doubted he would entirely wipe out any of the columns he'd designated—there had to be fifty or sixty thousand Bugs in each—but he could hurt them. *Besides, if I kill all of 'em, the others'll just disperse and—*

"Orders acknowledged, Generaaal," Varnaatha announced. "First strike will commence in five Standard minutes."

"All right—now we take the bastards!"

Captain Apollo Greene, TFMC, led the transport *Sequoia*'s assault shuttles in a sweeping turn. The "column" known as Alpha was actually many smaller columns, each about the size of a Terran brigade, and the air above them was thick with the armored helicopters Bugs used for air support. Greene had studied the data Operation Redemption's ground component had paid so high a price to obtain, and he respected those clumsy choppers' firepower. But they were out of their league against his squadron, and he grinned in wolfish anticipation.

"Boomer, your section takes right flank. Bucky, you're on the left. Anything in the middle belongs to me."

"Aw, hell! You *always* get the easy shots!" "Boomer" Weintraub grumbled in the resonant bass which had earned him his call sign. "Look how those buggers are piled together in there—you couldn't miss 'em if you tried!"

"Be nice, Boomer," Annette Sherman—known, for reasons Greene had never figured out, as "Bucky"—chided. "He has to take something he can hit, after all."

"Stow it," Greene growled around a grin, and checked his instruments. The squadron shook down into two sections of five and one of six shuttles each and fanned out, and his grin vanished. "Commence your runs and make 'em count!"

He put the nose down, and the squadron leapt from high subsonic speed to mach five. Targeting computers aboard each shuttle considered the constantly changing pattern of the enemy helicopters, murmuring to one another and sharing the targets out among themselves, and then the squadron screamed into attack range and the HVMs began to launch.

A hyper-velocity missile had no seeking system, and it needed none. At ten percent of light speed, no atmospheric target could move far enough between launch and impact to generate a miss if its initial targeting was on . . . and very few targets could survive a direct hit.

The Bugs had already met the infantry version of the HVM. If it had occurred to them that the Federation had a vehicle-launched version, they must have known what would happen to their helicopters, but they went to violent evasive action anyway. Perhaps they thought they *could* generate misses, that some small percentage of their aircraft could survive long enough to salvo their shorter-ranged missiles back. If they did, they were wrong.

The HVMs carved incandescent tunnels of superheated air like some pre-space concept of death rays, and fireballs glared above the

Bugs Varnaatha'shilaas-ahn had marked for death. Staggering concussions marched across their airspace in boots of flame, and Greene's squadron howled past above it. The sixteen shuttles killed fifty-eight helicopters in that single pass and lifted their noses, screaming back towards space to rearm, and exultant chatter filled Greene's earbug.

"Lord, did you *see* that!" Bucky Sherman shouted. "Like shit through a—"

Her voice chopped off, and Greene's eyes darted to his plot in horror as the icon of her shuttle flashed from green to scarlet. He wrenched his head around, staring at the visual, and his face went cold and deadly as the fireball fell away astern. Somewhere in that column below, a Bug missile crew had managed to get at least one bird off, and its explosion strewed Apollo Greene's friend and her crew across four square kilometers of jungle.

"Jesus," someone whispered, and Greene looked away from the falling fire.

"Back to the ship," he grated, and punched for the priority com circuit. Bug SAMs were better than projected, and he buried his grief and hatred under the cold formality of his report.

Lieutenant Sherman wasn't the only pilot lost in the opening air strikes, yet overall losses were minuscule. Aerial superiority missions swept the sky clean, and the ground strikes came rumbling in on their heels. Ripple-salvoed HVMs tore the hearts out of the designated formations, and other shuttles sowed the jungle around them with lethal cluster munitions. Surviving Bugs, those on the fringes of their columns, raced into the jungle, seeking safety in dispersal, but their flight took them directly into the waiting antipersonnel bomblets, and Varnaatha bared her fangs at her display as flame seeded the jungle and orbital observers tallied the results of her first attack.

"Seventy-six-plus percent kills over all, Generaaal! *Seeequoiaaa* reports a complete sweep on Alllphaaa-Two!"

"Good, Varnaatha. Tell them well done—and to get back down here and do it again!"

The massed air strikes continued pounding the Bugs, and despite his own experience, Mondesi found it hard to believe they were actually proceeding with their plan. Surely their columns were in communication with one another! Yet their sole concession to his aerial flail was to break up into smaller groups, each about the size of a TFMC regiment. But dispersal only slowed the destruction; it couldn't *stop* it, and the killing went inexorably on.

But perhaps they had no choice, Mondesi thought. They were on

their own, beyond any hope of support, and if they couldn't surrender—and, it appeared, they couldn't—the only other thing they *could* do was attack.

The first three columns were virtually annihilated short of their jump-off points, but three more got through, and Mondesi switched his aerial attacks onto them. This time Varnaatha sent every shuttle in on a single target, slamming down on it with a hammer of HVMs, napalm and cluster bombs that tore a thousand square kilometers into a smoking moonscape. The Bugs had reconcentrated for their attack, which made her task easier, but it also massed their SAMs, and her pilots paid for their success with five more shuttles.

Yet the column's destruction goaded the two survivors on. They seemed to have been waiting for the seventh and last force to reach its attack point, but they waited no longer. Instead, they launched something no Terran commander had seen in over two centuries: a mass charge.

Over a hundred thousand sentient beings burst from the jungle, hurling their unarmored bodies into the teeth of a prepared fire zone, and Mondesi's ground forces opened up with every weapon while orbiting warships poured in missiles from above. The jungle writhed, kilometer-wide expanses of vines and giant, spreading ferns exploding in a maelstrom of high explosives and HVMs, and *still* the Bugs came on! They didn't die by scores, or even hundreds—they died in *thousands*, yet even as they died, their own support troops opened fire, and nuclear-armed missiles shrieked through the carnage.

Navy air-defense teams fought back desperately. The Federation had long since abandoned surface-to-surface missiles slower than HVMs, for energy weapons doomed anything that moved slowly enough to be tracked. Yet there was one way they *could* get through, for enough of them could saturate the defender's tracking or firepower. Only one or two might break through, but if those one or two missiles carried nuclear warheads, they might well be enough.

Raphael Mondesi sat silent at his console as his support elements saturated the jungle with destruction and his antiair teams waged their battle against the missiles. There were more of them than he'd expected, and the Bugs' frontal assault had diverted his main firepower from their launchers. He could kill missile teams or he could kill infantry, and for all he knew, the infantry carried nuclear charges of their own. That would be of a piece with the rest of their apparent tactical doctrine, and if they did, he had to kill them as far from his own positions as possible. Which meant the air-defense crews were on their own, and he prayed they were good enough.

They almost were. A single Bug missile—just one—got past, and a fresh fireball glared as it scored a direct hit on the two companies of

Terran Raiders holding the center of Landing Zone Two's northern perimeter.

The kilotonne-range explosion was a ground burst. The Raiders directly in its path died instantly, but the men and women on their flanks were in combat zoots that shielded them from the radiation and initial thermal bloom. Vaporized vegetation, soil and humans mushroomed from the detonation, and the blast front ripped out like an enraged fist. It picked up entire trees, tore them to splinters, and hurled them outward in a shearing wave of "shrapnel" not even zoots could stop. More men and women died, and then the firestorm crashed over the survivors.

Some lived through it. Their zoots were smaller, faster and more heavily armored than the old Theban War equipment, and if they were very, very lucky, they were in a depression or the lee of some small swell of ground. One squad less than five thousand meters from ground zero actually made it through without losing a man, for their veteran sergeant had goaded them into digging their foxholes deep, driving them into what turned out to be a reverse slope at a sharp angle. But they were the exception. Two hundred Marines died in the explosion, with another three hundred wounded or incapacitated. For all intents and purposes, an entire battalion had been wiped out, and the dazed ten-man squad crawling out of its collapsed holes into a smoldering slice of Hell found itself all alone, directly in the path of the charging Bug infantry.

Raphael Mondesi swore viciously as LZ-Two's reserve—two platoons of Terran assault skimmers supported by two companies of Orion Raiders—rushed forward, for some of the Bugs had actually gotten through his supporting fire. It was impossible. *Nothing* could have lived in that inferno, but over six thousand of them had. They were shattered and broken, any trace of unit organization gone. They weren't an army; they were a mob, but they were an *armed* mob, and as long as any Bug remained on its feet, it continued to charge forward.

The isolated squad saw it coming. They were dazed and disoriented, suffering from dangerously high radiation doses, but their screaming sergeant cursed them into action. They hit their jump gear, bounding back to their alternate position, and each of them carried a full automatic flechette launcher. No unarmored Bug could survive a direct hit from their weapons, and they wreaked fearsome execution on the enemies streaming past the warheads' blast zone.

The enemy barely seemed to notice them. No one knew enough about how Bugs thought to know why, but perhaps their own disorganization was to blame, for no race, however ferocious, could have

coordinated its efforts after the pounding the attackers had endured. They came out of the smoke and dust and thunder on six evil, segmented legs, like nightmares given flesh. They were unarmored, and the radiation of their own warhead sleeted through blood and bone. They had to know they were doomed by such a massive dose, but it didn't matter, and they lunged forward in total, terrifying silence, killing anything in their path.

Wounded Marines, or those merely trapped in disabled armor, died screaming for help no one could give as Bugs fired into them at point-blank range, and the single intact squad cursed and shouted their hate, weeping as they poured fire into that swirling madhouse. Some of the Bugs noticed them at last and turned on them, but they, too, attacked as individuals, and the squad shot them down. It walled its position in their ripped and torn bodies . . . and watched in horror as Bugs with one and two and even three limbs blown away kept thrashing forward. More got in behind the squad, firing into its rear, and men and women who'd survived the fury of a nuclear warhead died as armor-piercing rounds riddled their zoots. Two went down, then a third. Two more. The five survivors rallied around their sergeant, firing desperately, knowing they were doomed, but the madness was upon them, too. They were as crazed as the Bugs, and they held their ground in the thunder and smoke, screaming their defiance, *daring* the Bugs to kill them as they blazed through their ammo.

A single Bug flung itself into their position in an impossible, prodigious leap. They couldn't shoot it without killing one of their own, and the sergeant dropped his launcher. His armored hands closed on the Bug's weapon. Exoskeletal muscles whined as he ripped it away, and the alien hurled itself upon him bodily, rearing high on two limbs to smash at him with the others. His zoot shrugged off the pounding attack, and he opened his armored arms to embrace its central body pod. The entire surviving squad heard his bellow of primal hate as he squeezed, and the Bug writhed in agony. Yet even as the sergeant's arms crushed its pod, even as fluids and splintered bones and crushed internal organs erupted like obscene fruit, *still* it was silent.

The sergeant hurled the corpse away. He snatched for his launcher once more as another Raider went down and swung it in an arc, hosing the Bug who'd fired, and then he shouted again—a wilder shout, of disbelief, not hate—as the first Terran assault skimmer whined through the smoke, bow guns blazing. Another came behind it, and another, and Tabby Marines swept forward with them.

Raphael Mondesi sagged in his chair, saturated with sweat. *Dear God,* he thought shakenly, *if this is how they fight on a captured colony world, what's going to happen if we ever have to hit one of their worlds?*

It was a terrifying thought, but he felt his staff's eyes upon him, sensed the shock which had shaken even Varnaatha's Orion militancy. That single warhead had hurt them badly—he doubted more than ten percent of the battalion it had hit had survived—but it was the only point at which his perimeter had broken, and their attackers were finished. Search and destroy teams were moving forward, covered by assault skimmers, and even as they moved out, Varnaatha's shuttles and orbiting starships turned their attention to the seventh and last column.

His plan had worked. That *had* to have been the bulk of the Bug combat troops on the planet. He'd sucked them out into a killing ground and annihilated them, and grievous as his losses might be, they were trifling compared to the enemy's. He told himself that firmly, almost fiercely, and he knew it was true, yet there was little comfort in its truth.

It's them, he thought. *It's the way they just keep* coming, *as if it doesn't even matter to them whether they live or die. We're not fighting soldiers; we're fighting something none of us ever truly believed existed. It's like trying to kill a hurricane, and, God help me, no exchange rate is "acceptable" against something like this!*

He drew a deep breath, then made himself turn to his staff with a fierce smile.

"All right, people, we've got the bastards now. We've proved we can stop anything they throw at us, and they can't have much left to throw. Angie," he looked at Major Windhawk, "instruct Least Claw Thaaraan to begin his drop north of Murphysville. We'll move out from LZ-Three to meet him, then reconsolidate and move east on New Cornell. In the meantime—"

He went on talking, brisk and confident, every inch the military commander who'd just scored a crushing victory, and felt the confidence flowing back into his staff.

Now if only *he* could feel it.

"Are you positive, Marcus?"

Vanessa Murakuma stared at her intelligence officer, and her shoulders sagged as he nodded grimly. *Dear God. Dear sweet God, we left over* six million *people on this planet. Marcus* can't *be right. He just* can't!

But he was, and she turned away as she saw her own horror in his eyes.

Eight thousand. Eight thousand one hundred and three. That was it—the *total* count of survivors on the planet Justin. Eight thousand brutally traumatized, filthy, terrified, human-shaped animals who'd been herded into holding pens and watched hopelessly as all the others who'd been herded in with them were marched away and *eaten.*

She closed her eyes and buried her face in her hands, and her body shook. Her fault. It was all *her* fault. *She* was the one who'd pulled out, left them, abandoned them to this atrocity.

"Vanessa." She shook her head fiercely, but the gentle voice refused to be rejected. "Vanessa!" it said more sharply, and hands gripped her wrists. They pulled her own hands down, and Marcus' face swam through her tears as she stared at him in mute anguish and *your fault, your fault, your fault* tolled through her brain.

"You couldn't help what happened," he said, kneeling before her walker. "No one could."

"I . . . I should've come back. Come back sooner. Gotten in here and—"

"You *did* come back." His voice was fierce. "My God, you came back *three times!* You damn near got yourself *killed* coming back, and you know as well as I do that you *couldn't* have retaken this system a day sooner than you actually did!"

"I should have found a way," she whispered. "There *had* to be a *way!*"

"There wasn't," he said more softly, and her tear-soaked face pressed into his shoulder as he put his arms about her. He hugged her close, alone with her in the briefing room, and if Regs said lovers couldn't serve together, then Regs could go to Hell. One hand stroked her red hair, and his own tears—tears of grief, of shared, irrational shame, and of anguish for the woman he loved—flowed down his cheeks as he murmured to her. "There wasn't a way, love. I wish there had been, but there wasn't. You did everything you possibly could—more than anyone else could ever have done—but there wasn't a way you could stop it."

"Then what use am I?" She clung to him, and the words choked her like slivered glass.

"You didn't stop it here," he told her, still stroking her hair, "and you didn't stop it on Harrison, no. But you *did* stop it on Clements, love. And in Sarasota and Remus and New Prague and Vernon and Walker. You stopped it when you ignored me before First Sarasota. We lost fourteen million people here and in Merriweather and Erebor, but you got *twenty-four* million out, and you saved another hundred million in Sarasota alone."

"It's not enough," she whispered.

"Of course it isn't," he said gently. "It'll never be enough. But it's what you've got, and horrible as it is, it's a magnificent achievement." She twisted in his arms with an ugly sound of vicious rejection, but he held her until her struggles eased, and he smiled through his tears.

"You'll never see that," he told her. "Oh, Vanessa! You're the one person in the galaxy who won't see it, whatever I tell you. But that doesn't change what it is . . . and it doesn't change what you have to do now."

"What?" she asked hopelessly, and he kissed her ear.

"You have to go on," he said quietly. "You've kicked these monsters out of Justin; now you have to *keep* them out, and after that, you have to go on leading fleets and commanding in battles. Do you remember what you told us before K-45? About the way this war would end?" She nodded against his shoulder, and he held her tighter. "Well, you were right, and you're going to be there to the bitter end, Vanessa Murakuma. You're going to be out in front of us, showing us it can be done, leading us—kicking us in the ass and by God *dragging* us forward—because we need you. Because we can't let you hand the job off to anyone who'd do it one iota less well."

"I can't," she whispered in horror.

"You can, and you will. Not alone—trust me, there'll be grief enough for a hundred admirals before this is over—but you'll go on. The only way the Bugs will stop you is to kill you, love, and the only way you'll let *yourself* stop will be to die, because, God help you, it's what you *have* to do and because we need you so desperately."

She clung to him, and the dreadful truth of his words crushed her like the weight of the murdered world her flagship orbited. He was right. She had to go on. She couldn't *not* go on, for she owed it to fourteen million ghosts, and she could not fail them again.

She drew a deep breath and nodded against his shoulder, then gave him one more fierce hug and pushed him away. She straightened in her walker and scrubbed her face like a child, wiping away her tears, and took the tissue he gave her with a watery smile. She blew her nose and took another breath, then turned her walker towards the hatch without another word.

Her staff was waiting on Flag Bridge. They needed her to tell them this holocaust was a triumph, and Marcus was right, God help her. It *was* a triumph. She knew it was—now she simply had to make herself believe it and transmit that belief to her officers.

It sounded so simple for something so agonizingly hard, yet she had no choice, and as the briefing room hatch hissed open, Vice Admiral Vanessa Murakuma smiled at her staff while her walker carried her forward into the ashes of victory.

CHAPTER TWENTY-ONE

The Xenologists' Best Guess

" . . . so they've authorized a complete resurvey." Marcus LeBlanc grimaced on Murakuma's terminal. Her own expression mirrored his, and not simply because of what he was saying. Marcus had been recalled to Nova Terra as Ivan Antonov's resident Bug expert before she was out of that damnable walker, and she resented it. Not that she'd been about to explain to Ivan the Terrible that his desire to "frock" Commodore LeBlanc to rear admiral and assign him critically important duties had put a monumental kink in her love life!

She felt her grimace smooth into a small, fond smile. At least Antonov had let her keep Marcus until Estelle Abernathy was fully up to speed as his replacement. They'd had time to say a lot of things that needed saying . . . and for her to begin to accept that just perhaps Marcus was right. Given the challenge she'd faced, perhaps she *hadn't* done too badly.

She realized the letter had gone on playing while she gathered wool, and she ran it back.

" . . . resurvey," Marcus said again. "Of course, it's kind of hard to blame them, but just between us, Admiral Antonov considers it pure PR. The Justin death toll hit civilian morale hard, and a lot of other worlds seem convinced there could be an unknown Bug warp point right next door to *them*, as well. This way the Powers That Be can convince the electorate they're Doing Something to keep them safe."

He grimaced again, then sighed.

"Maybe I'm being too cynical. Lord knows a lot of survey data needs updating—some of it's over two hundred years old—and just one unplotted warp point near any core world could make what happened to Justin look like a pillow fight. The problem is, any points like that are almost certain to be closed, or we'd have found them by now. And if they *are* closed, we're not going to find them anyway, and all the ships we've got busy looking for them could be better employed pushing out into unexplored space to find a flank route into Bug space."

He paused for a moment, then shrugged.

"Still and all, we might as well spend our time doing that. We're still gearing up, and it's going to be a while before we're ready to mount any offensives. And speaking of gearing up, you should *see* what the Nova Terra yards are turning out! I haven't been out to Galloway's Star, but I hear the yards out there are working even harder. It's going to be a while yet before you start seeing much new construction out there at the sharp end, love, but when you do, it'll knock your vac suit off. The new assault carriers are beautiful, and R&D's pulled out all the stops to get the new shields and armor into service. Well, you know they have, of course. By the time you screen this, you'll have started seeing some of the refits."

He paused and leaned back, smiling into the pickup.

"Enough shop talk—we've got more important things to discuss. And I wish we *could* 'discuss' them directly. You remember that little hotel at Crawford's Point here on Nova Terra? The one where we spent midterm break? Well, it's still there, and I'll be damned if old Matsuoka isn't still running the place! I mentioned you to him, and he remembers our visit—or pretends he does, anyway. In fact, he's invited us back if you ever get a long enough leave." He wiggled his eyebrows in his very best leer, and Murakuma surprised herself with a bright, sunny laugh—the sort of laugh she hadn't laughed since the Battle of K-45. "You're out of that walker by now, so figure out how to get back here for a visit. You could always confer with GHQ's planning staff or something during the day, and then during the night we could get to the *important* things.

"I hope you like the kimono," he continued more seriously. "Nobiki picked it out." Murakuma's eyebrows quirked at that. She hadn't quite had the nerve to mention Marcus to her children. They'd known him all their lives, but only as "Mother's friend, Marcus," and if they got the notion she was picking up an old affair which had predated her love for their father—

"She gave me a pretty hard time when she handed it over," Marcus went on with a wry grin. "Seems she and Fujiko think we're a bit slow—due to our extreme old age, no doubt. According to Nobiki, they've had a pool going on how long you'd take getting back together with Oji-san Marcus for over ten years now!"

"Attention on deck!"

The assembled officers rose as Murakuma, Anaasa, Saakhaanaa, and

Force Leader Darnash entered *Euphrates'* largest briefing room. The hatch was a tight fit for Darnash, and Murakuma had been prepared to allow him and his staff to attend the conference electronically. Not only was the briefing room claustrophobically confining for someone his size, but his clear, globular helmet, while a masterpiece of engineering, didn't look any too comfortable.

Yet Darnash had politely refused the offer. He was one of her officers; he would attend her meetings, and do so in person. That, as far as he was concerned, was that.

Now the massive Gorm made his cautious way around the table to the spot where two chairs had been replaced with a Gorm-style couch and lowered himself onto its saddle with every indication that he was completely at ease.

Murakuma gave him a small smile as he settled into position, then looked at her other officers. The haunted desperation which had been so much a part of earlier meetings had eased. Most of her officers—human and non—still looked grim, but they'd smashed a Bug fleet, driven the enemy from Justin, and held it without more than half-hearted sparring at the warp point for over three months. More to the point, the fortresses on the Sarasota side of the warp point had been reinforced to the point of near impregnability, and every single noncombatant had been evacuated. They could afford to fight their kind of battle if—when—the Bugs tried a comeback, and if they had to, retreat entirely out of the system without abandoning civilians to the enemy. It was, Murakuma thought more grimly, a sign of the sort of war this was that knowing they could "afford" to give up a star system with three habitable planets was actually a source of relief.

"All right, ladies and gentlemen," she said. "As you know, we've just received our first echelon of refitted TFN starships, and Rear Admiral Teschman brought along GHQ's latest update. My staff has evaluated it, and I'd like to begin with their reports. Captain Mackenna?"

"Yes, Sir." Leroy Mackenna stood behind the lectern against the briefing room's after bulkhead and brought up a huge holographic chart of the local warp lines.

"As you know, ladies and gentlemen, we now hold Sarasota in strength," he said, and the Sarasota System blinked. "As of this morning, we have fifty-two OWPs on the warp point, with a total fighter strength in excess of two thousand, and the minefields and energy platforms are being heavily reinforced on an ongoing basis. In short, we may now consider our rear secure."

Assuming, Murakuma thought, *that anything is "secure" where Bugs are concerned.*

"With that in mind, GHQ has reconfirmed our basic mission profile. Until we've fully reequipped with updated units, we're to stand on the defensive, retaining control of the Justin System, but we are authorized and directed to fall back on Sarasota rather than risk heavy losses. My understanding is that the fact that we *can* fall back is the reason we have not yet been more heavily reinforced. Our current strength is sufficient for a fighting withdrawal against any opponent, and GHQ's decision to send us only refitted units rather than committing additional *un*refitted ones will impose an unavoidable delay on offensive ops."

One or two officers frowned, but Murakuma wasn't one of them. Like any CO, she wanted as many ships as she could get, yet GHQ had a point. Fifth Fleet's order of battle now counted thirty-four fleet carriers and twelve CVLs, backed by thirty-two superdreadnoughts, eleven battleships, and thirty-four battle-cruisers. That was sufficient, given their monopoly on fighters, for any deep-space engagement, and she was entirely in favor of refitting the ships she would have to lead into battle. The new third-generation shields and advanced armors had been available even before the war—they simply hadn't been fitted because the civilians had balked at the cost. Now they *were* being fitted . . . and now the same civilians who'd screamed about the cost were screaming about the Navy's "inexcusable" delay in not having fitted them earlier!

Well, I can live with their stupidity as long as they let me have ships that can survive, she thought with a trace of bitterness. *And thank God they agreed to reconfigure the* Belleisles!

That refit was the most drastic so far proposed, and her own recommendations had been the deciding factor. None had come forward yet—the refitted battleships she'd so far received had simply been given shield and armor upgrades—but the *Belleisle-Bs* would give up their entire energy armament for a massed battery of standard missile launchers. They couldn't live in close combat with Bug superdreadnoughts anyway, and while they would still lack the range of the capital missile-armed ships, they'd be able to lay down devastating fire from outside the enemy's effective energy envelope. And if they *were* forced to close-range combat, a broadside of twenty-four sprint-mode missiles with AAM warheads would take the starch out of *any* opponent.

"—in the meantime," Mackenna was saying, and she shook herself back to attention. "Given the civilian death toll in Justin, GHQ has concluded there are no survivors in any of the Bug-occupied systems between here and Indra, and Admiral Antonov has no intention of sacrificing warships—and lives—to retake empty real estate. Fifth Fleet's function thus becomes that of holding Justin as our forward point of contact and as a security buffer for Sarasota while our accelerated survey activities seek additional points of contact. According to the theoretical astrophysics sections of both the Terran and Orion survey commands, the odds are high that we'll find some, given the general pattern of the warp lines in this sector. Should we do so, it will give us a second axis of advance and force the Bugs to divide their forces against more than one threat. Should we *fail* to do so," Mackenna's voice turned much grimmer, "we'll have no option but to reinforce Justin to the maximum possible extent and attack from here."

He said no more on that point, but every officer present knew how hideous casualties would be if the Alliance had to hammer straight ahead down a single, predictable line of advance.

"With your permission, Admiral," Mackenna continued with a glance at Murakuma, "I'll turn the lectern over to Commander Abernathy for a few moments, then let Commander Cruciero bring us up to date on our own dispositions."

Murakuma nodded—*exactly,* she thought, as *if we hadn't discussed it ahead of time*—and the newly promoted lieutenant commander who'd replaced LeBlanc as her staff spook rose. She looked ridiculously young—like a golden-haired schoolgirl in uniform—and her hands fidgeted a bit as she faced the briefing room full of senior officers, but her voice was clear and level.

"Admiral LeBlanc and the GHQ intelligence staff have put together a comprehensive briefing on the results of their examination of the material captured here in Justin," she began. "I've prepared copies of their complete download for each of you, so I'll simply hit the high points here. Please stop me if you have any questions.

"First, we've finally gotten some feel for the Bugs' technology. For the most part, they're somewhat behind us, as we'd surmised. That's the good news. The bad news is that they aren't *far* behind us. Based on known rates of R&D for our own races, GHQ estimates they'll need no more than eight months to duplicate our command datalink, even assuming they captured no intact installations to give them a leg up in any previous engagement."

A stir went through the briefing room. Not of surprise—it was a given that the Bugs realized how much their cruder datalink hurt them and were working to redress the balance—but at the thought of losing their greatest advantage in a missile engagement.

"The most puzzling aspect of the captured material, however, concerns the enemy's databases," Abernathy went on. "As you know, we secured several intact computers, both here and from destroyed enemy fleet units and dispatched them to Centauri, where Allied technicians and xenologists could examine them properly."

What Abernathy meant, Murakuma reflected, was that they'd been sent back to let *Orion* techs at them. In general terms, Terran hardware tended to be the best in space, but the Tabbies persistently—

and irritatingly, for some humans—produced the galaxy's best cyberneticists. If anyone could tickle the Bug computers into giving up their data, it was the Whisker-Twisters.

"Unfortunately," Abernathy said, "they've been unable to generate any meaningful output. They—" She paused as Anaasa raised a clawed hand. "Yes, Fang Anaasa?"

"They have generated *no* output?" The Orion demanded. "None at all?"

"I didn't say that, Sir. I said they've been unable to generate any *meaningful* output. They're convinced they're generating *something*, but no one's been able to figure out what it is."

"That's preposterous," Waldeck muttered. His face reddened as he realized he'd spoken aloud, and he shrugged. "What I mean is, if they're generating anything at all, the xenologists should be able to make *something* of it. They've got enough filters and computers to run it through, after all—and surely *some* of it is simple visual imagery!"

"I'm sorry, Sir, but it isn't—visual imagery, I mean," Abernathy said respectfully. "So far as anyone can tell, it's just so much electronic noise." Waldeck looked at her like a man who wanted to disbelieve, and she shrugged. "According to Admiral LeBlanc, Doctor Linokovich of the Xenology Institute hypothesizes that they're telepathic, and medical forensics may offer some corroboration. According to the autopsies, the Bugs are mute."

"*Telepathic?*" Carlotta Segram stared at Abernathy, then shook her head. "This is like some bad holodrama. You're telling us these things are *mind readers,* too?"

"No, Sir. That's the point. As you know, we've never been able to demonstrate reliable telepathy in humans. The Gorm—" she nodded to Darnash "—do have a telempathic sense, but though their *minisorchi* talent's existence has been conclusively demonstrated, no other race has ever been able to perceive it. The current theory is that the Bugs operate on a unique mental 'frequency' which they've managed to convert into electronic storage. Our problem is that we simply can't 'see' it. As Admiral LeBlanc puts it, we're like blind people trying to understand pink. But at least if we can't read *their* records, it seems unlikely they can read *ours.*"

"I wouldn't bet on that," Admiral Rendova murmured. "Our data outputs are all some form of visual information, and mute or not, we know these things have eyes."

Abernathy started to reply, but Murakuma's raised hand stopped her.

"That's certainly a point to bear in mind, Ellen. For now, however, all of this can only be considered an unproved theory. We'll just have to stick to our standard procedures for purging all databases which may fall into enemy hands and hope."

Rendova nodded soberly, and Murakuma waved for Abernathy to resume.

"For the moment," the lieutenant commander said, "the most immediate consequence is that, despite all the data we've apparently captured, we've been unable to learn a thing about the enemy except by direct observation. We still have no idea how large his imperium is, how his warp lines are laid out, or what his ultimate industrial and military potentials are. What we *do* know is that the Bugs aren't organized like any other species any of our races have ever met. They seem much more specialized by function, for example. The medical teams report distinct physiological differences between what GHQ is calling 'the warrior caste' and the other Bugs we encountered on Justin and Harrison. The 'warriors' are larger, stronger and tougher than the 'workers,' almost as though they were genetically engineered for combat."

"Lord! It gets stranger and stranger." Segram sighed. "Is GHQ saying they really *are* bugs? That we're up against some kind of hive race? Some sort of communal 'over mind'?"

"GHQ doesn't think so." Abernathy shook her head. "Our own ground forces' observation indicates they react as individuals. Not as individuals of any race we've previously met, perhaps, but still as individuals. The med teams' best guess—and it's only a guess, at this point—is that this species preselects individuals for societal roles at a very early point in life. It would appear the species differentiates physically as some Old Terran insects do: if fed one diet, they become workers; fed another they become warriors. If that's true and their society does preselect for function, then presumably it feeds them the diet and tailors their training to enable them to fill their selected roles most efficiently. The xenologists tend to agree, especially since both the 'warriors' and 'workers' we've seen so far are neuters. Xenology's best hypothesis to explain the Bugs' tactics is that this race has taken specialization to an unprecedented height. The *only* function of their warriors appears to be to fight; they have no other value to the race, since they can't procreate. That doesn't require that they be part of any 'hive mind,' and it doesn't prevent them from being imaginative—as they demonstrated in their Third Justin tactics—but it does mean they may regard themselves as completely expendable in the interest of their race."

"Perhappps they are notttt *necessssarily* unimaginatttive," Admiral Saakhaanaa put in, "yett they woulddd appearrr to *acttt* ass ifff they are."

"They certainly seem to stick to a plan once they've made one," Waldeck agreed.

"True, but they're not unique in that," Murakuma pointed out.

"Humans are pretty flexible, but there've been enough humans who insisted on 'sticking to the plan' even when it obviously wasn't working. Think about the Japanese military in World War Two—or the Communists in the old Soviet Union, or the 'social engineers' the West turned out in the twentieth century. Every one of them rode 'the plan' down in flames instead of changing it."

The various Allied officers looked puzzled, but they let it pass when Waldeck nodded. After all, everyone knew Humans were the galaxy's most complicated—and confusing—race.

"At any rate," Abernathy concluded, "research is continuing. No one expects any sudden breakthroughs, but anything they do come up with will be passed on to us as soon as possible."

"And in the meantime, *we'll* be the main laboratory," Murakuma agreed. She nodded for Abernathy to be seated and glanced at Cruciero. "Ernesto?"

The ops officer replaced Abernathy at the lectern and punched up a fresh hologram, this one a detailed breakdown of Fifth Fleet's order of battle.

"As you see, ladies and gentlemen," he began, "we're in much better shape these days, and GHQ informs us that industrial rationalization is proceeding as planned. Within another three months, Terran industry will be turning out expendable munitions—missiles and mines—designed for universal compatibility. Within another six, we'll be producing launchers and energy weapons which can be mounted aboard any unit of any Allied navy, as well. We'll pay a slight mass penalty for the additional control runs, but it should simplify our logistics tremendously."

Everyone nodded—or whatever his or her race used to indicate agreement—though there were some slightly sour expressions. The non-human officers found it irritating that Terran industrial productivity eclipsed their own by such an enormous margin that the Federation was the logical arsenal of the Alliance. Concentrating only on shipbuilding while the Federation produced their weapons would vastly simplify their own problems, but some of them—and particularly the Orions—resented humanity's industrial dominance. Yet some of the *humans* in the briefing room—like Leroy Mackenna—looked almost equally disgusted, for it was the industrial might of the Corporate Worlds which made it possible. Fringers like Mackenna might be grateful that capacity existed, but that made them no less angry over how the Corporate Worlds had manipulated the Federation's economy and laws to *create* it.

"In the meantime," Cruciero went on, "our own posture remains unchanged. As you can see from the holo, the Seventh Battle Squadron—"

He went on speaking, and Vanessa Murakuma tipped her chair back, expression attentive. The big news of the briefing had already been presented; all that remained now was the discussion of the nuts and bolts and their chance to display their confidence to one another. Those things were important, of course, and she would give them her full attention when the time came, but now, as Cruciero reported details she already knew only too well, she let herself concentrate on planning her next letter to Marcus.

CHAPTER TWENTY-TWO

"What *are* those things?"

Vice Admiral Murakuma closed her eyes and held the saki cup between her palms to inhale its sharp aroma. She'd been a sad disappointment to Tadeoshi's parents, despite her determined efforts to understand their culture. They'd welcomed her as warmly as they could, yet they'd never quite been able to forget she was *gaijin*. The fact that she'd asked them to raise her daughters after Tadeoshi's death rather than drag them from duty post to duty post with her had helped, but still that slight taint of the foreign barbarian lingered in their eyes.

Which made her father-in-law's gift all the more precious, for she *knew* how hard they'd tried to accept her . . . and how difficult that had been.

She opened her eyes and raised the cup to the holocube—the one of a laughing Tadeoshi on the Brisbane flight line—and then to the sheathed *katana* thirty generations of Murakuma *samurai* had borne. That blade was only in her keeping, to be passed to Nobiki on her thirtieth birthday as Tadeoshi had requested, and her eyes misted as they rested upon it. Then she sipped, and the saki burned down her throat, seeming to evaporate before it ever reached her stomach.

She savored the fiery taste which had come five hundred light-years from the planet Musashi. It was fitting that it should have been bottled on a planet named for Japan's greatest *samurai*, for she drank it in remembrance of warriors. Of her husband, who'd died training for the battles he never fought, and of those who'd perished in the First Battle of Justin one year ago today.

She sipped again, alone with the holocube and the sword which represented so much, and promised herself that blade would go to her daughter with its honor unstained.

554

✧   ✧   ✧

"They're up to something." Mackenna frowned across the conference table at Murakuma. "I *know* they're up to something."

"Demosthenes?" Murakuma said, and the Corporate World admiral shrugged.

"Leroy's right," he said, and Mackenna nodded vigorously. *Interesting,* she thought. *Once it was only "Captain Mackenna" and "Admiral Waldeck." I wonder if either of them even realizes how much his attitude has changed?* "They're burning too many pinnaces probing us," Waldeck continued, "and I can only think of one reason to do that."

"With all due respect, Admiral Waldeck, I'm not certain we can assume that," Ernesto Cruciero said politely. "It's been seven months since we kicked them out of the system. They haven't made a serious attempt to take it back yet, and we know how close one of their core systems is to us. If they planned an attack here, surely they could *already* have reinforced to launch it, and we've had similar upsurges before when no attacks were launched."

"Not to this extent," Mackenna countered. "Look at it—they've sent three waves of fifty-plus through in just the last two weeks. The CSP killed ninety percent of them, too. Even for Bugs, that's a lot of pinnaces to throw away if they're not planning *something!*"

"I don't categorically say they aren't, Sir. All I'm saving is that we shouldn't *assume* they are. As Admiral LeBlanc keeps saying, these things just don't think like we do."

Murakuma looked from one face to another. As a rule, she preferred to let subordinates debate without committing herself, for she got the fullest exposition of their views by letting them argue with one another rather than work, however unconsciously, to *her* viewpoint. But in this case they'd begun to rehash old positions, and all eyes snapped to her as she cleared her throat.

"Your point's valid, Ernesto," she said, "but Leroy and Admiral Waldeck have a pretty convincing argument. And the bottom line is that we're better off going to an enhanced readiness state when they're not about to attack rather than failing to do so when they *are.*"

"It's the SBMHAWKs and energy platforms that concern me, Sir." Cruciero's tone was diffidently stubborn. "We could put a lot of time on their clocks for an attack that never comes."

"That's true enough," Waldeck murmured, and Murakuma nodded. Energy platforms were maintenance-intensive compared to minefields. They tended to get temperamental if they were held too long at full readiness without periodic overhaul, and the same was true of the two hundred SBMHAWK pods deployed to cover the warp point.

"I know," she said, "but the first OWP strikegroups will be ready in five weeks. Once they're on-line, we'll be far less reliant on the platforms. I think we can stretch them to cover that five-week gap, then shut down for complete maintenance once the forts are in place."

Her juniors cocked their heads in consideration. Now that the Sarasota fortress shell was complete, the construction ships were assembling still more prefabricated bases in Justin. Given the Bugs' mass transit tendencies and the possibility of their developing their own SBMHAWKs, Murakuma had argued that Justin's forts should all be fighter-armed Type Fives or Type Sixes. They mounted no offensive weapons, but each OWP-5 could put seventeen fighter squadrons into space, while an OWP-6 could launch *twenty-seven,* and she intended to deploy them well back from the warp point and use their strikegroups to swamp any attack. Ten Type Fives were already operational, but she had no intention of exposing them to attack until she was confident of their ability to hold, for she refused to abandon their crews if her mobile units were forced back. Her five-week deadline would see another ten forts—all Type Sixes—on-line . . . and put the equivalent of seventy-four more fleet carriers into her defensive order of battle.

Until they were ready, however, and—especially—until their strikegroups had worked up, Fifth Fleet's mobile units had to shoulder the burden. And to do that, they needed the energy platforms and SBMHAWKs on-line the instant any attack came through.

"The platforms would be good for that long," Cruciero agreed. "They won't go much longer before effectiveness degrades, but they should make five weeks. The pods won't, though."

"They won't have to," Murakuma replied, "I want their tasking changed."

"Change their tasking?" Waldeck echoed, then his eyes narrowed. "You want to take them out of independent mode?"

"Exactly. If we slave them to the battle-line's fire control, they'll never go on-line at all unless we send the Fleet to general quarters."

"You'll cut way down on salvo density," Cruciero pointed out.

"Not really," Mackenna said. "We'll pick up anything we lose with better targeting. A *Matterhorn* can control up to ten pods—that's a fifty-missile salvo, enough to saturate the point defense of any ship without command datalink."

"And you've got twenty-five SDs, Demosthenes," Murakuma pointed out. "We can pound hell out of them in one firing pass even without a mass launch."

"I like it," Waldeck agreed.

"In that case, I think we can consider the matter decided. Ernesto, I'd like you to have the new fire plans to me by dinnertime."

✧   ✧   ✧

The Fleet was ready once more.

The delay between offensive operations had been far longer than pre-war planning had visualized, for the Fleet's doctrine was based upon seizing and maintaining the momentum, but the time had not been wasted. The last engagement had taught a lesson about underestimating the enemy, and the effectiveness of his attack craft—especially when used in numbers—had taught another. This attack force had barely eighty percent as many superdreadnoughts as the one which had been annihilated in the last engagement, but two-thirds of those it did have had been refitted with improved shields and armor, and they were only the beginning of the refit and construction programs, for less than forty percent of the Reserve had yet been mobilized. Every unit which was activated would receive the latest updates as it was taken from mothballs, and the Fleet had already begun laying down entirely new types to further redress its disadvantages. New battle-cruiser classes, every bit as fast as the enemy's vessels, would soon be available, as would new and heavier battle-line units designed to bolster the long suffering superdreadnoughts. And, of course, there was the other new type designed to answer the enemy's small attack craft.

Enough new and refitted units had come forward to make a fresh attack worthwhile, and even if it failed, the warp point linking this starless nexus to their target system had been so heavily fortified that no conceivable counterattack could take it. It was time to evaluate the new technologies in combat, and the massed ranks of capital ships came to full readiness behind the light cruisers of the Assault Fleet.

The two-toned priority signal warbled while Murakuma was working at her terminal. She opened a window to take the call, and Captain Decker appeared on her screen.

"Yes, Jessica?"

"We've got another pinnace transit, Sir—a big one," her flag captain said. "CIC makes it over a hundred, and they're hanging around for detailed scans, not making an immediate turn back for the point. The CSP's taking a lot of them out, but we're not going to get them all."

"Send the Fleet to battle stations," Murakuma said instantly. "Activate Alpha One and launch the ready squadrons. Then tell Leroy and Ernesto I'll be on Flag Bridge in five minutes."

She cut the circuit and wheeled from her terminal. *Two more weeks,* she thought bitterly. *All the bastards had to do was wait* two *more weeks, and I'd've had the forts in here, too!*

But they hadn't waited, and she opened her vac suit closet.

✧　　✧　　✧

The twelve surviving pinnaces broke back to rejoin the Fleet and beamed their data to the waiting starships. Evaluation was rapid, for the enemy had made few changes since the last probe, and the positions of the ships which mothered the small attack craft were noted. Only then were orders passed, and the Assault Fleet began its advance.

The light cruisers came through just as Murakuma dashed out of the intraship car into Flag Bridge. There was no time to give any orders, but that was why Fifth Fleet had battle plans, and Alpha One sprang into operation even as she jogged across to the master display. She stood with her helmet in the crook of her arm, and her jade eyes were intent as icons blinked in the tank.

Just under a hundred light cruisers flashed into existence. Fifteen exploded *out* of existence just as quickly, and the others spread out past the fireballs, deploying in the clear zone about the warp point. But this time Murakuma had the firepower for a classic warp point defense, and she intended to fight just that.

The primary beam platforms seeded among the mines held their fire—they were tasked for bigger fish—but a hundred and fifty laser buoys lashed out at just thirty enemy cruisers, and none of their targets survived. Nor were the lasers alone, for Fifth Fleet had twelve hundred fighters, and its heightened readiness state had increased the standing combat space patrol on the warp point to forty squadrons. Now the deadly little craft roared in, and Anson Olivera's *farshatok* had their priorities right. The *Cataphracts* were their natural enemies, and they peeled off to kill them while their transit-addled point defense fought to stabilize.

Degraded or not, the sheer volume of fire killed almost fifty fighters, but that was too little to stop Fifth Fleet's pilots. They rammed their attacks home, ripple-firing FRAMs at pointblank range, then pulled sharply away. The Bugs had sent twenty-four *Cataphracts* through the warp point; when the CSP broke off, two of them survived.

Murakuma's eyes flamed as two-thirds of the Bugs' assault wave was annihilated. Too little of it survived to clear lanes completely through the dense minefield, though they thinned it dangerously in two places, but the mine barrier was still intact when the last died, and she bared her teeth at the status boards. Waldeck had brought the waiting SBMHAWKs on-line, and she settled into her chair with hungry anticipation as she awaited the first Bug superdreadnoughts.

Assault Fleet courier drones told a disturbing tale. Despite its previous experience, the Fleet had underestimated the efficiency of the enemy's attack craft against ships whose systems were degraded by transit and which could not maneuver in the confines of the mines. But the purpose of this battle was largely to test the Fleet's new systems and its analysis of enemy capabilities. There could be no question of breaking off until those objectives had been attained.

"Here come the heavies," Cruciero said flatly, and Murakuma nodded. The Bugs were coming through dangerously tight—some superdreadnoughts actually made simultaneous transits, though this time the luck favored them and none were destroyed—and there were a lot of them.

"Bring up the jammer buoys," she replied, and thirty-five buoys, without a single weapon among them, came to life. They were pure electronic platforms with only one function: to jam Bug datanets. And even as they roused, the primary-armed energy platforms opened up. A hundred unstoppable beams ripped effortlessly through shields and armor, and fifteen riddled Bug superdreadnoughts blew apart as their magazines exploded.

The warp point was a cauldron of dying ships, and as the first wave of Anson Olivera's main strike came shrieking into it, Demosthenes Waldeck's battle-line began to fire.

Twenty of his superdreadnoughts controlled ten SBMHAWK pods apiece, feeding the pods targeting data from their vastly superior fire control. A single six-ship datagroup could—and did—send a perfectly synchronized salvo of three hundred missiles straight down the Bugs' throat before their defenses could stabilize, and more small, terrible suns glared. Terran *Dunkerque*, Orion *Prokhalon* and Gorm *Bolzucha*-class battle-cruisers added their SBMs to the holocaust, and more FRAM-armed fighters swooped in. Desperate Bug point defense stopped some of the missiles, killed some of the fighters, but it couldn't possibly stop them all, and human, Ophiuchi, and Orion howls of triumph echoed over squadron com nets as still more capital ships blew apart.

It was a massacre. Not even the *Archers* could reply effectively, for the jammer buoys smashed their datanets back, forcing each to fight alone, splitting their fire into individual salvos the Allies' datalinked point defense brushed aside with contemptuous ease.

The battle was disaster made flesh. The battle-line reeled, and even as it staggered, the enemy's shorter-ranged missile ships closed in to add their fire to the holocaust. For only the second time in the Fleet's history, orders went out to halt the advance before all of the battle-line had even made transit, for no starship could live in that vortex of warheads, beams and attack craft. But the enemy had closed to concentrate his fire, and even as the battle-line fell back, the third wave streaked through in the opposite direction.

✧　　✧　　✧

"What the—!" Carl Hathaway blinked as four hundred fresh lights spangled his display. They were far too small for starships, but their emissions were stronger than some corvettes, and they slashed through the carnage at incredible speed. "What the fuck *are* those things?" he blurted.

"Sir! We've got a new vessel of some sort!"

Murakuma's head whipped around at Cruciero's announcement. She looked down at her repeater plot, but the explosion of icons swamped its detail, and she shoved herself up to look at the master tank as the newcomers dashed into the minefields. Whatever they were, their emissions were powerful enough to attract the mines, but they were also impossibly fast. The mines were catching some, but most survived to streak straight towards her starships.

Anson Olivera took one look at the readouts and keyed his mike.

"Abort your runs!" he barked over the command circuit while Hathaway fought to get him data on the fresh threat. "All units, this is Ramrod. I say again, abort your runs! Leave the warp point to the battle-line and get on the new bogies!"

Hundreds of fighters acknowledged, but the newcomers were fast. Slower than fighters in clean condition, but far faster than they were with external ordnance mounted.

He glared at his display, watching the new threat run away from his pilots. They'd have to jettison. It was the only way to catch the bastards, and he opened his mouth to give the order.

"Sir!" Hathaway caught him before he could speak, and he darted a look at his tac officer. "These things' emissions are strong enough my missiles can lock them up!"

Olivera's eyes flashed, and he keyed his mike again.

"Ramrod to all units! Jettison FRAMs. I say again, jettison FRAMs, but any fighter with missiles attempt a missile engagement."

"Well?" Murakuma snapped. She knew she sounded angry, for she was, but not at Cruciero. He simply had the misfortune to be the man on the spot, and he shrugged helplessly.

"I don't know, Sir. They're bigger than fighters, but smaller than anything else with such powerful signatures. They're obviously warp capable, but their power levels are much higher than a pinnace's. It looks like a whole new drive system—something that crosses the line between small craft and starship drives. I'd guess they can run it flat out at settings that would burn out any other small craft's systems."

"What—" Murakuma began, then closed her mouth as the new vessels began to fire.

"Jesus Christ!" Olivera muttered. What the hell *were* those things? They weren't firing fighter missiles—they were firing full-sized standard ship-killers from ten light-seconds out!

But they weren't firing many of them, and his eyes narrowed. It looked like they could carry only four birds each, and the jammers were knocking back any datalink they mounted. That forced them to fire as individuals, which gave them a snowflake's chance in hell of getting through battlegroup point defense. But they seemed to realize that almost instantly. It was as if the first to fire had done so only to prove it wouldn't work, and half of them suddenly swerved straight in on TF 51's battle-line.

Demosthenes Waldeck shoved further back into his command chair and clamped his jaw as the small Bug warships charged his superdreadnoughts. They were far bigger targets than fighters—indeed, they could be killed by weapons which could never have engaged a fighter— but they were also lethally fast and a total surprise. No one had expected such a threat, and—his jaw clamped tighter as the readouts flickered—unlike fighters, they mounted point defense. That made them highly resistant to missile fire, and his missile-heavy battle-line was weak in energy weapons.

Half the Bugs howled down on his capital ships, but the other half broke suddenly towards TF 52. They seemed to ignore Anaasa's TF 53, but Saakhaanaa's Terran and Ophiuchi carriers were obviously priority targets. Yet the carriers were also well back, and carriers and their escorts were fast. The new Bug ships had no more than a fifty percent speed advantage, and Saakhaanaa had wheeled his ships almost instantly, racing away from the threat, slowing the closure rate while reserve squadrons spat from his catapults. Anaasa's fighters were launching, as well, cutting in from one flank while Olivera's antishipping strike charged up from astern.

But Waldeck had little time to watch, for the Bugs who weren't chasing carriers were lunging straight at *him*. Energy weapons and point defense blew dozens out of space, and fighters killed still more. The Bugs' point defense took toll of the fighters who closed with their onboard lasers, but the fighters were harder targets and the kill ratio was entirely in their favor.

Yet favorable kill ratio or no, they couldn't stop them all in the time they had . . . and neither could TF 51's energy batteries. At least forty survived everything Fifth Fleet could throw at them and hurled themselves headlong upon the capital ships. They didn't attempt to fire the missiles they carried; instead they rammed, delivering their antimatter warheads—and their own ships—in shattering concussions of flame and death.

There weren't enough to be decisive, thank God. They couldn't kill many of his ships, but they could—and did—wound them cruelly. TF 51 staggered under the blow, yet the Bugs' decision to split their attack between the battle-line and the carriers was crucial. "Only" three superdreadnoughts and a pair of battle-cruisers were actually destroyed, and had they thrown everything at TF 51, they *would* have killed many of its units; Waldeck was certain of that. As it was, they'd failed . . . and they were failing against the carriers, as well.

He wrenched his eyes away from his plot's appalling damage sidebars and snarled vengefully as shoals of Allied fighters closed in. Saakhaanaa's turn away had bought just enough time for them to mass, and they tore into the Bugs like demons. Dozens of Allied flight crews died, but the Bugs shriveled like spiders in a candle flame, and TF 52's escorts fell back astern of the carriers to pick off any Bug who leaked through the fighters.

A shaken Vanessa Murakuma sat in her command chair once more, watching her plot. She knew her victory had been decisive, but it would be a while before her emotions accepted that. The Bugs had lost their entire light cruiser force and over sixty superdreadnoughts before they broke off, yet their new weapon had crippled half of Demosthenes' battle-line, and her fighter losses were over two hundred. That might be far lower than the disastrous casualties they'd taken in the early days of the war, but it was still seventeen percent of her total fighter force.

So much for our "uncontestable" tech superiority. We had every conventional advantage there was. We should have annihilated their starships for minimal losses, and we did, but Lord God did they hurt us after that. And Battle Comp says some of those SDs had third-generation shields, too. She shook her head, eyes bitter as preliminary damage and casualty reports continued to crawl across her terminal. *They don't seem to do things the way we do, but the bastards are no slouches. Those gunboat things aren't as good as fighters, but we never thought of anything like them, and I can see some advantages to them. But the real point is how fast they got them into production. They couldn't have had them when the shooting started, or we'd already've seen them. Did they cook them up from some pre-war R&D program? Were they already close to producing them then, or are they a response to our fighters?* She shivered. *God, I hope they were working on them pre-war! If they weren't—if they actually developed an entire new weapon system from scratch in barely sixteen months—what else are they going to hit us with?*

She stared at the steadily scrolling reports and found no answer.

BOOK TWO

CHAPTER TWENTY-THREE

All We Can Do

TFNS *Euphrates'* Marine detachment, Vanessa Murakuma reflected, had had more practice than most at receiving exalted VIPs on inspection tours. Still, the Terran Marines—no Orion ones, for this visitor— came to attention in an exceptionally perfect line of black trousers and green tunics as the shuttle's hatch opened.

The woman who stepped through that hatch was known by sight, but not at all socially, to Murakuma, who'd been out of the War College and back in the Fleet before she'd become Sky Marshal. Hannah Avram lived on in her memories as a tall, slender sword-blade of a woman. Nowadays, middle-aged solidity had begun to make inroads despite all that antigerone treatments could do, but the image of a sword still came to mind, for she was still a living weapon, to be wielded against humankind's enemies.

Murakuma stepped forward and saluted with great formality. "Welcome to *Euphrates* and to the Justin system, Sky Marshal."

Avram returned the salute with equal punctilio, but there was no warmth in her dark eyes. "Thank you, Admiral. Now, perhaps we could find a place to talk in private."

Murakuma felt the bottom drop out of her elation at meeting one of the heroes of the Theban War. "Certainly, Sky Marshal. Please come this way."

"Now then, Admiral Murakuma," Avram began as soon as they'd detached themselves from the cloud of hangers-on and settled into the sanctum of *Euphrates'* flag quarters, "there are certain matters we need to address." She dropped with evident relief into one of the comfortable chairs, laying her attache case in her lap, and continued in the same clipped tones. "First, congratulations are in order. You've managed to reverse the course of this war by holding the Bugs and pushing them back, out of this system."

Murakuma felt a thawing of the chill Avram's manner had induced in her gut. "Thank you, Sky Marshal. That means a great deal to me." She indicated the well-equipped bar. "Would the Sky Marshal care for a drink?"

"Thank you, no. And secondly," Avram resumed in exactly the same tone, "just what the *hell* did you think you were doing, hazarding the persons of two members of the Grand Allied Joint Chiefs of Staff— one of them the chairman?" She raised a hand to forestall a defense Murakuma hadn't even formulated. "Oh yes, I know. Boys will be boys, and there's no fool like an old fool. And now that we've gotten those two platitudes out of the way, the fact remains that you had every right to turn down their doubtless piteous pleas to come along—turn them down with a Marine 'escort,' if necessary! That wasn't just your right, Admiral Murakuma—it was your *duty*!" She paused, looking annoyed with herself, and lowered her voice back to its original decibel level. "I know how Ivan Nikolayevich can be. But you could have told him to take any complaints to me. I'd have told him to grow up— some would say it's about time! He would have told me to stop being a Jewish mother, but that's not your problem. The point is that you should have realized, even if he doesn't, that he's got no business risking his life in combat operations."

Murakuma surprised herself with her voice's firmness. "May I speak, Sky Marshal?"

"Say your say," Avram grunted.

"First of all, I didn't yield to any entreaties or bullying on Admiral Antonov's part. It was *my* idea to invite him and Lord Talphon along."

Avram's dark brown eyes locked with her jade-green ones. "Well, Admiral Murakuma, I'll say this for you: you're not a bore." The Sky Marshal settled back and spoke conversationally. "So, you claim full responsibility for the idea of risking Admiral of the Fleet Antonov, and also Lord Talphon, a relative of the Khan—if *he'd* gotten killed in this little escapade, we might have had a *second* war on our hands." She cocked her head. "Care to explain why, Admiral?"

Murakuma drew a deep breath. "It was something Admiral Antonov said to me when we presented the ops plan for his approval. The people I'd already lost were . . . haunting me. He seemed to sense it, and he spoke directly to me, as though he and I were the only ones present who belonged to a kind of horrible fraternity—the only ones who could possibly understand."

"Yes, I know he can be like that, too," Avram murmured, almost too softly to be heard.

"And then," Murakuma continued "he said something that brought all my self-pity into perspective. He reminded me I still had the option of taking the risks I order others to take." (Unnoticed, and unconsciously on her own part, Avram shifted her left hand and fingered that which had replaced her right arm.) "So I still have something he lost a long time ago. And I felt a sense of obligation—a need to let *him* share it once more." She shook herself and gazed directly at the Sky Marshal with green eyes that had gone almost mischievous. "That's really all I can say in mitigation, Sir. Except perhaps for yet another platitude: all's well that ends well."

Avram held those eyes, unblinking, for so long that they almost wavered. But then a twinkle banished the Sky Marshal's glare, although nothing below the eyes softened. "I can perhaps understand your feelings, Admiral. But the fact remains that you took an unjustified chance with the lives of very important people. The consequences could have been very grim. More to the point, those consequences could have fallen on *me*! Don't you *ever* expose me to a risk like that again! Do I make myself clear?"

"Perfectly, Sir," Murakuma replied in a small voice.

"Good. And now, a couple of final points that could have been communicated to you through regular channels . . . but, since I was coming out here anyway—" The twinkle was back, this time accompanied by a very slight smile. Avram fumbled in her attache case and extracted an official-looking folder. "You're a full admiral now. We'll make the official announcement later." She allowed herself a moment to savor Murakuma's expression, then made a great show of having an afterthought and reached back inside the attache case. "We'll also make this official later." She extracted a small, flat box, deep-blue edged with gold, and casually tossed it to Murakuma, who seemed to come out of shock just in time to grab it out of the air.

The newly promoted admiral forced her maelstrom of emotions to subside—dear God, she'd only been a vice admiral for . . . how long?—and opened the box. The light caught the twenty-four karat gold of what lay within, but that wasn't what dazzled her as she gazed at the royal beast suspended from the multicolored ribbon. The Lion of Terra—highest decoration the Federation could bestow on its sons and daughters, conferring on its holder the right to take a salute from anyone in uniform who didn't possess it, regardless of rank.

After a time, Murakuma remembered where she was and lowered the box, revealing Hannah Avram, smiling an odd little smile. "I believe, Admiral," the Sky Marshal said, "That I'll have that drink now. Have you got any white wine?"

Murakuma's smile started out tremulously, but didn't stay that way. "Sure you won't make it Irish, Sir?"

✧　　✧　　✧

Rear Admiral Marcus LeBlanc leaned back, propped his feet on the desk, and ran a hand over the top of his head from front to back in a habitual gesture of weariness. The surviving hairs were insufficient to mar the sleekness, and for the thousandth time he wondered if that was because of wry realism, misplaced pride, sheer damned stubbornness, or just a lifelong aversion to putting himself in the hands of the medical profession.

"Are these the last of the reports?" he asked the offensively young ensign.

"Yes, Sir," Kevin Sanders responded, with more energy than he had any right to show this late in the working day. "We had to practically extort a final draft out of Dr. Kovac. But they're all here, ready to be correlated."

"Too damned late in the day to start doing it now," LeBlanc muttered. His gaze shifted to the window. They were at that point of their work-cycle where the end of the working day actually corresponded to the setting of Alpha Centauri A. As usual at this time of year in this particular part of Nova Terra, it was dipping behind the pale blue curve of Eden that loomed over the oceanic horizon like some titan-emperor's floating pleasure dome. LeBlanc's ad hoc organization of Bug specialists had been isolated here for reasons which he'd at least found good for a cynical laugh. The Powers That Be could stress "security" all they wanted, but they were far less concerned over Bug spies disguised as humans or fanatical human adherents of Bugism than that their citizenry might get wind of his team's . . . disturbing theories. Yet he couldn't deny that the island of New Atlantis was a lovely place, with its dramatic topography and the subtropical Terran vegetation that had pretty much pushed aside the less-evolved local stuff. Maybe too lovely; where reality presented such a gentle aspect, it was almost possible to forget what was happening in the universe beyond the white-sand beaches and regard the beings they studied as some fascinating abstract problem in xenology. Periodically, LeBlanc made himself view the tapes from Erebor.

Sanders followed his gaze. "Beautiful island, isn't it, Sir? I don't know about the name, though. I mean, there never was an *old* Atlantis!"

LeBlanc grinned. Sanders should know, coming as he did from Old Terra, which made him something of a *rara avis* in the TFN. He'd been working for Admiral Antonov's staff spook but had contrived to get himself detached to LeBlanc's outfit. The new-minted rear admiral was glad to have him; he had the kind of irreverent originality this project needed, and he was the sort to fit in well with this oddball half-military and half-civilian crew. In particular, he seemed to resonate well with the Tabbies, of whom there were quite a few here, along with a fair number of Ophiuchi and a couple of Gorm. Besides, LeBlanc liked him in the way people generally like those in whom they unconsciously recognize their own younger selves.

"Take a load off," the admiral said, gesturing at a chair. "Sorry you had to deal with Kovac—I know he can be difficult." He stretched hugely. "Late as it is, I suppose I need to try and make some sense of these reports tonight. The Director is sure to want a briefing." The Director of Naval Intelligence had arrived on Nova Terra less than a local day ago. So far she'd been kept busy at Allied Grand Fleet Headquarters, a quarter of the way around the globe. But she was bound to show up at New Atlantis, sooner rather than later.

"There's not much you can tell her about the databases, Sir," Sanders said as he settled into the chair. "We're still where we were when Dr. Linkovich had his initial insight. The Gorm have been trying to construct a model for electronic—'psychotronic'?—storage of psionic data patterns by analogizing from what they know of how their *minisorchi* operates. They're *sure* there must be such a model. But . . . Well, Gorm don't scream and smash the furniture. Not their style. But I can tell that that's exactly what they'd be doing if they were human.

"Trouble is, not even they have a 'unified field theory' relating psi to matter and energy. We humans don't have a clue; we've never had any real reason to be interested. So until some genius comes up with such a theory—which the Bugs must already have—we're just pissing into the wind."

LeBlanc stretched again, and rubbed his eyes. "Well then, we'd better concentrate on areas where we have a chance of accomplishing something. Like these new attack craft Admiral Murakuma encountered."

"Oh, yes." Sanders brightened, oblivious to the pain that had crossed LeBlanc's face at the mention of Admiral Murakuma. "That was what Kovac was working on. He gave me a running discourse while his flunkies were getting his 'extremely tentative and incomplete conclusions' printed out. I think I've got a pretty good—if elementary— idea of what he's driving at."

"Well, summarize for me. I'd like to hear the 'elementary' version before I tackle the full report."

"I fancy I'd like to hear it too, Ensign."

The clipped, British-accented voice from the doorway had a remarkable effect. LeBlanc was on his feet, fumbling to fasten his collar, while Sanders, who wasn't all that far removed from the Academy, was too busy trying to brace a bulkhead that wasn't there to be concerned with the state of his uniform.

"Why, er, Admiral Trevayne," LeBlanc stammered, "we weren't expecting . . . that is, we didn't know you were . . ."

Winnifred Trevayne waved a dismissive gesture, and occupied an empty chair. "Please be at ease, Admiral LeBlanc and Ensign . . . Sanders, isn't it? I remember you from your time on the Sky Marshal's staff." She steepled her fingers and gazed over them, sighting along the bridge of her keel-straight nose. Her coloring was dark, but that was the only vestige of the Jamaican fraction of her ancestry. "I suppose I should have given you some notice of my arrival. But I've only just been able to get away from Grand Fleet Headquarters. Besides, I couldn't face one more well-prepared reception." Her eyes surveyed the none-too-tidy office, finally settling on LeBlanc and Sanders, and her lips formed what in anyone else might have been suspected of being a smile. "Something rather refreshing about this place, actually. And now, Ensign Sanders, you were starting to say when I interrupted . . . ?"

Sanders took a deep breath. "Well, Admiral, our staff's concluded that the Arachnids have found a somewhat different approach to applying classic drive theory to small craft. We've always had a problem in applying the technology to smaller packages, because of the 'shallowness' of the inertial sump associated with small craft." The ensign was rapidly returning to his chatty norm. "For example, the version that made fighters possible paid for its compactness with a sump that was so much less deep that fighter performance, unlike that of starships, is degraded when carrying external ordinance, and—"

LeBlanc cleared his throat nervously. "I believe the Director is already conversant with these matters, Ensign."

Sanders had the grace to blush. "Er, sorry, Sir. We have a lot of xenologists around here who have to have things outside the biological and social sciences explained to them, and you sort of get used to . . . Well, let me cut to the chase. The data from Fifth Fleet suggests that the Bugs have developed a kind of intermediate drive for these 'gunboats,' too large for most small craft but with a sump almost as deep as a full-sized starship's. Their maximum speed is lower than an unloaded fighter's, but they can carry external ordinance without being slowed down."

"They must pay some sort of penalty," Trevayne mused.

"Oh yes, Sir. The penalty comes in the form of a high power requirement, with a correspondingly strong emissions signature. This, combined with its large size—for a small craft—means a gunboat can be targeted by ship-to-ship weapon systems. And it's not large *enough* to absorb the kind of damage those weapons dish out."

"That suggests it ought to trigger mine attacks as well," LeBlanc put in. "Actually, there's another piece of good news, as well. Analysis of the observational data confirms the supposition that, being larger than other small craft, gunboats can't use internal bays. Instead, they seem to be carried externally on ships. So rearming them must be

an EVA operation, and it doesn't take much imagination to see how awkward *that* must be."

"For openers," Sanders piped up, the other two's exalted ranks momentarily forgotten, "it means the mother ship's drive field has to be deactivated while they're doing it. The radiation would deep-fry somebody in a vac suit!"

He seemed about to say more, but Trevayne raised a hand. In the ensuing silence, she looked from one of them to the other and then back again.

"I'm afraid you're missing the point, gentlemen. You see, all the points of 'good news' you've adduced are outweighed by the one very large item of *bad* news." She met their eyes again, even more gravely than before. "The one, single advantage we've had up to now has been our somewhat superior technology. And we've assumed that that state of affairs will continue, that their tactical inflexibility must be accompanied by a lack of inventiveness. We can no longer make any such assumption. Since encountering our fighters, they've developed, produced and deployed a countervailing system. I'm not certain we could do so well in so short a period."

In the dead silence that followed, LeBlanc's quiet voice seemed almost raucous. "Uh, Sir, Admiral Murakuma speculated that the gunboats could perhaps be the end result of some R&D program they already had underway before the war."

"That, Admiral LeBlanc, is a classic example of whistling in the dark. It would be sheer folly for us to rely on it. Instead, we must assume there are more surprises in store. You and your people here must try and foretell what those surprises are going to be. You must try to deduce, on the basis of past experience, what they find most threatening in our technological tool kit and how they'll seek to counter it." All at once, her trademark crispness wavered, and she held a hand over her eyes as though to shield them, even though the office was only dimly illuminated against the twilight. "It's all we can do," she said, addressing someone other than LeBlanc and Sanders. "We really have no way of knowing what lies in wait."

Outside the window, the slow rotation of the twin-planet system sent the last light of Alpha Centauri A vanishing behind Eden. The sister planet shaded abruptly from sky blue to ultramarine, and the heavens grew dark.

CHAPTER TWENTY-FOUR

Broken Claws

Fourteenth Great Claw of the Khan Zhaarnak'diaano glowered into the small holo tank of his repeater plot. The worthless planets of the uninhabited Telmasa System orbited their K4 primary with a bland uselessness which mirrored his own mood all too accurately. Clan Diaano had once been famed for the warriors it produced in the Khan's service, but that had been before the Wars of Shame. It was not his clan's fault no chance had arisen to win back the honor lost in those disastrous wars, yet every one of his ancestors seemed to prowl the back of his mind, muttering balefully over their descendant's failure to seize glory by the throat in *this* war. For more than a full human year—almost two Orion years—it had raged, and *still* he sat tethered as a "rear area security umbrella" designed only to reassure civilians!

He growled and kneaded his claws in and out of his chair's padded armrests. Of course, very few of the Khan's warriors had so far been given the chance to measure themselves against these new foes—these "Bugs." Fang Anaasa and his pilots had won enormous renown for their rescue of the Human Fifth Fleet in the Third Battle of Justin, but no more of the KON's units had been rushed forward . . . for reasons which were one more ember in Zhaarnak's seething disgust.

Technology. Technology and experience. The Humans' R&D had—once more—outpaced the *Zheeerlikou'valkhannaieee's*, and so they were better equipped than the Khan's Navy. They had begun the war with better shields, better armor . . . better weapons. Even now their *technical missions* were busy throughout the Khanate, working to upgrade the KON's technology as if the *Zheeerlikou'valkhannaieee* were cubs who must be led by the hand. And though the Federation's last major war was an Orion century old, it remained more recent

than anything the *Khanate* could claim. Antipiracy operations, the suppression of a slaving outbreak in the Khithaar Sector, the short confrontation when District Governor Maashaar defied the present Khan's sire . . . those were all the "wars" the KON had fought since the Third Interstellar War, and so the Grand Alliance had agreed the Humans should lead the battle in the Romulus Cluster.

The great claw bared the tips of his fangs. Deep inside, a part of him acknowledged that it was the Humans who had first been attacked. Their warriors' blood had been the first shed, their civilians the ones butchered, and so it was right that they be given the honor of facing the foe. Yet another, deeper part of him could not accept that. Humans were *chofaki*. They *had* no honor. They were clever, yes, and skilled in the cold blooded execution of maneuvers, yet they lacked the warrior's fire. He had heard the arguments—*Valkha*, but he had heard them!—since the Theban War. *Minisharhuaak!* Of *course* they had shouldered their obligations in that war, but they had done so out of *fear*, Zhaarnak thought. It was they who had given the crazed Thebans technology in the first place, and they'd feared Liharnow the Great would loose the Navy upon them if they did not "step forward." And they had shown themselves *chofak* yet again in this war. What true warrior would have fallen back again and again, abandoning millions of his own civilians to certain death—to being *eaten* like so many *marhangi*?

He made his claws retract, and his mind replayed the official briefings like some endless, meaningless chant. The Humans had had no choice but to fall back. They had fought again and again, and not even Zhaarnak could deny the damage they had inflicted—assuming the reports were accurate. Yet that was the point. If the reports *were* accurate, then *why* had they been forced back? Almost four hundred superdreadnoughts—that was how many capital ships the Humans' Fifth Fleet claimed to have destroyed. *Four hundred!* The entire Orion *Navy* contained only four hundred and six starships, including even *destroyers*! Was he to believe the Humans had destroyed thirty times the KON's total tonnage without even *slowing* their enemies?

Ridiculous! Such inflated claims were the proof they were *chofaki*, dirt-eaters, beings so lost to honor they could not even recognize it as a concept! According to those same intelligence packets the Humans' ships were faster, their weapons longer ranged, their defensive technologies and datalink superior, *and* they had fighters! If they had destroyed so many ships, if they held such a tremendous tactical advantage, then why were *they* on the defensive? Oh, true, they had retaken Justin—finally, with Fang Anaasa's help—yet did they truly expect Zhaarnak to believe any opponent could absorb such losses and continue to *attack*?

He shook himself and rose. *Softly, Zhaarnak,* he told himself. *Softly. Whatever you may think, it is your duty not to show your officers your disgust. And be truthful. Would you be so ready to believe them* chofak *had they not brought such dishonor upon your clan?*

He twitched his ears brusquely, angry with that last thought, yet he could not quite reject it. His clan fathers had charged into battle in the Orion way in the Wars of Shame . . . and the Humans had slaughtered their commands in the *chofak* Human way. Perhaps the Terran Navy *had* taught the KON how wars were won, but what of *honor*? What of the battle sagas chanted when warriors were laid to rest? The Wars of Shame took those things from his clan, and even the meager redemption Clan Diaano had won in the Third Interstellar War had come on Human terms. It was the Humans who shared the strikefighter technology with the Khanate even before the Rigelians turned on the *Zheeerlikou'valkhannaieee.* It was the Humans whose industrial might had built entire *starships* for the Khan. Even Varnik'sheerino, the greatest fang of the last three centuries, had been forced to dance to Human terms, coordinate his plans with theirs!

Be honest. Be honest, Zhaarnak. Chofak *Humans may be, yet what you truly hate is that they never let your clan regain honor from them— only* with *them. There is no Human blood upon your claws, and you hate them for it.*

Well, perhaps that was truth, but truth was a bitter herb, and whatever cause he had to hate them, their showing in *this* war was cause enough for contempt.

He snorted and stepped into the intraship car. If he could not take his battlegroup to war, at least he would not sit here on his flag bridge like some clawless cub and watch an empty plot!

Least Claw of the Khan Shaiaasu'aaithnau sighed in relief as his six *Lahstyn*-class light cruisers headed for the warp point. Under other circumstances, he would have enjoyed exercising his first squadron command, but the Shanak System was and always had been as useful as a screen door on an airlock. It was lifeless, a cul-de-sac accessible only via a single closed warp point, whose sole claim to importance was that it lay adjacent to the *extremely* useful Kliean System. Unlike Shanak, Kliean boasted two habitable planets and an immensely rich asteroid belt. It was one of the Khanate's oldest and wealthiest inhabited systems . . . and the only reason Shaiaasu and his ships had just spent a thoroughly boring month resurveying Shanak.

He let himself relax as his lead ship entered the warp point, and lazy thoughts chased about his brain. He understood the panic behind his orders. If the rumors from the Human's Justin System were true, even the potential for a similar threat to a system like Kliean must be terrifying to the Khan's administrators. And, he admitted, the survey data on Shanak *had* been over four Orion centuries old. Improved instrumentation *might* have discovered a second warp point—it had not, but it might have—yet that had made the mission no less boring, and he felt abandoned so far from the front. Not that *Lahstyn*-class cruisers would have been much use in combat.

He purred a chuckle at the thought of his little survey ships leading a life-or-death attack. He had seen one of Humans' *Hun*-class cruisers. Now *there* was a survey ship! But the Federation was wealthy enough to build such vessels for survey work, and the *Zheeerlikou'valkhannaieee* were not. Indeed, he took a sort of perverse pride in his command's austerity. Humans might need big, comfortable ships; Orions did not. Not, he admitted, that he would refuse one!

He chuckled again, then braced himself as his own ship entered the warp point. *Acutar* seemed to twitch around him in the familiar stress of transit, and he carefully did not grunt in relief as the brief nausea eased. He gazed longingly into his plot at the blue dot of the planet Masiahn. He had relatives down there—and he wished he had time to visit them. Masiahn was one of the jewels in the Khan's crown, a beautiful world of mountains, forests, and swift, white-foaming rivers. The planet had an enormous tourist trade, and Shaiaasu would have loved to spend a few weeks there. The *jahar* hunting was excellent, and not many could mount one of the needle-tipped antler racks on his wall or claim he'd taken the beast with no weapon but his own claws.

But it was not to be. His squadron had completed this component of its mission, and he knew Great Claw Zhaarnak's reputation. The 109th Survey Squadron was an independent command, but the great claw was responsible for covering its operations, and Zhaarnak must be like a *zeget* with a thorn in its paw. Any mere least claw who wasted a single hour longer than necessary would regret giving him a target for his ire!

The cloaked cruiser watched the last enemy vessel disappear. It had been astounded when the enemy first appeared, for this system had always been useless. Reachable only via a closed warp point and with no outbound warp points, it had never attracted any attention. Yet doctrine was inflexible: any star system, however useless, must be picketed, and so this one had.

Now the cruiser waited, making absolutely certain of the coordinates of the second closed warp point through which the enemy vessels had vanished before it fired its courier drone home.

✧　　✧　　✧

Zhaarnak looked up from his paperwork as his com buzzed. He activated it, and Least Claw Daarsaahl'haairna-ahn, his battle-cruiser flagship's CO, looked out of it at him.

"Yes, Daarsaahl?"

"Least Claw Shaiaasu has reported, Sir," his flag captain—a term the KON had borrowed from the Humans, Zhaarnak thought sourly—twitched her ears derisively. "Having found nothing in Shanak, he is en route to Thraidaar. He will pass through Telmasa within the next two days."

"So he found nothing. Why am I not surprised?" Zhaarnak's ears mirrored the flag captain's sour humor. If Shanak had been cleared, the battlegroup would shortly be moved from Telmasa to Sak to cover the choke point there, and would *that* not be exciting?

He cocked his head in thought. Shaiaasu's message was for his information only, for the least claw was not technically under his command, but Zhaarnak *was* a great claw . . . and bored.

"Very well, Daarsaahl. Let me know when he arrives. We may as well run a tracking exercise on him. In fact, set up a few days of maneuvers. He can delay his Thraidaar survey that long, and we have been too long idle. Whether they let us fight it or not, there *is* a war on!"

"Of course, Great Claw."

"Good. In the meantime—" Zhaarnak surprised himself with a chuckle of true amusement "—I have more than sufficient paperwork to keep me occupied for the next several hours. Invite Theerah to join both of us for supper, and we can discuss the exercise plans over a haunch of *zeget*."

The freighter *Sellykha* was no swift *thirahk*. In fact, she was big, ugly, ungainly, and about as maneuverable as an over-age asteroid, but her captain loved her. The resource extraction ship had never been out of Kliean. She made her routine trips between the asteroid belt and the orbital smelters, earning her owners a steady if unspectacular profit, and if it was a boring berth, well, Shipmaster Faarsaahl'ynaara had *earned* a bit of boredom in the autumn of his life.

Still, it *was* a welcome diversion to be ferrying the small prospecting team to Shaylka's single moon. The outermost planet of the system was a typical ball of ice, but its moon was much more interesting. Its eccentric orbit had been noted during the original system survey, yet only in the last few years had anyone gotten around to taking a closer look at it. No one was prepared to suggest where it had come from or how Shaylka had captured it, but it appeared to be rich in transuranic elements, and *Sellykha*'s owners had gotten in the first claim on its mineral rights.

Faarsaahl padded down the bridge access tunnel—no intraship cars for work-a-day *Sellykha!*—while he wondered how much his employers would earn from those rights. It might all come to nothing, but there was at least the chance of a fat bonus, and his son-in-law and daughter had just presented him with his seventh, eighth and ninth grandcubs. Their home on Masiahn would need additional rooms, and he planned to give them a new wing for Jaathnaa's birthday.

He stepped onto the bridge, crossed to his command chair, and paused to check the engineering readouts. Number Two engine room had reported the recurrence of that irritating harmonic, and he wanted a detailed record for the yard techs. "Engineer's imagination" indeed! *This* time he would make those *thaarkoni* admit there was a problem and *do* something about it.

"Shipmaster?" He looked up at his fourth officers call. The youngsters ears were half-flattened, and he waved at his display. "Could you look at this, Sir?"

Faarsaahl crossed the bridge, wondering what fresh totally prosaic discovery Huaath had made. *You were young once yourself,* he chided himself, but the cub was so shiny and new Faarsaahl kept looking for milk on his lips.

"What is it?"

"I am not certain, Sir." Huaath peered intently into his display as his claws ticked gently over his panel. "I seem to be picking up some sort of drive field."

"A drive field? Out *here?*" Faarsaahl tried to keep the incredulity out of his voice.

"Yes, Sir. Its frequency matches nothing in our database, however." Huaath waved at his display. "Look for yourself."

Faarsaahl peered over the youngster's shoulder, and his spine stiffened, for there *was* a drive field out there. *Sellykha's* sensors fell far short of Navy standards, but the signature burned clear and sharp, and Faarsaahl felt his claws slip from their sheaths in sudden, terrible suspicion.

"Its vector?" he asked quietly.

"It appears to be inbound from Shanak," Huaath said, and Faarsaahl's belly knotted. He stared at the display for one more moment, then turned sharply to his communications officer.

"Get your transmitter on line!" The com officer blinked in surprise, and Faarsaahl bared his fangs. "Quickly! Alert Masiahn and Zhardak that unknown starships have entered the system!"

The com officer stiffened, whiskers aquiver in sudden understanding, and bent over his panel with frantic haste. Faarsaahl watched him, then turned back to his fourth officer and laid a clawed hand on the confused youngster's shoulder.

"Inform them that Fourth Officer Huaath'raamahl spotted them," he told the com officer quietly. "See to it that they know it was only his alertness which let us get the warning off."

"Aye, Shipmaster," the com officer said equally quietly, and Faarsaahl squeezed Huaath's shoulder. The cub still hadn't realized, he thought sadly. *Sellykha* had only a freighter's speed, but at least he could insure that Clan Raamahl knew it had a new father-in-honor.

Zhaarnak'diaano stared at his flag captain.

"What strength?" he demanded.

"The Governor had little data when he transmitted the alert," Daarsaahl replied flatly. "*Sellykha* was destroyed within minutes of sending her warning. Shipmaster Faarsaahl continued sending updates to the last, but he had seen only twenty or thirty light cruisers at that time."

"*Valkha*," Zhaarnak whispered. At least the message had reached him quickly via the interstellar communication network comsats that relayed light-speed transmissions between warp points, but his thoughts seemed frozen. Shanak. They had come from Shanak, but how—?

"They tracked Shaiaasu," he said softly. "They must have. But how did they *get* there?"

"There must be a second closed warp point." Daarsaahl's ears went flat as she spoke. "*Minisharhuaak!* Our own survey showed them the way!"

Zhaarnak shook off his paralysis and spun to his com section.

"Emergency priority, Juaahr! All units are to form on *Dashyr* for transit to Kliean. Then set up a conference link with the carrier commanders. Request an immediate update on squadron readiness states from *farshathkhanaak* Derikaal. Then send our own alert up the ICN. Request any available support—utmost priority." The com officer nodded, and Zhaarnak wheeled to his operations officer. "If this is only a probe, we may be able to stop it, Theerah. Configure Derikaal's squadrons for an antishipping strike. If we can destroy them or drive them back on Shanak, we have a chance to delay them long enough for someone else to get here."

"Who, Sir?" Son of the Khan Theerah'jihaal asked quietly.

"*Anyone!*" Zhaarnak snapped, then flicked his ears in apology. His fear and anger were not the ops officer's fault. Oh, no. It was the four *billion* civilians in Kliean who woke the terror at his heart, and he turned back to his console as the first carrier commander appeared on his com.

The Fleet continued its advance. Two more freighters had been destroyed. Both appeared to have been moving towards the Fleet, perhaps in an effort to acquire more data. If so, that was a good sign—an indication there were no enemy warships to oppose the attack.

Sensors continued to report. Both targeted planets blazed with the emissions of densely populated, high-tech worlds, and those same sensors had already detected the system's massive asteroid-based industry. That, too, was good. It indicated the wealth of resources waiting for the taking. Once its planets had been cleansed, this system would be a valuable prize.

Great Claw Zhaarnak's battlegroup raced through the warp point. Least Claw Shaiaasu's light cruisers screened the main force: six battle-cruisers and an equal number of *Mohrdenhau* light carriers. That was it. All Zhaarnak had. Twelve starships and one hundred and seventy-six fighters, and the great claw felt the agony of his own inadequacy as Zhardak and Masiahn glowed in his plot. Four billion. The number repeated again and again, tolling through his brain, and his eyes dropped to the icon of Shaiaasu's ship. He wanted to hate the least claw for letting this happen, yet Shaiaasu had only followed orders. He should have been more careful, but he had obeyed procedures. *And perhaps he, as you, saw his mission only as a distraction from his true duty. From his chance to win honor. And if he did, what does that say of you, Zhaarnak'diaano?*

"Transmission from Zhardak, Sir!" The com officer listened for a moment, and his ears went flat. Zhaarnak glared at him, part of him wishing Juaahr would suddenly be struck mute, yet he had to know. "Zhardak reports at least nine battle-cruisers and an unknown number of superdreadnoughts," the com officer said in a dead voice.

"*Shiaaahk!*" Daarsaahl whispered the savage oath, and Zhaarnak's claws drove deep into his armrests. This was no probe . . . and his battlegroup could never stop it. The light dots of the inhabited worlds drew his eyes like a black hole, and the same black hole sucked his soul into its maw as his earlier thoughts about warriors who abandoned civilians mocked him.

"Very well," he said after a moment, and the calmness of his own voice astonished him. "Update your force appreciation, Theerah." He looked down at the com link to his senior pilot. "Inform your squadrons, Derikaal," he said quietly. "Tell them—" He paused, searching for the words. "Tell them we are warriors. What we can do, we must, as the Khan expects of us."

"Yes, Sir," the *farshathkhanaak* said softly, and Zhaarnak looked at his flag captain.

"Take us to meet them, Daarsaahl."

The Fleet's sensors picked up the attack craft first, then the ships which had launched them, and the light cruisers fell back on the main force.

There were no gunboats to cover them, for this was a rapid reaction force, with none of the new units. But the enemy was still weaker, with less than two hundred attack craft and nothing heavier than a battle-cruiser to support them.

Eighty-Third Small Claw of the Khan Derikaal'zohkiir's fighters neared the enemy, and the *farshathkhanaak's* blood ran cold as he saw their true strength at last. Twenty-seven superdreadnoughts—a small force beside the ones waging such titanic combat on the Justin front, yet impossible odds for a single light battlegroup—were screened by nine battle-cruisers and thirty-three light cruisers, including a dozen of those the Humans had codenamed *Cataphract*. His fighter squadrons were a cub's toy against such power, but they were all Kliean had, and he forced his voice to remain calm as he designated targets.

"Ignore the cruisers," he told his pilots, knowing even as he did how many of them those cruisers would kill. "Mass on the lead superdreadnought division."

Acknowledgments came back, and he took his place at their head—the post of greatest honor and danger—as they shook out behind him. His two-seat command fighter was more austere than its Human counterparts, without a separate pilot. He remembered the arguments in which he had maintained the superiority of the Human arrangement, the times he had stressed how the extra position eased a strike commander's load, but today he was glad the controls were in his own claws . . . and it was not as if it would have mattered.

His pilots streaked into the Bugs' engagement envelope, and fireballs pocked their ranks. Fighter after fighter blew apart, but they held their course, howling down their enemies' throat in an attack they knew could only be futile. Yet it was an attack they had to make. They were Orions, and four billion civilians lay behind them.

A quarter of the enemy attack craft were destroyed short of the Fleet, but the survivors shrieked in on the leading superdreadnoughts, closing through everything the Fleet could throw at them, and salvoed their deadly FRAMs. Four SDs blew apart, and the attack craft tore through the formation, strafing with their onboard lasers, ripping at the Fleet in desperate fury.

Of the hundred and seventy-five who had attacked, eighty-one broke free to rearm, and the Fleet rumbled onward. Losses were higher than projected, but over half the attack craft had been destroyed. Their next attack would be weaker . . . and the one after that weaker still.

Zhaarnak sat bitterly in his command chair as the remnants of his third strike broke off. Derikaal had lived to lead the second, but the last had been led by a mere cub of the Khan, for no more senior officer had survived. Now his remaining fighters—all sixteen of them—fell back to their carriers . . . and the enemy continued remorselessly onward. Ten of his pilots had ignored orders and rammed capital ships, but it was useless. Useless. Their suicide runs had not even dented their targets. Only seven superdreadnoughts had been destroyed, and his battlegroup was hopelessly inadequate to stop the survivors.

"The fighters are rearming, Sir," Son of the Khan Theerah said, and Zhaarnak fought the need to scream curses at him. The fighters were *rearming*. What did Theerah think less than three squadrons could *do* against such firepower?

Every instinct shrieked to attack. That was the *Farshalah'kiah*, the Warrior's Way, which required him to die before he let these creatures murder his people's worlds, yet reason knew his battlegroup's death could not save Kliean. The system was doomed, unless reinforcements could somehow take it back, and there *were* no reinforcements. Kliean was too far from what all had assumed was the front. The bulk of the Fleet was busy deploying towards the known fighting or refitting for future deployment; only light forces like his were available, and if the enemy had massed so heavy a fleet this quickly, at least one of his main bases must lie in close proximity.

It should not be so, he thought bleakly. *We are caught like the Humans themselves, struck where we never expected it and naked under the enemy's claws. Yet there is* one *difference. The Humans had only colony worlds to defend . . . we* have *the entire Idnahk Sector.*

His blood was frozen. Four billion in Kliean, yes, but another billion and a half in Hairnow, yet another in Alowan, and over *thirty* billion within six transits of Sak. He looked upon the greatest disaster in the *Zheeerlikou'valkhannaieee's* history, and he could not stop it. Gods above, *he could not stop it!*

"Fall back, Theerah," he said.

"Sir?" The ops office stared at him, and Zhaarnak closed his fists, extended claws sinking a centimeter deep into his palms.

"Fall back," he repeated. His ops officer continued to stare at him, and Zhaarnak made himself meet that stare. "We cannot stop them," he said, wondering how he could speak so flatly while his soul died, "but we are the only force available. We must fall back to Telmasa. We cannot sacrifice ourselves here when our ships may make the difference in a warp point defense there."

"But, Sir, the planetary defense centers! If we fell back, joined with the PDCs—"

"The PDCs are antiques," Zhaarnak said, and his voice was no longer flat. It was harsh and ugly with despair and self-hate. "They lack even datalink! What they can do, they must, but our support would add nothing to their capabilities. We must fall back on Telmasa, where we *may* make a difference, not sacrifice ourselves where we know we cannot."

Theerah stared at him, still unable to believe what he was hearing, and Zhaarnak slammed a clawed, bleeding fist on the arm of his chair.

"*Minisharhuaak!* Must I repeat myself yet again? *Fall back,* Son of the Khan! We have an entire sector to consider!"

"I—" Theerah closed his mouth, then nodded curtly. "As you command, Great Claw." His voice was ugly, but the ugliness was directed less at Zhaarnak than at the knowledge that the great claw was correct, and Zhaarnak let it pass. Who was he to task another for the dishonor of insubordination when he had just abandoned four billion people to death?

Least Claw Shaiaasu listened in shock. *Fall back?* Abandon the system? *No!*

He stared into his own plot, seeing what Great Claw Zhaarnak saw, and knew what the great claw knew. The system was doomed—*doomed because of you, Shaiaasu'aaithnau*—and all the battlegroup could hope for now was to hold the Telmasa warp point until relief forces arrived.

But it couldn't. There were enough fighters in Hairnow and Alowan to replace the carriers' losses, but even with full hangar bays, they could never stop the Bugs—not in Telmasa, not in Alowan, not in Sak . . .

Humans had a word for what he had unleashed upon his people; they called it Juggernaut.

"Sir?" His exec's eyes met his, as sick as his own, and he looked past her, looked about him at his bridge officers, pictured all the other officers and ratings of *Acutar*'s company and the dishonor he had brought upon them all.

"*No!*"

Zhaarnak lunged upright as KONS *Acutar* changed course. She darted straight for the enemy, and as he watched, *Kilokharn* and *Kurv* wheeled to follow her, then *Faulhi, Nabahstahr* and *Zairoh,* until Shaiaasu's entire squadron streaked for the Bugs behind its flagship.

"Raise Least Claw Shaiaasu!" Zhaarnak roared, and his com officer punched keys. The great claw waited, watching in fury as his entire light cruiser element charged to its own destruction, and then Juaahr looked up.

"*Acutar* does not respond, Sir," he said.

Zhaarnak sank back into his chair, and to his watching officers, it was as if he aged a century before their eyes. He gazed into his plot, watching the first missiles streak towards the light cruisers—light cruisers which lacked even command datalink—and his ears were flat. *Curse you, Shaiaasu,* he thought numbly. *Curse you for doing what I long to do!*

Acutar staggered as the first missile slammed into her shields. Another followed, and a third. Her shields went down, and vaporized hull plating streamed astern, yet she never slowed, never hesitated. Her own launchers fired back as she entered their range, but they were pinpricks. The Bug leviathans shrugged them aside and poured a butchery of fire into Shaiaasu's squadron.

Kilokharn blew up, then *Zairoh,* but their sisters held their course, and Zhaarnak raised his open, blood-streaked hand. He thrust it towards the display, then closed it once more, digging his claws into his lacerated palm in salute even as his soul railed at the officers who had defied his orders. *Kurv* vanished, and beams began to fire, as well. *Nabahstahr* exploded, but *Acutar* and *Faulhi* continued their mad charge. They were broken wrecks, yet their drives survived, and they hurled themselves upon the enemy. A Bug light cruiser accelerated to meet *Faulhi,* and the two ships were blotted from the universe as they struck. Another light cruiser lunged at *Acutar,* but somehow Shaiaasu's ship evaded it. One ship—a single ship, out of an entire squadron—charged the massive target of its foes, and Zhaarnak looked up, watching the visual display, as *Acutar* struck her target and an enemy superdreadnought blew apart in a shroud of flame.

My claws are broken, Zhaarnak thought. *My honor is no more. I have failed my Clan Fathers and those who will follow me. I have failed my Khan. But in my dishonor, I may yet shield my farshatok.*

"Claw Daarsaahl."

"Yes, Great Claw?" his flag captain's voice was quiet, and Zhaarnak kept his eyes on the visual display's fading ball of fire.

"Make an entry in the log, Claw Daarsaahl. The decision to withdraw is mine and mine alone. I did not discuss it. I did not seek the concurrence of any other officer."

"But, Sir—" Daarsaahl began, only to stop as Zhaarnak raised a forestalling hand.

"Make the entry," he said softly.

CHAPTER TWENTY-FIVE

"May our claws strike deep."

"All right." Rear Admiral Raymond Porter Prescott looked at his subordinates with grim hazel eyes. "We reach Alowan in eighteen hours, and the Tabbies still hold it. Our job is to make sure they *continue* to hold until Great Fang Koraaza gets here."

Commodore Diego Jackson, commanding Task Force 23's light carriers, shook his head. "That's a tall order, Sir," he said quietly.

"Maybe, but that's the mission," Prescott said, and looked at his intelligence officer. "Bring us up to speed, Eloise."

"Yes, Sir." Commander Eloise Kmak had her notes on her terminal, but she didn't look at them. No doubt, Prescott thought bitterly, they were indelibly graven into her mind.

"The real surprise," she began, "is that there're any KON units *left* in Alowan. Given the Orion honor code—and, especially, his own record—I'm amazed Great Claw Zhaarnak fell back at all. The fact that he's managed to preserve his battlegroup essentially intact is even more astounding.

"As far as we can tell, he bled the Bugs badly in Telmasa, but they punched a simultaneous transit into his face. He got a little too close—that's how he lost the ships he did—but for the most part he used only his fighters. That was smart, Admiral. Very smart. They're his most replenishable resource; he was able to make good his losses in Klian from Hairnow, and the Alowan Fleet Base was able to replace those he lost in Telmasa. According to our latest reports, he has six Orion and three Gorm BCs, six CVLs, and eight *Gharbahg*-class CLs. That's not a lot, but the Tabbies did well to scrape up even that much after being surprised this way. GHQ and Idnahk Sector Command are trying to keep us updated on what else they may be able to find, but the situation's so confused no one's certain what is or isn't available. Essentially, we've sent out an 'all ships' signal. We'll take what we can get, but for now, we—and Zhaarnak—are it."

Prescott nodded slowly, for Kmak was right. It also meant his ten battleships, nine light carriers, nine battle-cruisers, five light cruisers and five destroyers represented a far heavier force than Zhaarnak's. *Not that it's heavy enough,* he thought, and his mouth twisted as he remembered the two battleships he *didn't* have. TFNS *Mars* and *Triomphant* had both lost too many engine rooms to keep up on the desperate, high-speed voyage from New Bristol, and he had no idea how the battle-cruisers *Ranseur* and *Pikeaxe* had managed to keep *their* drives on-line.

Maybe these bastards have a point using commercial engines. They may suck wind in a tactical *sense, but—*

"Given the larger strikegroups Tabby carriers carry and the partial squadrons they put aboard their capital ships, he actually has about sixty more fighters than we do," Kmak went on. "Our combined force will be able to put over three hundred into space, but we're very weak in capital launchers and, of course, we have no SD element. If we have to fall back on the Pairsag twin planets, we'll pick up another hundred and twenty fighters plus the Fleet Base's and PDCs' capital launchers, but that will also mean letting the Bugs range on the planets."

"We're not supposed to tie ourselves down, Sir," Commander Kenneth "Zulu" Sosa, Prescott's chief of staff, said.

"I'm aware of my orders, Zulu." Prescott didn't raise his voice, but most of his staff found someplace else to look. Every one of them knew it would be at least two months before Fang Koraaza'khiniak could reach Alowan. They also knew Zhaarnak and Prescott were under direct orders to continue falling back until he did. What they didn't know was whether or not Prescott intended to *obey* those orders, and he let the silence linger, then waved for Kmak to resume.

"My best appreciation is that things are going to get rougher, Sir. Bug doctrine is clearly to keep pouring it on until they hit something so hard they *have* to stop, and the Klean population size has to've told them they're into the Tabbies' core systems. Claw Zhaarnak's been lucky so far in not facing any gunboats, but it's unlikely they won't bring them along for an attack on Alowan.

"The only good news is that they may not yet realize the Hairnow System is there. The connecting warp point's a Type Two, so it won't be too hard to find, but it's over five light-hours out, and they've only had a couple of weeks to look for it. More importantly, Zhaarnak managed to destroy the ICN link to the system, so there're no comsat 'bread crumbs' to lead them to it. Additionally, they know where he went—he deliberately let them track him to the Alowan warp point—so we can at least hope they've concentrated on following him up."

"That was gutsy," Jason Pitnarau observed. Prescott's flag captain was short and stocky, and his almond eyes narrowed. "There's what—a billion people in Alowan?"

"Yes, Sir. But at least Alowan has some fixed defenses." Kmak's shrug was bitter. "Sak and Alowan are supposed to be the only way into the Kliean Chain; that's why both of them were fortified in the first place. But Hairnow was supposed to be covered by Alowan, so it has no local defenses, and there are a billion and a *half* civilians in that system."

"I didn't say it was *wrong*, Eloise, only that it took guts. He could've waffled and broken contact—left it to the luck of the draw. And if he loses Alowan, *someone* will damned sure blame him for 'leading the Bugs to it.'"

"He wouldn't still have a battlegroup if he were the waffling sort," Prescott said. "Eloise is right—it's amazing he managed to hold his command together at all."

"Yes, Sir." Kmak paused for a moment, then cleared her throat. "Ah, there are a couple of points to consider about the command structure, Sir," she said carefully.

"Such as?"

"Well, you're senior to Zhaarnak, and, well . . ." The intelligence officer drew a breath. "Sir, according to ONI, Zhaarnak *hates* Terrans. He may not react well when you supersede him."

"I'm aware of Zhaarnak's attitude, Commander." Prescott's tenor voice was toneless, but it was unlike him to use formal rank titles in staff meetings, and Kmak shut her mouth.

Prescott let his eyes circle the table, then spoke very slowly and deliberately.

"We're not going to tell him I'm senior." Several people stiffened, whether in surprise or from a desire to protest he didn't know, nor did it matter. "This officer has been, and remains, under tremendous strain. He's compromised his own honor to do the right thing—the smart thing. Fang Koraaza's approved his actions, and no doubt GHQ will, too, but he's a Tabby. An *Orion* from a clan whose honor has already taken a beating and who left four billion of his people on their own rather than dying in their defense, and you can bet your pensions there are *other* Orions who'll spit on his shadow for that. All right, he doesn't like Terrans. Well, some Terrans don't like *Orions*. I don't happen to be one of them, but I understand their attitude, and it's up to us to understand his. The smooth functioning of this task force in the defense of Alowan—which, I remind you, is also an *Orion* system—is our sole priority. If I can make it function more smoothly by letting him retain command, I'll do it . . . and given Orion traditions, I *can't* do it if he knows I'm senior. So understand me. Who's senior to whom stays right here in this compartment. It will not be discussed, even in casual conversation, with any other persons. Is that clear?"

Heads nodded soberly, and he waved a hand at Commander Alexander LaFroye.

"In that case, Alec, let's get to the nuts and bolts. I want contingency plans based on Zhaarnak's probable tactics so we can slot into *his* plans with the minimum of confusion."

"Yes, Sir." The ops officer brought blocks of information scrolling up his terminal. "In that case, Sir, the first thing to look at is the compatibility of our carrier elements, and—"

Great Claw Zhaarnak stalked out of the flag bridge intraship car into dead silence. He crossed to his command chair, hands folded behind his back, and stood beside it, glaring down into the repeater tank at the light dots of his reinforcements.

Humans, he thought almost despairingly. *What more can the gods do to me? Not enough to take my honor, not enough to fill me with nightmares of slaughter. No. Now they send the very* chofaki *who first destroyed my clan's honor as my "reinforcements."*

The thought burned like acid, and his stubborn self-honesty's insistence that he should be burning incense sticks for *any* reinforcement only made the it worse. It was the sheerest fluke that this Human great claw—this Prescott—had been close enough to respond. The Idnahk Sector had been colonized centuries ago, yet the Humans had found a closed warp point within it twenty of their years before. The protocols between the two imperiums had ceded it to the Khanate, since it lay in *Zheeerlikou'valkhannaieee* space, yet it linked the sector to *Human* space. Given the warp lines' crazed ingeodesics, the Human base at New Bristol was actually closer than any Orion base to Alowan, and this was the result. The KON was scrambling frantically to scrape up anything it could, but this task force—this *Human* task force—was the only organized unit available.

Zhaarnak watched it sweep closer and tried to feel some spark of hope, some belief that, with its aid, he might hold Alowan. But there was no spark. There was only the cold, drear sense of failure which had rilled him since Kliean.

He shuddered, mind filled with the ugly imagery the Kliean comsats had delivered to Telmasa before the Bugs drove him from it. The horrifying images of feeding Bugs, proving that the *Zheeerlikou'valkhannaieee,* too, were food for them. He closed his eyes, soul twisting in the icy wind at his center, and the stillness behind him made that wind even colder.

Do they hate me, my officers? Do they feel contempt for the coward who fell back rather than die? Do they understand why I did it? Or do they even care *why? My dishonor covers them, shields their names and their clans' names, but do they fear the taint which clings to mine?*

He turned away from his plot. The Human commander would arrive aboard *Dashyr* within the hour, and he must be in the boat bay to greet him.

Zhaarnak walked from Flag Bridge, and Son of the Khan Theerah watched him go. The great claw's spine was ramrod straight, yet Theerah sensed his despair and wished he knew how to fight it. He had been shocked by the order to abandon Kliean, and he understood the horror which haunted his commander, but the great claw had been correct. Theerah knew that now. Yet the way of the *Zheeerlikou'valkhannaieee* offered no way to *tell* Zhaarnak that, and so he watched the great claw in silence even as his heart burned to speak.

Raymond Prescott stood as his cutter's hatch cycled. He and his staff had changed into summer-weight uniforms in anticipation of the Tabbies' shipboard temperatures, and he flicked imaginary lint from his perfectly tailored cuff. A faint, fond smile curled his lips as the mannerism woke memories of his kid brother. Andy was twenty years younger . . . and totally unable to pass up any chance to tease him for the personal vanity he'd never quite overcome. And ever since Andy had attained captain's rank he'd taken to teasing Raymond over his "stalled career," too. Of course, promotion always slowed once an officer reached flag rank. Actually, Raymond had made captain earlier in his career than *Andy* had, and he was on the short list for vice admiral, but Andy had always been the feisty one, and teasing or no, Raymond wished he were here now.

No you don't—you want him to live. He felt his smile vanish into a grim, hard line, then inhaled deeply and stepped forward with Commodore Jackson and Zulu Sosa at his heels.

The Tabby side party snapped to formal salute, and a wild, swirling keen washed over him in place of the TFN's bosun's pipes. It was inevitable, Prescott thought, that a race whose language was often described as "a cat fight set to bagpipes" would develop *real* bagpipes as the favored instrument for its martial music. *Oh, well. At least it makes a change!*

He saluted the russet-furred great claw, and Zhaarnak returned his human-style courtesy with a stiff, formal Orion salute. It was always hard to read alien facial expressions, especially when the face in question featured a blunt muzzle, shoulder-wide whiskers, and a covering of soft, plushy fur, but Prescott sensed the exhausted belligerence behind that salute.

"Permission to come aboard, Sir?" he asked—and saw Zhaarnak's whiskers twitch as the request came out in High Orion. He knew he hadn't gotten it quite right, for human vocal cords simply couldn't hit the language's higher notes, but Prescott had the rare combination of perfect pitch and the ability to imitate almost any sound, and he waited while Zhaarnak grappled with the sheer shock of hearing a human speak the Tongue of Tongues.

"Permission granted, Ahhhdmiraal," he replied after a moment, and Prescott lowered his hand from the salute and gestured to his subordinates.

"Allow me to present Commodore Diego Jackson, my senior carrier division CO, and Commander Sosa, my chief of staff," he said in Orion. Zhaarnak bowed to each of them in turn, then rested one hand on the shoulder of the slender female officer beside him.

"Ninety-Sixth Least Claw Daarsaahl'haairna-ahn, my flag captain," he said, and waited while Sosa translated for Jackson, whose grasp of Orion was poor, to say the least. The flag captain returned Prescott's bow, and he reminded himself that a KON flag officer's flag captain was also his chief of staff. He was unfamiliar with Clan Haairna— no non-Orion could keep their sprawling clan structures straight— but Daarsaahl's pelt was the sable of the oldest Orion nobility, and she also wore the starburst of the *Valkhaanair'zegaair*, the equivalent of the Solar Cross, along with several lesser decorations. *Not just an aristocrat, but a good one*, he thought. The Orion patriarchal culture had persisted well into its interstellar stage, and even today, female Orion officers, regardless of birth rank, had to be a cut better than their male peers if they expected to advance. Daarsaahl, it appeared, was no exception to the rule.

"If you would accompany us," Zhaarnak said, "my staff is waiting to brief you." He paused, then continued more stiffly. "I regret that there is insufficient time to greet you with a proper meal, Ahhhdmiraal, but—" He broke off with an ear-flick shrug, and Prescott nodded.

"I understand, Sir," he said, and followed Zhaarnak and Daarsaahl to the intraship car.

"—so while we are not positive of the enemy's strength or plans," Theerah'jihaal finished his brief, "the addition of your carriers will let us mount a much stronger combat space patrol on the warp point. We do not know if we will be able actually to hold this system. Certainly we intend to try. The Sak fortresses rely upon the Pairsag Twins for support and maintenance; if we lose Alowan, we lose that support. More to the point, there are a billion civilians on the Twins.

And, of course, every system we lose is one more we must retake before we can relieve Kliean."

Zhaarnak kept his expression impassive as he watched his new allies' flat, naked faces. For the first time in his life, he wished he had made a serious study of them. He suspected this Admiral Prescott was skilled at evaluating *Orion* expressions, and that irked him. Human faces were far more mobile than he had previously appreciated, yet he was unable to interpret their mobility.

He watched Commodore Jackson as Sosa murmured a translation of Theerah's remarks into his flat, round ear and felt another flicker of resentment as the commander's translation reemphasized Prescott's ability to speak the Tongue of Tongues. It was convenient, but what business had a *chofak* learning the tongue of warriors? And why had he bothered? It could not have been easy, given the differences in their vocal apparatuses, so why take the trouble?

Now Prescott glanced at Jackson and raised an eyebrow. The commodore nodded, confirming his understanding of Theerah's presentation, and the admiral looked at Zhaarnak.

"I believe I understand your intentions, Sir," he said—still in the Tongue of Tongues, curse it, "and we can adjust our operations to conform with them. Commander Sosa has brought along chips detailing our current readiness states and com procedures. We will, of course, adapt our own protocols to yours, and, with your permission, I will send Commander LaFroye, my own operations officer, to *Dashyr* for more detailed conversations with Son of the Khan Theerah."

Zhaarnak flicked his ears in approval, but then his eyes narrowed as Prescott leaned back. Familiar with Human body language or not, the great claw recognized the look of someone about to suggest changes, and something inside him bristled in instant resentment. But he made himself wait. *Chofak* or no, this Human's task force was more powerful than his own. If Prescott wished to make suggestions, Zhaarnak had no option but to listen, however stupid they might be.

"One point which has not been discussed," Prescott said, "is that of equipment compatibility. As you know, our datalink is unable to mate with your own. This is unfortunate, and I understand your R&D people are working with our own to correct the problem, though it will not help us here. The point I would like to offer for your consideration, however, Sir, are the differences in our munitions and, particularly, our fighter ordnance."

Zhaarnak felt a fresh prickle of surprise at the Human's calm, respectful tone and raised one hand, palm uppermost and claws retracted, to invite him to continue.

"A support echelon from New Bristol will join us here as soon as possible, but the yard ships and freighters are slower than our warships and left later. They will not arrive for three more of our weeks, and the ordnance currently on hand is all we will have for that time. We were aware this would be true, so we have filled our own cargo holds with additional missiles which I would like to tranship to your Fleet Base. That would get them out of harm's way, and we can reammunition from the space stations following any engagement."

He paused, and Zhaarnak flicked an ear in agreement. That much, at least, was simple enough, but the Human was not yet done.

"Turning to the matter of fighter ordnance, our carriers can recover and launch one another's fighters. We cannot rearm your fighters, however, nor you ours. What I would suggest is that we redistribute our ordnance and life-support modules. If we were to transfer, say, half of our missiles, FRAMs, and life-support pods to your carriers and replace them with *your* hardware, it would be possible for any carrier to support any fighter squadron. Not only would this increase our tactical flexibility, but it would give us greater platform survivability through redundancy."

It was all Zhaarnak could do to keep his jaw from dropping. The Human's Orion was not perfect—he seemed incapable of reaching the proper notes for full emphasis, and his grammar was overly formal—yet that meant nothing beside what he had just suggested. The great claw glanced at Daarsaahl, seeing his flag captain's surprise—and approval—at the offer, and wondered why it had not occurred to him to make the same suggestion.

Perhaps it was because you let hatred blind you, he thought unwillingly. *Yet the offer has merit—great merit.* He gathered himself to speak, but before he could, Commodore Jackson leaned forward. His speech was incomprehensible to the great claw—*I must learn to understand them after all; chofaki or not, they are our allies, and it seems they may have something worthwhile to say after all*—and he waited while his own earbug translated.

"There's one other point I'd like to mention, Sir," the commodore said. "The Pairsag Fleet Base has a powerful fighter component, and it occurred to us during our discussions en route to Alowan that it might be worthwhile to consider staging those fighters through our carriers. With tenders and full life-support loads, they could make the flight to us well outside their theoretical range, and we could arm them once they arrive."

Zhaarnak looked at Theerah. His ops officer and he had discussed the same possibility but without a decision. Their carriers would have been badly overextended trying to support so many fighters, but if they adopted Prescott's suggestion about ordnance loads, it would be possible. It would also strip the Pairsag Twins of local fighter defenses, yet it would increase his own fighter strength—and hence his chance of actually holding the system—by almost fifty percent.

Theerah looked back, then flicked his ears, and Zhaarnak returned his gaze to Prescott.

"I believe these suggestions have merit, Ahhhdmiraal." It irked him that he still sounded faintly begrudging, and he made himself add, "It is a generous offer, and I thank you for it."

"'If my claws guard not your back, then whose claws shall guard mine?'" the admiral said softly, and Zhaarnak experienced yet another flicker of surprise at this Human's command of the Tongue of Tongues. How many years must he have studied the *Zheeerlikou'valkhannaieee* to have attained such insight into them? And, again, why had he bothered?

The great claw felt a nagging suspicion he would not like the answer to that question if he knew it. Not because Prescott had done so with sinister intent, but because . . . because . . .

He shook the thought aside. There would be time to consider it later—assuming any of them survived—and he pushed his chair back on its powered track and stood.

"Very well, Ahhhdmiraal," he said. "I approve your suggestions. Son of the Khan Theerah and Least Claw Daarsaahl will hold themselves in readiness to discuss the details with your Commaaaander LaaaFroyyye. In the meantime—" he hesitated, then made himself extend his hand in the Human manner "—welcome to Alowan. May our claws strike deep."

"May our claws strike deep," the Human agreed, and gripped his hand firmly.

CHAPTER TWENTY-SIX

"There are no *chofaki* here."

Zhaarnak looked up as his intelligence officer entered the briefing room. Nineteenth Least Claw Uaaria'saalath-ahn was young for her rank, especially as a female, but Zhaarnak had specifically requested her. She was a bit of a maverick, which scarcely endeared her to some superiors, yet she was also brilliant and the daughter of an old friend. And, he admitted with what he knew was old-fashioned sexism, she was most pleasant to look upon, as well. But now her expression caused him to put his display on hold, halting the play of the latest tactical plan Theerah and the Human LaFroye had worked out.

"Yes, Uaaria?"

"I have just learned something which should be drawn to your attention, Great Claw," she said with rather more than normal formality, and his ears pricked. "As you know, I requested background files on Ahhhdmiraal Pressscott and his senior officers from the Eyes of the Khan."

"I remember. Not that they told us much."

"No, Sir. But my request was bucked up to GHQ in Centauri, and the Humans provided the information we lacked."

"They did?" Zhaarnak was surprised. It remained difficult not to think automatically of Humans as *chofaki*, though he was being forced—to some extent—to modify his opinion as Prescott's task force shook down as TG 37.2 of the Grand Alliance's newly designated Task Force 37. Even so, he would not have expected their navy to provide such data.

"Yes, Sir." Uaaria almost seemed to squirm, then sighed. "Great Claw, he is senior to you."

"He—?" Zhaarnak sat as if struck to stone. Senior to him? The

Human was *senior* to him? Impossible! Surely he would have said something! But Uaaria did not make such mistakes.

"Are you positive?" he asked finally.

Uaaria's ears flicked, and Zhaarnak's thoughts floundered. If Prescott was senior, why had he not said so? Why had he always addressed Zhaarnak as "Sir" and accepted *Zhaarnak's* plans?

He looked back up at Uaaria. Young or no, she was a shrewd judge of character, and, unlike Zhaarnak, she *had* studied Humans as part of her intelligence training.

"Have you any theory as to why he has not told us so? Could he be unaware of the fact?"

"I doubt his ignorance, Sir," Uaaria said carefully. "Ahhhdmiraal Pressscott is clearly a student of our people. I feel certain he requested *your* dossier before reporting to Alowan."

"Then why?" Zhaarnak asked, and his eyes narrowed as the least claw hesitated. "Speak your thoughts, Least Claw," he said firmly, and she sighed once more.

"Great Claw, I think he knows your feeling for his people," she said softly. "I believe he chose to accept your authority because of it."

Zhaarnak leaned back in a welter of chaotic emotions. Astonishment. Confusion . . . and shame. If Uaaria was right, Prescott had deliberately renounced a command authority to which he was entitled. One of the *Zheeerlikou'valkhannaieee* might do such a thing, but only under very special circumstances which did not apply here. Part of the great claw longed to put it down to cowardice, to a *chofak's* desire to avoid responsibility, yet he had been forced to work too closely with Prescott over the last ten days to believe that.

No, he knew what the truth had to be: Prescott had done what he himself could not. The Human had sacrificed honor to the prejudices of another, accepting a lesser role, obedient to one he had the right to command, because he knew his legal subordinate hated his race. And he had not done so openly lest it underscore the great claw's prejudice and so dishonor *Zhaarnak*.

"I am sorry, Great Claw," Uaaria said, "yet I thought you should know. I—"

"No, Uaaria," Zhaarnak said quietly. "You did well in this. It is *I* who have done poorly."

"You have much on your mind and spirit," the least claw protested in his defense.

"Not enough to excuse insult to an ally," Zhaarnak replied, and fresh surprise filled him as he realized he meant it. That it was not simply the mouthing of a formality.

"There is no insult, Sir," Uaaria argued. "There would be insult only had you known."

"Which I now do," Zhaarnak pointed out. He looked back down at the frozen display and sighed. "Very well, Uaaria. Thank you. I shall com Ahhhdmiraal Pressscott and—"

He never finished the sentence, for even as he spoke the alarms began to scream.

"They're coming through, Sir!" Sosa reported as Prescott charged onto Flag Bridge. "Simultaneous transit—forty-plus CLs, but they seem weak in *Cataphracts*."

"Thank God for small favors, Zulu," Prescott muttered, and his mouth tightened as his plot confirmed Sosa's estimate. It also showed him something else, and his mouth tightened further as the first gunboat icons began to appear.

"Claw Zhaarnak's activated Alpha-Three," LaFroye said. That wasn't what the Tabbies called it, of course, but it was a designation humans could pronounce, and Prescott nodded.

"Acknowledge." He punched a stud and Diego Jackson's face appeared on his screen. "Alpha-Three, Diego," he said without preamble, wishing yet again that it had been possible to integrate TF 37's com net more fully. "Roll 'em out."

The Assault Fleet made transit with the leading gunboats. There were no energy buoys to flail them this time—a fringe benefit of pressing the enemy so hard—but there were sufficient mines to delay the light cruisers which survived transit. The enemy attack craft came slashing in, intent on killing the CLEs before their systems stabilized, and the gunboats went to meet them.

The gunboats were bigger, more vulnerable targets, but this time there were no jammer buoys to break their datanets, and while the attack craft were more heavily armed, their internal energy weapons could bear only directly ahead of them. The gunboats' internal lasers, however, had a command of over 270°, and their point defense systems had even more coverage. A dozen of them died in the first pass, but four-ship squadrons fired back at the attack craft driving in on them. Coupled with the cruisers' weapons, they killed at least as many enemy units for the loss of only seven CLEs, and that was a worthwhile exchange. The enemy had more carriers this time, yet none of his larger ones. He could not have many attack craft to expend.

"Their gunboats are more effective than expected, Great Claw," Theerah reported tersely. "Our CSP has lost heavily, but we have accounted for all but two *Cataphracts*."

"Here come the Humans, Sir," Daarsaahl said. Zhaarnak's eyes flicked back to his plot. Jackson's squadrons swooped past the survivors of his CSP, armed with missiles, not FRAMs. They opened fire from beyond the Bugs' range, and Zhaarnak snarled as fireballs glared. The gunboats' point defense might make them resistant to missile fire, but not resistant enough!

"The cruisers are moving into the mines," Theerah said, and then the ops officer's ears went flat. "Here come the superdreadnoughts."

The superdreadnoughts made transit in a tight chain. There were but thirty-eight, for the Fleet was still redeploying to exploit this axis, yet there were no enemy superdreadnoughts. Once his attack craft were gone, the battle-line would roll forward unstoppably.

Prescott watched Jackson's squadrons tear into the gunboats, but the cruisers were clearing the mines. There simply hadn't been time to emplace enough of them, and it looked like at least some light units would survive to screen the main force.

"The Tabbies are launching their reserve strike," LaFroye reported.

"Has Zhaarnak alerted the Fleet Base, Zulu?"

"Yes, Sir. The message went out—" Sosa checked a time display "—eight minutes ago."

Prescott grunted in approval, not that any of the Fleet Base fighters could reach them in time to stop the enemy from making transit. The Pairsag Twins were currently on the far side of Alowan from the warp point. It would take the alert message four hours to reach the Fleet Base, and the fighters would have needed a full day to make the flight out. That was beyond their range even with full life-support loads, but Theerah and LaFroye had arranged a resupply point with the orbital base's tenders. All they could do was replenish the fighters' life support, but that doubled their range. By the time TF 37 fell back to them, they'd be ready to stage through the carriers.

And we're going to have plenty of spare hangar space, the admiral thought grimly as the Tabbies hurtled in to attack the leading superdreadnoughts and the flashes of dying fighters speckled the visual display. The Orions broke through to salvo their FRAMs and five *Archers* blew up, yet their consorts caught the Tabbies in a crossfire between their own weapons and the gunboats, and Zhaarnak's pilots paid heavily for their success.

"They've cleared a lane, Sir," LaFroye said flatly. "They're breaking out."

The Fleet uncoiled directly towards the enemy starships, and those ships gave ground. They retreated steadily, remaining beyond missile range and sending in their attack craft again and again, but the battle-line forged remorselessly ahead. Battle-cruisers and the remaining light cruisers screened the superdreadnoughts against the attackers, and the enemy shifted targeting. He had no choice, for he must blow a gap through the screen just to reach the battle-line.

"They are no longer sending gunboats to meet our fighters, Great Claw."

Theerah sounded concerned, and Zhaarnak understood. The Bugs were saving their gunboats until his fighter strength was blunted. His pilots were his best defense against them; only after his strikegroups had been whittled away would the enemy commit them against his starships.

"Fighter losses?" he asked sharply.

"Forty-two percent for our own carriers. The Human loss rate is somewhat lower. I estimate they have lost perhaps thirty percent."

Zhaarnak flicked his ears in acknowledgment. The Human losses might be lower, but not because they were avoiding action. Their squadrons had not been harrowed by his own earlier losses in Kliean and Telmasa, and their experience showed. Even his carrier commanders admitted they were as good as any KON strikegroups, and they were spending themselves more wisely than his own *farshatok*, yet they fought as furiously as if it were *Human* worlds they defended.

If only the Bugs had fewer screening units! His strikes were costing their escorts dear, yet aside from that initial pass, only three superdreadnoughts had been destroyed.

"Inform *farshathkhanaak* Liaahk that he is to maintain a reserve of at least twenty percent. We dare not reduce our CSP below that."

"Yes, Great Claw," Theerah replied, and Zhaarnak looked at his com officer.

"Message from the Flag, Sir." Prescott turned his command chair at the com officer's announcement and waited. "Tango-Three-Delta, Sir."

"Acknowledge." Prescott looked at LaFroye. "Pass the order, Alec."

Fourteen battle-cruisers—three Orion, three Gorm, eight Terran—advanced against the enemy. The Gorm and Orion BCs were TF 37's only true capital missile ships, for the Terran *Broadswords* were configured primarily for closer action. They were attached solely to support and protect their longer-ranged allies, and as they closed, a fresh fighter strike went past them. Massed squadrons, half Terran and half Orion, tore down on the surviving Bug screen, and this time a heavy fire of SBMs came with them from the Allied battle-cruisers' external racks. The Bugs could use their point defense to stop missiles or fighters, not both, and ship after ship blew apart, yet the success came with a price. Another forty fighters were blasted out of space, and the battle-cruisers' attack had brought them in reach of the surviving *Archers.*

Missile salvos roared back and forth, matching superdreadnought shields and armor against the frailer battle-cruisers' superior point defense, and then a fresh wave of fighters slashed in. This time some of the gunboats came out once more, but not to engage fighters. Instead, they hurled themselves straight at the battle-cruisers, and cursing Orion and Terran squadron commanders diverted from their antishipping strike to claw around in pursuit.

They caught a dozen, but the rest got by. The battle-cruisers went to evasive action, firing furiously, and the Terran ships maneuvered between the gunboats and their allies, for the missile ships were weak in energy weapons. Two-thirds of the Bugs were blown apart; the other third got through, and they brought a surprise with them. They didn't have FRAMs, but their R&D *had* produced the cruder nuclear-armed FR, and a gunboat carried three times as many as a fighter.

TFNS *Arrow, Ranseur* and *Partisan* died as the gunboats poured fire into them. *Scimitar* and the command ship *Constitution* took heavy damage of their own, and despite all they could do, GSN *Bahlziak* fell astern, crippled and lamed.

Great Claw Zhaarnak watched the icons vanish. Once he would have felt only vengeful satisfaction at Human deaths; now he watched them dying like *farshatok,* deliberately drawing the enemy onto themselves to protect Orion ships. Dying under the orders of an Orion who was not even truly the senior officer of TF 37.

What now, Zhaarnak? The question seared through him. *Who knows the truth of honor? Those who die to defend their people . . . or those who die to protect* another's?

The Fleet ground onward. The enemy's battle-cruisers had suffered heavily. They had finished off the Fleet's battle-cruisers and two more superdreadnoughts, as well, yet three missile superdreadnoughts survived, and nothing the enemy had left could engage them. The rest of the Fleet formed around them, continuing its remorseless advance, and the enemy's attack craft came in in ever weaker waves. Soon it would be time to commit the gunboats once more.

Raymond Prescott scrubbed a hand across exhaustion-sore eyes. The battle had raged for almost two days, and losses were heavy on both sides. Heavier for the Bugs, but losses were *always* heavier for the Bugs . . . and never seemed to stop them. So far, TF 37 had destroyed sixty-three cruisers and battle-cruisers and eleven superdreadnoughts—

but that left twenty-seven superdreadnoughts, including those damned *Archers*. TF 37's fighters had been too weakened to get through to them, and even if they hadn't, killing them at this point would do little good. The whole point in killing *Archers* was to clear the way for Allied capital missiles and SBMs, and of TF 37's missile ships, only two Gorm *Bolzuchas* were still combat capable. Their strikegroups had suffered too heavily to take more losses trying for the *Archers* now, anyway, for their original three hundred and forty fighters had been reduced to eighty-eight, only fifty of them Terran.

He checked the time display again. Eleven more hours. The Fleet Base's fighters were already en route, and in about eleven hours, the Bugs were going to get a surprise when a hundred and fifty fresh fighters exploded into their faces.

It was time. The enemy's attack craft strikes had all but ceased. His strength must be nearly exhausted, and the order went out.

For just a moment, the exhausted plotting officers didn't believe their own instruments. But they had to, and frantic orders crackled as two hundred and thirty Bug gunboats and small craft screamed towards the Allied starships. Scratch-built squadrons, assembled out of the remnants of TF 37's original strikegroups, launched to meet them, but the attack roared in, and only Zhaarnak's order to maintain a reserve gave TF 37 a chance. The strength of his carefully husbanded fighters took the Bugs by surprise, and gunboats and kamikazes which had been targeted on battleships were diverted to the carriers lest still more fighters launch from them.

The Allied pilots were exhausted, their original squadron organizations long since wrecked. Pilots flew with whatever wingmen they could find, and Terrans and Orions streaked into the enemy together, flushing missiles into the gunboats, then closed with their lasers. They carved a river of fire through their enemies, but the Bugs outnumbered them more than three-to-one. Half died in the first pass, and even as they looped back, the remaining gunboats abandoned the slower antimatter-loaded cutters to streak ahead under maximum power.

Zhaarnak saw it coming, and there was nothing he could do. The Human carriers were better protected, for their smaller fighter groups and more advanced shields let them build in twice the defensive firepower of an Orion CVL, and Prescott's task group included a dozen CLEs and DDEs. But those escorts could not datalink with the Orion carriers. They did their best to protect their allies, yet good as it was, their best was not enough.

Defensive fire killed dozens of gunboats, but others tore through the formation, ignoring its battleships. More than half went after the Terran *Shokakus*, but only a handful of those got through. Four of the TFN carriers were damaged, yet none were hurt critically.

Not so the KON. The Bugs broke through their lighter defenses in strength, salvoing their close-attack weapons and following their missiles in to ram. *Bhutnothin, Burkhan* and *Falkyrk* were destroyed outright, and *Bathyr* and *Firmiak* took heavy damage. Every Orion carrier was hit, most badly, and engine rooms became infernos as kamikazes sent power surges ripping through abused drive fields. They fell out of formation while frantic engineers fought their damage, and Zhaarnak stared at the ruin of his carriers. His own task group had been gutted. Only its light cruisers and three battle-cruisers remained combat capable, and that was far too little to stave off the Juggernaut rolling down on his lamed carriers. The surviving fighters—all thirty of them—finished off the kamikazes before they completed the CVLs' destruction, yet he knew what he must do. He fought against it, but he had no choice, and he opened his mouth to order Prescott to abandon the doomed carriers and take his own command to meet the Fleet Base's fighters.

"The Tabby carriers are hurt bad, Sir." Alec LaFroye's fingers pressed his earbug as if to screw it bodily inside his head, and he grimaced. "Damage control's on it, but they need at least twenty minutes to get back enough drive rooms to stay away from the Bugs."

Prescott stared into his plot, eyes hard as the mind behind them whirred. Only eighteen Terran fighters survived, and his carriers hadn't gotten off unscathed. They had about eighty bays left, but over a hundred and fifty fighters were coming in from the Fleet Base. More to the point, those fighters were *Orion*, and, despite the transfers, his carriers were desperately short of Tabby ordnance after two exhausting days of battle. If they lost the surviving Orion fighter platforms, they wouldn't have the weapons to arm the Fleet Base's fighters once they got here.

"We've got to buy those ships some time," he said flatly.

"Sir, we don't have any orders from the Flag," Sosa pointed out. Prescott glanced at him, and the chief of staff looked back. The ex-fighter jock didn't like saying that, but it was his job to serve as his admiral's tactical conscience.

"I realize that, Zulu," Prescott said softly.

"Sir! Great Claw! The Humans!"

Zhaarnak's head snapped around at the semi-coherent shout, and his jaw dropped in disbelief. TG 37.2 was moving—not to break off as he had intended to order, *but to interpose between the Bugs and his carriers!*

It was insane! Prescott's battleships mounted only a single capital missile launcher each, and that only to deploy defensive missiles. He could engage the enemy only from within the Bugs' own weapons envelope, and he had *battleships,* not superdreadnoughts!

Even as he watched, the first missiles roared out, and capital force beams began to fire. The Humans' datalinked point defense blunted the missile salvos, but it could do nothing about energy weapons, and shields flashed and died as the suicidal pounding match began.

"Juaahr! Order Pressscott to break off!"

"Yes, Great Claw!" The com officer spoke urgently into his pickup, then stiffened. "Sir, Ahhhdmiraal Pressscott refuses!"

"Give me a direct link!" Prescott's face appeared on Zhaarnak's com screen instantly, and the great claw forced his voice to come out flat and level. "Break off, Ahhhdmiraal."

"I must respectfully decline, Sir," Prescott replied, and actually *smiled* as Zhaarnak's ears flattened in consternation. The image flickered as missiles and beams pounded the admiral's flagship, and Prescott shook his head in the Human gesture of negation. "You need those carriers. My own have too few weapons to support the Fleet Base's fighters."

"This is madness! You sacrifice your ships for nothing!"

"'My claws are yours, and your cause is just,'" the Human said softly. "'There is no dishonor in death—and no honor in flight.'"

Zhaarnak could not hide his shock as Prescott quoted the Warrior's Way. They were the final words of Shaasaal'hirtalkin, he who first formalized the *Farshalah'kiah,* second only to Craana'tolnatha among the fathers in honor of the *Zheeerlikou'valkhannaieee,* and even as Zhaarnak stared at him, the Human cut the circuit.

The great claw dropped his eyes to the plot, and his fists clenched as the outnumbered, outgunned Humans engaged their foes. Shields flashed and died, warheads and beams ripped at hull plating. Prescott's battle-line was trapped in the heart of a furnace, and *still* it held its ground, drawing the enemy's fury down upon itself while the carrier crews fought to repair their drives.

A battleship died, then another. A battle-cruiser followed them, and Prescott's flagship shuddered as her own shields went down. Armor shattered under the pounding beams, yet no Human ship turned away. They stood and died at their admiral's side, thundering back at their massive enemies for five minutes, eight, ten. . . . For twelve endless, terrible minutes they held alone, until the surviving Orion carriers were able to get back underway.

Then, and only then, they, too, began to pull away from the enemy once more, but four battleships and three more battle-cruisers of the

Terran Federation Navy had died. Every surviving ship was damaged, some critically, yet Raymond Prescott had done what he set out to do . . . and Zhaarnak'diaano would never think of Humans in the same way again.

The Fleet continued its pursuit until a sudden infusion of fresh attack craft assailed it. The enemy battleships had inflicted damage out of all proportion to their relatively small size, and the fresh attack craft struck at the worst possible moment. There were few gunboats left, and the Fleet—busy reorganizing its crippled data-groups—was caught unprepared. Six already damaged superdreadnoughts succumbed to a blizzard of FRAMs, several of those which survived were badly wounded, and the Fleet called off the pursuit. It knew where the enemy was headed, after all . . . and it also knew reinforcements were en route.

"The scanner buoys confirm it, Great Claw," Least Claw Daarsaahl said wearily. "Twenty-four additional superdreadnoughts have joined the enemy. At present rate of advance, they will enter range of the Twins in seventy-one hours."

"Escorts?" Zhaarnak'diaano asked.

"Thirty battle-cruisers and approximately fifty light cruisers," Daarsaahl said flatly. "They appear to be accompanied by many additional gunboats, as well."

"I see." Zhaarnak drew a deep breath, and closed his eyes. Five days had passed since the first attack withdrew, and he'd let himself hope. Now that hope died.

"Has Ahhhdmiraal Pressscott been informed?"

"They were his sensor buoys, Sir," Daarsaahl said with a flicker of weary humor, and Zhaarnak's own ears twitched in bittersweet amusement. *Human technology,* he thought. *Must they* always *be better than we?*

"Your orders, Great Claw?" his flag captain asked, and Zhaarnak shrugged.

"There will be no retreat this time," he said. "Lord Khiniak will not arrive for another month. If Great Claw Eaarnaah's fortresses can hold Sak until he arrives, his force should be powerful enough to retake Alowan. But if the Bugs can take Sak first, or even mount a warp point defense of Alowan in strength, he will pay heavily to break in. I know only one way to weaken them for him, and I doubt the enemy realizes how powerful the fixed defenses are. Between us, the bases and our ships can cripple this force before we are destroyed—perhaps even inflict sufficient delay to prevent an invasion of the Twins before Lord Khiniak relieves them."

"And the Humans?" Daarsaahl pressed in a gentle voice.

"I will not insult their honor," Zhaarnak said softly. The flag captain gazed at him a moment longer, then nodded, saluted, and withdrew without another word.

Zhaarnak returned to his terminal, staring sightlessly at the reports which had just become so meaningless, then cleared the screen and brought up a visual of TF 37's battered remnants.

Eleven wounded light carriers, only three of them Orion, hung in orbit about the twin planets, supported by six damaged battleships—all Human—and eleven battle-cruisers—three of them Human. With the missile batteries of the Fleet Base and the PDCs, they would give a good account of themselves, yet they were doomed. Zhaarnak knew it, and he knew Prescott knew it, but the Human had not even suggested the withdrawal of his units. *Horned Viper* had been hit hard in her stand against the enemy battle-line. Commander Sosa was dead, Commander Kmak was badly wounded, and Prescott himself had suffered minor wounds to the head and leg. Many of his other ships had been damaged, as well, and unlike Zhaarnak's ships, none of them could tie into the massive point defense nets provided by the PDCs.

It did not matter. The Human support ships had not yet arrived, yet Prescott's exhausted crews had torn into their repairs with what limited help the Fleet Base technicians could provide. Most of their shields had been restored, many of their weapons had been put ba online, and the munitions Prescott had off-loaded earlier had suff to refill their surviving magazines. Yet their armor was riddle their repairs were fragile. It would take little fresh poundin them back out of action, but Raymond Prescott would no the Pairsag Twins. As Zhaarnak, he knew relief could r time . . . but that every enemy ship destroyed killing b would be one less to bombard the Twins or contes entry into Alowan.

And, like me, he cannot abandon still more civil' do worse than die with such "chofaki," the grea And as Prescott himself said, "There is no di honor in flight."

"Here they come, Sir," Jason Pitn nodded. His flag bridge was a sham battleship had been destroyed ov Alec LaFroye onto *Horned Vip*

Now he rubbed the bandag ing the master plot's ominou plans springing into purposeful— Pairsag Twins. He doubted the Bu,

powerful the local defenses were, but when they found out, it was going to be ugly.

No doubt the PDCs would draw a heavy bombardment, which was why the Federation seldom mounted offensive weapons on inhabited worlds, and once the Bugs realized what they faced, they would abandon any plan to come in piecemeal and throw everything they had straight at the huge, heavily armed Fleet Base . . . and what was left of TF 37.

Glad you weren't here after all, Andy, he thought, then smiled crookedly at *Dashyr's* icon. *For a bigot, you're not too shabby, Zhaarnak'diaano. I suppose a man could do worse.*

"How long, Alec?" he asked.

"Seven hours," LaFroye replied, and Prescott astonished himself with a chuckle.

"Right on our original projection," he observed. "Remind me to congratulate CIC."

"Of course, Sir," Pitnarau said with a small smile of his own, and they returned their attention to the plot as the minutes leaked away. The Bugs slid closer and closer, inching towards engagement range— and then, suddenly, they stopped.

Prescott straightened in his chair. He hissed as his wounded leg protested the movement, but it was a distant pain. There was no reason for them to stop. They'd advanced across the system for days, and the one thing Bugs *didn't* do was hesitate about committing to action!

But they *were* hesitating. And then, as abruptly as they'd stopped advancing, they turned away! *All* of them turned away—gunboats, cruisers, superdreadnoughts, the entire fleet!

"What the *hell*?" Pitnarau was staring into the plot in disbelief, and Prescott shook his head. A part of him was actually angry at the Bugs for stopping when he'd made up his mind to die. *Get in here and* get *it over with, you bastards! Isn't it enough for you to kill us without screwing around this way?!*

But they were still moving away—moving away at maximum speed.

"— ! The buoys are picking up— My God, Sir!"

"— at?" Prescott snarled, taking out some of his confusion on the lieutenant who'd just spoken. The young woman shook her— punched commands into her console.

"— t your repeater, Sir," she said, and Prescott dropped his gaze — lay.

"— other of God!" he whispered.

"— r fresh Orion ships were headed in from the Sak warp — ot *just* ships. Over a hundred fighters led the way, a

combat space patrol sweeping the way for twenty fleet carriers and fourteen superdreadnoughts!

"It can't be," he said softly. "Koraaza's still over a month out, and he doesn't have anywhere *near* that much firepower to begin with! Those people can't *be* there!"

"Well, for people who don't exist, they look mighty good to me!" Pitnarau said jubilantly.

In fact, Prescott was right. That huge relief fleet not only couldn't be there, it wasn't. Or, rather, it wasn't what it looked like. The massive task force was actually only three battleships, five CVs— *not* twenty—and five CVLs, and twenty-one battle-cruisers and heavy cruisers. They weren't part of Lord Khiniak's force. Indeed, many weren't even combat ready. They were simply everything the Tabbies could scrape up—convoy escorts, training ships, vessels snatched out of the Bureau of Repair's hands, *anything*. None of the CVLs had any fighters, the battle-cruisers' magazines were less than two-thirds filled, and two battleships still had repair techs aboard, but they all mounted third-generation ECM, and the Tabbies had it on-line in deception mode.

A bluff, Prescott thought two days later as he stood in *Horned Viper's* boat bay. *The whole thing was a colossal* bluff! *I don't think I'll ever play poker with a Tabby.*

He smiled at the thought, then straightened, leaning heavily on his cane, as the Orion cutter settled into its cradle and the side party came to attention.

Great Claw Zhaarnak'diaano stepped out into the twitter of bosun's pipes. He saluted sharply, and Prescott ignored the pain in his leg as he came to attention and returned the courtesy.

"Permission to come aboard, Sir?" the Tabby yowled to Captain Pitnarau.

"Granted, Sir," Pitnarau replied, and Zhaarnak stepped over the line on the deck.

The pipes fell silent, and deafening quiet filled the bay as Zhaarnak crossed to Prescott. He stopped and gazed into the admiral's eyes for a moment, then drew his *defargo*, the honor dirk of an Orion warrior. The wickedly keen blade gleamed in his hand, and he spoke quietly.

"When I was told Human ships had arrived to support me, Ahhhdmiraal Pressscott, I accepted them only because I had no choice, for such aid was an insult to my honor and that of my clan. Any allies were better than none, yet I swore to my clan fathers that the day I no longer needed your assistance I would spit upon your shadow. I would not challenge you as I would one of the

Zheeerlikou'valkhannaieee, for I knew you would not accept challenge if I offered it, and it would only insult my honor further if you had."

Prescott's mouth tightened, but he said nothing. He simply stared into Zhaarnak's slit-pupiled eyes, waiting, and the Orion moved his ears slowly back and forth.

"Humans are cowards and *chofaki,* Fang Pressscott. I did not *think* they are; I *knew* they are, as surely as I know my own name . . . but what I knew to be true was a lie, and black dishonor to your people." He flipped the *defargo* to extend its hilt to the Terran, the formal gesture of a liege man to his lord, and his eyes met Prescott's unflinchingly. "There are no *chofaki* here, Clan Brother. There are *only farshatok.* Your honor is our honor, and if ever Clan Diaano can serve you or yours with treasure or blood, we are yours to command."

CHAPTER TWENTY-SEVEN

"It *is* about honor."

The command balcony of the great orbital station looked out over an expanse of control consoles and computer terminals. Beyond them was a great, curving transparency showing the sun of Idnahk, its glare suitably stepped down. It was by the reflected light of that sun that Tenth Great Fang of the Khan Koraaza'khiniak, *Khanhaku* Khiniak, could see with naked eyes the ships of his command—that which was to be the Grand Alliance's Third Fleet.

Those ships had been straggling in since shortly after the ships of the enemy the Humans called *Bugs* had entered the Kliean System with their cargo of nightmare. The Navy had begun assembling all available ships here at the sector capital immediately after Zhaarnak'diaano sent forth the alarm. Then, with the delay built into all interstellar communications, had come the response of the Grand Allied Joint Chiefs of Staff. They'd recognized at once that the war had acquired a second front even more squarely within the domain of the *Zheeerlikou'valkhannaieee* than the original one was within Human space. So a new Fleet—a fleet of the Khanate, just as Admiral Murakuma's was a fleet of the Federation—had been added to the Alliance's organizational structure, and the Khan had honored Koraaza by entrusting him with its command.

Still, he reflected, it would have been nice if Third Fleet had been anything more than an organization chart when he arrived here. The ancient Terran military theorist Sun Tzu—who had finally won acceptance in Koraaza's service despite the seeming contradictions between his precepts and *Farshalah'kiah*—had observed that numbers alone confer no advantage in war, and the ever-increasing number of ships whose flanks reflected the light of Idnahk's sun had built up to an impressive total—essentially everything in the sector capable of move-ment—but had never functioned as a fleet before. His hastily assembled staff would have been lucky to get all of them moving in the same direction on the same day, and any sort of coordinated maneuvers would have been impossible without the merciless exercises Koraaza had laid on. But those indispensable exercises had required still more time, and time was precisely what Zhaarnak'diaano—and, to an even greater extent, the civilians of Hairnow and any surviving Telmasans— did not have.

It was, thought Koraaza, who was something of a military history enthusiast, a lesson the Terrans had taught the *Zheeerlikou'valkhannaieee* in the Wars of Shame. His people, too long accustomed to expanding at the expense of unworthy opponents and therefore inclined to take the old hero-sagas literally, had thought of ships as individual swords to be wielded by the champions who commanded them. They had forgotten the long-term coordinated training necessary to provide the fleet and squadron organization which was to a navy as tempering was to a blade.

The thought of Terrans brought a smile to Koraaza's lips. He knew Zhaarnak'diaano, and when he'd heard that the first, crucial reinforce-ments that could be gotten to the great claw were *Terran* units, he'd seen disaster looming. Zhaarnak might not be quite so reactionary as his father in most things, but he seemed determined not to excel the old *Khanhaku* Diaano in unreasoning hatred of Humans—which would have been impossible—but to equal him. Koraaza had known, with a horrible sinking certainty, that Zhaarnak would not only bring about military calamity but also dishonor the Khan by insulting an ally. The latter had worried the great fang almost as much as the former, for however much he consciously rejected the narrow and rigid *Farshalah'kiah* of his ancestors in favor of modern rationalism, he could no more free himself of it than he could free himself of those ancestors' genetic legacy.

So it had been with incredulous relief that Koraaza had read Zhaarnak's last few reports, with their steady change in tone. He was looking forward to meeting this Human great claw (or *rear admiral* as they called it in their unpronounceable tongue) who had brought about that which he would once have unhesitatingly declared impos-sible, and in little more than three local days, he and Third Fleet would set out to do just that.

The communications officer broke in on Koraaza's thoughts. "Your pardon, Great Fang," said the young son of the khan (*lieutenant commander,* Koraaza thought, his mind continuing to crank out title equivalencies in the outlandish Terran rank structure), "but Gover-nor Kaarsaahn requests a moment of your time."

Koraaza's whiskers twitched with annoyance. As long as Third Fleet was located within the Idnahk Sector, and most especially while it was assembling at the sector's capital, a degree of jurisdictional friction between the fleet commander and the sector governor was inevitable. In this case, differences in temperament made the situation worse than it had to be. He turned resignedly to face the holo imager, and moved within the pickup, "Put him on," he ordered, and the governor of the Idnahk Sector seemed to flash into existence.

"Governor Kaarsaahn," Koraaza greeted, touching clenched fist to chest in salute.

The huge orbital station could accommodate the bulky holo imager for which warships had too little space to spare, but it was in geostationary orbit around Idnahk. About a quarter of a second passed while the message came and went, imposing a delay which was barely noticeable, yet spoiled the illusion that Kaarsaahn was here on the command balcony rather than in his palace on the surface. He responded to Koraaza's salute with a courtesy that verged on unctuousness.

"Greetings, Great Fang. I have no wish to disrupt your busy schedule, but I have not yet received confirmation that you have dispatched to Great Claw Zhaarnak the orders we agreed on. I'm sure you have done so . . . as we agreed," he added with pointed repetition. "But I felt obliged to confirm it personally."

Koraaza sighed inwardly. He *had* agreed, albeit with a reluctance that had caused him to put off actually keeping his promise. "Your pardon, Governor, but the press of my duties has prevented me from actually sending the dispatch. I have, however, prepared the necessary orders to Great Claw Zhaarnak: stand on the defensive in Alowan, attempting no counteroffensive before I arrive." He drew a breath. "Governor, I will of course send the orders if you insist on holding me to my promise. But perhaps we should reconsider. Remember, every day the enemy is left undisturbed in Telmasa is another opportunity for him to discover the Hairnow warp point. Some aggressive raiding, at Zhaarnak's discretion, might distract the enemy from survey activities."

Kaarsaahn's habitual blandness was beginning to look a little frayed around the edges. "As I argued at our previous discussion, Great Fang, we have no way of knowing that the enemy has not already discovered the Hairnow System. More to the point, until Third Fleet arrives in Alowan, Great Claw Zhaarnak's force is the sector's only defense. It cannot be hazarded on premature adventures. And, while I have hesitated to raise this point before, I fear Zhaarnak's 'discretion' cannot be relied on in this matter." He hastily raised a clawed hand. "Yes, I know you are honor-bound to defend a fellow officer. It does you credit. But consider: his withdrawal from Kliean ànd Telmasa flew in the face of his temperament as well as *Farshalah'kiah*. The fact that he had no choice cannot possibly compensate in his own mind. He is bound to be biased towards reckless displays of courage, seeking to wipe out the stain—however illusory—on his honor. Under the circumstances, the knowledge that your command will soon depart Idnahk may well goad him into such an action—independently—rather than encourage him to hold fast."

Koraaza opened his mouth to hotly declare that Zhaarnak, like all officers of the Khan, was well aware of his paramount duty to defend the race's inhabited worlds . . . then snapped it shut. For Kaarsaahn, damn him, had a point. Zhaarnak *was* aggressive by nature, and any imagined disgrace *would* make him even more so. He might not do anything culpably stupid, but he might well overestimate his own strength in order to rationalize his need for action. And according to the latest reports, that strength was insufficient for any serious attempt on Telmasa.

No, Zharnaak's guilt over the worlds he had been forced to leave to their deaths could not be allowed to imperil still more worlds. It was a truth to which the *Zheeerlikou'valkhannaieee* had never really become reconciled: the higher one climbed on the ladder of rank, the more often honor had to be sacrificed on the altar of duty. Koraaza himself had yet to accept it gracefully.

"Your points are well taken, Governor," he said leadenly. "I will send the orders."

Raymond Prescott began to rise, struggling with his wounded leg, as Zhaarnak'diaano entered the briefing room, but the great claw waved him back.

"Sit, Great Claw." The Orion title came more naturally to Zhaarnak than the Terran one, and he smiled a fang-hidden smile as Prescott sank back. "After all," he added dryly, "it is *I* who should rise when *you* enter."

"Nonsense," Prescott said. "The task force is overwhelmingly *Zheeerlikou'valkhannaieee* and Gorm—and the fixed defenses are *wholly* Orion. If only because of communication problems, you must retain command."

"You are a strange being, Great Claw," Zhaarnak said. "Are all Humans like you?"

"We humans are a pretty confusing lot," Prescott replied with a smile. "But, yes. I think most of my people are much like me where it matters."

"Then it is my loss that I have not made myself more familiar with them." Zhaarnak's tone was serious, not a polite formula, and Prescott bobbed a small Orion-style bow. Then Zhaarnak inhaled sharply and lowered himself into a chair.

"You have seen Least Claw Uaaria's report?"

"I have."

"And your opinion?"

"I believe she may have a point," Prescott said after only the briefest hesitation. "While any rational foe might have avoided action against Claw Daairaah's apparent fighter strength, the Bugs have appeared willing to date to accept total annihilation in order to inflict attritional losses. And even if they believed Daairaah's force was overwhelming, they could have forced *us* to engage on their terms—or abandon the Twins and the Fleet Base—before he intervened."

"True." Zhaarnak tipped his chair back, claws kneading its armrests gently. "So why decline to attack? Unless, of course, Uaaria is correct."

Prescott nodded, wishing fervently that Eloise Kmak were still available. But while she was expected to recover fully, she would be out of action for months. He'd borrowed Lieutenant Commander Cruikshank from Diego Jackson to replace her, but Cruikshank was less comfortable with the Orion language. He also lacked Kmak's unorthodox imagination, and Prescott had always preferred intelligence officers who thought outside the boxes of conventional wisdom. He missed Eloise badly . . . but it seemed Least Claw Uaaria had the same ability.

He cocked his own chair back in thought. As Zhaarnak said, the Bugs had to have known they could carry through against the Twins. Based on every other battle they'd fought, that was precisely what they *ought* to have done, and Uaaria had been the first to ask why they hadn't.

The only answer she'd been able to come up with was that, for some reason, *this* time they were unwilling to risk crippling losses. That was very unlike them, yet they couldn't have *expected* to contact the Alliance in Shanak, which suggested one possible explanation. If this contact had been as unexpected for them as for the Alliance, then they must have attacked with whatever was available. And if it was all an opportunistic response to an unanticipated opening, they might well have broken off because there were no—or very few—additional mobile units behind them. And if that were so . . .

"I think we must assume, tentatively, at least, that Uaaria is correct," he said finally. "If she is, it might also explain why they have not reinforced and attempted Alowan a second time."

Zhaarnak flicked his ears in agreement. Over a Terran month had passed since the enemy had pulled back, and during his inactivity Lord Khiniak's forces had completed assembling. They would reach Alowan within two weeks, and more reinforcements had arrived in the meantime than Zhaarnak had believed possible. Orion, Gorm—even a few additional Human starships had come in, and some, like the Gorm superdreadnoughts *Clerdyng* and *Dathum,* had been totally unexpected. They had been beyond New Bristol, in Human space, when the call went out, and communications had been so chaotic no one had realized they were responding. Which was probably as well. If anyone *had* realized, they would no doubt have been diverted to Idnahk.

The Human support ships had also arrived and labored mightily. Zhaarnak was deeply impressed by how rapidly they had put the wounded Human ships back into action, yet the other thing they had achieved was almost more important. The joint Human-Orion R&D teams had finally determined how to make TFN and KON command datalink interface, and the Humans' mobile shipyards had worked out jury-rigged field modifications. No doubt the "official" version would be much neater, but the Human techs' crude version worked. The ships under Zhaarnak's command could now be formed into battlegroups on a tactical basis rather than being forced to operate as separate national units, and the value of that would be difficult to exaggerate.

He was not certain he could have stopped a full-scale warp point assault, but Idnahk and New Bristol had sent up sufficient fighters to refill every hangar in Alowan. With that much fighter strength, backed by his hybrid battle-line and, if necessary, the fixed defenses, he felt confident he could hold the system, even if he were forced to concede the warp point.

And that is why Uaaria's theory is so convincing. The Bugs must realize we are straining every sinew to reinforce, and they would not have given us time to do so unless they had to.

"If," Zhaarnak said very carefully, "the enemy is, indeed, too weak to attack us, is it not possible he might be weak enough for *us* to attack *him*?"

He watched Prescott's face. He was learning, gradually, to interpret Human expressions, but nothing he had so far learned was of much help at the moment, and he wondered how Prescott would have fared across the *eschaai* table. *Probably quite well. I doubt even another Human could tell his thoughts just now.*

"I suppose," Prescott said after a moment, "that the possibility must exist. Of course, if we suggested as much, our superiors would no doubt find the evidence insufficient . . . particularly with such heavy reinforcements en route. I suspect they would order us to hold our position until relieved rather than risk our ships on any such hypothetical speculation by a mere least claw."

"Your command of the Tongue of Tongues is most impressive, Great Claw Pressscott," Zhaarnak remarked, "and your assessment of Sector

Command's probable reaction is astute. We are, of course, merely discussing possibilities, and I feel sure Lord Khiniak would be more, ah, *adventurous* than Governor Kaarsaahn. Unfortunately, it is Kaarsaahn who holds final authority."

"I see." Prescott pursed his lips. "My people are not unfamiliar with such situations," he observed, "and we have a saying we sometimes use. 'What your superiors do not know about, they cannot countermand.' The translation is not exact, but I believe the meaning comes through."

"Indeed?" Zhaarnak gave a purring chuckle. "Interesting. There is a similar saying among the *Zheeerlikou'valkhannaieee:* 'Actions taken *without* orders are not taken *against* them.'"

"Perhaps our peoples are more alike than most think," Prescott replied, then met Zhaarnak's eyes levelly. "But however that may be, what we are considering constitutes a grave risk. Not simply to our commands, but to Alowan. If we attempt Telmasa—" Zhaarnak's ears twitched at the confirmation that they *were*, in fact, thinking the same thing "—and take heavy losses, we may expose this system to a *Bug* counterattack."

"Truth," Zhaarnak said seriously. "And I cannot and will not order you to support me in this. Not only are you my superior, despite your willingness to allow me to retain command, but the risk to your ships and personnel would be great—as would the risk to your career." Prescott made a dismissive gesture, but Zhaarnak continued in the same earnest tone. "Do not make light of it, Great Claw Pressscott. I think Human and *Zheeerlikou'valkhannaieee* admiralty boards are alike in that much. Success justifies all, yet failure blots out even past accomplishments."

"There is a time to consider careers," Prescott said, "and one to consider duty."

"You speak truly," Zhaarnak said. "And you are also correct about the risk to Alowan. Yet I cannot forget Kliean . . . or Hairnow. We do not know if the enemy has discovered Hairnow exists. Even if he has, he may not yet have had time to wreak much damage there, but he has been in possession of Kliean for over three of your months, and there are four billion of my people in that system. If we could retake Telmasa before Lord Khiniak arrives here, he would begin his own operations only one warp point assault from Kliean, not two. And if the enemy has not, in fact, learned of Hairnow's existence, we would protect another billion and a half of my people. Those are the prizes against which we would hazard our commands."

Prescott leaned back, eyes hooded, and considered the Tabby's quietly impassioned plea. And plea it was, he thought. The Alowan Fleet Base had produced a few dozen SBMHAWKs, but it was only now getting into full production. Yet New Bristol had stripped its own magazines bare and rushed the weapons forward. Over two hundred *TFN* pods had reached Alowan, and only the lavish use of those pods could possibly get them into Telmasa intact. Without Prescott's support, Zhaarnak couldn't possibly attack; even with it, the odds against success would be high.

Yet Zhaarnak was also right about Kliean and Hairnow. Every day that passed could be the literal difference between life and death for millions of Orion civilians, and he suddenly realized there was one argument Zhaarnak *hadn't* made.

Honor. Zhaarnak'diaano had pulled out of Kliean and Telmasa rather than fight to the death. His successful defense of Alowan might have vindicated his decision, yet honor and vindication weren't necessarily the same thing—particularly to a Tabby. But if he fought his way back into Telmasa, that, coupled with the Battle of Alowan, *would* cleanse his honor.

Yet he hadn't made that argument, and, as he looked into Zhaarnak's eyes, Prescott realized he *wouldn't* make it. Not because he felt it would have no impact on a Terran, for by now he knew how intimately Prescott had studied Orion culture and the *Farshalah'kiah*. He knew Prescott would understand the centrality of honor—his clan's, even more than his own—to any Orion, but his concern was with lives, billions of them. Orion or no, Zhaarnak'diaano had set his honor aside. Indeed, he was risking even greater dishonor, for if he made the attempt and *failed*, all too many of his fellows would consider him a total, feckless bungler. Very few Terrans would have understood the immensity of the self-sacrifice he was prepared to embrace . . . but Raymond Porter Prescott was one of them.

"'Death is lighter than a flower, but duty is heavier than a mountain,'" he said softly. Zhaarnak's ears cocked questioningly, and Prescott smiled. "A saying from Old Terra, Great Claw, from some of my people I think you would have understood."

"This is not about honor," Zhaarnak said quietly, but Prescott shook his head.

"No, Great Claw. It *is* about honor . . . and duty. One may sometimes clash with the other in the eyes of others, but it is *our* eyes we must consider here."

He held the Tabby's slit-pupilled eyes for a moment, then punched a code into his com without looking down. A moment passed, and then a voice spoke from the terminal.

"Yes, Sir?"

"Great Claw Zhaarnak and I are in Briefing Room A, Alec," Prescott said. "Please collect Cruikshank and join us. We have an operation to plan."

CHAPTER TWENTY-EIGHT

A Good Day for It

The Fleet waited far behind its heavy cruiser screen, for it was uneasily aware of its exposure. Pre-war doctrine would have moved its entire strength into range of the warp point; as it was, the decision to defend the system at all had come hard. The Fleet was too weak to risk a conventional deployment against missile pods, and the temptation to fall back to the first system it had seized was great. Yet the advantages of holding here—if it could—were also great. At best, it would win time for its reinforcements to arrive; at worst, the enemy still had no idea where the second closed warp point in the contact system was . . . and if the Fleet had not yet received the warships it needed, it had received the new missiles to support its gunboats.

This time it was an Orion show, and Raymond Prescott leaned on his cane on *Horned Viper*'s patched up flag bridge as Task Force 37 headed for the Telmasa warp point.

He and Zhaarnak had agonized over their timing, for if they failed and Uaaria's theory was wrong, Alowan would certainly be counterattacked. The Fleet Base's fighter strength had been tripled, and tenders were prepared to ferry fighters from Sak to Alowan to replace losses, which should give the base a chance against whatever the Bugs had left after destroying TF 37, yet neither Prescott nor Zhaarnak could free themselves of concern for the system. That was why they'd waited almost another week. Lord Khiniak must be en route now, and despite their burning need to relieve Hairnow, they'd delayed to buy a little more time for him to arrive. They were still cutting it close, but if, in fact, the Bugs hadn't yet discovered Hairnow, the risk was worth it.

And whatever happened, he thought grimly, TF 37—and especially its Tabbies—would take a lot of killing before it went down. Of the eighty-plus ships in his display, sixty-two percent were Orion. It had taken the assistance of his mobile shipyards to get them all ready in time, but thirteen of TF 37's twenty-one carriers and fourteen of its twenty-one battle-cruisers were Orion. Combining their battle-line units' light fighter components with their carrier strikegroups, the Tabbies also accounted for eighty-three of the task force's hundred and ten fighter squadrons, and they'd managed to scare up four battleships, as well. Of course, KONS *Ambrych* had repair techs onboard even now, but the battleship's captain insisted she was ready to fight, just as the COs of the CVLs *Rohrdenhau* and *Vohlghar* insisted *their* ships were. Neither carrier had had a single fighter embarked when she arrived, and two of *Vohlghar*'s catapults were iffy, but no Tabby was going to sit this one out. They'd seen the imagery from Kliean. They *knew* what was happening there—and might be happening in Hairnow, as well— and the Devil himself wouldn't stop them.

Prescott understood that, and he was glad he'd insisted Zhaarnak retain command. The Battle of Alowan had earned his personnel enormous respect from their Orion allies, but as he'd told the great claw, TF 37's composition made it unthinkable for him to demand command authority. Not only was it a predominately Orion force, but he himself was the only one of his officers who could actually speak Orion, and he'd been hard pressed to find enough Orion-cognizant personnel just to fill the critical communication slots aboard his ships.

But Zhaarnak had done a little reshuffling of his own personnel when he reorganized his task groups. Prescott's TG 37.2 had given up its CVLs, its surviving battle-cruisers, and two of its DDEs, to Zhaarnak's TG 37.1. It made sense to combine all the carriers in one force, and the *Broadswords'* energy weapons and short-ranged missile batteries would be more useful covering the fighter platforms against gunboats than going toe-to-toe with *Archers*. And Prescott couldn't complain about what he'd gotten in return: two GSN superdreadnoughts—*Gormus*-class ships with heavy energy batteries and no capital missiles, perhaps, but still formidable units; four Orion battleships; seven Orion and Gorm battle-cruisers (all missile ships); and seventeen Orion heavy and light cruisers to supplement the four *Swiftsure*-class CAs New Bristol had scared up. Despite the pounding his original command had taken, his new task group was far more powerful, and every one of its allied ships had at least one com officer who understood Standard English.

Even so, I'm glad I reminded my tac officers to stay away from contractions, he mused. Contractions and homonyms, neither of which the Tongue of Tongues used, could give English-cognizant Orions enormous trouble, and with their emotions running as high as they were—

Of course, our emotions are pretty high, too. I probably should have looked closer at Mexicano's readiness report—I'm pretty sure Captain Trayn did a little creative editing to get in on this one—but a battleship's a battleship, and we need everything we've got.

He limped from the plot to his command chair, and settled back with a sigh of relief. A yeoman hung his cane on the shock frame for him, and he brought up his link to CIC. The senior plotting officer looked up as it came on-line, but Prescott only nodded to him. Commander Huyler nodded back and returned his attention to his own console, and Prescott checked the time.

Thirty-two minutes.

"Very well, Great Claw Pressscott," Zhaarnak said formally. "Engage."

"Yes, Sir." Prescott looked at Alec LaFroye, his acting chief of staff as well as his ops officer, and nodded. "Launch your birds, Alec."

"Aye, aye, Sir!"

LaFroye punched a stud, and one hundred and twenty Terran SBMHAWK pods carried six hundred AAM-warhead SBMs into Telmasa in a single mighty wave.

None of the Orion pinnaces which had probed Telmasa had survived, which suggested a massive gunboat CSP beyond it, and Least Claw Theerah had suggested programming at least some pods to go after those gunboats, but LaFroye had countered that they didn't know for certain that the pods would track on them. Even if they would, it would have required at least one full pod to insure the destruction of each gunboat, which could easily spread them too thin.

The TFN pod techs swore their birds would home on gunboats, but they had to admit they couldn't prove it, and LaFroye was right about the dispersion effect. More, he and Theerah agreed the Bugs would have used their heavy cruiser "OWPs" to cover the warp point, and the Terran had successfully argued in favor of targeting the pods on them. In return, Zhaarnak had decreed that only half their total SBMHAWKs would be used in the first strike. Six hundred missiles should account for the cruisers, especially when surprise was (hopefully) complete; the remaining pods would be held back to cover a retreat at need.

Now the SBMHAWKs vanished, and TG 37.2, Grand Alliance, accelerated towards the warp point on their heels.

The sudden eruption of missile pods caught the Fleet unaware, for the enemy had ceased expending reconnaissance pinnaces six days ago, and the Fleet had taken his inactivity to indicate he had no thought of an attack.

The gunboat CSP was only thirty units strong, and many were out of position to intercept before the pods stabilized. Less than a dozen pods were picked off before the survivors fired, and most of the cruisers were still rushing to general quarters when the missiles came in.

In direct contravention of normal tactics, Zhaarnak and Prescott had chosen to send TG 37.2's lighter ships through first. They had no choice, for they had too few capital ships to expose them to the first, terrible embrace.

Only eleven of the Bug cruisers Allied intelligence had codenamed *Danger* survived the opening bombardment, and all were damaged. Four had not yet brought their offensive weapons on-line when the first Allied cruiser appeared, but the other seven opened fire instantly, and each mounted no less than sixteen of the short-ranged plasma guns. TFNS *Ammiraglio di St. Bon* and *Peder Skram* died without getting a shot off, and TFNS *Eidsvold* and KONS *Debniha* fired only a single broadside apiece before following them into destruction. But each of those broadsides finished off an active Bug CA, and their consorts flooded forward, firing savagely. Within ninety seconds, every Bug starship on the warp point was dead.

Yet that left the gunboats Theerah had wanted to target. They came slashing in with heavy loads of close-attack missiles, driving in through the thunder of the Allied missile launchers to launch at point-blank range, then closed to ram. Only a few got through, but a few were too many. KONS *Athnak*, *Noizuwha*, *Vhertygho* and *Pilko* were destroyed outright, and the air-bleeding wreck of TFNS *Voltaire*, the only Terran CA to survive, turned to limp back to Alowan.

"The cruisers have cleared the warp point, Sir," LaFroye reported, and Prescott nodded grimly. Returning courier drones tallied the dreadful price his lead waves had paid, but they'd done their job, and their sensors confirmed that the nearest superdreadnought was over two light-minutes out. That was good, because he needed all the time he could get to clear lanes through the mines. Only the TFN's ships could fire the internally launched AMBAM, yet each of his battleships mounted only a single capital missile launcher. Designed to deploy decoy enhanced-drive missiles as a defensive measure, those seven launchers were all he had to fire AMBAMs, and if the Bugs had been close enough to hammer his battle-line while it was still pinned down on the warp point, the entire operation would have had to be scrubbed.

But they weren't, and he nodded to Captain Pitnarau's com image.

"Take us through, Jason."

✧　　✧　　✧

It was disturbing that the enemy had finally realized it made more sense to lead attacks with expendable units, for that indicated he was evolving better tactics, but the battleships which followed suggested he had no superdreadnought element of his own. In turn, that suggested he had not been strongly reinforced. If that was true, the new missiles should make it relatively easy to hold this system after all, and the Fleet launched its ready-duty gunboats in a solid wave.

"They're moving in on us, Sir. Looks like they're sending in the gunboats first."

"Understood." Prescott acknowledged LaFroye's report almost absently. It was the ops officer's job to make it, but there was nothing Prescott could do about it. The *Belleisles* were clearing mines as fast as they could, but they were taking much longer than *Matterhorn*-class superdreadnoughts would have. "Have all the cripples cleared back to Alowan?"

"Yes, Sir. *Doushai* and *Juzavahn* didn't want to go, but they're clear."

"Good." Prescott watched his escorts form up to screen the battle-line and shook his head. *Tabbies! Neither of those ships had more than two launchers left, and they* still *wanted to stay!*

"Three more salvos and Alpha Lane will be through the field, Sir," Pitnarau reported.

"Beta and Charlie?"

"They're badly behind," Pitnarau admitted, and Prescott frowned.

"Forget them, then. We need maneuvering room. Move us out through Alpha now."

The enemy's units—including a mere two SDs—streamed through the minefield gap before the gunboats could attack. Some of his ships launched attack craft, but there were no more than thirty of them, and eighty gunboats streaked to meet them.

"Here they come," LaFroye said, and *Horned Viper* twitched as TG 37.2 belched missiles. The understrength fighter squadrons from the Tabby battleships and battle-cruisers raced towards the gunboats as well, and fireballs pocked the Bug formation. But the kill numbers were lower than they should have been against such fragile targets, and the strike came on grimly. *That damned point defense of theirs,* Prescott thought bitterly, and looked at Pitnarau.

"Zulu Four, Jason."

"Aye, aye, Sir. Executing Zulu Four."

TG 37.2 turned away from the gunboats, maneuvering to hold the range open while missiles and Tabby fighters tore into them. The vector shift seemed to surprise the Bugs; they lost precious seconds correcting, and the defenders used those seconds well. Only twenty-one attackers broke through, and they flung themselves upon the two Gorm leviathans which dominated Prescott's formation. But a *Gormus*-class was a dangerous opponent for anyone, especially something the size of a gunboat. Heavy energy batteries and shoals of missiles exploded into the Bugs' faces, backed by the point defense of the entire battle-line. GSNS *Dathum* lost most of her shields and took some armor damage, but she and her sister, supported by the four Orion battle-ships datalinked to them, blew the gunboats into vapor before they could ram.

"All right!" someone shouted from CIC, but Prescott's face was carved iron, for another wave was coming in, and this one was three times as strong.

"Looks like we find out if the techs were right, Alec," he said quietly, then raised his voice. "Zulu Five, Captain Pitnarau!"

The first mass strike was a disappointment, but it seemed to have confused the enemy. He recoiled, turning still further away, foolishly circling around behind the warp point. If he meant to retreat, he should have reversed course down his cleared lane and escaped the system entirely. Surely he did not expect the Fleet's own mines to deter its gunboats!

Apparently he did. He was trying to use the mines as a shield, and no doubt they would kill a few gunboats. At their speed, IFF gear was not fully reliable, and some mines were likely to attack them. But not enough to make any difference, and once they reached the warp point, they could block the enemy's retreat and swamp any additional enemy starships if they tried to make transit to support the units already in the system.

"Launch!" Prescott said, and a dozen courier drones flicked through to Alowan just as the gunboats hit the minefield. Six or seven were blown apart by their own mines, but the others screamed across the field to attack TG 37.2, and this time more got through. Most of the Tabby fighters were destroyed in a wild melee amid the mines, but they took out another forty gunboats first, and the Allied battle-line's missiles and energy weapons met the survivors furiously.

The Bugs slashed in, ignoring the screen to go after battleships, and once more, the two superdreadnoughts acted as magnets for their fury. But before they could reach their targets, a fresh wave of SBMHAWKs erupted from the warp point behind them.

The timing wasn't perfect. The pods were supposed to have caught the Bugs before they penetrated TG 37.2's perimeter, and they launched late. But the techs had been right. They *could* target gunboats, and the delayed launch actually increased their effectiveness, for gunboats, too, had blind spots, and the missiles drove straight up them.

One entire flank of Prescott's formation was a solid wall of glaring detonations as SBMs chased the Bugs in among his starships. Two of his battle-cruisers got in the way of their own SBMs and took hits that shook them to their keels, but their shields held, and their tactical officers went right on pouring fire into the Bugs.

Dathum's last shield went down, and two gunboats got through with ramming attacks, as well, damaging her drive and ripping at her hull. Her armor buckled, but she shook off the damage, holding her station. KONS *Fikhar* was less fortunate. A tornado of missiles battered the Tabby battleship's shields flat, smashed her armor, and tore deep into her hull. She staggered *in extremis,* and her agony drew the attention of other gunboats. They howled in, ramming again and again, and suddenly one of them reached her magazines. Every antimatter warhead detonated at once, and the fireball licked away another half dozen Bugs as she died.

Fikhar was gone, and three of Prescott's battle-cruisers were mangled wrecks, but the combination of TG 37.2's defensive fire and the unexpected SBMHAWKs proved decisive. The remnants of the Bug strike broke off, fleeing back to its own battle-line, and Prescott drew a deep, shuddering breath. He'd been hurt, but the core of his task group was intact and that *had* to have been the bulk of the Bugs' gunboats.

Of course, he thought as the enemy superdreadnoughts started forward, *that leaves the* rest *of their damned fleet!*

"Damage report from *Dathum?*" he demanded.

"She's lost an engine room, but she's still as fast as we are," LaFroye replied. "Damage control is bringing her shields back up now. Her armor's a sieve, but most of her weapons are in one piece, and Captain Haarmak says he's still combat capable."

"Good. We're going to need him. Com, send the second-flight drones."

The gunboats had proved less effective than anticipated, and the proof that the missile pods could target them had grim implications for future actions. But the enemy remained too weak to meet the Fleet's battle-line head on, and thirty-eight superdreadnoughts and three battle-cruisers started forward, screened by their light cruisers.

"Great Claw Pressscott has done well," Zhaarnak purred, studying the drone readouts. He and his Human ally had structured TG 37.2 as a mace to smash through the shell of the defenses, but TG 37.1

was a rapier, and it was time to bring it into play. "We will advance, Theerah."

Twenty-one carriers and their escorts scorched into the warp point at max.

The Fleet paused as fresh enemy units suddenly materialized and began launching attack craft. The gunboats were still fleeing back to the twelve battle-cruisers detached to rearm them, and the Fleet could not reach the warp point before these new enemies completed transit. It could neither seal the point against them nor afford to be destroyed if the new missiles proved ineffective, so it turned ponderously away, retreating until it saw how well the new technology worked. There would be time to return to the warp point if the missiles fulfilled predictions.

Raymond Prescott heaved a surreptitious sigh as Zhaarnak made transit, molested only by a handful of gunboats. Stragglers from the last Bug strike tried to penetrate to the carriers, but the old cliché about the snowflake in Hell came to mind as the Tabby squadrons pounced on them.

The task groups made rendezvous, and Prescott scratched the unshaven side of his head as he studied the plot. The Bugs were moving slowly *away* from the warp point rather than trying to close. They'd never done that before, and something seemed to crawl down the back of his neck as minutes dragged past without a single offensive act out of them. Zhaarnak held his own force on the warp point while his recon fighters swept outward to assure him no cloaked Bugs waited to pounce, but somehow Prescott was sure none did. Yet if not, what *were* the bastards up to?

"Great Claw Pressscott?" He turned from the plot to his com as Zhaarnak appeared on it.

"Yes, Sir?"

"My pilots have swept a light-minute sphere without contact. Least Claw Theerah and Commmodorrre Jaaackssson agree it is time to launch the next phase. Do you concur?"

"Of course, Sir. However . . ." Prescott paused a moment, rubbing his upper lip, then shrugged. "I urge caution," he said. "They are not reacting in usual fashion, and I distrust an enemy who does exactly what *I* want him to do."

"Most surprises represent only misinterpretations of known data," Zhaarnak agreed. "Yet if they wish to stand, we can only attack and discover what it is they wish us to misinterpret."

"Truth, Great Claw. Strike deep."

✧   ✧   ✧

The enemy was finally ready, but his delay had been helpful. The gunboat's greatest tactical limitation was its inability to dock internally. To rearm, it must return to its mother ship's external rack, and the mother ship must shut down her drive to reload its ordnance racks. The enemy probably had not learned that—yet—but his tardiness was still of immense value.

Though not, it was to be hoped, as much value as the new missiles.

The *Zheeerlikou'valkhannaieee* would launch the first strike. It was less a matter of honor than of practicality, for there were far more Orion fighters, and the chance of confusion between pilots who couldn't speak one another's languages had to be minimized. The less numerous Terrans were detailed as the task force's covering CSP for the opening phase. Once the Bugs had been hammered a time or two and their gunboats had been finished off, Commodore Jackson's strikegroups could be used to help complete their destruction.

Besides, there would be more than enough action to go around.

Raymond Prescott watched three hundred Tabby strikefighters arrow into the attack. Least Claw Theerah and Zhaarnak had studied Fifth Fleet's combat reports intensively. They knew how dangerous the *Cataphracts* were, and they'd taken a page from Admiral Murakuma's book: their pilots would go for the screen, using longer-ranged FM2s to pick off the *Carbines, Cannons, Cleavers* first, then go for the *Cataphracts* with FRAMs.

It was a good plan—and it came apart the instant the fighters tried to execute it.

The attack craft flashed closer. Their targets were obvious, and the screen adjusted its formation slightly. There were only eighteen Cataphracts, *and two dozen* Carbines *formed a solid wall between them and the enemy, daring him to waste his fire upon them.*

Farshathkhanaak Iaouusa'hairniak led the attack. Gee forces drew his lips back, baring his fangs, and his eyes glowed as the Bugs shifted formation. The *dairshnahki* were actually moving his designated targets out where he could get at them!

Wait! What was th—?

Iaouusa never finished the question as the very first Bug AFHAWK ever used in action scored a direct hit on his fighter.

Prescott slammed his fist down on the arm of his command chair. AFHAWKs! The bastards had AFHAWKs! No *wonder* they hadn't tried to attack! They'd been waiting to spring their ambush when *Task Force 37* attacked!

Surprise was total. It shouldn't have been. He and Zhaarnak should have allowed for the possibility, but so little time had passed since the Battle of Alowan that such a radical shift in the tactical balance hadn't even occurred to them, and Zhaarnak's pilots paid a fearful price. The missile-heavy *Carbines,* suddenly infinitely more danger- ous than the *Cataphracts,* poured devastating fire into the lead squad- rons, and the fighters had *known* they were beyond threat range. None had even taken evasive action . . . and seventy-one died in the first, terrible salvo.

The survivors reacted like the elite pilots they were. They broke instantly, in apparently total confusion, only to drop into the Orion version of the TFN's "Waldeck Weave." They twisted their base vec- tors together in a tangle of competing target sources to confuse the enemy's fire control, and despite their shock, carried through against their targets. Some managed to break lock, maneuvering hard against the AFHAWKs which had acquired them; others were less fortunate, but none turned aside, and the survivors salvoed their missiles into their briefed targets.

The Bug screen writhed as the Orion fire struck. Half the *Carbines* were destroyed outright, and most of the rest were damaged. But *none* were supposed to have lived, and the kills had cost three times the projected losses. Worse, the cost of killing the *rest* of their fleet would be still higher, for the entire Bug battle-line was belching AFHAWKs.

The Orion survivors broke off to rearm—and reorganize around their casualties—and the Bugs waited until they had been recovered for rearming . . . then sent all two hundred remaining gunboats in to kill the carriers while they were helpless in their bays. But Diego Jackson's CSP charged to meet them. The carriers' escorts and the battle-line raced to interpose between them and the gunboats, rak- ing the incoming strike with fire, but it was Jackson's outnumbered fighters who broke the attack's back.

They paid for it with sixty-one Terran fighters, and they didn't stop them all. That was perhaps the most terrifying thing about a mass suicide attack. When the attackers were intent on dying anyway, some *always* got through. The leakers slammed into TG 37.1 like hammers, and the Tabby fleet carriers were their primary targets, *Ytarible* tore apart under a hurricane of missiles and kamikazes, and *Celshakhan* and *Itumahk* were hit hard, especially *Itumahk.* Half the big carrier's hangar bays were reduced to ruin, taking their fighters with them, yet she was luckier than the CVLs *Ghiurdauni* and *Rymanthhus.* Both light carriers disappeared in the terrible glare of nuclear fusion, and the Terran *Bonhomme Richard* went with them.

But agonizing as the personnel casualties were, fighters losses were worse. Coupled with the effect of that first, dreadful AFHAWK broadside and the CSP's dogfight, half of TF 37's total fighter strength had been written off in less than twenty minutes . . . and those fighters had been Zhaarnak's main battery. His entire plan had been based on staying beyond shipboard range and battering the enemy to death with fighter strikes, but if the Bugs had AFHAWKs . . .

"I fear we must increase our fighter loss projections by at least a factor of two in light of the enemy's possession of the AFHAWK, Great Claw," Least Claw Theerah said heavily. He sat with his commander before a subdivided com screen which held the faces of Diego Jackson and his ops officer as well as Raymond Prescott and Alexander LaFroye. "Given the losses we have already suffered," he went on somberly, "I cannot guarantee success if we continue the attack."

"Wait a minute, Theerah." It was a sign of the least claw's concern that he didn't even wince as Jackson's atrocious Terran accent mangled his name. "We're hurt, sure, but we're not out of this yet. Your boys and girls kicked hell out of their *Carbines,* and *my* people finished off virtually all their gunboats. We can still take these bastards!"

Theerah let his earbug translate, then sighed. "I admire your spirit, Commmodorrre, but I am not certain I share your confidence. Our surviving strikegroups are badly disorganized. It will take hours to restore their efficiency . . . during which the enemy will reach the warp point. The prudent course would be to withdraw to Alowan to reorganize, yet I fear that is impractical."

"Truth, Least Claw," Prescott said. "We have exhausted our SBMHAWKs. Without them, we cannot force a return to the system once we retreat."

"On the other hand," LaFroye pointed out, "we *have* knocked hell out of their gunboats. If nothing else, we've insured that they can't take Alowan before Lord Khiniak arrives."

"I didn't come here to lose, Alec," Prescott harshly. "I came here to relieve Hairnow!"

Zhaarnak hid a flicker of bitter amusement. *How odd. Humans say we do not know how to give ground, yet it is Theerah who counsels caution and Humans who reject his words!*

"Damn right," Jackson growled. "I have *had* it with these things, and I *want* their asses!"

"I realize that, Sir." LaFroye said respectfully, reminding himself Jackson was a fighter jock by training and inclination. "I'm simply pointing out that we've already achieved our minimum objective."

"You are correct, Commmannderrr LaaaFrrroye," Zhaarnak said, "as are you, Theerah. Yet as Great Claw Pressscott says, I did not come here to lose. So I ask you. Is Commmodorrre Jaaacksssson correct? *Can we complete the enemy's destruction?*"

The least claw sat silent for several seconds, eyes straying to the plot on which the Bug battle-line advanced towards the warp point. If TF 37 meant to retreat before the enemy's missiles could command the point, it must begin its withdrawal within the next fifteen minutes.

Theerah disliked being the voice of caution. It felt unnatural and somehow sordid, yet it was also his job, and he closed his eyes and thought furiously. Then he sighed.

"I do not know, Great Claw," he said finally. "Certainly we can do them great damage, but to *destroy* them will require our battle-line to accept action. We cannot do it with fighters alone."

"We can hack that," LaFroye said, "but only if we take their SBMs and capital missiles out of the picture. They only have nine *Archers*. Can the fighters get in and kill them first?"

"Commmodorrre?" Theerah asked quietly, and Diego Jackson bared his teeth.

"We can do it," he said confidently. "It'll cost us, but we can do it."

"In that case, Great Claw, I think we can do it," LaFroye said. "They don't mount CMs in anything else, and we've got nine capital missile battle-cruisers. We send the fighters in to kill the *Archers*, then empty the battle-cruisers' magazines into them from outside their range. Instead of outright kills, we concentrate on knocking down their datalink, then the battle-line pounds them with standard missiles from outside effective energy range and closes with the fighters in tight, like Admiral Murakuma did in Leonidas, and kicks their guts out from the inside."

"Theerah?" Zhaarnak asked.

"It should work, Great Claw," the least claw said. "Yet casualties will be very heavy, and for us to attempt it, we must first complete our strikegroups' reorganization. That will require us to allow them to reclaim the warp point, so if it does *not* work, none of our ships will escape."

"Lord Khiniak will reach Alowan in six days," Zhaarnak murmured as if to himself. "Even if we are destroyed, his strength will hold the system, and if we do sufficient damage to the enemy, he will retake Telmasa with ease." His eyes flicked to the icon of the Hairnow warp point, and his ears flattened. He gazed at it for several seconds, then inhaled sharply.

"Very well, Commmannderrr LaaaFrrroye, you have convinced me. We shall send our worst damaged ships back to Alowan and attempt your plan with the remainder. And if we fail," he raised one clawed hand, palm uppermost, and closed it slowly into a fist, "then we shall end like *farshatok*." He smiled thinly. "It is a good day for it, war brothers."

CHAPTER TWENTY-NINE

The Tips of Our Claws

Tenth Great Fang of the Khan Koraaza'khiniak, *Khanhaku* Khiniak, CO Third Fleet, stood behind the side party in KONS *Ebymiae*'s boat bay and watched the cutter dock. It was a Human cutter, and Lord Khiniak found that entirely fitting as he glanced about the cavernous boat bay at the officers and ratings of his new flagship. He had shifted his lights to *Ebymiae* only six days before, on his arrival in Telmasa, for she was the sole Orion battleship to survive Second Telmasa. She *deserved* her status, and he felt a pride in her which only the *Zheeerlikou'valkhannaieee* could fully have understood.

Or perhaps not, he told himself, thinking of the officer he was about to greet.

The hatch opened, and the pipes skirled. They did not offer the KON's normal honors; instead they played *Suns of Splendor,* the anthem of the Terran Federation.

Two officers walked forward into that music. One was a tall, russet-furred Orion; the other a shorter, battered-looking Human who leaned heavily on a cane. His uniform bore the brand-new insignia of a TFN vice admiral, but one side of his shaven head showed a freshly healed, cruel-looking scar, and his immobilized left arm hung useless. He moved slowly, in obvious pain, and the Orion at his side tried not to hover attentively over him.

"Task Force Thirty-Seven, arriving!" the intercom announced. That, too, was not usual Orion protocol, and Lord Khiniak saw surprise—and pleasure—in the Human officer's face.

The newcomers halted, and the Human looked down at his cane, then gave a crooked Human smile and braced painfully erect. He handed the cane to his companion, who took it gingerly, and saluted the son of the khan at the side party's head.

627

"Permission to come aboard, Sir?" he said in the Tongue of Tongues, and the son of the khan's salute would have done the Khan himself proud.

"Permission granted, Fang Pressscott!" he replied loudly, and Lord Khiniak stepped forward as Zhaarnak returned Prescott's cane. Lord Khiniak carefully did not note the Human's relief—or his small sound of pain—as he reclaimed his prop, but the great fang neither saluted Prescott nor offered his hand in the Human greeting his guest could not return while leaning upon it. Instead, he gave a much deeper Orion bow than usual.

"I am most pleased to meet you, Fang Pressscott," he said. "And to greet you once more, Great Claw." This time he did extend a hand, and Zhaarnak took it. They brought their free hands flashing to one another's faces in a warrior's salute, and Lord Khiniak smiled. "You bring great honor to us all, both of you. In the name of all the *Zheeerlikou'valkhannaieee* and of my Khan, I thank you."

Raymond Prescott watched Zhaarnak from the corner of one eye. The Tabby actually looked embarrassed, and Prescott waited for him to speak. But the cat seemed to have Zhaarnak's tongue—despite the pain of his wounds, the cliché made Prescott smile—and so he cleared his own throat.

"Honor comes to those who act with honor, Great Fang," he said for them both, "and it was our *farshatok* who brought honor to us all."

"Well said, Fang Pressscott," Lord Khiniak approved, then looked up. He clicked his claws, and a gorgeously bejeweled least claw stepped forward with a small, gem-crusted casket. Lord Khiniak took it in his own hands, and for all the solid weight of its precious metals and jewels, it seemed far too light for what it held as he turned back to his guests.

"Fang Pressscott—" no Orion would ever again greet this Human by his TFN rank "—Great Claw Zhaarnak, I bring you these as token of the honor you have earned. I speak in this as *hirikolus'ni'hami*, with the mouth of my Khan, and my hand is his hand."

Prescott and Zhaarnak stiffened and squared their shoulders almost in unison. Technically, every member of the Orion military was *hirikolus'ni'hami*, oath-sworn to the *Khan'a'khanaaeee*, but Lord Khiniak's formal emphasis carried another, deeper meaning. It was the ancient meaning, that of a liege man and war captain who, in this moment, literally *was* the Khan, a physical avatar for his distant war-lord and hence for every Orion who had ever been or would be born.

He opened the casket reverently, and Prescott heard air hiss between Zhaarnak's fangs as Lord Khiniak lifted out a ribbon of deepest midnight blue, the imperial color of the Khanate. A magnificent golden starburst hung from it, broad as a Terran coffee cup yet delicate, exquisitely wrought like living, dancing flame, and a huge, blood-red ruby glittered at its heart.

The great fang returned the casket to his aide, who held it on open palms while his superior turned once more to face the Terran.

"Fang Pressscott, in the name and stead of my Khan, I beg you to accept this in the name of all the Human warriors who so valiantly perished defending the *Zheeerlikou'valkhannaieee*." Khiniak paused, then allowed a very small flicker of amusement to flaw his solemnity as he added softly. "We have consulted with your Navy and government, though we asked them not to inform you of our request and spoil our surprise, and they have approved."

"I—" Prescott paused to clear his throat. "I would be honored, Great Fang."

"Good." Lord Khiniak settled the ribbon about his neck, then slapped him gently on the cheek with his claws. "In all our history, only two warriors not of our own race have received the *Ithyrra'doi'khanhaku*, and both were of our Gormish *farshatok*. Your name will be added to the Khan's own clan fathers in honor, and you are no longer human alone, Raaaymmonnd'pressscott. By the blood you have shed and the lives you have saved, you are *Zheeerlikou'valkhannaieee*, as well, *Khanhaku* Pressscottt, and while our people endure, we shall not forget."

Prescott bowed deeply, but he said nothing. He wasn't sure he could have trusted his voice if he'd tried to, nor was it the Orion way to indulge in flowery speeches. Few words but heartfelt ones were the Orion ideal. The more profound the occasion, the less they spoke of it, and he felt Zhaarnak quivering with emotion beside him.

Lord Khiniak gazed at him for a moment. Then his hand dipped into the casket once more for a smaller, equally beautiful copy of the star about Prescott's neck. This one was sized to fit an Orion officer's harness, and the great fang turned to Zhaarnak.

"As Fang Pressscott, so you, Great Claw," he said quietly. "You are named no longer Zhaarnak'diaano in the records of our clans, but Zhaarnak'telmasa, First Father of Clan Telmasa, and our Khan has personally charged me to welcome you to his fathers in honor."

Zhaarnak gripped his *defargo's* hilt so hard the tips of his claws emerged as Lord Khiniak removed the golden starship which marked him as an officer of the KON and snapped the star into its place. He would never again wear that starship, for the *Ithyrra'doi'khanhaku* would serve in its place . . . just as it would forever answer any slur upon his honor for retreating from Kliean.

Lord Khiniak finished affixing the medal, then stood back with a bow.

"And now, war brothers, join me in my flag briefing room. I would hear our situation from your own mouths."

"—and so we did," Zhaarnak finished quietly. "Commmannnderr LaaaFrrroye was correct; we did have the firepower . . . and as Theerah had warned, the cost *was* heavy."

Lord Khiniak flicked his ears in slow agreement, pondering the vagaries of Fate. His tardy order to stand fast had reached Alowan seven hours *after* TF 37 launched its attack. Had he sent it when Governor Kaarsaahn first instructed him to, the task force would neither have attacked nor suffered such casualties. And Third Fleet would have paid an even more terrible cost when *it* discovered the enemy's AFHAWKs.

He glanced into the repeater plot at the icons which been added to his own order of battle. They were agonizingly few, for ninety percent of Zhaarnak's and Prescott's fighters had died in Second Telmasa, and their battle-line had been savagely battered. The superdreadnought *Dathum* had perished . . . along with the battleships *Ambrych*, *Fikhar*, *Colossus*, *Mexicano* and *Umaghoz*. Virtually every surviving capital ship was little more than a wreck—Prescott's *Horned Viper* had barely survived, and her flag bridge had been reduced to an abattoir. TG 37.2's battle-cruisers had been almost as heavily hammered, and the entire task force had been reduced to impotence.

But in return, TF 37 had destroyed every Bug starship in Telmasa . . . before the enemy discovered the warp point to Hairnow. A billion and a half civilians had been saved, and his own command faced only a single warp point assault to reach Kliean once more.

"You should not have done it, war brothers," he said softly at last. "You should not have, knowing I was coming. Yet it is well you did— very well, indeed. Thank you."

"We could not have done it without our Human *farshatok*," Zhaarnak said, and Lord Khiniak nodded, hiding his amusement at hearing such words from an old-line fire-eater such as he who had been Zhaarnak'diaano. He could hardly wait for Zhaarnak'*telmasa's* next interview with *Khanhaku* Diaano. Clan lord or no, the old man would find cold welcome from Zhaarnak if he started on one of his anti-Human harangues now.

"Truth, Great Claw," the great fang said, and turned to the human. "I am glad your own Navy has rewarded you with promotion, Fang Pressscott, and deeply regret that your fresh wounds will prevent you from serving with us when we return to Kliean. I trust they are less severe than original reports indicated?"

"The leg will be fine in time," Prescott replied. "As for the arm?"

He gave a human shrug. "The surgeons have not yet given up hope, but I fear they have little to work with. And it may be as well if I leave *Horned Viper* . . . I seem to attract too much fire for her good."

Lord Khiniak gave a purring chuckle at his wry tone. It was amazing how well this Human spoke the Tongue of Tongues. Given Zhaarnak's original prejudices, the gods had smiled upon the *Zheeerlikou'valkhannaieee* indeed when they sent this man to them.

"We shall hope she suffers less in Kliean," he replied, "but I shall be honored to have her with us, and from all I have heard, Ahhhdmiraal Jaaackssson will lead your *farshatok* well."

"Diego is a good man," Prescott agreed, "and he certainly deserves the promotion."

"Yes. Well." The great fang stood. "I thank you both for the briefing. Now I have other duties to attend to before we dine. Please remain here as long as you wish. Should you have any needs, my aide will remain on Flag Bridge and will be happy to attend to them."

He waved them both back into their chairs as Prescott struggled to rise, then left with a graceful bow.

Zhaarnak rose and crossed to the holo display, gazing at the ships which spangled it. A hundred and twenty starships, led by eighteen Gorm superdreadnoughts and eleven Terran and Orion battleships, glowed in its depths, supported by eight fleet carriers and thirteen CVLs. Over seven hundred fighters rode those icons—fighters which now knew the enemy had AFHAWKs and would not be surprised again, and that knowledge, he knew, was almost as important to the Grand Alliance as the relief of Hairnow. It was a mighty force beside the one he and Prescott had led into Telmasa, and still more warships were en route. The Idnahk Sector had been saved, and as he stared at the lights, he felt the Human who had truly made that possible behind him.

"We did it, war brother," he murmured. "We truly did . . . and I never thought we could."

"Indeed?" Prescott's chuckle turned Zhaarnak from the display, ears cocked, and the Human laughed. "You hid your doubt well, Great Claw. Did I hide mine equally well?"

"Well enough *I* never saw it," Zhaarnak replied. "But the price, my friend. Gods, the price was high!"

"By the tips of our claws," the Human agreed more somberly. He pushed himself up and limped over to the holo on his cane. "We did it by the tips of our claws," he repeated softly.

"Truth." Zhaarnak turned his head, studying Prescott while the Human looked into the display, then cleared his throat. "There is something I would ask of you, Fang Pressscott."

"Ah?" The Human's round-pupiled eyes looked at him from their flat, alien face, and Zhaarnak flicked his ears in agreement.

"We have seen much, you and I, and in the seeing, I have learned even more. About your people, and about myself. I have not enjoyed my lessons, yet learn them I have, and it is my honor to have learned from one such as you." The Human's face darkened with the blush Zhaarnak had learned indicated embarrassment, but he went on quietly. "Many years ago, I met Lord Talphon at a conference, and, to my shame, I regarded him with contempt, for he had sworn *vilkshatha* with a Human. Yet I know now why he did so, and so I ask this of you, little though I deserve it after so many years of foolish hatred." He drew a deep breath. "War brother, will you swear *vilkshatha* with me?"

CHAPTER THIRTY

Blind in the Dark

"I have grown to hate my work."

Son of the Khan Shaairal'haairaa looked up as Small Claw Maariaah'sheerino spoke. Survey Flotilla 80's commander was tipped back in his chair while he nursed a beaker of *chermaak*. He flattened his ears in an expression of abject misery the most skilled actor could not have bettered, and Shaairal purred a soft chuckle.

The Orion term *maavairahk* was not one of approval when it was borrowed from humanity in ISW-3. That remained true for the majority of the KON's officers even now, but it certainly fitted Maariaah. Yet maverick or no, he was also one of the best survey officers the KON had ever produced, which explained his rank at such a young age. Well, that and his status as the great-great-grandcub of one Varnik'sheerino, the greatest First Fang in Orion history. Personally, Shaairal suspected Maariaah had deliberately developed his iconoclastic persona *because* of his lineage, for it could not be easy to bear such a name. Besides, Varnik himself had been a *maavairahk* in his day, even if the Tongue of Tongues had not then boasted the word.

But whatever the small claw's motives, Shaairal recognized a cue when he heard one.

"And why is that, Small Claw?" he asked respectfully.

"Because it is so *boring*," Maariaah said plaintively. Other ears cocked on *Harkhan*'s bridge as Shaairal's officers and the small claws staff listened. The KON's survey crews were a tight-knit fraternity in which officers such as Maariaah inspired a sense of camaraderie rare outside the strikefighter community. "We go through the warp point, we look around, we hunt for fresh warp points, and, if we find one, we go through *it* and start all over again. Think of it, Shaairal. If we had but reactor mass enough, we could sail forever without ever reaching the end of it all." The small claw quaffed *chermaak* and shook his head mournfully. "There is too much emptiness in the universe, and I have already seen half of it."

"Perhaps so," Shaairal made his voice as sympathetic as he could, "but you should not think of it in that way, Sir. Instead, think of all the emptiness you may yet be the first to see."

"Oh, *thank* you, Son of the Khan! You have a gift—indisputably, a gift!—for encouraging your commander."

"Thank you, Sir," Shaairal replied as a chorus of chuckles ran around *Harkhan*'s bridge.

"You are welcome."

The small claw let his command chair swing upright and set his *chermaak* aside, satisfied the byplay had taken some of the tension out of Shaairal's bridge watch. Not all of it—a little tension kept people on their toes—but enough that he could now put it aside and get down to business. *And,* he thought, *it could be very serious business, indeed.*

"Are we prepared, Son of the Khan?" he asked the flag captain.

"We are, Sir. The escort and fortresses are all at action stations."

"In that case, proceed to that fresh emptiness you promised me."

Shaairal began giving orders, and Maariaah left him to it. His own eyes strayed to the master plot, and he felt his claws try to ease from their sheaths. Survey Flotilla 80's eighteen cruisers were almost lost amid the multihued lights of their escorts, and like every other person aboard *Harkhan*, Maariaah devoutly wished those icons were somewhere far, far away.

But they were not. Four months—*No, three* standard *months,* he reminded himself, for the Grand Alliance had decided to use Human date conventions—had passed since Lord Khiniak's reconquest of Kliean demonstrated the consequences of the botched Shanak survey. Four billion dead, an entire star system's habitable planets reduced to so much useless, irradiated wasteland. It was a lesson the Alliance would not forget, and what had begun as a war of honor to succor an ally had become something else for the Orion Navy . . . which had no equivalent of the Human concept of "turning the other cheek." The fury the Kliean Atrocity had waked was impossible to exaggerate, and the consequences for the race which had wreaked it would be unimaginable.

But Kliean had also shaken the Alliance to its core. The millions who had perished in the Romulus Cluster had been bad enough; the death toll in Kliean was obscene, and a wave of panic had washed outward from it. If it could happen to Kliean, it could happen *anywhere.* It could not, of course. Maariaah knew that, but few civilians truly grasped the realities spacers took for granted. All they knew was that the planets of Kliean would lie lifeless for thousands of years.

Maariaah understood their fear, but he hated how the war had slowed as governments strove to calm the panic. Every nook and cranny was to be fortified; minefields were to be sown about every warp point, however far from the front; and massive covering forces were to be organized at nodal positions. It all amounted to an enormous diversion of industrial effort and priceless warships from offensive duties, and the impact on future operations would be profound.

And it is all so pointless, he thought moodily. *Even if the fears are correct, the sheer size of the fleets these Bugs commit will make a mockery of our efforts. We cannot fortify every system sufficiently to stop them, and so all our efforts will do nothing but divert desperately needed strength into public relations activities which ultimately accomplish nothing.*

Maariaah was not alone in his feelings. Both the Human Antonov and First Fang Ynaathar had protested the new directives, but in vain. The political leaders—*Zheeerlikou'valkhannaieee* and Human alike—refused to heed them, and even in the Khanate, warriors had no choice but to obey orders.

And in this particular case, Maariaah conceded unhappily, those directives actually made sense, for the warp point SF 80 was about to explore was in a terrifying location. It lay in the Rehfrak System . . . a sector capital with a population even greater than Kliean's had been.

The small claw's lips wrinkled with disgust as he considered the long dead commander of the original Rehfrak survey. Type Eleven warp points were elusive, but the instruments of the time had been quite capable of locating them. It would have required a considerable investment in time, however, and Claw Faairnaas had been in a hurry. He had skimped on the survey—a cursory reading of his log made that plain—and this was the result: an open, unsurveyed warp point at the heart of one of the Khanate's oldest, wealthiest and most heavily populated sectors.

Well, at least Rehfrak, unlike Kliean, had been fortified for over three Orion centuries. Once the initial panic passed, three dozen powerful OWPs had been towed to cover the newly discovered warp point, and the KON had assembled over a hundred warships to support them.

Quite an escort for one lowly survey flotilla, Maariaah thought, then tensed as *Harkhan* began to move towards the invisible hole in space. Soon enough, they would know if all this military might was no more than the wasted effort Maariaah devoutly prayed it was.

✧　　✧　　✧

The transit surge passed, and Maariaah's ships vanished into cloak. After Shanak and Kliean, the Alliance had no choice but to assume the Bugs maintained pickets in every explored system, however useless. Henceforth, every survey force would operate only in cloak, which made sense but was expensive in both equipment wear and time. A cloaked vessel could not use active sensors, which cut its sensor reach by seventy percent, with a consequent increase in the time required to cover a given volume. Using larger survey forces could offset some of that, yet every ship added to a flotilla also increased the odds that it would be detected, despite its ECM.

And, of course, a Bug picket in precisely the right place might pick them up on transit, before they could bring their cloaking systems up, setting all their efforts at stealth at naught.

But in this case, Maariaah decided, it was unlikely any picket was present. Their entry warp point was a Type One five light-hours from the G8 component of a binary system. Component B was a dimmer K8, almost six light-hours from Component A and five hundred light-minutes from *Harkhan* as the light cruiser emerged from warp. But the important point was that Component A had a planet at six light-minutes, well within its liquid water zone. It also boasted a large asteroid belt at twenty-one light-minutes, with all the industrial advantages that offered, yet there were no artificial emissions, and the Bugs would surely have developed such prime real estate . . . had they known of it. No one, least of all Maariaah'sheerino, was going to assume anything—not with the bleeding wound of Kliean so fresh—yet he felt an undeniable easing of the tension about him as his officers worked their way to the same conclusion.

"All units' ECM is up, Small Claw," Shaairal reported, and Maariaah flicked his ears in approval.

"Well executed, Son of the Khan. Transmit my thanks to all units—discreetly, of course."

"Certainly, Sir."

"And while you are about it, set up our initial spiral," Maariaah added. "We will proceed cautiously, but the sooner we begin, the sooner we can move on to still more emptiness."

Survey Flotilla 80 prowled stealthily about Component A. The warp points of a binary system were invariably associated with the more massive star, moving in their own, fixed relationship with it. The math which described the phenomenon always made Maariaah's head ache, but he was grateful for the way it reduced his survey area. By his most conservative estimate, however, the task would still consume at least two months, and more probably three, and he bent his attention on ways to keep his personnel alert as they settled in for the duration.

What had happened to Kliean made that easier, but nothing could fully offset the sheer, mind-numbing tedium of their task. No one who had never participated in a first survey could truly appreciate the sheer immensity of any star system, and warp points were elusive prey.

Days passed, then weeks, and the cloaked ships continued their methodical activity, winnowing space for the tiny gravitational eddies which might indicate yet another warp point.

Maariaah was sound asleep when the alarm wrenched him from dreams of his wife and cubs. He lurched upright on his sleeping mat, stabbing for the com button even before his eyes opened, and light flared in his darkened cabin as his terminal came on-line.

"Bridge," a taut voice said, then changed as the officer of the watch recognized the small claw. "*Chaarkhan* has just reported detection of what may be an unknown starship, Sir!"

"*May?*" Maariaah repeated sharply.

"Yes, Small Claw. If it is, it, too, is cloaked."

An icy fist squeezed Maariaah's stomach, and he made himself pause. It would do neither his image nor the crew's nerve any service to appear flustered, and so he kept his voice level.

"Location?"

"Thirty-one light-minutes from *Harkhan* at zero-six-three, two-five-one, Sir."

"Do we have a vector?"

"No, Small Claw. It appears to be stationary."

Either that, or the dairshnakhu *saw* Chaarkhan *and went dead,* Maariaah thought grimly. *If he truly exists at all, he is pretending to be a hole in space and waiting for us to make a move.*

"Is Son of the Khan Shaairal there?"

"I have just arrived, Small Claw," Shaairal's voice said, and *Harkhan's* captain's face replaced that of the duty officer. "The flotilla has implemented standing orders, Sir."

"Good. I am on my way. Do nothing but observe until I arrive."

Maariaah's mind raced as he killed the com, scrambled from his mat, and reached for his harness. *Chaarkhan* might have detected only a sensor ghost, but he dared not assume anything of the sort. Yet how should he proceed? His standing orders had brought the entire flotilla to a halt, which reduced its drive signatures to a bare minimum and made its cloaking systems far more effective, but ships which did not move could not close to obtain better data.

The one thing he absolutely could *not* do was send word back to Rehfrak. Courier drones could not cloak, and a drone's vector would give the Bugs—if there *were* any Bugs!—a bearing on the flotilla's entry warp point. No, he must somehow determine whether or not the enemy was present, first. Then, if he had the firepower, he must destroy any pickets before *their* drones reported *his* presence. If he could not destroy them, he must somehow break contact with at least one of his ships and send it back to Rehfrak with word of the danger.

Whatever he did, the next few days would not be pleasant.

"There it is again, Sir," Observer First Cheraahlk said.

Maariaah raised a hand, stopping the flotilla's senior engineer in mid-report, and watched Cheraahlk lean forward. The observer babied his passive sensors and computers as he worked the elusive contact, and then his ears flattened in disgust.

"*Shiaaahk!*" He looked up, expression apologizing for the oath, but Maariaah waved it off. The last six days had been even less pleasant than anticipated. The unknowns—and there was no longer any doubt *someone* else was in the system—were fiendishly elusive, and Cheraahlk was his best sensor officer . . . and more than entitled to an occasional curse.

"Did you get any more on him?"

"Not much, Small Claw," Cheraahlk said apologetically.

"Anything at all will be welcome," Maariaah assured him.

"Observe your plot, please, Sir," Cheraahlk requested, and a crimson icon appeared on the small claw's repeater display. The observer replayed his entire brief track on it, and Maariaah watched it slide across the very edge of the sensor envelope and then vanish once more. "His instrumentation must be at least as good as our own," Cheraahlk said. "He knew we were here—not our precise location, but our general position—and came in for a closer look, then broke back out before we got a good lock. I think it was Unknown Three this time, Sir, but it could have been one we have not seen before."

Maariaah flicked his ears and keyed a replay command. The icon slid across the display once more, and there was something damnably familiar about it. Its maneuver was not one a ship of the *Zheeerlikou'valkhannaieee* would have employed, yet he had the maddening sense that he had seen it—or one like it—before.

He replayed it again and muttered a mental curse of his own. That sharp yet graceful turn *was* familiar . . . and Cheraahlk was right. The unknown's scanners must be at least as good as *Harkhan's*. Probably better, for she had not picked it up until it was well into its sensor run.

Any cloaking field leaked a little energy, and the emission patterns which oozed through it were distinctive, and so far, Survey Flotilla Eighty had made tentative IDs on at least five unknowns. Their antics demonstrated that they knew Maariaah's command was present, yet they had launched no attacks, and every battle report Maariaah had seen suggested that the Bugs *should* have attacked by now, if only to draw his fire. Such a maneuver would almost certainly result in the destruction of the attacking unit, yet it would absolutely confirm the presence of his own units and give hard locations on the ships which fired. Given the enemy's willingness to sacrifice starships, Maariaah had anticipated just such an attempt for days now.

Yet it had not happened . . . and there was that nagging sense he had seen such a maneuver before. But where? Try as he might, he could not recall, and it was driving him mad.

He leaned back in his chair and folded his hands across his belly, tapping his claws together while he thought. There was a limit to how long he could let this game of hunt the *marhang* continue. Whether the Bugs knew it or not, *he* knew they posed a deadly threat to Rehfrak, and his overriding responsibility was to alert the sector capital.

He thought a moment longer, then beckoned Shaairal to his side and spoke quietly.

"Cheraahlk is correct, Shaairal. Whoever this is, his instrumentation is excellent. We are unlikely to pin him down without assistance, and we must warn Rehfrak. We dare not use a courier drone, so we must use one of our ships."

"Risky, Small Claw," Shaairal murmured. It was not a protest, simply a consideration of the difficulties, and Maariaah flicked his ears in agreement.

"Truth, Son of the Khan, yet I see no option. We will detach *Fraikhal*, *Mhote*, and *Shergha*. *Shergha* will be our courier, and the other two will accompany her to the warp point and screen her. She will hold position just clear of the warp point while they run a sweep around it, and she will make transit only when they report all clear."

"With your permission, Sir, I will add *Jhusahk* and *Timkhar*," Shaairal replied. "Daughter of the Khan Deaara has the next best observer after Cheraahlk himself, and I trust her judgment."

"An excellent thought," Maariaah agreed, "and—"

"*Communication laser!*"

Both officers whirled to the com officer in shock. The young cub of the Khan raised a hand, cupping his ear bug as if to somehow hear better, then looked up in total disbelief.

"Someone is lasing us, Small Claw! It—Sir, it appears to be a standard Alliance com protocol!"

An *Alliance* protocol? Maariaah looked at Shaairal, and the son of the khan gave an ear flick of helplessness. Was it possible the Bugs had somehow cracked a captured Allied database when the Alliance had persistently failed to crack theirs?

"Put it on intercom," he ordered, and a voice rattled the speakers.

Maariaah read Standard English, but his understanding of the spoken language was poor, and he looked at Shaairal for a translation.

"He says 'Unknown vessel, this is the Terraaan vessel *Maaashhaaanaaa*. Identify yourself or be fired upon.'"

"*Maaashhaaanaaa?*" Maariaah repeated. "What sort of ship name is that?"

"Sir, I have her on our shipping list," Shaairal's tactical officer reported. "According to the file, she is one of their *Hun*-class survey cruisers."

"*Hun*-class, is it?" Maariaah wished—not for the first time—that all TFN ships could have such easily pronounced names rather than the clumsy sounds Humans kept inflicting on the poor things. But the thought was only a flicker on the surface of his mind, for the *Huns* were survey ships, like his own *Harkhan*. Was it truly possible—?

"Sir, the challenge is repeating," the com officer said nervously, and the assistant tactical officer spoke almost in the same breath.

"Captain, I am picking up fire control emissions from at least five sources!"

"Very well," Maariaah said far more calmly than he felt. "Com, reply 'This is the *Zheeerlikou'valkhannaieee* cruiser *Harkhan*,'" the cub of the khan acknowledged and Maariaah looked at the tac officer. "If this is a ruse, he will fire the instant he receives our reply. Be ready."

"Aye, Small Claw."

A moment of intolerable tension hovered, and then the voice came from the speakers again. It spoke much more slowly this time, slowly enough even Maariaah could follow it.

"*Harkhan*, this is Captain Josepha Vargas, TFN, commanding Survey Flotilla Two-Five-One. You've had us worried," it said.

CHAPTER THIRTY-ONE

Hell's Gate

Small Claw Maariaah watched his plot's icons and tried—unsuccessfully—not to feel envious. His *Lahstyn*-class cruisers represented the best compromise the Khanate could afford: well equipped to avoid detection, yet extremely austere, without even command datalink. The KON simply could not divert sufficient funding to build the numbers of survey ships it required if it opted for any more sophisticated design, but the Terran Federation could . . . and had.

Maariaah was senior to Captain Vargas, the Human survey force commander, yet his ships, for all their numbers, made a poor showing beside her command. TFNS *Belisarius*, her flagship, was one of the new *Guerriere-B* command battle-cruisers, with the control systems to provide a datanet for her entire flotilla, and her actual survey ships were all *Hun-Bs*, refitted with military engines. It reduced their strategic speed but gave them the tactical fleetness to outrun any Bugs they happened across—just as *Belisarius'* datalink gave them an excellent chance of outfighting any picket cruisers which crossed their path. And what Maariaah envied most of all, perhaps, was TFNS *Caravan*, an armed freighter built on a converted *Dunkerque*-class battle-cruiser hull and equipped with cloaking ECM as well as a light missile battery. *Caravan*'s cargo capacity was the final support element which allowed the TFN to mount long-ranged, sustained survey operations which the KON simply could not match.

And the crowning element in Maariaah's ignoble envy were the eighty brand-new second-generation recon drones in *Caravan*'s capacious holds. The Humans had finally gotten warp-capable drones into production, and the all but invisible robots let Vargas probe warp points at greatly reduced risk of detection . . . and without exposing her own ships to hostile action.

It was, he thought, a lesson in the advantages of affluence, and not even the fact that the Humans were shipping thousands of the new RD2s to the Khanate completely eased its sting.

Yet for all that, Vargas had reached the system Maariaah had named Zaaia'pharaan, in honor of his maternal granddam, only after his own flotilla. Zaaia'pharaan lay at the extreme end of a frontier warp line Vargas had been engaged in extending, and so was of far less value to the Federation than to the Khanate. No doubt the Humans would have ceded it to their allies for that reason alone, but under the Treaty of Mattar, a system belonged to whoever reached it first, and Vargas had readily acknowledged the *Zheeerlikou'valkhannaieee's* prior claim on Zaaia'pharaan.

Still, they were allies, and they were here, and he and Vargas had decided to operate in concert. Once they had realized they were playing catch-as-catch-can with allies rather than enemies—*or, rather, once* Vaaargaaas, *with her superior instrumentation, realized it,* the small claw reminded himself sourly—they had not taken long to complete their sweep of the system. They had found no sign of enemy vessels, but they *had* detected two additional warp points, and they would soon make the first move to explore them.

In the meantime, Rehfrak had been brought up to date. Vargas' relief at having a powerful fleet in support distance had been unmistakable, but the Human least claw had also realized why Maariaah was so nervous. She had no more desire than he to show the Bugs the way to Rehfrak, and it was she who had suggested that the fleet element remain in the sector capital rather than advance to Zaaia'pharaan. Under the circumstances, it was more important to keep the Rehfrak connection secret than to protect the survey ships. In the event that the enemy was encountered and managed to track them, the Humans had agreed that their combined force would fall back on *Human* space, leading the Bugs away from Rehfrak. Given that no inhabited Human system lay within twelve transits, the Federation had far more depth to play with. As to who held title to any additional systems they jointly discovered, that would be up to the diplomats, although Maariaah suspected the Khanate's possession of Zaaia'pharaan would give it the inside track.

"Caaaptain Vaaargaaas reports that she is prepared to deploy the first drone flight, Sir," Shaairal reported, and Maariaah flicked an ear in acknowledgment.

"Instruct her to proceed," he said.

"All right, Mal," Josepha Vargas said. "We've got an audience of Tabbies just waiting to see how well our new toy works. Let's not embarrass ourselves."

"I think that can be arranged, Sir," Commander Malcolm Klesko replied, "but please remember these things are still on the temperamental side."

"I'll be totally sympathetic," she assured him. "Right after I skin you out and salt down the hide."

"You're so understanding," Klesko sighed, but he grinned as he spoke. The RD2 was his baby, for he'd been assistant project officer on the team which finally got it into production. That was why Vargas had specifically requested him, and getting her request granted was a major coup for her. Yet they both knew he was right. The new drones were—or would be, once they got the kinks out of them—an enormous boon to Survey Command, but they were still a new system, and the conditions under which they had to operate were harsh.

Although larger than courier drones, they were smaller than anything else which had ever been capable of making even a single transit, and single transits were useless for survey missions. They had to get through the warp point, look around, *and* come back. So far, about one in three was getting home, but only one survivor in ten brought back any useful data; the internal systems of the other nine were hopelessly addled by the brutal stress of a first-transit through an uncharted warp point. R&D promised the failure rate would drop, but the most optimistic success rate projected, even for the fully matured technology, was no more than forty to fifty percent.

"Just do your best," Vargas said, and Klesko nodded before he keyed his boom mike.

"Final systems check," he said crisply.

"All green, Sir," Ensign Michaelson replied instantly.

"Very well. Activate the first flight."

"Activating now," Michaelson confirmed, and Klesko watched his display.

The RD2s were too large to launch from XO racks. Instead, they had to be deployed from a cargo hold, preflighted in space by vac-suited technicians, and then sent on their way. It was all very complicated, but Klesko felt a glow of satisfaction as the first ten drones brought their drives on-line, headed for the warp point in a chain of glittering icons, and one by one vanished.

"Telemetry lost," Michaelson reported, exactly on the tick, and Klesko nodded and tipped his chair back to keep an eye on the time. All they could do now was wait.

✧   ✧   ✧

"Those are very difficult sensor targets, Small Claw," Observer First Cheraahlk said in tones of deep respect.

"Good," Maariaah grunted. "Perhaps the enemy will find them equally difficult to detect," he added, and other officers flicked their ears in sober agreement.

"I wonder if Caaaptain Vaaargaaas would sell us a few?" *Harkhan's* tac officer mused.

"I shall ask her," Maariaah assured him with a purring chuckle. "Of course, we would also have to rent *Caravaaan* to haul them around for us!"

"I have nothing else to spend my exorbitant salary on, Sir," the tac officer replied, and a wave of laughter rippled around the bridge.

Malcolm Klesko checked the time—again—and nodded. Assuming the warp point didn't lead to a black hole or something equally drastic, he should see something just ... about ... *now.*

"Transit beacon!" Ensign Michaelson sang out, and Klesko grinned. "I've got another one—No, wait ... Correction, Sir. I have a total of four beacons!"

"Outstanding!" Klesko replied. A forty percent return rate was the highest they'd managed yet, but he reminded himself not to start celebrating too soon. The mere fact that his babies had returned didn't mean they'd come home coherent, and he began inputting commands.

The first drone was a disappointment; his techs *might* be able to overhaul the systems for reuse, but the memory core was a compete write-off, and he moved on to number two.

Aha! *That* was better. The second-stage astro data was shot, which meant the drone could provide no information on whatever lay beyond the warp point, but first-stage memory was intact. That gave him a readout on the grav stresses, and even if the other two drones contained no data at all, he'd be able to program the second flight for a much gentler transit, which would enhance the chance of obtaining recoverable data by at least a factor of ten.

He tapped a key, downloading the grav data to Plotting, and let the astrogation techs play with it while he moved on.

Drone three was a complete write-off. He doubted there was even much point in trying to salvage components, but he handed it off to Michaelson's crew anyway. They might get *some* use out of it, and the things were expensive enough to make the effort worthwhile.

Despite the blank on number three, Klesko felt decidedly cheerful as he turned to number four. The grav readout alone justified all the hard work R&D had put in on the system, and—

His thoughts broke off as the drone's memory downloaded to his display. He stared at it for a moment, trying to convince himself he was really seeing it, then looked over his shoulder.

"Captain," he said very, very quietly, "I think you'd better look at this."

The tension hit Small Claw Maariaah and Son of the Khan Shaairal like a fist as Josepha Vargas' exec led them into TFNS *Belisarius'* briefing room. Neither was particularly skilled at reading human expressions, but their hosts' taut, unnatural stillness required little skill.

"Thank you for coming, Small Claw," Vargas said quietly, rising to greet the visitors.

"No thanks are necessary, Caaaptain," Maariaah replied after Shaairal had translated. "Your vessel's data systems are far better suited to processing and displaying this information."

Vargas dipped her head in a small bow and waved the two Orions to chairs. She waited until they were seated, then nodded to Klesko.

The commander cleared his throat—he was more accustomed to dealing with machinery than Tabbies, and he was very much the man on the spot—and brought the holo unit up. A small-scale display of the system beyond the warp point appeared, and he picked up his light pencil and spoke slowly, allowing Shaairal time to translate for the small claw.

"As you can see, gentlemen, we don't have much detail," he began. "The drones' sensors are the best we can build into such a small package, but they aren't very powerful compared to a full-sized starship's. Nonetheless, I think the imagery speaks for itself."

He used the light pencil to pick out the icon of the drone's entry warp point.

"This is a Type Fourteen closed point. That's the good news. *This—*" the light pencil moved to the two innermost orbital shells of the G3 primary "—is the *bad* news."

The Human, Maariaah thought, had a distinct talent for understatement. The planets lay at six and ten light-minutes respectively, well within the liquid water zone, and they were a solid glare of high-level emissions. Worse, the closed warp point lay little more than a light-hour out, well below the system ecliptic. That had given the drone an excellent look "up" at its environs, and the space between the star's asteroid belt and those planets was heavy with drive fields.

Bug drive fields.

The small claw shivered. Undoubtedly, most of those drives belonged to freighters and resource ships, but there were over two hundred. Gods alone knew how many the drone had *not* seen, and, for the first time, Maariaah realized emotionally, not just intellectually, how massively the enemy exploited star systems. That many ships suggested an industrial base *at least* five times as great as that of any Orion system he had ever seen . . . and it lay two transits from Rehfrak.

Fathers of Sheerino, he thought numbly. *The very thing every Allied strategist dreams of finding, a closed warp point in the very heart of an enemy core system, and it lies* here.

"It's an El Dorado, gentlemen," Klesko said, "and I wish to God it was anywhere else."

"Truth, Commaaander," Maariaah said softly.

"Small Claw, this system belongs to the Khanate," Josepha Vargas said. "Whatever the Joint Chiefs ultimately decide, the immediate decision must be yours. Shall I send the second-flight drones through or suspend operations pending the decision of higher authority?"

Maariaah gazed at the holo—at the priceless axis of attack which was also the very gate of Hell for Rehfrak—and knew the Human captain was right. The decision *was* his.

"How confident are you that your drones have not been detected?" he asked.

"Mal?" Vargas said.

"I'm totally confident that no one actually observed their transit, Small Claw," Klesko replied. "This drone's systems came through in remarkably good shape. If anything had been close enough to spot such a small signature, the drone would have picked it up, even if it was cloaked. But we lost six drones somewhere in-system. The odds are vanishingly small that *we* could ever find them once power exhaustion takes their telemetry links off-line. The only way I could be sure of finding them would be to trigger their homing beacons, and the Bugs can't do that without the access codes. But there is a chance someone could literally stumble over them."

"Not a high one, I should think," Shaairal put in. "There appears to be no traffic near this warp point—not surprisingly, given how close to the primary it lies. One does not find many warp points so close in, and it also lies below the ecliptic. Surely there is only a very small chance any of their ships would come close enough to it to pick up such low-signature objects."

"No doubt you're correct, Sir," Klesko agreed, "and that's exactly what we designed the drones to accomplish. But 'unlikely' isn't 'impossible.' There is a chance, however slight."

"And if we insert additional drones, we increase that chance," Maariaah observed.

"True." Vargas sighed. She leaned back in her chair, one hand toying with a lock of short brown hair, and let her worried eyes sweep her own officers, then looked directly at Maariaah.

"Small Claw, there's going to be enormous pressure to use this warp point as soon as possible—especially from my people," she said flatly.

"We've been totally on the defensive from Day One, and so far we've taken far more damage than we've inflicted. No doubt some of your own fangs will feel the same way, but you and I both know what a double-edged sword this is." Maariaah was unfamiliar with the metaphor, but he grasped the implications instantly when Shaairal translated, and he gave a vigorous human-style nod. "Is your Navy in a position to guarantee Rehfrak's security if this operation goes sour?" she asked bluntly.

"No." Maariaah's reply was equally blunt. He disliked admitting that, but it was only truth, and the stakes were too great for anything less.

"Neither can we," Vargas said. "We're a long way from the closest Terran naval base, and our covering force is no more than a heavy task group." She looked around once more, then nodded sharply. "Under the circumstances, I recommend against deploying the second flight."

"I concur, Sir," Shaairal said, and Maariaah flicked his ears in agreement, profoundly relieved by the human's attitude.

"I think that wise," he said after a moment. "We can always send more probes through later, and I would feel much better with powerful support forces in position first."

"As would I." Vargas looked back at the holo and sighed. "I've been looking for exactly this since the war started. Now I've got it, and I wish to hell I didn't. Or that it was somewhere out back of beyond. But at least this time we found *it* instead of them finding us, Small Claw."

"Truth," Maariaah said again, and bared just the tips of his fangs. "It is nice to be on the finding end for a change, is it not?"

"As long as it doesn't turn around and eat us after all, Small Fang," Vargas said very quietly, eyes still on the holo. "As long as it doesn't turn around and eat us."

CHAPTER THIRTY-TWO

Questions of Command

Kthaara'zarthan gazed at his *vilkshatha* brother, and shook his head slowly in what he'd learned was a gesture reflecting sorrowful contemplation of the depths of Human evil.

"I fear you have let it go to your head, as you Humans say, Eeevahn'zarthan."

Ivan Antonov grinned at him. Kthaara's pronunciation of his first name certainly came closer than the butchery—roughly, EYE-van—committed by native speakers of Standard English. "Come, Kthaara Kornazhovich," he said in a mollifying tone. "You know me better than to think I'd let my head be turned by this 'Grand Alliance Commander in Chief' nonsense. The only advantage it has is that, because some people *are* stupid enough to take it seriously, it lets me cut through the bureaucratic shit and get some things done more expeditiously than I used to as simple chairman of the Joint Chiefs of Staff."

"Like appointing yourself to command the offensive to be launched from Zaaia'pharaan," Kthaara accused.

Antonov smiled. "Be honest, Kthaasha. Is it the Khan's agreement to cede Zephrain?" (He used the human compromise with the impossible handle Maariaah'sheerino had given the system.) "Is that what's really bothering you?"

"It is not my place to question the Khan's decisions," Kthaara huffed. Then he relaxed with the suddenness that could still catch Antonov by surprise after sixty years. "And besides, I have to admit that this one makes sense. It is just so . . . well, unprecedented."

Antonov nodded, understanding Kthaara's feelings. The Orions were a conservative lot. And the agreement *was* extraordinary. But so was the dilemma the Khan and his advisers had found themselves in. Their very genes—to say nothing of the white-hot memory of Kliean—had cried out to them to use Zephrain for an offensive into what was clearly part of the Bug industrial heartland. But with the thought of Kliean had come the chilling realization of what could happen if a Bug counterstroke penetrated to Rehfrak. And the Khanate, unlike the Federation, could not spare the industrial capacity to undertake a massive new program of defensive construction.

So the Khan had stunned his Terran allies by offering to cede Zephrain to them in fee simple, in exchange for their pledge to fortify it—and also Rehfrak itself—beyond any reasonable possibility of danger should the offensive go awry. The Federation had accepted, and agreed to postpone the attack until the work of castramentation was complete. And so the freighters had begun to ply the route to Zephrain, laden with modular components of Fortress Command's prefabricated orbital weapons platforms and with the myriads of cheap but lethal mines that would envelop the crucial warp points with clouds of death. Those freighters' databases, like those of all Allied ships that would operate in Zephrain space, were innocent of all knowledge of the warp link to Rehfrak; secrecy, as much as firepower, would shield the Khan's subjects.

The titanic project was by no means complete, but it was far enough along for Antonov and his staff to begin planning the offensive that would set out from an impregnable Zephrain. And to name that offensive's commander . . .

Antonov smiled again. "Don't mope, Kthaasha. You know I wouldn't do it if I didn't have you to leave here as acting chairman of the Joint Chiefs. As it is, I know I won't have anything to worry about." (Kthaara gave the brief low-pitched growl that was the equivalent of a human snort.) "And besides, you ought to be happy with my choice for a battle-line commander."

The ebon Orion brightened slightly. "Ah, yes: Least Fang Raaaymmonnd'pressscott—or Raaaymmonnd'*telmasa*, as he is now entitled to be known. A most impressive officer . . . for a Human. And one with whom you should feel something in common."

"True. Not every human has sworn *vilkshatha*." In point of fact, aside from Antonov himself, Prescott was the *only* one who had. That had been just before he'd left for Alpha Centauri, to recover from his wounds and provide Grand Fleet with the benefit of his experience. So, unlike his *vilkshatha* brother, he'd missed the brutal slugging match of Second Kliean, when Lord Khiniak had retaken the system . . . and a remark Antonov had made during the Theban War had come back to haunt him. "Even a small planetary population is hard to completely extirpate, short of rendering the planet uninhabitable," he'd said, and the Bugs evidently agreed, because that was precisely what they'd done—and the population of Kliean had been far from small. All at once, the Khanate of Orion had lost interest in counting the cost. The Bugs had found that out when they'd returned to Kliean two and a half months later.

Third Kliean had been a see-saw exercise in mutual slaughter, with Third Fleet stopping the attempted reconquest and following the defeated Bugs back to Shanak. The Gorm, no less than the Orions, had felt the need to avenge the ghosts of Kliean; they had volunteered to take their first newly produced gunboats into Shanak in simultaneous transits—the first time the Allies had used that mad tactic. But Third Fleet, weakened by short-range plasma-gun fire and wholesale suicide attacks, had lacked the strength to seize Shanak and hold it against newly arriving Bug reinforcements. So the war in the Kliean chain had settled into the kind of standoff that Vanessa Murakuma already knew only too well.

There was no longer any serious debate in the Grand Alliance over the reimplementation of General Directive 18—the genocide directive that had been invoked only once before. The screech of static that had answered Third Fleet's communications hails in Kliean had put an end to *all* such debate in the Khanate, and the few human dissenters like Bettina Wister were now isolated even within their own Liberal-Progressive Party. The only problem had been the lack of any apparent way to effectuate the directive with the war stalemated on both fronts . . . until the discovery of Zephrain.

Antonov shook free of his thoughts. "*Da*, you're right. Vice Admiral Prescott and I share something unique among humans. And we also share something else: frustration. You know how much it's galled him to be absent from the battles at Kliean."

"Naturally." Kthaara nodded—a Human habit that had become second nature to him. "Anyone worthy of being asked to swear *vilkshatha* can only feel like a caged *zeget* when wounds or duty keep him from his *vilkshatha* brother's side in a desperate battle."

"There's more to it than that," Antonov said grimly. "He felt his place was at the head of his own personnel at Second Kliean. When he learned Rear Admiral Jackson had died there . . . well, there's a common phenomenon called 'survivor's guilt.'"

"It is not unknown among my own race," Kthaara remarked. "But we tend to deal with it by seeking vengeance against the killers of whomever we feel somehow died in our place. Least Fang Pressscott should find no lack of opportunities for vengeance when we launch our offensive from Zaaia'pharaan against these . . . these . . . I will not even call them *chofaki*, for it does them too much honor and dilutes a perfectly good insult." The Orion's voice remained so controlled that few humans would even have realized he was controlling it. But

Antonov did, and he didn't interrupt the few heartbeats of silence that followed. Then Kthaara smiled his teeth-hidden carnivore's smile. "And now, back to business. I believe we are due at the staff conference soon."

"Attention on deck," Raymond Prescott said quietly, as senior officer in the conference room.

"As you were," Antonov rumbled as he and Kthaara moved to their seats. He looked around the table and at the holo dais where the image of Marcus LeBlanc had come to attention and was now resuming its seat as the actual Bug expert was doing in New Atlantis. "Admiral LeBlanc, I believe I saw you in deep discussion with Captain Kozlov a moment ago. I trust this means you have completed your analysis of the observational data from Second Kliean."

"Yes, Sir," LeBlanc affirmed. "In essence, we've confirmed the surmise of Lord Khiniak's people. The Bugs have learned to launch antifighter missiles from their gunboats. It surprised Third Fleet, which was the principal reason for our heavy fighter losses." (Prescott, outside the holo pickup and thus unnoticed by LeBlanc, winced.) "There's nothing mysterious about it; we've known all along that the gunboats could mount standard missiles as external ordinance, so there's no real engineering obstacle to fitting them with AFHAWKs. It's just one more indication that the Bugs are capable of more flexibility and inventiveness than we'd like them to have."

"That doesn't worry me as much as the sheer damned determination with which they fought," said Antonov's chief of staff. Captain Blanton Stovall was a scion of one of the TFN's "dynasties": families, mostly Russian or North American (like Stovall's) in origin, but including a fair number of Europeans, in which Federation service had been a tradition for as long as there'd *been* a Federation. A stocky, sandy-haired type, he was as stolid and imperturbable as he looked.

"You can't really use terms like 'determination' or 'courage' in connection with the Bugs, Captain," LeBlanc admonished. "They're not applicable—"

"Indeed not," Kthaara muttered, unheard by anyone but Antonov.

"—because for virtues like those to have any meaning, there has to be the option of *not* acting that way."

"Oh, yes, I understand all that, Admiral LeBlanc. It just disturbs me that whatever they use as a substitute seems to work altogether too damned well."

Antonov cleared his throat. "This is aside from the point, gentlemen. I wish to defer consideration of Admiral LeBlanc's conclusions until later. First, we need to take up an organizational matter. The command structure for the offensive from Zephrain is now complete, with one exception: a commander for the carrier component. None of the possibilities we've discussed to date have been satisfactory, for various reasons. The floor is open to suggestions."

"I have one, Sir," Raymond Prescott said quietly. The newly named commander of Task Force 21 was flanked by his chief of staff, Captain Anthea Mandagalla—a very tall, very black woman from the planet Christophe—and Commander Jacques Bichet, his ops officer. "From any number of standpoints, I believe the best possible choice would be Least Fang Zhaarnak'telmasa."

Antonov gave Prescott an intense look. The visible signs of his wounds were now mostly gone. His hair—prematurely iron-gray, shading to nearly white at the temples—had grown back enough for a haircut that was short but even. And he had so adjusted to his prosthetic arm that it seemed as entirely natural to others as it usually did to him. There was still the barest hint of a limp when he walked. But when, as now, he was seated, it was easy to forget that he had been seared by forces of a kind that normally left no survivors, however scarred.

"Some might argue, Admiral Prescott," Antonov spoke mildly, "that yours is not an altogether unbiased recommendation."

"I'm aware of that, Sir. But my special relationship with Least Fang Zhaarnak doesn't alter the facts. His record in Alowan and Telmasa speaks for itself. And even if it didn't, the *Ithyrra'doi'khanhaku* would." Of course, Prescott didn't mention the blue-and-gold ribbon nestled among the rows of colorful cloth on his own left breast. The Orions didn't use ribbons to represent medals on service dress uniforms, and the TFN had had to hastily design one for a decoration it had never expected to see awarded to a human. "Furthermore, Sir, I would ask you to consider his more recent record. I refer in particular to the great moral courage he displayed during the Third Battle of Kliean ... as Lord Khiniak himself has acknowledged."

Everyone present understood what he meant. Koraaza'khiniak had decided to withhold a considerable percentage of his SBMHAWK inventory from the initial strike into Shanak, looking ahead to the problem of securing the warp point after his fleet had transited. Zhaarnak had protested, respectfully but vehemently, doubting the adequacy of a first SBMHAWK wave that should have been ample against a normal enemy. Events had proven him right.

A cleared throat broke the silence, and Antonov turned to his ops officer. "Yes, Commander?"

Armand de Bertholet leaned forward with the eagerness, tinged with impetuosity, that he seemed to bring to everything he did. He was a younger son of one of the noble families of Durendal, and while cosmopolitan experience had long since worn away whatever aristocratic affectations he might have once possessed, he was inescapably a product of a culture that embodied a romantic worldview and valued dash. Not all Fringe Worlds had been settled by groups with roots sunk deep into pre-space Terra's ethnic topsoil. Some of the pioneering societies had been frankly artificial ones, cultures built around an idea rather than a sociopolitical reality. Antonov sometimes thought they *all* were, in greater or lesser degree; but some, such as the neo-feudalism of Durendal, were more obvious about it than most.

"If I may, Sir," he said, "I'd like to add another argument to Admiral Prescott's. It is essential that the tactical command structure for our offensive include representation of our allies of the *Zheeerlikou'valkhannaieee*." He wasn't as much of a "Tabby expert" as most of Antonov's staffers, but he made a creditable effort at pronouncing the name. "And what better field for that representation than the fighter operations at which they are admittedly preeminent? At the same time, Least Fang Zhaarnak has demonstrated an ability to work in close conjunction with humans—a necessity in what will, inevitably, be a predominantly human expedition."

"Commander de Bertholet has a point, Sir," said Midori Kozlov. It was unusual for the staff spook to outrank the ops officer, as Kozlov outranked de Bertholet, in the TFN, and the fact that intelligence officers were restricted line—specialists outside the direct chain of command—further muddied the waters. If Kozlov and de Bertholet had been the only two officers left alive aboard a ship, he would have been in command, and she made it a point not to stomp too hard on his toes. "Least Fang Zhaarnak's adaptability to cooperating with humans is all the more remarkable in light of what we know of his lifelong attitudes." She gave Kthaara a half-apologetic look.

"We are all adults here, Captain Khozzloff," the Orion said with a smile. "As such, I doubt if any of us are shocked by the fact that intelligence services take an interest in their allies as well as their enemies. I would be surprised if you did *not* have dossiers on senior officers of the Khan."

"Your attitude is much appreciated, Lord Talphon," Kozlov replied, trying to match his suavity.

"And furthermore," Kthaara went on, "you are absolutely right. Least Fang Zhaarnak has indeed demonstrated a capacity for growth—one which I doubt you can fully appreciate, not being directly acquainted with those of my race who belong to his father's school of thought." He turned to Antonov. "I concur: Least Fang Pressscott's suggestion is eminently sound. Zhaarnak would be an ideal choice for carrier commander."

"Lord Khiniak won't want to lose him," Antonov rumbled. "In fact, we won't need courier drones to hear him bellowing. Still, he'll have to admit Zhaarnak could do more good in a war of movement, which is what we have a chance of turning this one into when we attack from Zephrain. He's wasted on a deadlocked front. Yes." He brightened. "As I was saying earlier, Kthaara Kornazhovich, this 'Grand Alliance Commander in Chief' business has its uses when it comes to getting things done. Of course, I'll go through First Fang Ynaathar." The Khanate's senior officer had, of necessity, been named second in command when Antonov had gotten his new title. "But yes, we'll have him report here as soon as possible."

He gave Raymond Prescott a sideways look and noted the seemingly intensifying life in that face. Yes, he reflected, Zhaarnak would make an excellent carrier commander. But, just as importantly, Prescott would make an even better battle-line commander with Zhaarnak present. Antonov knew full well what it meant to have one's *vilkshatha* brother guarding one's back, and as he gazed surreptitiously at the one human with whom he shared that knowledge, he knew that whatever enhanced that man's attainment of his full potential was very much worth doing.

CHAPTER THIRTY-THREE

"Security is relative."

Commander Nobiki Murakuma had found that being the older daughter of one of Battle Fleet's rising captains—and then of one of its more respected junior admirals—was a burden for someone determined to make her career on her own, but being the daughter of Vice Admiral Vanessa Murakuma was worse. The newsies had dubbed her mother "The Savior of Sarasota," and every time Nobiki turned around some fresh infernal busybody wanted a "background interview." And the *questions* they came up with!

She shook her head as she checked the status boards in Sky Watch One, the massive orbital station which coordinated the Centauri System's fixed defenses. She loved her mother, but truth to tell, she'd seen more of her since joining the Navy than she had as a child. Vanessa Murakuma's daughters were Navy brats, and they'd learned early that an officer went where she was sent. They'd understood there was seldom any way to take children along, and no one could have given them a more secure (if sometimes confining) childhood than their grandparents. Their mother's slender, very un-Japanese beauty, long absences, and infrequent appearances had imbued her with a sort of glamorous magnificence which joined with the Murakuma tradition to make it inevitable they would follow her into uniform, and both of them were proud of her, yet they had few of the mother-daughter childhood memories civilian families seemed to take for granted.

The newsies appeared unable to grasp that. They kept plaguing Nobiki for background when, frankly, they could have gotten better information from the public record! Fortunately for Fujiko, her Survey Command duties put *her* safely beyond their reach. Nobiki had no such luck. She wished Captain Hammani would let her tell them where to go, but someone from Public Information had gotten to her CO and stressed the necessity of cooperating with the press, and—

An anomalous reading caught her attention, and she frowned. Her eyes darted back across the boards, and her frown deepened. Surely that couldn't be right!

She punched up her traffic files. There was a lot of data, for Centauri was always busy. Every starship to or from Sol had to pass through it, and powerful Home Fleet detachments were permanently on station to support the heavy fortifications guarding The Gateway—the single warp point from Centauri to Sol which was humanity's door to the stars. Despite the apparent confusion of ships moving about the system, its traffic was meticulously regulated . . . yet none of the information in her files explained what a ship would be doing out *there*.

She rubbed her chin, thinking hard. There were Fleet exercises underway—three of them, in fact—but only one involved cloaked units, and she plugged a query into the system, then swore softly as the computers refused to answer. *Well, of course they did,* she scolded herself. *Admiral van der Gelder is supposed to be sneaking up on us, after all.*

Still, there was no good reason for van der Gelder's big, new CVAs to be stooging around out in Theta Quadrant. Which added to her mystification, but didn't offer any answers.

She turned back to the scanner ghost. It wasn't much, but with a little enhancement . . .

She hummed as she worked. Sensor glitch was the most likely explanation, but it was also possible someone had decided to throw an additional surprise exercise at them—a sensor shell test, perhaps. Centauri's open warp points had been plotted three hundred years before, but the TFN had always worried about closed warp points in strategic systems, and especially in *this* one. Like all core systems, it had been provided with a sphere of scansats three light-hours from the primary to provide warning in the unlikely event some unfriendly soul *did* find a closed point in—

Nobiki Murakuma's thoughts froze as the computers beeped. She stared at the analysis of the enhanced datum, held by shock for just a second, and then a flashing hand punched a com key.

"CIC, Captain Hammani," a tenor voice said in her earbug.

"Captain, this is Murakuma in Plotting," Nobiki replied, and the professionalism of her own voice amazed her in a distant sort of way. "Sir, according to my board, we have a cloaked Bug force operating in unknown strength in Theta Quadrant."

The survey flotilla slid stealthily in-system. It was a powerful force, for the Fleet believed in surveying in strength, yet detection would doom it; that much had been evident from its first long-range scan. A light cruiser had been dispatched homeward the instant the entry warp point was identified as a closed one, fulfilling the most critical component of its mission, but the Fleet needed more data. The survey ships' total destruction would be a paltry price for a strategic prize of this magnitude, and so the main body swept onward, passive sensors busy. Eventually, it would be detected, attacked, and—undoubtedly—destroyed, yet it would learn a great deal first.

The enormous chamber at the heart of Sky Watch One—officially "Alpha Command," but known to its denizens simply as "the Pit"— was the Centauri System's nerve center, and an icy hand squeezed Fleet Admiral Pederson's heart as an alarm howled. He whirled to Main Plot's huge tank just as CIC updated it, and his mouth tightened. A dozen lurid icons flashed crimson, and for just an instant he could only stare at them. Then he punched a stud.

"CIC, Hammani," a harassed voice said in his earbug.

"Gold One," Pederson identified himself tersely. "Talk to me."

"It's confirmed, Sir." Hammani's voice was flat. "We don't have a definitive count. So far, we make it at least six light cruisers, nine or ten battlecruisers, and three superdreadnoughts. From their apparent formation, there are more of them, though. We just haven't seen them yet."

"Jesus Christ, Yassir! How the *hell* did they get this close before we spotted them?"

"Obviously their entry point was too far out for the buoys to pick them up on arrival, and they went into cloak immediately. We didn't even get a sniff till they actually crossed the shell perimeter. On the other hand, I doubt *they* spotted the buoys. The ones we've nailed crossed the line almost perpendicularly, and they wouldn't have given us stern aspects if they could help it."

"Well, thank God for small favors," Pederson muttered, watching the blood-colored icons creep across the tank with near imperceptible speed.

"Yes, Sir. I'd say every credit we ever spent on scansats just justified itself."

"Damn straight. And now what say we blow their asses straight to hell?"

"Sounds good to me, Sir."

"All right." Pederson inhaled deeply, then nodded to himself. "We'll go with Sigma-Three. Send Admiral MacGregor the alert signal and download their loci and vectors. This far in, they'll never be able to outrun her, and—"

"Excuse me, Admiral," a new voice said in his earbug. "I have a Priority One for you."

"Not now, Jeffers," Pederson replied testily. "Tell whoever it is I'll get back. Now, Yassir, as I was—"

"Admiral, I think you'd better take it now. It's Admiral Antonov, Sir."

"*Antonov?*" Pederson looked across the Pit at Hammani, and the captain raised both hands in bafflement. *Damn it, has he added omniscience to his talents? How the devil did even Ivan the Terrible find out about this so fast?*

"Go ahead and alert MacGregor, Yassir," he decided, "but have her hold position until I get back to you. Check?"

"Check, Sir."

"Thanks." Pederson inhaled and sat back down. "All right, Jeffers. Put the Admiral on."

There was a moment of silence, and then an earthquake bass rumbled in his ear.

"Admiral Pederson?"

"Speaking, Sir."

"I understand we have visitors."

"You might put it that way, Sir. I'm just about to send them a welcoming committee."

"I thought as much," Antonov said. "That's why I commed. Admiral, it is imperative that you do nothing—nothing at all—to tell them they've been detected."

Pederson's eyed widened. This was the *Centauri System*—the one, perhaps the only, star system short of Sol itself which humanity simply could not afford to lose—and Antonov wanted him to sit by and do *nothing?*

"Sir," he said, gripping his self-control in both hands, "with all due respect, these ships are already close enough to start getting solid reads on our inner defenses, and even if we hit them as quickly as possible, we won't be able to keep them from getting their drones off. We can't let them amass any more data than they already have!"

"Yes, we can," Antonov replied flatly.

"But, Admiral—"

"I am not in habit of repeating myself." Antonov's voice had gone still deeper, and every senior flag officer knew it was a bad sign when his Standard English started losing definite articles. But Oscar Pederson was the system's commanding officer, and the Admiralty hadn't picked a weakling to run its most critical Fleet Base.

"Admiral Antonov," he said very formally, "I am the system CO. In my judgment, it is vital to destroy this force as rapidly as possible, and I intend to do so."

"You will *not.*" Pederson heard the grumble of shifting tectonic plates in the words. "You will do nothing at all until I reach Alpha Command."

"Sir, I realize you're the *Alliance* Commander-in-Chief, but, again with all due respect, this is a Terran system, and I am responsible for its security."

"Security is relative, Admiral Pederson," Antonov said coldly, "and there is more at stake here than a single star system—even this one. I am not interested in official chains of command, and I will repeat myself one last time. You will take *no action* until I arrive. If you desire, I will have Sky Marshal Avram confirm that order before you and I discuss it personally."

The menace in that last sentence was unmistakable, and more than one TFN officer had brought his career to a catastrophic end by irritating Ivan Antonov. Yet Pederson hovered on the brink of defiance for a long, fulminating moment.

"Very well, Sir," he said at last, in his iciest tone. "I will obey your instructions, but I do so under formal protest and request that you confirm them to me in writing on your arrival."

"As you wish." Antonov's voice was still cold, but there was respect in it as well. Pederson waited for him to say something more, but he heard only the click of a disconnected circuit, and he snarled a silent curse as he turned to glare back down into the tank.

The survey force continued inward, holding its velocity down to .03 c to reduce emissions leakage. Its passive sensors began delivering data on the inner system, and this was the first time the Fleet had encountered such enormous, obviously pre-war fortifications. Combined with the sheer numbers of drive fields swimming about the system's depths and the glaring energy signatures of two habitable planets, their presence amply confirmed the value of its find.

The ships spread wider to cover a greater volume, whispering across the light-seconds to one another with whisker lasers. Each unit's courier drones were configured for continuous download of not only its own sensor data but also that of every ship in communication with it. The priceless information came in slowly, but it came, and the drone memories began to fill up.

"How's your signal strength, Nobiki?" Captain Hammani asked in Nobiki's earbug, and she shrugged, still staring down into her display while her skilled fingers caressed her console.

"Sir, I've got three extra computer sections tied in to help with signal enhancement, but it's still extremely weak. They're moving very slowly, and I'm still hanging onto the ones I had at least strength-three reads on, but two weaker ones have already dropped off the plot. If they get ten or twelve more light-minutes in-system, the buoys are going to lose them completely."

"Understood." There was a moment of silence, and then Hammani spoke gruffly. "You did well, Commander. Very well. Your mother would be proud of you."

Nobiki blinked, but before she had to think of a response, she heard the click of a closed circuit.

Oscar Pederson turned just a bit too quickly as Ivan Antonov entered the Pit, but he managed—somehow—to keep his anger out of his expression as the massive Russian stalked towards him, trailed by Commander Kozlov and Rear Admiral LeBlanc. Kozlov's uniform was immaculate, but the Alliance commander-in-chief's "Bug specialist" looked as though he'd dressed in a hurry. There was nothing sleepy about LeBlanc's expression, however, and he stepped to one side, peering down into the main tank as Pederson greeted Antonov with frigid formality.

"Admiral." He clipped the title off just short of insubordination, and Antonov gave him a very hard look. Then the ex-sky marshal's expression softened micrometrically.

"Admiral Pederson." He studied the Centauri System CO for a moment longer, then sighed. "I believe I owe you an explanation," he said in the tone of a man clearly unaccustomed to making even oblique apologies. "I have no intention of allowing this force to inflict damage on the Centauri System, and I appreciate your concern over the data they are undoubtedly obtaining. But I have a far more pressing long-term concern: the location of their entry warp point."

Pederson felt his icy fury thaw slightly—very slightly—but it didn't show in his reply.

"I considered that, Sir. Unfortunately, it must be a closed point. That means there's no way we can detect it, and they certainly won't show us where it is."

"Not knowingly, no," Antonov agreed readily, then beckoned. "Admiral LeBlanc, if you please," he rumbled, and Marcus LeBlanc turned from the tank to the two senior officers.

"Yes, Sir?"

"Your evaluation of the enemy's objective?"

"Sir, they're obviously trying to get a fix on the inner system."

"And their probable course of action?"

"They'll keep coming in until they're positive they've been detected," LeBlanc said confidently. "The one thing we know about Bugs is that their units' survival is completely secondary to their missions. They'll hang on until they *know* we see them, then send word back."

"How?" Antonov prompted, watching Pederson's face closely.

"If they've left a picket on the warp point, they *could* use com lasers, Sir. But from what we've seen of them, they'll probably use drones if the range is more than a light-hour or two."

"Precisely," Antonov said.

"Even granting that Admiral LeBlanc is correct, we can't even detect drones at ranges in excess of twelve light-minutes," Pederson objected. "That means we can't possibly track them to their exit warp point." The logic of his own statement was unarguable, yet there was a new note, almost a questioning one, in his voice, and Antonov gave him a sharklike smile.

"Unfortunately for the Bugs, Admiral Pederson, we *will* be able to track them."

"How?" Pederson demanded, and the sharklike smile grew colder.

"I believe Fang Kthaara is coordinating an exercise in which Admiral van der Gelder is tasked to penetrate your defenses?"

"He is," Pederson said slowly.

"Well, I have just been with Fang Kthaara, monitoring the exercise. So unlike you, I know where van der Gelder is at this moment, and Fang Kthaara has already sent her a change of orders. If we can keep these *pizdi* creeping in on us for another four to five hours, she will be able to cut in *behind* them. With a very little luck, her fighters will be able to track any drones the enemy launches. While they will lack the endurance to follow them all the way back to their entry point, we should be able at least to determine its general bearing. If so, we will know which areas to saturate with additional scansats to insure that we *will* detect the next ship to make transit."

"I see," Pederson said in a very different tone. He rubbed an eyebrow for a moment, thinking furiously, then gave a slow nod. "I see," he repeated, smiling back at Antonov for the first time, "and I withdraw my request for written confirmation of your orders, Sir."

"*Korosho!*" Antonov grinned, then nodded to the tank. "In that case, Admiral, let us consider which of your units will make the best beaters when the time comes to start the quarry."

Vice Admiral Jessica van der Gelder stood on TFNS *Thor*'s flag bridge, gray eyes intent as she studied the vectors threaded through the main display. The scansats' tenuous readings were fading, but the Bugs' courses had been plotted with care. Given how steadily they'd held those courses and their clear belief they were still undetected, a direct back plot *should* give a bearing to their warp point. Unfortunately, she couldn't be certain of that.

She frowned and folded her hands behind her, pacing slowly while she wished she had more fighters. Each of her six assault carriers was half again the size of a *Borzoi*-class CV, but they were *assault* carriers, designed to take fighters through defended warp points. Most of that tonnage had gone into tougher defenses, not larger strikegroups, and if she spread her strength too wide watching for courier drones, she wouldn't have much left to help swat Bugs.

Her frown deepened as metronome-steady paces took her up and down, up and down, her flag deck. Examination of enemy wreckage had confirmed that Bug CDs were a tad slower than the Alliance's, with a top speed of just under .2 *c*. They were faster than any starship, but an F2R recon fighter with two life-support pods could pace them. Unfortunately, even with the pods its endurance would be only seven and a half hours. If the warp point was, say, five light-hours out and the Bugs launched from *two* light-hours out, their drones would take twice that long to reach the point. Her escorting battle-cruisers' pinnaces had a months endurance each, but they could barely hit .12 *c*. They had *time* to catch the drones, but, unlike her fighters, they lacked the legs.

Lord Talphon's orders indicated Admiral Antonov would settle for a definite bearing, but the firepower the Bugs had brought to bear for *fringe* systems made just thinking about what they would commit against a target like this enough to freeze the blood. Centauri's defenses were massive, but *no* defense could stop an enemy willing to lose enough starships *and* able to get into the system unopposed . . . and mankind's birth world lay one transit away beyond The Gateway.

No, she thought, *we need to know* exactly *where it is. We need to be able to camp on it with the whole damned Home Fleet and blow* anything *that comes through it into dust bunnies. But how do I find it when their drones are either faster or longer ranged than anything I've got to track them with?*

She paused. *Wait a minute. Wait a minute! The pinnaces have plenty of time on their clocks, and the fighters . . .*

"Andrushka!"

Commander Andrei Kulnozov, her ops officer, looked up.

"Yes, Sir?"

"Current range to the enemy?"

"Twenty-six light-minutes," Kulnozov answered, and van der Gelder smiled. They were still far beyond the range at which scanners could detect a target as small as a pinnace drive field.

"All right," she said crisply. "I want every pinnace loaded with fighter scan packs and launched immediately. Get with CIC and work out a conical pattern along the Bugs' backtrack, then assign vectors that will spread the pinnaces to cover it and send them out-system at max."

Kulnozov frowned for a moment, then nodded. "Of course. And we'll hold the fighters until they actually launch."

"Exactly. We use the fighters to track to the limit of their endurance.

The drones'll be on a least-time course, so we'll have steady vectors to pass on to the pinnaces. With their head start, they should be able to stay with them out to as much as six light-hours."

"If they've left a picket with gunboats out there, pinnaces will be sitting ducks," Kulnozov pointed out, and van der Gelder nodded.

"Arm them with FM3s. That'll let them shoot back, and the Bugs won't expect the extra range. I know its risky, but locating that warp point is worth losing all of them."

"Agreed." Kulnozov nodded and began giving orders, and she turned back to her plot.

Rear Admiral Hansen Lutz sat in his command chair aboard TFNS *Orinoco,* watching a holo display even more intently than van der Gelder. Unlike van der Gelder's command, Task Group 12 had no carriers, which could prove painful if the Bugs threw in a gunboat attack. But TG 12 *did* have seventeen SDs, including five *Chimborazo*-class "escort" superdreadnoughts, the first dedicated capital ship anti-missile/anti-fighter platforms the TFN had ever built. BuShips and BuPlans had debated the SDE concept for over five years before the Bugs' use of kamikaze small craft and gunboats provided the final impetus to build them. They carried no energy armament or capital missile launchers, but each could put sixteen standard missiles—or AFHAWKs—into space in a single broadside, and their point defense outfits were massive. If he couldn't have carriers, *Chimborazos* were certainly the next best thing. He allowed himself a thin smile at the thought while he watched the display. TG 12 and Rear Admiral Wilson's TG 22 had been chosen to play beater because they were conducting routine training ops in the right general positions. Since the alert had come in, they'd altered their headings—as casually as possible—to close on the Bugs. Not directly; their present headings angled to meet well inside the enemy. Hopefully that would encourage the Bugs to assume their maneuvers really were routine, but the enemy was so far in-system that his lower tactical speed would make him easy meat when Lutz and Wilson showed their true intentions.

The survey force noted the approaching enemy and slowed still further. The two groups of starships were obviously headed for a rendezvous well beyond any range at which units in cloak could be detected. Their firepower was more than sufficient to crush the entire survey force, yet it seemed evident the enemy still had no idea the surveyors were there to be crushed. Had he done so, those ships would have rendezvoused outside the survey force to cut it off from retreat, and every other drive source within detection range continued serenely upon its way. Nor was there the least sign of concern from the fixed defenses. Given his apparent blindness, it might even be possible for the survey force to complete its mission and withdraw without losses.

Ivan Antonov sat motionless, watching the plot. The last few hours had been nerve-wracking, and the scansats had lost lock on the last enemy unit sixteen minutes ago. CIC had projected their positions based on the last hard data . . . but those positions were *only* projections.

He checked the time. Kthaara had relayed Vice Admiral van der Gelder's decision to deploy her pinnaces three hours ago. Transmission lags meant those pinnaces had been underway for two hours before Kthaara found out about them, and she'd dropped them thirty-one light-minutes out from her present position, so they should be thirty-eight light-minutes out-system from point of launch. That should be far enough . . . and it was going to have to be.

He took one last look at his "beaters." TG 12's superdreadnoughts were sixteen light-minutes from the Bugs' projected positions; TG 22's four fleet carriers, five superdreadnoughts, and ten battle-cruisers were a bit further out, but they were also twenty percent faster than Lutz's command, for all of Wilson's SDs were the new *Athabasca-* and *Borneo*-class ships. Antonov still wasn't thoroughly convinced of the concept behind the *Athabascas* and their command ship consorts, yet their speed certainly made them ideal for their present mission.

The class had been conceived as a way to provide heavy escorts which could stay with carrier groups under maximum power. Matching the speed of Gorm battle-line units without using engine tuners had been a technically audacious concept, but the new ships had drawbacks. From a material viewpoint, the worst was cost. Building superdreadnoughts with battle-cruiser speed required a drastic reduction in mass. It had proved possible to design low-mass substitutes for everything except armor, but the new systems were hideously expensive, and drive power still had to rise to unprecedented levels. Which led to the design's major *tactical* drawback: lack of internal volume. For all intents and purposes, the *Athabascas* could mount little more than a battleship's armament simply because of the squeeze effect of those massive drive rooms.

The same research had provided the hulls for the new *Scylla* and *Thor*-class CVAs, but superdreadnoughts were main combatants, not fighter platforms. Antonov would have preferred to give them heavy capital missile outfits and turn them into bigger, tougher versions of the tried and tested *Dunkerque* battle-cruisers, but he'd been retired for over ten years when the design was finalized, and BuShips had given them shorter-ranged armaments. There were arguments both ways. Using standard missile launchers had let the designers cram in a decent hetlaser broadside and a missile armament little lighter than the new *Chimborazos,* but only at the expense of conceding the long-ranged missile envelope to any enemy, and—

He shook free of his thoughts and looked at Admiral Pederson. "Very well, Admiral. You may begin your attack."

The approaching starships abruptly altered course and went to full power. The survey force came to a halt while tactical sections projected the new vectors, but the projections weren't really required, for the enemy's shields were coming up as well. Worse, one group was already launching attack craft. It would never have done that if it had not had a target for them, yet there was no panic. This, after all, was the reaction the survey force had initially anticipated, and sensors had already ascertained that there were new and unfamiliar ship types in both enemy groups. It would be as well to gain data on them before launching courier drones.

It was unfortunate that the survey force's units were so dispersed. Its detachments would be unable to offer one another much support, but at least the closer of the enemy groups appeared to have no attack craft to fend off a gunboat strike.

Just under two hundred gunboats erupted from cloak along a vast arc, heading straight for TG 12, and Admiral Lutz swore as CIC reported the numbers. That many gunboats meant the enemy's strength had been substantially underestimated. They were going to be a handful even for *Chimborazos,* but at least their launch points pinpointed the locations of the starships from which they'd come, and red icons glowed in his plot, marking those locations.

TG 22's fighters altered course, streaking towards the closest enemy starships, and Lutz watched them go. He couldn't fault Erica Wilson's decision. The two task groups were too widely separated for her fighters to intercept the gunboat attack before it hit him, but he was going to miss their support.

"The enemy's launched gunboats at Admiral Lutz, Sir!" Kulnozov said sharply, and van der Gelder nodded. Carrier Group 19 had been able to sneak in closer than she'd dared hope, but she was still too far out to detect drone launches. She drummed on the arm of her command chair, chewing her lower lip, and her thoughts were bleak.

If I launch now, I might distract them—get them to recall their strike to deal with me *and leave Hansen alone. But it would also tell them I'm here, and if they know that, they may not launch drones. It's unlikely, but it* is *possible, and getting them to launch is the whole point.*

She chewed harder, fighting the instinct to come to TG 12's assistance, and said nothing.

The enemy's attack craft would reach the survey force well before its gunboats attacked the other enemy force, and there were many of them. It was unlikely the battle-cruisers they were about to engage would survive the strike, and so they launched their drones now.

"I have drone separation! Multiple drone separations!"

The pilot's taut report crackled from the flag bridge speakers, and Erica Wilson nodded.

"Inform Admiral van der Gelder," she told her com officer sharply.

Thirty-two endless minutes ticked past while van der Gelder and Kulnozov watched the gunboats bearing down on TG 12. The Bugs had covered a third of the original distance to Lutz's ships, and TG 12 was still coming to meet them. It had to, if it was to attack the starships beyond them, and the tension of watching that drawn out approach to carnage had tightened every pair of shoulders on *Thor*'s flag bridge. Then van der Gelder's com officer looked up suddenly.

"Admiral Wilson reports drone separation, Sir."

"Time?" van der Gelder snapped.

"Twenty-six minutes ago, Sir."

"CIC has the vectors," Kulnozov reported with a vicious smile. "They're coming right down our throat!"

"Excellent!" van der Gelder's smile matched his. "Launch Captain Ghandra's strike."

Consternation struck the survey force as a fresh, even more power-ful wave of attack craft abruptly appeared behind it, but understand-ing followed instantly. The enemy had known the survey force was here all along! This fresh assault could only mean he had herded the survey force into a trap . . . and that enemy vessels were in position to engage its courier drones.

But the survey force had no way of knowing how many cloaked starships were back there. Two hundred attack craft were already charg-ing to the attack, yet hundreds more might still lurk aboard their mother ships. That many attack craft could easily destroy every drone which had already launched, and it was imperative that at least one get through.

Under these new circumstances, there was only one way to be sure it would, and every survey ship belched its full load of courier drones, sending out such a dense cloud of them as to guarantee saturation of the enemy's ability to engage them.

✧   ✧   ✧

"Admiral van der Gelder's launched, Sir!"

"How nice," Hansen Lutz said drily. The com message was thirty-four minutes old, and Jessica's launch wouldn't do a thing about the gunboats howling towards him, but he supposed it meant Antonov's plan had worked. At the moment, however, he had other things to worry about. TG 12 was still headed for the enemy at max, closing with the gunboats at a combined speed of over .23 c, and the range was down to thirty-six light-seconds.

"There go Admiral Wilson's jocks, Sir," his ops officer reported, and Lutz nodded. He had another two and a half minutes before the Bugs hit him, and he looked at the repeater plot tracking Wilson's strike. Its data was fourteen minutes old, but he felt vengeful pleasure as he watched it. His sensors still couldn't see the cloaked Bug starships, but Erica's pilots could, and fireballs began to glare as the fighter jocks laid into them with the new, longer-ranged FM3.

The bastards won't like that *toy,* he thought, for the new missile had both more range than the AFHAWK *and* better penetration aids than earlier fighter missiles. Its warhead was the same, but more would get through, and pilots didn't have to fly down the Bugs' throat to deliver it.

"Here they come, Sir," the ops officer said grimly, and ten *Matterhorn*-class superdreadnoughts began slamming SBMs into the oncoming gunboats.

"Sixty-one minutes," Kulnozov said, and van der Gelder nodded. Assuming a velocity of .2 c, the drones had covered just over twelve light-minutes.

"Roll out the recon fighters," she said, and thirty F2R fighters spat from Carrier Group 19's assault carriers. They carried no weapons, only their internal sensors and a pair of life-support pods, and she and Kulnozov had timed things perfectly. Barely forty seconds after the last recon fighter launched, their scanners picked up the first drones and they swerved in pursuit.

And now, Jessica van der Gelder told herself coldly as she leaned back in her command chair, *we can kill these vermin.*

CHAPTER THIRTY-FOUR

Into the Unknown

Kthaara'zarthan was an exceptionally tall Orion, and the species' legs were longer in proportion than those of homo sapiens. Still, he had to hurry to keep up with Antonov as the burly Grand Alliance commander in chief strode along the corridors.

"Why do I have the feeling that we have been through this before, and not so very long ago?" he grumbled.

Antonov gestured dismissively without breaking stride. "The arguments for my taking personal command still apply, Kthaara Kornazhovich. We're just moving things up a little—"

" 'A little'!"

"—and launching our offensive from right here, rather than having to go to Zephrain to do it." He grinned over his shoulder. "You must admit the logistics have improved."

"An amusing concept," Kthaara growled. "I trust the inhabitants of this system—and of Sol!—who have suddenly awakened to find themselves on a war front, are equally amused."

"Well, then," Antonov replied serenely as they reached the bottomless-looking abyss of the drop shaft, "we'll just have to push the front away from them, won't we?" Then he addressed the low-grade brain that handled the shaft's routing. "Ground floor."

They stepped off the edge, and the tractor-beam-like effect took them, lowering them swiftly downward with no sensation of motion. Floor after floor shot upward past them, but Antonov didn't notice, for his thoughts were on the incredible turn of events in Centauri space.

The Bugs had been wiped out, of course, and with little loss. Even Admiral Lutz's BG 12, which had suffered the heaviest damage, hadn't

668

lost a single ship. Best of all, their closed warp point of entry been pinpointed, and that single fact had changed the strategic picture beyond recognition. The universe might have suddenly become an even more dangerous place, but it also offered a new opportunity. And Antonov had all of Terran Home Fleet, plus the beginnings of Second Fleet here at Centauri, with which to take advantage of that opportunity. To have failed to seize the moment was simply not in him.

The drop shaft deposited them on the ground floor with all the impact of falling leaves. Admiral Ellen MacGregor awaited them there, and Antonov nodded to her as she joined him and Kthaara. Mac-Gregor had transferred to Centauri from her position as second in command of Home Fleet to take over the newly designated Allied Fourth Fleet, although calling it a "fleet" at the moment was stretching a point. Along with Oscar Pederson, the short, sturdily built brunette would be responsible for holding the fort here in Centauri, but the enormous warship tonnages already diverted to the fighting front, to various nodal reaction forces, and to bring Antonov's Second Fleet up to strength for "Operation Pesthouse" would leave her shorthanded. The KON had promised to divert at least one heavy task force to support her, yet she couldn't be very happy about her available order of battle, which was why he'd asked her to accompany him to his new flagship for discussions. If she had concerns, he wanted to know about them—just as he wanted any insight she could give him into the capabilities of the squadrons he'd poached from her.

Marine guards fell in around them as they proceeded across the public area towards a side entrance and the skimmer waiting to take Antonov and MacGregor to the space field. They'd covered about half the distance when the commotion began at the main entrance, off to their right.

"Admiral Antonov! Admiral Antonov!" His heart sank at that shrilly nasal voice, and sank even further as its owner broke free of the cluster of arguing flunkies and guards and advanced towards him, trailing a cloud of media types. "As elected representative of the People of Nova Terra, I demand to speak to you!"

It was, he reflected, miserably bad luck that the Bug incursion had come between sessions of the Legislative Assembly. Otherwise Bettina Wister would have been on Old Terra, not tending the farm among her constituents. He firmly suppressed his impulses, for with the holocameras whirring away he had to be civil. And he didn't deign to notice Kthaara's amusement.

"Assemblywoman Wister," he greeted mildly. Too mildly. People in the lobby who knew him blanched, although Wister remained oblivious. "As you can see, I'm somewhat rushed just now. But you can contact my public relations officer at—"

"Oh, no!" Wister struck a pose for the cameras. "There'll be no coverup by the Military Establishment this time, Admiral! I am reliably informed that the ravening, genocidal Bug hordes that the Navy *inexcusably* allowed to enter this system launched courier drones, presumably carrying navigational information."

"I seem to recall, Legislative Assemblywoman Wister, that you are on record as objecting vociferously to the 'unenlightened' use of the term 'Bugs' for our opponents in the current unpleasantness. I believe your objections were voiced in the course of the debate in which you opposed reimplementation of General Directive 18."

"Cheap shot!" Wister shot back, face half-turned to the cameras. "Typical of the mean-spirited attacks with which the Navy seeks to divert the People's attention from its failure to totally exterminate these galactic vermin—as I have advocated from the first! But as I was saying, I have it from reliable sources that some of the Bugs' courier drones were allowed to escape!"

"Presumably, Legislative Assemblywoman Wister, your 'reliable sources' are our own press releases, for that has never been a secret. Our first priority was to locate the warp point from which the Bugs had emerged. The need to concentrate on this objective meant that some of the courier drones did, indeed, escape. This was perhaps regrettable, but not disastrous given that we now know where any subsequent attackers must appear and can therefore defend against them."

"Yes," Wister replied with a theatrical sneer, and Antonov's eyes hardened. The fact that self-serving politicos disgusted him didn't mean he didn't understand them, and she clearly had no interest at all in anything he might say. She was proceeding along her own script for the press's benefit, and the sound-byte opportunity of the Navy's "failure" was simply too good for her to pass up. Especially now. Her public stance had undergone a remarkable change from obstructionism to frothing-at-the-mouth enthusiasm when *her* precious constituents found themselves on the front line. It seemed the prospect of hanging could concentrate even Nova Terrans' thoughts. What a pity nothing *short* of that could do the trick!

"I'm aware of the Navy's feeble excuse that the Bugs entered through an unknown warp point," she continued. "I am also aware that you are now departing with large forces, leaving Alpha Centauri undefended, naked before these murderous alien hordes! As a member of the Naval Oversight Committee, I promise you there will be a full investigation of your failure to defend the civilian populace of this system."

If I squash this svolochy as she deserves, it will only serve her own ends, Antonov told himself, and forced his deep, rumbling voice to remain calm and reasonable.

"Since you are aware of so much else, Assemblywoman Wister, you must be aware that we have taken steps to secure this system against attack, and that additional reinforcements have already been ordered by Sky Marshal Avram herself to join Admiral MacGregor—" he indicated the woman beside him "—here in Centauri in my absence."

"Nor will the inquiry stop there," Wister raved on without a break. She was pleased to note the expression on the Orion's face. As a rule, she despised the Orions who had invaded Centauri since the Alliance's activation almost as much as her own militarists, but such a broad, *toothy* smile could only be one of sympathy and encouragement. "We will have answers, Admiral! Answers to the larger question of why the Navy, in well over two years of war, has not wiped out these inhuman monsters to the last foul creature! There will be a thorough housecleaning of—"

"Major Lin!" It wasn't so much Antonov's increased volume that caused Wister to stop short. It was more a kind of subliminal, almost subterranean vibration in his bass voice.

"Sir!" The Marine major in charge of security hurried over and snapped to attention,

"Major, this area is to be cleared at once. The entire building is off-limits to unauthorized personnel until further notice from Lord Talphon. Now, get this *pizda* out of here."

Lin gulped. He'd been around Ivan the Terrible long enough to know that what the admiral had called Wister was the equivalent of an English-speaker's use of the word "asshole." But he also knew that the idiom—used without regard to the gender of the individual in question—translated literally as "cunt." Luckily, Wister's blank look suggested she was unaware of that fact. "Yes, Sir!" he rapped.

Antonov started to turn to go, then paused with the movement half completed. When he spoke, his voice was mild again. "You know, Ms. Wister, there is a mistaken proverb which tells us that those who are ignorant of the past are condemned to repeat it. In fact, they're *lucky* if they're allowed to repeat it. More probably, they're condemned to something even *worse* than the past. This is doubly true of those who believe that their ignorance somehow makes them morally superior to those who don't share it." He turned back and faced Wister squarely, looking at her as he might have looked at something disgusting in a plate of food. "I go now to lead brave men and women into what will be, for many of them, death. They go willingly, out of devotion to a state which unfortunately is not worthy of it. But, as someone once said, it is the quality of the passion that matters, not its object." He turned on his heel and strode away through a thundering silence.

Behind him, Bettina Wister held her head high as she was led away. It was a lovely image for the cameras, she thought: a small, harmless *civilian* woman between two huge, hard-faced Marine guards. It was even more than she'd hoped for, and she hid her triumph behind an expression of outraged dignity, already considering the most effective way for her staffers to cut and edit the recordings.

The type K0v orange primary star of this system (its remote red dwarf companion was quite invisible) reflected feebly from the flanks of Second Fleet's ships. Ivan Antonov stood on TFNS *Colorado*'s flag bridge and gazed at the view screen. One volume of space was much like any other, he supposed. But there was something special about this particular expanse of nothingness. For he was looking at original, pre-war Bug space. He was the first human since Commodore Lloyd Braun to look on such space—and the first ever to look on it as a conqueror.

Admiral van der Gelder's Task Force 22 had led the way through the warp point from Alpha Centauri behind the new fourth generation SBMHAWKs that had blasted a path through the warp point covering force . . . including the gunboats, whose point defense was useless against the sprint-mode missiles the new pods could carry. Raymond Prescott had transited in her wake. His Task Force 21 included his own veteran light carrier force from the Kliean campaign as well as the cream of the new-construction fast superdreadnoughts and refitted battle-cruisers. It was like a weapon forged for his hand, and he'd wielded it like a *kendo* master. He'd swept around behind the defenders and driven them into the waiting jaws of van der Gelder's battle-line and Vice Admiral Taathaanahk's fighters, many of them Ophiuchi-piloted and operating from the new assault carriers, and the Bugs hadn't stood a chance. They'd died with their usual horrifying obliviousness to personal survival, inflicting whatever damage they could on an enemy who possessed the prohibitive fire-control advantages of command datalink. And now Antonov stood in the midst of a fleet that was verging on euphoria at the lightness of its losses, waiting for the reports from the drones that had sped on ahead to spy out the system he'd already dubbed Anderson One in honor of his old friend.

"We're getting preliminary readings, Admiral." Blanton Stovall spoke from behind him. "No indication of any habitation—all the planets are useless rockballs or gas giants anyway."

Antonov tried not to show his disappointment Too bad the first conquered Bug system should turn out to be an undistinguished accumulation of cosmic detritus. *Come, Vanya,* he chided himself. *What did you expect? To transit from Alpha Centauri directly into the capital system of the Tsar of all the Bugs?*

"One lucky break—we think we've already inferred the general location of one warp point," Stovall went on. "It's in the inner system, which is why the drones picked it up so quickly, while looking for life-bearing planets. We're putting it on the display now."

Antonov turned to the holo tank in which the system's features were winking to life as fast as their existence was confirmed. The icon of a warp point had begun to blink off and on, fairly close to the system primary.

"The search for warp points must take first priority," he rumbled. "We must secure this system against counterattack as quickly as possible."

Stovall nodded in understanding. The Bugs, by fighting to the last ship and not even attempting to flee, had deprived them of any indication of where more of their kind might be expected to appear. This newly discovered warp point might be the gateway to the enemy's heartland, or it might not. And any pickets at other warp points would, of course, have departed by now, before anyone was close enough to detect their departure.

"We'll be prepared to act on any data we receive, Sir," Stovall said confidently. "Now that Admiral Chin's fleet train has transited from Centauri, our post-battle repairs are well in hand."

"Good. Keep me informed of any—"

"Admiral!" Armand de Bertholet's voice came from the flag bridge's com station, where he leaned over an operators shoulder. "New reports from the inward-bound drones indicate . . . Well, you can see for yourself in the tank."

Antonov did. A short distance outward from the inner-system warp point, but still almost six light-hours from Second Fleet, tiny red icons were popping out like smallpox.

"Bogies," Stovall said unnecessarily.

"Quite a few of them," added Midori Kozlov, joining them. "They can't have already been in this system."

"Of course not," de Bertholet said emphatically. "Their vector shows they've come from that inner warp point. And if their velocity's held constant, they must have emerged from it—" he fiddled with his wrist calculator "—just as we were mopping up the last of the defense force."

"Good timing, from our standpoint," Stovall put in drily.

"But I don't know how valid that constant-velocity assumption is," Kozlov said. "They're moving at what has to be the pace of their slowest ships. They're also keeping a very tight formation, from what we can tell. All in all, I'd say they're advancing very cautiously."

"Wouldn't you, in their place?" De Bertholet's rhetorical question was almost challenging. For reasons doubtless related to his upbringing, he had a way of carrying off remarks that in anyone else would have sounded like sheer bravado. Even his appearance helped; he always kept within grooming and uniform standards, but he still managed to have the kind of looks that had once been called "Byronic," a word whose root no one remembered. He turned to Antonov and Stovall, body language fairly shouting urgency. "Admiral, we must engage them without delay!"

"I think we should amend that to 'Without *unnecessary* delay,' Commander," Stovall spoke in mild reproof. "We've still got some repairs in progress, and I believe we can afford to complete them."

"Get me reports from the ships in question, Commodore Stovall," Antonov ordered. "Also whatever data the drones can provide on this force's composition. Like you, I'd rather complete repairs before we advance. But the important thing is getting those *svolochy* out of this system."

"And so," Midori Kozlov concluded her presentation, "before the Bug force departed through the warp point we were able to make a definitive estimate of its composition, at least by mass equivalents: forty-two superdreadnoughts, ten battle-cruisers and thirty light cruisers."

"A considerable force," de Bertholet commented. "Still, distinctly inferior to ours, even without our tech advantages. Small wonder they fell back when we advanced."

"What about the warp point?" Antonov growled.

"Pinpointed, Sir," Stovall reported. "A fast covering force has been dispatched there as per your orders."

"All right." Antonov swept the staff meeting with his eyes. "So we're now sitting on the warp point the Bugs used to enter this system. What about our search for still more warp points?"

"No results as yet, Sir. But there wouldn't be, at this point. We'll need time for some extensive survey work to satisfy ourselves that there are no more open warp points." Stovall paused and gave a wry half-smile. "And of course there's no telling about *closed* warp points; but that's true anywhere—as we've all been reminded lately."

"Very well." Antonov turned to Kozlov. "Commodore, what is your interpretation of the astrographic and military situation in which we find ourselves?"

"Well, Sir, the military situation is that we've secured this system at very little cost, and that the force the Bugs put into it was so inadequate to face us that it withdrew rather than follow their usual practice of accepting extravagant losses if any appreciable damage can be inflicted in exchange. It seems probable that that force was the only one they *could* put into this system; if they could have deployed enough strength to stop us, they surely would have. This in turn suggests we're in a rather lightly defended area."

"Which won't *remain* lightly defended," Stovall put in grimly.

"Exactly my own conclusions," Antonov stated. "So now I wish to pose the following question: should we proceed deeper into Bug space?" He looked around and decided he'd better recognize the operations officer before he burst. "Commander de Bertholet?"

"I think, Admiral, that we've been given a priceless opportunity." De Bertholet leaned forward as though to physically impart greater force to his words. "But it's an opportunity that won't last. As Commodore Stovall has pointed out, the Bugs must have sent for reinforcements. We've caught them off balance, but we must press on without hesitation before they've had time to regain that balance. This is a crucial moment in history!"

"Now hold on, Commander," Stovall spoke in his slow, deliberate way, rather like a harmonica following a trumpet. "Let's not forget we're in an unsurveyed system. We don't have the slightest idea where we are."

"With great respect, Commodore, we do know one thing, because the Bugs themselves told us." De Bertholet indicated the conference room's small replica of the flag bridge's holo tank. "By falling back through that warp point, they showed us the way to what they consider most vital to defend—which can only be their centers of population and industry."

"That's sheer inference," Kozlov protested.

"But a reasonable one," de Bertholet shot back. "Why would they have withdrawn into some dead-end warp chain? And why would they have been there in the first place? Remember, they emerged from that same warp point."

Stovall shook his head slowly. "I don't know, Admiral. Let's not let success go to our heads. It's true that we didn't have many outright ship losses, but a fair number of our ships took varying degrees of damage. And Admiral Taathaanahk lost a lot of fighters when they entered the Bugs' defensive envelope. We'll want to replace those losses."

"Of course, Sir," de Bertholet conceded. "But as soon as those matters are seen to, we should advance without further delay. This opportunity is absolutely unique."

"So are the potential dangers," Kozlov argued. "Until we've thoroughly surveyed this system, we can't be sure there are no other warp points. And if there are, there's no guarantee they lead to 'dead-end warp chains,' as some of us are assuming a little too readily. We'd be leaving ourselves vulnerable to being cut off from our base by an attack from an unexpected direction."

De Bertholet's face darkened a half shade, but his self-control was unimpeachable. "I can't deny that what I'm proposing contains an element of risk, Commodore. But if we insist on a total absence of risk, we'll never move at all. As Commodore Stovall intimated, there could be closed warp points here, and no amount of surveying will ever reveal them. It didn't at Centauri—and we've been there almost three hundred years!"

He stopped abruptly, and no one else spoke, for they all knew Antonov well enough to recognize the brooding look he'd assumed. It meant he was through listening to advice or arguments and had assumed the burden of decision that none of them could share.

Well, Vanya, now's when you earn your salary. For a moment he allowed himself to wish he had Kthaara with him. But then he dismissed the thought. After all, he knew exactly what the frosted-sable Orion would say: *Attack!* And, he thought with growing conviction, Kthaara would be right.

Antonov was far from unaware of the danger of a victorious force letting its *élan* do its thinking for it. And de Bertholet was, by nature, the very voice of *élan*. But his point, stripped of the theatrics, was compelling. For the first time, they had the initiative; it was worth taking terrifying risks to keep it.

And yet . . .

His thoughts came back to the conference room, and his eyes met those of his staff. "Commodore Stovall," he rumbled, "proceed to implement repairs. Make arrangements to begin probing the system beyond this warp point with recon drones. And commence operational planning for a full-scale advance through the warp point after those repairs are completed and our fighter strength is replenished." He studied their reactions. De Bertholet could scarcely contain his elation, and Kozlov looked glum. But Stovall's worried look seemed no more than what he knew was expected of him; he was no more capable of *not* wanting to press on through that beckoning warp point than he was of not voicing all possible objections to it.

"And," Antonov continued, "while we're in the process of ferrying fighters from Alpha Centauri, I myself will be returning there briefly, to put my proposed course of action before the Joint Chiefs." For a moment he let himself enjoy their expressions of almost comical surprise. "Yes, I'm sure it seems out of character. But consider: if Commodore Kozlov's nightmare of a flank attack on this system through an undiscovered warp point comes to pass while Second Fleet is off somewhere deeper in Bug space, the Bugs will be one warp transit away from Centauri, two from Sol—and Old Terra."

He gauged their expressions again. They were surprisingly alike, and he wondered what these disparate people had felt at the words 'Old Terra.' Stovall? Indian summer in the Alleghenies, perhaps. De Bertholet? Surely a montage of images from what historians called the Cavalry Revolution and romanticists knew as the Age of Chivalry. Kozlov? Hard to say. But for all of them, as for every member of the far-scattered progeny of Adam and Eve, it meant something inexpressibly holy . . . not that anyone would have dreamed of putting it that way.

Antonov shook his head heavily. "No . . . there are some decisions which no one has a right to make alone."

"I gather, Admiral Antonov, that your staff was divided on the question."

"True, Fleet Speaker Noraku," Antonov acknowledged. He permitted himself a tight smile. "It would be remarkable if they hadn't been. I picked them with that in mind. I want lively debate, not sycophancy. My chief of staff, Captain Stovall, is cautious and deliberate by temperament. So I sought out an operations officer with opposite inclinations."

"Ah, yes," Kthaara nodded. "The young commander with the totally unpronounceable name. I like him."

"You would," Hannah Avram remarked. Strictly speaking, she wasn't a member of the Joint Chiefs. But to not invite her to this meeting would have been out of the question. She turned to Antonov. "Yes, your Commander de Bertholet *does* seem to be a firebrand. But I think he—and you, Ivan Nikolayevich—are right about pressing on with Pesthouse. Especially now that Ellen's reinforcements have arrived here at Centauri. Even if the enemy does break into Anderson One behind you, this system will be secure."

"Agreeeeeeed," said Admiral Thaarzhaan. "Ssstill, ittt issss a gaaaaamble. Ssssecond Fffleet would be aaaadvancing into unknownnnnn space, withhhh no notion of the ffffffforces it may fffface."

"Come, we have already been over the arguments." Kthaara's voice was impatient. "Second Fleet's tactical speed advantage should suffice for it to disengage if it finds itself faced with a force too strong to fight. Of course, we cannot ignore the potential threat to this system, and to the Human home world. But Sky Marshal Avraaam is confident she and Ahhhdmiraal MaacGrrregor can guarantee their security. In fact, she and our chairman, both of whom are Human, favor the operation." He paused for the barest heartbeat. "There comes a time when we must not let risks blind us to opportunities, especially when the opportunity is a fleeting one."

"I concur," Noraku stated.

"Asss do I," Thaarzhaan said, a little less emphatically.

Antonov settled back in his chair with a silent sigh. So it was settled. Second Fleet would forge on into the unknown.

"Thank you," he said with unwonted quietness. "I would not have been able to embark wholeheartedly on this without your unanimous support." He rose to his feet. "And now, I must make preparations to return to Anderson One without delay. The offensive must commence as soon as our repair and resupply operations are complete."

Kthaara gave a short growl. "Naturally our chairman is eager as an unleashed *zeget* to return and reassume the command to which he has appointed himself!"

Avram laughed, and Noraku and Thaarzhaan gave their respective races' equivalent indicia of amusement, as the tension evaporated. Antonov smiled, all innocence. "But, Kthaara Kornazhovich, it is *my* plan; surely you must agree that I should be the one to put it into effect."

Kthaara gave him a baleful look. "Trust you to come up with such an argument, Eevaahn'zarthan." He stood and faced his *vilkshatha* brother. "Yes, I understand perfectly. And while you are gone, I shall busy myself thinking of an appropriate way to make you pay for your practice of leaving me behind to handle all me boring administrative work. You have always had a tendency to . . . what is the Human idiom?"

"Pull rank," Avram supplied.

"Now, Kthaasha," Antonov soothed. "There'll be plenty of fighting for everyone before this is over. And don't be like this. It's not as though you're never going to see me again." And, with a jauntiness that was somehow not inappropriate despite his age, Antonov was gone.

CHAPTER THIRTY-FIVE

"What else are we to do?"

Jessica van der Gelder's superdreadnoughts emerged into the new system amid the final reverberations of the SBMHAWK-spawned holocaust among its warp point defenses.

Antonov wasn't advancing into the altogether unknown. RD2s had established that this system was heavily populated, which tended to confirm the conclusions de Bertholet had drawn from the Bugs' avenue of retreat. They'd also provided enough data on the defenders to satisfy Antonov that his fleet train's SBMHAWK inventory would suffice to blast a path through them.

Now he stood on *Colorado*'s flag bridge as the superdreadnought advanced in van der Gelder's formation (he wasn't about to depart from a tradition which dated back to the First Interstellar War; the supreme commander would go in with the first waves) and saw that view confirmed. Some of the dying glows of SBMHAWK warheads were actually visible to the naked eye in the expanding clouds of vaporized metal they'd wrought, and the holo tank told an ever-elaborating tale of smashed or crippled fortresses. Extensive minefields remained, but Second Fleet's AMBAMs had already cleared paths through them.

TF 22 forged ahead, and Admiral Taathaanahk's TF 23 was already beginning to transit. Soon Raymond Prescott would bring TF 21 through. But Antonov, staring fixedly at the holo tank, had eyes only for the scarlet icons in Second Fleet's path.

"Commodore Kozlov," he rumbled without shifting his eyes, "have you been able to reach any conclusions regarding the mobile Bug forces?"

"Yes, Sir. Now that our leading elements have begun to exchange

679

fire with them, we're getting harder data. These have to be the same ones that withdrew from Anderson One just ahead of us. The force composition by ship classes is an exact match—too exact for coincidence."

"So they haven't been reinforced yet," de Bertholet breathed. "We've caught them still trying to mobilize against us. This force is still all they can put in our path; it must be under orders to stand and fight this time because this is an inhabited system." He turned to Antonov, his excitement barely under control. "Admiral, this could be the beginning of the end of the war! If we can continue to advance, continue to keep them off balance—"

"Excuse me, Admiral." Kozlov didn't often interrupt de Bertholet, and something in her tone caused even Antonov to turn away from the plot to face her. "We're starting to get some disturbing tactical analyses from the ships most heavily engaged. They're receiving precisely coordinated time-on-target fire from as many as six Bug ships at once."

The silence lasted less than a heartbeat before de Bertholet broke it. "But . . . but that's as many ships as one of our own battlegroups! D'you mean to suggest . . . ?"

"I'm not the one suggesting it, Commander. The data speak for themselves." She jerked her chin toward the tank and the midair columns of luminous figures that told the tale of damage well beyond what they'd allowed for at this stage of the engagement. "And," she continued, "why should it be such a surprise? Admiral LeBlanc's been telling anyone who'll listen that it was only a matter of time. The Bugs have seen command datalink in action often enough, and it doesn't require any basic technology beyond their demonstrated horizons. It's just that we've come to take our monopoly for granted, as though it were somehow in the nature of things—"

"Thank you, Commodore," Stovall cut in quietly but authoritatively. He understood her accumulated frustration at the immemorial reluctance of line officers to listen to the intelligence community until after its forecasts had become fact, but this wasn't the time for her to get uncharacteristically worked up about it. "Admiral, we can defer interpreting these data until later. But it's clear that, at a minimum, our projections have erred on the optimistic side where Bug fire control is concerned. Should we implement our contingency plan for breaking off engagement?"

"*Nyet.*" Antonov's voice held absolutely no invitation to debate. "Signal Admiral van der Gelder to press her attack with maximum aggressiveness. And raise Admiral Taathaanahk as soon as he's transited; it is imperative that he begin launching fighter strikes as quickly as possible." He met his staffers' eyes, each in turn. The Theban War lay beyond living memory for their generation, and day-to-day contact tends to rub away the patina of legendry. But all at once the tales they'd grown up on came crowding back, for this was the man who had advanced through every defense like an unstoppable force of nature, grimly disregarding casualties as he gained his objectives... and the nickname Ivan the Terrible.

All at once, those tales seemed very real.

"Aye, aye, Sir," Stovall said quietly.

Antonov turned back to the tank and watched van der Gelder's task force advance into a holocaust of fire unprecedented in its intensity. It soon became apparent that at least a dozen of the Bug superdreadnoughts belonged to the missile-heavy *Archer* class. Even with the defensive firepower of her new SDEs, van der Gelder didn't relish missile duels with six-ship battle groups of those behemoths; she ordered her ships to close to beam range while trying to stay outside the zone in which plasma guns were truly deadly. It was a difficult balancing act, performed while nervously awaiting the onset of gunboats on suicide runs.

But no kamikaze attacks came, and the reason became apparent when Taathaanahk's fighters entered the fray. The Bugs, perhaps out of confidence in the way their new datalink technology enhanced their firepower, had held the gunboats back as anti-fighter escorts, adding their loads of AFHAWKs to the tremendous defensive fire from the tight enemy formations.

Losses continued to mount, and periodically *Colorado*, fighting in TF 22's battle-line, shuddered for a sickening instant. Calls for damage control began to reverberate through the great ship, but Antonov never flinched. He held grimly to the rail that surrounded the holo tank and stared at the battle the tank revealed, as though it was a living being with which he was in silent communion, broken only to bark occasional orders.

Finally the balance commenced to tilt. Ships continued to emerge from the warp point, as did the reserve SBMHAWKs, which came under the control of Fleet command. Their firepower, and Second Fleet's overall numerical superiority, began to tell. Almost abruptly, the Bugs broke off in an orderly retreat, and van der Gelder's shaken task force left the job of harrying that retreat to Taathaanahk's already weary fighter pilots and Prescott's newly arrived ones.

"Admirals Taathaanahk and Prescott both report heavy fighter losses," Stovall reported as the fighting receded out of missile range and a palpable air of relief suffused *Colorado*. "The volume of anti-fighter missile fire seems unabated."

"It will abate as the attacks continue to be pressed." Antonov was as impervious to the flagship's new mood as he had been to the earlier tension. "Their magazines aren't infinite. And the attacks *must* be pressed without letup. Make that very clear to Taathaanahk and Prescott. Losses are secondary; we have nearby sources of reinforcement, which they apparently do not."

Stovall swallowed hard. "Aye, aye, Sir."

"Oh, and one other thing, Commodore. As soon as practicable, I want recon drones dispatched sunward. We already know there's a planet here that's a high-energy population center. It must be quite close to a dim sun like this one. We will, of course, proceed there as soon as the Bug forces are cleared from the system."

"You mean, Sir . . . ?"

"Yes." Antonov's expression was absolutely unreadable. "Our orders are clear. We are about to become the first in well over a century to implement General Directive 18."

The staff conference room had a wall screen. Antonov had decreed that it be left on, and eyes kept straying to the planet Harnah—everyone was calling it that by now, even though this system had officially been named Anderson Two. Beyond the world's blue curve was the bone-white crescent of its moon. That moon, like the oxygen-rich atmosphere, represented a triumph over the odds. Harnah orbited just outside the zone in which the orange sun's tidal force would have stopped the planet's rotation and stripped away any natural satellites, but close enough to that relatively feeble fusion furnace for water to exist as a liquid in which life could arise.

And why do you keep letting your mind wander into this astronomical blagadarnost, *Vanya?* Antonov unflinchingly answered his own question: *Because you'd rather think about that, or anything at all, than about what you've found here on this lovely blue planet.*

Things had gone according to plan. Task Forces 21 and 23 had herded the Bugs out of the system with relentless fighter strikes. They'd never broken that dense defensive formation, but the Bugs had withdrawn minus a quarter of their capital ships and most of their light cruisers. Better still, the warp point through which they'd done their withdrawing had been pinpointed and was now heavily guarded against any counter-stroke. Meanwhile, TF 22 had proceeded behind a cloud of recon drones, following the spoor of that which the Grand Alliance had condemned to death.

They'd been prepared for swarms of gunboats to rise from the planet in suicidal fury . . . yet none had. There were only orbital defenses—fortresses and the kind of elaborate military/industrial faculties one would expect around a highly developed planet. Antonov had waited until some of the other task forces' carrier formations had joined him, then finished off the orbital works with SBMHAWK bombardments and fighter strikes. And the planet had lain open to them with its two or three billion Bugs . . . and something else.

The wait for the carriers hadn't been a very long one, but it had allowed time for an extensive survey of the surface. In the course of mapping targets, one of Midori Kozlov's subordinates had noticed vast enclosures that were clearly stockyards for meat animals—six-legged vertebrates like all the planet's higher land fauna. But something had bothered him, a wrongness he couldn't quite put his finger on. Kozlov hadn't been able to put her finger on it either, at first. She'd demanded greater and greater magnifications of the imagery. . . .

No one could ever forget the moment when the screen had shown one of the meat animals, the foremost third of its body held erect, making marks on the wall of a shed with a crude implement held in one of its forefeet.

After the planet's sky had been cleared of all opposition, more detailed reconnaissance had commenced, using aural sensors that were the highly evolved descendants of an earlier century's shotgun mikes. And they'd all watched the meat animals, most of them almost reverted to a hexapedal habit, go about their rudimentary socialization under the leadership of the class that had somehow halted their degradation just short of the loss of writing. The computers were still trying to crack the spoken language, and had analyzed a few of the sounds. One of those sounds was "Harnah" for "world," and so it had become in the minds of the horror-stricken humans who gazed at the overgrown ruins of what had clearly been cities, occasionally adorned with sculptures of the proud centauroids who'd built them.

Kozlov's self-consciously flinty voice roused Antonov from his reverie. She hadn't been the only one to turn green around the gills as realization dawned. In retrospect, perhaps, the discovery was inevitable; in every other sense it had been unthinkable. Justin and Kliean had told the Grand Alliance the Bugs regarded them as food sources, yet some deep-seated part of the Alliance's analysts had seen that as an act of opportunity, like the pre-space practices of strip-mining or clear-cutting watersheds. The notion that even Bugs would actually raise sentient beings as a self-sustaining herd of meat animals had not occurred to them . . . *perhaps,* Antonov reflected grimly, *simply because it was so utterly unacceptable.*

"There's no room for doubt," Kozlov was telling the staff and various senior officers. "They're the descendants of the city builders, the original inhabitants of Harnah. Indications are that their civilization was no more advanced than early twentieth-century Earth's. Vacuum tube electronics and hydrocarbon-burning internal combustion engines. They never stood a chance when the Bugs arrived."

Raymond Prescott shook his head slowly. "Are you sure? I mean . . ." He gestured vaguely, and they all knew what he meant, for they'd all watched the occupants of those vast, fetid, dung-choked pens as they shuffled listlessly about.

"Quite sure, Admiral Prescott. Granted, they're incredibly degraded. We have no way of knowing how long they've been . . . livestock. Quite a while, from the condition of the ruins. But they're still sentient—they haven't had time to evolve away from it, even though the capacity to feel such things as rebelliousness must be decidedly contra-survival in their circumstances."

"So," Stovall said in the voice of a man trying to awake from nightmare, "they *know* that they're going to be . . . ?"

"Yes." Kozlov nodded jerkily. Her color was poor, and her voice was that of a machine. "There will have been a strong natural selection in favor of those willing to go on living—and bringing forth offspring— as a domesticated food source."

They were all silent for a few heartbeats, each of them alone in hell with the new-found knowledge that there are worse things than extinction. But they weren't really alone at all, for the human inhabitants of the Bug-occupied worlds seemed to fill the room.

Finally, Antonov cleared his throat. In that silence, it was like a thunderclap. "Thank you, Commodore Kozlov. And now, ladies and gentlemen, we must consider the effect of these findings on our plans to carry out General Directive 18."

De Bertholet's head jerked upward, as though emerging from his private vision of horror. "Ah, Admiral, I don't understand. Surely no one can now doubt the wisdom of reactivating the Directive." The sick look on his face began to give way to one of fury. "The universe must be cleansed of these monsters! We're dealing with an abomination beyond humanity's conception of evil. By comparison, Hitler was a naughty boy, the Rigelians mildly maladjusted!"

"Agreed, Commander. But the Harnahese present a complicating factor. There are, Commodore Kozlov estimates, several million of them scattered among the Bug billions. It isn't always easy to tell just *where* they are, for the 'ranches' where they're bred are interspersed with those devoted to raising other, lower animal species native to this planet." He leaned forward, and his voice dropped to a basso fit for a Mussorgsky chorus. "I am under orders to exterminate the Bugs wherever I find them. But I am neither ordered nor authorized to commit genocide upon *another* sentient race. And I am disinclined to do so—especially in this case." He smiled slightly. "The older one gets, the harder it becomes to believe in any kind of universal ethical balance—divine justice, if you will. But one doesn't like to take chances! And should I happen to be wrong in my skepticism . . . well, if anyone in the universe has suffered enough, the Harnahese have."

Stovall broke the awkward silence that followed. "Admiral, the fact remains that we, like all Alliance forces, are subject to the general order to extirpate all Bug populations. And the Harnahese presence here poses a moral dilemma only if we limit our tactical options to scorching the surface clean of life. Perhaps there are other alternatives."

"I've considered those alternatives, Commodore. General Nagata, please summarize our discussion on the subject."

Brigadier Heinrich Nagata, the senior Marine officer embarked with Second Fleet, came unconsciously to a seated position of attention. "Sir, ever since Justin we've known how tough the Bugs can be in a ground action. And this is the first time we've ever contemplated fighting them on the surface of a long-established planet of theirs, with hundreds of millions of workers available to soak up fire." He paused awkwardly, unaccustomed to presenting arguments *against* going in. But he plowed ahead. "Second Fleet as presently constituted doesn't even incorporate a real landing force. We didn't anticipate needing one. With the reactivation of General Directive 18, it was assumed that any Bug-inhabited worlds would simply be smashed from orbit. All I've got are the ships' regular Marine detachments. There's simply no way I could hope to go down there and selectively wipe out three billion Bugs while preserving the Harnahese."

Kozlov looked up in agony. "We're only two transits from Alpha Centauri, three from Sol. Maybe we could bring in more surface forces—"

"You're talking about Marines, Commodore!" Nagata snapped. "Do you have any conception of how many of them would die, even if we brought in the whole damned Corps?"

"I'm sorry, Brigadier. I know what they'd have to face. But what *else* are we to do?"

Antonov's voice cut the exchange off like a battleaxe. "That cannot be our decision. A policy is going to have to be hammered out for dealing with this world—and others like it. Our surprise is merely a result of wishful thinking; we should have anticipated such situations."

"How coulddd we hhhave, Admiral?" Taathaanahk asked quietly. "Admittedly, we hhhave alll haddd to accusssstom ourselves to whattt the Buggsss do to the inhabitants of conquereddd worrrlds. But the nnnotion of sssentient beingsss rrraised from birthhh as . . ." He couldn't continue. It was the first time any of them had seen the avian lose his composure.

"I suppose," Raymond Prescott grated, "we've simply assumed—*had* to assume—that the Bugs gorged on the conquered human populations until they'd finished them off. We never let ourselves consider that they were keeping some as . . . as breeding stock. Children, probably . . ."

A low sound, more primal than any spoken language, suffused the compartment. Antonov cut it off.

"For present, I have decided how we will proceed." They all noticed the loss of definite articles; a few knew him well enough to realize the stress level that implied. "Commodore Stovall, I want staff to plan surgical strikes aimed at destroying all spaceport facilities and major industrial centers and military installations on surface, as well as any remaining space-based industry. And no, I don't expect you to guarantee these strikes won't kill a single Harnahese; only a politician could be so fatuous. We'll strand Harnah's Bug population on planet, where it can be left to await Alliance's decision. Our next courier drone will inform Centauri of this course of action—and of my assumption of full responsibility for it."

He stood up abruptly and stalked out of the room before the rest of them could rise. They were left staring at the view screen, at the lovely blue planet.

"Yes, Admiral Antonov, the Joint Chiefs—with Sky Marshal Avram's hearty concurrence—fully endorse your handling of the Harnah problem. They wished me to convey that to you in the most emphatic terms." Rear Admiral Jamal Moreno beamed at Antonov. He'd only just arrived at the head of reinforcements that included factory-like repair ships, even more welcome than the warships to a heavily damaged Second Fleet.

"So," Stovall asked, "have they decided what to do about Harnah?" He, de Bertholet and Kozlov sat with the two admirals, bathed in the simulated ruddy light of Anderson Two's primary. One entire bulkhead of *Colorado*'s flag lounge was a holo projection, and the cozy compartment seemed open to space in a way that someone from an earlier era would have found disconcerting.

"Not yet," Moreno told him. "They're still thrashing out the problem. It's hoped that genetic engineering may provide the answer: a tailored virus that's deadly to Bugs but harmless to indigenous Harnahese life. They want me to bring back biological samples, which shouldn't be hard to obtain given your absolute control of the planet's sky."

The staffers looked at each other, clearly uncomfortable with the idea. Which, Antonov thought, was a measure of the effect this war was having on its participants. Three years earlier, they wouldn't have been uncomfortable; they would have been glassy-eyed with shock.

The making of microorganisms to order had been a simple matter as far back as the twenty-first century. At first, few had appreciated the horrific potentialities of the djinn crouching within the shiny new bottle.

But a few *very* close calls had brought humanity to the realization that, as Howard Anderson had once remarked, "a nuke is just a big bubble-gum pop by comparison." The problem, of course, was microbes' susceptibility to mutation, combined with their eyeblink-brief generations. Tailored bioweapons could evolve out from under whatever limitations had been engineered into them with terrifying speed, and the youthful Federation had decided, with rare unanimity, that the djinn must never be let out. The matter had been beyond debate for centuries, and the Orions, on whose original home world it *had* been let out, were even more emphatic.

"Well," Antonov said gruffly, "with Lord Talphon running the Joint Chiefs, I know any experiments along these lines will be conducted under *extreme* safeguards. We'll send expeditions down to collect your specimens. But now," he continued in a tone that closed the subject, "the Harnah issue is out of our hands. We need to turn to the question of Second Fleet's next move."

De Bertholet looked alarmed. "Surely, Admiral, there can be no question! Once again, we've had our avenue of advance marked out for us by retreating Bugs, and the recon drones have confirmed there are no fortresses guarding the next system. It must be an uninhabited system which doesn't rate large-scale fixed defenses."

"Still," Kozlov said dubiously, "the drones also indicate the Bugs have been surrounding the warp point with minefields and laser buoys. And the mobile forces we drove out of this system have been reinforced up to somewhat more than their original strength."

"In absolute terms, yes," de Bertholet retorted. "But relative to our forces, including the reinforcements Admiral Moreno's brought, they're weaker than they were." He turned back to Antonov with a look of urgency. "Admiral, the enemy can't fail to recognize the threat Operation Pesthouse represents. They would surely have poured in more reinforcements to contest our next transit—*if they could!*"

"This is just more of the same argument you used when we entered *this* system," Kozlov protested.

"And it's just as valid as it was then! Either we're in a poorly defended frontier region, as we originally theorized, or—" a feverish gleam of excitement entered his eyes "—they're so heavily committed on the established fronts that they're coming to the end of their resources! If the former, then we should press on and gain as much ground as possible before reinforcements finally arrive from their main bases, as ours finally arrived in the Romulus Chain. If the latter . . . then they have no massive reserves left to place in our path!"

Stovall spoke in his slow, deliberate way. "I find myself in agreement with Armand, Admiral. In light of what we've seen here, we have a moral responsibility to pursue any course of action that promises a quick end to this war—and to the Bugs!" Kozlov shot him a surprised look, and he smiled with the self-deprecating humor that was so much a part of him. "Yes, I know; we North Americans have always been suckers for anything marketed as a 'moral responsibility.' But look at it from the narrowly tactical standpoint. Here we have a significant force of Bug capital ships which, since they have command datalink, must be among their newest construction or retrofits. And we're in a position to annihilate them!"

"Actually, Commodore," Antonov said in the quiet voice that often surprised people, "I'm less interested in annihilating them than in forcing them to retreat." He smiled into their surprised faces. "You see, I still want to see which *way* they retreat. While I'm not yet prepared to let myself believe in Commander de Bertholet's second possibility, I am firmly convinced the Bugs are in retreat towards their centers of population." He paused, then spoke as much to himself as to the others. "I've made myself remain alert to the possibility of some kind of trap—even more than I ordinarily would, given the alienness of the mind-set we're dealing with. But, damn it, these creatures can build starships! However weird they are, they must be *rational*. That's been true of every technologically advanced race we've encountered. Even those whose philosophies were incomprehensible or repugnant to us, like the Rigelians, were capable of acting rationally in pursuit of those philosophies' goals. But the Bugs have now given up a planet inhabited by over three billion of their own race. I cannot believe rational beings would do such a thing—particularly after *they* initiated the saturation bombardment of planetary populations—if they had *any* other option. And no rational fleet commander would willingly leave this large a force in a position where it didn't stand a chance of survival!"

"Exactly, Sir," de Bertholet urged. "They aren't strong enough to stop us, but sixty-six capital ships and thirty-six light cruisers are too much for *anyone* to consider expendable."

"Still Admiral," Kozlov spoke up, "I'm worried about the possibility of flank attacks. It's a danger that grows as we advance further into enemy space. The latest news from Anderson One should remind us of that."

"What?" Antonov looked up, blinking away his preoccupation. "Oh, yes; the third warp point our survey turned up. They're reasonably certain they've found all the warp points that are there to be found, correct?

"Yes, Sir."

"Well, then, we'll take most of the ships off survey operations in Anderson One and form them into a flotilla to explore the warp chain beyond this new warp point. We'll make sure we won't be taken by surprise."

Kozlov looked worried. "I'd hoped we could bring some of those ships forward to join us here in Anderson Two, Sir. With all our present survey assets occupied searching this system for warp points, we won't have many survey-equipped craft to take with us into the next one."

De Bertholet waved the point aside. "Let's worry first about fighting our way into it—Anderson Three, I suppose we'll call it. Plenty of time for survey after we're in possession."

"I suppose so," Kozlov said, not sounding altogether convinced.

Antonov only half-heard the exchange. He was examining the problem from every possible angle, seeking any sources of danger he'd missed. For the life of him, he couldn't think of any. Unless . . . but no. Such a mentality was simply inconceivable.

The dark, silent ships hung in space, awaiting the arrival of the enemy who had, unbeknownst to them, named this system "Anderson Three"— this system that the ships were destined never to leave. But that was a matter of no moment to them. That it could even be a consideration was simply inconceivable.

CHAPTER THIRTY-SIX

"I *want* them to escape."

Ivan Antonov's recon drones had told him of the dense minefields that surrounded the emergence warp point in Anderson Three, and of the fifty-seven heavy cruisers that covered those minefields. So he knew how intense an SBMHAWK bombardment was needed to burn a path through those defenses for Second Fleet.

The drones had also confirmed that the enemy's heavy units were being held well back from the warp point. As usual, that placed them outside SBMHAWK range, but Antonov didn't mind, for it allowed him to revive a classic tactic of carrier warfare.

This time, the first ships to enter the hostile system were Admiral Taathaanahk's assault carriers. The instant carbon- and silicon-based brains had reoriented themselves from the wrongness of warp transit, the electromagnetic catapults flung scores of fighters into space. Then the CVAs executed a tight turn and began vanishing back into the warp point from whence they'd come. Once back in Anderson Two they would turn again and re-enter Anderson Three, where their fighters would presumably be ready for rearming after fulfilling their task of covering the emergence of the subsequent assault waves.

It was the sort of maneuver which would have been flatly impossible in the days of reaction drives. Even today, such a turning radius was beyond the capabilities of any other ships in the new super carriers' size range—superdreadnoughts and the very largest freighters. But the maneuver worked, and the superdreadnoughts of Task Force 22 emerged into the unaccustomed environment of friendly-controlled space.

They faced an enemy who was behaving very oddly. Gunboat deployments were promptly detected, and TF 22 braced itself for kamikaze attacks. But none came, and the Bugs hung back in uncharacteristic hesitation while the bulk of van der Gelder's ships—including *Colorado*—transited unmolested. Only then did they close to long missile range.

Antonov had expended almost all his fourth-generation SBMHAWKs to clear the warp point, but he retained a substantial reserve of third-generation pods. These now transited and came under TF 22's control. They went far toward redressing the balance between fifty-six Bug superdreadnoughts and about thirty Terran ones. But the former *did* have command datalink now.

"Admiral," de Bertholet suggested after a time, "should we order the fighters to attack in support of the battle-line?"

"*Nyet*," Antonov answered absently. He knew what was bothering the ops officer. The initial missile exchanges had favored Second Fleet—but those loss ratios included the results of the SBMHAWK increment to TF 22's firepower, and couldn't be expected to continue after the missile pods were gone. Still . . .

"No," he repeated. "For now, we'll continue to hold them back as a shield against gunboat attacks. It's too soon to risk heavy fighter losses. Admiral Taathaanahk's carriers are due back shortly, in conjunction with Admiral Prescott's ships. When we have our entire carrier strength in this system, it will be time to launch a massive, coordinated strike."

Time wore on, and the anticipated gunboat attack failed to materialize. But the shift in the statistics of carnage after the SBMHAWKs ceased to be a factor was as per expectations. The Bugs were playing it very cagily, keeping the missile duel at long range and drawing back gradually as more and more Terran superdreadnoughts emerged. Antonov sensed a mood he didn't like on the flag bridge, a kind of nervous incomprehension of such a radical departure from the Bugs' "normal" suicidal eagerness to close to the shortest possible range. As Taathaanahk's and Prescott's carriers transited one by one, he found himself fretting as well. But the delay gave de Bertholet time to coordinate with TF 23 ops, and it was a very purposeful wave of over seven hundred fighters—Antonov was still holding back his defensive screen—that streaked away towards the silent black ships.

They encountered a nasty surprise: Bug gunboats in a purely defensive stance. The small craft drew as much blood as possible with their externally mounted anti-fighter missiles, then pulled back into a defensive envelope around their capital ships. Strictly defensive formations were rare in space warfare, and this proved to be a very strong one. Frustrated, stung by their losses, and still under orders to avoid excessive losses while still in Anderson Three's outer system, the fighters withdrew for rearming.

That operation reminded Antonov of a possibly decisive advantage that still remained to him, if he only exploited it. He proceeded to do so, ordering Second Fleet to press the missile duel, allowing the Bugs no respite in which to shut down their drives in order to rearm the gunboats. So it was with their internal weaponry alone that those gunboats faced a fresh assault by fighters laden with missiles and freed of their earlier tactical constraints.

Taathaanahk's pilots went relentlessly in, the humans hurling missile strikes at the gunboats while their Ophiuchi comrades covered them against the anticipated counterattack by those gunboats. But the Bugs stubbornly refused to be drawn out of their defensive hedgehog, and the Ophiuchi were denied the dogfighting at which they were the acknowledged masters. Instead, the fighters pressed their attack home into the defensive envelopes of the Bug capital ships' massive energy weapons and numerous missile launchers, grimly accepting whatever losses it took to blast the gunboats out of the equation.

"And," de Bertholet concluded his report to a hastily convened staff meeting, "the last of the squadrons have reported in or are accounted for. They're all en route back to their carriers, and the loss figures can be regarded as definitive." He indicated the columns of color-coded numbers on the display screen of the small conference room just off *Colorado*'s flag bridge.

Antonov eyed those figures with scant favor. He'd been forced to jettison his original guidelines for what constituted acceptable fighter losses, and he didn't like it. Still less did he like the way the Bugs— *sans* gunboats but still formidable—were continuing to be coy. Their tight formation held back just outside missile range, five and a half light-hours from the K type primary star of this undistinguished binary system whose details the probing RDs were gradually filling in on the plot. They'd already ruled out any high-tech population centers, and Antonov caught himself sighing with relief that there'd be no Harnah here. He shook the thought aside and glared anew at the red icons representing the Bug force, not giving battle but impossible to ignore.

He grew aware that de Bertholet had finished. "Thank you, Commander. Now, Commodore Kozlov, have you been able to form any rationale for the enemy's behavior?"

"We've all been thrashing that one out, Sir. The consensus seems to be that they're being cautious about risking ships equipped with their new datalink technology. Also, they may not have settled yet on a tactical doctrine for utilizing that technology."

"You mean," Stovall queried, "they're still experimenting, and right now they're impressed with its defensive possibilities?"

"That accounts for the observed facts while minimizing assumptions."

She gave one of her infrequent smiles. "I'm not sure Bugs shave with Occam's Razor. But it's the best I can do at present."

Antonov continued to glare at those red icons. "If they won't come to us," he rumbled, "we'll go to them. With our tactical speed advantage, we can force engagement. But before we do, I want our emergency repairs completed. There should be time, because I also want us to wait until the fleet train can rendezvous with us and replenish our depletable munitions."

"Aye, aye, Sir." The relief on Stovall's face was palpable. "Might I suggest that we also consider some organizational adjustment on the battlegroup level? Our losses—especially the five superdreadnoughts—have resulted in some imbalances."

"An excellent suggestion, Commodore. See to it that—"

What brought Antonov up short was the sudden jerk of Midori Kozlov's left forearm. He recognized the reaction of one who was being given an emergency jolt by a wrist communicator—an entirely unexpected jolt, for she'd left orders not to be interrupted. She gave Antonov an embarrassed look.

"Answer it, Commodore Kozlov," he said mildly.

She complied, with the device on minimal volume and held close to her ear. Whatever she was hearing caused the blood to drain from her face. But she reported to Antonov in level tones.

"Admiral, one of our drones has detected hostiles transiting into this system through a warp point located almost directly between us and the system primary—and only about eighty light-minutes from us. CIC designates them Force Two, and they'll be appearing on the display directly."

She'd barely stopped speaking before the fresh icons started blinking into existence. The reporting drone was very close, and data on their force composition began to roll in quickly.

"Lordy," Stovall broke the silence. "This is like Anderson One all over again!"

"Not quite, Sir," Kozlov said, her eyes still fixed on the unfolding data. "There, the second Bug force didn't arrive until we had finished wiping out the system's defenders. *This* force has appeared when we're just *preparing* to do so."

"Precisely, Admiral," de Bertholet said, in rare agreement with the spook. "And on their present vectors the two forces will rendezvous before we can complete the repairs and resupply you've ordered."

Antonov nodded absently as he studied Force Two's composition: eighteen superdreadnoughts and twenty-four battle-cruisers. He could continue as planned, and then a rearmed, repaired Second Fleet would face defenders reinforced by those forty-two fresh ships—which, he had to assume, possessed command datalink. Or he could strike now and seek to defeat the two enemy fleets in detail. Given those alternatives, his choice was clear if far from easy.

"Commodore Stovall, as soon as the fighters have rearmed, all elements of Second Fleet will advance to attack Force One. Our objective is to annihilate it before the new arrivals can make contact." He raised a hand in a gesture which foreclosed any discussion. "Yes, I know, we're battered and depleted. Well, they're also battered and depleted. I want there to be nothing but cooling plasma for Force Two to rendezvous with!"

It was a haggard staff that reconvened in the same compartment. Antonov, as usual, seemed elementally impervious to both fatigue and horror, but the others showed the strain of the battle whose reverberations had just died away.

"Are all ships now accounted for?" the admiral asked without preamble.

"Yes, Sir," de Bertholet acknowledged. His left arm hung in a sling; one of *Colorado*'s lurches from a near miss had sent him staggering against a stanchion with shoulder-dislocating force.

"Then report on Fleet's status."

"Aye, aye, Sir. We lost nine superdreadnoughts outright, in addition to the five we lost in the earlier fighting. At that, it could have been worse; as our tactical analysis suggested, they were concentrating their fire on the SDs. Twenty-seven took moderate to heavy damage, but we've only had to order one of them back to Anderson Two—that's *Colima*. *Colorado* got off very lightly, in spite of . . ." He ruefully indicated his arm. "They didn't pay nearly as much attention to our lighter units, but we still lost seven battle-cruisers, with another thirteen damaged."

"And fighter losses?" Antonov had a pretty good idea of what he was going to hear, and he didn't relish it.

"Forty-seven percent of our embarked strength." A chorus of gasps ran around the room. "However, the positive side is that we've fulfilled our objective. All but two of the enemy are confirmed kills, and those two—both battle-cruisers—are believed to have withdrawn into cloak."

"What about Force Two?'

"Its status is unchanged, Sir. It completed the course-reversal that it commenced as the battle here reached its final stages, and is continuing to withdraw to its entry warp point at its maximum speed. Your orders as to the pursuit are being carried out: TF 22's faster, relatively undamaged ships are being temporarily reassigned to Admiral Prescott. He and Admiral Taathaanahk probably won't be able to intercept it before it transits, but it's been made clear to them that their first priority is to locate that warp point."

"Good. The rest of us will follow as quickly as possible. And now, Commodore Kozlov, what interpretation do you place on the enemy's actions in this system?"

Midori Kozlov ran a hand through her hair in a characteristic gesture of discomfort. "Admiral, I was discussing this with Commander de Bertholet just before this meeting convened. And while I'm still not altogether comfortable with the conclusion, I can no longer see any reason for *not* concurring with him. A force that powerful—but still manifestly insufficient to stop us—would never have been ordered to stand and fight to the last ship if there were any alternative. It would have either been reinforced or withdrawn to participate in an eventual counterattack, if the resources for such reinforcement or such a counterattack existed. What finally convinced me was the behavior of the reinforcements they *did* put into the system. They tried desperately to come to the aid of the defending force and didn't turn tail until it became unmistakably clear that they couldn't make any difference to the outcome."

"Thank you, Commodore. Does anyone else wish to offer any thoughts?" For once, there was silence, as de Bertholet left well enough alone and no one else sought to disagree.

Antonov examined his own thoughts. Advancing into the unknown like this, overconfidence was the great enemy. From the first, he'd made himself think in terms of the possible trap, the low-probability contingency, the worst-case scenario. But there seemed no rational alternative to the conclusion that they'd broken into the territory of an enemy who was, at least locally, vulnerable. And anything de Bertholet and Kozlov agreed on must be virtually beyond dispute!

"Thank you, Commodore," he said aloud. "I believe your analysis has merit. But for now, we will continue the pursuit."

"The recon drones are beginning to report back, Admiral," Stovall reported.

Antonov grunted. They'd followed the fleeing enemy across Anderson Three's outer system, narrowing the gap but, as he'd more than half expected, unable to overhaul them. The Bugs had transited without slowing down, and Antonov, still wary of ambushes, had ordered recon drones sent ahead to probe the warp point. He wasn't about to charge through in pursuit with no idea of what lay ahead, especially with Second Fleet in a strung-out configuration as the slower ships proceeded towards the warp point even more slowly than usual in order to allow those of their number who'd suffered drive damage to remain in formation.

In a surprisingly short time, Kozlov crossed *Colorado*'s flag bridge and reported to Antonov. Beneath her usual reserve, he thought he could sense a sternly suppressed excitement. But that was typical of the way she'd been acting in this system. She hadn't even come to him with her usual requests for more of their thinly stretched survey resources to explore it for warp points. Doubtless that was why he'd never quite gotten around to ordering it. *Must see to it,* he started to tell himself. But then Kozlov spoke.

"Sir, an unusually large number of drones have reported back— the reason why will become apparent shortly—so we've been able to flesh out our information quickly. What's on the far side of the warp point is a class G single-star system, but with no evidence of habitation. And the Bugs haven't stopped after transiting; they're continuing on across the outer system—the entry warp point is about twenty-three light-minutes from the primary. And . . ." She paused with the air of someone saving the best for last. " . . . the warp point isn't defended. It *isn't even mined.*"

De Bertholet couldn't contain himself. "Admiral! This is the final proof! We *must* have broken through the enemy's defensive shell."

Antonov understood perfectly. Every star nation's defensive doctrine—and there had, God knew, been no indication the Bugs disagreed—called for routinely mining warp points that led inward from the frontier towards the core worlds, turning every system into a barrier to at least delay an invader. Thus the *absence* of mines meant Second Fleet must have entered regions where the Bugs felt entirely safe from attack. They'd burst into a defensive vacuum.

He forced his excitement to heel. "You say they're proceeding across the outer system?"

"Yes, Sir. Their vector takes them even further from the primary, out between two gas-giant orbits. There *can't* be anything out there but another warp point."

"Towards which they're in headlong flight!" Triumph clanged in de Bertholet's voice.

"Still," Stovall cautioned, "we can't rule out the possibility of cloaked enemy units. The drones couldn't have detected them." Antonov knew the chief of staff well enough to recognize the signs of the same predatory excitement that was infecting the rest of them, but being the voice of caution had become a self-imposed duty for him.

"Nevertheless, Commodore, we will transit without delay and proceed in pursuit. But because the point you've raised is a valid one, we'll keep the fleet together as we do so, and not allow the faster ships to open up too much distance between themselves and the main body."

"That will slow us considerably, Sir," de Bertholet pointed out. "Especially given the fact that a number of our superdreadnoughts are even slower than usual due to drive damage."

"I'm aware of that, Commander. But I can accept it." Antonov smiled tightly. "You see, I'm not really interested in catching these Bugs. I want them to escape, showing us the location of the next warp point as they do so."

The last of the Fleet reemerged into normal space-time, leaving behind the swirling combat of gunboats and fighters in the system it had fled.

There had never been any real danger of being overhauled by the enemy's main body in the stern chase across that system. That main body had held tenaciously together, and on at least one occasion the swifter ships had clearly been ordered back as they began to leave their slower sisters too far behind. But the enemy's tiny attack craft had ranged far ahead, and many ships bore the marks of their harassing attacks. The gunboats had been expended to fend off those tormentors, and the remaining ones had been left behind.

The Fleet had been concerned by the possibility that the enemy would, despite everything, overtake it before it could transit, for that would have prevented it from performing that which had been its function from the first: to show the enemy this warp point which he himself wanted so badly to be shown.

But things had gone according to plan. Now nothing must be done to alarm this inscrutable foe into changing his plan. Which meant, among other things, that no action must be taken against that small exploratory force whose precise location at any given time had proven so annoyingly difficult to pinpoint.

The disorientation of warp transit subsided, and the heavens stabilized into a pattern bereft of a sun. Rear Admiral Aileen Sommers, commanding Survey Flotilla 19, ordered herself not to be disappointed.

Captain Feridoun Hafezi, her chief of staff, was standing close enough to read her mind. Teeth flashed in his neatly trimmed black beard. "We already knew this was a starless warp nexus, Admiral. The recon drones told us as much."

"Oh, I know. But we've been exploring this worthless warp chain for almost two months, and the only thing to be said for it is that since every system's had just two warp points, there's never been any question where to proceed next. It would've been nice to find something interesting for once. And the fact that our first transit was also into the middle of nowhere makes this almost like rubbing it in."

They'd departed from the conquered system Ivan the Terrible had dubbed Anderson One shortly after its third warp point had been located, entering that first starless warp nexus through a closed warp point. Since then they'd forged on through two systems, both barren— the first a miserable little binary of two red dwarfs, but the second a single star glowing with the yellow light that *ought* to portend life.

"Yes, that last system was a real letdown," Hafezi said, continuing to track her thoughts. "But even if it had had a planet of the right mass at the right orbital radius, it wouldn't have been any good. We knew that star was really young as soon as we got the figures on its rotation rate."

"True. And if there *had* been a life-bearing planet, it probably would've been a solid, writhing mass of Bugs. Still . . ." Sommers started to run a hand through her hair, then remembered that the longish growth—oddly colored, basically dark but with blond streaks—was pulled tightly together at the back of her head. Irritably, she turned away from Hafezi and walked the few steps required to cross the cramped flag bridge of a *Thetis*-class command battle-cruiser like *Jamaica*. She stood in front of the view screen and listened as one ship after another reported successful transit.

In her early forties, Aileen Sommers was young for her rank. She was of medium height and had a figure which none of the men in her life—she'd never married—had been able to describe in terms that helped with a certain deeply buried insecurity. It had been self-evident to them that there was absolutely nothing mannish about her, but rather that she looked like exactly what she was: a very strong woman. In fact, this was self-evident to everyone . . . except her.

Hafezi rejoined her, rubbing the tip of his hawklike nose. Sommers had a weakness for historical holodrama, and her mental image of her chief of staff always included a snowy burnoose and flowing white robes. Which was inaccurate, of course. Hafezi's ancestry was Iranian, not Arab, and it was an important part of him. The third son of a highly respected imam, the captain was proud of the role his family had played in rebuilding—and humanizing—Old Terra's Middle East after the carnage of the Great Eastern war.

"I wonder what's happening with Second Fleet?" he asked now, not expecting an answer. It was the flotilla's staple topic of conversation, and had been ever since they'd departed Anderson One in a different direction from that followed by Antonov's fleet. They'd learned of the outcome in Anderson Two and the discovery of Harnah by courier drone while still surveying that first starless warp nexus. Since then . . .

"Too bad we can't still get courier drones," Hafezi resumed.

"True, but there's nothing to be done about it," Sommers replied. "We've gone too far for drones to have a prayer of reaching us without nav buoys at the warp points." *And,* she didn't need to add, *emplacing such buoys would have been like advertising the flotilla's position with bells and strobe lights for any cloaked Bug pickets that might be lurking in the systems through which they'd passed.*

It was an extension of the same consideration which had led GHQ to issue orders to operate permanently in cloak. Some of the survey specialists hated the way that slowed their work, but Sommers, Captain Kabilovic, and the rest of the "gunslingers" backed it enthusiastically . . . especially after events in Zephrain.

A report distracted Hafezi's attention for a moment. Then he turned back. "Everyone's completed transit, Admiral." An instant later, a status board update verified his words.

Sommers studied the board. Survey flotillas these days were weightier than they'd been in prewar days, but SF 19 was even more powerful than usual, since no separate covering force was available. Besides *Jamaica*, Sommers commanded three other command battle-cruisers to weld her firepower into datagroups, and that firepower included five *Dunkerque*-class missile-armed battle-cruisers, but the centerpiece of the gunslinger array was Captain Kabilovic's fleet carrier *Staghound* and the two attached Ophiuchi *Zirk-Coaalkyr*-class CVLs. Five *Atlanta*-class CLEs provided defensive support for the main combatants, and two *Wayfarer*-class freighters carried extra ordinance as well as recon drones, maintenance materials and everything else required for long-term self-sufficiency.

All of the above were along to protect and nurture the five *Hun*-class cruisers which did the actual survey work . . . and whose crews could perhaps be excused for occasional insufferableness about being the *raison d'etre* for what was, on prewar standards, a not insignificant fighting force.

"All right, Feridoun," the admiral said briskly. "Let's recover the drones; waste not, want not. Then we can commence surveying for warp points. At least we've no planets to check out."

"That's putting the best possible face on things, Sir," Hafezi muttered. Then he brightened. "Maybe there won't *be* any other warp points, and we'll be able to turn back and report that this is a dead-end warp chain. Then maybe we'll be sent somewhere *interesting*."

CHAPTER THIRTY-SEVEN

"They're not our drones!"

The entire auditoriumlike room rose to attention as Ivan Antonov entered, with Stovall in tow. He took his seat and looked out over the full staff and the senior flag officers and their own chiefs of staff—a sea of TFN black and silver varied by the Ophiuchi and their multicolored feathers. The latter were famous—or infamous, depending on one's viewpoint—for their uncomprehending rejection of military punctilio in all its manifestations, but they'd risen to their feet along with everyone else out of simple courtesy, and respect for the supreme commander.

"As you were," Antonov rumbled. "I trust you've all familiarized yourselves thoroughly with the plan for Operation Xenophon. I realize your time has been limited—as was the time Commander de Bertholet and the rest of the staff had to prepare it." Stovall's face showed satisfaction at the implied compliment even as it showed exhaustion—he had suitcases under his bags. It was certainly true that their time had been limited; Second Fleet had only been here in Anderson Four nineteen standard days, and there had been much else to compete for their attention, notably repairs to battle damage.

"I wish," Antonov continued, "to review the considerations behind our planning. After we secured this system and invested the warp point the Bugs had revealed to us in the course of their withdrawal, we probed that warp point with recon drones. Our probing revealed that the next system has the kind of dense minefields whose absence surprised us in this one. This made it out of the question to press on directly through the warp point. Instead, the decision was made to recoup our strength for a carefully prepared offensive against that system, which clearly is the holding position we've all been expecting

700

to encounter. And subsequent probes have reported that the Bug defenders have been reinforced by eighteen superdreadnoughts, suggesting that the Bugs are frantically trying to shore that position up. We cannot give them any more time to do so.

"It is for this reason that our schedule has been moved up, and the commencement of Operation Xenophon set for tomorrow."

Antonov paused and ran his eyes over the faces. He saw worry on many of them, and he understood it fully. "This decision was not an easy one. I am well aware that Second Fleet is weaker than it was before the last battle; only five fresh superdreadnoughts have arrived to offset the cripples we haven't had time to repair." The concern on Jessica van der Gelder's face intensified, for a disproportionate number of the absent cripples back in Anderson Four with Admiral Chin and the Fleet Train came from her task force. At least she'd gotten Chin's battleships in partial recompense. "But on the positive side," Antonov continued, "our fighter groups have been brought back up to full strength, and our SBMHAWK supplies replenished. Furthermore, the tactical equation should be changed in our favor by the new capital missiles." He saw some of the faces brighten a bit, for they'd all been impressed by the new missile package, with its enhanced penetration aids and evasive maneuvering capabilities. After their experience with datalinked Bug point defense, they were more than willing to accept the tradeoff of some payload capacity.

"Before we take up a detailed discussion of the plan, are there any questions' concerning the larger picture?" Antonov scanned the gathering. "Admiral Prescott?"

"Just one thing, Sir. I'm a little concerned about the allocation of our survey assets since SF 24's departure."

There was a murmur of unease. As if they hadn't had enough on their minds here in Anderson Four, a third warp point had come to light, not far, as interplanetary distances went, from the one through which they were preparing to hurl Operation Xenophon. So most of the scout cruisers which had somewhat belatedly set to work in Anderson Three had been rushed forward, and a new flotilla had been organized. It had vanished into the newly discovered warp point only two days before.

"I'm concerned," Prescott repeated, "by the de-emphasis of Anderson Three's warp point survey."

"Commander de Bertholet," Antonov said, turning towards the ops officer, "would you like to respond?"

"Our survey assets are finite, Admiral Prescott, and became even more so when Admiral Sommers' SF 19 was detached in Anderson One. The ones we've got left have become stretched ever more thinly as we've advanced further into enemy space. We've simply had to assign priorities and make choices. When the third warp point turned up here, we had no alternative but to explore beyond it in force. And there may be still others; we haven't completed the survey of this system. I assure you that the search for additional warp points in Anderson Three hasn't been abandoned. We just have fewer ships to do it with."

Prescott said nothing further, for de Bertholet's explanation was unexceptionable. But his face said he wasn't altogether satisfied. *Yes,* Antonov thought, *I too wish we'd started surveying Anderson Three earlier, or had longer to do it before launching Xenophon.* But, he told himself, that was water over the dam. "Thank you, Commander," he said aloud. "And now, if there are no further questions, let us turn to the order in which the first wave's ships will transit."

"General signal from the Flag, Sir. Prepare to execute Xenophon."

"Understood. Anna?" Raymond Prescott glanced at his chief of staff. Captain Anthea Mandagalla studied her display a moment longer, ebon face intent, then nodded.

"We're ready, Sir—and Admiral Taathaanahk's just confirmed *his* readiness."

"Good." Prescott returned his attention to his plot and the diamond dust of SBMHAWK pods awaiting their brief moment of thunderous splendor. That itchy sense of concern he'd felt since Operation Pesthouse began was back, like the irritating phantom itch of the fingers he no longer had, but that was hardly surprising.

And the bastards are still falling back, he reminded himself, and it was true. Yet he knew a part of him would be happier when Second Fleet finally ran into something so hard it *had* to stop. Considering the wear on its systems, it—

"Execute Xenophon!" the com officer snapped, and hundreds of SBMHAWKs began to vanish.

The waiting gunboats had learned a great deal about the enemy's new missile pods' capabilities, and they knew what to do when the first made transit. Every one of them turned instantly away from the warp point at maximum power, racing to escape the pods' acquisition envelope before the deadly, sprint-mode close assault missiles could launch.

It was the first time they had used the tactic, and it worked for many of them. Those it did not work for were doomed, for all the CAM-armed pods launched against them, and the unstoppable weapons blotted them from the universe. Yet more than half the total CSP survived, and the survivors reversed course as quickly as possible, driving in on the warp point once more.

The heavy cruisers of the warp point defense force fared less well.

They were further back, with more time to bring their defensive systems on-line, but they were too slow to evade, and other pods belched standard SBMs against them. Their new datalinked defenses allowed them to destroy hundreds of incoming missiles, and several actually survived. But they were battered and broken, cripples which could inflict little damage upon the enemy. Whatever might be achieved would depend upon the CSP's survivors.

The volume around the warp point was the vestibule of Hell. Bug cruisers blew up, pod-launched AMBAMs streaked outward into the minefields and waiting laser buoys, and TF 23's big, powerful CVAs erupted into an inferno of exploding starships, gunboats, mines, and energy platforms. Surviving laser buoys poured fire into TFNS *Charybdis* and *Succubus,* Vice Admiral Mosby's lead carriers, but this was the sort of attack they'd been *designed* to lead. Their massive armor was rent and buckled, but it held, and Mosby watched her plot stabilize. She felt the whiplash shudder as a full group launch spat from *Thor*'s catapults, more fighter icons erupted from her other carriers, and then—

"Clear decks!" Her ops officer's voice was a bit shriller than usual, but she didn't blame him.

"Turn us around," she replied, and even as *Thor* wheeled to lead the Terran and Ophiuchi carriers back through the warp point, she glanced at her com officer. "Prepare to upload to Admiral Taathaanahk and *Colorado* as soon as we make transit."

She turned back to her plot and winced. The pod-launched AMBAMs had killed most of the Bugs' laser platforms before they could fire; coupled with the CVAs' sheer toughness, that meant most of her ships were going to make it out safely. But the Bugs' new maneuver had saved a lot of their gunboats, and her rearmost units were going to take some heavy hits.

The CSP's own evasion maneuver had carried it beyond immediate striking distance. The nearest gunboat was still far out of range when the big, new carrier vessels made transit, and all of them had launched their attack craft before the defenders could engage them. Nor did the starships linger. Having launched their broods, they wheeled back to the warp point, fleeing with their sensor scans of its environs even as their attack craft howled in to engage the CSP. Dozens of gunboats blew apart, but here and there they broke through, and not all the starships could escape before they were engaged.

Returning carriers spilled from the warp point, transiting with reckless speed and dangerously tight spacing. Most made it safely, but

Dryad and *Norn,* last in the formation, took a heavy pounding from the gunboats which broke through. Once again, *Dryad*'s massive shields and armor stood her in good stead, and she escaped with relatively minor damage. *Norn* was less fortunate, and Ivan Antonov's hard face was expressionless as the shattered, air-streaming wreck staggered from the warp point. A handful of gunboats followed her through, but the massed fighter squadrons covering this side of the warp point made short work of them.

"*Norn*'s taken heavy personnel casualties, Sir," de Bertholet reported. He looked up from his console, and his voice was grim. "Commander Lafferty's assumed command. He's her astrogator—third in the chain of command."

Antonov merely nodded, his face betraying none of his own awareness of what a hell the interior of that ship must be just now. Clearly, more of the Bug CSP had survived than anticipated.

"We are fortunate the damage is no worse," he rumbled. "Pass the word, Commander de Bertholet. We will wait ten minutes before sending the next wave through. That should give Mosby's fighters time to clean up the last gunboats."

"Yes, Sir."

"What do we know of their other forces, Commodore Kozlov?"

Kozlov's eyes were locked on her own display, and she didn't look up as she spoke.

"The main body seems to be hanging extremely far back, Sir. They're over seventy light-minutes out, right on the edge of the CVAs' sensor envelope, so our readings are tentative, but it looks like about sixty ships. Plotting and CIC are still trying to refine their data. At the moment, at least seventy percent of them appear to be superdreadnoughts."

"Um." Antonov leaned back in his command chair and rubbed his chin. That would give them near parity with his own battle-line, but they were enormously outnumbered in escorts. *And, of course, they have* no *carriers. But if they're so far back, why can we see them at all? Why aren't they hiding in cloak?*

De Bertholet sensed his mood. "Sir?"

"I'm simply wondering why they should be so obvious. I don't object to enemies who tell me where they are . . . unless they have something nasty planned for me."

"I was just thinking the same thing, Sir," Stovall said. "It occurs to me that a little caution might be in order."

"Precisely." Antonov shook himself like an irritated bear. "We will take the battle-line through, but we will not advance until we have brought the entire fleet up in support. And we will do so with a fighter shell fifteen light-minutes out in all directions."

✧   ✧   ✧

The enemy attack craft finished off the last gunboats and crippled heavy cruisers. They took losses of their own, but their casualties were minor compared to the carnage they wreaked. When the enemy's heavy units began to transit at last, the space about the warp point was clear of all save the tattered remnants of minefields which could scarcely even inconvenience him.

The waiting deep space force watched from seventy-one light-minutes as ship after ship streamed from the warp point. The enemy's ship-launched mine-killing missiles completed the task of clearing lanes, and fresh waves of attack craft fanned out to cover his flanks as he began to advance. The deep space force watched . . . and then it began to retreat.

"That's affirmative, Sir," Kozlov announced from her station. "All elements of the enemy main body are withdrawing. They're on a vector which, if unchanged, should take them along this projected course." She made adjustments, and a red line appeared in the flag bridge's holo tank. It was a course that made sense only if the objective was to reach another warp point. *God knows there's nothing else to reach,* Antonov thought; the local primary star was a blue giant, shining palely in a view screen which automatically stepped down its brilliance in deference to human eyes. The recon drones hadn't even bothered scanning for planets.

Maybe the lack of anything to defend explained this unBuglike behavior. Still . . .

"Shall we pursue, Admiral?" de Bertholet asked, breaking into his thoughts.

"*Da.* But we will continue to observe all defensive precautions. Anyone who breaks formation without orders will hear from me!"

"That will hold us down to the speed of the slowest superdreadnoughts." De Bertholet carefully made it an observation, not a protest.

"We will proceed even more slowly than that, Commander. Our drives have been overworked in the course of this campaign, without the opportunity for a proper overhaul. I don't wish to abuse them further. We will pursue at a speed which allows us to keep the Bugs under pressure with fighter strikes. Greater speed than that is neither necessary nor, perhaps, desirable."

"What do you mean, Sir?" Stovall asked.

"Their failure to engage their cloaking ECM still disturbs me. If there's any kind of trap awaiting us, I want to be sure our ships still have their full tactical speed capability available. For this reason, I'd rather not push our drives to their limit just now. If, on the other hand, there's nothing more here than meets the eye—if, that is, it's a simple case of the Bugs retreating because a useless warp nexus like this isn't worth fighting for—then I don't *want* to overtake them before they've shown us the warp point through which they intend to escape."

"They're falling back, Sir!" Captain Mandagalla sounded as if she couldn't quite believe her own report. *Crete* and the rest of Prescott's fast superdreadnoughts and battle-cruisers led Second Fleet towards the enemy, covered by the smoothly practiced strikegroups of TF 21's CVLs, and Prescott felt his matching surprise as his plot confirmed his chief of staffs report. They *were* falling back, and that itch of worry stirred again.

It wasn't the first time the Bugs had retreated, yet he couldn't quite quash the itch. They *couldn't* retreat fast enough to avoid action forever, and given the massive gunboat force those ships must mother, the logical move would have been to linger just beyond SBMHAWK range, then rush the warp point behind a wall of gunboats and kamikazes. They probably couldn't have *stopped* Second Fleet—especially if Antonov had deployed reserve SBMHAWKs—but it would certainly have been their best chance to hurt it badly. So why hadn't they?

"Anything from the recon fighters, Jacques?" he asked sharply.

"No, Sir," the ops officer replied. "They're over ten light-minutes out already. If there were anything out there, they'd have seen it by now."

The cloaked battle-cruisers watched from fifty light-minutes out as the enemy moved to pursue the retreating deep space force. He was not moving at the full speed of which he was capable. That was good; it would take him longer to overtake and destroy his targets.

The battle-cruisers waited until the last enemy vessel had cleared the mines, then began their stealthy advance towards the warp point at twenty thousand kilometers per second. It would take them over twelve hours to reach their destination, but that had been calculated from the outset. They were too few in number to affect the outcome of the battle to come, anyway . . . and perfectly sufficient for their mission.

Commander Francis Lafferty, acting CO of the brutally wounded CVA *Norn*, let himself sink into the astrogator's command chair with a carefully suppressed groan of exhaustion. He was just as happy Captain Duk's chair had been destroyed by the hit which killed her. He'd liked the captain almost as much as he'd respected her; sitting in her chair would have seemed a slap at her memory, yet Regs and tradition alike would have left him no choice if it had survived her.

At least we've got the command deck pressurized again, he thought bitterly. *That's more than half our compartments can say.*

Norn would fight again, thanks entirely to the engineers who'd designed her for maximum survivability, but Lafferty felt another wrench of anguish as he thought of the hundreds of people who wouldn't be aboard when she did. The anguish only intensified when he added the already confirmed losses her strikegroup had suffered, and he jerked himself away from that painful subject and looked at the visual display. TFNS *Hyacinth,* the *Dunedin*-class CLE detached to stand by the big assault carrier, floated in its depths like a reminder there were still friends in a hostile universe, and just seeing her was an enormous psychological relief.

His com panel chirped, and he pressed the key. "Bridge, Comman— Captain speaking," he corrected himself with a grimace.

"We've got Drive Four and Five back on-line, Sir." Lieutenant Driscoll, *Norn*'s senior surviving engineer, had worked nonstop for twenty hours since the rest of Second Fleet had left the CVA behind to lick her wounds. Her dirty face was etched with deep lines on the com screen, and Lafferty wondered if she would ever look young again.

"Good work, Jeanette," he said sincerely, and was rewarded by a wan smile. *Norn* could make half her designed speed now, and he turned his chair—one of the irritating things about its location was that it *required* him to turn to see his bridge crew—to face his helmsman. "As soon as Lieutenant Driscoll signals readiness, take us to maximum available. I'll feel better with a little more space between us and the warp point."

"Aye, aye, Sir," the helmsman replied.

Lafferty was just turning back to his panel when the acting tac officer spoke.

"Drones transiting the warp point," he announced, then paled. "They're not ours, Sir!"

Lafferty jumped out of his chair and crossed to Tactical, and his face went as pale as the tactical officer's as he saw not simply dozens but scores of drones streaking past his ship.

"Vector?" he snapped.

"They're heading straight up the chain, Sir," the tac officer said grimly, and Lafferty's stomach froze. A few drones passed close enough for *Hyacinth*'s point defense to kill, but ninety percent got through, and he could think of only one reason for the Bugs to be sending them.

"How many drones do *we* have left, Com?" he demanded.

"Uh, ten—no, twelve, Sir, but two are damaged. I don't know how reliable they are."

Lafferty's mind raced. With no way to know what course Second Fleet had pursued since his own ship had been detached he couldn't use courier drones to alert the Admiral from here. He could warn the Fleet Train and Alpha Centauri, but to warn Antonov—

He faced the implications squarely, then drew a deep breath. "Stand by to record."

"Standing by, Sir."

"'Enemy courier drones have just been dispatched past this ship,'" Lafferty told the pickup in a flat, overcontrolled voice. "'They are headed up the chain towards Centauri. I repeat, towards Centauri. I will attempt to advise Admiral Antonov.'" He started to say something more, then stopped himself. Anyone who received that message wouldn't need him to tell them the Bugs wouldn't have launched drones unless there was someone to receive them.

Someone lurking along Second Fleet's only line of retreat.

"Got it?" he said instead.

"On the chip, Sir."

"Very well. Append our log and be sure the location and time chops are current, then transmit it to *Hyacinth*. Inform Commander Watanabe that I want him to download it to his drones, then launch half of them for Centauri and the other half to Admiral Chin."

"Aye, aye, Sir. And our own drones?"

"Download the same message and set them for a circular search pattern. Tag their beacons with an all-ships signal and lock in the Code Omega release sequence."

"But—" the com officer began, then closed his mouth as Lafferty met his eyes. He hesitated a moment longer, then nodded. "Aye, Sir," he said quietly, and Lafferty stared down into the plot. He felt the tac officer beside him and tasted the other man's fear as he worked through the logic Lafferty had already followed to its terrifying conclusion.

"We don't have much speed," Lafferty said almost thoughtfully. "If whoever sent those drones is covering the warp point, we'll never be able to outrun them. But if we take *Hyacinth* back through with us, one of us may be able to get a transmission—or at least a drone— off to the Admiral."

He didn't add "before they kill us," but the tac officer swallowed audibly, then nodded. Unless there was time for Plotting to get them a bearing on the rest of Second Fleet, they couldn't even use lasers or give their drones a definite vector. They *might* have time for an omnidirectional transmission, but in twenty hours, Antonov could have moved as much as a hundred light-minutes. That was too far for an omnidirectional message—and if the Bugs who'd launched those drones were directly atop the warp point, it would take far longer than they were likely to have to get the com lasers a bearing. Which meant it would all come down to the twelve drones *Norn* still had, and on a blind search pattern. . . .

"I want as many nonessential personnel as possible off both ships first," Lafferty said quietly. "Tell *Hyacinth* to fill up her small craft, then fill ours, as well. Cram them in as tight as you can without overloading their life support, then get back to me."

"Yes, Sir," the tac officer said just as quietly. "I'll see to it."

The enemy fleet had moved well beyond its sensor range of the warp point in pursuit of the deep space force. It was safe to launch gunboats now, and the battle-cruisers deployed one hundred and twenty of them.

TFNS *Norn* and TFNS *Hyacinth* made transit. They survived for twenty-three seconds . . . far too short a time for their sensor systems to stabilize or their transmitters to come on-line.

Even with the auto-launch Omega sequence on-line, only five of *Norn*'s drones got away. Pouncing gunboats killed two, and the other three fled blindly into the depths of the system.

CHAPTER THIRTY-EIGHT

Heralds of Armageddon

Rear Admiral Michael Chin strolled onto the battle-cruiser *Psyche*'s flag bridge with a pleasant sense of repletion. Chin was a small man whose careful tailoring couldn't disguise a slight tubbiness. That caused him the occasional moment of depression, but he was also a cheerful extrovert who liked his simple pleasures, and breakfast had hit the spot nicely. His silver-chased coffee mug bore the crest of TFNS *Prince George*, whose ship's company had presented it to then-Captain Chin on the day he made commodore, and he sipped from it as he ambled across to Commander Maslett, his ops officer.

"Good morning, Sir."

"Morning, Andy." Chin took another sip while he studied the plot. Second Fleet's support ships lay in Anderson Four, near the warp point to Anderson Three, prepared to retreat towards Centauri at need, and a few small craft plied back and forth on routine missions. "Looks quiet," the admiral went on. "Anything more from Admiral Antonov?"

"Not since his initial drones," Maslett replied.

"Huh." Chin lowered his mug and pulled on his nose with his left hand. He was basically Second Fleet's grocer at the moment, but epicurean or not, he was also an experienced—and good—Battle Fleet flag officer, and the enemy's antics puzzled him. There had to be a reason the Bugs were falling back instead of counterattacking, but he was damned if he could think of one. Unless they knew reinforcements were coming and they were trying to rendezvous before Antonov hit them? But if that was the case, why not cloak? A star system was a huge hiding place, and Second Fleet knew the locations of none of Anderson Five's other warp points. If Chin had commanded an inferior system-defense force and known reinforcements were coming, *he* certainly would have stayed cloaked till they got there. He would have taken up a position near the reinforcements' entry warp point and hidden until they arrived to join him—and without carriers, he would have gone right on hiding until he actually engaged the enemy.

Of course, *these* defenders were Bugs, and no one—with the possible exception of Marcus LeBlanc—was prepared even to try to explain how their minds (if any) worked. It was also true the hammering they'd taken over the last five months might have shaken them into panic-born stupidity, he supposed, but it still seemed odd.

Well, that was Antonov's problem, and Chin could think of few people better suited to handle it. His own problems were more prosaic, and he grimaced as he glanced at the icons of the damaged units which had replaced his tried and tested battleships. He'd hated giving up BG 30, but he supposed it would have been churlish to complain when he'd been given eight SDs in exchange. It would have been nice if those SDs hadn't been chosen because they'd been so badly shot up, but whatever shape their armor might be in, his repair ships had gotten most of their *internal* systems back on-line. And, he reminded himself, damaged or not, a superdreadnought was still a superdreadnought.

He smiled at the thought, nodded to Maslett, and headed for the com section to catch up on the day-to-day details of his command.

It was getting on towards lunch, and Admiral Chin was updating reports on his briefing room terminal when a signal warbled at him. His head snapped up as the priority of the two-toned signal registered, and he stabbed at his com key.

"Yes?"

"Sir, we've got drones transiting to Anderson Three." It was Commander Guthrey, his chief of staff, and the report on Chin's display vanished as he opened a window to the com system. Guthrey's face replaced it, and his expression was as tense as his voice. Chin raised an eyebrow, and Guthrey's mouth tightened.

"They weren't ours, Sir," he said quietly, "and we make it at least fifty of them."

"Headed *up* the chain?" Chin's question was sharp, and Guthrey nodded grimly.

Chin felt as if someone had just punched him in the belly. It didn't take a mental giant to realize the Fleet Train was directly in the path of whatever might respond to those drones.

"Did we kill any of them?' he demanded.

"A few, Sir—not many." Guthrey shrugged. "We only had a light CSP out, and they took our pilots completely by surprise and blew past us before anyone could really respond."

"Damn." Chin said the word softly, then closed his eyes and made himself think. If only their survey efforts hadn't fallen so far behind! The Navy still knew virtually nothing about Anderson Three, but the data on One and Two was piling up. If there was an undiscovered Bug warp point back there, and the courier drones said there was, then it was most probably in Three—which put it right on top of Rear Admiral Michael Chin.

He sat for perhaps forty-five seconds, mind flashing through possibilities and options, but he had too little information to assess the former . . . and far too few of the latter.

"Alert the Task Force," he said. "Send the escort to GQ and tell the service ship skippers we're moving out in ten minutes. Then have Astrogation plot a course to take us into Anderson Three and on a sharp dogleg back to Anderson Two."

"A dogleg's going to increase our transit time," Guthrey warned.

"I know. But they wouldn't call in the troops unless they thought they had enough to deal with all of Second Fleet. That means *we* sure as hell can't fight them, but if we make transit quickly enough, we *may* be able to get far enough away from the warp point to hide from them."

"Yes, Sir." Guthrey still didn't like it, but he nodded sharply.

"As soon as you've passed those messages, fire up the com sats to Centauri and—"

"Excuse me, Sir." Andrew Maslett's voice cut into the circuit. "We're picking up more drones, and this time they're ours."

"From Admiral Antonov?"

"No, Sir. Most of them are headed up-chain, but five are coming straight for us, and their beacons say they're from *Hyacinth*. Com is querying them, but they're still six light-minutes out."

"From *Hyacinth*?" Chin's eyes met Guthrey's. The chief of staff shrugged in helpless ignorance, and Chin's jaws clamped tight. *Hyacinth* was only a CLE, so why would *she* dispatch drones to him? If Second Fleet had been engaged, any message should be coming from Antonov or one of his subordinate flag officers, not a light cruiser's skipper!

"All right," he said again. "Pass the rest of those orders, Stan, but hold the message to GHQ until we've had a chance to read *Hyacinth's* drones."

"Yes, Sir."

"I'll see you on Flag Bridge in two minutes," Chin concluded, and cut the circuit.

"We've got the drone download, Sir," Maslett said. Ten dragging minutes had passed since the drone beacons had been picked up. Most of the Fleet Train was already into Anderson Three and headed for

Centauri, but *Psyche* had lagged behind to recover the drones, and Chin turned to his ops officer with painfully divided emotions. Part of him burned with impatience for the message's contents, but another part wanted to delay the moment as long as possible, as if not knowing could somehow keep whatever it said from being true.

"Very well, Andy. Let's see it," he said quietly, and the small com screen at his command chair bunked to life with Commander Lafferty's brief message.

Chin watched it with mingled relief and frustration. At least his worst fear—that Second Fleet had been annihilated, leaving *Hyacinth* its sole survivor—had been disproved, but Lafferty's warning had been dispatched two days ago. God only knew what had happened since!

At least Lafferty was in position to see the drones coming, he reminded himself, *and we're tied into the comsat chain to Centauri. From the timing, the bastards waited until Antonov was too far out from the warp point to see them* go. *That means this probably* is *an ambush, but* Norn saw it coming. By now she's warned Antonov, and we can alert Centauri a hell of a lot faster than if we had to rely on drones of our own.

"At least we've got some warning," he said quietly.

"Yes, Sir." Guthrey didn't add "for what it's worth," but Chin heard it anyway.

"Update our sitrep, then get it off to Centauri," the admiral went on. "Be sure to append our projected course, and inform Sky Marshal Avram we'll try to evade on our way home."

"Yes, Sir."

A brisk nod dismissed his staffers to their jobs, and the message flashed at light-speed along the chain of satellites Second Fleet had emplaced across Anderson Three. That chain stretched all the way to Centauri, and the message, slowed only briefly at each manned warp point relay station, would reach Centauri within little more than twenty-three hours. Unless, of course, the Bugs had already cut the chain somewhere ahead of the Fleet Train.

Chin leaned back in his command chair, eyes cold as he watched the icons of his command run for safety. His covering force consisted of only eight damaged superdreadnoughts, eleven battle-cruisers, five of them damaged, and five Ophiuchi CVLs, with only a hundred and twenty fighters embarked. That was all he had to cover thirty-three mammoth freighters, transports, and mobile shipyards, and there were well over a hundred thousand Allied personnel aboard those waddling service ships. If Bug gunboats got loose among them . . .

He made himself push the thought aside, but it was hard. He spared one more moment for a silent prayer for Second Fleet's warships, then turned to face the far grimmer task of trying to save his own command.

✧   ✧   ✧

The long-anticipated courier drones arrived at last, flicking past the massive warp point fortifications, and the starships stirred as the robotic messengers summoned the Fleet to battle. Ninety-eight warships, fifty of them superdreadnoughts and six the new, more powerful battle-line units which were finally ready for action, streamed through the warp point in a long, sullen chain of destruction and advanced into the enemy's rear.

The attention signal jerked Michael Chin awake. He sat up in his sleeping cabin, rubbing his eyes, and a leaden hammer pounded the back of his forehead. Three exhausting days had passed, and he felt every one of them. A glance at the chronometer told him he'd gotten only about three hours in the sack. It wasn't enough, yet it had taken all his willpower to get even that much. He grimaced and punched the key, accepting the com call audio only.

"Talk to me," he said harshly.

"Plotting's picked something up, Sir." Andrew Maslett sounded grim. "Looks like about two hundred gunboats."

"On an attack vector?" Chin was surprised he could sound so calm when his mouth was suddenly a kiln.

"Not yet, Sir. They're over a light-hour out, and it looks like they're still sweeping for us, but with all these freighters and transports—"

Maslett left the rest unsaid, and Chin swung his feet to the decksole.

"Understood." He rubbed his forehead. A light-hour. Even if the Bugs headed in to the attack, they'd take almost seven hours to reach him. Of course, he wouldn't know they'd even started in for an hour or so after they did, but naval officers were used to thinking in those terms.

His best defense would be his fighters, but they'd be outnumbered something like two-to-one. Some of the Bugs were going to get through. He clenched his jaw and made himself accept that, but his brain was coming fully awake, and he felt it pushing out to other considerations.

Andy was right. He had his warships cloaked, but the gunboats were certain to spot his service ships. When they did, they'd attack . . . and he hoped they would. They wouldn't be here unless there were, indeed, heavy enemy forces somewhere between him and safety, and that meant the *worst* thing they could do was take their time. He had a chance, however slim, against this many gunboats, but he needed another eighty-four hours to make it back into Anderson Two. If the bastards settled for shadowing his starships while one of them went back and whistled up still more gunboats, they could guarantee their ability to swamp his defenses.

"Okay, Andy," he said finally. "Alert the task force and have Commodore Haasnaahr arm his fighters for an anti-gunboat strike. If they head our way, we'll hit them as far out as we can and try to bleed them before they enter the escorts' engagement envelope."

"Yes, Sir. Shall I alter course?"

"No point," Chin sighed. "They know where we're headed. Our only hope was to get far enough off a least-time course they'd miss us entirely, and we didn't make it."

"Yes, Sir," Maslett said very quietly.

"Send an update to Centauri. You'd better get a flight of drones off, too—a heavy one. For all we know, they've already taken out the relay and put a CSP on the Anderson Two warp point. Append our current tac data and inform the Sky Marshal my intentions remain unchanged, and I'll see you on flag bridge in twenty minutes."

"Sir, it might not hurt to get a little more—"

"I appreciate the thought, Andy, but I'm not going to get back to sleep. I might as well sweat it out up there with you." Chin's lips twitched in a parody of a smile Maslett couldn't see. "Ask Chief Reynolds to make sure we've got plenty of coffee. It's going to be a long night."

The units which had detected the enemy's starships represented less than a quarter of the Fleet's total gunboat strength, but that strength was deployed in widely spread search groups, and much could happen in the time it would take to recall and assemble it all. Despite the fifty-light-minute range, the enemy's emissions signatures made it clear these were support ships. They would be unarmed and only weakly shielded, yet it was remotely possible they might somehow slip away. Under the circumstances, there could be only one decision.

One gunboat turned back to the Fleet and a second was sent back to its home system. Six more were detached to keep the enemy under observation, and the remaining hundred and ninety-six altered course sharply towards the enemy.

"Well, they see us now," Commander Guthrey said flatly.

Chin simply nodded, then looked at Maslett. "ETA?"

"CIC makes it roughly three and a half hours, Sir."

"Um." Chin folded his hands behind himself and rocked in place. The Bugs' decision to detach some of their number was ominous, but the rest were coming in, and he tried to feel glad he at least had a chance to whittle them down before they called in a really heavy strike.

"Tell Haasnaahr to launch in two hours, Stan," he told Guthrey quietly. "I want them hit fourteen light-minutes out, but we can't afford losses this soon. His pilots are to use FM3s and stand off. Once they launch, their speed will get them back here with thirty minutes to rearm, reorganize, and swap off flight crews before the *Bugs* get here, and their job this time out is to whittle the bastards down, not to stop them dead. Be sure they understand that."

The gunboats continued their run. The enemy had made no attempt to alter course—not that it would have helped—but he had launched attack craft. There were barely half as many of them as there were gunboats, but their presence proved there were warships out there, as well. They were cloaked, not visible on sensors, yet none of the enemy's main fleet could possibly have gotten this far since the summoning drones were launched. No doubt they were no more than the support echelon's escorts, in which case they could not be particularly powerful or numerous. It was likely the gunboats were about to lose heavily, but if the attack craft were foolish enough to close, they would lose, as well. And whatever happened to this strike, others would close in soon.

"There they go."

Chin didn't look up. He was certain whoever had spoken didn't even realize he had, and his own attention was locked to the fourteen-minute-old icons in the plot.

Squadrons began to flash from green to amber as they salvoed their FM3 missiles from just outside the Bugs' point defense envelope. It was like some bloodless simulation . . . or would have been, if every man and woman on *Psyche*'s flag bridge hadn't known what would happen when the "simulation's" survivors reached the task force.

The long launch range didn't help. It reduced accuracy by almost fifty percent, and the fighters needed at least five hits to saturate the Bugs' point defense and guarantee a kill. That took most of a squadron's entire missile load at this range, and he had only twenty squadrons.

Bug icons began to vanish, and he felt the hungry approval of his officers and ratings. The fighters were doing a little better than projected; some of the squadron COs had clearly opted to ignore orders and split their fire between multiple targets—no doubt they'd figured out how unlikely they were to survive to be reprimanded—and this time disobedience was paying off.

The last fighter salvoed its ordnance and broke off, still never having entered the Bugs' range, and he waited while Maslett tallied the results.

"Twenty-seven, Sir," the ops officer announced. "They're down to a hundred sixty-nine. They'll be entering our capital missile envelope in twelve more minutes."

"Turn the support ships away," Chin directed. "Let's slow their overtake."

"And the escorts?"

"We'll stay right where we are, Andy." Chin smiled mirthlessly. "According to the boffins, their gunboats' sensors aren't as good as our recon fighters', and they're probably pretty fixated on the support ships right now. Let's see if we can't play road block."

"It's worth a try, Sir," Maslett agreed with a matching smile.

The enemy changed course at last. There was still no sign of his warships—the attack craft had vanished aboard their cloaked mother ships—but it was likely the escorts were waiting somewhere between the gunboats and their prey. Yet they could not engage the gunboats without revealing their own positions when they fired, and the massed squadrons bored in for the kill.

"Here they come, Sir," Maslett muttered, and Chin glanced at his com link to Commodore Haasnaahr aboard OADCS *Zirk-Cothmyriea*.

"Ready, Haasnaahr?"

"Yesss, Sssir," the fierce-beaked Ophiuchi replied, and Chin nodded.

"Good. Inform Admiral Triam she may engage, Andy."

"Aye, aye, Sir."

Five battle-cruisers and five superdreadnoughts began slamming CMs into the gunboats. Their fire control was far better than any fighter's, and their capital missiles were *much* harder to stop. Gunboats tore apart, and Chin watched the fireballs sweep closer. The incoming missiles told the Bugs where the firing ships were, and they altered course to race straight for them.

"Now, Haasnaahr!" Chin snapped, and a hundred and twenty Ophiuchi fighters suddenly launched *behind* the Bugs. Splitting off those carriers and their escorting *Broadswords* had been a gamble, but now the fighters launched at such short range they were already in firing distance—and the gunboats' blind spot—before the Bugs even realized they were there.

Shoals of FM3s streaked out, unopposed by the point defense the Bugs couldn't bring to bear, and the *Broadswords'* heavy broadsides came with them. Over eighty gunboats died in barely forty seconds, and the Bug formation came apart. There were still almost a hundred of them, and half looped back, looking for the carriers. Most of the others continued their runs on the battle-line units, but perhaps twenty ignored carriers and superdreadnoughts alike, racing across the escorts' engagement envelope to pursue the support ships.

The escorts did their best to nail the evaders, but they had to defend themselves, as well, and thirteen Bugs got away clean. Chin swore viciously as he watched them go, but the ones actually engaging his warships were like spiders in a flame. The Ophiuchi pilots fired their last missiles and drove into them with internal lasers, and the close-range plot dissolved into a swirl of dogfighting madness. Ship-launched missiles continued to reach out into the carnage, homing on the more powerful emissions of the gunboats' hybrid drives, and the Bugs were slaughtered.

But some of them closed to FRAM range before they died, and TFNS *Scharnhorst* found herself targeted by at least a dozen. FRAMs smashed the battle-cruiser's shields flat, and then, despite her wild evasion maneuvers, two gunboats rammed her cleanly. All three vessels vanished in an intolerable glare, and the last two gunboats swerved to attack her sister *Guam,* only to be bounced and killed barely a thousand kilometers short of target by an Ophiuchi fighter squadron.

And then, suddenly, it was over. *Scharnhorst* was gone, but she was the only warship Chin had lost. It looked like Haasnaahr had lost twenty or thirty irreplaceable fighters, but the rest of the escorts were intact. In fact, none of the survivors reported more than minor damage, and he let himself smile with cold pleasure. They'd massacred the bastards, and badly as *Scharnhorst's* loss hurt, it could have been far, far worse.

He opened his mouth to congratulate his people, but Maslett spoke before he could.

"Captain Hardiman's just reported, Sir," the ops officer said quietly. "I'm afraid we've lost *Dover, Cromarty,* and *Columbine.*"

Chin winced, his satisfaction suddenly ashes in his mouth. *Dover* and *Cromarty* were bad enough—the mobile shipyards had each carried a crew of fifteen hundred—but *Columbine* had been a transport, with over five thousand Fleet replacement personnel on board.

"Shit," someone said bitterly behind him. Chin began to turn to see who it was, when a com rating stiffened at her panel, and he looked at her, instead.

"Excuse me, Sir," the young woman said. "Commodore Haasnaahr reports that *Cestus* has just picked up another strike seventy light-minutes astern and closing."

"How many?" the admiral asked Maslett harshly, and the ops officer queried CIC. Chin watched his shoulders tighten before the commander turned his chair to face him.

"Plotting says at least three hundred, Sir—and another group's coming in from port. They're still too far out for a count, but they may be even stronger."

"Christ," someone whispered, and Chin's mouth tightened. Six hundred more—at least. Given the gunboat complements Bug superdreadnoughts mothered, that meant there were *at least* fifty capital ships out there somewhere. Their obvious mission was to close off Second Fleet's retreat, and he doubted they'd let themselves be diverted from that to chase down his task force. But they didn't *need* to divert from it. They could use only their gunboats and destroy every ship he had without even slowing their own progress towards Anderson Five.

"Get the fighters rearmed," he heard himself say, "then bring the service ships back inside our point defense umbrella and have Commodore Hardiman deploy his SBMHAWKs. Stan, you and Astrogation work out a course to take us away from the group to port. We need to tempt them into hitting us as two separate strikes rather than one big one."

"Yes, Sir," Guthrey replied.

"Com, record for transmission to Second Fleet."

"Recording, Sir."

"'Admiral Antonov, this is Rear Admiral Chin. We've engaged and destroyed approximately two hundred enemy gunboats, but we have what appears to be another six hundred on our scanners. I stress that these are how many we've *seen*; there may well be more out there. The numbers we've observed suggest at least fifty capital ships are headed your way. All I can do is try to get my command out; I cannot provide any security for your rear. I've dispatched messages to Centauri and hope and believe a relief force will be organized ASAP, but I can't guarantee even that much.'" He paused, trying to think of some encouraging thing he could add, but there was nothing. "'Good luck, Sir,'" he said softly instead, and nodded to the com officer.

"I want that downloaded to every drone in the task force. Hold back *Psyche*'s own drones, but program all the others for a maximum spread pattern in Anderson Five. And be sure you append full log downloads. Admiral Antonov has to know what's coming up his backside."

"Aye, aye, Sir," the com officer said, and Chin turned back to his staff.

"All right, ladies and gentlemen," he said flatly. "Now we have to find a way out of this. Any suggestions?"

CHAPTER THIRTY-NINE

The Trap Springs

Everyone on TFNS *Xingú's* flag bridge had learned the inadvisability of bothering Sky Marshal Avram—not that most of them would have been inclined to do so in any circumstances. Even now, with the relief force assembled and ready for departure, she still paced in a veritable fury of impatience, occasionally turning to the view screen and glaring at Alpha Centauri A and the distant orange flare of Alpha Centauri B for reminding her by their presence that she hadn't yet departed the system.

Stop being such a goddamned kvetch, she chided herself. Admiral Chin's warnings of disaster had arrived only two standard days before, and this relief force—seventeen superdreadnoughts, ten battleships, eleven battle-cruisers and twelve heavy cruisers—had been organized slightly sooner than humanly possible. She would have preferred a heavier force—especially some carriers—but this was all that was available out of the Home Fleet elements immediately at hand. She'd commandeered virtually every one of Admiral MacGregor's mobile units—aside from those currently undergoing scheduled overhauls—and waiting for anything more to arrive from Sol would take time they didn't have. *And,* she thought grimly, *we've already picked Sol so bare for Pesthouse and Fourth Fleet that waiting wouldn't add anything worthwhile to my strength, anyway.*

No, she couldn't really complain about the pace of the preparations. And she'd had to waste less time than she'd feared shouting down various old ladies of both genders who'd gotten their undies in a bunch at the notion of the Sky Marshal taking personal command. No, she wouldn't have been in such a vile mood, except . . .

As though to rub it in, a com rating looked up. "Sky Marshal,

720

Admiral Mukerji sends his apologies for the delay and reports that all elements of his command are ready for departure."

No good deed goes unpunished, Avram philosophized to herself. If she hadn't blocked Agamemnon Waldeck's attempt to put him in command of Fifth Fleet over Vanessa Murakuma's head, Vice Admiral Terence Mukerji would have been shipped off to the Romulus Chain. As it was, he'd been at Centauri in circumstances under which there was no way she could escape having him as her second in command.

"My compliments to Admiral Mukerji," she said through gritted teeth, "and if he's *quite* ready, perhaps we can proceed." Her staff took the hint; orders began to go out, and the ships of the relief force began to swing out of their orbits around the Nova Terra/Eden binary planet and set their courses for the Anderson One warp point.

Avram commanded herself to calmness. There was no way to know what had happened to the Fleet Train since Chin had dispatched his drones. Even less could she know what had happened to Second Fleet. But in all this fog of imponderables, she held fast to one datum. Norn had fired off her drones about six standard days ago, and surely she'd sent them to Antonov as well as to Chin. With an ease bred of two days' constant repetition, Avram ran the mental calculations: at their best speed, Bug superdreadnoughts would take a hundred and ninety hours to cross from one warp point to the other in Anderson Four— *after* transiting from Anderson Three. So Antonov ought to have at least a week's warning. Given that . . . well, if Ivan Nikolayevich couldn't extricate Second Fleet from Anderson Five and be well on the way back towards Centauri, nobody could.

The enemy's support echelon had proved a much tougher opponent than anticipated. The first gunboat strike was annihilated for very little return, and the second suffered just as badly for even scantier results, for the enemy's freighters had carried large stores of missile pods. The support echelon had deployed hundreds of them to cover its flanks, and the gunboats had not even seen them . . . until their CAMs launched.

The third strike had done much better. The enemy had exhausted his pods against the second, and the third destroyed at least six of his warships and a third of his freighters, but once again it took heavy losses. Indeed, losses were so severe that the gunboats which had been detached to seal the warp point through which any enemy effort to dispatch relief forces to his trapped fleet must enter the system had been diverted against the stubborn support ships.

The diversion, while irritating, created no problems. In effect, the fleet simply exchanged its gunboats for the blocking force's, which, after striking the enemy's support ships, would continue on to overtake it before it left the system. The exchange had delayed blockage of the warp point by some hundred hours, but the new gunboats had ample time to reach their position, for the enemy could not even begin responding until warning drones reached him.

Unfortunately, the support echelon proved a still dangerous foe when the fourth strike went in. Barely twenty percent of its support ships survived the attack, and reports on warship losses—while less definite— indicated its escorts had been hit equally hard. But before they died, they killed almost half their attackers. The Fleet would be going into battle with its gunboats badly understrength. Even more irritatingly, it had been impossible to send in a fifth strike without prohibitively delaying either the warp point blocking force or the Fleet, and the surviving enemy ships had managed to slip away into the depths of the system.

In the long run, it mattered little. Badly damaged, low on ammunition, and trapped between the blocking force and the fleet contingents about to annihilate their main fleet, those ships had nowhere to run. Eventually they would be hunted down, and the Fleet refused to allow them to further divert it from its primary mission.

Ivan Antonov's plot flashed with fury as another fighter strike crashed into the enemy. The Bugs' futile attempt to evade him had ended in a cataclysm of violence, and his face was hard as he watched the death toll rise.

It was fortunate he'd decided to bring the battle-line into action, for the Bug gunboats' AFHAWKs had inflicted brutal losses on the fighter jocks of the first strike. Unfortunately for the Bugs, losses hadn't been brutal enough. Once their AFHAWKs were exhausted, the gunboats had been easy meat, and while the escort fighters were exacting their revenge, the battle-line had closed to SBM range of the main enemy force. Second Fleet had taken ugly losses of its own, but the second, FRAM-armed strike had been waiting on the catapults when the first was launched. Antonov had sent it in along with the missiles, and the need to stop both fighters *and* missiles had fatally overloaded the Bugs' point defense. Not that it had been quick or simple, for Antonov had declined to close to energy or even standard missile range. He'd lost his monopoly on command datalink, but he had more heavy launchers than the enemy this time, and despite his initial strike's losses, he also had an enormous fighter strength. He'd used both to batter the enemy for almost thirty hours at long range before he finally committed to close action, and his eyes glowed coldly as the fighters blew through the final gunboats and swept over what was left of the Bug starships.

"I think it's almost over, Sir," de Bertholet said quietly. "We only lost about twenty fighters this time."

"*Da.* All that remains is the cleanup," Antonov agreed. He rose from his command chair and stretched hugely. "You did well, Commander." His eyes swept the rest of his flag bridge crew. "You all did. Commodore Stovall, please pass my thanks to the entire Fleet."

"Of course, Sir." Stovall hid a smile. Ivan the Terrible truly had mellowed, he thought.

"Good." Antonov walked closer to the main plot and gazed into it, rubbing his jaw in thought as de Bertholet stepped up beside him. "Still nothing from the recon fighters?"

"Not a word, Sir." The ops officer tugged on an earlobe, then shrugged. "Shall I move them further out?"

"No." Antonov shook his head. The recon fighters watching Second Fleet's flanks were already at fifteen light-minutes. If he pushed them much further out, he'd have to spread them so thin they might miss a cloaked enemy, and fifteen light-minutes would give an hour and a half of warning before even a gunboat launched from cloak could reach attack range. Against *uncloaked* attackers, the warning time jumped to almost ten hours.

He shoved his hands into the pockets of his uniform tunic and thought. He'd lost few ships in the engagement, but several were damaged, and the engineers' reports on drive reliability were even worse now. This particular bunch of Bugs had declined to show him the next outbound warp point and, deep inside, he was just as glad. He needed to regroup, bring up reinforcements, get his rear properly surveyed, and, above all, service his drives before he advanced again.

"We will remain here for seventy-two hours once the enemy has been mopped up, Commander de Bertholet," he said finally. "That will give us time for shipboard resource repairs and to reorganize our strikegroups."

"Yes, Sir."

"We will, of course, be somewhat more vulnerable while we do so," Antonov continued thoughtfully. "So once the strikegroups have reorganized, I think we *will* push the recon shell a bit further out. Inform Admiral Taathaanahk that I want a third of his regular fighters fitted with external sensor packs to expand the shell to twenty light-minutes."

"Yes, Sir."

"Good, Commander," Antonov murmured. "Good."

The dispersed attack groups slowed their advance. The enemy had destroyed the decoy force, but now he sat motionless. His high tactical speed always made him difficult to engage on the Fleet's terms, and the attack groups were grateful for his lack of activity. The longer he sat, the better, for the fourth and final attack group drew closer with every hour. Any one of the four could engage the enemy's total force on terms of near equality; with his retreat sealed and vast numbers of gunboats coming up from adjacent systems, his inferiority would be crushing.

And best of all, he did not even know he was in danger.

"I think you'd better look at this report from Captain Trailman, Sir," Jacques Bichet said.

Raymond Prescott raised a hand at Lieutenant Commander Ruiz, his logistics officer, interrupting their discussion of TF 21's increasingly strained resources, and turned to Bichet with a slight frown. Vincent Trailman, TF 21's *farshathkhanaak,* outranked Bichet, but the two of them had been friends since the Academy. It was unlike the ops officer to refer to him by anything other than his given name, and the ops officers voice was strained. "See what, Jacques?"

"One of Vincent's fighters just picked it up," Bichet said grimly. "It's a courier drone beacon." Prescott's eyebrows rose, and Bichet voice went lower. "That's not all, Sir. According to the ID string, it's from *Norn*—and it's Code Omega."

"*Code Omega?*" Prescott snapped upright in his chair, and Bichet jerked a choppy nod.

The stocky admiral stared at his ops officer in horrified disbelief. *Norn* had been left safely behind in Anderson Four—damaged, yes, but in no danger. Unless . . .

"Where is this drone?" he demanded, and Bichet consulted his memo pad display.

"According to CIC, it's just under twenty light-minutes out—that's from the fighter shell; it's forty light-minutes from *Crete*—at one-niner-one, zero-three-three, Sir. That puts it right on the very limit for a drone beacon's omnidirectional broadcast range, and signal strength comes and goes. Plotting and Com agree that *could* mean its on a circular search. We lose strength as it heads away from us and pick it up when it closes again."

"A circular search." Something icy crawled down Prescott's spine. He could think of only one explanation for an Omega drone from *Norn*. But that was impossible . . . wasn't it?

"All right," he made himself say. "Pass the information to the Flag and inform Admiral Antonov I'm detaching *Pyotr Veliky* and *Ramilles* to recover the drone. Then get hold of Captain Yukon and Captain Shariz. I want them cloaked—this could be some sort of decoy ploy, and I don't want them sucked into anything. After you talk to *them,* tell Vincent I want a fighter sweep in the direction of the drone. If there's anything out there, that may draw its attention away from *Veliky* and *Ramilles.* If they don't, I want them close enough to support the battle-cruisers."

"Aye, aye, Sir." Bichet hurried off to give the necessary orders, and Raymond Prescott leaned back in his chair and worried.

Antonov sat facing his three task force commanders on the split-image screen. Prescott had summarized the message of *Norn*'s drone, but that was only for the benefit of van der Gelder and Taathaanahk, for its contents had already been downloaded to *Colorado*. So Antonov had already gone beyond what the others were going through now, and could step in quickly to fill the numb silence with his decisive bass.

"Thank you, Admiral Prescott. Now, we must consider the implications of this. Clearly, our information is somewhat out of date, inasmuch as the drone was launched approximately one hundred and eighty hours ago. A lot can happen in almost seven standard days. But we know this much: *Norn* and *Hyacinth* were destroyed here in Anderson Five, so some Bug forces must already be here, doubtless in cloak, in addition to the force—clearly a very powerful one— moving in from somewhere behind us." *From Anderson Three*, he silently corrected himself. *Through some warp point we never found because our survey was too little and too late.* He dismissed the thought; the *pizdi* might have entered some other system through a closed warp point. And self-reproach was hardly the most useful mental exercise just now. "The fact that they've committed this force suggests that there is also a major force waiting ahead of us, intended to be the other jaw of a trap."

"I quite aaaagree, Ssssir," Taathaanahk said with a calmness drawn from that *naraham*—inadequately translated as "detachment"—that was one of the four pillars of his culture's *Taainohk* philosophy. "I thhhhhhink we mussstttt asssssume they knnnnow their owwwn capabilities—annnd they ccccccertainly knnnnow *ours,* fffor thisss cammmpaign hasss given themmm ample opportunity to asssssessss our strength. They woulddd hhhardly hhhave sssprung thisss trappp unlessss their forrrces were sssuch asss ttto allow a rrrreasonable expectation of sssuccesssss." The Ophiuchi admiral paused as though to invite disagreement. None came. "I therefore sssuggest thattt our firssst priority ssshould be to exxxtricate Sssecond Fleet wiiithout delay."

"I concur," van der Gelder said, blinking the haunted look from her eyes. "We should head back now, hard and fast. With our tactical speed advantage, we can leave whatever's waiting ahead of us eating our dust and blast our way out before the blocking force has had time to settle into a defensive posture behind us."

"Unfortunately, Admiral van der Gelder," Antonov rumbled, "we can take as a given that the blocking force is coming from at least as far back as Anderson Three. Unless we get out of this system without any sort of observation by the Bug units that destroyed *Norn* and *Hyacinth*—which is sheer wishful thinking—the Bugs will send courier drones through the warp point ahead of us. With that warning, the blocking force will form up and await us on the far side of whichever warp point is most convenient. And without Fleet Train's SBMHAWK stores, we're in no position to mount a warp point assault." He left unspoken the probable fate of the Fleet Train, and watched their reactions. Prescott seemed unfazed—he'd had even longer than Antonov to adjust to the new facts. But he could recognize the signs in van der Gelder, and the subtler ones in Taathaanahk, as the implications began to sink home.

"However," he went on before the silence could stretch too thin, "I agree that we should retire into Anderson Four as promptly as possible, if we can do so without heavy losses. Once there, we'll have the warp point in our rear, as it were; we can hold it against whatever forces are here in Anderson Five while letting the blocking force cross Anderson Four and come to us."

"Alssso, Sssir," Taathaanahk observed, "we'll be able to ussse our ffffighters and AFFFFHAWKs to interdict any courrrier drrrones sssent thhhrough the warrrp pppoint, thusss preventing their ffforcesss from mmmounting a cooooordinated attack."

"Yes!" Van der Gelder leaned forward with new animation. "That would give us the opportunity to defeat them in detail. Especially considering the probability—which I consider high—that Home Fleet has dispatched a relief force."

"They woulddd hhhave had to orrrganize one vvery quickly," Taathaanahk said dubiously.

"If I know the Sky Marshal," van der Gelder rejoined, "she scraped together everything at Centauri that could fly and energize a beam and sent it off—or, more likely, *led* it off—without waiting for reinforcements from Sol. She knows when time is of the essence! So the relief force may not be as big or as well-balanced by ship types as we might like. But if it can hit the Bug blocking force from the rear in Anderson Four while it's heavily engaged with us . . ."

"Even if no such relief force arrives," Prescott put in, "our speed advantage means that all we'd have to do is break through the blocking force to escape. And we may as well face the fact that 'escape' has become our objective." Then a thought seemed to come to him, and he faced Antonov squarely. "But, Sir, I seem to recall that you implied that this is all contingent on our being able to transit from this system back to Anderson Four 'without heavy losses.' "

"Your recollection is correct, Admiral Prescott. You see, we've been assuming that the main threat still lies ahead of us. But there is no justification for such an assumption. What has happened so far suggests a very well-prepared operation with formidable forces behind it. And given the greater numbers of warp points normally associated with massive stars like this one, I consider it entirely possible that there are already one or more large Bug formations here in Anderson Five. Some of them may well be in a position to intercept us as we retire towards Anderson Four, and if we have to fight our way back through this system, those of us who escape to Anderson Four may be too weak to mount a warp point defense against their pursuers."

For several heartbeats, there was silence. The others, even Prescott, had clearly not allowed themselves to explore the full dimensions of the nightmare in which they found themselves.

"Therefore," Antonov finally said, in a voice that only seemed loud, "we will commence our withdrawal to Anderson Four. If we can get back through the warp point with minimal resistance, well and good. But if we detect powerful Bug forces so situated as to be able contest our passage, we will remain here in Anderson Five until the blocking force has been drawn into this system."

"Sssir," Taathaanahk said with uncharacteristic hesitation, "wwwe don't knnnow the sssize of the blllocking ffforcccce. What ifff they cccan divide it, sssending one ffforcccce on into thisss sysssstem and llleaving another in Aaanderson Fffour to hhhold the warrrp pppoint?"

To everyone's astonishment, Antonov actually grinned. "Admiral Taathaanahk, I wouldn't worry about that if I were you. If the Bugs have *that* many ships in the blocking force, then—" a fatalistic Slavic shrug "—we're fucked anyway." Prescott and van der Gelder smothered a guffaw and a giggle respectively. "But assuming that we *do* have a fighting chance, I prefer to take that chance in a war of movement in this system."

No one looked altogether happy, but no one argued. "And now," Antonov resumed, "I wish to announce the following restructuring of our forces for the withdrawal. Admiral Prescott, I am detaching your task force's CVLs; they go to Task Force 23. But in exchange you will get Admiral Taathaanahk's twelve *Borzoi* class fleet carriers."

Prescott and Taathaanahk both looked puzzled. "Hardly an exchange I can complain about, Sir," the former admitted. "But . . . can I keep Captain Trailman, my *farshathkhanaak*?"

"*Nyet.* I think it best that he remain with the strikegroups he knows, and which know him."

"Very well, Sir." Prescott knew better than to argue. "But . . . may I ask the reason for the swap?"

"The reason, Admiral Prescott, is that the *Borzois,* unlike your *Shokakus,* have cloaking ECM. You see, when we begin our withdrawal,

I'm going to detach you from our main body. And after being detached, I want your entire command to go into cloak."

The puzzlement on Prescott's face intensified—but only for a moment. Then understanding dawned. And he and Antonov exchanged a grin.

As she'd found herself doing more and more since they'd entered Anderson Two, Hannah Avram let her eyes wander towards the view screen, and thought of the planet, thankfully invisible with distance, that lay within that orange primary's meager liquid-water zone. *We thought we had all the time in the world to figure out a solution to the Harnah problem,* she thought bleakly. So the Bugs were still on that planet, albeit with their space capabilities in ruins. And if the Alliance was forced to give up this system, they'd simply continue to herd their sentient meat-animals for God knew how long.

Her mind recoiled from the thought with disgust, and she turned from the conference room's view screen. Even this meeting, wrestling with the problem of organizing her hastily assembled force while underway, was a welcome refuge from the ghosts of those centauroids.

The staff, with their terminals flanked by untidy stacks of hard copy, filled the compartment. The senior flag officers attended electronically, and had taken up a fair amount of time bickering over who got which ship for which task force. But now Terence Mukerji was striking a new note, and she sighed inwardly as she composed herself to hear him out.

"Of course I can understand your orders to remain in cloak after we transit to Anderson Three, Sky Marshal," he was saying in his unctuous way. "And also your policy of using RD2s to probe the Anderson Three warp point and all subsequent warp points before we transit. After all, this system is the last one we can be certain the Alliance still controls. But we must consider that the Bugs may be— indeed, very probably are—sending blocking forces to bar at least one of these warp points."

"Then what's your point, Admiral?" she demanded, reining in her annoyance. "It's precisely to warn us of such a force that I ordered the probing of the warp points. But in this fluid situation, the blocking forces may not be in place as yet. That's why I insisted on haste in assembling this force."

"Yes, Sir," Mukerji murmured. "And why we didn't wait for additional forces to arrive from Sol."

Avram resolutely held her temper and continued as though the interruption hadn't taken place. "Likewise, remaining cloaked between transits will maximize our chances of advancing up this chain undetected *if* we can make it through the warp points before opposition crystallizes." She had to put up with Mukerji, whose most obvious talent was that of knowing which politicians to cultivate. More than once, she'd listened to Agamemnon Waldeck praise him as "an officer with a sound awareness of the political realities," and somehow refrained from gagging.

"Ah, yes, Sky Marshal. To be sure. At the same time . . . well, I would be derelict in my responsibility as second in command if I failed to point out that such a swift, undetected passage may carry its own risk."

"Precisely what are you talking about, Admiral?"

"Simply this, Sky Marshal. If enemy blocking forces of sufficient strength arrive in position *after* we've transited, and if we find that Second Fleet has already been destroyed or rendered too weak to be of assistance, then we would be trapped ourselves." Mukerji paused and, misinterpreting Avram's silence, pressed on. "So might I suggest that a more deliberate advance, coupled with attempts to ascertain Second Fleet's status, might be in order? This way we could avoid the possibility of, as it were, throwing good money after bad." He paused again, awaiting appreciation of his witticism. But what he saw in Avram's expression decided him against continuing. As the pause stretched and stretched, the noises in *Xingú's* conference room died, one after another, until there was utter silence.

Avram broke it. "Understand me, Admiral Mukerji . . . and everyone else in the sound of my voice. Rescuing Second Fleet is our *only* consideration. We will pursue any course of action that offers a possibility of doing so, and to that end, I'm prepared to risk the loss of this entire force. We are all expendable!" She glared directly at the pickup and noted out of the corner of an eye that Mukerji's face, normally the color of weak coffee, seemed to have acquired an extra dollop of cream. "Is that unmistakably clear, Admiral Mukerji?" *You pusillanimous turd,* she silently added. Without waiting for a reply, she cut the connection. Then she swung her glare towards the staff. With comical abruptness, the hubbub resumed. Avram spared a moment to look back towards the view screen, where the distant stars gave no sense of motion although she knew that they were proceeding towards the Anderson Three warp point with all the speed their drives could provide.

You would've squashed him flat long ago, Ivan Nikolayevich, she thought as she gazed at those frustratingly motionless stars. *But I'm not you. Nobody is. Is that why I'm prepared to risk this force for any chance of getting you out alive? Or is it because Second Fleet is the cream of the TFN, and its loss is unthinkable? Either way, I'm making a logically unexceptionable decision, on the basis of cold calculation. Of course I am. Got to keep telling myself that.*

✧   ✧   ✧

"Red Seven-Two's picking up something ahead, Skip."

"What?" Commodore Lucinda Chou, officially Special Operations Officer for Fighter Operations but known to one and all as Second Fleet's *farshathkhanaak,* crossed quickly to her assistant's console. Chou would vastly have preferred to be out in her own command fighter, but *Thor's* CIC was the only logical place for her to be. Simple communications lag would have made it impractical for her to coordinate her recon shell from a point on its periphery.

"Not sure yet, Skip," Commander Ashengi replied. "Looks like a cloaked starship, but it's way out at thirty light-minutes. Seven-Two got dead lucky to pick up anything at that range."

"Maybe they've got a malfunctioning ECM suite," Chou murmured. She turned and looked into the huge holo tank—eight times the size of the one on *Thor's* flag deck—and rubbed her chin. The tiny light code was barely inside the perimeter of even CIC's plot, but it was almost squarely between Second Fleet and the Anderson Four warp point. That icon might be a sensor ghost, and she wanted to believe it was, but she didn't.

"Inform Admiral Taathaanahk and the Flag, Aucke," she said quietly. "Then set up an armed recon sweep. The Admiral may just want someone to go take a closer look at this."

Commander Aathmaahr led his mixed Terran-Ophiuchi strikegroup towards the contact. Aathmaahr had been a pilot—one of the elite *Corthohardaa,* whom the Terrans called "the Screaming Eagles" from the stylized *hasfrazi* head of their insignia—for over twenty Terran Standard years, but he'd never seen combat until the Bugs attacked. Now he'd seen more than he'd ever wanted to, and there seemed no end in sight. *Well,* he corrected himself, *there is one possible end, but I will defer it as long as possible.*

He clicked his beak in a grim chuckle and checked his instruments. Like most of his people, he felt disdain for the slower, clumsier gunboats. They were dangerous, yes, but they could never match a fighter's dogfighting maneuverability, and Aathmaahr had made ace (a Human concept the OADC had adopted with enthusiasm) in his very first engagement against them. Of course, that had been before they started carrying AFHAWKs. Trying to go in close now would be even more costly, but squadron for squadron, and despite their point defense, gunboats were still no match for fighters armed with FM3s.

Yet they can *kill us,* he reminded himself, remembering how the human Chou had become Second Fleet's *farshathkhanaak.* That post had been Captain Ythaanhk's . . . until he met one of the gunboat-launched AFHAWKs head on. Not that Chou wasn't a satisfactory

replacement. She was less gifted than an Ophiuchi behind the controls, but she certainly understood fighter ops.

He checked his sensors again and shook off his daydreams. His strikegroup was beyond the recon shell perimeter now, and if that sensor ghost was truly a starship, his arrow straight course towards it would draw a response soon.

His fighters streaked onward, laden with three missiles each, and a worm of tension coiled within him. Surely the Bugs realized his purpose, and virtually all Bug starships carried gunboat racks. Only their pure missile platforms retained conventional XO racks, instead, and—

"Talon Leader, Talon Green One," a human voice crackled in his earbug. "Do you see what I see at zero-zero-zero?"

"Afffffirrmatttive, Grrreeen One," Aathmaahr replied. He felt a spike of pique that Lieutenant Brahman had gotten his report in before any of his Ophiuchi pilots, but it was distant and far away. The icons of Bug gunboats were blinking onto his plot in shoals, hundreds of them, with the instantaneous solidity possible only to small craft launching from cloaked starships.

Well, they've seen us, a small voice said deep within him.

"Aaaalphhhha One," he said to his tac officer, and Lieutenant Dahrmaar clicked his beak in assent. Long, strong fingers tapped at his console, flashing the order to the rest of the strikegroup, and Aathmaahr's squadrons closed in around his own fighter. The Bugs had left their launch just too late, he thought grimly. They were launching across a broad arc, which gave an indication of their fleet's deployment, but it also meant they needed time to concentrate. No more than fifty or sixty gunboats could intercept him short of the icon he'd come to examine, and he had forty-eight fighters to throw against them.

Even odds are in our favor, he reminded himself as his pilot rammed the drive to full power, and took his strikegroup straight down the enemy's throat.

Attack Force One had waited eight days for the enemy. His long delay—probably to make repairs—had given the dispersed attack forces ample time to spread out to envelop him, whatever course he finally took, but it was obvious he had detected them at last. Fortunately, he had sent in only a fairly weak force of attack craft; unfortunately, the powerful reinforcements the core systems had sent up to support the attack forces' organic gunboat components were seventy light-minutes astern of Attack Force One . . . and so were the escort cruisers which were most effective against attack craft. Their inability to cloak had dictated their deployment, for it had been essential to hide the attack forces' presence from the enemy as long as possible.

But the enemy knew now, and com lasers sent their summons flashing astern at the speed of light. Even so, the message would take over an hour to be received, and Attack Force One's own gunboats raced to meet the enemy.

The fighters held their missiles until the last moment, then punched every bird straight down the Bugs' throat at a range of five and a half light-seconds—a half light-second beyond the range of their AFHAWKs. Aathmaahr was only peripherally interested in killing gunboats; his mission was to determine what the enemy had in the way of starships, and he flung everything he had at the only foes between him and his objective.

Forty-eight fighters salvoed a hundred and forty-four missiles. Seventy acquired lock and homed for the kill, and point defense engaged them as they closed. Thirty-four were destroyed short of their targets; thirty-six went home, and fifty-six percent of the gunboats died. But then the survivors salvoed *their* ordnance, and a hundred and twelve AFHAWKs came streaking back.

The strikegroup split apart, each squadron maneuvering hard in the Waldeck Weave and its Ophiuchi equivalent. There were enough missiles out there to kill the entire strikegroup twice over, but the Bugs had fired too soon. Accuracy was poor at that range, and the fighters' evasive maneuvers made it poorer. "Only" seventeen of Aathmaahr's fighters were blown apart, and the thirty-one survivors swept back in, drives howling, to tear into the twenty-eight remaining gunboats with internal lasers. Eight more fighters died, but they took all of the gunboats with them, and Aathmaahr led his shrunken group past the tumbling wreckage of friend and foe alike.

"One passs!" he cautioned his pilots as they swept in towards the range at which no ECM could hide a starship from them. There would be time for no more—not with the other gunboats closing in vengefully from all sides—but without their missiles, his fighters had a forty-five percent speed advantage. They could get their look, then evade and—

His thoughts broke off in disbelief as the Bug starship appeared suddenly on his sensors. Impossible! *Nothing* was that big! But the lumbering behemoth refused to vanish. It hung against the starscape, armored flanks studded with cavernous weapon bays, and he shook himself.

"Ffffalll backkk!" he barked over the com. "Tannngo Two!"

The twenty-three surviving members of SG 371 turned and fled for their carrier. Behind them, the stupendous ship they'd come so far to find ground steadily onward with its consorts.

CHAPTER FORTY

Even Legends Die

TFNS *Colorado's* flag bridge was deathly silent as the holo of an unbelievable starship hung in the tactical display. It wasn't a real visual, just computer imagery generated from the fighters' sensor data, but that made it no less terrifying. Twice the size of a superdreadnought, it hung there like a curse and chilled every heart with the firepower it must pack.

Too bad LeBlanc isn't here, Ivan Antonov thought distantly. *He keeps insisting Bugs don't think like we do, and here is the proof. Three entire fleets, counting the one we just destroyed. Over five* hundred *starships— a hundred and sixty of them superdreadnoughts—God only knows how many gunboats, and the surrender of a populated star system just to bait a trap, and I walked straight into it.*

He glared at the image, feeling the sickness and self-disgust at his core, then closed his eyes and sucked in a deep breath.

No. It can't all have *been a trick. They would have required omniscience to deliberately* let us see them *in Centauri just to lure us here. No. They set this up only after we destroyed their covering force in Anderson One, yet that makes it no better. I have led three quarters of Home Fleet into a death trap.*

He opened his eyes once more and made himself think.

"Estimates on firepower?" he asked de Bertholet quietly.

"Impossible to say, Sir." The ops officer seemed almost grateful for the technical question. "We've never even considered building something that size, so I don't have any idea how much mass its engines eat up. At a guess, I'd say it probably has about a sixty or seventy percent edge over a superdreadnought in weapons' tonnage. It can't be a lot more, even as big as it is; the support systems for its crew have to be scaled up, as well."

"So it has *only* a seventy percent individual superiority, eh?"

Antonov's wry voice was poison dry, and de Bertholet surprised himself with a bark of strained laughter. He smoothed any sign of levity from his face instantly, but Antonov only produced a wintry smile without taking his eyes from the display.

"Unless their construction rate is far higher than our own, it must have taken at least two years to build such vessels," he spoke as if only to himself, then nodded. "Yes, that would make sense. Especially since they lacked command datalink at the outset. They couldn't match our datagroups' size, so they built bigger individual units to even the firepower." He frowned, rubbing his chin. "Yet why wait this long to commit them? Unless their breakthrough into modern datalink came as a surprise to them?" He cocked his head, then nodded again. "If that were the case, then they would have had to refit with the new command systems before committing them—possibly even redesign their entire armaments. We know they prefer specialized designs, after all. . . ."

He gazed at the holo a moment longer, then turned away. A raised hand summoned Stovall and Kozlov to join de Bertholet at his side, and he folded his hands behind him as he faced his senior staffers grimly.

"The level of threat has just risen," he said flatly. "We lack even the most imperfect estimate of the firepower this new class represents, nor do we know how many of them the enemy has. We have seen only one. There may be dozens, or they may have only a handful; the only way we can discover which is to engage them."

Stovall nodded with matching grimness. The others simply waited, eyes and mouths tense.

"Unfortunately, we must assume that whatever force their drones summoned *also* has such units. If this is true, a warp point assault against them becomes even more unacceptable. Nor can we risk a head-on engagement with the enemy force we have detected. If we take heavy losses against the single force we *know* about, we weaken ourselves—perhaps fatally—against any additional enemies."

He paused, and Stovall frowned. "You're correct, of course, Sir," he said slowly, "but they're between us and the warp point. To me, that suggests they must have had us under observation the entire time, probably with cloaked light cruisers, or they couldn't have positioned themselves so precisely. Assuming that's true, they have the advantage of knowing where we are. If we let them choose the time and place to hit us—" He shrugged, and Antonov nodded.

"True enough, but we have advantages of our own. Our ships' drives may be less than fully reliable, yet while they last, we retain our speed advantage, and for all we know, this new class is still slower. With a fighter shell posted sufficiently far out, we should be able to detect them—even cloaked—soon enough to evade them."

"While our drives last," Stovall conceded.

"And," Antonov went on, "if they bring up light cruisers to screen their formations against our fighters, they'll become much easier to track, since their fleet-type CLs can't cloak. The same is true of their gunboats, the only vessels with sufficient speed to overhaul us. In short, they cannot force us to commit to close action until and unless we *allow* them to."

"But, Sir," de Bertholet said quietly, "sooner or later, we'll simply run out of supplies, or our drives *will* pack in. All they have to do is sit on our exit warp point long enough, and we'll have no choice but to come to them sooner or later."

"Precisely," Antonov said, and his staff blinked at his icy, armor-plated smile. "And that's why we must keep them from deciding to do just that. We must draw their attention and be certain we hold it—be certain they keep *trying* to overtake us rather than give up and fall back on the warp point—until the final component of their trap makes transit."

"That could take another ten or twelve days, Sir," Stovall said, "and they're going to be throwing every gunboat they can at us the entire time."

"Understood. It will be up to our fighters and escort vessels to hold them off. It will be difficult, and our orders must stress the absolute necessity of conserving ammunition, yet it is the only hope I see. We *must* stay alive long enough for their full force to arrive and then break out at a time of *our* choosing." He paused and swept his eyes slowly from face to face, and his deep voice was a subterranean rumble when he spoke again. "Whatever we may do, our losses will be heavy. Accept that now, for it is inevitable. But we *must* get whatever we can out of this trap."

One by one, his staff nodded. He was right. The task he proposed to accept was virtually impossible—evading multiple enemy fleets while playing matador to all of them would require maneuvers no navy had ever trained for—yet it was the only chance Second Fleet had. And if any flag officer in the Terran Navy could pull it off, the man before them was that officer.

"Very well," Antonov said. "We will alter course, Commander de Bertholet. Turn us away from them and take us above the ecliptic. We will begin by heading away from the warp point."

"Yes, Sir."

"Before altering course, however, detach Admiral Prescott. He knows what I want him to do, but it is essential the Bugs not see him separate from us, so he must go immediately."

"If they *do* have us under observation from cloak, they'll see him drop off their scanners, Sir," Stovall said.

"We'll take the entire Fleet into cloak simultaneously," Antonov replied. "Any scout ships must be outside our present fighter shell, cloaked or not. That means they're too far out to track us in cloak even with known starting positions . . . but they will be able to track our *fighters*. Let them think they've panicked us into a useless attempt at concealment. The picket fighters will maintain their positions relative to the flagship as we move away, and TF 21 will go dead in space. The enemy will track the fighter shell and be drawn after us; once we're well clear, Admiral Prescott will bring up his drives and proceed with his mission."

"And when they send in their first strikes?" the chief of staff asked, "if they have a good count on us now, they're likely to realize someone's missing, Sir."

"A risk we must take, but the Fleet will remain cloaked throughout. Their gunboats shouldn't be surprised if they can't see all of us at any given moment. With luck, they'll assume that's where Prescott is—just out of sight in cloak, but still with the rest of the Fleet."

"Yes, Sir." Stovall nodded. It was a gamble, but, then, so was Antonov's entire plan. And who knew? It might even work.

Clearly the enemy had finally divined the nature of the trap—or a part of it, at least. It was a pity; the Fleet had hoped to keep him in ignorance until the final units arrived. But the possibility had been allowed for. That was why Attack Force One lay directly between him and his escape warp point.

But he appeared even more confused than the Fleet had anticipated. The cloaked light cruisers which had watched cautiously from a light-hour beyond his formation now saw his entire force of starships disappear. ECM had been a matter of some concern when the plan was formulated, for it was possible the enemy might somehow creep past the Fleet to the warp point in cloak. But though his ships might have disappeared, his sphere of attack craft had not. They moved off across the system, swinging away from Attack Force One and—though the enemy could not know it—almost directly towards Attack Force Three. Of course, it was possible he was actually trying to creep away in a totally different direction while his attack craft decoyed the Fleet, but it was unlikely. He persisted in his inexplicable refusal to sacrifice units for tactical advantage, and that shell represented at least a third of his total strength in attack craft.

Attack Force One adjusted its position slightly, swinging to port and climbing above the ecliptic to stay between the enemy and escape, but it made no effort to pursue. There was no need. Eventually Attack Force

*Three or Attack Force Two would make contact . . . and in the mean-
while, the time had come to commit the gunboats at last.*

"Looks like it's working, Sir," Anthea Mandagalla said quietly. "If
they knew we were here, they'd be doing something about it."

Raymond Prescott nodded without taking his own gaze from the
huge tank. He and his staff were in *Crete*'s CIC, not on Flag Bridge,
to take advantage of the master plot's size, and he chewed his lower
lip as a massive wave of gunboats streaked past his command. The
reorganized TF 21—sixteen fast superdreadnoughts, twenty battle-cruisers,
and ten fleet carriers—lay motionless, wrapped in the invisibility of
their ECM. The nearest gunboat was over twenty light-minutes distant, so the ECM probably wasn't even necessary, but it was impossible to know where the Bugs' cloaked *starships* might be, and he
recalled Andy's account of his mission in Justin before Operation
Redemption. *This seems to be becoming a Prescott speciality. Let's hope
we don't have to do it* too *often!*

He watched the gunboats streak away after the rest of the fleet, then
glanced at Bichet.

"We'll give them another hour, Jacques." His mouth twitched a taut
smile. "If this works at all, we've got plenty of time, so let's take it
easy and hold those emissions down, shall we?"

"Dear God . . . *eleven hundred* gunboats?"

Midori Kozlov had barely spoken above a whisper, but Antonov
heard her distinctly in the hush that had fallen over *Colorado*'s flag
bridge. He ignored her as he studied the holo tank in which the two
incoming swarms of gunboats showed as fuzzy amoebas of red light.
Any meaningful display of individual craft was out of the question.

They'd detected the first wave-front of six hundred gunboats sweeping in from astern, and everyone had remained steady—it wasn't as
though they hadn't been expecting something of the kind. But now
the fighter screen had detected this new force approaching on a different bearing. Kozlov's reaction, and the stunned silence from everyone
else, told Antonov he needed to dispel the psychologically devastating sensation of being caught between two forces.

"It appears," he said very distinctly, "that the enemy's timing is a
little off."

"Sir?" Stovall tore his gaze from the plot.

"Observe, Commodore: the force approaching from astern is so much
closer that we should have no trouble dealing with it in detail. Of
course," he added thoughtfully, "it won't remain so if the present vectors
remain unchanged; in fact, they're probably counting on the rate at
which we're closing with the second force." He swung to face Stovall.

"We will alter course away from the second gunboat flotilla's bearing. At the same time, have the fighter screen recalled and rearmed with FM3s; the change in course provides an optimum opportunity to do so, and I believe we have sufficient time."

"Aye, aye, Sir." Stovall turned to de Bertholet. "Armand, see to it." As the ops officer busied himself with the necessary orders, the chief of staff turned back to Antonov and spoke more quietly. "Sir, there may be a risk inherent in this evolution. What if they have yet *another* force, waiting in cloak just beyond the fighter shell's detection range? We'll be vulnerable to a gunboat strike launched by such a force while our fighters are away striking the known forces."

Antonov smiled and replied in an equally quiet voice. "I'm glad you're thinking in terms of additional enemy forces, Commodore Stovall, because I haven't wanted to mention the possibility out loud; I don't think it's what most of our people need to hear at the moment. But I'm more and more convinced that the possibility is very real. We know nothing about this system's warp points, or about the forces the Bugs have put through them. Therefore," he continued in a more normal volume, "I intend to hold a quarter of our total fighter strength in reserve to deal with any unexpected threats."

The fighters of the shell returned to their carriers for rearming while the shoals of gunboats continued to crawl across the light-minutes, and Second Fleet turned to meet the closer of them. The carriers still with the fleet's main body were up to about eighty percent of maximum hangar capacity—a total of seven hundred and seven fighters—and five hundred and thirty streaked away, laden with third-generation fighter missiles.

The strain mounted on the flag bridge as the fighters crossed fifteen light minutes to make contact with the Bugs, then ratcheted up to new levels of tension as the report of the strike crept across that distance at the speed of light. Then the messages arrived in a rush, and it was as though an emotional dike had burst.

"Over two hundred and fifty kills!" de Bertholet whooped to make himself heard over the hubbub. "And not a single fighter lost!"

"And," Stovall added more quietly, "they all followed orders and turned tail before they came into AFHAWK range of the enemy." He grinned weakly, looking drained. "Fighter pilots are such hot dogs you can never be sure."

"Yes." Antonov nodded ponderously, standing like a rock amid the jubilation, as impervious to it as he'd been to the earlier stunned apprehension. "They'll have time to return, rearm, and go out for another strike."

"What about the reserve fighters, Sir?" de Bertholet asked, brought back down to earth by the admiral's stolidity.

"Continue to hold them in reserve, Commander. We'll need them soon enough."

The fighters returned, and the flag staff, past its emotional peaks and valleys, coordinated the rearming and the launching of a second strike smoothly. Once again five hundred and thirty fighters went out, and once again they decimated the Bugs from beyond AFHAWK range. This time they returned with the gunboats close behind them, but less than a hundred of those gunboats remained, and swept into AFHAWK range of the screen's escorts with a self-sacrificing futility that would have been appalling in any other species. There was barely time to receive the report of that fact before the last of them had been blasted into oblivion.

"Not a single casualty on our side," de Bertholet breathed, almost reverently.

"And now," Antonov said, still unmoved, "as soon as the fighters have rearmed, I want them launched against the *second* gunboat strike force."

For a moment, silence reigned. No one had been thinking of that other incoming wave of five hundred gunboats.

"Ah, shall we signal the carrier commanders to expedite the rearming, Sir?" Stovall inquired.

"*Nyet*," Antonov snorted. "They have enough on their minds right now without having pompous admirals and officious staff *zalyotniki* tell them their jobs. They'll get the fighters turned around as fast as it can be done." He scowled. "Unfortunately, by then there won't be time for them to intercept the enemy at long range. So, Commander," he continued without a break, turning to de Bertholet, "I think it's time to launch the reserve fighters. And yes, Commodore Stovall, I know there's a risk involved. But risk avoidance has become a luxury— one which is going to be in shorter and shorter supply." He paused, considering. "On reflection, I think we'll hold back the fighters that are now being rearmed until the reserve fighters have returned, and then send them all out in a combined strike. They've just conducted two long-range attacks without a break, and pilot exhaustion is a factor we don't need."

The hundred and seventy-six fighters of the reserve were off the mark quickly enough to intercept the second wave of gunboats ten light-minutes out, where they killed seventy-five of them with FM3s before returning to their carriers.

"We're only going to have time for one more strike, Sir," Stovall reminded Antonov as the rearming neared completion.

"*Da*," the admiral acknowledged. "And they won't be able to get all the remaining gunboats from outside AFHAWK range." He thought in black abstraction for a heartbeat or two. "After they've expended their

FM3s, I authorize one, repeat *one* pass with lasers. Afterwards they're to return directly. We can't afford heavy fighter losses at this stage. There'll be no unrestricted dogfighting, as dearly as I know the young fools would like it." He turned away and gazed into, and beyond, the plot. "The young fools," he repeated in a voice that held infinite sadness.

The gunboats were three light-minutes out when a hurricane of missiles from Antonov's still-undiminished fighter force blasted two hundred and sixty-six of them out of existence. But the others came on, and this time the fighters didn't wheel to flee. They drove in, taking so little time to close that they lost only a few of their number to the AFHAWKs the Bugs were finally able to bring into play. Then the two forces interpenetrated at an unthinkable relative velocity, and that instant of interpenetration was marked by a brief but searingly intense exchange of energy weapon fire in which a hundred and twenty gunboats died. Then, too fast for thought, the fighters were through and commencing the turning maneuver that would take them back to their carriers.

"Sixty-seven fighters lost," Stovall observed grimly as the last squadrons reported in.

"But only thirty-nine gunboats left," de Bertholet breathed. "And *still* they come on!"

It was true. No more discouraged by losses than any other force of nature, the Bugs drove into the warships' defensive envelopes. Five managed to make attacks before the AFHAWKs obliterated them; none of those attacks even penetrated shields to scratch material defenses.

At the moment of the last gunboat's demise, a strange release of emotion swept *Colorado*'s flag bridge. Stovall caught himself cheering with the rest, and turned an abashed face to Antonov. Amazingly, the admiral was actually smiling a little. He let the smile linger a second, as though savoring it like the last rose of the season, before relinquishing it.

"They won't make that kind of mistake again in coordinating their attacks," he rumbled, shaking his head slowly.

"But, Sir . . . *eleven hundred gunboats!*"

"True. But to get them, we shot away ninety percent of our FM3s. The remaining ones won't last long when the next gunboat wave comes."

"If there is one, Sir. Maybe they've shot their bolt."

"You believe that about as much as I do, Commodore. No, they'll be back. And when they do, our fighters will have to meet them armed with short-ranged munitions. Which means they'll have to get through the gunboats' AFHAWK envelope before they can even use their weapons. And when they do get to fire, they'll be doing it at the gunboats' own most effective range."

Stovall started to open his mouth, then closed it and looked around the flag bridge. The shouting was over, but the cheerful back-slapping and story-comparing was still in progress.

Antonov laid a restraining hand on his arm. "Let them enjoy it while they can, Commodore," he said gently, in a voice no one would ever have expected to hear from Ivan the Terrible. "They'll only have a little while."

The fleet had not anticipated such savage losses. The new, longer-ranged missiles of the enemy's attack craft offset the gunboats' defensive missile capability, and the timing which had sent the first two strikes in separately had denied them mutual support.

But none of the destroyed units had come from the Fleet's organic gunboat strength; all had come from one of the adjacent systems, and despite the two botched attacks, a total of almost three thousand remained.

The Fleet would use them more wisely henceforth.

"That's a hundred and sixty kills," de Bertholet declared, looking at the board.

"So," Midori Kozlov said quietly, "that only leaves eleven hundred and forty."

They'd detected the thirteen hundred incoming gunboats twenty hours after the destruction of the earlier waves. This time, Flag Bridge hadn't been blanketed by an aghast silence. It was as though these people had moved beyond all such emotions by now. They simply functioned as modular components of a machine whose purpose was survival.

Antonov's last FM3-armed fighters had gone out and performed what everyone knew would be their last cost-free slaughter. Now they were on the way back, to be rearmed with external laser packs. As they drew closer, the admiral and his staff held a hurried colloquy.

"We can turn them around in time to launch all six hundred and forty remaining fighters for another long-range strike, Sir," de Bertholet reported. "Perhaps we could simultaneously engage with SBMs. They weren't designed as gunboat-killers, I know. But it can be done. And keeping the enemy as busy as possible would help compensate for the fighters' lack of FM3s."

"I've considered that, Commander, but our stocks of SBMs are low. We used many of them against the Bug defensive force that lured me into this system." Antonov's voice remained level as he implicitly assumed full responsibility. "Remember also the SBM's greater vulnerability to point defense." The admiral smiled at de Bertholet's crestfallen look. "Nevertheless, your idea of coordinated missile and fighter strikes has merit. We will hold the fighters back until the enemy is within capital missile range. We still have an abundant supply of those."

So it was that the Bug gunboats approached to within fifteen light-seconds of Second Fleet before the fighters—all that Antonov still possessed—swooped in. The Bugs had a brief time to take advantage of the unaccustomed opportunity to use AFHAWKs, and they made the most of it, killing two hundred and sixteen fighters. But then the deadly little craft were in among them, and swarms of capital missiles came with them, overloading point defense that might otherwise have engaged fighters at what passed for knife range in space combat. The fighters took fearful vengeance, their finely coordinated squadrons going through the serried ranks of gunboats like mowing machines. They slaughtered nine hundred while the missiles that weaved through the defensive laser-lattice claimed another hundred and fifty. On Second Fleet's view screens, as revealed by remote pickups, the rapid-fire immolations resembled a dense swarm of fireflies.

Ninety gunboats got through, and before the fighters could reverse course and catch them they were among the ships. In the brief time left to them, they swarmed around and destroyed two assault carriers, a battleship, two battle-cruisers, and . . .

"Sir, Rio *Grande* reports failure of all major systems!" De Bertholet might as well have saved his breath, for another of TF 22's ships was downloading a view of Admiral van der Gelder's flagship, and on a small screen at his station Antonov watched the superdreadnought die.

"*Dosvedania*, Jessica," he breathed as the searing, strobe-like series of explosions seemed to merge into a single transcendent one.

"*Rio Grande* Code Omega," de Bertholet finished, even more unnecessarily.

It was the gunboats' final, dying blow, and a subdued flag bridge watched the damage totals begin to arrive. Cheering, like terror, had seemingly been left behind in some previous life which held room for things besides grim desperation.

The enemy was resilient, but this time he had been hurt. The distance between the attack forces made coordination difficult and time consuming, and, once again, losses had been heavy. But the gunboats were not intended to destroy the enemy. It would be good if they could, yet their true function was to wear him down. To batter his starships, grind away his attack craft, and force him to expend ammunition before the battle-lines engaged.

And they were succeeding. The enemy had lost thirty percent of his attack craft, and so few of them had attacked with missiles that his ammunition must be running low.

It would be difficult to launch another strike like the last. Attack Force Three's organic gunboat component had been effectively eliminated. Attack Force One and Two retained theirs, but those forces were widely separated, making coordination between them all but impossible. The last three hundred system-based gunboats would be committed, but the two attack forces would retain their integral strength until the decisive moment.

"That's the last of them, Sir." De Bertholet managed to make the report fairly crisp, even though, like everyone else, he'd only been able to catch fitful catnaps during the sixty hours—it only seemed like an eternity—since Prescott's task force had split off.

The three hundred gunboats had been detected thirty-one hours after the last attack. Once again, Antonov's fighters—four hundred and twenty-three in number now—had intercepted at close range in coordination with capital missiles. And again the attackers had been wiped out. But it had cost seventy-eight fighters as well as the ship losses beginning to appear on the board.

"Thank you, Commander," the admiral acknowledged, never removing his eyes from the unfolding toll. A CVA, five battle-cruisers, two light carriers, seven light cruisers . . . He finally shook himself and turned to assess his staff's haggardness. Gazing back at him, they saw only bedrock steadiness.

"You will note," he began, ignoring the losses they'd just taken and indicating the strategic display of the system, "that since we initially changed course in response to the first gunboat attack our continued course changes have had the net effect of bringing us around in a three-quarter circle, almost two hundred and seventy degrees relative to our original course. I believe it is now time for us to begin working our way back toward that original course."

Midori Kozlov shook herself as though to shake loose from webs of fatigue and despair. "Back toward the Anderson Four warp point, Sir? You think the time has come when . . . ?"

Antonov saw the nascent hope in all their faces. They knew the desperate plan that lay behind the *totentanz* whose measure they'd been treading. So they knew that the order to set course for the warp point would promise an end to their nightmare . . . one way or another.

"*Nyet.* I'm as certain as I am of anything in the universe that Admiral Prescott is carrying out his orders. But as for the Bug blocking force . . . No. We have a while yet. But it isn't too soon to start working our way onto the heading, very gradually and without being obvious about it."

✧　　✧　　✧

Raymond Prescott sat on his flag bridge once more as Task Force 21 made its final turn and slunk stealthily towards the warp point. His ships' high designed speed had made this slow, careful approach even more frustrating, yet that slowness had not only reduced the power of his drive signatures, substantially easing his ECM's task, but given his passive sensors ample time to sweep the space before him . . . and the Bugs had been careless.

He bared his teeth as he glanced into his plot once more. The Bugs "knew" where Second Fleet's units were, and so the two battle-cruiser datagroups guarding the warp point "knew" they were far beyond any enemy's sensor range. One of them had taken its ECM down— probably only to repair some fault, since it had come back up seventy-one minutes later—but that had been long enough for TF 21 to obtain a firm fix. With that datum in hand, Prescott had swept a bit wider of the warp point, and his sensor sections, working outward from the ship which had so obligingly revealed itself, had spotted its consorts, as well. It was entirely possible there were other ships watching the warp point, but Prescott was privately certain any others would be light units. He had the battle-cruisers, now, and his own *Dunkerques* were cycling continuous targeting updates just in case. When the time came—

"Drones transiting the warp point!" There was an instant of silence, and then, "They're TFN birds!"

Prescott's head jerked up at the sudden announcement, and Anthea Mandagalla's eyes met his, glowing like pools of flame in her space-black face. He looked back into the plot, watching scores—hundreds— of drones fan out in what was obviously a search pattern, and felt his own powerful surge of hope. But—

"They're from Admiral Chin," Com said flatly. "We're reading their beacons clearly."

Chin, Prescott thought, all elation vanished. He made himself sit motionless, refusing to show how terribly he'd hoped they were from an approaching relief force, and a dreadful premonition gripped him. He knew what those drones were going to tell him.

"Are any of them heading our way, Jacques?" he asked quietly.

"Yes, Sir."

"How many?" Prescott kept his eyes on his plot as the cloaked battle-cruisers opened fire on the drones. They killed many of them, but they were concentrating on the ones headed in Second Fleet's direction, and Prescott was on the far side of the warp point from the rest of the fleet. The ones which broke out and away from the point were of no concern to the enemy, for no one was out there to receive them . . . they thought.

"About ten, Sir. Some may change vector—there's no way to know what sort of search pattern they're programmed for—but on present headings, at least five will pass within a light-minute or less of the task force."

"Thank you." Prescott thought a moment longer. Recovering one of those drones was out of the question; he couldn't afford to have one of them simply disappear if the Bugs were tracking it. But it was possible they might shed some light on whatever was coming down the Anderson Chain, and that possibility justified a certain amount of risk. "Commander Hale."

"Yes, Admiral?" *Crete*'s senior com officer looked up from her console.

"Can you trigger the com laser on one of those drones and order it to upload to us without terminating its beacon?"

"Without terminating the beacon?" Hale frowned. "I think so, Sir. I'll have to rewrite a couple of lines in the standard interrogation package, though."

"Can you do it before they make their closest approach?"

"No problem, Sir," she said confidently.

"In that case, I want you to trigger the closest drone. Get with Plotting first. Make certain no known enemy positions will be in the transmission paths—from the drone, as well as us—when you do it. It's imperative that the enemy not realize what we've done."

Hannah Avram knew the feeling was irrational. In any real sense, the space here below (arbitrary term!) Anderson Three's primary sun was no more empty than the plane in which its barren planets and ruddy ember of a companion orbited. But she couldn't shake off the feeling of being adrift in a realm of cold dark nothingness where the soul could lose its way.

The relief force had only just left Anderson Two and its tragedy-haunted planet behind and entered Anderson Three when Tracking picked up a massive gunboat formation proceeding from what must be the undiscovered warp point in this system toward the one they'd just transited. Some anxious hours had passed, but the gunboats had proceeded singlemindedly on course, and Avram had breathed a sigh of relief as she realized they were just too late to detect her.

After the last gunboat icon vanished off the edge of the plot, Admiral Mukerji had shattered the residual silence on *Xingú*'s flag bridge with a request for an electronic conference. "Sky Marshal, in light of what we've just seen, and what it suggests about the sheer scale of Bug activities along the Anderson Chain, may I suggest we send courier drones ahead to alert Admiral Antonov of our estimated time of arrival? This would enable him to plan his operations with a view to being as close to the Anderson Four/Anderson Five warp point as possible at that time. Surely having our two forces in a position to combine their efforts would maximize the chances of success."

And of your personal survival, Avram had thought. But she'd held her tongue. Mukerji's suggestion, whatever motivations lay behind it, wasn't totally irrational. Still . . .

"No, Admiral Mukerji. We have no way of knowing Second Fleet's status, so Admiral Antonov might not be able to act on that information."

"Still, Sky Marshal, what harm can it do?"

"Simply this, Admiral: to reach Admiral Antonov, the drones would have to pass through whatever Bug forces lie ahead of us, and might very well be detected. The enemy's ignorance of our presence is the greatest advantage we possess, and the need to preserve that advantage outweighs the speculative benefits of alerting Second Fleet to our approach. In fact, I'm about to order a course change to take us on a dogleg to the Anderson Four warp point."

"That will add to our flight time, Sky Marshal."

"So it will. But I'm willing to accept that as the price for removing any possibility of random encounters with Bug forces like the gunboat flotilla we just observed."

Her orders had been carried out. Like many—though by no means all—warp points, those connecting Anderson Three to Anderson Two and Four both lay in the same plane as the system's planets. The course change would, indeed, lengthen her passage time. But it would also take her force well outside that plane, keeping it beyond the sensor range of any Bugs shuttling between Anderson Three's known warp points as it proceeded towards the Anderson Four warp point. She reminded herself of that and tried not to let impatience gnaw holes in her gut.

"That's it, Sir," Stovall reported. "They've all been accounted for."

"And this time our losses are minimal," de Bertholet added, gesturing at the board. "Admiral, this was the weakest gunboat attack we've faced so far. Could it be . . . ?"

All the staffers looked at Antonov, and he read the hunger in their eyes. They wanted him to tell them that this latest attack's feebleness represented a ray of hope in the world of unrelieved blackness they'd inhabited for what seemed as far back as memory could reach.

But he couldn't. *Unless I'm very much mistaken, this wasn't a real attack at all. They were just probing, trying to gauge how much fire-power we've got left without expending too many gunboats to do it.* And yet he wouldn't say so aloud, for letting his people have a straw of hope to grasp for couldn't hurt and might possibly help.

So he held his tongue. But gazing at these people, all so much younger than he (*Who isn't?* he thought with a moment's wryness), he saw that it had been a waste of silence. They knew.

As she gazed at the sensor readouts, Hannah Avram thought of Rear Admiral Michael Chin and remembered the *bon vivant* she'd known. Did he still live at all?

The relief force had, on her orders, stayed on full sensor alert even in these regions far outside the system ecliptic, where no Bugs could reasonably be. Her caution had reaped an unexpected reward, for they now had an answer to one of the questions that had been plaguing them since their departure from Centauri: the fate of the Fleet Train.

The further they'd proceeded, the more they'd settled into the glum conclusion that nothing remained of Chin's command except debris dissipating into the void. But the sensors had brushed against what could only be survivors sheltering out here in the deeps far from any warp point—all too few survivors. Avram didn't even let herself think about the personnel losses that the absence of so many repair ships and transports implied. She couldn't, for she had a decision to make.

She made it. "Commodore Borghesi," she addressed her chief of staff, "inform Ops that I want to detach a couple of battlegroups to rendezvous with those survivors while the rest of us continue on course for Anderson Four. They're to convey my orders to Admiral Chin . . . or whoever's in command."

"What orders are those, Sky Marshal?"

"I want them to take up a position, at least ten light-hours from any warp point, and wait for us to return to this system with Second Fleet." Avram pointedly omitted any qualifiers. "At that time, we'll contact them by courier drone—keeping our presence concealed will no longer be a factor then—so they can rejoin us as we retire to Centauri."

"Aye, aye, Sir." Borghesi went to summon the staff and Avram took a last look at the meager tally of fugitives. She didn't really want to divide the none-too-abundant forces she was leading to Second Fleet's rescue. But the tatters of Fleet Train needed additional cover if they were to have any chance at all of surviving. And, unless she was very much mistaken, their morale needed any boost it could get.

"From all the information available to us, it is my judgment that the Bug blocking force will enter this system from Anderson Four in the immediate future."

Ivan Antonov looked at the half-circle of his staffers' faces and watched their reactions as his words sank home through layers of fatigue into their dulled awareness.

Stovall shook his head like a punch-drunk boxer. "You mean . . . ?"

"*Da.* The time has come to set course for the Anderson Four warp point." Antonov quickly raised a forestalling hand. "Let us be in no doubt as to the gravity of our position. Look here." He turned to the system holo display with the tiny icon of the local blue giant star at its center. In terms of the arbitrary "north" the computer had assigned as a frame of reference, Second Fleet lay about a hundred and forty light-minutes to the south-southeast. The warp point that represented their road home was due east of the star at a distance of slightly over a hundred and ninety light-minutes, placing it somewhat less than three light-hours to their northeast.

"From the vectors of the gunboat strikes we've sustained, Commodore Kozlov and I have been able to infer the approximate configuration of the enemy forces that have been sending them. We believe there are three elements. One has to be about here." He pointed a hand remote and a fuzzy scarlet icon winked to life due south of the star, describing with Second Fleet and the warp point a straight line. "We're less certain about the other two, but they must be in these general areas." A pair of the indeterminate red indicators, oscillating to denote even greater uncertainty, appeared in regions bracketing Second Fleet's present position and the first part of its course to the warp point. "We'll be able to lead the first one a stern chase. The problem will be the other two; they'll try to close in and engage us as we pass."

"Our speed advantage should enable us to slip out of any envelopment, Sir," de Bertholet stated confidently. "Despite the wear and tear our engines have sustained."

"I hope you're right, Commander. However, it can't hurt to throw off the enemy's calculations concerning our capabilities in that area. For this reason, I want to proceed at slightly less than our best speed. Fast enough to prevent the force to our southwest from overhauling, but slow enough to make the Bugs think our engines are in even worse shape than they are."

Midori Kozlov managed a smile. "The technique is called 'disinformation,' Admiral."

Antonov smiled back. "I know, Commodore. My ancestors—and some of yours—were once noted for it."

Attack Force One watched the enemy turn for the warp point at last. He had managed to work his way between Attack Force Three and Attack Force One, too far distant for either to engage. Attack Force Two was astern of him, and too slow to catch up, and his strategy was now obvious. Badly as he had been hurt, he still hoped to outrun the Fleet and escape through the warp point, and his timing was good—or would have been, if not for Attack Force Four.

But Attack Force Four was almost here. Attack Force One had kept it fully advised with periodic courier drones, and now it sent off another flight. The Fleet's fresh strength would arrive knowing precisely where to look for the enemy . . . and sweep in from the warp point, meeting him head-on. And so Attack Force One let its doomed foes run. It and Attack Force Three closed in from either flank, angling inward while Attack Force Two sealed the rear of the net, and the long, weary pursuit was almost over.

The last three and a half days had been the worst of Raymond Prescott's life, worse even than the desperate days in Telmasa. For eighty-six hours, his ships, a full third of Ivan Antonov's total combat strength, had sat silent and still, watching Bug courier drones come and go but doing *nothing* while their consorts fought for their lives. The battle was far too distant for his sensors to pick up the starships, gunboats, and fighters fighting it, but nuclear and antimatter explosions were glaringly evident, even at extended ranges, and there'd been too many of them.

But at least they mean there's still somebody *left . . . and they're headed this way at last.*

He nodded at the last thought. The Admiral was beginning his run. He was still thirty hours out, but he was coming in, and Prescott felt his inner tension winding still tighter.

And he knew something Antonov didn't. Chin's drones had reported not only the massive strength of the gunboat strikes which had ravaged the Fleet Train but their *timing*.

The Bugs didn't use light-speed communication relays between warp points. Presumably, that—like the cloaked pickets they seemed to leave everywhere—was a security measure, intended to deny any enemy a "bread crumb" trail to their inhabited systems. The fact that they hadn't attempted to destroy the comsat chain Jackson Teller had left in Erebor might also suggest that the notion simply hadn't occurred to them, which might be the best news of this entire disastrous affair. If they didn't realize Second Fleet had established a comsat chain in its rear, they were almost certain to have significantly overestimated the time Centauri would require to respond. If that were so, any relief fleet was likely to arrive long before they expected it. But the important point just now was that the Bugs relied *solely* on courier drones as their only means of coordinating at interstellar distances, and *Chin's* drones had told Prescott how long the Bugs had taken to come within sensor range of the Fleet Train. And *that* data gave him a good idea, given the top speed of courier drones and gunboats, just how far the Bugs' warp point into Anderson Three had been from Chin—and thus from the warp point to Anderson *Four*. Which meant that, unlike Ivan

Antonov, he *knew* the Bugs would be arriving within the next four-teen hours . . . and that Ivan Antonov had timed the climac-tic maneuver of his career perfectly. Now it was up to TF 21 to be certain it worked.

Ivan Antonov stared fixedly at the plot. It wasn't that he hoped to see anything there that he didn't already know. It was just that it was expected of him: Ivan the Terrible, displaying total, inhuman con-centration and impassivity.

So instead of looking for hidden meanings in the display the computer constantly updated—a silicon-based *idiot savant* compul-sively pawing its abacus—he let himself covertly contemplate the young people with whom he shared Flag Bridge, and the rest of *Colorado*, and the rest of the fleet.

So *young*. . . . Those youthful faces truly were from another time, another world, yet if any of them were to live, their survival depended upon him. They trusted him to get it right, and for just an instant, as their trust crushed down upon him like an extra layer of fatigue, he felt the weight of every endless year of his unnaturally extended life and knew he was too old.

He shook free of the thought. Surely all the experience one accu-mulated in a century and a half must count for something! Anyway, if the antigerone treatments really were a colossal counter-evolutionary mistake, humanity would simply be replaced by something that wouldn't make such errors, for it wouldn't deserve to survive. . . .

"*Now don't go Russian-nihilistic on me, EYE-van.*" Antonov's lips curved in a smile no one else noticed as he heard the voice echoing across the gulf of seven decades. *No, Howard, I won't*, he thought. *I can't afford to just now. I brought these people into this, and it's my duty to get as many of them as possible out of it.*

And, it ought to be possible to get a fair number out . . . if only the timing was right.

Dear God, bozhe-moi, *please let my timing have been right.*

Attack Force Four had reached its final warp point. A fresh shower of courier drones went ahead, announcing its arrival, and its warships prepared for transit. Its losses against the enemy's support echelon left it thirty percent understrength in gunboats, but it still had over four hundred. The ships without gunboat groups would be left behind—someone had to watch the warp point—and the others would join the attack on the enemy's fleet.

"Ships transiting the warp point!"

The announcement from Plotting wasn't loud, yet it cracked like a whip in Flag Bridge's silent tension. Prescott handed his coffee cup to a steward and spun his command chair to face his plot, and his mouth tightened as the deadly stream of Bug warships flowed into existence.

The escorts came first: thirty-six light cruisers, *Cataphracts* and *Carbines* in a tighter transit than any Terran admiral would countenance. They made no effort to scout—after all, a dozen battle-cruisers had been watching the warp point for over twenty days—but flowed out into a spherical screen, and then the first of those stupendous warships followed them. One, two, five—*eighteen* made transit, and behind them came twenty-four superdreadnoughts, and after them the battle-cruisers. One hundred and three starships burst through the flaw in space and formed up, and Raymond Prescott realized he was actually holding his breath as he waited.

Then they began to move, and a fierce exultation flared within him. Six of the new leviathans and half the superdreadnoughts remained behind, but the others—*all* the others, even the battle-cruisers which had picketed the warp point for so long—headed in-system, and they were already launching their gunboats.

"All right, Anna, Jacques," he said flatly. "Pass the standby signal. Those big bastards are the priority targets, then the SDs."

"Twelve of the new . . . mobile fortresses. At least a dozen superdreadnoughts. The battle-cruiser and light cruiser totals should be available soon." Midori Kozlov's voice was an inflectionless drone as she studied the sensor readouts like a soothsayer peering into the depths of a crystal ball and read off the tally of the Bug forces sweeping forward to intercept them.

"How many have been left to cover warp point?" Antonov's tightly controlled voice might have fooled anyone who didn't know him well enough to notice the loss of definite articles.

"Unknown, Sir. We're still too far out."

"No matter. It is time." The admiral swung his bearlike bulk to face de Bertholet. "Commander, deploy the fighters."

All the fighters Second Fleet still possessed had been at alert for hours, their pilots holding exhaustion at bay with drugs and adrenaline. Now they launched as one and took up flanking positions against gunboat attacks.

At the maximum speed it could manage and still keep formation, Second Fleet arrowed directly towards the massed ranks of death coming to meet it.

"All right, people," Prescott murmured, eyes locked to his plot. TF 21 had crept in even closer, moving at glacially slow speed. They were barely half a light-minute from the warp point, directly behind the ships facing the rest of Second Fleet, and any Orion would have envied his fang-baring smile. "This is what we came for. Let's make it count. Are you ready, Jacques?"

"Ready, Sir." The ops officer half-crouched over his console, like a runner in the blocks, and his hands rested lightly, ever so lightly, upon it.

"Execute!" Raymond Prescott snapped.

The ships on the warp point watched the enemy running headlong into the waiting tentacles of the rest of Attack Force Four. Given his speed, some of his units might actually win through the waiting inferno, but the detachment waited to sweep up the broken pieces as they came to it. The attack force's gunboats were two-thirds of the way to the enemy, and—

Four hundred and three SBMs exploded from empty space as TF 21 flushed its external racks. Another hundred belched from the *Dunkerques'* internal launchers, and their targets had had no inkling those ships were there. Thirty seconds passed before light speed sensors even detected TF 21's launch, and there was no time to react, no time to take evasive action or bring active defenses on-line. Raymond Prescott's birds were in terminal acquisition, screaming in on their targets at .8 *c*, and then the universe blew apart.

All five hundred of those missiles were directed at just six targets, for TF 21 had no idea how much damage those unfamiliar monsters could absorb. But however mighty their shields, however thick their armor, they were no match for that devastating strike. The vortex blazing on the warp point momentarily rivaled the blue giant furnace at the system's heart, and when it cleared, the ships which had been at its core no longer existed.

The Bugs reeled under the totally unexpected blow, and even as they fought to adjust to it, fresh salvos roared in from the *Dunkerques* and ten *Borzoi-C*-class fleet carriers launched three hundred and sixty hoarded fighters. Those strikegroups had been made fully up to strength before they were attached to TF 21, even at the expense of the exhausted, over-strained squadrons which had fought to protect Second Fleet's main body for ten heartbreaking days. Their pilots had sat in their ready rooms, ready for instant launch if TF 21 had been detected yet knowing—for they were veterans all—what their fellow pilots had endured while they sat inviolate in cloak. Now it was their turn, and the key to Second Fleet's survival lay in their hands.

They streaked in, drives howling, vision graying, and behind them came the rest of TF 21. The *Borneo*-class superdreadnoughts had no capital launchers, but they had heterodyne lasers and standard missile launchers, and they were fast. Raymond Prescott brought them in at 30,000 KPS while the *Dunkerques* lay back, pouring in SBMs and capital missiles, and the totally surprised Bug starships fought around in desperate turns to meet them.

It took the fighters three minutes to reach them—three minutes of frantic maneuvers while the *Dunkerques* hammered them with another six hundred missiles. Point defense stopped many of the follow-up birds, but the battle-cruisers got two more massive salvoes in virtually unopposed first, and three Bug superdreadnoughts were destroyed and two more damaged before the fighters even arrived.

AFHAWKs roared to meet the strike, but the Bugs had sent their escorts forward with the rest of their attack force. TF 21 lost thirty-seven fighters; the other three hundred and twenty-three, armed with full loads of FRAMs, carried through. There were ten superdreadnoughts and twelve battle-cruisers on the warp point when they began their runs; when they finished them, there were three air-streaming, shattered, half-molten wrecks, staggering half-blind towards TF 21 as if in some instinct to hurl themselves bodily upon their enemies.

But they never had the chance, for TF 21's enraged fighter jocks came screaming back. They had no external ordnance, only their internal lasers, but that was sufficient.

The warp point lay half a light-hour behind Attack Force Four; by the time it realized its detached units were under attack, every one of them had been dead for over twenty minutes.

The attack force had no idea how many enemy ships were astern of it. Its sensors showed a horde of attack craft sweeping back from the warp point, disappearing as they rejoined their mother ships to rearm, but no enemy starship had emerged from cloak. There couldn't be many vessels back there—surely the other attack forces would have known if any significant portion of the enemy fleet had eluded them!— and yet there must be a powerful force. The blazing speed of the detachment's destruction, even of the mighty new units, was proof of that, and Attack Force Four dared not be caught between an enemy of unknown strength and the survivors streaming towards it. It must know what it faced, and there was only one way to learn that.

The gunboats which had almost reached Second Fleet arced suddenly away, for they had the speed—and numbers—to reach the warp point once more and spread out, find the enemy, determine the nature of the threat.

Com lasers and courier drones spilled from the attack force to alert the other forces, but it would take yet another half hour for that information to reach the closest addressee. By the time it did, the diverted gunboat strike would be a sixth of the way back to the warp point.

The starships hesitated a moment longer, and then Attack Force Four turned to follow its gunboats. It was still closer to the warp point than the known enemy forces, but given its slower speed, the prey it had come to kill might actually be able to beat it there. Yet it had no choice. The enemy had smashed the barricade which was supposed to hold him pent; if it was not replaced, then all of his ships might yet escape.

Everyone on *Colorado*'s flag bridge had seen photos of distant nebulas where hot young stars blazed through the glowing clouds of cosmic dust from which they'd had their birth. Now they gazed at the main screen where the spectacle at the warp point was displayed: explosions so intense they must surely gnaw at the fabric of space itself but veiled by a surrounding haze of superheated gas, a nebula of man's creation. And there was utter, awed silence in the presence of a cataclysm that seemed beyond the powers of any save the Maker of Stars to wreak.

But then, after a time lag that the distance differential reduced to almost nothing, the four hundred incoming gunboats swerved away in hundred-and-eighty-degree turns and began to recede into the blackness. And all at once the silence shattered into a million fragments as all the pent-up tension released itself. Such were the cheers and the weeping that they hardly waxed any further when, minutes later, the enemy starships also turned back.

"Prescott *did* it, Sir!" Stovall turned exultantly to Antonov . . . and what he saw stopped him. Boulder-impervious to the storm of emotion around him, the admiral was staring at the tank in which the red icons of the enemy, having completed their turning maneuver, were racing for the warp point ahead of Second Fleet's green ones. He consulted his wrist calculator with scowling concentration, then faced Stovall.

"It appears, Commodore," he said quietly, "that our speed advantage won't quite suffice to overtake and pass the blocking force before it gets back to the warp point—at least not by any significant margin. Note also—" he indicated another portion of the tank, astern of the green icons "—that the Bug forces pursuing us have launched what must be their entire remaining gunboat complement."

"They won't catch us, Sir," Stovall stated emphatically.

"No, they won't . . . unless we slow down as a result of damage sustained when we catch up with the blocking force just short of the warp point. This leads me to two conclusions, Commodore Stovall, neither of them pleasant."

"Sir?"

"First of all, we will need our fighters to help us fight our way past the blocking force. *All* our fighters; we don't have enough left to send any to Admiral Prescott's assistance when the blocking force's gunboats get back to the warp point."

Stovall swallowed. He hadn't thought that far ahead. But the admiral was right, of course. Prescott would have to stand alone against those four hundred gunboats for as long as it took.

"Ah . . . and the *other* conclusion, Sir?"

"That we *cannot* slow down as we pass the blocking force, for if we do the gunboat waves pursuing us will catch up. Not for *any* reason. Therefore, you will pass the following general order: any ship that falls out of formation from battle damage is to be left behind."

For an instant, it simply didn't register on Stovall. Then he felt his head shaking slowly in mute denial. "Uh, Admiral Antonov, Sir . . . excuse me, but I thought I understood you to say that we are to *abandon our cripples.*"

"That is precisely what I said, Commodore, and I am not in the habit of repeating orders."

Stovall felt a flush spread from his ears and neck, and he didn't care, because before he could even think of stopping himself he blurted out the unsayable. "*No! By God*, Sir, you can't! Every tradition—"

"Commodore Stovall!" Antonov's voice had dropped whole octaves and it seemed to reverberate through the chief of staff's entire body, not just his eardrums. No one else had been able to make out precisely what they were saying; but everyone, in the immemorial manner of subordinates, found something else to be doing with silent concentration. Antonov's voice dropped to a near-whisper. "You will transmit the order, Commodore. Otherwise I will relieve you and order Commander de Bertholet to do so."

"But . . . but, Sir, the crews of those ships! I mean, if we were fighting any normal race—Orions, or even Thebans—it would be different! But—"

"Do you think I like it, Commodore? But understand this: not all of us are going to escape. If we insist on trying to rescue everyone, we will save *no one.* Accept that fact! And let me clarify my order—by 'any ship' I mean to include this one!"

Stovall started to open his mouth again. But then he felt the heat start to recede from his face. For Antonov was right. Oh, maybe not right in a human way . . . but that way offered no hope of survival for any of them.

All at once, for the first time, Stovall truly understood the origin of the nickname "Ivan the Terrible."

"Aye, aye, Sir," he said expressionlessly, and turned towards the com station.

✧   ✧   ✧

Four hundred gunboats swept towards the warp point. Behind them, the gunboats of Attack Forces One and Three streaked after Second Fleet, fifteen hundred strong, but they would still be over twenty minutes behind Ivan Antonov when his ships made transit.

If they made transit, for Attack Force Four still lay between him and safety, and Raymond Prescott locked his shock frame and sealed his helmet as the gunboats came in. The freshly arrived Bug force had also detached its light cruisers—his sensors had the uncloaked vessels clearly, watching them race towards him behind the gunboats— and CIC reported sensor ghosts which might well be cloaked vessels coming with them. *Battle-cruisers,* he thought. *Those have to be battle-cruisers. Well, we knew they've used military drives for some of their ships all along; it's about time they tried to produce a "fast wing" to match our Dunkerques.*

"Launch the fighters," he said quietly.

The gunboats roared onward. Their less powerful sensors were beginning to pick up the ghostly traces of cloaked vessels . . . and then there was something besides ghosts on their displays. Three hundred and fifteen attack craft exploded into space, and they knew they were doomed. The enemy's known attack craft strength had been so reduced they had intended to rely on internal weapons to beat off interceptions, and none mounted AFHAWKs. But there was nowhere else for them to go, and their mission remained unchanged. They must locate and identify the enemy's starships, and they streamed in to the attack.

"Attack sequence X-Ray," Captain Kinkaid announced. Acknowledgments came back, and she altered course slightly, leading her massed strikegroups to meet that phalanx of gunboats. She wasn't driving in as fast as she could have; there was no need, with the enemy coming to her, and so no point in putting the extra wear on her drives. She smiled at the thought—the smile of a hunting wolf—and looked at her tac officer.

"Targeting laid in, Sir," Lieutenant Brancuso announced crisply. "We've got good solutions. Launch range in . . . thirty-one seconds."

Raymond Prescott's fighters salvoed over nine hundred FM3s. Fireballs pocked the Bugs' formation—only a few, at first, but growing in the space of a breath to a forest fire that reached out from the front of that massed wave of gunboats, swept back along its flanks, and ate into its heart. Two hundred and seven died, and the survivors' datanets were shattered. They were no longer squadrons; they were broken bits and pieces, individual craft still charging forward, and Terran and Ophiuchi pilots closed with lasers. They had to enter the Bugs' point defense envelope to engage them, but gunboats were much bigger targets, and, unlike the Bugs, the Allied datanets were intact. Entire squadrons stooped upon their prey, lasers blazing in coordinated attacks on single targets, and Captain Kinkaid, covered by her own carrier's strikegroup and hovering just beyond the melee to coordinate the attack, realized *none* of the bastards mounted AFHAWKs!

"*Kill 'em!*" she snarled, and led SG 211 to join the slaughter.

The cruisers and battle-cruisers racing ahead of the rest of Attack Force Four watched their gunboats die, but some of them had gotten far enough in, lasted long enough to pierce the enemy's ECM and get contact reports off. Attack Force Four's detached screen knew what it faced, and the odds were less uneven than it had feared. The enemy had superdreadnoughts and almost as many battle-cruisers, but the screen had thirty-six light-cruisers to support the battle-cruisers, and the attack craft would have too little time to rearm for an anti-shipping strike. The screen could not kill all those enemy vessels, but it could hurt them badly . . . and that was all it truly had to do, with the rest of Attack Force Four coming up from astern.

"Here they come, Sir," Bichet said through gritted teeth as the fighters' relayed sensor data showed TF 21 the cloaked Bug battle-cruisers. Apparently the gunboats had done the same for the enemy, for those battle-cruisers began to belch SBMs. Their targeting wasn't perfect, but it was good enough, and point defense began tracking as they streaked in.

"I think we'll codename these 'Antelope,' Jacques. Appropriate, given their speed, don't you think?" Prescott's tone was almost whimsical, however intent his eyes, and Bichet nodded.

"From their salvo densities, they look pretty much like *Dunkerques,* Sir," Lieutenant Commander Ruiz put in. The logistics officer spoke with unnatural calm, refusing to let her admiral out-panache her, but her BuShips background showed in her professional assessment.

"Yes, they do," Prescott agreed as *Crete* began spitting countermissiles. His *Dunkerques* fired back at the Bugs. They could match the enemy's battle-cruisers almost one-for-one, and his fighters had nearly completed reforming after the gunboats' massacre, but the Bugs had a solid phalanx of *Cataphract-* and *Carbine*-class CLs. He couldn't send his fighters in against that kind of firepower with only their lasers . . . but he couldn't let the Bugs push him off the warp point, either. He *had* to hold it until the admiral arrived.

"Instruct the fighters to break off, Jacques," he said. "Recover and rearm them ASAP."

"Aye, aye, Sir."

"In the meantime, I believe *we* have an appointment with the Bugs," Prescott added calmly, and TFNS *Crete* led TF 21's superdreadnoughts straight at the enemy.

The enemy came to meet the screen, and the battle-cruisers realized they had erred by concentrating on the enemy's superdreadnoughts. Very few missiles had penetrated those ships' massed point defense, and the enemy's battle-cruisers had used their own immunity to batter the screen painfully. But the superdreadnoughts appeared to mount no capital launchers. They were closing into standard missile range, which would allow even the screen's missile-armed light cruisers to engage them. In the meantime, the battle-cruisers shifted fire to the enemy's battle-cruisers and prepared to switch from capital missiles to CAMs as the range fell.

At what seemed a crawl in the holo tanks, Second Fleet gradually overhauled the Bug blocking force in their race to the warp point.

Neither Antonov nor any of his officers could avoid a teeth-gritting awareness of the irony involved. If they'd had all the time in the world to kill Bugs, they would have been in an ideal position to close in on those enemy starships from their "blind zones" and eat them alive. But, in the here-and-now, fifteen hundred gunboats would have arrived during the meal. So they had to press on, past those Bug ships.

Nor could they afford the time-wasting course change to give them a wide berth as they passed. No, they had to pass within close range of undamaged, undepleted enemies that included those new behemoths.

They'd just have to take it until they could pull ahead.

TF 21 closed to standard missile range, hammering the Bugs with antimatter warheads, and the superdreadnoughts' powerful hetlasers ignored the battle-cruisers. Instead, they swiveled with deadly precision and blew every missile-armed CL apart with a single massed broadside. Then, and only then, did they turn to the battle-cruisers— just as the Bugs began firing CAMs.

In ninety-one seconds, twenty-three Bug battle-cruisers and seventeen more light cruisers ceased to exist . . . but they took the superdreadnoughts *Erie* and *Koko Nor* and the battle-cruisers *California* and *Howe* with them. Only six of Raymond Prescott's SDs escaped totally unscathed, and three more of his battle-cruisers were little more than air-streaming wrecks. But he held the warp point, and he looked back at the master plot as the Bug battle-line rumbled down upon him.

One edge of the Bug formation was an incandescent furnace of warheads and energy fire as Antonov's battered ships overtook it. The Bug superdreadnoughts and new, monster ships were forty percent slower than the Allied battle-line, yet it took an agonizingly long time for the Allied ships to begin to draw ahead of them, and Prescott bit his lip as icons flickered and danced with CIC's estimates of damage. The brutal pounding the rest of Second Fleet had endured while TF 21 held station on the warp point was all too evident in the two sides' weight of fire. Ivan Antonov had more ships than his opponent, but his carriers were little more than mobile targets, and many of his capital ships had been beaten into near impotence. Those which could still fight held station on *Colorado,* pounding back at the Bugs with desperate fury, and the hideous firepower of those new, monster ships slaughtered them methodically.

One of the new ships blew up, but the smaller Terran superdreadnoughts were paying at least a two-to-one price to kill them, and the ships Antonov's combat-capable units fought to protect were losing as well. The CVAs *Dragon, Gorgon, Horatious* and *Zirk-Sahaan* blew up or staggered out of formation, and the Bugs seemed to realize it wasn't necessary to *destroy* their enemies outright. As soon as any ship was lamed, they shifted to another target, battering at them, trying to cripple their drives and slow them until their own leviathans could resecure control of the warp point or the other attack forces' pursuing gunboats could overhaul.

The toll of dying ships rose hideously, and Prescott clenched his fists, chained to the warp point by his orders. The faster units of the main Bug formation were close enough to range on his own ships now, and his rearmed fighters launched while his starships bobbed and wove in evasive action and salvoed their own missiles. The battleship *Prince George* blew up in the heart of Antonov's formation, and her sister *Spartiate* lost a drive room and fell back—then turned to join the equally lamed superdreadnoughts *Sumatra, Kailas,* and *Mount Hood* and engage the enemy more closely. They could no longer escape; all they could do was make their deaths count by covering sisters who could still run, and Prescott's eyes burned as they drove into the enemy.

The battle-cruiser *Al-Sabanthu* tore apart, and Vice Admiral Taathaanahk died with his flagship. The CVLs *Arbiter* and *Shangri-La,* a part of Prescott's own task force for so many long months, exploded, and *still* the carnage went on and on and on.

But the Bugs were losing ships, too, he told himself fiercely. Five superdreadnoughts and now three of their new monster ships were gone, and others were damaged. His own fighters arrived, tearing into the enemy, ripple-firing FRAMs, vanishing in hateful spalls of fire as AFHAWKs or energy weapons or point defense snatched them out of space, yet it was working. *It was working!* Hideous as Second Fleet's losses were, some of its units were breaking into the clear, running ahead of the storm, already vanishing through the warp point while Antonov personally coordinated the rearguard and TF 21 engaged the handful of faster Bug ships foolhardy enough to come within its reach. *Crete*'s flag bridge crackled and seethed with combat chatter and orders as Prescott and his staff fought to impose some sort of order on the chaos, and then—

"Sir!"

Prescott's head snapped up at the anguish in Jacques Bichet's voice. He looked at his ops officer, and Bichet's face was white.

"Sir, *Colorado*'s lost three drive rooms!"

Raymond Prescott felt the blood drain from his face. He spun back to his plot and saw the jagged, flashing band that indicated critical damage about the fleet flagship's icon. Somehow, even now, it seemed impossible. It *had* to be a mistake. Ivan Antonov was a legend . . . *but even legends die,* a small, numb corner of Prescott's brain whispered.

"Recall the fighters." He didn't recognize his own voice. "Get them aboard for transit."

"But, Sir, the—"

"*Get them aboard!*" Prescott barked, without even turning his head. And then, "Com, get me the Flag."

Even now the range was sufficient to impose communications lags, and he waited—his heart an ice-wrapped knot—until an image stabilized on his display. He looked past Antonov's helmeted head into the anteroom of Hell. *Colorado*'s flag bridge was a depressurized shambles, littered with bodies—bodies, Prescott was numbly certain, of men and women he'd come to know well—and one side of Antonov's vacsuit was spattered with blood.

"You did well, Admiral," Antonov said quietly. "Thank you."

Prescott wanted to scream, to curse the other for *thanking* him, but he didn't. Instead, he forced his voice to work around the lump which seemed to strangle him.

"Sir, we can hold a little longer," he said. "Keep coming. We can get you out!"

Seconds ticked past while the message sped towards *Colorado,* and he saw two more of the cripples covering Second Fleet's retreat wiped from his display before Antonov replied.

"Negative, Admiral Prescott," he said almost calmly. "You are now Second Fleet's commander, and your responsibility is to your people. Recover your fighters and make transit." His eyes stared into Prescott's for a moment, and then he said, very softly, "You can do no more here, Raymond. All you can do is get the rest of our people home. I count on you for that."

The screen went blank as Antonov cut the circuit, and Raymond Prescott bowed his head.

"We can't recover all the fighters before the Bugs get here, Sir," Jacques Bichet said. "Over sixty are too far out to reach us in time."

"We'll have to leave them," Prescott said drearily.

"But—"

"I said we'll have to leave them." Prescott interrupted Bichet's sharp protest, and his voice was so flat with pain the ops officer closed his mouth with a snap.

Prescott felt Bichet's presence, but he couldn't take his eyes from the plot. Not even when his carriers flashed through the warp point, or when his battle-cruisers followed. Not even when his own flagship headed into the warp point. He stared into it, watching the last, abandoned units of Second Fleet's rearguard and their tattered umbrella of dying fighters as the pursuing Bugs closed for the kill.

The last thing Raymond Prescott saw before *Crete* vanished into the warp point herself was TFNS *Colorado*, her weapons destroyed, her broken hull trailing atmosphere and water vapor and debris but no life pods—never a life pod—as she redlined her surviving engines . . . and disappeared in an eye-tearing boil of light as she rammed one of those new monster ships head-on.

CHAPTER FORTY-ONE

The Road Home

The enemy had escaped.

It was not possible, yet he had. The Fleet had paid heavily to bait the trap, to close it behind him, to draw him in and expose his core systems to counterattack, and still almost half his warships had escaped.

Attack Force Four turned vengefully on the handful of cripples which remained in the system. The enemy's lamed vessels were no more than wrecks, yet they fought to the last, and when their final weapons were gone, they closed in agonizingly slow ramming attempts. Few succeeded, but each of those who did took yet another starship with it, and so the Fleet stood off and smashed the final units with missile and energy fire.

But when the last died, the Fleet's quandary remained. The plan had called for the enemy to perish here, *and he had not. A review of the tactical data indicated that most of his escapees were damaged—many critically—and his losses in attack craft had been even heavier, proportionately, than in starships. Yet those starships remained faster than the Fleet's battle-line, else they had not escaped at all. The handful of new, fast battle-cruisers might be able to overtake, as could the light cruisers of the other attack forces, once they reached the warp point, but by that time the enemy's capital ships would have had many hours to make emergency repairs. Superdreadnoughts, even damaged, would be more than a match for such light units, and if the enemy had detached yet another sacrificial rearguard to cover the warp point, the Fleet's starships would pay a hideous price to pursue him.*

Yet there might still be an answer. The gunboats of Attack Force One were barely twenty-five minutes from the warp point, with those of Attack Force Two only an hour behind. If Attack Force Four's survivors took those gunboats under command, they could be thrown through the warp

point in a single wave fourteen hundred strong. The enemy's decimated attack craft could not stop such a mighty force, and gunboats had the speed to run down any starship.

The decision was made, and Attack Force Four closed on the warp point, licking its wounds and reorganizing its shattered datagroups whil(it awaited the gunboats.

Crete emerged from the warp point. Too much grief and heartacl filled her flag bridge to permit of any sense of elation, but Raymor Prescott dragged himself up from the depths of his own despair. ten days—no, in twelve *hours*—he'd gone from Second Fleet's m(junior task force CO to its commander in chief. That terrible respc sibility was his, now, and he felt it grinding down upon him.

"How many fighters made it out, Jacques?"

His voice was quiet, but Bichet flinched. Prescott had no idea I much grief had leaked through his self-control, and the ops offi cleared his throat.

"I'm not certain, Sir. Captain Kinkaid made it—looks like *farshathkhanaak* for the fleet now—but I'm not even sure how I of the *carriers* got out. I'm trying to get reports now, but the r(the fleet's command structure is shot to hell, Sir."

"How many aboard *our* carriers?" Prescott pressed.

"I make it two hundred, Sir," Bichet said softly. "Roughly."

Prescott winced, then drew a deep breath.

"Relaunch half of them immediately. I want them on the warp as an antigunboat CSP. Rearm the other half with FM3s, if \ have enough. Each strikegroup will have fifteen minutes to ¡ nize its own squadrons, then I want them in space again. A as *they* launch, recall the first half to rearm and reorganize.

Bichet nodded, and Prescott turned to his chief of staff.

"Anna, your job is to find out what's left of the other tasl I want a head count, and I want to know exactly what mun and weapons—everyone has. Sandy," he switched to Ruiz, " complete inventory of what *we* have left, too. Work with Ann me a complete picture of the entire fleet ASAP."

The logistics officer nodded, and Prescott turned back to M

"Get me that info fast, Anna," he said with quiet urge Bugs'll be after us any minute, and I need to know what ¡ to fight with."

"Yes, Sir." Mandagalla's ebon face was grim. "What about ¡ reorganization?"

"That'll have to wait until we know what we've got. J; ops officer looked up from his console at his name, "fo¡ assume whatever TF 21 has left is all we've got. You're a

reorganize battlegroups as you see fit. We'll fine tune your OBs later . . . if we get the chance."

"Aye, aye, Sir," Bichet replied, and Prescott turned back to his plot as his staff dived into the frantic effort of discovering how much of Second Fleet had survived.

He already knew the numbers were going to be bad.

The last gunboat had finally arrived. Attack Force Four spent several more minutes rechecking its new battlegroups. Over half its ships had been destroyed, and another ten percent were too damaged to be committed, but it remained a powerful force—and far closer to intact than its enemies could possibly be. It was time.

"Gunboats making transit!" *Crete*'s tactical officer snapped.

Prescott's raised hand interrupted Captain Mandagalla's report as he wheeled back to the plot. Icons already spangled it, but the Bugs had given him eighty-one priceless minutes. Every surviving fighter— three hundred and seventy-one of them, barely thirty percent of Second Fleet's original fighter strength—had been rearmed and stationed directly atop the warp point. TF 21's carriers' combined magazines had retained only two hundred and six FM3s. They were mounted aboard a hundred and three fighters; the others had been fitted with three additional laser packs and one life support pod each. Most of those flight crews were exhausted, and every squadron was a scratch-built, jury-rigged improvisation. They were far, far below their usual standards of effectiveness . . . but they were also waiting in ambush.

The gunboats blinked into existence, and the fighters tore into them like demons. Missiles brushed past transit-addled point defense, and the rest of the fighters screamed in with their massive external laser armaments. They killed almost four hundred gunboats in their first pass, and another seventy before the Bugs' systems restabilized . . . but that left almost a thousand.

The fighter jocks wanted to loop back yet again, but Prescott's orders to Captain Kinkaid had been both clear and nondiscretionary. She broke off, using her superior speed to draw clear, and streaked after the rest of Second Fleet.

Prescott watched them come, and his heart was cold. They'd done better than he'd dared hope and lost only twenty-three of their own to do it, but the gunboat force was far stronger than expected. He'd had time for a brief conference with Antonov's exhausted battlegroup COs, and after the enormous hard kills Second Fleet had scored, it had seemed impossible for even Bugs to have that much left.

But they did, and it was coming straight for him.

"All right, Jacques. Go to Ivan Two," he said flatly.

"Aye, aye, Sir." Bichet's orders went out, and TF 21, supported by all the rest of Second Fleet's combat-capable superdreadnoughts and battleships—all twelve of them—dropped further astern of the other survivors. None of those ships' crews expected to survive the next hour . . . but that wasn't their job. All they were supposed to do— all they could *hope* to do, with their depleted magazines and battle damage—was throw up a roadblock. When the fighters reached them, half would peel off to support them; the rest would continue to the fleeing carriers to provide the survivors with whatever frail protection they could after the roadblock died. But Raymond Prescott knew one thing with absolute certainty: if he could draw the Bugs down on his command, few of them would survive his last fight to go after his cripples.

"Enemy ETA forty-seven minutes," Bichet announced quietly, and Prescott nodded.

"Anna, contact Admiral Mosby. I know her. Make absolutely certain that she understands she is not, under any circumstances, to send the other fighters back into this."

The gunboats recognized what the enemy intended, but they were willing to accept his sacrificial gambit, even at the price of their own destruction, for those had to be his last combat-capable units. With them gone, there would be nothing to prevent the other attack forces' new, fast battle-cruisers from overhauling and smashing his wounded ships on their long road home.

"ETA twenty minutes," Bichet announced. Prescott nodded acknowledgment without looking away from the plot. *At least it won't take long against this many of them,* he thought. *I wonder—*

"Sir! Admiral Prescott!" The sudden shout jerked his attention to his com officer, and his eyebrows flew up as he saw the wild exultation transfiguring Commander Hale's face. "Sky Marshal Avram!" she blurted. "*Sky Marshal Avram is on the priority channel!*"

Hannah Avram's heart twisted as her cloaked starships streaked past the first staggering, broken wrecks. She could feel the agonized exhaustion with which those ships clawed towards home. Second Fleet hadn't been *defeated*; it had been shattered, yet its survivors fought on, and she remembered Second Lorelei. This was the second time she'd seen the wreckage of a Terran Fleet, and heartbreak warred with pride as she watched that wreckage which had refused to die.

"I have Admiral Prescott, Sir," her com officer said.

"*Prescott?*"

"Yes, Sir." The com officer sounded stunned, as if he couldn't believe his own words. "Admiral Antonov is dead, Sir."

It hit Hannah like a fist, and even through her shock, she knew it would hit every other Terran officer—and all of their allies—with equal ferocity. But for now she was grateful for her shock. It kept the news from being real while she grappled with what she had to do, and she turned to her com screen as Raymond Prescott's exhausted, harrowed face appeared upon it.

"I'm coming in cloaked from your zero-zero-six, zero-zero-niner," she said flatly. "I have seventeen superdreadnoughts, ten battleships, eleven battle-cruisers, and twelve heavy cruisers, but no carriers. Keep coming; I estimate contact in twenty-three minutes. Stay alive, Raymond. Keep them bunched and concentrating on you until I can hit them by surprise, but *stay alive!*"

Raymond Prescott turned away from his com screen.

"Jacques, new orders for Kinkaid! *All* of her fighters stay with us."

"Yes, Sir!"

Icons shifted wildly as the fighters which had already passed *Crete* broke back towards her. The gunboats were only sixteen minutes out; he had to survive for five minutes, and without those other fighters, he wouldn't.

Minutes limped into eternity. His own sensors hadn't picked up the Sky Marshal yet, but he knew she was there . . . and the Bugs didn't. He watched the gunboats sweeping closer. Ten minutes out. Eight. Six. Kinkaid's fighters smashed into them head-on, and the plot was ugly with the fireballs of dying gunboats and allied pilots. His *Dunkerques* began punching SBMs and capital missiles into the Bugs, and the furnace roared hotter. Four minutes. Two. *Crete*'s missile batteries began to fire, and then the madness was upon him.

TF 21 and its supporting, scratch-built battlegroups writhed under a tsunami of gunboats. Ships twisted and danced in wild evasion maneuvers, and the visual displays were a kaleidoscope of explosions. The battleship *Timoléon* was the first to die, then the superdreadnoughts *Ellesmere* and *Namcha Barwa*. *Crete*'s sisters *Titicaca* and *Lake Michigan* followed, then the battle-cruiser *Arizona* and her squadron mate *Moltke*. But even as they were pounded to pieces, they fired back in an orgy of mutual destruction and hate. It went on and on, seconds stretching into hours and minutes into eternities, and *Crete* staggered again and again. Her shields were down, her armor shattered, her breached hull belching air, but somehow she lived and killed and killed and killed . . .

And then, suddenly, Hannah Avram was there. Her undamaged,

unshaken ships slammed into the Bugs like the hammer of God, and they flushed their XO racks as they came. The gunboats had been so intent on their prey they never even saw her coming, and the fresh hurricane of fire took them totally by surprise.

It was the Bugs' turn to die, caught between two fires. But they, too, struck back. The superdreadnoughts *Luzon* and *Palawan*, the SDEs *Mercedari*, *Tasmania*, and *Paricutan*, and the battleships San *Genera* and *Terrible* had raced all the way from Centauri to Anderson Four in just fourteen days only to die, but they accomplished their mission. The Bug gunboats burned like a prairie fire, and in their ashes lay the survival of what remained of Second Fleet.

Yet there was one last, agonizing price for the Terran Federation Navy to pay. Even as Hannah Avram's ops officer announced success and she turned to her com link to *Crete*, one last flurry of gunboats evaded every weapon targeted upon them in their death runs. They salvoed their external ordnance and followed it in, tearing deep into TFNS *Xingú*'s armored hull, and Raymond Prescott's com screen went blank with terrible, sudden finality.

The gunboats' destruction was final. The Fleet had no idea how many enemy starships had come to their fellows' rescue, nor of how they could have avoided the blocking gunboat force which should have stopped them, but there was no point in sending battle-cruisers and CLs against such heavy units without battle-line support. Courier drones were sent ahead, alerting the forces still between the enemy and home, but although the waiting gunboats might harass them, they were too weak to stop them.

The trap had failed . . . but not completely. The enemy had been decisively crippled, and all four attack forces would pursue as rapidly as possible. The Fleet would arrive on his heels, and this time it would send no mere survey force into the system from whence he had come.

CHAPTER FORTY-TWO

Road With No End

"No question about it, Sir," Feridoun Hafezi reported with as much briskness as any of them could manage these days. "They've entered the system in force this time—fourteen battle-cruisers."

Rear Admiral Sommers nodded and looked around the haggard faces of Survey Flotilla 19's staff—the faces of people who had, in all probability, just been condemned to death. Irritatingly, at this moment when she had far better uses for it, her mind flew back in space and time to their fourth warp transit from Anderson One, and she couldn't repress a wholly inappropriate smile.

"Well, Feridoun, remember when we'd just transited into that starless warp nexus and you hoped that maybe we could go someplace where things would be more interesting?"

The chief of staff grimaced. "Yes . . . I did, didn't I? Now I finally understand why combat veterans never seem to mind being bored!"

It had been just after that, with their warp point survey of that stretch of space still in progress, when they'd become aware of the Bug forces closing in behind them. Where they could have come from along this barren warp chain, and what their presence implied about the fate of Second Fleet, were questions Sommers hadn't had the luxury of contemplating. Instead, she'd had to make an impossible decision. Trying to fight her way home through enemy forces of unknown size hadn't even been an option; SF 19 was no battle fleet. Forging on into the unknown on the one-in-a-million chance of finding a warp chain that doubled back to Allied space had seemed an equally preposterous alternative. But it had been the only alternative she'd had, and she had ordered the *Huns* to redouble their efforts to find a second warp point.

They'd succeeded . . . just as one of the probing Bug gunboats stumbled onto the cloaked Terran ships. It sounded the alarm before it died, and they'd been unable to prevent the packs of pursuing gunboats from observing them as they fled towards the newly discovered warp point They'd emerged into the domain of a red giant that had long since incinerated any planets it might have possessed. Without even pausing for breath, Sommers had ordered her *Huns* to spread out in a desperate quest for warp points while the gunslingers turned at bay against the pursuers they'd known would be through the warp point close behind them.

Her fighters had sent the initial wave of gunboats reeling back through the warp point. Then the *real* pursuit burst on them in mass simultaneous transits of gunboats and cruisers, followed by waves of battle-cruisers. Sommers' combatants had battered them back through the warp point again, winning priceless time for the scout cruisers' frantic search for a warp point.

TFNS *Inca*, which had found the way out of the last system, had repeated her feat while there was still time. Sommers had ordered the flotilla toward the newly discovered warp point, but fresh Bug gunboats had poured into the system just as the fighter screen she'd left behind had come to the end of its life support and begun to withdraw. A desperate dogfight had swirled across the red giant's sky, and the damaged battle cruiser *Kalinin*, her crew evacuated, had been left behind to an attention-distracting self-immolation. But the flotilla had, in the end, managed to transit undetected, leaving behind the cooling plasma that had been the gunboats which might have pinpointed the escape-hatch warp point. And Sommers had been able to breathe again, in the feeble light of the type M red main-sequence star into whose system they'd materialized.

Ten days had passed before the Bugs found their way into the new system and sent clouds of gunboats probing into it while their battle-cruisers sat watchfully on the warp point. Sommers' ships, in cloaked battlegroups built around the *Huns*, had commenced a nerve-racking game of cat and mouse as the search for yet another new warp point went on.

Then, three days after the Bugs' arrival, four of their gunboats blundered into Sommers' carriers and freighters. Hastily launched fighters had blasted them out of space and then rendezvoused with their carriers beyond scanner range. SF 19, reprieved once more, had resumed its cloaked maneuverings. But the Bugs, with their enemies' presence in the system positively confirmed, had intensified their search. And now, three days later, they'd been reinforced, bringing their total in-system strength to thirty-two battle-cruisers and God knew how many gunboats. . . .

"Yes," Sommers said, dragging her mind back to the staff meeting, "I believe the situation has ceased to be desperate and become serious." A couple of people smiled. "We now need to decide what changes, if any, to make in our survey procedure." She indicated the display screen. It was no holotank, but two dimensions were all that was required to display the orbital plane of this system's cold, worthless planets. It showed the warp point through which they'd entered and on which the Bug battle-cruisers now squatted sullenly, a hundred and twenty light-minutes out from the red star on a bearing about thirty degrees "east" of the display's arbitrary north. Other icons showed the elements into which SF 19 had been divided, probing in regions closer to the system primary. "The floor is now open to suggestions. Yes, Feridoun?"

The chief of staff cleared his throat. "Admiral, in my considered judgment, the arrival of more Bug battle-cruisers lends added force to the argument I've made before."

In private, Sommers mentally interjected. Now it seemed he'd decided to go public. "Why is that?" she asked aloud.

"Operating in the inner system, so close to our entry warp point, maximizes our vulnerability to detection by the battle-cruisers there. The presence of additional battle-cruisers makes the risk we're running an even more unacceptable one."

Sommers decided not to make an issue of Hafezi's arguably improper use of the word *unacceptable.* "You're aware of the basis for my orders."

"Yes, Sir: you're firmly convinced that the warp point we're looking for is a Type Seven, all known examples of which occur within ninety light-minutes of their system primaries." Hafezi drew a deep breath. "Admiral, I have utmost respect for the extensive survey experience on which you base this . . . hunch. But I must point out that only nine percent of all open warp points are Type Sevens. And *all* the other ninety-one percent are located at greater distances from their primaries—usually at considerably greater distances. I therefore recommend that we discontinue our inner-system survey and turn our attention to the outer system, where the probability of finding a warp point is eleven times greater and where we can perform survey operations beyond the enemy battle-cruisers' sensor range."

Sommers restrained an angry retort—she *had* opened the floor to suggestions, and Hafezi hadn't quite strayed over the line into insubordination. "There's something in what you say, Commodore. But I would remind you that the Bugs, presumably following the same line of logic as yourself, have sent their gunboats to the system's outer limits and begun a gradual inward sweep. And while gunboat sensors aren't as powerful as those of battle-cruisers, there are a lot more of them."

She held the chief of staff's eyes. "At any rate, that is all secondary. The central point is that the region we're in now is the place to find a Type Seven. And that, in *my* 'considered judgment,' is precisely what we're looking for."

Hafezi's eyes didn't waver. "I respectfully disagree, Sir."

They continued to lock eyes while the rest of the staffers tried to be inconspicuous and Sommers wondered why the chief of staff was so determined to make this a contest of wills. *Could it be,* came the unwelcome question, *because I'm a woman?*

Feridoun came from a tradition of educated cosmopolitanism; serving under a Westerner wouldn't gall him. But a woman . . . ?

It wasn't even that she was a Western woman. There was a strain in Islam which had always equated *Western woman* with *whore,* but he'd no more have any truck with that than Sommers would with the trashier elements of the West's past. Indeed, an Islamic woman might actually have been worse, summoning up from his mental background certain assumptions about the proper roles of the sexes that not even his austere and intellectualized form of Islam had ever entirely exorcized.

But none of that mattered, for Sommers was in command, and she had to *stay* there if they were to have any hope, however forlorn, of survival. Attempts to command by committee—or COs who waffled when decision time came—were a prescription for disaster Aileen Sommers had no intention of following. *And,* she thought grimly, *given that a Type Seven is our only real chance to get out of this system alive, I'm not about to debate logic-versus-instinct with* anyone.

"Your objection is noted, Commodore, and you may have it on record in any form you wish. Nevertheless, we will continue to conduct our survey as per my orders. Is that clear?" Sommers' final question was not just for Hafezi, for her eyes swept over the entire staff.

Only one other pair of eyes wavered under that regard. Commander Arabella Maningo, the logistics officer, looked left and right as though searching for something that wasn't there. When she spoke, her voice was at first quiet to the point of inaudibility and level to the point of expressionlessness, only gradually taking on a high quaver. "What does any of this matter? Even if we do find a warp point and get through it, we'll just be one more system further away from home. And then we'll have to find *another* warp point, and then another, on and on forever, and eventually our ships will wear out and our life-systems will degrade—"

"That will do!" The bullwhip crack in Sommers' voice brought Maningo's head jerking up, eyes blinking, and the fog of incipient hysteria in the compartment seemed to dissipate. "I know that pressing on into the unknown is a bleak option. But it happens to be the only option we've got! And it's *not* hopeless. Remember, the Federation and its allies comprise one hell of a lot of warp nexi. It's not at all out of the question that we'll happen onto one of them. And we're equipped for long-term independent operations. Our maintenance resources won't give out any time soon . . . assuming that *you* manage to do your job."

Maningo's eyes flashed and her jaw clenched. *Good,* Sommers thought. Better anger than the lugubrious despair that would overtake them if they let the nightmare vision of suffocating in their own wastes, lost in an infinity of cold dark emptiness, take up residence in their heads. She found herself half-wishing that the Bugs would find them—this waiting was killing them as dead as combat could, and taking longer about it.

She shook the thought away and met all their eyes again. "We will continue to pursue whatever avenue holds out any hope of survival. That is our minimal obligation to our personnel. Giving up is not an option we are permitted!" She made sure none of those eyes met hers, either in defiance or with a mute plea to let them all lie down and die, before she adjourned the meeting.

The Bugs found them midway into the second watch of the following day.

Sommers and Hafezi were both on the flag bridge, maintaining a mutual politeness which was brittle in its frigidity, when the sensors erupted in electronic panic. A dozen gunboats, sweeping out of the blackness into close sensor range of *Jamaica*'s own battlegroup. They were also within missile range of the group's two battle-cruisers.

"Get them!" Sommers snapped as the gunboats turned tightly to escape with their news. But missiles were already arrowing forth from *Jamaica* and *Roma* as per standing orders. Nine were blasted apart, yet three got beyond the missiles' reach. Sommers and Hafezi looked at each other wordlessly, all differences forgotten. By unspoken consent, they turned to the system display in which the four tiny battlegroups and the skulking cluster of carriers and freighters swam. Of course there'd be no change in Bug dispositions yet. But as soon as those surviving gunboats' messages could speed across the light-minutes . . .

She stared for a moment at the icon that represented her own little battlegroup—in addition to the battle-cruisers she had the *Hun*-class scout cruiser *Uzbek* and the CLE *Marblehead*—and then turned to Hafezi. "Feridoun, I want the battlegroup to proceed on this course." She used her remote, and a string-light grew in the holotank.

"*Away* from the others, Sir?"

"That's right. We're the only ones whose location the Bugs know. I want to draw them away from the rest of the flotilla."

"We'd stand a better chance of defending ourselves if we joined forces, Sir. Especially with the carriers—"

"Negative. Even combined, we wouldn't stand a chance against the Bug forces in this system. No, the other groups' best defense is invisibility. Which means, among other things, that the carriers are *not* to launch their fighters, in support of us or for any other reason. It would maximize the Bugs' chances of detecting them, and their lack of a command ship to datalink their point defense makes them peculiarly vulnerable." She gave the chief of staff a hard look. "Carry out your orders, Commodore."

"Aye, aye, Sir," Hafezi said without a perceptible pause.

Jamaica's battlegroup swung into its new course, and as the minutes crept by the scarlet lights of incoming gunboats began to pop into existence on Sommers' plot like a rash breaking out. *No way,* she thought. *They've got us. No self-deception. And no searching Feridoun's face for reproach.* She straightened her back and gazed at the viewscreen on which the approaching death was, of course, not to be seen. *At least the others will have more time for a search. It's still not impossible that some of them could—*

"Admiral!" The voice from the com station was almost unseemly in its loudness. "Priority signal from *Thémis*. They've found it, Sir!"

"Found it? Found what?" Sommers blinked away her oppressively dark thoughts and fought to shift mental gears.

"A warp point, Sir! A Type Seven, located . . . well, they're downloading it now, Sir."

In the holotank, to the "east-northeast" of the primary star at a distance of about sixty light-minutes from it, the icon of a warp point winked into life like the electric signpost of a doorway out of Hell.

"Admiral! You were right!" It never for an instant occurred to Sommers to suspect Hafezi of brown-nosing. There was nothing in his face but relief and unaffected congratulation. "We can turn around and make it out before any of the gunboats reach us."

"No." Sommers' quiet monosyllable wiped the chief of staff's face clean of every expression but bewilderment. "Our other groups are all closer to it than we are—and we have no knowledge of the Bugs' strength in their vicinity." She shook her head. "No, we'll continue to try to draw the Bugs after us. Order all other elements of the flotilla to clear the system ASAP."

For a moment that stretched, Hafezi stared at her. Then he spoke levelly. "Admiral, have you considered the effect this order will have on our personnel's morale? There's no way we can keep the rumor from circulating through this ship that a warp point's been found."

And that I'm slamming that doorway out of Hell shut in their faces.
She forced herself to smile. "Feridoun, you've been a naval officer long
enough to know that the only antidote to rumor is forthrightness."
(Although, her familiar imp reminded her, some officers *never* learned
it.) "I'll address the crew, and have it patched through to the other
three ships. I'll tell them the situation, and explain to them that this
is the way to maximize the chance of survival for *some* of our people,
and that it is therefore our duty."

"With great respect, Admiral, are you *sure* it's our duty? Are you
certain this doesn't go just a little beyond it? Is it possible that
you're . . . trying to prove something?"

"I'll ignore that last question, Commodore. But as to the nature
of our duty . . . yes, this is my interpretation of it. And my interpretation is the one that counts, isn't it?"

"Of course, Admiral. I'll give the necessary orders." Hafezi turned
to go, then paused and faced her, and a smile flashed in the beard
he'd managed through everything to keep as precisely sculpted as
ever. (She recalled the Prophet's admonition to the faithful to grow
beards so as not to be mistaken for Romans but to trim them so
as not to be mistaken for Jews.) "By the way, I meant it: you were
right and I was wrong, and those who *do* get out of this will owe
their lives entirely to you." Then he was gone before she could think
of a response.

The battlegroups led by *Thémis* and *Belvedera* had transited the
newly discovered warp point, and both times *Jamaica* had rung with
cheering that had promptly subsided as they'd all gone back to awaiting
the approaching gunboats. Finally, the red and green icons crawled
together in the holotank, and time seemed to accelerate.

Twenty-odd gunboats swept in from the blackness, sprinkling the
battlegroup with missile fire that point defense could deal with. Then
they came on through a storm of second-generation close assault
missiles, seeking self-immolation. Three of them survived long enough
to find it.

A starship's first line of defense against collisions—intended and
otherwise—is its electromagnetic shields. Its second line of defense
is its space-distorting drive field, without which any physical impact
at such velocities would be totally and spectacularly fatal. It is only
after both of these are overloaded that the occupants are affected in
any way, for any violence—however horrific—that expends itself
against them has no physical medium through which to transmit shock
waves to the ship itself. Thus Sommers, Hafezi and the rest of the
flag bridge's complement sat in their cocooning shock frames and felt
no concussion as the gunboat that had approached far too swiftly to

be seen was consumed. They also saw nothing, for the viewscreen went black at the moment of impact. When it came back on, a few bits of still white-hot debris could briefly be glimpsed as they spun away and were swallowed by infinity.

"*Roma* got two kamikazes, Sir," Hafezi reported. "Fortunately, there was an interval between them, and there was no physical damage. A near thing, though; she took a lot more shield overload than we did."

"Tell them to get the shields restored as quickly as possible," Sommers ordered. "Same goes for this ship. The next wave—" she waved at the plot "—isn't going to be nearly as easy."

Hafezi moved away. But he was intercepted by the duty com rating. (In a quiet voice; he'd had words with them about blurting things out.) He turned back to Sommers with a frown.

"Admiral, we've gotten a signal from Captain Kabilovic. They've detected a Bug gunboat force vectoring in on the carriers and freighters. In light of the overwhelming probability that they've been detected, he's asking for permission to launch his fighters."

She had to smile. "Yes, that's the way Milos would put it. Permission granted, of course." She sighed deeply. "Well, Feridoun, there's no further point in trying to draw the Bugs off them, is there? Get us headed for the warp point at max. We'll rendezvous with Milos on our way."

For an absurd instant, Hafezi actually looked embarrassed by the fact that the course of action he'd recommended had turned out to be the only viable one. But it only lasted an instant. Then he was off, and Sommers was left looking at the holotank in which the Bug battle-cruiser formations at the entry warp point had moved off station and proceeded to intercept this newly detected group of prey.

Even Hafezi was looking a little disheveled—he'd developed a nervous habit of running his fingers through his beard—as they approached their rendezvous with the carriers.

It had been a terrifying chase. For a while it had looked as though the battle-cruisers that had been pursuing them—faster than Bug battle-cruisers had a right to move—would be able to swerve aside and intercept the carriers at a time when the fighters were otherwise occupied. But then the third survey battlegroup, led by TFNS *Imperieuse,* struggling to reach the warp point, had maneuvered into the Bugs' blind zone and given them a serious load of missiles up the ass. The subsequent degradation in Bug fire control suggested that they'd gotten the command ship—*something* had to go right every now and then—and the subsequent demolition of the unreasonably fast battle-cruisers had followed as a matter of course.

Stung, the Bugs had diverted their available gunboats to the new threat, and TFNS *Caio Duilio* had vanished in multiple fireballs of kamikaze attacks. But Sommers had used the time that had been won and was now coming into datalink range of the carriers—

"Incoming gunboats!"

With practiced precision, they all flung themselves into their command chairs and locked their shock frames. Sommers and Hafezi had a chance to make quick eye contact before the flood of data and horror flowed over them.

The gunboats were barely even bothering with extended-range missile fire anymore. With nightmarish persistence, they sought out ramming targets, and this time they came in a wave that swamped the little battlegroup's defenses. With almost physical pain, Sommers watched the readouts that told of *Uzbek*'s cataclysmic destruction, of damage to *Roma* and *Marblehead,* of one course after another of *Jamaica*'s own shields giving up in showers of sparks and clouds of acrid smoke as their generators overloaded . . .

"Incoming!"

As though struck by a war-god's hammer, *Jamaica* shuddered as a gunboat's death agony smashed down the last of her shields and rended hull metal. Sommers barely heard the apocalyptic noise, for her vision began to dim as she was whiplashed back and forth within the life-saving confines of her shock frame. Then came another hammer-stroke, and another, and another . . .

Her next awareness was of shouting that seemed to come from a great distance. She shook her head to clear it, tasting the brassy tang of blood. Vision returned, and she found that the shouts hadn't been coming from so far away after all. In fact, Hafezi's face was only a few inches from hers, and those of the medics crowding in behind him weren't much further. At first she thought the ship was still shuddering, but it was only Hafezi, shaking her.

"Aileen . . . er, Admiral, are you all right?"

Why does he look so frantic? She wondered with a small fraction of her returning consciousness. Most of it took in the fact that she was still on *Jamaica*'s flag bridge—a flag bridge that was still functioning. The next fact to register was that Hafezi's faceplate was open, as was hers. So they had air. She tried to sit up, and found she had to shake her head again.

"Yes . . . yes, I'm all right. What about the ship?"

"Damage control has things in hand," Hafezi reported. She wondered why he looked weak with relief, and decided it must be because the ship had come through. "Most of our internal systems are all right, and the rest will be soon. But we haven't much in the way of armor integrity left."

"And the others?"

"You know about *Uzbek. Marblehead isn't* much better off; she's got one engine room left, but not much else. *Roma* is in about the same condition we are."

Sommers struggled upright and waved away the medics. "We won't survive the next wave," she muttered. She forced her brain to think and her voice to firm up. "I see we've got a little time left before that next wave's ETA. Let's use it. I want to incorporate the carriers into this ship's datagroup; we can use their point defense. That's our first priority."

"Aye, aye, Sir. But . . . Admiral, you need to let them take you to sickbay and have a look at you."

"No time. Now, our second priority is to get *Marblehead*'s survivors evacuated. Send our small craft and *Roma*'s. What's the status of the fighter groups?"

"*Staghound*'s squadrons are back aboard the carrier, rearming. Same goes for most of the Ophiuchi. But two of their squadrons got through to *Imperieuse* and her battle group. That's why three of those ships still live, although *Imperieuse* is badly damaged. The Ophiuchi are still there."

"Good. Signal *Imperieuse* and order them to make a beeline for the warp point. Move!" She stood up and smiled at Hafezi and the hovering medics. "See, I'm fine."

They departed, still looking dubious. It was only then that she carefully lowered herself back down into the command chair and closed her eyes to shut out the swirling universe.

The situation was somewhat frustrating. Half the Fleet's available gunboat strength was still in the system's outer reaches, and could not arrive in time to be a factor. And after suffering that costly surprise, the battle-cruisers would be kept together—which meant the new fast ones wouldn't be able to take advantage of their speed . . . and that it would take the formation a long time to bring the enemy within missile range.

But did they have that time? The enemy had obviously discovered a warp point; his headlong flight could have no other destination. But where was that warp point? There would be no way of knowing until the enemy ships began to vanish.

So there was no time to organize the gunboats into a single overwhelming wave. The scattered elements must continue to make piecemeal attacks. Even if they couldn't destroy the enemy before he made transit, they must at all costs stay in contact so as to observe that transit.

"*Nürnberg* is Code Omega, Sir."

Sommers nodded absently, her soul as dulled to pain as her body had become after the repeated kamikaze impacts that had begun to tear *Jamaica*'s vitals. The flagship couldn't complain; *Roma* had taken even worse damage.

But the chase was coming to an end—the temporary sort of end that was the only kind that seemed possible for them anymore . . .

"*Boise* has transited, Sir," Hafezi reported quietly.

Sommers nodded again. She couldn't bring herself to rejoice. They'd made it to another warp point, true. But the Bugs would follow them, for they would pinpoint that warp point from her ships' transits. So it would be the same all over again in yet another system. . . .

She straightened. "Get the carriers through as soon as possible. The battle-cruisers will form a rearguard. *Jamaica* will, of course, be the last to transit."

"Aye, aye, Sir."

Roma died just short of the warp point. So did the freighter *Voyager*, despite everything the battle-cruisers could do to shield her. But then the last battered half-wreck was through, and *Jamaica* was coming up on the hole in spacetime through which she would sail into . . . what?

Hafezi turned to face her. "You did it, Admiral. You got us out of this system."

No one else was in earshot, and she finally let bitterness enter her voice. "Yes . . . for what?" She indicated the plot, with the swarming red icons that would follow them through the warp point.

Hafezi shook his head. "It doesn't matter, Aileen. You did your duty, and a good deal more besides." His eyes held hers, and he reached out a hand and gripped hers, hard, in a motion that his body shielded from all eyes on the flag bridge.

She returned the pressure, wordlessly because there were no words, and smiled tremulously at him.

"Stand by for transit!"

Their hands were still clasped as TFNS *Jamaica* vanished from the system of the red sun.

CHAPTER FORTY-THREE

"I wish I could spare more."

"I'm afraid that's it, Ellen," Oscar Pederson said wearily. He ran a hand through his hair and leaned back in his chair aboard Sky Watch One, gazing into the system schematic displayed above his desk. It was littered with the wildly scrambled icons of Fortress Command units, and Ellen MacGregor sat in the flag briefing room of TFNS *Amaretsu*, studying its twin from the other end of their conference link.

"I wish I could spare more," he went on, "but if it comes apart on you, I'll need everything I've got just to fend them off Nova Terra and Eden—not to mention this side of The Gateway."

"I understand, Oscar," MacGregor replied in a sympathetic tone. It was a bit hard, just at the moment, to sympathize with anyone but herself, yet she didn't envy Pederson a bit. They held the same rank, but he was Fortress Command while she was Battle Fleet, and that gave her command authority in Centauri until Hannah Avram's return. If she ordered him to give up still more fortresses, he'd have no recourse but to obey, and part of her wanted to do just that— especially since she was busy *leaving* the system at the moment with every warship she could scrape up. She was also leaving the warp point mother naked in her absence, but if she *didn't* take those ships forward into Anderson Two, the gunboats on that system's warp point to Anderson Three would have a field day against Second Fleet's survivors. Uncovering Centauri didn't make her any happier than it made Pederson. But the very fact that she was leaving only gave added point to his responsibility for all of Centauri, not just the Anderson Two warp point, in her absence, and she refused to second guess his dispositions.

"It ought to be enough," she told him now, lips pursed as she continued her study of the schematic. Alpha Centauri was the second most heavily fortified system in human-held space, with powerful fortress shells and minefields on each of its eleven open warp points. Fortress Command had begun assembling fresh forts to cover the system's newly discovered *twelfth* warp point even before Second Fleet's departure, and a potent shell of eighteen fortresses had been "borrowed" from the other warp points to cover it while its own OWPs were built. Pederson had personally overseen both the siting of the forts and the beginning of the new minefields, and since the new warp point was a closed one, he'd been able to emplace the mines directly atop it. That would deny an attack any clear zone into which it might transit, and he'd ringed the mines with independently deployed energy platforms, including both laser buoys and primary beam platforms, for good measure. With that backing, MacGregor had felt thoroughly confident of even her badly understrength Fourth Fleet's ability to guarantee Centauri's security in Second Fleet's rear.

But that was the critical point: she'd expected to cover Second Fleet's *rear,* and like everyone else, she'd thought she had months to perfect her defenses. Second Fleet was driving the Bugs back, after all, and even if the enemy managed to mount a counterattack, Ivan Antonov's warships would be between him and Centauri. At the very least, Antonov would be able to slow him down and buy time for MacGregor and Pederson to dig in behind him.

That comfortable assumption no longer applied, and Pederson had every minelayer in the system employed in the frantic placement of more mines and platforms. It was going slower than MacGregor would have liked—(*of course,* she thought wryly, *it* couldn't *go fast enough to make me* happy!)—but that wasn't because the weapons weren't available. Mines and energy platforms were being *produced* at a staggering rate by the system's spaceborne industry, and even if they hadn't been, she and Pederson could have raided the other warp points' long established defenses for them. No, the problem was that there were only so many minelayers, and their crews, however skilled, could physically position weapons only so quickly. They were working till they dropped, but the mine densities needed to blunt a Bug attack simply couldn't be built up overnight.

Which was why she was having this conference. Pederson and his staff had stripped ten of Centauri's eleven open warp points of virtually all their OWPs and commandeered every available tug in Centauri and Sol to reposition those forts. Both he and MacGregor were aware that the Grand Alliance was straining every nerve to reinforce Fourth Fleet, and even if MacGregor lost control of the outer system, the forces rushing back towards Centauri would almost certainly regain it in time. But it was Oscar Pederson's job to see to it that there were still live humans on the system's planets when that time came—not to mention his responsibility to protect Centauri's mammoth orbital industrial infrastructure and provide the maximum possible cover for The Gateway. Humanity's home system was even more heavily fortified than Centauri, but Centauri was Sol's buffer and glacis. That had been the bedrock of the TFN's strategic planning ever since there'd *been* a Federation Navy, and that—and Pederson's local concerns here in Centauri—had governed his proposed OWP redistribution. The majority were bound for positions around the system's twin planets to bolster Sky Watch One and the other orbiting space stations. Those not headed there had been divided equally between The Gateway and the closed warp point beyond which Hannah Avram's relief force was—*must* be—leading Ivan Antonov's survivors towards safety. Once they were all in position, MacGregor would have seventy fortresses, with something like a thousand fighters embarked, to bar the Bugs' passage into Centauri.

And a damned good thing, too, she thought mordantly, *'cause I sure as hell don't have anything* else *to do the job with!*

She grimaced at the familiar thought. The Federation was enormous, and ships took months to travel from its core to its borders. Those vast distances had always spread the TFN far thinner than raw hull numbers might suggest to the layman, for a starship could be in only one place at a time, and that simple fact was the crux of Ellen MacGregor's problem.

Home Fleet, as the biggest single concentration of Terran warships, had been heavily raided in the war's opening phases. As every available forward-deployed unit had been rushed towards threatened sectors—the Romulus Cluster, originally, and then Kliean——Home Fleet units had been redeployed to fill the vacuum created by their departure. Then the need to build up nodal reaction forces throughout Allied Space had put still more strain on the Alliance's navies, and once again, Home Fleet had been tapped to help make up the required numbers. MacGregor understood the logic behind that. Given Sol's position at the very core of the Federation, it had certainly seemed as unthreatened as any star system was likely to be, and the needed ships had to come from *somewhere.*

But then the Bugs had stumbled into Centauri and Operation Pesthouse had been mounted—from Centauri—ten months before it was scheduled to kick off from Zephrain. Half the units originally earmarked for Second Fleet had already been en route to Zephrain, so the cupboard had been bare when GHQ started looking around for the muscle Pesthouse required, and its eye had fallen yet *again* on Home Fleet. All of which meant that, at this moment, Ellen

MacGregor had precisely forty-seven starships, headed by only six superdreadnoughts, nine battleships, and Home Fleet's last eleven carriers and assault carriers, to support those seventy OWPs. More were coming as fast and hard as they could, but they weren't here yet, and she didn't even know precisely how many were on their way. And however many there might be, neither they, nor the forts, nor the minefields were on the warp point *now*.

She shook herself and produced a crooked half-smile for Pederson's benefit.

"It ought to be enough," she repeated. "And it damned well *better* be, hadn't it?"

The attack forces' courier drones confused the blocking force gunboats, for they clearly suggested that the enemy had somehow gotten a relief force through the warp point the gunboats were charged to block. Surely that was impossible. The attacks on the enemy's support echelon had put the blocking force behind schedule, true, but not enough for that. Unless, of course, the Fleet had misjudged the enemy's initial deployments. The Fleet had been unable to scout the intervening systems before attacking, after all. It was possible that the enemy's "relief force" had actually been a routine reinforcement echelon which had already passed through the blocking force's system of responsibility en route to the front when the trap was sprung, and the fact that it had included none of the attack craft mother ships made that seem even more likely.

But whatever had happened, the courier drones had reached the blocking force well before the enemy's survivors, and this time the gunboats would be waiting.

Captain Jeremiah Dillinger, MacGregor's chief of staff, and Commander Fahd Aburish, her operations officer, flanked her as she gazed at the holographic representation of Anderson Two in CIC's holo sphere. The icons representing *Amaretsu* and the core of Fourth Fleet's limited striking power floated in the sphere, and MacGregor felt her staffers' unhappiness—especially Aburish's—at being here. She couldn't blame them, yet she saw no alternative to her deployment. So far, the enemy appeared not to have entered this system. She couldn't be positive of that, but the interstellar comsats were still intact as far as the Anderson *Three* warp point, and the cruisers and destroyers she'd deployed to picket the known warp points in One and Two reported no enemy activity in-system. Unfortunately, she'd also brought along five *Wayfarer*-class freighters with heavy loads of RD2s to mount a watch on the Anderson Three side of the warp point, and the drones had made it clear the enemy was maintaining a massive gunboat screen there. If Antonov and Avram were going to break through that screen with acceptable losses, MacGregor was going to have to help clear their way.

That was why she'd brought Fourth Fleet forward . . . yet she dared not move any *further* forward before Second Fleet arrived. The fact that gunboats were warp-capable prevented her from putting her ships right on top of the warp point, so she had to hold them far enough back to give her time to get her fighters launched before any surprise gunboat strike could reach her. Which, she conceded silently to Aburish, gave her the worst of both worlds. This deep into Anderson Two, she ran a very serious risk of being cut off from her retreat to Centauri if the Bugs managed to run still another ambush force in behind her, yet she was compelled to do nothing constructive until Second Fleet arrived. *If* Second Fleet—

She chopped that thought off and folded her hands behind her while she made herself rethink the strategic situation yet again. If Second Fleet managed to get back more or less intact, Antonov should have an excellent chance—with Fourth Fleet's support—of holding Anderson One. She hoped so, anyway. If he couldn't, then the Navy was going to have to write off all of Survey Flotilla 19, as well. Admiral Sommers might know where Anderson One's third open warp point led by now, but no one else did, and she was much too far out for anyone who hadn't already surveyed the warp line to find her. Yet whatever the future held, what had already happened to Second Fleet was a grimly pointed reminder that there might be other warp points no one knew about, and a part of MacGregor wanted desperately to pull back to One. But her starships would have required seventy-six hours just to cross Anderson Two to the Anderson Three warp point, and that was simply too long a transit time for her pickets to call her forward when the drones indicated Second Fleet's arrival was imminent.

"Time remaining?" she asked after a moment.

"Assuming Sky Marshal Avram had to proceed clear to Anderson Five before turning for home, she should reenter Anderson Three approximately one day from now," Aburish replied. "That would put her on the Anderson Three-Anderson Two warp point in—" he consulted his calculator "—one hundred twenty-six hours."

"I see." MacGregor grimaced at the holo sphere once more. "This waiting is beginning to get just a bit tedious," she observed.

"Sir, I'd like to point out—" Aburish began, but her raised hand stopped him.

"We've already been over it, Fahd," she said, her husky alto quiet but firm, "and the answer's still the same. I recognize the risk I'm running, but we can't know what shape Admiral Antonov's carriers are in . . . or if he's been engaged in a running battle all the way back to us. But the recon drone reports *do* make it clear the Bugs on this warp point are holding tight rather than moving forward to meet him, and we've got almost five hundred fighters aboard *our* carriers. If we hit the bastards from behind while he and Sky Marshal Avram hit them from the front, we should be able to blow the door open before they know which end is up."

"And if they trap us the same way they ambushed Admiral Antonov, Sir?" Aburish wasn't giving up, but his resigned tone said he already knew how his admiral would reply.

"There has to be some limit to even the Bugs' total strength," MacGregor said, "and if *I* were the Bug lord high admiral, I'd've committed everything I had to smashing Second Fleet. The fact that they're using nothing but gunboats to cover this warp point may well indicate that they figured the same way, but even if they do have another ambush force, and even if there is an as yet unknown warp point in Two, they'd have a hell of a time coordinating another attack into *our* rear. And let's face it, Fahd: if we don't get Second Fleet back to Centauri, the ships we have with us won't make all that much difference by themselves."

"I suppose not," Aburish sighed. "I just hope we're not throwing good money after bad."

"Well, if I've made the wrong call, I'm sure Antonov or Avram will tell me in no uncertain terms," MacGregor snorted. "In fact, it would probably be something of a relief if I could get them mad enough to replace me!"

Another gunboat squadron had reported still more of those irritating sensor ghosts, but, as with all earlier such reports, they had been unable to run them down. The ghosts' persistent refusal to either go away or let themselves be tracked down was worrisome, for it suggested that the enemy was up to some new technological trick, yet that was a secondary concern for now, for the retreating enemy would reenter this system shortly. The gunboats would have preferred to go to meet him, but that, unfortunately, was impossible. There were still at least some surviving enemy ships in this system, and it seemed extremely likely there were at least some in the next system up the chain. But the ambush which had been supposed to destroy the enemy's entire fleet had skimmed off almost every available gunboat. The eight hundred still guarding the warp point had made the journey from the nearest core system under their own power, operating without tenders or mother ships. That meant the external ordnance they now mounted would be all they had, and they dared not be drawn into wasting that ordnance on any diversionary target. That was why they had not advanced further up the chain towards the enemy's core systems, where they would almost certainly have been engaged and forced to expend their munitions.

But their wait would end shortly, and they began to stir, spreading their outriding squadrons a bit wider to insure that no ship could evade their sensors' sweep.

"They're definitely up to something, Sir," Aburish said tautly. "Look here . . . and over here on the other side of their formation, as well." He jabbed a light pencil at the display generated from the latest RD2 sweep. "Looks like they're expecting company."

"And just about on the button for your time estimate, Fahd," Dillinger noted. "It's got to be the Sky Marshal and Admiral Antonov."

"Agreed." MacGregor rubbed the tip of her nose. "Are the SBMHAWKs ready?"

"Yes, Sir. Standing by and targeted," Aburish said crisply.

"All right," she said. "Given how they're adjusting their position and that no one's turned up to reinforce them, I think we have to proceed on the theory that this force is all they've got." That, as she was painfully aware, could turn out to be a fatal assumption, yet she had no choice but to make it. "I want the probe schedule accelerated. Put a flight through every ten minutes."

"That's going to burn through the available numbers in a hurry," Dillinger pointed out, "and it's also going to increase the chance of their being spotted."

"Those are risks we're just going to have to take, Jeremiah. We've got to know when they get ready to commit, and the probes' sensors are good enough they should see Second Fleet by the time the bad guys do. When they do—"

Ellen MacGregor looked at her senior staffers, and her smile would have chilled a shark.

There they are, Sir," Anthea Mandagalla said wearily.

"I see them," Raymond Prescott replied. The last week had been as terrible, in its way, as Task Force 21's agonizing wait for Second Fleet to break back towards it in Anderson Five. He and his staff had managed to reorganize the remnants of Ivan Antonov and Hannah Avram's ships into what looked like battlegroups, but they were nothing of the sort. Despite all emergency repairs could do, eighty percent of those ships were totally unfit for combat, their "battlegroups" no more than defensive huddles, tied together by jury-rigged datanets in the hope of fending off at least a few incoming missiles.

But now someone whose ordeal had been even more hideous than Second Fleet's had appeared on their sensors: Michael Chin's surviving support ships, covered by the battle-cruisers Hannah had detached on her way through. They were precisely where they were supposed to be, and they moved steadily towards rendezvous with

Prescott's tattered command as it headed for the warp point to Anderson Two.

"We've got Admiral Chin's strength report, Admiral," Commander Hale reported, and Prescott looked at her. "He says he has seven fighters to support the Sky Marshal's battle-cruisers," the com officer said quietly. "His own escorts are fit only for defensive action."

"Seven," Jacques Bichet repeated softly. "Sweet Jesus, they got hammered even worse than we thought."

"There's been a lot of that going around," Prescott replied with bitter humor, then shook himself. Chin's seven fighters would bring his entire surviving fighter strength up to one hundred and ninety-two. But at least he saw the icons of TFNS *Anchorage* and *Lisbon* in the plot, and those had been two of Antonov's ammunition colliers.

"Inform Admiral Chin that we're critically short of ammunition," he told Bichet. "Tell him we're especially short of fighter munitions and capital missiles. I'm sure the bastards already know we're here, and without the fighter strength to maintain a recon shell, we can't be sure there aren't cloaked fleet units out there. I suspect we'd already have heard from them if they *were* there, but we can't be certain, so I don't want to halt the fleet for very long. On the other hand," he smiled bitterly, "we don't have that many fighters or combat capable ships left. Chin should be able to organize enough shuttles to get what we have resupplied on the fly."

The enemy appeared on the gunboats' own sensors at last. The escapees from the ambush and the survivors of the support echelon had made rendezvous, and they were coming straight for the warp point. Well, it was not as if they had a choice, and the gunboats began to stir. Now that they knew where both the enemy's forces were, they would swarm out and envelop him, spreading themselves too widely for his surviving attack craft to intercept in strength.

"Looks like you called it, Sir," Bichet said. "They're going to wait on the warp point, then come at us on a broad front to spread the fighters."

"And if we send Kinkaid in on a preemptive strike, we guarantee her people will be too far out to support the battle-line when the gunboats she doesn't catch make their runs," Prescott agreed. "Well, we knew it was coming. Let's just be grateful they don't seem to have any regular warships to support them."

"I'm *trying* to feel grateful, Sir," Mandagalla said, "but it doesn't seem to be working."

"That's because—" Prescott began, only to be cut off by a sudden shout from Plotting.

✧ ✧ ✧

The gunboats' first warning was the sudden emergence of missile pods in their rear. And not just any pods. These were the new type, loaded with close assault missiles, and they seemed to know exactly where each gunboat was. They vomited their deadly cargoes with devastating accuracy, and point defense was useless against the sprint-mode capital missiles.

"*All right!*" It was hardly a professional report, but Prescott felt no inclination to reprimand Bichet, for whoever had planned that attack had demonstrated impeccable timing. He and his command were still five light-minutes out, but the Bugs had been moving away from the warp point when the pods erupted in their rear. Over half of them had been destroyed, and even as they died, the first assault carriers came through the warp point. TFNS *Amaretsu*, *Ajax*, *Minotaur*, and *Wizard* led the way, followed by the Ophiuchi *Zirk-Sefmaara* and *Zirk-Siraacan* and five Terran fleet carriers. Missile-armed fighters spat from their catapults, and then the precious carriers wheeled and fled back towards Anderson Two. The remaining gunboats hesitated, clearly torn between continuing toward Prescott or turning on the fighters in their rear. But their hesitation was brief. They were outnumbered by the newly arrived fighters now, and the carriers' prompt departure deprived them of any starship targets on the warp point. They swerved back onto their original courses, racing for Prescott's command, and he smiled cruelly.

"Launch the fighters, Jacques. Then reverse course."

"Aye, aye, Sir," Bichet said with an answering smile.

The gunboats charged the enemy they had awaited for so long, but that enemy was no longer advancing. Instead, he expelled his own attack craft and then fell back, holding the range open, and the gunboats were doomed. They were slower than the attack craft swarming out from the warp point in pursuit, and they were armed with FRAMs and standard missiles for antishipping attacks, not AFHAWKs.

The attack craft killed the last of them four light-minutes short of their intended victims.

Fifteen days after assuming command of Second Fleet, Raymond Prescott sat still and silent on his flag bridge, eyes burning, as the survivors of Operation Pesthouse limped brokenly back into Centauri. Half of his remaining capital ships were under tow, abused engines crippled beyond repair, and only eight ships—eight, out of Second Fleet's entire initial order of battle and Hannah Avram's relief force—were undamaged. He thought of Hannah and his eyes burned hotter, yet he'd done it. With her help—and Ellen MacGregor's—he'd obeyed Ivan Antonov's last order and gotten his people home.

But the price, he thought. *Dear God, the* price!

His memory replayed Ellen MacGregor's shocked disbelief when he informed her that *he* was Second Fleet's senior surviving officer . . . and that Hannah was dead as well. And her disbelief had turned to horror as his exhausted voice numbly detailed the Navy's losses. Thirty-two superdreadnoughts, eleven assault carriers, six fleet carriers, three light carriers, five battleships, thirty battle-cruisers, ten light cruisers, eleven *hundred* fighters, and twenty-eight support ships had been destroyed outright, and the ships which could still fight wouldn't have made three battlegroups. In three hundred years, the Terran Federation had never been more decisively defeated—nor lost so many splendid ships.

And people.

He closed his eyes, clenching himself against the pain. The people. He still didn't have definitive casualty figures, but there were already over two hundred thousand confirmed dead, and all of it—*all* of it!— for a campaign which ended with the Alliance right where it was when it began. The Pesthouse disaster had crippled the offensive capability of the TFN. God only knew how that would affect the strategic balance, yet even more frightening than that was the dreadful firepower of those new, monster ships. GHQ had decided to name them "monitors," for like the original ironclads of Old Terra, they were as slow and clumsy as they were terrifyingly well armored and armed. But slow or not, there was nothing between them and Centauri.

He sat gazing into his plot, drained and exhausted, and fear pulsed deep inside him. They would be coming for Centauri, those monitors. He knew it. And somehow the Alliance would have to stop them without three-quarters of Home Fleet . . . or Hannah Avram or Ivan Antonov.

Somehow.

CHAPTER FORTY-FOUR

The Black Hole of Centauri

The Fleet made its way back along the warp chain down which the enemy had been lured. There was no opposition, yet even with damaged units under tow, the enemy was too fast to overhaul, and the blocking force had been trapped and expended for minimal results. Its extermination had further weakened the Fleet, but now the survivors of all the attack forces had gathered, joined by the first of the special ramming units. It was the most powerful force the Fleet had ever assembled—not simply in this war, but ever—yet its catastrophic gunboat losses imposed delay. It dared not confront enemy attack craft without a powerful gunboat force, and so all of those massive starships waited while the small craft it needed were rushed to it.

Hundreds of feet scuffed as Ellen MacGregor's senior officers rose, and she crossed the auditorium stage with a brisk, determined stride and her jaw set in a confident jut. Her staff followed, and she deliberately refrained from looking over her shoulder at them. She'd made the public demeanor she expected of them clear in terms no one could possibly have misunderstood.

She reached the lectern between the long conference table and the edge of the stage and turned with parade ground precision to take her place behind it. Her staffers seated themselves at the table behind her, joining her second in command and *his* staff, and she took a moment to turn and smile tightly at Raymond Prescott. He looked less harrowed and exhausted than he had. That still left a lot of room for improvement, but however exhausted he might be, at least he'd evinced none of the bleak despair or outright panic which hovered over Centauri's inhabited planets like an evil fog. *He's got a hell of a lot better right to feel those things than certain other people, too,* she told herself. *Like that son-of-a-bitch Mukerji.*

She allowed herself a fleeting, sharklike grin at the thought of the political admiral. All of Operation Pesthouse's surviving flag officers—except one—had distinguished themselves during Second Fleet's grim retreat. Mukerji hadn't. In fact, an iron-voiced Prescott had been forced to relieve him when he'd revealed the soft, panicky center most of his peers had always suspected was there. Agamemnon Waldeck had, predictably, objected in the strongest terms and even gone so far as to propose Mukerji for command of TF 43, the orbital forts covering the Anderson One warp point. MacGregor, however, had been unimpressed by the Naval Oversight Committee chairman's arguments and, backed to the hilt by the Joint Chiefs of Staff, had confirmed Prescott's decision and sent Mukerji packing with an alacrity she knew would have delighted Hannah Avram. It had certainly delighted *Mukerji* (in the short term, at least), for it had gotten him out of Alpha Centauri and away from the Bug juggernaut he confidently expected to hammer the system flat. It was probable that he would get over his panic once he was certain his own hide was safe, but while it was remotely possible that Waldeck's patronage might be able to find him *some* form of employment one day, MacGregor's scathingly brutal assessment of his state when she approved his relief should keep him from ever again commanding in action.

But her grin faded as she turned back to face the well-filled auditorium, and she scolded herself for dwelling on Mukerji. He'd proven how amply he deserved to be slapped down, yet she knew the savagery with which she'd done that slapping owed even more to her own reaction to the loss of Ivan Antonov and Hannah Avram than to her longstanding contempt for him.

Well, what if it did? she asked herself coldly. *The son-of-a-bitch had it coming, and if kicking his ass is the only thing I do to compensate for my own sheer, howling terror I'm at least in better shape than certain of my esteemed political masters! Or, for that matter,* she added grimly, *than most of my military subordinates.*

"Be seated, ladies and gentlemen," she invited, and feet scuffed once more as her officers—primarily Terran and Ophiuchi, but with a few Tabbies and even a handful of Gorm scattered among them—did whatever their respective species described with the verb "sit."

She let her eyes sweep their tense, silent ranks and felt their anxiety like a barely contained forest fire, probing at the firebreaks she'd labored to erect around it. Ellen MacGregor knew about war, for she'd gone straight from the Academy into the closing stages of the Theban War, yet in all her years of service, she'd never sensed anything quite like this. There was a brittleness to her subordinates, a stunned desperation overlaid by lingering disbelief. That was especially true of the Terrans out there, for it was *their* fleet which had been so savagely mauled, but that same brittle, disbelieving fear—resignation, almost—clung to the nonhumans as well. Hannah Avram had been perhaps the most respected human officer of her generation. Her loss would have been a blow under any circumstances; coupled with Ivan Antonov's death, it had hit the Alliance squarely between the eyes with staggering power. For sixty years, the navies of the Grand Alliance—*all* of them, not just the TFN—had regarded Antonov as the galaxy's greatest living naval commander, the admiral who stood alone as the only true heir to Howard Anderson and Varnik'sheerino. He'd been more than simply the military commander of the Grand Alliance. He'd been its icon, its living war banner. Now that banner had fallen, and with its destruction, the Bugs had destroyed the certitude of the officers who'd followed it into battle.

And the way they did it only makes it worse, MacGregor conceded. *They sucked us in—all of us, not just Antonov—and then jumped us with those godawful monitors. Maybe if we'd really* listened *to LeBlanc it wouldn't have hit us so hard, but we didn't. Despite the gunboats, despite the Assault Fleet, despite the plasma gun, we never truly believed—not deep down inside—that the Bugs could out-innovate us. We were so sure they'd have to play perpetual technological catch-up that it never occurred to us they might actually produce something that gave them the advantage in hardware, and we were just as confident of our ability to outthink and outfight them. They were simply a huge, unthinking, elemental force, not an opponent capable of analysis and strategic innovation.* She snorted mentally. *Yeah.* Sure *they were!*

She shook off the thought as she realized her audience had settled into its chairs (or whatever). Ten days had passed since Raymond Prescott led his crippled fleet back to Centauri, and MacGregor sometimes thought she, Kthaara'zarthan, Oscar Pederson, and Prescott were the only four people in the galaxy who realized how priceless those days had been. In addition to her role as Fourth Fleet's CO, she'd found herself tapped as the Federation's acting representative to the Joint Chiefs of Staff, but that responsibility, at least, had been one she could entrust to other hands. She knew enough about Tabbies to recognize how terribly his *vilkshatha* brother's death had hit Lord Talphon, but he'd let neither grief nor his hunger for *vilknarma* divert him from his duties as the Joint Chiefs' new chairman. He and his nonhuman colleagues had worked beyond exhaustion to squeeze out every possible reinforcement for Centauri, but they'd remained tactfully distant from the purely human side of the situation. Especially the political one.

MacGregor deeply appreciated their efforts to bolster Fourth Fleet, and she understood why they'd stepped aside from the political aspects of the crisis. She only wished she could do the same, but that was out of the question. She and Pederson had worn themselves hoarse trying to quell the panic of such notable war leaders as Bettina Wister (who'd left the very morning after Prescott's return—with indecent haste—for an emergency Assembly session on Old Terra . . . thank God!) without success, yet their own officers were almost worse. They might not run around in circles waving their hands and squealing like that political whore Wister, but their numb lack of anything resembling aggressiveness made MacGregor feel as if she were swimming in tapioca. Perhaps it was only her imagination, but things certainly looked better to *her* than they had ten days ago! Fourth Fleet had acquired sixteen more superdreadnoughts and nine more battleships, counting new arrivals and the combat capable survivors of Second Fleet and Hannah Avram's relief force. Some of those survivors were still being worked on by the repair ships, but all were fit for service under emergency conditions, and if her minefields weren't yet as heavy as she wanted, they were five times heavier than they *had* been. All of that should be evident to every person in this auditorium from Jeremiah Dillinger's daily status reports. Yet try as she might, the bulk of her officers seemed unable to drag themselves out of their slough of despond, and she was getting more than a bit tired of it.

Well, she thought, *if this news doesn't get them off their butts, our morale's in even worse shape than I thought!* She inhaled deeply, propped her forearms on the lectern, and leaned across it to address the assembly in clear, crisp tones.

"Thirtieth Least Fang Harniaar and his task force will arrive in Centauri at approximately 0730 local tomorrow," she told them, and a stir, more sensed than seen, rustled through the auditorium. It wasn't strong enough to call relief, but MacGregor decided to regard it as headed in that direction.

"His arrival will increase our battle-line strength by twenty-seven percent, double our battle-cruiser strength, and increase our mobile units' combined fighter strength by eighty-four percent," she went on briskly. "In fact, our order of battle will be stronger in every unit category, except superdreadnoughts, than Second Fleet was for Pesthouse. And with the additional support of Centauri Sky Watch plus the advantage of a defensive position directly atop a warp point, our effective combat power will be *at least* six times as great!"

She smiled fiercely, but there were no answering smiles from her audience, and she felt her own congeal. That frozen, singing tension remained. It was as if her officers couldn't quite make themselves believe in their own advantages, as if some inner part of them could see anything she said only as an effort to jolly them along. She felt their misgivings mocking her . . . but she felt something else, as well, and a dangerous light flickered in her dark brown eyes. She closed her mouth, firm lips tightening in an ominous line, and glared at the silent rows of officers for a long, smoldering moment. And then, deliberately, she stepped around the lectern. She walked to the very edge of the stage and put her hands behind her, gripping them fiercely together as she glared out at Fourth Fleet's command structure, and her voice was harsh.

"All right, ladies and gentlemen," she half-snapped and half-snarled. "Let's get this out in the open, shall we?" Her hard, contemptuous tone sent another stir through the audience—one of uneasy surprise this time—and she smiled a thin, unpleasant smile. "Oh, come now! *Surely* someone out there would like to address the point so obviously on everyone's mind!"

No one spoke, and she rocked on her toes, bouncing up and down in short, sharp arcs that reminded the humans in her audience of the flick-flick-flicking tail of an irate tigress.

"No? Then *I'll* address it," she told their silence flatly. "We—and by 'we' I mean, specifically, the Terran Federation Navy—got our ass kicked. To date, counting all known losses, the Bugs have destroyed almost three hundred and forty TFN ships. In case some of you haven't run the figures, that's twenty-eight percent of our prewar hulls and over *fifty* percent of our prewar tonnage. Oh, and let's not forget the sixty-four capital ships out of action for major repairs or the 'combat capable' units of our own fleet which still have unrepaired battle damage. Then there's Pesthouse itself. In addition to most of Home Fleet, we've lost Admiral van der Gelder, Admiral Taathaanahk, Sky Marshal Avram, and Admiral Antonov. Worse, we lost all those ships and all those people because we fucked up. We walked right into it— all of us. We and our allies saw what we wanted to see, what the *Bugs* wanted us to see, and we screwed up by the numbers, didn't we? Be honest, ladies and gentlemen," she invited scathingly. "We've just been guests of honor for the biggest cluster-fuck in our mutual histories, and all of us, and especially every *Terran* officer in this auditorium, are scared to death, aren't we?" She glared at the assembled officers, chin jutting aggressively, shoulders squared, eyes snapping, and still no one spoke.

"Well, we've got *reason* to be scared," she went on in a marginally gentler voice. "We've been hammered, we've lost our best commanders and our most experienced units, and we're it—the entire mobile defense force—for Centauri *and* Sol. And just to make things worse, the Bugs have acquired command datalink *and* introduced an entirely new ship type bigger and nastier and lots, *lots* tougher than anything we've got. Does that just about sum it up?"

Again, no one replied from the auditorium seats, but this time a voice spoke up behind her.

"Yes, Sir," Raymond Prescott said with poison-dry wryness. "I guess that *does* sum it up, just about."

MacGregor turned her head, and he smiled crookedly at her. It was a battered and tired smile, but far from a beaten one, and she smiled back.

"I'm glad to hear that, Admiral Prescott," she told him. "I was beginning to think we might have a *serious* problem here." Prescott's smile became a grin, and a few people in the audience actually chuckled. The laughter sounded surprised, as if its authors couldn't quite believe they'd produced it, but it was real, and MacGregor swung back to face the seats.

"All right, people," she said, and her voice had replaced its brief humor with adamantine determination, "let's cut to the chase. The Bugs are coming. When they get here, they're going to throw a simultaneous assault transit into our faces at a time of their own choosing. They're going to cover that assault with hundreds, probably thousands, of gunboats, and they're going to back it up with superdreadnoughts and these new 'monitors' of theirs, and the bastards will have command datalink. Taking everything into account, this will probably be the most powerful warp point assault in history. And do you know what's going to happen when they launch it?"

Not a voice spoke, and she swiveled her head, sweeping her eyes across them all in slow, remorseless arc, as she let the silence stretch out. Then she snapped it.

"What's going to *happen*, ladies and gentlemen, is that we're going to reduce their fancy new ships, and their gunboats, and their assault fleet—and them—to plasma. We've got the ships, and the forts, and the fighters, and the weapons we need, all backed up by the greatest industrial capacity in the known galaxy, and we are damned well going to turn the Centauri System into a Bug-eating black hole. People, I don't give a good *goddamn* what *they* have. All I care about is what *we* have, and we are going to mine that warp point until I can frigging well walk across it! We're going to cover it with energy platforms, and missile pods, and forts, and capital ships, and combat space patrols, and we are fucking well going to *kill* any Bug that sticks its ugly snout through it! And if any of you think we're not going to do those things—or if even *one* of you gives me any less than a one thousand percent effort—being eaten by Bugs will be the *least* of your worries! *Is that perfectly clear?*"

The silence was different now—a ringing stillness, crackling about her, and she nodded.

"Good," she said mildly. "In that case, let's get down to the nuts and bolts of just how we're going to do that, shall we?"

❖   ❖   ❖

Raymond Prescott tipped his chair clear back, stretched and yawned hugely, and propped his heels on the briefing room table to survey his staff wearily.

"Does that just about cover it, Anna?" he asked, and Captain Mandagalla scrolled back through the notes on her own terminal.

"Just about, Sir," she agreed after a moment. "Admiral LeBlanc's agreed to your request to assign Captain Chung as your staff spook— I understand there was quite a bit of competition for his services; Admiral Trevayne even wanted him on Old Terra—and he'll be reporting tomorrow morning. And you've got that com conference with Admiral MacGregor, Admiral Chamhandar, and Fang Harniaar tomorrow, as well. I think we've got most everything nailed down in preparation, but Jacques and I don't have the latest readiness updates yet."

"Um." Prescott rubbed his eyes with his organic hand and wished he could scrub away his fatigue. But it was better than the retreat from Anderson Five had been. He told himself that at least six times a day, and one of these days he was actually going to begin believing it.

He smiled—or grimaced, at least—at the thought, and then again, more naturally, at the memory of now MacGregor had kick-started her officers. He was probably the only other officer in Fourth Fleet who could truly understand how she must feel, given that he was also the only other officer who'd suddenly found himself in the shoes of both Ivan Antonov and Hannah Avram, and he hadn't envied her a bit as she struggled with her subordinates' shattered morale. Her decision to transfer her flag from *Amaretsu* to the hastily repaired *Xingú* had been a statement of her determination to carry on for Hannah, and Prescott had done his dead level best to support her by projecting the confidence she needed from him, but they'd both been fighting a losing battle . . . until she decided to kick ass. *Ivan Antonov couldn't have done it better himself,* he thought, *and if there truly is an afterlife, he and Hannah must be laughing their asses off watching MacGregor. I hope they are, anyway. They deserve it.*

He drew a deep breath, unaware of how his smile had softened, then shook himself.

"All right, then!" he said briskly. "You and Jacques can fine tune the readiness numbers for me before the conference, Anna, but leave it until tomorrow. For right now, I think we can all use some sack time."

The last gunboats arrived under their own power. There were barely two thousand of them, yet the Fleet dared delay no longer. The system beyond the warp point boasted massive industrial capacity. It could undoubtedly build attack craft very quickly and in large numbers. Further delay was thus likely to work in the enemy's favor, despite the new ship types.

"—so as I see it, we've actually got two objectives here, Lord Kolaas," Admiral MacGregor said to Least Fang Harniaar. "First, of course, we have to hold Centauri and protect The Gateway. But just as important, it seems to me, is the need to knock the Bugs back on their heels in a way that every citizen of the Grand Alliance can understand."

She paused, watching the Orion commander of Task Force 42 on her split com screen in *Xingú*'s flag briefing room. The least fang had surrendered twelve superdreadnoughts to Prescott in return for the same number of Terran and Ophiuchi carriers and assault carriers, for it had gone without saying that he would command Fourth Fleet's strikefighters. Now he combed his whiskers with his claws, slowly and thoughtfully, then nodded in a human gesture of agreement.

"You are, of course, correct Ahhhdmiraal MaaacGregggorr," he yowled in the Tongue of Tongues. "Your people have been understandably anxious"—MacGregor's tips twitched wryly at the Tabby's choice of words—"since the failure of Operation Pesthouse, but my own have been equally stunned by Second Fleet's losses and their implications for the future conduct of the war."

He paused, and Raymond Prescott and Vice Admiral Ira Chamhandar nodded in grim understanding from their own quadrants of MacGregor's screen. From the outset, the Grand Alliance had tasked the TFN as its primary offensive striking force. The Terran fleet, bigger and more powerful than any of its allies and supported by the most potent industrial machine in the galaxy, had been the only logical choice for the role. But whatever happened when the Bugs attacked Centauri, the TFN would be launching no new offensives any time soon. Simply replacing its lost hulls—and training the personnel to man them—would require at least a full year, and replacement alone wouldn't be enough. The Bugs' now possessed both command datalink and those new, mammoth monitors, and for all MacGregor's brave words, no one really knew if a monitor-led assault *could* be stopped. Even if it could, any sustained offensive would require the Grand Alliance to build vessels of matching weight and power, and that was going to add a minimum of eighteen more months to the wait.

"Given those implications," Harniaar went on levelly, "you are quite correct, Ahhhdmiraal. I do not know if it is possible to damage the *enemy's* morale, but it is imperative to restore our own with a resounding success here. And, of course, it would be most desirable to inflict sufficient losses upon the enemy to induce *him* to abandon further immediate offensives."

"Precisely," MacGregor said, "and that's why—"

The shrill, atonal scream of *Xingú*'s General Quarters alarm cut off whatever she'd been about to say.

Two thousand gunboats and a hundred and fifty light cruisers erupted into Centauri space. Fourth Fleet's RD2s had kept a cautious eye on the Bugs in Anderson One, but it appeared the Bugs had realized that. They might not know precisely how it was being accomplished, but they'd allowed for the possibility, and their starships sprang almost instantly from normal standby procedures to all out attack. There was virtually no warning before the gunboats roared off their external racks and the assault fleet's light cruisers lunged for the warp point. Only the fact that the Bugs had been forced to hold their forces beyond SBMHAWK range of the warp point bought Fourth Fleet any time at all, but the first gunboat still burst into Centauri less than fifty seconds after the recon drones which warned of its coming.

Yet Ira Chamhandar's command fort had already sounded the alarm, and the combat space patrol on the warp point was alerted. MacGregor's starships, twenty-five light seconds from the warp point, received the warning fifteen seconds later than Chamhandar, and they were still charging to battle stations when the first Bugs appeared, but the warning was sufficient for the ready duty carriers and Orion battle-line units to launch. Three hundred and twenty fighters streaked towards the warp point, flashing in to join the two hundred forty-strong CSP, and then the mines began to detonate.

Twenty-one light cruisers interpenetrated on transit. That was a somewhat higher percentage than usual, yet it would have been acceptable . . . normally.

But these were not normal conditions, for the Fleet had never encountered such mine densities before, and the new datalink systems' ability to coordinate point defense conferred no advantage. This was a closed warp point. The enemy could place mines directly atop it, and he had. There was no clear zone, no space in which transit-addled electronics could recover. The deadly mines streaked in to blow ship after ship out of space; the fortresses which had been at immediate readiness added their fury to the holocaust; attack craft streaked in, salvoing missiles at the gunboats; and a bright, terrible sphere of flame blazed about the warp point.

"My God, Sir!" Commander Aburish sounded as if he couldn't believe his own readouts. "It looks like—It *is*, by God!" He wheeled to MacGregor with a savage smile. "According to Plotting, Admiral, we've just scored a one hundred percent kill on their cruisers!"

"Outstanding!" MacGregor bared her own teeth, then shook herself. "Gunboats?"

"Harder to say, Sir. Several hundred, at least, but they're much harder mine targets. The CSP caught them with their point defense degraded and nailed a lot of them, and our own strike is on its way in, but—" He shrugged, and MacGregor nodded, then flicked her eyes to Raymond Prescott's portion of her com screen.

"The battle-line will advance to support the forts, Admiral Prescott," she said formally.

The area about the warp point became a wild, swirling melee as fishtailing fighters and gunboats spun and snapped at one another. The standing combat space patrol had exhausted its missiles, but the human and Ophiuchi pilots closed grimly with their internal lasers. The gunboats had suffered terrible losses in the initial strikes, and despite their speed and relatively tiny size a small percentage had been picked off by mines, as well. But half of them had carried AFHAWKs, and all of them had their own internal weapons. Fighters began to die in the vicious, fiery spits of deep-space death, and then the first Bug superdreadnought rumbled through the warp point.

An incandescent halo racked the huge ship's shields as the minefield attacked, but the assault fleet's light cruisers had not died entirely in vain, for they'd drawn in many of the mines directly atop the closed warp point, thinning the field's density. What remained was sufficient to wound the Bug leviathan cruelly, but not to kill it outright, and even as it wallowed in its agony, a second and third superdreadnought followed it into Centauri space. More mines streaked to attack *them*, as well, but with steadily diminishing power, and Ira Chamhandar's eyes were hard.

"Release the pods to local fire control," he told his ops officer coldly. Fresh orders flashed out from his command fort, and the energy-armed Type Three and Four OWPs closest to the warp point acknowledged their instructions. Their fire control activated the shoals of SBMHAWKs slaved to it, firing them in individual, carefully controlled salvos, vomiting sprint-mode capital missiles against the air-bleeding wrecks which had survived the mines' fury, and space itself shuddered as antimatter warheads tore at their targets.

The gunboats realized what was happening, and half of the survivors swerved for the fortresses. But the OWPs' energy weapons flamed in response, and the stupendous "escort" fortresses—two-hundred-thousand-tonne bases designed and armed solely to kill missiles and fighters . . . or gunboats—smashed them by the score even as Allied fighters raced up their wakes. Space was littered with the hideous debris of what once had been gunboats, yet some broke through to hurl themselves bodily upon the forts with full FRAM loads. Shields flashed, armor vaporized, and men and women died as the blast ripped deep into the fortresses' compartments.

"They're getting through to the forts, Sir," Anthea Mandagalla said tautly.

"How bad is it?" Prescott demanded, never taking his eyes from his own plot. His heavy missile ships were almost in range to begin punching SBMs and capital missiles into the holocaust on the warp point, and a sort of deep, visceral horror gnawed at his guts as he watched still more superdreadnoughts transit unflinchingly into the maelstrom. *Nothing* should just keep coming that way, yet they did, and for all its fury, the warp point crucible was less terrible than it had been. The mines were being worn away—not swept, but *absorbed*—and the fortresses had expended most of their missile pods . . . or died.

"It could be worse, but it's not good," Jacques Bichet answered for the chief of staff. "CIC estimates hard kills on forty superdreadnoughts, but they've taken out six forts completely, and a dozen more are badly damaged."

"Admiral Chamhandar's released the Alpha Group energy platforms, Sir!" Commander Hale called out, and then Bichet nodded decisively.

"SBM range, Sir!" he announced sharply.

"Fire as you bear," Raymond Prescott said harshly.

The warp point was a sphere of fiery death, far worse than the Fleet's projections. But the Fleet had allowed for the possibility that its estimates might err. It had sent sixty superdreadnoughts through the invisible hole in space, and courier drones told the tale of destruction which had awaited them. But another fifty superdreadnoughts waited in reserve, backed by the new, larger ships, and those who had led the way had weakened the mines and begun the destruction of the enemy's fortresses.

The attack would continue.

"That's fifty superdreadnoughts confirmed destroyed, Sir," Fahd Aburish said, and Ellen MacGregor nodded silent acknowledgment. *Fifty*, she thought almost calmly. *That's six more than our entire superdreadnought strength, and the bastards are* still *coming through!*

Xingú staggered as a Bug SBM exploded against her shields. The fleet flagship was a part of Prescott's TF 41, and the Bugs had almost two dozen intact superdreadnoughts—most the missile-heavy *Archers* or the new *Arbalest*-class command ships—in Centauri. Those ships were all damaged to greater or lesser extent, but they were also missile armed, and the survivors had command datalink. Their salvos were as heavy as the ones thundering down upon them, and they were concentrating their fire on Fourth Fleet's battle-line.

Stupid of them, MacGregor thought. *They've got to clear the forts out of their way before they can even think about moving in system, and tonne-for-tonne, an OWP is a hell of a lot more heavily armed than a superdreadnought or a battleship!*

"Admiral Chamhandar's released the Alpha Group platforms, Sir," Aburish said, and MacGregor smiled an ugly smile.

The invading Bug starships had absorbed the fury of most of the mines within a half light-second of the warp point, winning at least a limited space in which their consorts could deploy and fight. But the mines had been only a part of Ellen MacGregor and Ira Chamhandar's fixed defenses. Now Chamhandar's command fortress transmitted yet another activation code, and two hundred-plus laser buoys flamed as one. A solid phalanx of X-ray lasers sleeted through the Bugs, ignoring shields to rip deep into armor and alloy, and a baying cheer echoed from *Xingú's* CIC as every single enemy ship on the warp point blew apart.

But the cheer faded almost instantly, for *still* the enemy came on, and he was no longer sending in *Archers.* He was sending through primary-armed *Augers,* force beam-armed *Avalanches,* and deadly, short-ranged *Acids* with their massive plasma gun batteries. TF 41's missiles tore at the new targets, Least Fang Harniaar's TF 42 sent massed fighter strikes screaming down their throats, and Chamhandar's surviving energy-armed fortresses rained fire on them. Yet not even that concentrated torrent of destruction could keep those Bug capital ships from firing back as they died, and Ellen MacGregor's face went white as twenty-one more fortresses—and over a hundred thousand men and women—were wiped out of existence.

"Permission to release the Beta Group platforms?" Chamhandar asked hoarsely, his own expression tight with anguish as he watched his people die, but MacGregor shook her head.

"Denied," she grated, and anger flashed in Chamhandar's eyes. He started to say something more, then clamped his jaw, nodded curtly and turned back to his own staff, and MacGregor understood his rage. But she had no choice, for the Bugs had not yet committed a single monitor. It was possible they wouldn't, that they were saving them, or that they had fewer of them than MacGregor had feared, but she dared not count on that. Any navy which would sacrifice entire fleets and surrender an entire world inhabited by its own species just to bait a trap was entirely capable of sacrificing scores of superdreadnoughts just to wear down the defenses before it launched its decisive blow. And if that was what the Bugs were doing here, she would need every Beta Group platform she had.

✧   ✧   ✧

The superdreadnoughts' losses continued to mount, and those losses spelled the probable defeat of the master plan, for without them, it was unlikely the Fleet would be able to carry through against the defenses which must have been erected around the target system's inhabited worlds. But failure to achieve all of the plan's objectives did not preclude attaining some of them, and the Fleet appeared to retain the capacity to at least cripple the forces defending the warp point. The fragmentary reports from its lead elements indicated that the enemy's fortress shell had taken severe losses, and the mines and energy buoys which covered those fortresses had been sufficiently depleted to offer a zone in which only the enemy's attack craft and starships could effectively engage.

It was time to send in the true *attack.*

"Oh, *shit!*" Prescott's head snapped around as Bichet spat the vicious obscenity, and his ops officer looked up to meet his eyes.

"Here come the monitors, Sir," he said grimly.

"The enemy have committed their monitors, Least Fang," Harniaar'kolaas' flag captain said in a flat voice, and the least fang flicked his ears in acknowledgment.

"Understood, Least Claw," he said, and looked at his operations officer. "What is our fighter status?"

"We retain roughly four hundred of our own and two hundred Human fighters still aboard ship but tasked for antishipping strikes," the ops officer replied. "Another two hundred are returning to rearm, and a strike of approximately three hundred is about to enter attack range. And we have—" he paused to check a display "—one hundred and two Ophiuchi fighters armed for gunboat suppression holding just outside the outer minefield shell."

"Hold the present strike and launch the reserve," Harniaar ordered. "We will send them in together, with the Ophiuchi for cover."

"That will delay our attack, Sir," the flag captain pointed out quietly, and Harniaar flicked his ears once more.

"Truth. Yet these are not superdreadnoughts. We will require massed strikes to penetrate their defenses, and I prefer a meaningful blow, even if I must delay its delivery."

"And in the meantime, Sir?"

"And in the meantime, Least Claw, it will be up to Ahhhdmiraal Chaaamhaaandaaar," Harniaar replied softly.

"Activate the Beta Group but do *not* fire!" Ira Chamhandar snapped. He didn't have to ask MacGregor again, for this was the threat against which Fourth Fleet's CO had reserved those energy platforms. The fact that she'd been right to hold them this long didn't make him feel any better about the people he'd lost to the superdreadnoughts, yet his teeth skinned back from his lips as he watched the Bug giants flowing into existence on the warp point. They floated in a hole among the mines—a hole their superdreadnoughts had carved with their own deaths—and their massive batteries began to smash fortresses and Allied capital ships methodically, but still Chamhandar held back. He could only do this once, and he made himself wait . . . and wait . . . and *wait* until no less than two dozen of those mammoth vessels had emerged. Then, and only then, he gave the order, and four hundred more independently deployed energy platforms fired. Not laser buoys, this time, but primary and particle beams that smashed implacably through even monitors' shields and armor. Of the twenty-four monitors on the warp point when they fired, only five survived, and Fourth Fleet closed for the kill.

The lead wave's monitors had been devastated. It was clear now that the system could not be taken, but it was equally clear that the enemy was closing on the warp point. He was approaching with every starship he still possessed, and he would undoubtedly commit his full remaining attack craft strength, as well. The opportunity thus remained to inflict heavy loss upon him, and the Fleet changed its deployment. The second-wave monitors refitted with the new datalink systems were pulled from the assault queue, but the fifteen more expendable monitors still equipped with the old-style datalink moved to the front, accompanied by seventy-six battle-cruisers, eighteen light cruisers, and all of the new ramming ships.

"Holy shi—!"

The fighter pilot's exclamation was chopped off by the explosion of his fighter, and Raymond Prescott flinched as his plot changed abruptly. And insanely. Even after Pesthouse, he couldn't believe—not on any deep, emotional level—that *anyone* would do something like *that!*

But the Bugs *had* done it. One moment space about the warp point was all but empty as the fighters and Prescott's own missiles finished off he last Bug cripples. The next moment, over a hundred warships flashed into existence in a stupendous simultaneous transit. Not light cruisers, but *battle-cruisers* and even *monitors!* Perhaps a dozen of them interpenetrated and perished, but the others survived, and even with their systems impaired by transit, they belched a hurricane of missiles and beams into Chamhandar's bleeding fortresses.

"Take us in, Jacques!" Prescott heard someone else say with his own voice. "Missile platforms stay back; everything else closes *now!*"

✧   ✧   ✧

"Fang Pressscott is closing, Sir!" Harniaar's flag captain snapped, and Harniaar bared his fangs. Of course Fang Prescott was closing! His *farshatok* aboard the fortresses were dying, and no holder of the *Ithyrra'doi'khanhaku* would let them die alone. Nor could any officer of the *Zheeerlikou'valkhannaieee* fail to follow where such a one led.

"Send in the fighters, Least Claw," Harniaar said. "Then release our escorts."

Ellen MacGregor sealed her helmet and double checked her shock frame as *Xingú* joined Raymond Prescott's charge. Fleet commander or no, that was all she could do now ... unless she chose to order Prescott off, and that was unthinkable. A part of her was actually content, for her battle plan had worked. Even for Bugs, this simultaneous transit *had* to be a last gasp by an assault which had failed, yet the carnage had been so vast—and was about to become so much more terrible still—that she could feel no sense of triumph. Later, perhaps, if she lived, she might feel such things. For now, there was only hatred and the need to kill.

She stabbed one last look at her display, saw the faster battle-cruisers and *Athabasca*-class superdreadnoughts pulling ahead of their consorts. Bug battle-cruisers came to meet them, and a corner of her brain cringed as yet more Bug ships raced straight for Chamhandar's closest surviving forts. Most died in the intervening minefields, but the staggering power of the explosions which killed them came from something far more potent than mines or even the fury of their own antimatter warheads. Only four reached their targets, but for each which did, a Terran fortress died.

Sweet Jesus, MacGregor wondered almost numbly. *What are those things? The bastards must've packed them to the deckhead with antimatter!*

But it was only a passing thought, for *Xingú* had caught up with the madness on the warp point, Harniaar'kolaas' fighters on her heels, and there was no more time. No time for anything but killing.

Pause in the Storm

Kthaara'zarthan rose from the Terran-style chair behind his desk as Ellen MacGregor and Raymond Prescott walked into his office. A week had passed since the Battle of Alpha Centauri, and the RD2s had confirmed what was happening in Anderson One.

The Bugs were digging in. Their minelayers were emplacing their own mines—and, undoubtedly, energy buoys—on their side of the warp point. Powerful mobile forces, including still more of their monitors, hovered watchfully behind the minelayers, but they remained carefully beyond SBMHAWK range of the warp point. No one was prepared to predict that they would stay on the defensive forever, but the implications were clear, and Kthaara bowed to the two officers who had been most responsible for stopping the enemy dead.

"Ahhhdmiraal MaaacGregggorr, Fang Pressscott. Be seated, please," he invited. His guests obeyed the polite command, and he resumed his own seat and regarded them levelly across the desk. "You have done well, both of you," he said quietly. "The Grand Alliance owes you and your *farshatok* more than it can ever hope to repay, and I—" he paused to look directly into Prescott's eyes "—owe a deeply personal debt, for I cannot doubt that among the *chofaki* you and your warriors slew were those responsible for my *vilkshatha* brother's death. There will be more blood balance before this war is over, yet you have exacted the first *vilknarma,* and for that I will be always in your debt."

MacGregor looked a little embarrassed, but Prescott only nodded soberly, and Kthaara flicked his ears twice, then cocked his chair back.

"You have also," he went on in a less emotionally charged voice, "bought the Alliance some additional time. Had the enemy succeeded in taking Centauri, he might well have carried through against Sol. Even if he had not, we would have been forced to retake Centauri at any price, and the losses his monitors might have inflicted against warp point assaults or in deep space could have been devastating. As it is, and despite the losses Fourth Fleet suffered, he has clearly abandoned attacks on this system for the immediate future. By the time he feels secure enough to attempt them once more, we will have three or four times your strength waiting on the warp point for him. I do not think—" he bared his fangs in a lazy, hunter's grin "—that he will enjoy any future attacks on this system even as much as he did his last."

"But that doesn't mean he won't make them, Sir," Prescott pointed out quietly. "And all he has to do is get lucky once."

"Truth, Fang Pressscott," Kthaara acknowledged. "And it will remain true until we are able to take the offensive to *them* once more. Hopefully," a cold, bleak hatred glowed in the Orion's slit-pupilled eyes, "on *our* terms this time,"

"You're referring to Zephrain, Sir?" MacGregor asked, and her eyes were troubled when Kthaara nodded. "With all due respect, Sir, I'd think that what happened here—what *almost* happened here—gives even more point to the fears of what might happen to Rehfrak if we attack through Zephrain and fail."

"Truth," Kthaara agreed once more. "There are many who would agree with you, Ahhhdmiraal, and I share your views in great part, as well. There will be no precipitous attacks. This war has lasted for three and a half of your years, almost seven of my people's, and the ghosts of Kliean will not soon be forgotten by any of us. It will take time to prepare our blow, for we must first build our own monitors. Yet I feel it is particularly important that I, as the *Khan'a'khanaaeee's* representative to the Joint Chiefs, press for the earliest possible date for such an attack. Above all, we dare not allow these creatures leisure to press their own exploration until *they* find the equivalent of Zaaia'pharaan and a blow such as the one you have just stopped falls unopposed upon one of our core systems. I recognize the need to prepare carefully, however hard inactivity comes to one of the *Zheeerlikou'valkhannaieee* in war, yet we must not allow ourselves or our superiors to forget that the breathing space you and your valiant warriors have bought can be only a pause in the storm . . . and that it must be allowed to linger no longer than absolutely necessary."

He gazed at the two human admirals, and they nodded back soberly.

"I am glad you agree," he said after moment, "for you both will have major parts to play. From what I have heard from your admiralty, you, Ahhhdmiraal MaaacGregggorr, will soon be confirmed as Sky Marshal *and* designated as the Federation's permanent representative to the Joint Chiefs." MacGregor hissed in shock, sitting suddenly very straight in her chair, and Kthaara gave another lazy Orion smile. "You have earned it, Ahhhdmiraal," he told her. "Besides, you remind me in many ways of a younger Eevaahn'zarthan . . . although you still have much to learn of the proper way to describe politicians. Still," he permitted himself a purring chuckle, "your new position will no doubt provide sufficient exposure to them to hone your vocabulary."

"I—" MacGregor started to speak, then closed her mouth and settled for a nod, and Kthaara looked at Prescott.

"For you, Raaymmonnd'telmasa, there will be another task," he said quietly. "As you know, our original plan for the Zaaia'pharaan operation would have placed you in command of its battle-line under Ahhhdmiraal Antaanaav while Zhaarnak'telmasa commanded its carriers. That will not now be possible, but after much discussion with my colleagues of the Joint Chiefs, we have decided that *you* will command the entire operation in Eevaahn's place. I believe he would have wished it that way . . . and I can think of no officer whom *I* would prefer to see in that position. Fang Zhaarnak will, of course, be made available to you as your second in command."

"Thank you, Sir," Prescott replied in the Tongue of Tongues, and Kthaara nodded, then inhaled deeply.

"None of that will be happening anytime soon, however," he said more briskly. "In the meantime, I feel confident that we can keep both of you suitably busy right here, overseeing Centauri's defense and helping me kick the *droshokol mizoahaarlesh* of our various research and shipbuilding commands into action. And, I fear," he bared just the tips of his fangs, "making occasional public appearances with our highly respected political leaders."

Prescott groaned aloud, and Kthaara laughed.

"Come now, Raaymmonnd! I can even promise you a special treat this afternoon, for First Fang Ynaathar's personal representative will be passing through Centauri tomorrow, and he has been invited to address your Naval Oversight Committee. I realize how much you dislike interviews and politician's speeches, but I believe you and Ahhhdmiraal MaaacGregggorr will both take particular pleasure from Fang Ulaahkhaa's speech. You see, Fang Ulaahkhaa has served as a member of our equivalent of your Naval Oversight Committee, and I fear he is somewhat of the old school. He is also known to share Eevaahn'zarthan's view of politicians, and he continues to be known for the, ah, *blunt*, plainspoken fashion in which he expresses his views. I mention this only because I understand that both Msss. Wisssterr and Mr. Waaaldeccck will be attending his speech, and—" the big Tabby's smile took on an almost seraphic quality "—I will be most interested to hear how the interpreters render his remarks for them."

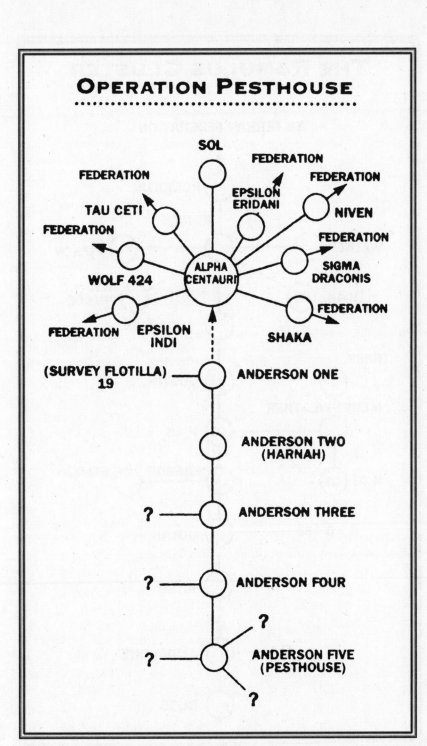

OPERATION PESTHOUSE

SOL

FEDERATION

FEDERATION

EPSILON
ERIDANI

FEDERATION

TAU CETI

NIVEN

FEDERATION

ALPHA
CENTAURI

FEDERATION

WOLF 424

SIGMA
DRACONIS

FEDERATION

FEDERATION

EPSILON
INDI

SHAKA

(SURVEY FLOTILLA)
19

ANDERSON ONE

ANDERSON TWO
(HARNAH)

?

ANDERSON THREE

?

ANDERSON FOUR

?

?

ANDERSON FIVE
(PESTHOUSE)

?

THE ROMULUS CLUSTER

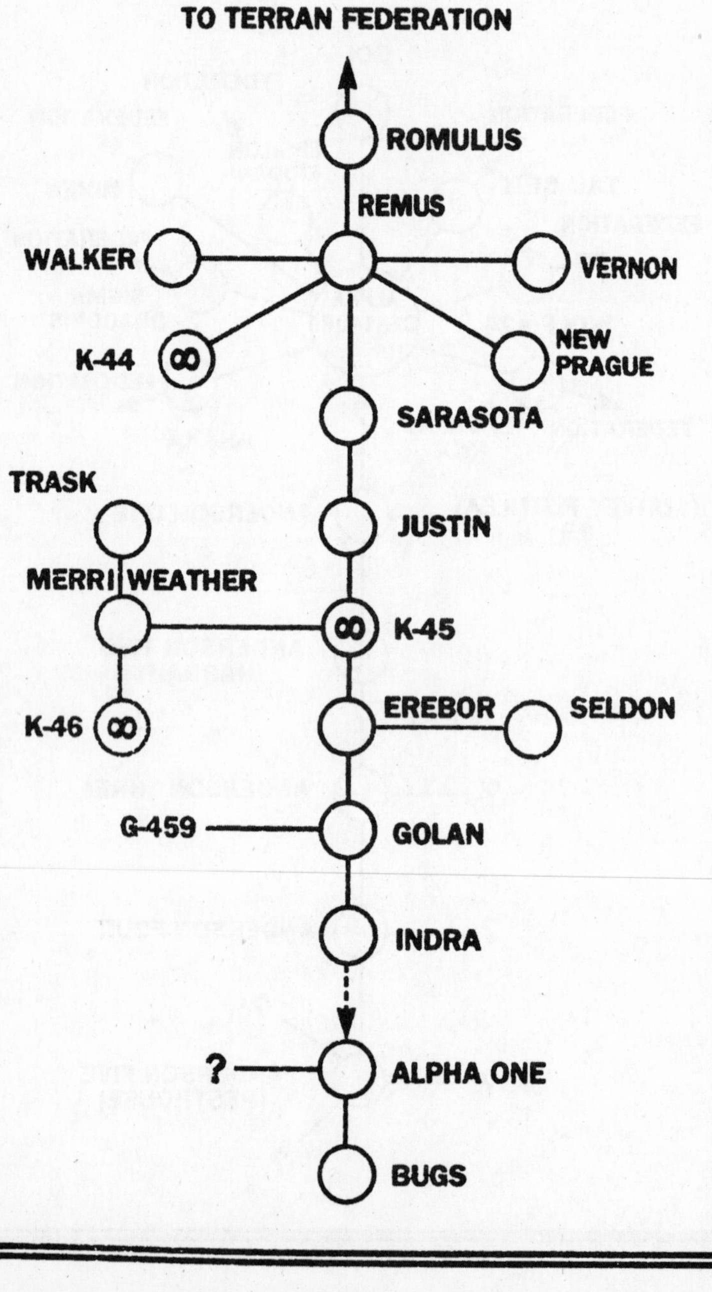

TO TERRAN FEDERATION

ROMULUS

REMUS

WALKER — VERNON

K-44 ∞ — NEW PRAGUE

SARASOTA

TRASK

JUSTIN

MERRIWEATHER — K-45 ∞

K-46 ∞ — EREBOR — SELDON

G-459 — GOLAN

INDRA

? — ALPHA ONE

BUGS

THE KLIEAN CAMPAIGN

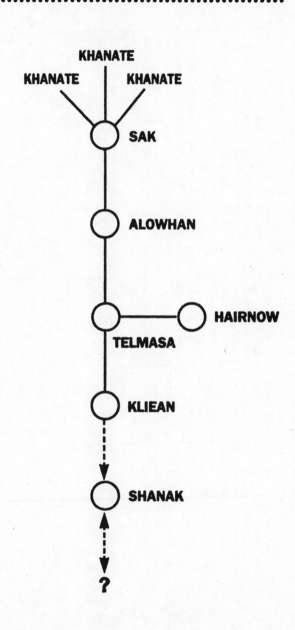